THE SECOND GEORGE FELSE OMNIBUS

THE SECOND GEORGE FELSE OMNIBUS

Ellis Peters

Black is the Colour of My True Love's Heart
The Grass Widow's Tale
The House of Green Turf

WARNER FUTURA

A *Warner Futura* Book
First published in this omnibus edition in 1995 by
Warner Futura

This omnibus edition copyright © Edith Pargeter 1995

BLACK IS THE COLOUR OF MY TRUE LOVE'S HEART
first published by Collins in 1967
Published by Futura in 1988
Reprinted 1988, 1989, 1990

Copyright © Edith Pargeter 1967

THE GRASS WIDOW'S TALE
first published by Collins in 1968
Published by Futura in 1991

Copyright © Edith Pargeter in 1968

THE HOUSE OF GREEN TURF
first published by Collins in 1969
Published by Futura in 1992

Copyright © Edith Pargeter in 1969

The moral right of the author has been asserted

A CIP catalogue for this book
is available from the British Library

ISBN 0 7515 1187 0

Phototypeset by Intype, London
Printed and bound in Great Britain by
Clays Ltd, St Ives plc

Warner Futura
A Division of
Little, Brown and Company (UK)
Brettenham House
Lancaster Place
London WC2E 7EN

Contents

Black is the Colour of My True Love's Heart

Chapter 1

The girl with the guitar-case was standing alone at the Belward-ine bus-stop when Arundale parked the car before the station entrance, and went in to collect the records Professor Penrose had left behind. She was still standing there when he came back and stowed the battered box under the bonnet of his grey Volkswagen. She had the green-railed enclosure to herself. She didn't know it, but the Belwardine buses were independents, and waited for neither man nor train, and there wouldn't be another for more than half an hour.

Arundale was not a man who went out of his way to offer people lifts. It was the guitar-case that stirred his sense of duty; but for that he would hardly have been aware of her at all, for only one woman really existed in his life, and that was his wife. This girl was perhaps nineteen or twenty, tall, slim, and of striking appearance. Her face was thin, richly coloured, with long, fine-drawn features and large, calm, fierce eyes as blue as steel. Her great fell of heavy brown hair coiled and spilled round her face with a dynamic life of its own, and was gathered into a waist-long braid as thick as her wrist, interwoven with narrow strips of soft red leather, as though only tethers strong enough for horses could confine it. She had a duffle bag slung over her left shoulder, and wore a duffle coat carelessly loose over a charcoal-grey sweater and skirt of deceptively plain but wickedly expensive jersey. She stood carelessly and splendidly at ease, but her face was intent and abstracted. She looked like a fate in the wings, imperturbably waiting for her cue; and that was what she was. But all he saw was a long-haired girl with a guitar, and an inescapable and rather tiresome duty. He had delegated this course to his deputy; it was annoying that he should be obliged to ferry in the strays.

She looked at him, and found him looking at her. Without hesitation and without mercy, as the young will, she took all decisions out of his hands.

'Excuse me,' she said in a voice unexpectedly cool and limpid, the voice of a singer off-duty, 'could you tell me how often these buses run?'

She could pitch that superbly soft and confident note clean across the station approach at him, but he had to move nearer in order to reply without a sense of strain.

'I'm afraid they're not very frequent. In the evening there's a forty-minute interval. Perhaps I could be of service to you. I'm going that way myself.'

'I've got to get to a place called Follymead,' said the girl, measuring him without haste or prejudice. 'It's a sort of musical college, they're having a weekend course on folk music. Maybe you know the place.'

'I know it,' he said. Who could know it better? But for some reason, or for no good reason at all except lack of interest in her, he didn't tell her how closely he was connected with that curious foundation. 'I can take you there with pleasure. It would be much quicker than waiting for the bus.'

She gave him the quick scrutiny wise girls do give to middle-aged gentlemen offering lifts, but it was a mere formality; his respectability, his status, and the store he set on keeping it, were all written all over him. He was fifty-five, and still an impressive figure of a man, even though his frequent games of tennis and squash could no longer keep his weight down as low as he liked it. He had a businessman's smooth-shaven face and commanding

4

air, but a don's aloof, quizzical, slightly self-satisfied eyes and serious smile. He thought well of himself, and knew that the world thought well of him. She couldn't be safer.

'Really? I shouldn't be taking you out of your way?'

'Not a yard, I assure you.'

'Then thanks very much, I'll be glad to accept.' And she let him take the duffle bag from her, but she held on to the guitar-case, and herself stowed it carefully on the rear seat of the car before she slid into the front passenger seat with an expert flick of long legs. 'My train was late. I only made up my mind to come at the last moment.'

'You're not actually taking part in this folk-music course, then?' he asked, casting a glance behind at her instrument as he started the engine.

The girl followed the glance with a thin, dark smile. 'Oh, that! I just happened to have it with me when I made up my mind to come. No, I'm not on the programme. Just one of the mob.'

'You came to study the form?' he suggested helpfully. He was surprised, all the same, for the guitar-case was old and much-carried, and her speaking voice promised a singing voice of quality.

The small smile tightened, burned grimly bright for an instant, and vanished. 'That's about it,' she agreed, her eyes fixed ahead. 'I came to study the form.'

'But you *are* a folk singer?'

'I'm a ballad singer,' she said, with the crisp and slightly irritable intonation of one frequently forced to insist upon the distinction.

His eyebrows rose. Rather dryly he said: 'I see!'

'I'm sorry,' she said, softening, 'I didn't mean to sound touchy, but it's a sore point with me. I've never claimed to be a folk singer. I'm not even sure I know exactly what a folk singer is, and I'm dead certain too many people use the term to mean whatever they want to persuade the world *they* are. About a ballad singer you can't be in much doubt, it's somebody who sings ballads. That's what I do, so that's what I call myself. How far is it to this Follymead place?'

'Nearly five miles. We'll have you there in a quarter of an hour.'

The streets of Comerbourne slid by them moistly in the April dusk. Neon-lit shop-fronts, all glass and chrome, gave place to the long, harmonious Georgian frontage of Crane Place, and that in turn to the two smoky lines of hedges streaming alongside like veils, just filmed with the green of new leafage, and the sinewy trunks of beeches, trepanned with metal reflectors. April had come in cold, angry and wet, trampling and tearing the heavy late snow with squalls of rain, and bringing the flood-water rolling down the Comer brown and turgid from the hills of Wales. But this evening had fallen quiet and still, with a soft green afterglow in the sky, and a hazy, glow-worm look about the first side-lights wavering along the road.

The girl gazed ahead steadily, her fine brows drawn together, her profile intent and still. She watched the budding hedges swoop by her, and the compact villages come and go, and made no comment. Her mind, somewhere well ahead, grappled already with the unknown realities of Follymead; but when it came it was none the less daunting.

A deep half-circle of grass swept inward on their left, the tall grey-stone wall receding with it. The drive swung in towards huge, lofty gate-posts that almost dwarfed a tiny hexagonal lodge. The wrought-iron gates stood wide open, and on either side, on top of the yard-thick posts, an iron gryphon supported a toppling coat of arms. Beyond, acres of park-land stretched away in artfully undulating levels that owed very little to nature.

'This is it?' asked the girl, staring out with astonished eyes at the monsters pole-squatting ten feet above the roof of the car.

'This is it.' He had already turned the car inward towards the open gates.

'Oh, just drop me here at the entrance. I can walk up to the house.'

'With your luggage? It's nearly a mile. In any case, this is where I'm going. I should have told you before,' he said, condescending rather complacently towards apology. 'My name's Arundale, Edward Arundale, I'm the warden of the college.'

'Oh?' She turned her head and gave him a full, penetrating look, probing with candid curiosity, and some distrust. 'I see! Then it was you who arranged this course?'

'Not exactly, no. My deputy's running this one. I've got some outside engagements that are going to take me away for most of the weekend. In any case, this isn't really my field. My wife's the enthusiast for folk music. And your lecturer is a don from our parent university, Roderick Penrose. No, I'm staying strictly in the background. Penrose forgot a case of recording tapes at the station, that's why I offered to run in and fetch them for him, otherwise I shouldn't have had the pleasure of offering you a lift. The guitar, you know. As soon as I saw it, I thought you must be headed for Follymead.'

'Lucky for me,' said the girl, 'that professors live up to their reputation for absent-mindedness.' She peered out unbelievingly at the fantasies of Follymead unrolling along the drive. The dusk softened their outlines and colours, but there was no missing them. In a clump of cypresses on top of a hill too artfully rounded to be natural, the pallor of a Greek temple gleamed, a hotch-potch of Doric, Ionic and Corinthian in flaking plaster. Distant on the other side of the drive the tamed park gave way to a towering wilderness of crags, with the mouth of a cave neatly built in at a high level, no doubt for the hermit without whom no Victorian poetic landscape would be complete. A coil of river showed in angry silver among the folds of greensward, an arched bridge where certainly no bridge had been necessary before the landscape gardeners got busy. Somewhere ahead, on a still higher viewpoint, the jagged outline of a ruined tower

7

posed self-consciously against a sky now darkening to olive-green.

'No pagoda?' said the girl disapprovingly; and suddenly there was the pagoda, prompt to its cue, peeping out of the trees behind the heron-pool. She laughed abruptly and gaily. 'Who in the world built this place? Beckford?'

'It was built by a highly-respected family named Cothercott.' The tone was a reproof, for all its forbearance, and all the chillier because she had surprised him by knowing about Beckford, and had got the period exactly right. Follymead was within ten years or so the same vintage as Fonthill Abbey and Strawberry Hill and all its neo-Gothic fellows; and she hadn't even seen the house yet. 'They had more money than was good for any family, and spent it on building their private world, as so many others were doing. And like most of their kind they dwindled away for want of heirs, and the last of them left Follymead to the county, about twenty years ago. With a very good endowment fund, luckily, or it would have been impossible to use it. As it is, by charging a fairly economic fee for board and tuition, we can contrive to keep out of the red. The place is considered a very fine example of its period,' he said forbiddingly, lest she should be in any doubt where he stood, 'and the grounds are justly famous.'

The girl was as capable of delighting in fantasy as anyone else, but she had not, until then, been disposed to take Follymead seriously. She took a sidelong look at the regular profile beside her, the austere cast of the lips, the smoothset, humourless eyes; and she saw that Edward Arundale took it very seriously indeed, perhaps not for its own sweet sake, perhaps because it was an appurtenance of himself, and sacred accordingly.

'So they turned it into a residential music college,' she said. 'I shouldn't have thought there'd be enough demand for that sort of thing.'

'There wouldn't be, locally, but from the beginning I've made it my policy to turn the place into a national asset. We draw on the whole country. We've got adequate space for conferences and festivals, as well as providing our own courses and recitals. It's taken a few years to establish us properly, but I think I can say we've achieved national recognition now. International, even.'

His voice had taken on the smoothness and richness of an occasion; she felt herself acting as audience to a lecture, and remembered the time-table:

5.00 p.m. to 5.30 p.m. Students assemble. Tea will be available on arrival.

5.30 p.m. Conducted tour of the house, optional.

6.45 p.m. Assemble for dinner. The warden, Dr. Edward Arundale, M.A., F.R.C.M., will welcome artists and students to Follymead.

She wondered if it was always the same address of welcome, suitably modulated, or if he ever made allowances for the sceptics, and admitted to the possibility that this kingdom he inhabited was a monstrosity. And yet, was it? She found herself almost tempted to enjoy a fantasy so uninhibited, as somebody had enjoyed creating it. Not reverently, like the warden, but exuberantly, with all the abounding energy and ingenuity of the eighteenth century, no holds barred. And who cared what a plethora of turrets might be jangling overhead, as long as the acoustics in the music rooms were right?

'It was particularly suitable to use it for music,' said Arundale, unbending a little. 'It so happens the Cothercotts were a musical family, and they left us a very fine collection of instruments with the house. We had to restore the organ, but the other early keyboard instruments are splendid.'

Clearly this *was* his field; he still sounded like a lecturer, and perhaps he always would, but at least there was the warm flush of enthusiasm in his voice now. But he didn't enlarge; she was merely one of the folk-singing clan, he could hardly expect her to be interested in the Cothercott virginals and the perfect little

9

table spinet by Holyoake. And in any case, the car was just rounding the final, planned curve of the long drive, and the house would be waiting to take the stranger's breath away, as it had been designed to do.

Here came the curve. The bushes shrank away on either side, the great, straight, levelled apron of lawn expanded before them, and the house, nicely elevated on its three tiers of terraces, soared into the dusk and impaled the sky with a dozen towers and turrets and steeples and vanes, tapering from steep gables above row upon row of mullioned windows silvered over with the faint afterglow, as calculated and stunning as some monstrous stage-set at curtain-rise. There were tall, glazed oriels, rounded rose-windows, tight, thin arrow-slits; there were battlements, and pediments and conical roofs, and galleries, and even gargoyles leaning darkly from the corners of the towers. It was so outrageous as to be almost beautiful, so phoney that it had its own kind of genuineness. For one thing, it hadn't happened by mistake, or through sheer over-enthusiasm. The effect it produced was the effect it had been made to produce, and no chance horror. And it had been built well, from a lovely light-grey stone, and with a certain assured symmetry. There had been a mind behind its creation, as well as money, and an individual, cool and sinister mind at that. The owner or the architect?

The girl sat silent, staring in fascination and disbelief tensed in resistance, as the car approached along the pale ribbon of tarmac between the planed acres of grass, and the pile of Folly-mead grew taller and darker and vaster with every yard.

'Impressive, isn't it?' said Arundale, aware that she hated being impressed by mere stone, mortar and glass; he could feel how furiously she was bracing herself against it. 'Walpole stayed here several times. He described it as a house where drama was a permanent upper servant, eccentricity a member of the family, and tragedy an occasional guest.'

'And comedy?' said the girl unexpectedly. 'They named it

Follymead, not Nightmare Abbey. Maybe it took them by surprise, too, when they saw it finished.'

He drew the car round to the foot of the sweep of stone steps that led to the terrace. Lights winked on, one by one, along the great glazed gallery on the first floor, running the whole length of the house-front. Through the windows they saw a gaggle of people passing slowly, peering round them with stretched necks; earnest elderly ladies, bearded, shaggy young men with pipes, ascetic students in glasses, broad-barrelled country gentlemen with time on their hands and a mild musical curiosity, eager girls peering through their curtains of limp long hair.

'They're just taking parties round on a tour of the house,' said Arundale, opening the door for his passenger. 'Leave your luggage, I'll bring it in when I've run the car round to the yard. You just trot in and join them. Formalities later.'

She reached in again for her guitar, all the same, and straightened up to look at the lighted windows above them. The party passing had halted for a moment, all their faces turned up to some painting hung very high on the inner wall. Only their guide faced the windows as she went through her recital; a very young girl, surely no more than fifteen or sixteen, slight and pale, with wings of mouse-brown hair framing a serious and secretive face, a face full of doubts and hesitations and flashes of uneasy animation, as early-April as the weather outside, and her own difficult season. Something in the fine, irresolute features, the set of the eyes and carriage of the head, made the newcomer turn and look again at Arundale; and she was not mistaken, the likeness was there, allowing for the years and the toughening and the entrenchment, though maybe he'd never possessed the possibilities of passion which the girl in the gallery certainly had, and didn't know yet what to do with.

'That must be your daughter, surely?'

His face stiffened very slightly, though he gazed back at her with polite composure. 'My niece. Unfortunately my wife . . . We have no children.' He snapped off the sentence briskly, like a thread at the end of a seam. A sore subject, she was sorry she'd embarked on it, however innocently. She was just wondering how to ride the punch, and whether his voice was always so constrained when he spoke of his wife, when he turned his head to look along the necklace of lighted windows, as willing to evade complications as she, and said in a very different tone: 'Ah, there is my wife now, with the next party.'

She had thought him without passion, but evidently he had one. This was quite another voice, warm and proud and soft, heavy with unguarded affection. No, his wife's childlessness was only a shared sorrow, not at all a count against her, or a shadow between them. The girl looked up, following his devoted, secret smile, and saw a woman caught for a moment under the full brilliance of one of the chandeliers. She was slender and fair and elegant in a plain dark dress, with pale hair piled on her head, and a swimming, wavering walk that seemed to balance the silvery coils like a conscious burden. Her eyes were dark and large, her colouring richly fair, her face bright and animated almost to the point of discomfort. She talked and gestured and passed, and the medley of students and guests passed after her, consolingly ordinary, unhaunted and content.

The girl stood fixed, watching her go without a smile, and for some moments without a word. When the pageant had passed she stirred, and moistened her lips.

'She's beautiful,' she said at last, with deliberation.

This time she had said the right thing. She felt the evening filled with the glow of his pleasure.

'Some excellent judges have thought so,' he admitted, a little pompously, more than a little proprietorially.

'I have a feeling that I've seen her somewhere before,' said the girl in a cool, distant voice.

'It's quite possible. You're a ballad singer. Audrey has some close friends in folk music circles.'

The girl with the guitar-case suppressed a faint and private smile. 'Yes . . . yes, I'm sure she has,' she said gently, and turned from him and ran up the stone steps towards the great doorway.

Miss Theodosia Barber, Tossa to her friends, was an implacable hater of all humbug, and a merciless judge of all those who seemed to her tainted with its unmistakable sweet, self-conscious odour. At rising nineteen she could afford to be, her own pro-ceedings being marked by a total rejection of falsity. She had weighed up the celebrated Dickie Meurice, disc-jockey, compère and television personality extraordinary, before they had even reached the armoury and his third questionable joke. Give him an audience of twenty or so, even if they were by rights young Felicity Cope's audience, and he'd have filched them from under her nose within minutes, and be on-stage. Doubtful, rather, if he was ever off.

'Licensed clown,' said Tossa fastidiously into Dominic Felse's ear, as they followed the adoring giggles of the fans into the long gallery. 'All *he* ever goes *anywhere* for is to advertise the product. I bet he cracks wise in his sleep, and has a built-in gadget to record the level of applause. What's more, he won't stop at much in the cause. Watch out, anybody in the business here who has a reputation to lose.'

'Could be several people in danger, then,' said Dominic criti-cally, eyeing the group that surged amorphously before them, and seeing celebrities enough. And this was only one party of three perambulating the house on this conducted tour. Over by the window shone the cropped red heads of the Rossignol brothers; less vulnerable, perhaps, by virtue of being French, identical twins, and tough as rubber, not to say capable of con-siderable mischief themselves if they felt like it, but all the same this folk music business was an international free-for-all, these days, and no one could count himself immune. The new young American, Peter Crewe, stood close to his guide, earnestly follow-ing everything she had to say, and turning his bright, weathered face faithfully from portrait to portrait, staring so solemnly that if there was anything to be discovered about the Cothercotts from those calculated approximations, he would surely discover it. Malice might well bounce off such innocence as his, but it might also take a strip of hide with it at every rebound. There was Celia Whitwood, the harp girl – the second witticism this evening had been at her expense, and she hadn't relished it. And yet this licensed clown, as Tossa called him, could draw the fans after him with a crook of his finger, and have them hanging on his lips ready to laugh before he spoke. An extraordinary force is television for building or destroying public figures, without benefit of talent, desert or quality.

'I wonder who was the genius who thought we needed a compère for this weekend?' said Tossa, sighing.

'Somebody shrewd enough to know how to fill the house,' said Dominic simply. 'He fetched the fans in, didn't he?'

And he had, there was no doubt of that; but not only he, as Tossa promptly pointed out.

'You think all those kids fawning round Lucien Galt came for the music?'

'*I* wouldn't know, would I?' responded Dominic crisply. 'Did *you*?' The slight edge to his voice, and the faint knife-prick of disquiet that went with it, startled him. He was accustomed to immensely secure relationships in which jealousy would have been an irrelevant absurdity, and the indignities a lover can inflict on himself came as a surprise to him, and an affront. As for Tossa, she wasn't yet used to the idea that someone could be in love with her, and she wasn't alert to possible pitfalls; she missed the smarting note and took the question at its face value.

'Idiot!' she said cheerfully. 'Are you lumping me in with that lot? Not that I can't see their point,' she added honestly, studying the lofty male head islanded among hunting girls. 'At least he looks and sounds like a real person. Take his microphone away, and he's still *there*.'

Lucien Galt certainly could not easily be ignored, even thus hemmed in at close quarters by his unkempt admirers. The black

14

head tossed impatiently, the lean, relaxed shoulders twitched, like a stallion shaking off gadflies, and for a moment his face was turned towards the two who discussed him. Dark as a gypsy, with heavy brows and arrogant eyes, built like a dancer, light-framed and quick in movement, intolerant of too close approach, and scornful of adulation as of any other stupidity, he carried his nature in his looks, and took no trouble to moderate its impact. He slid from between the ranks of his fans and put the width of an inlaid table between himself and them, leaning with folded arms and braced shoulders against the damask-panelled wall. He had put Felicity off her stride by the abrupt movement; he caught her eye, and apologised with a brilliant, brief smile that transformed his saturnine face for an instant. And that was the only move he had made to charm, and no more to him than a brusque gesture of politeness.

He was twenty-three years old, and already an artist on a world scale. In what other field can you climb the peak so fast? Or so suddenly slither all the way down it again and vanish? Or, once vanished, be so completely forgotten?

'You couldn't say he went out of his way to please, could you?' whispered Tossa. 'He as good as tells them they're a bore and a nuisance, and they lap it up and come back for more. And just look at the other one, working at it every minute, ladling out the honey like mad. He must just *hate* Lucien.'

Considering she had never set eyes on either of the pair before, it was a fairly penetrating observation; but all Dominic noticed at the time was the easy way the name Lucien came to her tongue. The popular music world deals in Christian names, of course, and there's no particular significance in it; still, he noted it, and was annoyed with himself for the resulting smart. Ever since he'd brought his girl home from Oxford with him for the Easter vacation, to meet his parents for the first time, he'd been discovering in himself nervous sensitivities he'd never suspected before, like broken nails forever ready to snag in the fine threads of this most difficult of all relationships. It wasn't doing his vanity any good.

'Theirs is a cut-throat world,' he said sententiously. 'Still, he looks as if he can stand it.'

'Oh, I should think he's pretty tough,' she agreed serenely.

'With a name like that,' said Dominic, involuntarily rubbing the sting, 'he'd have to be.' Who knew better than he did the hard training to be derived in early schooldays from having an unusual and provocative name? As if being a policeman's son wasn't enough in itself to keep a boy on his toes!

'From what I read somewhere, he was brought up in an orphanage, right from a baby. His parents were killed in the buzz-bomb raids on London at the end of the last war. They say he thinks the world of his home, though, and goes back there regularly. Not at all a deprived child type. And yet you never know,' said Tossa thoughtfully, 'maybe that does account for the way they say he is.'

'*I* haven't been reading him up,' said Dominic patiently. 'How *do* they say he is?'

'Oh, like he looks. You-be-damned! Terribly independent, won't compromise, won't pretend, a real stormy petrel. The way I heard it, his agent and the recording people, and all the ones who have to work with him took to calling him Lucifer instead of Lucien.'

Lucifer leaned with folded arms against the wine-coloured damask panelling of the long gallery, under the carved black ceiling and the Venetian chandeliers. Rankly dramatised Cothercott portraits hung cloaked and hooded about him, the expensive, perilous and eclectic accumulations of generations of Cothercott collectors were elegantly displayed along the walls at his back, their often lovely and sometimes repulsive furniture fended off teenage girls from too close contact with him. The dark, rich, Strawberry Hill colours, the heavy gilding, the assured and lavish use of black, all framed him like one of the family pictures. He

16

looked at home here, and in his element, a little sinister, a little dangerous, treacherously winning, like the house itself.

'Now you can't,' Dickie Meurice was saying persuasively, his incandescent smile trained at full-tooth-power on the warden's niece, 'you really *can't* ask us to believe that all these characters were models of industry and virtue. Just take a look at 'em!' He waved a hand towards the family portraits deployed along the wall, and indeed half of them did look like romantic poets and half like conspirators. Even the ladies appeared somewhat overdressed in conscious merit, as though they had something to hide. 'Every one of 'em straight out of the wanted file. There ought to be profiles alongside. Don't tell me they got the fortune that built this pile out of honest trade.'

'Ah, but I think that's just what they did,' said Felicity with animation, 'and just what they didn't want you to believe about them. They much preferred to put up on their walls something that looked like degenerate aristocrats who'd never done a day's work in their lives.'

She had abandoned her usual recital already, derailed by Meurice's facetious comments, and begun to indulge her own suppressed feelings about this formidable place; but it wasn't at Meurice she was looking, and it wasn't for him she was lighting up like a pale, flickering candle, her serious grey eyes warming into brilliance. She gazed wide-eyed at Lucifer, leaning there against the wall with his dark brightness dulling the painted faces on either side of his head, and her small, grave face reflected his slight, sardonic smile like a mirror. She was the teenage fan with a temporary and precarious advantage, and she was using it for all she was worth, bent on catching and holding his attention now or never, and reckless as to how pathetically she showed off in the attempt. She had begun this tour, as on all the other similar occasions, very poised, very grown-up, a world-weary sophisticate aged fifteen and a half, but the first time he had looked at her the shell had begun to melt, and let in upon her all the hurts and all the promises of the untasted world of maturity, and from the time that he had smiled at her she had thrown away everything else and bent herself to make an impression. Once for all, and now or never. She hated being fifteen, but she wouldn't always be fifteen. She looked rather more, she hoped, even now. And he was only twenty-three himself. She knew all about him, he'd been written up lavishly since he became famous, and she hadn't missed a single article about him if she could help it.

'Take this one – William Henry Cothercott the third. He looks like Byron turned bandit, I know, but he hadn't a line of poetry or an act of violence in him. He made a pile out of the early railway boom, and he had some ships that weren't too particular whether they carried slaves or not, when other cargoes didn't offer, but that's the worst we know about him. They even started collecting more curious things than harpsichords, just to give the impression they were a lot of romantic damned souls. There are some very naughty books you won't get shown, but I doubt if they ever really read them. And all these rapiers and knives and things, here along the wall – those are part of the effect, too, just theatrical props. That fan – you wouldn't know it had a dagger in it, would you? And this silver-headed walking-cane – look! The head pulls out, like this . . .' She showed them, in one rapid, guilty gesture, six inches of the slender blade that was hidden inside the ebony sheath, and slid it hurriedly back again. 'Straight out of "The Romantic Agony",' she said, purely for Lucien's benefit, to show him how well-read she was, and how adult. 'Only it doesn't mean a thing, they were still nothing but stolid merchants. Not a mohawk among the lot of 'em. They never stuck so much as a pig.'

'And yet somebody put the devil in this house,' said Lucien with detached certainty.

'Maybe somebody here among us,' suggested Dickie Meurice, turning the famous smile on him, 'brought that aura in with him.'

Lucien turned his head and looked him over again at leisure, without any apparent reaction. He knew who he was, of course. Who didn't? He had even worked with him on two occasions. It couldn't be said that he had ever really noticed him until now, and even now he wasn't particularly interested. In such a narrow gallery, however, you can't help noticing someone who is so full of quicksilver movement without meaning, and makes so much noise saying nothing. Lucien, when not singing, was a dauntingly silent person, and spoke only to the point.

'I doubt it,' he said indifferently. 'This is built-in. More likely to have been the architect. What was he like? Who *was* he? Do they know?'

'His name was Falchion. Nobody knows much about him, there are only two other houses known to be his work. We think he must have died young. There's a story,' said Felicity, recklessly improvising, and looking even more passionately truthful and candid than usual, 'that he was in love with one of the Cothercott daughters. *That* one . . .' She pointed out, with deceptive conviction, the best-looking of the collection, confident that no one would notice that she belonged to a later generation. 'She died about the time the house was finished, and he was broken-hearted. They used to meet in this gallery while he was working on the features in the grounds, and she's supposed to haunt here.'

She had Lucien's attention, and she didn't care whether he knew she was lying or whether he believed her. Maybe it would be even more interesting to be seen to be lying. In many ways this whole set-up was a lie, even though Uncle Edward was a genuine scholar and a genuine musician, devoted and content with his sphere. In a sense, only what was utterly and joyously false had any right to exist in this setting, phantasms were the only appropriate realities in this shameless fantasy.

'She comes in daylight, not at night,' said Felicity, loosing the rein of her imagination, but holding fast to Lucien Galt's black and moody stare. 'She comes to meet him, and she doesn't know she's dead, and she can't understand why he never comes. She's

19

still in love with him, but she's angry, too, and she's only waiting to meet him again and take it out of him for leaving her deserted so long . . .'

'She's making it up as she goes along,' said Tossa very softly in Dominic's ear. 'What a gorgeous little liar!'

'It's this place,' Dominic whispered back. 'It would get anybody.'

'Has anyone actually seen her?' asked Peter Crewe, round-eyed.

'Oh, yes occasionally, but it only happens to people in love.' Felicity turned, and began to pace slowly and delicately towards the great oak door at the end of the gallery; and they all caught the infection and walked solemnly after her, their steps soundless in the deep carpet. 'You may be walking along here some day, just like this, going to put fresh flowers in that stone vase there on the pedestal. Not thinking about anything like ghosts. With the sun shining in, even, though it could be just at dusk, like this. And you're just approaching this door when it suddenly opens, and there she is, confronting you . . .'

And suddenly the oak door opened, flung wide by a hand not accustomed to doing things by halves, and there she was confronting them indeed, with head up and eyes challenging, a tall, brown, imperious girl with a great plait of dark hair coiled like an attendant serpent over one shoulder, and a guitar-case in her hand.

Felicity rocked back on her heels, startled into a sharp and childish giggle of embarrassment. The procession at her back halted as abruptly, with a succession of soft, clumsy collisions, like a Bank Holiday queue of ambling cars suddenly forced to brake sharply. It would all have been a little ridiculous, but for the composure with which the newcomer marched into the gallery and looked them over, undisturbed and unimpressed. Her glance passed over the whole group in one sweep, riding over their heads and rejecting all but the tallest. She found

Lucien, alert, dark and still against the wall. There she fixed, and looked no farther.

Tossa, watching from the fringe of the group, literally saw the flash and felt the shock as their eyes locked, and her fingers reached for Dominic's sleeve. The tension between those two set everyone quivering, even those who were too insensitive to understand why. And yet they could hardly have maintained a more stony assurance, calmer faces or stiller bodies. Only for the briefest instant had the daggers shown in two pairs of eyes now veiled, and cool. The girl's face wore a newcomer's polite, perfunctory smile, she was looking clean through Lucien and failing to see him, she had excised him from her field of vision. But the pressure of Tossa's fingers, alert and excited, directed attention rather to Lucien himself. So far from crossing the stranger out of his notice, he was staring at her frankly and directly, trying to see deep into her and read some significance into what he saw; but if he was getting much information out of that closed and aloof face, thought Tossa, he must be clairvoyant. The glint in his eyes might have been alarm, or animosity or, curiously, elation. He might, for that matter, be the kind of person who would find a certain elation in the promise of a stand-up fight.

The instant of surprise and silence was gone almost before they had recorded it. The girl with the guitar turned to Felicity, and was opening her lips to speak when the high, self-confident voice of Dickie Meurice gave tongue smoothly and joyously:

'Well, well, well! Just look who's here!' And he danced forward with arms outspread, took the girl's hands in his, guitar and all, and pumped and pressed them enthusiastically. Her dark brows rose slightly, but she tolerated the liberty without protest.

'Hullo, Dickie, I didn't know you were going to be here.'

'I didn't know *you* were. For goodness sake, why didn't they have your name on the prospectus?'

'They didn't know I was coming, and I'm not here to perform. I came as a student, like anybody else.'

21

'Come off it!' said Meurice, laughing, and tapped the guitar-case. 'You think you're the sort of girl who can take her harp to a party without anybody asking her to play? Not while I'm around!' He laid an arm familiarly about her shoulders, and turned her to face the company. 'Don't you know who we've got here? Just about the greatest ballad singer this side of the Atlantic, that's who. Ladies and gentlemen, I'm proud to present to you none other than the great Liri Palmer.'

Chapter 2

Edward Arundale made his speech of welcome in the small drawing-room before dinner, against the sombre splendour of black, white and heavy gilt décor that might have been specially designed to render him more impressive. He expressed his pleasure at having so intelligent and enthusiastic a company beneath the roof of his college, outlined the origin and history of the Follymead foundation, wished them a very pleasant and productive weekend, and deeply regretted that he himself wouldn't be able to enjoy the whole of it with them, since tomorrow afternoon he had to leave to fulfil two speaking engagements in Birmingham, and would not be back until Sunday evening. After this evening, therefore, he would be handing over direction of the course to his deputy, Henry Marshall – Mr. Marshall, who was young, anxious and only too well aware of being on trial, smiled nervously – and Professor Roderick Penrose, whose name and reputation were certainly known to everyone interested in folk music. Mr. Arundale wouldn't claim that folk music was the professor's subject; he would prefer to describe it as his passion and if he held some unusual and controversial opinions on it, the discussion during the weekend would be all the livelier.

Professor Penrose, who was seventy-five, bursting with energy, and just beginning to take full advantage of the privileges of age, notably its irresponsibility and licence, grinned happily, fluffed up his clown's-tufts of grey hair with eager fingers, and licked his lips in anticipation. He couldn't wait to get his carnivorous teeth into all the sacred cows of the cult.

Then they trooped in to dinner in the neo-Gothic vaulted hall, still hung with Cothercott tapestries and lit by great torches (electric now) jutting from the gold and scarlet walls. Audrey Arundale, dazzlingly fair in her plain black dress, sat beside her husband, looked beautiful, kept a careful watch on the conversation, and said and did all the right things at all the right moments. That is what the wives of the Edward Arundales are for, though they may also, incidentally, be loved helplessly and utterly, as Audrey was loved.

She was fifteen years his junior, and looked even younger. He had never grown tired of looking at her, never lost the power to feel again the knife-thrust of astonishment, anguish and delight that possession of her beauty gave him. He still hated to leave her even for a day.

'I wish you were coming with me,' he said impulsively in her ear. The young people were getting into their stride, you could gauge the potential success of a course by the crescendo of noise at their first meal together. He smiled at her quickly and reassuringly. 'No, I know you can't, of course. I wouldn't take you away from this, I know how much you're going to enjoy it.'

'It's just that I really began it,' she said apologetically. Her voice had something of the quality of her eyes, hesitant and faintly anxious, as though even after twenty years of backing him up loyally, first as the revered head of Bannerets and now here, she was still in doubt of her own powers, and still constantly braced to please. 'I've really got to see it through, after getting Professor Penrose and all those others into it, haven't I?'

'Of course, my dear, I know. But I shall miss you. Never mind,' he said, letting his hand rest for a moment on hers, 'let's enjoy this first concert together, anyhow. It looks as if you're going to have a success on your hands, by all the signs.'

The noise by then was almost deafening but there were those who observed that Lucien Galt wasn't contributing much to it, and neither was Liri Palmer.

'Tomorrow,' said Professor Penrose, rubbing his hands, 'will be time enough to begin haggling about all the usual questions, such as definition and standards, what's permissible and what isn't, who has it right and who has it wrong. Tonight we're going to enjoy ourselves. We have here with us a number of recognised artists in the field, whose judgement of their material *ought* to command respect. Let's ask them, not to tell us, but to show us. We'll get them to sing their favourites, songs they take as beyond question or reproach. And then we'll examine the results together, and see what we find.'

'Now you got me scared,' said Peter Crewe plaintively, and got a mild laugh from under Dickie Meurice's nose; but his time was coming.

'Mr. Crewe, you are probably the safest person around here. We shall see! Don't let me cast any shadows. I'm retiring into the audience as of now.' The professor, a born chameleon, was taking on colouring from his American artist without even realising it. 'Here and now I hand over this session to an expert at putting people through hoops. Mr. Meurice, take over.'

Mr. Meurice rose like a trout to a fly, and took over gleefully. The professor retired to a quiet corner beside the warden and his wife, and sat on the small of his back, legs crossed, looking at his specimens between his skidding glasses and his shaggy brows, and grinning wolfishly.

'There's really no need of any introductions at all tonight,' said Dicke Meurice, beaming. 'If you people down there didn't know all about all these people up here, you wouldn't be here at all. All they need me for is to name them in order, and you could tell me everything I could tell you about them. Maybe more! I dare say there's something even I could learn, this weekend. So let's not waste time listening to me, but get on to the music. Ladies first! Celia, will you lead the way? You all know Celia Whitwood, the girl with the harp. It makes a change from guitars, doesn't it?'

It got a ripple of delight from his fans, but it was a very gentle joke for Dickie Meurice. 'I thought he'd be cruder,' Tossa confided in a whisper.

'He probably will,' returned Dominic as softly, 'before he's done. Just feeling his way. He's no fool. This needs a different approach from a disc-jockey session.'

Celia Whitwood settled her instrument comfortably, and sang 'Two Fond Hearts' and 'By the Sea-Shore', both in Welsh, translating the words for those who did not know them. She had a small, shy voice, and at first was uncertain of the acoustics in the great yellow drawing-room, but by the end of the first song she had the feel of the space about her, and was using it confidently. She followed with 'The Jute-Mill Song', and made her harp do the mill noises for her. Peter Crewe sang 'Times are Getting Hard', 'I'm Going Away' and 'The Streets of Laredo'; Andrew Callum contributed two Tyne-side colliery songs and 'The Bonny Earl of Moray' from across the border. And Dickie Meurice continued bland, bright and considerate, as though his judgement, too, was on trial.

'All playing safe,' remarked Tossa disapprovingly.

The Rossignol twins began with a ballad-like thriller, grim and dramatic, 'Le Roi a fait battre tambour'. They were twenty, flame-headed, of rather girlish prettiness but more than male toughness and impudence, and decidedly disturbing to watch, for one of them was left-handed, and one right, and they amused themselves by trading on this mirror-image appearance to such an extent that it had now become second nature. They followed with a lullaby in a dialect so thick it was plain they felt sure not even Professor Penrose would understand a word of it. 'Quarrel with that!' said their innocent smiles. Then they consulted each other by means of two flicks of the eyebrows, cast a wicked glance at the professor, and broke into the honeyed, courtly melody of the fifteen-century 'L'Amour de Moi'. They sang it like angels, with melting harmonies as gracious as the flowers they sang about. The professor nodded his ancient head and continued to smile.

'Well, they trailed their coats, anyhow,' said Dominic.

Lucien Galt began with 'Helen of Kirkconnell'. There was no doubt from the opening that here was an artist of stature, first because nature had given him a voice of great beauty, a warm, flexible baritone that would have been attractive even without art, and second, because he had the rare gift of total absorption in what he did, so that he lost them utterly while the song lasted. He *was* the bereaved lover hunting Helen's murderer along the water-side, and hacking him in pieces for her sake. The voice that had been all honey and grief over her body could find gravel and hate when it needed them. He was all the more compelling because everything he did was understated, but the passion vibrated behind the quietness with an intensity that had them holding their breath. He seemed surprised when they applauded him; probably for the duration of that experience he had forgotten they were there.

Next he sang 'The Croppy Boy', a venturesome choice for somebody without a drop of Irish blood; nor did he attempt to put on the Irish. He sang it like an Englishman possessed by the guilt of England past, and with an unexpected simplicity that made the child-soldier's last innocent confession almost unendurably touching:

> ' "I've cursed three times since last Easter Day,
>   At Mass-time once I went to play,
>   I passed through the churchyard one day in haste
>   And forgot to pray for my mother's rest".'

By the time he reached:

27

' "Good people who dwell in peace and joy,
    Breathe a prayer and a tear for the Croppy boy",'

he had several of the teenage girls in tears. That startled him,
too, but he was disarmed. It was the first time Tossa and Dominic
had seen him look kindly at his fans.

'And what's the third one to be?' asked Meurice amiably.

Lucien thought for a moment, his lip caught between his
teeth, his fingers muting the strings of his guitar. He looked
across the rows and rows of expectant students, and Dominic,
turning his head to follow that glance, caught a glimpse of Liri
Palmer's chiselled profile and great coil of brown hair. She sat
at the back of the assembly, attentive and still. There was no
reading anything into her face.

Lucien began to sing. They all knew the air as 'Believe me if
all those endearing young charms', but that was not what he was
singing.

' "My lodging is on the cold, cold ground,
    And hard, very hard is my fare,
    But what doth me the more confound
    Is the coldness of my dear.
    Yet still I cry, O turn, love,
    I prithee, love, turn to me,
    For thou art the only one, love,
    That art adored by me.
    I'll twine thee a garland of straw, love,
    I'll marry thee with a rush ring,
    My frozen hopes will thaw, love,
    And merrily we will sing.
    Then turn to me, my own love,
    I prithee, love, turn to me,
    For thou art the only one, love,
    That art adored by me".'

'That ought to fetch her,' whispered Tossa, shaken, 'if anything can.'

Dominic was astonished. He hadn't noticed this incalculable girl of his following any significant glances, and yet it seemed she knew very well what was going on. He wished he did. There was certainly something, and there was a tension in the air that threatened more; yet nobody else seemed to have noticed anything. Maybe all the girls took that declaration to themselves, and applauded it accordingly; and it was just possible – wasn't it? – that that applied to Tossa, too.

'Now hold your horses a minute,' beamed Dickie Meurice, fanning down the applause. 'We haven't finished yet. Oh, yes, I know that's all we promised you, but we've still got a card up our sleeve, you'll find. Some of you know it already, but to most of you it'll be great news. Do you know who's been modest enough to come along to this course as a student? She's right there among you at this moment, maybe some of you talked to her at dinner and never realised. Liri . . . Liri Palmer! It's no use trying to hide back there. I know where you are.' She hadn't moved, not even a muscle of her disdainful face. She didn't want to be haled out of her anonymity, but she certainly wasn't hiding even from the crack of doom.

'Yes, folks, that's the whole secret. Liri Palmer is here among us. There she sits! Now you give her a big hand, and maybe she'll surrender.'

He was growing by the minute, expanding to fill the twenty-one inch screen that wasn't there, to dominate the cameras, the emotions and the events of this evening. This was what he'd been waiting for.

'Come along, Liri, don't cheat us. You can't blame us for wanting you. Come up here where you belong, and let us hear from you.'

Every head had turned by this time, even the slowest of them had located her, even those who knew nothing about her had identified her by the glutinous stares of the others. Someone began to applaud, and all the rest took it up like a rising wave.

'Come on, Liri, we're all waiting just for you.'

She rose from her chair, but only to gain a hearing. 'I came to listen, you must excuse me. And I haven't got my guitar down here.'

'Lucien will lend you his guitar, I'm sure. Come on, you can't disappoint everyone. Lucien, don't just sit there, help me out. If *you* ask her, I'm sure she'll come.'

Lucien Galt was seen for once out of countenance, and that in itself was astonishing. He sat shaken and mute, staring across the array of hopeful faces to where Liri stood braced and annoyed, her brows drawn down in a formidable scowl. It was Lucien who flushed and stammered.

'Yes, Liri, please do. You'd be giving everyone so much pleasure.'

There could have been no milder invitation, but what happened next was more like the formal acceptance of a challenge.

'Very well,' said Liri abruptly, 'since *you* ask me.' And she walked fiercely up the gangway between the goggling fans, and stepped up on to the concert dais in the great window-embrasure, where the artists sat. She took the offered guitar, sat down on the forward edge of Dickie Meurice's table, and stroked the strings, frowning. There was a moment of absolute silence, while she seemed to forget they existed, and only to be gathering herself for a private outburst. Then the whole drawing-room shook to the shuddering chords she fetched out of Lucien's instrument, and she lifted her head and poised her silver-pure entry with piercing accuracy, like a knife in the heart:

'Black, black, black, is the colour of my true-love's *heart*!
His tongue is like a poisoned dart,
The coldest eyes and the lewdest hands . . .
I hate the ground whereon he stands!

30

Black is the Colour of My True Love's Heart

'I hate my love, yet well he knows,
I love the ground whereon he goes,
And if my love no more I see
No one shall have his company!

'Black, black, black, is the colour of my true-love's *heart* . . .'

An achingly sweet voice, so rending in its sweetness as to corrode like an acid when she used it like this, as if all the frightening possibilities of her nature, for good or evil, could be molten in the furnace of her feeling, and pour out in that fine-spun thread of sound to purify or poison. She sang with such superb assurance that they all accepted it as the only rightness, only realising afterwards how she had changed words to her own purposes, and torn the heart out of the song to leave it the antithesis of what it was meant to be. As if she turned the coin of love to show hate engraven in an almost identical design.

The silence was unnerving, but it did not unnerve her. She stood up, and the applause began, noisily and violently, with almost guilty fervour, to cover the pause which should not have been there. She laid down the guitar on the table.

'It doesn't sing properly for me. I'll use my own tomorrow, if you don't mind.' There was an empty chair behind the semicircle of artists; she slid by them and took it, abdicating from public notice before they had stopped approving her, and giving them no acknowledgement.

The incident was over before half of those present fully grasped that there had been an incident. But with the end of the applause the numbness wore off, and the shock reached them all.

In the front row old Miss Southern, as innocent at seventy as she had been at seventeen, leaned anxiously to her neighbour. She had come to this course in the hope of hearing again 'Early one morning', 'The Oak and the Ash', 'Barbara Allen', and all the songs she had been taught at school – sometimes in bowdlerised versions! – and nobody could put anything over on her where the canon was concerned.

'But she got it wrong,' she whispered. 'It's *hair*. "Black is the colour of my true-love's *hair*." Do you think we ought to tell her?'

'*No!*' hissed her neighbour, appalled. 'For heavens' sake!'

'But perhaps she got it from one of these degraded variants, you know. I learned it at school. It's "*hair*", not "*heart*". Shouldn't we . . .?'

Half the front row had heard this last agitated utterance. Professor Penrose came up off the small of his back with the agility of an ageing monkey, but without any appearance of haste or concern, and demonstrated his right to be in charge. His old voice had all the power and command it needed, and he, at seventy-five, was not innocent at all.

'Well, I'll admit I did issue a sort of challenge,' he said, scowling amiably round the half-circle of tense and quiet singers, 'to our young friends here, and they certainly took it up. We'll go into details tomorrow morning. All I'll say now is that we've just had a very ingenious demonstration of one of the essentials of folk song, and that is its ability to change and renew itself. Folk music is organic. It adapts itself to answer the needs of expression of those whose natural music it is. Once it becomes static it has begun to die. One of its chief functions is to be the voice of the otherwise inarticulate, and don't you forget it. As for you,' he said severely, wagging a finger at the Rossignol twins, who gazed back at him with benign smiles, 'I'll deal with you tomorrow. Toss a sophisticated little court-pastoral melody at me, would you, and hope for me to fall over my own feet telling you it isn't a folk song! Of course it's a folk song! The people took what they wanted where they found it, as well as creating it for themselves, but don't doubt it became truly theirs. From the court, was it? So was the *carmognole*! So was the *Ça ira*! Go collecting in the more rural parts of Bohemia, and you'll find themes of Mozart sung to folk poems, and if you go back far enough you'll find they were genuine folk songs almost before Mozart was dead, and those who heard them carried from the distant towns and took them for their own use never knew or cared what seed they were cultivating. And don't think you can faze an old hand like me by bouncing off into Auvergnat *patois*, either. I knew that lullaby before you were born.

'All right, let's break off there for tonight, and think over what we've heard. Tomorrow I hope you won't be afraid to disagree with me, there's room here for a lot of different opinions. If you think "My lodging is on the cold ground" can't be a valid folk song because the words are by John Gay, and have the ring of the theatre rather than the village, you stand up for your views. We probably shan't come to any firm conclusions, but we might uncover some very interesting ideas. As well as hearing some very fine singing and playing, I may say, if they live up to tonight. And now let's all adjourn to the small drawing-room for coffee.'

And they went, swarming out of the great room and along the corridor, so bemused by his persuasive tongue that they were almost convinced nothing fiery and violent had ever passed between those two people now silently following. Just a clever bit of impromptu theatre, to show that folk music was alive and adaptable to a human situation today, no less than two hundred years ago. All the same, there was something still quivering in the air, electric and disquieting; something that moved the left-handed Rossignol twin to murmur to the right-handed Rossignol twin, as they climbed the staircase:

'Do you know, *mon vieux*, I think perhaps this weekend is going to be not so boring, after all.'

She hadn't reckoned fully with his ruthless ability to rid himself of unwanted company, and had supposed that if she hung back until all was quiet he would be swept into the small drawing-room and the coffee conversation by the crowd of eager fans that swarmed about him, enthusing, flattering and angling for position. But when she came to the turn of the stairs, alone, treading on the fringes of the distant clamour, he reached out from the folds of the velvet curtains and caught her by the arm, pulling her to a standstill face to face with him.

'Liri, I want to talk to you.'

His voice was taut and very low, his face flushed and dark and convulsed with pride. She tried to wrest her arm out of his grasp, and instinctively gave up the attempt, knowing she could not do it by force and he would not let her go.

'*I* don't want to talk to *you*. Let go my arm.'

'Liri, don't be like this, I tell you I've *got* to talk to you . . .'

'You did talk to me,' she said through her teeth, 'just now. You talked and I answered, and I've said all I've got to say to you. Now get away from me.'

'I don't believe it! If that's all you've got to say to me, why did you come here at all?'

'Why shouldn't I?' she demanded fiercely. 'I came as a student, like anybody else . . .'

'That's a lie,' he said bluntly. 'You came because you knew I should be here, you must have, you couldn't have known the course was on at all without knowing I was part of it. You followed me here. Why, if you've got nothing to say to me now you're here?'

'You!' she said, suddenly rigid with quiet fury. 'You think the world goes round you. You think you can play what tricks you like, and no one has the right to kick. You wouldn't know what I have against you, would you? Oh, no! Listen just once more, and then I never want to see you or hear your voice again. I'm finished with you! I don't know you, I don't want to know you, you mean nothing to me, and you never will mean anything again. Now take your hands off me.'

'The devil I will, till you listen to *me* . . .'

Lucifer blazed, and the answering fires burned up in Liri's eyes. She would have liked to swing her free palm and hit him resoundingly in the face, but in the quietness where they were, and sharp above the still ferocity of their voices, it would have brought the curious running as surely as a pistol-shot. There were other ways. She stooped her head suddenly, and closed her teeth in his wrist.

He never made a sound, but his startled muscles jerked, and in the instant of surprise when his grip relaxed she tore herself free, eluding the recovering lunge he made after her, and slipped away from him up the staircase.

By one of the coffee-tables in the small drawing-room they were just getting used to applying the term to an apartment about as large as a tithe-barn – Dickie Meurice had gathered his court about him, and was exerting himself to be at once king and court-jester. He, at least, was having a successful evening. Things were shaping up very nicely. He didn't miss Liri's entry, or fail to hug himself with satisfaction at sight of her high colour and burning eyes; but he let her alone. So far from having anything against her personally, he was just beginning to find her interesting. She might be a tigress, but she had looks and style; she made most of the girls look like mass-produced dolls. There might be a bonus in it for him if he could make certain that her separation from Lucifer was permanent.

Lucien Galt came into the room with his usual long, arrogant step, his head up, his brows drawn together into a forbidding line. He crossed to the coffee-table and helped himself without a word or a look for anyone, and then stood balancing the cup in his hand and looking round until he found Liri, in a group surrounding Professor Penrose, in the far corner of the room. He watched her frowningly, attentively, without a thought for all the curious, covert glances fixed on him. It was like him not to bother to dissemble for them; the most offensive thing about him was that he made no concessions to his public. In Meurice's catalogue of sins that was blasphemy.

And, damn him, here came the girls, just the same! He could stand there and look through them as though they didn't exist, and they came edging in on him like cats, purring and rubbing themselves against his knees. The Cope kid among the first of them, of course; she'd got it badly. Pale as death, tight as a bow-string, swallowing her desperate shyness in still more desperate bravery.

'Mr. Galt, you were wonderful! I know you must be tired of hearing it, but I do mean it, I really do!'

'Fabulous! I mean, that Irish song . . . I *cried*!'

'I always listen to your broadcasts . . . I've got *all* your records. But to hear you *live*, that was just out of this world. Mr. Meurice, wasn't he *marvellous*?'

Dickie Meurice slid unobtrusively nearer, merging his own adorers into the rival group; that way, there was always a hope of annexing them all, or at least being credited with them all, when Lucifer lost his patience and swooped away, picking his feet fastidiously out of the syrup of their idolatry like a hawk ripping himself loose from birdlime. He was certain to do it, sooner or later.

'He was indeed,' said Dickie sunnily, and smiled into Lucien's frowning stare. 'If anybody got the message tonight, he did!' The bright, hearty, extrovert voice pushed the small, private barb home, and felt it draw blood. 'Nice performance, Lucien, boy, very nice.'

'Yours?' said Lucien laconically. 'Or mine?'

'Now, now! No bitchery between colleagues, old boy.' His blue eyes, wide and hard and merciless as a child's, fixed delightedly on Lucien's lean brown wrist, the one that supported the coffee cup. The oval of tiny, indented bruises, strung here and there with a bead of blood, marked the smooth skin with an interesting pattern of blue and purple. 'Well, well!' sighed Meurice, shaking his blond head. 'And I was always taught that eating people is wrong!'

Lucien looked down at his own battle scar, and raised his brows in sheer astonishment. He had felt nothing since she ran from him, and never even looked to see if she'd marked him.

Observing the evidence, and hearing the small, indrawn breaths and the blank, brief silence, he would have hidden his wrist if he could, but it was too late for that. He let it sustain the sudden, avid weight of their curiosity, and looked over it at Dickie Meurice with a cool indifferent face.

'Really? You must have quite a job reconciling that with the tone of your TV programme, I should think. The only time I watched it, it was pure cannibalism.'

The circling girls shrank and gasped. They looked from Lucien's stony composure to Dickie Meurice's fair face, suddenly paling to bluish white, and as abruptly flushing into painful crimson. If there was one point on which he was sensitive, it was his programme. There was no parrying that straight stab with a joke, and the killing stroke didn't come to him.

'Except that some of the meat you were gritting your teeth on was carrion,' said Lucien with detachment, 'so I suppose the term hardly applies.'

He turned at leisure and laid down his cup, wasted a polite moment for any come-back, and hoisted an indifferent shoulder when none came. Without haste he walked away, weaving between the shifting groups of people; and Felicity Cope turned like a sleep-walker, and followed him.

'I never invited him to be my guest,' said Meurice, collecting himself. 'Maybe that colours the view.' And he offered them his quirky smile and intimate glance, and got a slightly embarassed murmur of response; but it was too late to repair the damage, and he knew it. He had been discomfited before his loyal and scandalised fans, something no public personality can ever be expected to forgive. Something heroic would be needed to restore his authority.

'Between you and me,' he said, his voice earnest, confidential and sad, 'we have to forgive Lucien almost any crudity just now. God knows I wouldn't want to score off the poor devil while he's all knotted up the way he is over Liri. Don't spread this, of course, but I think it's as well if some of you know the facts.

You can help to smooth the way if you understand what's going on.' His tone was all warmth, consideration and kindness; and no one could do it better when the need arose. 'You see,' he said, 'up to a couple of weeks ago Lucien and Liri . . .'

His voice sank to a solicitous whisper, drawing their heads together round him like swarming bees to their queen. He made an artistic job of it, and sighed at his own cleverness. 'What a situation! And here we are over the weekend, stuck with it! No, don't misunderstand if I let Lucien get away with murder just now. I figure he's got more than enough on his mind, without my turning on him as well, just because he takes his soreness out on me. My shoulders are broad, I can take it.'

They shifted and glowed, worshipping. They murmured that it was really big of him to look at it that way. They promised faithfully that they'd keep his confidence. And within minutes they were dropping off from the edge of his circle to spread the news.

The girl with butterfly glasses peered through the brick-red fringe that came down to the bridge of her nose, and her short-sighted eyes glistened. She had relayed the tale four times already, and it got better every time. Her fellow-missionaries were circulating with equal fervour round the room, avoiding only the august vicinity of Edward and Audrey Arundale, whose position, among this largely under-twenty assembly, remained very much that of the headmaster and his wife, and effectively froze out gossip. The only other islands immune from this industrious dirt-washing were where Lucien Galt moved aloof, abstracted and tense, with Felicity faithful at his elbow, and where Liri Palmer sat withdrawn and alone. Every other soul in the room must be in the secret by now.

' . . . madly in love,' said the girl breathlessly, 'and then it all blew up in their faces, just two weeks ago. They had a terrible row. *She* broke it off, but *he* was just as mad with her. Well, you can imagine what a fight between those two would be like. So they parted, and they haven't seen each other since, not until today. And now suddenly she turns up here, where *he's* got an engagement for the weekend. Just as if she's following him . . .'

'How do you know all this?' asked Tossa sceptically.

'Dickie told us. He knows them both well, he's worked with them before. You can be sure it's quite true. If you ask me, she's come to make mischief if she can.'

'She certainly didn't seem to be in any conciliatory mood,' admitted Dominic, 'when she laid off just what she thought of him, tonight.'

'She didn't, did she?' Delighted eyes blinked behind the butterfly glasses and the curtain of hair. 'It's thrilling, really, because when you come to think of it, she actually *threatened* him! She said if she couldn't have him, nobody should. And did you know? – they had some sort of a brush before they came in here. No, honestly, I'm not making it up! She *bit* him!'

'Oh, go on!' said Tossa disbelievingly. 'People don't go round biting each other, not even the folk element.'

'All right, if you don't believe me, take a look at his left wrist. You'll see the marks there, all right.' Her voice sank to a conspiratorial whisper, drunk with the pleasures of anticipation. 'You don't suppose she really came here to try to *kill* him, do you? I mean, she as good as *said* . . .'

'No,' said Dominic flatly, 'I don't suppose any such thing. One minute you're telling us she gave him the push, and the next that she's carrying a torch for him, and will see him dead before she'll let anybody else have him.'

'Well, they could both be true, couldn't they?' said the girl blithely, and went off to spread the news farther.

'And the devil of it is,' said Tossa, looking after her with a considering frown, 'that she could very well be right. They're getting good value for their tuition fees this time, aren't they?'

'Now don't you start!' protested Dominic. 'Don't forget this has all come from Dickie Meurice, and you said yourself he must hate Lucien, so what's odd about his drumming up all the trouble he can for him? But it's just a load of personal spite. It won't come to anything.'

The Arundales, dutifully circulating among their guests, were approaching this quiet corner by easy stages, the image of a successful, efficient, socially accomplished college head and his eminently suitable and satisfactory wife. 'Now I ask you,' said Dominic, low-voiced, 'how on earth could melodrama muscle in on any party of theirs? It would never get past the secretary's office.'

Half an hour later he was not quite so certain.

The party broke up early. The warden had no way of ensuring that his houseful of young people would stay in their four-bedded rooms, even when he had got them there, but he could at least set a good example, and hope that they would take the hint and follow it. Felicity had already been detached unwillingly from Lucien Galt's side and edged away to bed. A few of the older people had drifted off to their rooms, and more were on their way, pausing to nose along the library shelves for bedside books. The Arundales completed their tour of all the groups left in the drawing-room by half-past ten, said a general good night, and strolled out along the gallery towards their own rooms. And so powerful was the compulsion of their authority that Lucien Galt, who happened to be with them at the time, fell in alongside and left with them, and half a dozen others wound up their conversations and followed.

'Not that I shall get to bed for an hour or so yet,' observed Arundale with a rueful smile. 'I've got to address the Vintners' annual dinner tomorrow night, on adult education in general and Follymead in particular, and I haven't got my ideas in order yet. We're hoping to get an annual grant from them, of course! And on Sunday after noon there's a conference of clerical and lay educationalists, on the use of leisure – a big subject, and very much in the news just now. I'm afraid it must all sound rather boring to you,' he said, glancing across his wife's fair head at

Lucien Galt, with more of patronage than apology. 'At your age the problem of leisure is largely a matter of getting enough of it – no difficulty in filling it.'

'I don't find it boring at all,' said Lucien politely. And indeed, the dark profile he turned to the view of Dominic and Tossa, strolling a yard or two behind, did not look bored; the tight lines of it had eased and warmed, his colour was high and his eyes soft and bright. A slightly hectic gaiety touched him, perhaps from the salutary effort of making conversation, perhaps from the secret activity of his mind. He looked at Audrey Arundale, walking between them, and from her to her husband, and said with warmth: 'I think what you're doing here is fine, and I'm glad to be associated with it.'

Mrs. Arundale turned her head a little at that, and her dutiful, acquiescent smile, which seldom left her lips and never lost its faint overtone of anxiety, flushed into something proud and animated with pleasure.

'I'd like to think it's fine,' said Arundale, accepting the bouquet. 'I know it isn't enough. I can only hope it has some effect.'

At this point Dominic's thumbs pricked, surely quite unjustly, as he told himself. But who had ever heard Lucifer go out of his way to pay a compliment to anyone before? He sounded quite sincere, and probably he was, but even so it didn't seem in character that he should say it. And the slight prick of wonder and curiosity suddenly reminded Dominic of that alleged mark on Lucien's left wrist. That was why he happened to glance down at the right, or perhaps the wrong, moment, and see what Tossa failed to see.

The three in front were walking close together, the flared skirt of the woman's dress rustling softly against her escorts as they moved. Lucien's left hand, carried loosely at his side, suddenly uncurled its long fingers, and delicately and deliberately touched Audrey's hand between their bodies, and in instant response she opened her fingers to accept him. They clasped hands ardently for an instant, and as quickly and smoothly drew apart again.

Their steps had never faltered, their faces had not quivered; only the hands embraced and clung and separated with passion and resolution, as though they had an independent life of their own, or had drawn down into themselves, for one moment, all the life of these two people.

In an unexpected but natural reaction, Dominic looked round hastily and almost furtively, to see if anyone else had been watching and seen what he had seen. But Tossa, thank goodness, was looking up at the elaborate pendants of the Venetian chandeliers, now turned down discreetly to a quarter their full power, so that the long gallery was almost dim, even in its open walk; and the view of anyone coming along behind must have been blocked completely by their bodies. No, nobody! He was almost relieved as if he had risked being caught out in some embarrassing misdemeanour himself, and by luck rather than desert survived undetected.

Then a minute, sudden refraction of light drew his eyes sharply to the deep alcove where one of the Cothercott portraits hung. Someone was sitting there, so still that but for the ring she wore he would never have found her. But when he had once found her, her eyes burned brighter than the reflection from her ring. She sat motionless, the long, heavy plait of hair coiled on her shoulder. Her face was as fixed as ice, her nostrils flared wide. She was neither surprised nor disconcerted. She had seen only what she had been prepared to see, something against which she was forewarned and forearmed; but it was at the same time something she would never forget or forgive, and something she would not endure without retaliation.

They moved on, and Liri Palmer watched them go, and never moved. No one saw her but Dominic; no one but Dominic knew what she had seen.

Chapter 3

'I hope,' said Professor Penrose, casting a lightning glance at his watch, which showed twenty minutes past twelve, and lifting the tone-arm delicately from his precious disc of Moravian Slovak recordings, 'that we've at least established a basis for the *name* of our subject. I hope we can agree that it should not be merely "folk", but "music", too. Beware of the fanatic who finds everything phoney that isn't sung without accompaniment by an eighty-five-year-old in a public bar . . . without voice, too, as a rule, and who can wonder at it? No, we've disposed of that. We've surely demonstrated that there are places in the world where performances of the utmost virtuosity can be truly "folk", because the heritage of that particular people is a musical sensitivity which we, here in England, associate only with privilege, training and sophistication. Never lose sight of that humbling fact, and beware of subscribing to purely English standards – or should I say, British?' He cocked an eye at Andrew Callum, and grinned. 'But they're two different things, as I'll show you this evening. The Celtic fringe has the drop on us poor English in so many ways, you'll find. Puritanism has a lot to answer for.'

He slammed shut the huge book of notes at which he never even looked, though he opened it religiously at the beginning of each session.

'Now be off with you and get ready for lunch. This afternoon is free, and I understand the deputy warden has arranged two excursions for us in the locality. I'll be going with one of the parties myself, so one of the coach-loads, at least, will have to behave. And the rest of you I'll expect here at five, fit and ready for action. Mind you're not late. Away with you, and wash! Gong in five minutes!'

They took their tone from him, and rushed for the doors in a furious babble of argument and controversy. It was becoming clear now that the professor, from the recesses of his own antiquity, regarded them all as eighteen years old at most, and liked them that way. They'd had a deliriously happy morning with him; the afternoon was to be in every sense a holiday, and the evening a continued delight. He had his class exactly where he wanted it.

The first coach, headed for Mottisham Abbey and the antiquities of West Midshire, and captained by the professor, hummed away down the drive prompt at two o'clock. Tossa and Dominic watched it go from the highest view-turret at the front of the house, up among the fantasy of chimneys and gargoyles and leads that lived a film-cartoon life of its own over the heads of the music-students. A scarlet beetle, scurrying along a thread of pale gravel, it rounded the planned bend in the drive, and vanished from sight. In a few minutes more the second, bound for the region of geological curiosities in the north-east of the county, followed it, Henry Marshall no doubt still anxiously counting his chickens. When it was gone, it seemed to them that the whole house had been evacuated, and they were alone with the fairy-tale threat that had driven the others away. Only then did they become aware of the large bird-population of Follymead, the inhabitants of this roof-world. The noise of starlings and martins and pigeons was all the music left to them. Somewhere in the park a green woodpecker was beating out his staccato rhythms like a drummer.

'You're sure you didn't want to go with them?' asked Dominic, shoulder to shoulder with Tossa at the open window.

She shook her head vehemently. 'No, this is better. You know all those places, and we hardly know this at all. It's all ours now.'

'Oh, there must be a few others who chose to stay.'

They saw one of them at that moment, crossing the pale forecourt far below them, a tiny, foreshortened human creature, walking rapidly but progressing slowly. It was astonishing how long it took him to cross the open court and set foot on the grass path that led away into the park, downhill towards the river, glimpsed in a few specks of silver through the trees.

'Lucifer was in no mood for excursions, evidently,' said Dominic.

The small, dark speck achieved form and proportion as it receded; it no longer looked as if it could be smudged out of existence, like a May midge, by the pressure of a finger. And in a moment a second figure came bounding down the steps to the gravel, and set off full speed in pursuit, a thin little figure with a child's long-legged and angular movements. She caught him up before he reached the trees. He checked and turned for a moment with a formidable suggestion of impatience, but then he set off again, and she fell into step beside him. They disappeared together where the trees engulfed the path.

'I shouldn't!' said Tossa in a warning whisper, and shook her head over what she certainly couldn't help.

'Maybe you would, if you were Felicity. Actually he's been remarkably forbearing with her so far, considering his reputation. She was under his feet all last night, and he stood it nobly.'

'It won't last. She'll be due for a shock pretty soon if she doesn't get out of his hair.' Tossa looked after them with perplexed sympathy. 'She's a queer little thing, isn't she? Rather sad, really. I was talking to that nice elderly maid in the buttery this morning. She says Felicity's mother is Mr. Arundale's younger sister, she's a widow, not all that badly off, but the querulous sort, and it seems she's inclined to think her distinguished brother owes her a living. She farms the girl out on Follymead every holiday as a sort of junior secretary, and has her hang around the Arundales all the time she isn't at school.'

'Hoping she'll come in for whatever they've got to leave, some day?'

'Well, that's what Mrs. Bremmer says, anyway. After all, they've got no children of their own, so it's a reasonable hope. And in the meantime, at least she's making them provide for her nearly half the year. But what a life! I mean, it isn't as if she was dumb. She isn't at all, she's rather too bright, if anything, she must know very well what goes on. Not too good for an intelligent adolescent,' said Tossa, wise at nineteen, 'knowing she's being used to prise hand-outs out of her relatives, and her mother cares more for her prospects than her company. No wonder she's gone cagey. You can see right away that she's all the time waiting for the world to hit out at her. That's why she puts on the sophistication so thick, to pretend things don't hurt.'

Dominic listened to this with the more respect because not so long ago Tossa herself had been in a somewhat similar relationship with the world at large, and her actress-mother's procession of husbands in particular; and with the more tenderness and pleasure because her tone now indicated a quite remarkable degree of recovery. He was a little dubious of crediting himself with the change, but the fact remained that he had happened to Tossa just at the right time to assist the process. If she was right, then young Felicity Cope was all set to be a pushover for a grand passion; and if it went right it would liberate her for good, even if it afterwards went the way of most adolescent loves. But he couldn't persuade himself that she was going to get anything but disaster out of Lucifer.

'Felicity!' he said thoughtfully, and made a wry face. 'Whoever christened her that has something to answer for.'

Tossa leaned out from the window to look down dizzily on to the terraces below. 'Look, there's Liri, too.'

'So she didn't want to go sight-seeing, either.'

Black is the Colour of My True Love's Heart

Liri, in a red sweater bright as a drop of blood, crossed the terrace and walked slowly down the steps. On the drive she hesitated for a moment, and then set out briskly across the grass towards the distant hillock on which the fake ruin stood. She walked as one who has decided on an objective, rather than as one who is going somewhere with a purpose, and her chosen course was taking her steadily farther and farther away from the copse that had swallowed Lucien and Felicity. The damp grass showed the silvery line of her passing, lengthening along the sward; and it might also have been ruled there, it was so uncompromisingly straight.

'Let's go down and have a look at the grounds,' said Tossa, turning away abruptly from the contemplation of that lance-like wake, 'while we've got the place more or less to ourselves.'

They went down, and the house was wonderfully hushed and quiet about them. True, there were still one or two people around. The staff must be still washing up after lunch, Edward Arundale in his private quarters was collecting what he needed for his drive to Birmingham, there were two elderly ladies placidly reading in the gallery, and two more strolling between the flower-beds in the shelter of the enclosed garden; but with the withdrawal of some seventy people the whole house was changed, had reverted to its cat-sleep with eyes half-open, and lay deceptively still and harmless and helpless in the faint, stormy sunshine of April.

There was room in the grounds of Follymead to lose a thousand people, and still believe yourself alone. They walked away from the drive, turning towards the arched bridge that spanned the river in the distance. Crimson and orange alders showed the winding course of the stream, even when the flood-water itself was hidden from them. Clustering woods drew in to complete the picture like a blackcloth; and out of the trees, while they were still some hundred yards distant, came Felicity, her head down, her fleet, child's running muted to a stumbling, rapid walk. She didn't notice them until the sound of their feet whispering in the grass, and the hint of a shadow at the edge of her vision, made her fling up her head with a wild, wary gesture, like a startled colt.

She said: 'Oh! . . . Hullo!' and her face put on its armour, settled narrow, clean-arched brows and quivering; irresolute mouth into arduous but instant serenity. 'Going for a walk?'

'Why don't you come with us?' suggested Tossa impulsively, and her eyes signalled apology to Dominic for a rash generosity he might not approve. But the girl was so solitary and gauche, and her grey eyes looked out so defensively from behind the delicate, half-formed face, like lonely wild things in hiding. 'You know all the best places. We haven't seen anything yet.'

'I'd love to, thank you . . . but I can't. I've got to go in now. I've got some jobs to do for my uncle in the office. I only came out to run down and have a look at the swans' nest. There's a pair nesting down there under the alders, on a tiny island.' She pointed rather jerkily, turning her face away from them. 'But be careful if you go to look, don't go too near, will you? The pen's all right, but if the cob's there he can be rather dangerous.'

'We saw you come out,' said Dominic casually, and saw the faint colour flow and ebb again in her solemn face, and the grey eyes in ambush flare into panic for an instant. 'We hoped you were going to have an afternoon off, you spend enough time indoors. Can't the work wait for today?'

But she did not want it to wait, that was clear. She began to sidle round them, intent on escape. 'No, I'd rather get it done. Things like the press-cutting book and the photographs get into arrears very easily, you see, and we don't just keep them for interest, the record's needed for reference. But, look, if you go on this way, along the river, you'll come to the summer pavilion, and from there you can work round through the woods to the pagoda. There used to be a heronry there at the pool, but the last pair flew away last year. You will excuse me, won't you?' She was backing away from them towards the house, ten yards distant before she stopped talking, and turned, and broke into a run.

48

The feverish sound of her voice clung unpleasantly in their ears as she dwindled, sometimes running, sometimes walking hastily and unsteadily, her track a shaky line in the wet grass.

'It seemed only fair to let her know we'd seen her,' said Dominic dubiously, meeting Tossa's eyes. 'She hadn't said anything that *couldn't* be true, up to then.'

'I know, I was glad you said it. I don't think we'll go and look for the swan's nest, somehow, do you? It'll be there, of course. She's quick, she wouldn't give herself an excuse that could be knocked down just by going and looking.' Tossa stooped and picked up from the grass a couple of tiny, cross-shaped blossoms that had fallen from Felicity's hair as she combed it nervously with her fingers. 'Lilac . . . look, what a colour! So deep, and really almost pure blue instead of purple . . .'

She stood for a moment holding them, and then turned her palm and let them fall again sadly into the turf. 'I suppose he turned on her. Something happened.'

'I suppose so,' said Dominic. 'Probably told her to run away and play with her dolls.'

'Isn't it hell,' sighed Tossa, 'being fifteen?'

The coach parties came back hungry and in high spirits just after half-past four, and tumbled up the steps into the hall for tea. The noise, now that they had sorted themselves out into congenial groups and had plenty to talk about, was deafening. Arundale, if he had been there to hear, would have been satisfied of the success of the course by the soaring decibel count. There were no clouds, no shadows, no disagreements, no clashes of temperament, and nobody even wondered why; until five o'clock struck, and Professor Penrose came in to hasten the laggards along to the drawing-room for his next lecture, and looking round the emptying room, suddenly asked:

'Where's young Galt?'

He was not with the other artists, already on station in the

49

window-embrasure of the yellow drawing-room. He was not in the hall, lingering with the scones and tea–cups. And now that the question arose, he hadn't been in to tea at all.

'He wouldn't stand us up purposely, would he?' asked the professor shrewdly, and in a tone which required confirmation of his own views rather than information.

'Surely not,' said Dominic, abandoning his self-imposed task of loading the huge tea-trolley; and: 'No!' said Liri Palmer at the same instant, and still more positively, even scornfully.

'No, that's what I thought. Boy's a professional. No, I don't think he'd welch on a session. So *where is he?*'

There was a dead silence. No one had anything to volunteer. There were only a handful of them left there, in the strewn wreckage of tea, a china battlefield.

'He didn't come out with us this afternoon,' said Henry Marshall. 'Was he with your party?'

'No.' The professor sounded a little testy. Lucifer was not the kind of person who could pass unnoticed on board a coach.

'He stayed here,' said Dominic. 'Tossa and I saw him go out, soon after the coaches left. He started off towards the river, by that path that dives into the trees.'

'And you haven't seen him since?'

'No. Felicity just might have. She was down that way this afternoon, we met her coming back.' No need to say she'd followed Lucien from the house; she knew there were others who knew, she'd be able to answer questions and keep her secrets, too.

'Shall I go and find Felicity?' offered Tossa, to fend off any other messenger.

'If you wouldn't mind, my dear. No need to broadcast anything – not yet, anyhow.' The professor smiled at her, but he was not quite easy in his mind, even then.

'No, I won't.' And in a few moments she returned from the drawing-room with Felicity. The girl was pale, her eyes huge and opaque as grey glass, her mask slightly and frighteningly out of drawing.

'Felicity, we've lost Lucien Galt.' The professor was placid and gentle. 'Maybe he's just loitering about somewhere with a stopped watch, maybe he's gone to sleep in the summer-house, or something daft and simple. But we'd better have a look for him, perhaps, just in case. I hear you were down by the river this afternoon, did you see anything of him? I'm told he'd gone that way.'

'I . . . we went out together,' said Felicity in a thin thread of a voice. 'He was just ahead of me when I went out, so I caught him up and we went together. We went downstream on the other side, but only as far as where the paths cross. You know, by the baby redwood tree. Then he went on across the loop, I think . . . anyhow, I crossed over again by the stone bridge, and left him there.' She looked from the professor to Dominic and Tossa, and moistened her lips. 'I met Miss Barber and Mr. Felse when I was coming back.'

'And you weren't out again? And you haven't seen Mr. Galt come back to the house?'

She shook her head vehemently. 'No. I was indoors all the rest of the afternoon. I had some work to do for Uncle Edward.'

The whip of the warden's name stung Henry Marshall into full awareness of his responsibilities. Arundale was in Birmingham by now, and the whole load of Follymead came down on his deputy's shrinking shoulders. The social load was enough, but that he was prepared to tackle. This was something that hadn't been on the agenda, and he didn't know what to do.

'He must be in the grounds,' he said unhappily. 'Apparently he simply went out for a walk. I suppose there's always a possibility that he may have had an accident, just an ordinary fall. It's not so difficult to break an ankle, or something like that, along the river-banks. Professor, I really think you'd better get on with your lecture, and try to manage without him, if you can, while some of us have a hunt through the park for him.'

'I think I had,' agreed the professor dryly, one ear cocked for the rising noise of conversation drifting in from the distant drawing-room. 'I'll tell them nothing about this. Better keep it to the few of us here, until we know what we're about.'

They agreed, in a subdued murmur.

'You find the lad,' said the professor, swooping towards the door. 'I'll keep this lot quiet.'

When he was gone, there were just five of them left in the room, Tossa, Felicity, Liri Palmer, Dominic and Marshall. It wasn't the party they would have chosen. Three of them women, and two of those tense and anxious already. Liri was unquestionably durable, but Felicity looked brittle as glass, ready to shatter. Dominic touched her hand lightly, and urged her with a frown and a silent shake of his head to leave the search to them. Nevertheless, they were still five when they went out in the green, misty, pre-evening light to quarter the grounds for Lucien Galt.

The path by which Lucien and Felicity had vanished in the early afternoon sank itself deep in groves of diverse trees, artfully deployed, and reached the river at some distance from the house. A narrow footbridge with a single handrail brought Dominic to the other side. The largest of the three weirs that controlled the passage of the Braide through the Follymead grounds lay upstream, and here the waters rolled brown and high and fast, seamed with currents, and tossing twigs and branches from hand to hand as it rushed along. The spring rains had been heavy after heavy snows, the sodden grass of the banks fermented with brownish foam, and strained at its roots, streaming out like dead hair along the taut surface of the water. On the other side the path turned downstream, at first close to the bank; but in a little while it plunged into woodland again, and left the waterside to take a short cut across one of the artificial loops into which the Braide had been contorted by Cothercott ingenuity.

Dominic turned with the path. Almost certainly Lucien had

come this way with Felicity this afternoon, just as she had said. She had reappeared from the copse on the other bank, having recrossed by the arched stone bridge two or three loops downstream, the bridge which was designed as a part of the Follymead stage-set, to be seen in exactly the right place in that elaborate landscape when viewed from the drawing-room windows. Somewhere between this spot and that bridge she and Lucien had parted company. Dominic walked the widening ride, fenced off now on the water side by a barrier of old, ornate iron posts and fine chains, and his feet were silent in last autumn's rotting leaves.

It didn't follow, of course, that Lucien need be anywhere in this quarter now; in the time between he could have been anywhere in the grounds, or even several miles out of them. There was so much of Follymead that the five of them had had to spread themselves out singly in order to cover it all; and it was hardly surprising that Felicity had set off, at first, in this direction. But she had drawn back when she had seen Dominic heading the same way, and gone off voluntarily to thread the shrubberies and gardens on the other side of the house. Liri and Tossa were patrolling the more open ornamental park-land, one on either side the drive to the lodge. Where Marshall was he didn't know; probably in the distant preserves which were going to be the worst job of all if they were forced to make a real search of it.

The river was out of sight now, somewhere away on his right hand; but here came a small cleared space where another path crossed his, and the right turn here must surely close in on the Braide again, and bring him to the bridge. And here was Felicity's baby redwood, just inside the railed enclosure, an infant of about fifty or sixty, probably, with the characteristic spreading base and narrow, primitive, aspiring shape. He leaned over the chain fence and stuck his thumb into the thick, spongy bark. So here it had happened, whatever had happened between them . . . here or somewhere close by, she wouldn't bother to be

53

accurate to a few yards. And after that nobody had seen anything of Lucien again. Though there was always the comfortable possibility, of course, that he had simply decided to be irresponsible this evening, and gone off to the pub in the village to see what entertainment was offering locally.

Dominic would have liked to believe it; but whatever Lucien Galt might not have been, he seemed to be a conscientious professional who delivered what he promised. And again, and more disturbingly, the prosaic solution didn't chime with the atmosphere of this fantastic place.

He hesitated at the crossing of the two paths, and then turned right, as Felicity must have done when she took her broken heart and hurt pride in her arms and ran away from the débâcle. And twenty yards along, with the chain fence still accompanying him on his right, he came to an enormous scrolled iron gate in it, massive with leaves and flowers, twice as tall as the fence. Evidently the gate was a survival from some older and far more solid fence, long taken down for scrap. To judge by the gate itself, it dated from the high days of iron, maybe around 1800 or even earlier, stuff that could go neglected for centuries before it even began to corrode seriously. It hadn't been painted for a long time, and it sagged a little on its hinges, but swung freely when he pushed it. The bracket into which the latch should drop was still fixed immovably to the gate-post, as big as a bruiser's closed fist; but there was no latch hanging now in the wards.

The elaboration of the approach suggested that this patch of woodland by the river bank enshrined one of the features of the grounds. He went through the gate on impulse, and down to the riverside. He could see the distant gleam of sullen light on the water in broken glimpses between the trees; and the belt of woods thinned suddenly and brought him out on an open stretch of grass, ringed round every way with shrubs. Even across the river the woods lay close here, the alders leaning over the bank. A nice, quiet, retired place, carefully made, like everything here. Nature had abdicated, unable to keep up the pace. The cluster of rocks that erupted on the bank had been placed there by man, artfully built up to look as natural as the eighteenth century liked its landscape features to look. Dominic crossed the thirty yards or so of open meadow that separated him from it, and found that the face the rocks turned towards the Braide was hollowed into a narrow cavern, with a stone bench fitted inside it. The inside walls were encrusted with stucco and shells, and overgrown with ferns, and there had once been a small spring there, filling a little channel in the stone floor and running down to the river. There was only a green stain there now, and a growth of viridian moss.

He looked round the grotto dubiously, and was turning to leave it when he saw, between the stone and the river, the first raw scars in the grass. The ground was soft and moist, the grass still short, but lush enough to show wounds. Feet had stamped and shifted here, with more pressure and greater agitation than in mere walking. Close to the edge of the flood, gathering in concentrated force here before leaping the third weir, there was a patch of grass some two yards across that had been trampled and scored, the dark soil showing through. Here someone's foot had slipped and left a slimy smear.

Dominic approached cautiously, avoiding setting foot on the scarred place. Close to the water the grass shrank from a bare patch of gravel and stone; and there were two darker spots on the ground, oval and even and small, a dull brown in colour. He stooped to peer at them. It had rained briefly in the morning, but not since. These were therefore more recent than that rain; and they looked to him like drops of blood. He went down on one knee carefully to look more closely, and put his supporting hand on something hard that shifted in the grass. He made an instinctive movement to pick it up, and then took out his handkerchief, and handled his find delicately through the linen. A small silver medal, worn almost smooth, some human figure, maybe a saint, on one side, and on the other what seemed to be

55

a lion rampant. From the ring that pierced it above the saint's head a thin silver chain slid away like a snake and slipped through his fingers; he caught it in his other hand, and saw that it had not been unclasped, but broken.

He had seen it before, or at least something so like it that in his heart he knew it was the same; round, worn, plain, of this very size, why should there be two such in Follymead at the same time?

This morning, at Professor Penrose's lecture, Lucien Galt had worn an open-necked sweater-shirt, and several times he had leaned forward to attend to the professor's record player for him. He had then been wearing this medal round his neck. Dominic had noticed it because it had seemed at first out of character; and then, and more acutely, because it was entirely in character, after all, that he should wear it as he did, without a thought for either display or concealment, as naturally as he wore his eyelashes. And the thing itself had an austerity that made it singularly personal and valid, like a silver identity bracelet round a sailor's wrist in wartime. Not for show, but not to be hidden, either; something with a right to be where it was.

He stared at it in the fading light, and he knew it was the same. He looked at the sky, which was ragged with broken clouds, and then went and found some large leaves of wild rhubarb from the waterside, and laid them over the drops that were possibly blood, and the trampled ground, in case of rain. He found a sharp stone and drove it into the turf where he had picked up the medal. That was all he could do.

Then he went to find Henry Marshall.

'I'm not sure about the blood,' said Dominic for the fourth time. 'I *am* sure about the struggle. Two people – or more than two, but it looks like two – were fighting there. And *this* was in the grass, and Liri says it was his, and I say so, too. And that's all we've got, between the five of us.'

They were in the warden's office, with the door tightly shut.

Dinner was over, without them; they had sandwiches and coffee in here, but no one had done more than play with them. Liri sat bolt upright, pale and calm, her mouth tight and her eyes sombre. Felicity, mercifully, had been manoeuvred out of the council by Tossa, and driven in to the evening session, where she would have to mingle and be social and keep her mouth shut. She didn't even know exactly what Dominic had found, though maybe she guessed more than was comfortable. Someone would have to keep an eye on her, and it looked as if the some-one would have to be Tossa. But Felicity had resources of her own, and whatever she couldn't do yet, she could keep secrets. At fifteen it's an essential quality; one's life depends on it. She wouldn't give anything away.

'We can't leave it at that,' said Dominic reasonably.

'No, I realise that, of course.' Henry Marshall was barely thirty, none too sure of himself after four months under Edward Arundale's formidable shadow, and at this moment in an agony of indecision. 'But we have no proof at all that anything disas-trous has happened, no proof of a crime, certainly. And you must understand that this establishment is in a curiously vulnerable position. If a scandal threatened our reputation it might cut off funds from several sources, as well as frightening away our actual student potential.' He dug his fingers agitatedly into his straw-coloured hair, and his black-rimmed spectacles slid down his long young nose. 'A bad period of some weeks could close us down. It would be cataclysmic. As long as we run steadily on a moderate backing we're perfectly safe. But any interruption of any long duration would finish us. And that would be a real national loss. I know we must follow this up. But I most protect Follymead, too. It's what I'm here for.'

'I still think we need the police,' said Dominic. 'For that very purpose. You want to avoid scandal, of course, but it would be a worse scandal if you concealed what turned out to be a criminal matter. To cover Follymead, I'm afraid you've got to hand this job over to the proper people.'

And that was the whole crux of the matter, the thing that was tearing the deputy warden apart. He was terrified of calling in the police, perhaps to find it had all been unnecessary, and even more terrified of bearing the responsibility for not calling them in, should the affair turn out to be serious after all. Above all he was afraid of trying to contact Edward Arundale, and for good reason. Arundale was a man of decision, who would know how to deal with every situation, and he would be highly intolerant of any deputy who couldn't handle affairs himself in an emergency. Marshall hadn't been here long, this was his first assignment on his own responsibility; and he wanted, how he wanted, to keep his job.

'We have so little to go on,' he said in agony.

'We're not competent,' said Liri Palmer tersely, 'to say whether it's little or much. That's the whole point.'

Dominic looked at Tossa, and found her looking at him, with the clear, trusting, eager look by means of which she communicated her sense of adoption into his family. He knew what she was thinking, and what she wanted him to do and say. It was having lost her own father so early, and suffered such frustrations and vicissitudes with stepfathers since, that had made her attach herself so fervently and gratefully to Dominic's beautifully permanent, stable and reassuring parents. And especially to George Felse. He wasn't at all like her adored professor father, but he gave her the same sense of security. She would have taken all her own problems to him, it was natural she should think of him immediately in this crisis. Even if he hadn't been a policeman, she would have wanted him; but he was, and that was the solution to everything.

An exchange of glances like that, radiant with confidence, could turn Dominic's bones to water with gratitude and astonishment. He had brought her home in the common agonies every man feels in bringing together two jealous and valued loves; he wasn't yet used to the staggering bliss and relief of his total success.

'If I could make a suggestion,' he said, with all the more care and delicacy because of his own conviction of undeserved grace, 'I could get my father to have a look over the ground.' He caught Tossa's glowing glance, and trembled; he still couldn't quite believe in the accumulation of his luck. 'He's a detective–inspector in the county C.I.D. I'm sure he'd be willing to come out here, if you'll let me call him. Then you'd have covered yourself and the college, in case there *is* something in this. And we could ask him to treat it as a quite private matter until he's satisfied that there's a case for official investigation. In either case, you'd be protected.'

Henry Marshall took his head out of his hands, and gaped unbelievingly but gladly at his salvation. Arundale himself couldn't do better than this.

'You think he'd come? On those terms?'

'I'm sure he would. It's better for them, too, if they have notice of these things in time to judge. If it turns out to be something quite harmless and on the level, so much the better. May I call him?'

'Please do,' said Henry Marshall thankfully. 'Perhaps you could meet him at the lodge, when he arrives? You *do* drive? Take the station wagon down and wait for him. I'll talk to Professor Penrose, and see to everything here. We shall be most grateful. *Most* grateful!'

Chapter 4

George Felse swore, but with resignation, listened, and came. Dominic was not in the habit of going off at half-cock; he had been a policeman's son too long for that. If the affair turned out to be a mare's-nest after all, there was no harm done; and if it didn't, far better to take a close look at the circumstances as soon as possible, rather than after the scent had gone cold.

'Save it,' he said, cutting off the details. 'I'm on my way, we'll have all that when I come.'

It took him twenty minutes to drive from Comerford to the Follymead gates; there wasn't much on the roads at this hour, and the going was good. The college station wagon was parked just behind the lodge, already turned to point back up the drive, with Dominic and Tossa waiting beside it.

'We thought it might be better if you leave the car here at the lodge,' said Dominic. 'Just in case there's somebody who knows it.'

'In that case,' said George reasonably, 'the somebody would be even more likely to know me.'

'Yes, but we hope you'll be able to stay out of the general view. There's only a handful of us know what's happened. If anything *has* happened. And that way, if it all turns out to be nonsense, there's no fuss, and nobody's made to look a fool. It seemed the best thing. It's this second-in-command, you see, he's left holding the baby, and he's terrified of calling the police, and terrified of not calling them. Whatever he does is probably going to be the wrong thing.'

'So I'm the working compromise. He realised that if there does turn out to be anything in it, it becomes an official matter?'

'If there's anything in it, the fat's in the fire, anyhow. Yes, of course he understands that. Even Arundale couldn't help that.' Dominic climbed into the driving seat of the station wagon, and set it rolling up the long, pale drive, bordered now, by fitful moonlight and scurrying cloud, with phantoms of Cothercott ingenuity even more monstrous than by day. 'Is Bunty very mad at me? I'm sorry about it, but honestly, this business . . . I don't like the look of it.' He had only recently taken to calling his mother Bunty, and it didn't come quite naturally yet, but using the old, childish form of address had suddenly become as constricting to him as a strait-jacket. He'd never so much as given it a thought until Tossa entered the house; but it still hadn't occurred to him to work out the implications.

'Not with you. Maybe with your missing folk-singer, for his bad timing. Cold, Tossa?' She was between them on the broad front seat, and shivering a little in spite of the camel-coloured car coat in which she was huddled.

'No, it's just tension, don't mind me.' She relaxed against George's shoulder, reassured by his presence. There were going to be times when Dominic would feel a little jealous of George, who, after all, was only forty-five, and tall and slim, and not that bad-looking as middle-aged men go. 'I'm glad you're here. I don't like this much, either. There are too many over-developed personalities around, things *could* happen.'

'Well, let's hear it.'

Dominic told it, as succinctly as he could, and Tossa added an occasional comment. There was no time for all the background detail now, only for the facts. Nevertheless, glimpses of personalities emerged, and they were seen to be, as Tossa had said, a little distorted, drawn from a world where bizarre and

61

improbable things could happen. The moon came out and silvered the pagoda roof, beyond the heronry where there were no herons, and picked out like a lance-thrust the black entrance of the hermit's cave, distant in its concrete rocks. Anything was believable here.

'With a house full of about eighty people,' said George, 'he thinks he's going to be able to keep this secret?'

'If it has to be a full-scale investigation, no. But long enough for you to have a look at the set-up and judge, yes, I reckon with luck we might. Because almost everybody was right away from here all afternoon, you see, with these two coach-parties. They left before we saw Lucien Galt go out into the park. And they came back only just on time for tea, and came milling in all together. They're out of it. They *can't* know anything.'

'That leaves how many? More than enough.'

'Not really, because the staff were working indoors as usual, and they're sure to be O.K. Mostly they'd be in pairs or more all the time, what with washing up after lunch, and then preparing for tea and dinner. We were here, of course, you know about us. Then there's Felicity, that's the young one I told you about, Arundale's niece. And Liri Palmer . . . she was in the grounds, too, we saw her start off towards that phoney ruin, over that way. And we four, and Mr. Marshall, are the only ones who know about what I found by the river, so far. Then there's Professor Penrose, he knows about Lucien being missing, but he doesn't know the rest yet. He'd just got them all into the drawing-room for his after-dinner session when we came back to the house.'

'And you think all that lot can be trusted to keep it dark?'

'We can only try. Yes, I think we might.'

'Even the girl? This Felicity?'

'Yes,' said Tossa positively. She cast a quick glance at Dominic, and went on, encouraged: 'She has a special reason for keeping quiet. Dominic didn't tell you quite all about her afternoon. Oh, he told what we know, but not what we *think* we know. You see, she's an odd child. But no, it *isn't* odd to be like that, not at her age, it's not odd at all. She's awkward and tense and self-conscious, and she's a sort of poor relation here, and things are pretty much hell for her, even though everybody means well. And this weekend she's gone right overboard for Lucien Galt, that's all about it. That's why she followed him out this afternoon. And when we met her coming back, we felt pretty sure he'd got fed up with having her round his neck, and sent her off with a flea in her ear. So if she seems to be covering up, that's what she's covering. And whoever tells more than they need about this afternoon, it won't be Felicity.'

'I see,' said George, touched by what she had omitted rather than what she had said. 'Don't worry, I'll leave her her dignity.'

'I know,' said Tossa warmly.

'What about the mere fact that one of the artists has missed two sessions? I suppose he should have appeared in all of them? Aren't quite a number of people going to wonder about that? Even if they don't notice *your* absence from the audience.'

'I don't think we need worry about that. We sit wherever we happen to find a place, it's liable to be different every time, and if you're not along there now, why shouldn't you be somewhere at the back? They won't wonder about us, among so many. But about Galt it is rather different. We left that to the professor. Unless he saw a need, I don't suppose he's told them anything at all, just sailed on as if everything was just as it was meant to be. But if he thought they were beginning to do some serious wondering, I bet he could hand them an absolutely first-class lie.'

'He may have to. Keeping it quiet suits me, too. I don't want seventy excited people tramping all over the place and getting in the way, any more than the county or the warden want their cherished college to get the wrong sort of advertisement. Will they still be in at the lecture now?'

'Should be. We ought to have half an hour yet.'

63

'We'll go down to this grotto of yours first, then. Can we slip in by a back door afterwards, and dodge the house-party?'

'Yes, easily, from the back courtyard, where the garages are. There's a covered passage to the basement stairs, and the warden's office is quite near the top of the staircase. The front's all gilt and carpeting and ashlar, but the back stairs is a little spiral affair. Pity,' said Dominic, 'about the light. But there's a huge torch in the glove-pocket here.'

'I want to take a look at the marks tonight, lift a sample, if possible. It's going to rain before morning.'

'He covered them,' said Tossa, promptly and proudly.

'I should hope so,' said George; but he smiled.

They swept round the dramatic bend in the drive, and the house rose superb and staggering in the bone-white moonlight to take their breath away. The long range of the drawing-room windows blazed with light, flooding the lowest of the terraces; the class was still in session.

Dominic drove round the wing of the house and into the courtyard, and there they locked the station wagon and left it, taking the torch with them. The whiteness of moonlight on the pale, complex shapes of stone here was hard and dry as an articulated skeleton, the windows glared like empty eye-sockets. Dominic led the way down to the footbridge, and in the spectral, half-fledged woodland he switched on the torch. The great, gaunt gate towered in its inadequate fence, a few yards beyond the redwood tree. They came out on the blanched greensward by the grotto. The noise of the river, more deadly than by day, reached for them, a humming, throbbing, low, ferocious roar, a tiger-cat purring, and just as dangerous and beautiful.

Carefully Dominic circled his ring of rhubarb leaves, and lifted them. The little pool of the torch's light moved in deep absorption all around the area, an eye of warmer pallor in the cold pallor of the moon.

'All right, cover them again,' said George at length. 'Where's this stuff that may be blood?'

Black is the Colour of My True Love's Heart

The two heavy drops seemed to have shrunk since early evening, but even by this light they were there, clearly visible. They had no colour now, only a darkness without colour; but they had a clear form. Liquid had dripped, not directly, but in flight from a body in motion. One was flattened on open stone, immovable; but the second was on hard ground. George took a pen-knife to it, patiently and carefully, and pared it intact out of the ground, while Tossa held the torch for him. He had brought pill-boxes with him for such small specimens as this.

'Tomorrow morning, early, I'll go over all this open ground. Maybe Mr. Marshall can find me a tarpaulin, or something to drape over this. Now where was this medal and chain you found? Yes . . . I see.'

Behind them the river roared as softly as any sucking dove, and they felt it there, and were not deceived into believing it harmless. The sound had a curious property, it seemed to be one with the vast outer silence which contained it. At night, in the grounds of Follymead, Pan and panic were conceptions as modern and close as central heating, though what they distilled was a central chill. Dominic folded his arm and his wind-jacket about Tossa, and felt her turn to him confidingly. She wasn't afraid; she only shook, like him, with awareness of chaos, braced and ready for it.

'All right,' said George, in a soft, surprised and gentle voice. 'Let's get back to the house and talk to Mr. Marshall.'

'We must have tests made, of course,' said George, installed behind the desk in Edward Arundale's private office at the top of the back stairs, 'but I think I ought to say at once that this is almost certainly blood.' The little pill-box with its pear-drop shape of dull brown on fretted gravel lay in his palm; he shut the lid over it and laid it aside. 'I needn't tell you that blood in that quantity could come from the most superficial of injuries. But we're faced with the fact that Lucien Galt has not reappeared or sent any message. Those who know him say he wouldn't cheat on a commitment. I regard this as good evidence. They know what to expect of him; they didn't expect this, and they don't accept it. He was regarded as in many ways a fiendishly difficult colleague; but he didn't give short weight once a bargain was struck. We must also face the face that the Braide in flood ran a yard or so from where these tell-tale marks were found. If there was a struggle there, as appears to be the case, then the loser may only too easily have gone over the weir and down the river. I am putting, of course, the gravest possible case, because we can't afford to ignore it. We must take into account *all* possibilities.'

Henry Marshall licked his dry lips and swallowed arduously. 'Yes, I realise that. I . . . may I take it that you will assume responsibility for whatever inquiries are necessary? I want, of course, to co-operate as fully as possible.'

'I should prefer to keep this inquiry quiet, as long as that's possible. I gather you feel the same way. Let me have this office for my own use, and keep the course running. Can you do that? I've already talked to Professor Penrose, he's quite willing to work them as hard as possible, and it looks as if they're enjoying it. Concentrate on helping him, and keep the course afloat between you, and we ought to be able to get them out of here on Monday evening none the wiser about what's been occupying us. They'll have enough to think about.'

'I shall be very grateful,' said Henry Marshall, in the understatement of the year. 'You understand my position . . . this is the first time I've been left to run a course single-handed. It would be disastrous if we allowed our students to panic and the course to disintegrate. Not only for me. I'm worried about myself, naturally, I don't pretend I'm not. But I'm honestly worried about Follymead, too. We *are* worth an effort, I give you my word we are.'

He was an honest, decent, troubled young man, not very forceful, not very experienced, but George thought Arundale might have done very much worse.

'I'm sure of that. I want to use discretion, too. But you understand that if there has been a tragedy here, if there has been a crime, that can't be suppressed. The moment I'm convinced that it's a police matter, it will become official.'

'I couldn't, in any case, agree to anything else,' said Marshall simply. 'I'm a citizen, as well as an employee afraid for his job. But there's no harm in hoping it won't come to that.'

'None at all. I've got the list of people who stayed here this afternoon, instead of joining one or other of the sight-seeing parties. Tell me if there's anyone who should be added.' He read off the list. It included four elderly ladies, all local, and therefore all acquainted with the local antiquities, and disposed to vegetate in the Follymead libraries or gardens rather than to clamber over castles; but they had booked in in pairs, and almost certainly had hunted in pairs this afternoon. With luck there would be no need to involve them. A little casual conversation – Tossa might help out here – would eliminate them. 'I realise that Mrs. Arundale will have to be told, eventually, about this inquiry. Is there anyone else who stayed here?'

'Yes,' said Marshall. 'Mr. Meurice should have gone with my coach this afternoon. He cried off at the last moment. I may be wrong, but I got the impression that he changed his mind because he found that Miss Palmer was staying.'

'It wouldn't be such an unheard-of thing to do,' agreed George. 'No one else?'

'Not that I can think off.'

'Then as time's getting on, I wonder if you'd get Felicity Cope in to me first. I won't frighten her. I believe she knows already about Mr. Galt's disappearance.'

'She knows,' said Marshall, pondering darkly how much, indeed, Felicity did know. 'You won't frighten her. She's a very precocious young woman.' It sounded like a warning; it also sounded, paradoxically, as if he felt sorry for her. George made a mental note to beware of that attitude; it might, he reflected, be the most demoralising thing in the world to feel that everyone was sorry for you.

'I know I'm difficult,' said Felicity, in a very precise and slightly superior tone. 'I *have* difficulties. I don't know how much you remember about being my age?' She gave him a sidewise look, and was arrested by the nicely-shaped growth of the grey hair at his temples; it gave him a very distinguished look. He had nice eyes, too, deep-set and quiet; it would be hard to excite him. It must be so restful, she thought, clutching at distant, desirable things to suppress her memories of anguish, to be with people who've known nearly everything, and can't get feverish any more.

'More than you'd think,' said George earnestly. He was on the same side of the desk with her, almost within touch; he knew quite a lot about making contact. 'And I have a son – that's going through it again, you know, only with one experience to build on. Not a daughter, I wasn't that lucky. My wife couldn't have any more children. We badly wanted a girl.'

'Really?' said Felicity, side-tracked. 'Uncle Edward is terribly unhappy, too, about Aunt Audrey not having any children. He's extremely fond of her, but it's always been an awful disappointment to him.' She tightened suddenly, he saw her face blanch. Her eyes, momentarily naked and vulnerable, veiled themselves. No one can be more opaque than a girl of fifteen, when she feels the need to defend herself. Why did she? From what?

'You know Lucien Galt's gone missing,' said George practically. 'It looks as if you were the last person to see him, here at Follymead. He didn't say anything to you, did he, about running out? After all, something could have happened to call him away.'

'No,' said Felicity, with a fixed, false smile. 'He didn't say anything about leaving. Nothing at all like that.'

'What did you talk about on your walk?'

'Oh, about the course, and the songs we had in the morning session. Just things like that.'

Black is the Colour of My True Love's Heart

'Miss Barber and my son were a little disturbed about you . . . did you know? They had a feeling you were unhappy . . . upset . . . when they met you this afternoon. They'd have felt better if you'd agreed to go with them. *Was* there anything the matter? You know, it's a kindness to confide in people. We *do* worry about one another, that's what makes us human. Tossa's had her difficulties, too, you mustn't be surprised if she has a feeling for other people's crises.' Careful, now! She had shied a little at the word he had chosen; her eyes, blankly grey, fended off his too great interest distrustfully. 'I'm not being clairvoyant,' he said patiently. 'You told me a moment ago you have difficulties. You wouldn't have mentioned them if they hadn't been on your mind.'

She looked down into her lap, clasping and unclasping her hands in a nervous pressure. The small, thin, beautifully-boned face was subtle and still, but it was a braced and wary stillness.

'I made my mistake,' she said, in a dry and careful voice, 'being born into a clever and distinguished family. It *is* a mistake, when you turn out to be the plain, dull, nondescript one. Uncle Edward – everybody knows how brilliant he is. And my mother – she's his sister, you know – she has an arts degree, and she paints, and sings, and plays, she can do everything. It's only because of her ill health, and because she happened to make a rather unfortunate marriage, that she didn't become a scholar and celebrity like him. Aunt Audrey isn't an intellectual, like them, of course, she doesn't come from such an intellectual family. Her people were tradesmen who'd just got into the money. She went to a terribly select boarding school, and all that – Pleydells, I expect you've heard of it? – but she didn't get any great distinctions, they took her away before her final exams. I've never understood why. Maybe they weren't interested in academic success, all they wanted was the cachet. But she was everything else, you see. It's enough to be so beautiful, don't you think so? She's beautiful, and she knows how to do everything beautifully, even if she doesn't do it so terribly well. Me, I'm well-read, and I'm not stupid, but that's all I've got, and in our family it just isn't enough. Even things I can really do well, I find myself doing so badly . . . It's . . . a personal thing. I try too hard, and over-reach myself. It isn't easy, being the one without any gifts at all. I can't see any future ahead of me, except playing second fiddle all my life to someone. I *know* I have moods! Wouldn't you have moods?'

Most of which was her mother speaking; and the faithful repetition of the threnody of complaint only went to show the helpless and vulnerable affection she had for her mother. She hadn't yet turned to doubt any of that, or pick it to pieces as some young people can and do, and find all the flaws in it. There was a lot of undeserved loyalty wrapped up in this rather pathetic package.

She caught his eye, and her pale cheek warmed a little. She liked the thick, strongly marked eyebrows that yet stood so tranquilly apart, with none of the menace of those brows that almost meet over the bridge of the nose. She minded his penetrating glance less than she had expected, and yet she was afraid of it.

'I suppose I'm a psychiatric case, really,' she said rather loftily, 'only nobody's done anything about it, so far.'

'On the contrary, I think you're a completely normal adolescent who has suffered from rather too much adult companionship,' said George candidly, and smiled at her astonished, even affronted stare. 'Abnormalities *are* the norm, when you're struggling out of one stage and into another. Let's face it, Felicity, you're not grown-up yet, you're only growing up. I haven't forgotten how damned uncomfortable it is. I've seen it happen to others. You're not doing too badly. Just don't take any of your elders too seriously. Above all, don't take any of them as the gospel. Not even the psychiatrists, some of them need psychiatrists too. Is that what was troubling you, this afternoon?'

He had brought her back to the matter in hand none the less firmly for the gentleness of his manner; but she didn't hold it against him, she knew she had to face it. The long, fair lashes lay on her cheeks. Her face was set, and she wasn't going to show him her eyes.

'It makes it worse that I have been so much with grown ups. I still am. They expect me to act like an adult, and yet they don't treat me as one. They get the work out of me, and then expect me to be in bed by ten. I did try to confide. I . . . I didn't choose very well. He hadn't got time to listen to me. I thought . . . he's only twenty-three, and women are so much more mature . . . I thought we could be contemporaries but he . . . I saw it wasn't any good,' said Felicity with dignity, 'so I went away and left him. But you'll understand, I didn't want to talk to anyone after that.'

'I do understand. You left him . . . where?'

'Just under the redwood tree,' she said firmly, 'where the paths cross.'

'You took the path to the bridge? And left him standing there?'

'Yes,' she said, with the flat finality of a slab of stone being laid over a grave.

'Let me be quite certain . . . he was then at the cross-roads, and outside the fence that rails off the riverside enclosure with the grotto?'

'Yes,' she said, with the same intonation.

'You didn't look round to see where he went from there?'

'I didn't look round at all. I'd been dismissed, I went,' said Felicity, with completely adult bitterness.

'And that was the last you saw of him? You don't know where he went from there?'

'I do now,' said Felicity. 'I didn't then. That was the last I saw of him.'

She looked up. Her eyes were enormous in fear and grief, greedy for reassurance. Of this terror and this hope there was no doubt whatever. 'Mr. Felse, do you think something happened to him? You don't . . . you don't think he's . . .?'

'I don't think anything yet,' said George. 'I hope he's simply suffered a crisis of his own, and run away from whatever was on *his* mind. Don't think he's exempt at twenty-three. Maybe he was so full of his own problems he couldn't spare any consideration for yours. If we can find him, be sure we will. Now you go to bed, and leave it to us. If you've told me all you know, there's nothing more you can do.'

'I've told you all I know.' She got as far as the door, and looked back. Her face was mute and stiff, but her eyes were full of haunted shadows. 'Good night, Mr. Felse!'

'Good night, Felicity!'

And all that, thought George, watching her go, sounds like truth, and nothing but truth. But he still had an uneasy feeling that truth, with Felicity, was an iceberg, with eight-ninths of its bulk under water.

'I'd better tell you at once,' said Dickie Meurice, settling himself at his ease and spreading an elbow on Edward Arundale's desk, 'that of course I've realised what this is all about, even if there's been no official admission that anything's wrong. Old Penrose has given the impression that everything's proceeding according to plan, and he had no intention of using Lucien Galt in to-night's lectures. Without even saying so, which is pretty good going, but then, he's a deep old bird. But I know too well what Lucifer costs. If they bought him at all, they wanted him onstage the whole weekend. And I know *him* too well to miss the moment when he absents himself from among us. He went off, voluntarily or otherwise, between lunch and tea. And *you're* here to cover the management, in case it turns out he didn't disappear voluntarily. Solicitor? Or private trouble-shooter?'

'County C.I.D.,' said George without expression but not without relish, and saw with satisfaction the instant recoil, quickly mastered but not quickly enough.

Dickie Meurice tapped his cigarette on the arm of his chair, and stared, and thought so hard that his blond countenance paled. He said carefully, lightly: 'You don't mean you've found him? You've got a genuine police case? This is official?'

'Not yet. If everybody co-operates it may not have to be. No, *we* don't know yet where Lucien Galt is. Do *you*, Mr. Meurice?'

'Why should *I* know?' The smile a little strained now, the voice demonstrating involuntarily its disastrous tendency to shrillness.

'You had, it seems, about the same chance of being the last to see him, this afternoon, as any of the others who passed up the sight-seeing trips and stayed at Follymead. Were you?'

'Look,' said Meurice, persuasively, leaning forward with the look of shining candour that meant he was at his most devious, 'if this is on the level, if it's a police job, of course I'll co-operate.' He had made up his mind rapidly enough where his interests lay, and that they were already involved; tweak that string occasionally, and he'd co-operate, maybe even a bit too much. 'Tell me what you expect of me, ask me whatever you want to know, and I'm with you.'

'I expect you to keep this strictly to yourself until, or unless, publicity becomes inevitable. Only a handful of people know about it, and it's better for all concerned that it should remain that way. Better for Follymead, better for all these people attending the course, better for the artists involved, and better for me. Publicity may be very good business in your profession, of course, but only the right kind of publicity. And as you happen to be one of those who stayed at home today . . . Though of course, you may be able to account for every minute of your time, and provide confirmation of your account . . .'

The artless, concerned smile became even more winning and anxious to help. So he couldn't account for his time; and he would play ball, though perhaps not strictly by the rules.

'I don't need that kind of publicity, I can't use it. I'll keep it quiet, don't worry. What can I tell you?'

'You were going on one of these coach-trips, I gather, originally. What made you change your mind?'

'I thought I could use my time better here. There's no chance to talk seriously to anyone at this sort of affair, with seventy or eighty people milling around in a communal spree. And there was someone I wanted to talk to. And she didn't go, so I didn't go.'

'Liri Palmer?'

'That's right. I thought there might be a good opportunity of cultivating her company while the place was virtually empty.' He was being very frank, very open; an honest man would have looked less eager, and sounded a good deal less forthcoming. 'I like Liri. She's wasting herself on a heel like Lucien Galt, whether she loves or hates him. I wanted to tell her so, and get some sense into her. I don't know whether they've told you what's in the background between those two, or what happened last night?' He didn't wait to be answered, he told it anyhow; no one could do it better. Maybe he wanted it on record officially that someone, and not himself, had threatened Lucien Galt's life; if, that is, you cared to take that impromptu revision of a song as a serious threat. He liked Liri Palmer – or did he? – but he liked Dickie Meurice a lot better.

'I see you don't exactly love Galt, yourself,' observed George.

'That's no secret. Why should it be? He's treated Liri badly, and the rest of his profession didn't christen him Lucifer for nothing. But I didn't set eyes on him all this afternoon,' he said firmly. 'The last time I saw him was at lunch.'

'But you did see Liri?'

'Yes, I hung around in the gallery until she went out, and gave her five minutes start. Just after two o'clock, that would be. She made for that artificial ruin on the hillock across the park, and I came along shortly afterwards and found her there. I tried to get her to write off Galt and spend her attention on something better worth it – me!' A gleam of apparently genuine self-mockery shone in his eyes for an instant; it was the nearest he had come to being likeable, but in all probability he was merely experimenting to find out what attitudes would recommend him to George.

74

'Was she amenable?' asked George, with a wooden face.

'Metaphorically speaking, she spat in my eye. Nobody was going to put Liri off her grudges or her fancies.'

'And which was this?'

'At that stage, I'd say practically all grudge. She'd been badly hurt, and she can be an implacable enemy. I saw I was getting nowhere, so I gave up and came away. There was hardly anybody about, I'm afraid, I can't bring witnesses, but I give you my word I was back in the walled garden soon after three o'clock, and I didn't leave there until I came in to tea. There are archery butts there. I was practising all by myself until four, and then I came indoors to wash. And that's all. Not a very productive afternoon.'

'And you left Liri there at the tower. When would that be?'

'Maybe about twenty minutes to three. She was sitting there alone, nobody else in sight that I noticed.'

'You wouldn't see very much of the river's course from there?'

The winsome blue eyes lit with a flare of intelligence that was not winsome at all. 'Well, not from the ground, that I do know. There are tall trees in between, all you see is a gleam of water here and there. But there's a stairway up that tower,' he added helpfully. 'I haven't been up there, but I should think you'd get a pretty good view with that added height. Not that she showed any signs of making use of it,' he concluded fairly, 'while I was there.'

'Well, thank you, Mr. Meurice, you've been very helpful. If we should have any difficulty in filling in the details of the afternoon, I'm sure you'll do your best for us again. And you will keep the matter confidential?'

Give him his due, he could take a double-edged hint as well as the next man. He promised secrecy with almost unnecessary fervour, and departed, having done his level best to plant the suggestion that, if something had really happened to Lucien

Galt, Liri Palmer had made it happen. Who else, after all, had threatened his life?

George sighed, grimaced, and sent for Liri Palmer.

'Oh, he was there, all right.' Liri crossed her long and elegant legs, and declined a cigarette with a shake of her head. 'He was doing his best to make up to me, but I wasn't having any. What it adds up to is that he was inviting me to join in an all-out attack on Lucien's professional position. A lot of dirty work goes on in the record business, and popular disc-jockeys have a lot of influence. With a few like-minded assassins as dedicated as himself, Meurice could ruin a man.'

'And you were not interested?'

Her lips curled disdainfully. 'If I decide on assassination, I shan't need any allies. I told him where he could go.'

'Yesterday, I hear, you made what could be considered as being a threat against Galt, about as publicly as possible.'

'Oh, that!' A tight, dark smile hollowed her cheeks, but she was not disconcerted. 'Dickie made sure you knew about that, of course. He needn't have worried, I'd have told you myself. Yes, it's true. I did that.' She sounded faintly astonished now in looking back at it, as though it had become irrelevant and quite unaccountable in retrospect.

'Did you mean it?' asked George directly.

'Did I mean it . . . Yes, at the time I probably did. But even then what I really had in mind was not action so much as a declaration of my position. All the rest of them just happened to be there,' she said, with an arrogance Lucifer himself could not have bettered. 'It was nothing to do with them.'

'Then you didn't act on it, this afternoon?'

It was the first direct and deliberate suggestion that Lucien Galt might have suffered a murderous attack, might, in fact, be dead at that moment. She received it fully, thoughtfully and silently, and betrayed neither surprise nor any other emotion. What she thought, what she felt, she kept to herself. Like her private communications in song, they were nothing to do with anyone else. This was a young woman accustomed to standing on her own feet, and asking no quarter from anyone.

'I didn't see Lucien this afternoon. He never came near me, and I didn't go looking for him. I sent Dickie Meurice away, and stayed up there at the folly until it was time to come in to tea.'

'Not, I feel, without some sort of occupation?'

Her smile warmed a little, but remained dark and laden. 'I was wrestling with an idea for a song. It didn't work out.'

'Miss Palmer, I've gathered – and not only from Meurice – that a little while ago your relations with Lucien Galt were very close indeed. Would you mind telling me the reason for your break with him?'

'Yes,' said Liri, directly, firmly, 'I would mind. It's a private matter between him and me, and I want it to stay that way.'

He accepted that without question. 'Then, if you're good at keeping things private, keep this interview, this whole investigation, between the few of us. This weekend may as well run its course without a general alarm, if it can. And there's one more thing I'd like to consult you about.'

He laid upon her knee the small box in which he had placed the silver medal and chain. 'My son found this at a certain spot by the river. Maybe you've already seen it.'

She took up the box in her palm, and touched the little disc gently with one long finger. 'Yes, I've seen it. Dominic showed it to us – the few of us who knew. It's Lucien's. He always wore it.'

'Always? As long as you've known him?'

'Yes, from the first time I met him. He said he'd worn it ever since he was a child. It was the one thing he had that belonged to his father.'

'He told you that himself? And how long have you known him?'

'Just over two years now. Yes, he told me himself.' There had been confidences between them then, and confidence. He was

77

not, by all accounts, a person who talked about himself, or indeed much of a talker on any subject. 'He wouldn't have much left from his parents, obviously, after their shop was flattened by a buzz-bomb. You know about the Galts? They had a newsagent and tobacconist business in Islington. It was one of the last bombs of the war that got it. Both his parents were killed. He grew up in a children's home.'

'I know what's been published about him,' said George.

'That's all most of us know. He loved his foster-parents at the home, though, there wasn't any warping there. He still goes back there pretty regularly.' She looked up suddenly; her face was pale and still. 'He *did*,' she said, and closed the box carefully over the silver medal.

'Mr. Marshall has told me,' said Audrey Arundale in a low, constrained voice, 'about this affair, and about your great kindness in coming here privately to help us. We're very grateful to you. My husband would wish me to thank you on his behalf, as well as my own. I feel – you'll understand and excuse me – terribly lost without him.'

She stood in her own rose-and-white sitting-room, herself a white rose ever so slightly past her most radiant bloom, fair and frightened and gallant, terribly lost without Edward. She was used only to things that went smoothly; things that went hideously off the rails bewildered and confused her.

'Please sit down, Mr. Felse. I feel so guilty at making use of you in this way, when we have really nothing to go on. Is there anything you want to ask me?'

'As a matter of form, I should like to know how you spent this afternoon, whether you saw anyone, and what time your husband left. I want to form as full a picture as possible of the hours between lunch and tea.'

'I understand, yes. I was indoors all afternoon. Edward was here with me until just before three o'clock, then he went out to the car, to load it for his trip. I can't say exactly what time he got off, because I didn't see him go. I think he wanted to pick up some books from the library, but that wouldn't take long. I should think he was away by a quarter past three. After he left I was in here writing letters.' She made a faint gesture of one hand towards the neat little pile of them, lying on her writing-desk. 'I didn't go down to join the party at tea, I had it in here. I didn't realise that Mr. Galt was missing, though I noticed, naturally, that he didn't take part in the five o'clock session. He hasn't come back, of course.' Her anxious face hoped against hope for reassurance.

'He hasn't. On the contrary, we've found certain traces which suggest that we have a serious matter on our hands.'

'May I know,' she asked hesitantly, 'what they are?'

He told her. She turned half aside from the mention of blood, and seemed for an instant to want to withdraw absolutely from this place and these events, which obeyed no rules in her ordered existence, and made chaos of her security. She reached out blindly and briefly with one hand for Edward, who had always been there, but Edward wasn't there. She said, though with dignity and quietness, exactly what George had felt sure she would say:

'Don't you think we ought to contact my husband and tell him what's happened? I wouldn't think of suggesting it in any normal circumstances, when Harry's in charge, but these aren't normal circumstances. This is more than the mere responsibility for the present course, it's a question of the responsibility for Follymead as an institution. Edward can't delegate that, not in such a serious matter.' She looked across the room at Henry Marshall, who had sat silent throughout this exchange. 'I'm sorry, Harry, I ought to have left it to you even to make the suggestion. I know you would have done.'

No mistake about it, that fancy boarding school of hers had done pretty well by the tradesman's daughter, even if she hadn't distinguished herself in examination, like Felicity's illustrious kin. No wonder Marshall looked at her with something like devotion.

'Mr. Felse and I have already recognised the need to put this matter on a proper footing. Obviously I hoped and believed we should have some word from Mr. Galt, or that he would turn up again with his own explanation, but after so many hours without news it becomes rather a different case. Yes, I think we should call Dr. Arundale.'

'I think perhaps I'd better do it,' said George, 'if I may. Where will he be at this hour?'

The clock on the desk said ten-forty. 'It's a guild dinner,' said Audrey. 'He's staying overnight with the chairman afterwards, but they won't be very early. I should think they're still at the Metropole. I have the number here.'

George dialled and waited for his connection. It was very quiet in the room; even the clock was almost silent.

'Hotel Metropole? I believe you've got the Vintners' annual dinner there tonight? Is the party still in session? Good! Would you ask Mr. Arundale to come to the phone? That's right, Edward Arundale – he's their speaker tonight.' He waited. Audrey felt behind her for the arm of a chair, and sat down very slowly and silently, never taking her eyes from George's face. It felt so still that she might have been holding her breath.

'Hullo, is that . . .? Oh, I see. No, I didn't know that.' There was a long, curious pause while he listened, and the faint clacking of the distant voice that was, surprisingly, doing all the talking. 'At what time was that?' And again: 'You're sure? You'd know the voice? No, that's all right, I'm sorry to have disturbed you, I'll contact him there. Thank you! Goodbye!'

He cradled the receiver and held it down in its rest, and over the hand that pinned it in position he looked up gently at Audrey.

'Mrs. Arundale, I'm afraid this is going to be a surprise to you. Even a shock. Mr. Arundale isn't there. That was a man named Malcolmson speaking to me, the president of the Vintners' Guild. Mr. Arundale cancelled his engagement, they had to whip up a substitute speaker at a minute's notice.'

'But . . . that's impossible!' she said in a soundless whisper. 'Why should he cancel it? He said nothing to me. He took his notes . . . and the references he needed for tomorrow . . . everything. I didn't know anything about this . . . I didn't know . . .'

'All the same, he did it. There's no doubt at all about this. He says Mr. Arundale rang up to explain and apologise, this afternoon, just about three o'clock. He says he's known him for eight years, he knows his voice on the telephone too well for any possibility of mistake. It was your husband himself who called. An emergency, so he told him, here at Follymead, that made it impossible for him to leave as planned. Naturally Mr. Malcolmson didn't question it, however inconvenient it might be for him.' He lifted the receiver again; distant and staccato, the dialling tone fired its dotted line of machine-gun bullets into the silence. 'Can you give me the number of someone who'll know about this conference tomorrow? The secretary?'

She got up from her chair and moved to the pedestal of the desk like a creature in a bad dream. Her fingers fumbled through the pages of a notebook, and found the entry. The secretary was the vicar of a suburban parish, and his voice, when he answered, sounded young and crisp and agile.

'I'm sorry to trouble you at this late hour, but I'm clearing up a few arrears of business for Mr. Arundale, and the notes he's left me don't make it clear whether he managed to call you about the conference tomorrow. Have you already heard from him today?' No need to sound the alarm yet; this would do better than candour.

'Yes, he telephoned this afternoon,' said the distant voice promptly. 'We're very sorry indeed that we shan't have him with us tomorrow, after all, it's a great disappointment. But I know he wouldn't have called it off if he could possibly have avoided it.'

'No, of course not. About what time did he ring you?'

'Oh, I suppose shortly after three. It might even have been a little earlier.'

'Thank you,' said George, 'that's all I wanted to know.'

The telephone clashed softly in its cradle.

'He telephoned there, too, and cancelled his engagement. Wiped out all his arrangements for the weekend. And yet he took the car and left, at about the time he was expected to leave, and without mentioning to anyone that he'd changed his plans. So where has he gone? And why?'

Marshall let his hands fall empty before him; there was nowhere he could get a hold on this, and no way he could make sense of it. 'I don't know. I don't understand anything about it.'

Audrey stood motionless, her eyes enormous in shock and bewilderment. In an arduous whisper she asked: 'What must we do?'

'I don't think we have any choice now. We still have no real evidence of anything either criminal or tragic, but we have two unexplained disappearances, occurring at much the same time, and we can't ignore them, and we can't afford to delay. Lectures had much better continue as though nothing's happened. If we can get through the weekend without making this affair public, we'll do it. There'll be the least possible obtrusion. But I've no alternative now,' said George, 'but to inform my chief. From now on, this becomes an official police matter.'

Chapter 5

As soon as he was back in Edward Arundale's office, with the door closed on the distant and cheerful din of the house-party and the close and fearful silence of the warden's apartments, George telephoned his chief. Detective-Superintendent Duckett was Midshire born and bred, with all the advantages of having come up from the uniformed branch the hard way. It meant he not only knew his job and his own subordinates, but also all the complex social pressures of a conservative county; sometimes, in his less tolerant moments, he called it a feudal county, and nobody had a better right. The first thing he said was: 'Thank God your boy was there!' And the second: 'Can you still keep this dark?'

'Yes,' said George, with fair certainty that he was telling the truth. 'We've no body, no proof of a crime, only a very, very fishy situation that still may confound us by coming out blameless. Let's hope it does. In the meantime, we've every right to behave as if nothing had happened, on the surface, provided we dig like moles underneath. Only seven people know anything about my being here to investigate Galt's disappearance, though they must all know by now that he's gone. That can't be helped. Only Marshall and Mrs. Arundale know that Arundale's apparently run out.'

'That suits me, and it'll suit the Chief Constable still better.

He's a prime backer of that outfit at Follymead. The place balances its budget and fends off the tax-payers by luck, faith and act of God. What can we dig for you?'

'It's going to be pretty sticky,' said George honestly, 'in any case. Don't forget one of the parties concerned is the warden. What we're going to find is anybody's guess, but what I've got here is a nasty situation in which two people have vanished, one apparently without warning and involuntarily, the other with evidence of premeditation. No bodies, no known motives for any violence, but some evidence that there *was* a struggle, that there *were* injuries. If there's a link between these two people, I want to know about it. I'm not so simple as to believe that they could both take off into the blue at the same moment, and no connection between the two events. It's against the law of averages. Now, these two are public persons. I'd like reports on their backgrounds. I want to know if there could be a link between them, and if so, what it is. And brace yourself, in case what comes out goes against Arundale. Because *he's* the one who planned his departure, not the boy.'

'If he slung the kid in the river,' said Duckett with admirable directness, 'neither you nor I can get him out of the resultant mess, George, my boy. With luck we might get Follymead out of it. Knock off fifty per cent for over-enthusiasm, and still the place is worth preserving.'

'I think so, too. All right, at first light I'm going down to look over the ground again, carefully. I hope to have some specimens for the lab boys, and I don't care if we do have to pull 'em back from their Sunday hobbies.'

'Right, and first thing tomorrow I'll have Scott turned loose on their histories.' He was silent for one pregnant second. 'How's the flood level?'

'High,' said George. 'I reckon anything that went in there would bounce that last weir like a cork, and be out of the grounds long before now. We're past the fancy curves at that point. The next real check is the bend by Sandy Cliff, the other

84

side of the main road. Anything can happen with this sort of spring flow, but I should start dragging there. That's where he's most likely to come ashore.'

George went down to the riverside in the first light of morning. The threatened rain had fallen in the small hours, while he had slept uneasily and briefly in Arundale's office, declining the bed Marshall had offered him. The dawn sky was tattered with filmy clouds and fitful brightness, and the grass was saturated and silvery against the river's turgid brown. Slanting light picked out in deep relief the wounds in the turf, still dark, fresh and soft from the protection of Marshall's plastic car-cover. George went over the ground carefully, inch by inch. There was only one clear print, and that of only the sole of a shoe, stamped into the raw clay, a composition sole cross-cut in saw-tooth grooves for grip. A well-shaped shoe with a good conservative toe, maybe size nine; the kind two-thirds of the men in the house probably wore, half of them in this size. All the rest of the tracks were trampled over, crossed and blurred by the resilience of the grass, but in sum they were there, and their implications unmistakable.

He found one other thing. One of the stamping feet, driving in a heel deeply, had left behind in the print one of last autumn's leaves from the ride, one of the old ivy leaves, rubbery even in decay, that drop with their naked, angular stems, and lie long after the rest of the woodland loss is mould. This one had been cupped round the edge of the shoe's heel, and remained so, pressed into the turf; and something that was not water, something hardly visible at twilight against its brown colouring, had splashed into it later, and gathered in the cup. Warm and sheltered under the plastic sheeting, it had remained moist. Not so much of it, maybe, as they take from your thumb for a blood test; but possibly as much as the lab boys would need in order to group it.

George extracted the moulded leaf gingerly, and found another little box for it, propping its edges with cotton-wool and keeping it upright. There was nothing else here for him. He covered the bruised ground again, and prowled along the very edge of the water; it seemed to him that it had risen a shade higher in the night with the new rain, but he had seen it last night only by moonlight and torchlight. Certainly in this green, moist dawn, full of the drippings and whisperings of water, that concentrated brown flood was impressive. No finding anything in that without dragging, or going down into it; not until chemistry did its work, and it surfaced again, and judging by the force of this current that would be miles downstream. The coiled curve by Sandy Cliff just might bring it ashore, as he had said to Duckett; but even there the water would be over the summer beach and burrowing hard under the cliff, and whatever it carried might continue downstream with it.

George made his way thoughtfully back to the house, mapping this part of the Follymead grounds mentally as he went; and in the warden's office Dominic was waiting for him.

'Hullo!' said George with unflattering surprise. 'Whatever got you up at this hour?'

'I thought of something that may be important. I meant to be up earlier, but I had to be careful. I've got the Rossignol twins in my room, and they can hear the grass growing. I didn't want to bring the whole hunt down on you. But it's all right,' Dominic said in hasty reassurance, 'I left them dead asleep.' He looked from his father's face to the small box carried so carefully in his hand. He didn't ask any questions about it, and George didn't volunteer anything.

'All right, what's on your mind?'

'It was on my mind, too, half the night. You know how it is when you know you've seen something before, and can't for your life think where or when? I woke up suddenly this morning, and I'd got it. That medal . . . could we have another look at it, and I'll show you.'

The pill-box that contained it was locked into the top drawer of Arundale's desk. George extracted and offered it. Dominic remembered to turn it with the tip of a ball-pen when he wanted to refer to the reverse, as he had remembered not to handle it directly when he first found it. He shivered a little with clinging sleepiness and the chill of the morning.

'You see here, this side, that formalised figure in armour, with a nutshell helmet like the Normans in the Bayeaux tapestry, and a long shield with a sort of spread eagle on it . . .? I suddenly remembered where I'd seen it before. You can't mistake it once you do get the idea. That's Saint Wenceslas. Yes, I'm quite sure. He always looks like that. You ask Tossa, she'll tell you the same, we got to know the form last year, when we were in Prague on holiday. And the other side . . .' He turned it delicately to show the lion rampant with a forked tail. 'This I *can* show you, right here. I should have known it on sight if it hadn't been quite so worn. Look! By pure luck I happened to have this still in my jacket.'

He held it out triumphantly, a small badge, questionably silver, unquestionably the same rampaging lion, with feathery fringes like a retriever, and double tail bristling.

'Lieutenant Ondrejov gave me that, before we left Liptovsky Pavol, last year. You see, it *is* the same. This is the Czech lion. And Saint Wenceslas is the chief of their patron saints, and doesn't belong to anyone else. I bet you anything you like this medal originated in Czechoslovakia.'

George measured the two small heraldic creatures, and found them one. 'Now why,' he wondered aloud blankly, 'should Lucien Galt be wearing a Czech medal?'

'I wish I knew. But that's what this is.'

George stared, and thought, and could not doubt it. This was, according to Liri Palmer, the one thing Lucien had that had belonged to his father. That didn't, of course, determine to whom it might have belonged earlier. It was wartime, Galt could perfectly well have had some chance-met friend among the self-exiled Czechs who formed, at that time, the most articulate, the most reticent – the two were compatible! – and the most nearly

English component of the European armies in Britain. Maybe they swopped small tokens before the unit moved out for D-Day; and maybe the medal acquired value because its giver didn't come back. There were such things, then, unexpected friendships that went deeper than kith and kin.

'Well, thanks very much for the tip. It's certainly curious.' George pocketed the trophy along with his other specimens. 'And since you are up, how about running me down to the lodge and bringing back the station wagon afterwards?'

'Yes, of course.' He brightened perceptibly at the thought of being useful. 'You're going in to headquarters? Is it official, then?'

'It's official, but it's still not for publication.'

'Shall I meet you at the lodge again when you come back?'

'No need. I'll drive up by the farm road at the back, and put my car in the yard there. I might need to get out and in quickly, later in the day.'

'Is there anything I can be doing?'

'Yes, but you won't like it much.'

'I still might do it,' said Dominic generously, 'seeing as it's for you.'

'Be on the spot here, then, attend everything, and help to keep everybody occupied and out of our hair. Have a word with Professor Penrose, and ask him to lay on a session after lunch, too, even if it wasn't in the programme. Keep everybody's nose hard against this folk-music grindstone, and try to make the whole weekend pass off without anything of this business leaking out. Get the professor to ask Liri Palmer to take part in every session. If the stars back him up, the rank and file won't want to miss anything.'

'And in the meantime,' Dominic asked soberly, perceiving one answer for himself, and not much liking it, 'what *will* they be missing?'

'Maybe nothing. But I don't want them down by the river. They wouldn't get to the grotto, anyhow, I shall have a watchdog on duty. But I'd rather they didn't know that, either, so keep them hard at work here in the house.'

'We can but try. Anything else?'

'Keep your ears open. I'd like to know what sort of comments they're making. The professor will probably have to tell them some tale about Galt being called away, but, even so they'll have their own theories. I want to know what they are, and who starts them. And anything else you notice that may be of interest.'

'When shall I see you, then, to report? Hadn't we better have an arrangement?'

'Come down to the grotto as soon after lunch as you can, and come on the quiet. If I'm not there, Price will know where to find me.'

'There it is, then,' said Duckett, shuffling the typed pages across the table, 'and much good it does us.'

And there it was, compressed, bald and completely barren, the fruit of Scott's interim researches into the past history of Edward Arundale and Lucien Galt. And nothing could be more above-board.

Arundale, only son of an illustrious academic family, one sister, five years younger; father a historian, mother a specialist in Oriental languages, both dead; his school, his college, his degrees, all listed, all impeccable; a distinguished teaching career, culminating in the headmastership of Bannerets, which he held for fifteen years, and after that this appointment as warden of Follymead. Married in 1946 Audrey Lavinia Morgan, only child of Arthur Morgan, of Morgan's Stores, a chain of groceries covering the south of England. The bride, it seemed, was then twenty years old, and Arundale, thirty-five. Her father's money was recent and plentiful, *his* father having merely run two modest suburban shops, and limited his ambition to getting elected to the local council. Arthur, or maybe Mrs. Arthur, had bigger ideas for their offspring. Audrey had been sent to Pleydells, a good boarding-school in North London, though evacuated to

Scotland during the war years, which must have been Audrey's period. It seemed that the Morgans were then on the climb, bent on equipping their daughter for an outstanding marriage. Maybe Arundale's was the kind of lustre they valued and wanted. No university career for Audrey, no mention of any special academic qualifications; just as Felicity had said, quoting, no doubt, her aggrieved mother. Her upbringing had been aimed at marriage, not a career. Edward supplied all the scholarly distinctions necessary, she provided him with a hostess well-trained, conscientious and lovely to look at. All very satisfactory, and nowhere a shadow on it. Their life at Follymead was constantly in the public eye, and the public eye doesn't miss much.

That was Arundale. And in the other file, this boy from a children's home, bright, handsome, aggressive, disdainful, intolerant of adulation, and single-minded about his art. Lucien Galt, born 1943, son of John James and Esther Galt, who kept a small newsagent's shop in Islington. Parents killed by a V-2, one of the last to fall on London, son taken into public care and brought up in one of a group of cottage homes in Surrey. Good school record, early development of musical ability, apparently well adjusted, never in anything worth calling trouble. Not interested in staying on at school, already set on music. Left at fifteen, and worked as a garage hand and mechanic until he broke into the record business, broadcasting and television, all in the same month, at the age of nineteen. Made a tremendous success as a folk singer, several European tours behind him, heading for a South American tour very soon. Said to be still on the warmest terms with his former foster-parents at the home, visiting them regularly, and being credited with several gifts to the present household. Considered difficult in the entertainment world because there are songs he won't sing, engagements he won't accept, places he won't go, and indeed nothing he will do except what he wants to do.

And all they knew of him, to add to that dossier, was that he had worn a silver medal on a chain round his neck, that he had told Liri Palmer it was all he had of his father's, and that he had left it lying in the grass by the river when he vanished from Follymead.

'Not a thing in common between them,' said Duckett, 'and not a thing to show that they'd ever clapped eyes on each other before Friday night. How can you get to the point of murder in only twenty-four hours?'

'How do you even get to the point of being on fighting terms in only twenty-four hours? With their kind of contact and at that kind of place?'

'There's always the classic way,' said Duckett disgustedly. '*Cherchez la femme!*' He wasn't serious, of course; Arundale's past was so rigid with rectitude that the idea of connecting him with a *crime passionnel* managed to be almost funny. Besides, there was only one woman in his life, apparently, and that was his equally blameless wife, to whom he'd been married for twenty well-matched years. 'Putting him on one side, just for argument, I gather there are others who might be capable of pushing this lad in the river?'

'Several, I'd say. The girl has all the necessary fire and guts, and Meurice hates him enough, given the opportunity. And either of them *could* have been there with him at round about the right time.'

Duckett breathed pipe-smoke heavily through his brigand's moustache, and drummed a thick fingertip on the edge of his desk. 'Well, I'll keep Scott on the job. If we take anything out of the river,' he said grimly, 'you'll be the first to know about it. What can Scott most usefully be doing for you?'

George considered, frowning at the meaningless pages that yet must hold somewhere a more substantial image of the persons to whom they applied. 'Seems to me that if Galt had anything to confide, the people he'd turn to would be his foster-parents, this house-father and mother – Stewart, the name seems to be. It might be worth a drive down there to see if they can shed any light. With a lot of luck he may have gone to them, or at least got in touch with them – *if* he's alive, if this is some other sort of trouble that's caught up with him. And Scott could call in on this service garage where the boy worked, that's another possibility, if a thin one. Then there's his business agent, of course. Send Scott down there, have him comb out the lot, all the people he might have turned to if he's alive and in trouble.'

'Right, I'll see to that. We can't put out a call for Arundale or the car,' said Duckett reasonably, 'unless we do bring the body ashore. It would be as much as my life's worth to compromise that set-up for nothing, so let's concentrate on finding the boy – dead or alive.'

George was smoking a cigarette moodily by the river, watching a methodical sergeant take casts – probably useless – of the one clear shoe-print and the indentation of the heel, when Dominic came to report. The dragging of the Braide had not yet reached the Follymead boundary, more than a quarter of a mile away; nor, so far, had it netted them anything more than driftwood, two long-abandoned eel-traps, and an old bicycle frame. By the quantity and size of the driftwood you could gauge the violence and indiscipline of the spring. The Braide ran down to the Comer, which was a river with its feet in the mountains; this was a tamed park stream by comparison with what the Comer brought down out of Wales. Any more rain, and Comer-water would be backing up from the confluence, churning up the muddy counter-current until they both spilled out over the whole expanse of the low-lying fields. Lucien Galt might yet fetch up on somebody's doorstep.

George heard them coming through the trees, not one, but two, a boy and a girl talking briefly, in subdued and serious voices. He should have thought of that possibility, of course, but it came as something of a revelation that Dominic should have reached the point of taking it for granted that any privilege given to him automatically extended to cover Tossa, too. 'They' were to be deflected by any means from this area by the river; but Tossa was not 'they', Tossa had become 'we'. It was not quite so clear whether she also took it as her right. The moment they emerged from the trees she slipped her hand from Dominic's and hung back, silent and tentative, but very much on the alert. She caught George's eye and moved nearer, encouraged. Under the ornamental trees that circled the grotto she halted; the tiny blue crosses of lilac blossom drifted down into her dark hair, as the branches threshed uneasily in a rising wind.

'Well,' said George, 'how are things going?'

'All O.K., so far. Everybody's come along to the lectures, and they all seem to be enjoying themselves. I told the professor what you said, and Mr. Marshall, too. It's working smoothly enough up to now. Nobody's let anything out to the others, and they don't suspect anything's wrong. The professor made a sort of vague apology for Lucien's having to leave, but he managed not to say anything definite about the reason. But you were right about the rumours. There's a murmur that Lucien ran out because he couldn't take the Liri situation . . . You know, she'd followed him here with a grudge, and the astmosphere was tense, and he preferred to duck out. It makes good sense, and it tickles them, so they like it. And it lets the professor out, too, because of course the authorities would simply have to accept whatever excuse Lucien offered, even if they thought privately he'd run for cover from a situation he couldn't manage.'

'That ought to serve pretty well,' agreed George with a wry smile. 'Go along with it. Who started it?'

'Well, I'm pretty sure it came from Dickie Meurice in the first place. That way, you see, he makes a good show of helping you to keep the thing wrapped, and at the same time he churns up a little more dirt to stick to Galt when he does reappear. *If* he does reappear,' he corrected himself, very soberly.

'He will,' protested Tossa, her eyes fixed confidently on George's face. 'Won't he? This is just something quite stupid, that only *looks* like that sort of trouble, isn't it?'

93

'We hope so,' said George gently. 'You keep on thinking so. What about this afternoon?'

'That's all fixed. We're in session again at two–fifteen. We slipped out by the back way as soon as we got away from lunch, and came down through the trees. Nobody's any the wiser.'

'Good! Has Felicity attended this morning?'

'We sat with her,' said Tossa, 'the first time. I think she only came at all because nobody can talk to her while there's a lecture going on, or people singing. She looks terribly wretched and sick. She dodged us in the second session, after coffee. And as soon as we're out of the music-room she goes off somewhere out of sight. I'm worried about her. But she doesn't want anybody, she only wants to be left alone.'

'Keep an eye on her,' said George, 'all the same. Did Mrs. Arundale show up?'

'Yes. She looked pretty pale and anxious, too,' said Dominic, 'but she's keeping the thing rolling. It must be rather awful for her, having something like this happen, especially when the warden isn't here. I bet she'll be glad when he comes back to-night.'

George said nothing to that; there was no need to burden them with even more secrets to keep, however trustworthy they might be. As for accounting for Arundale's non-return this evening from those meetings in Birmingham, leave that bridge to be crossed when the time came.

His mind had been much on Audrey Arundale, ever since he had talked to Duckett this morning. *Cherchez la femme*, indeed, but what an unlikely woman to look for at the heart of a *crime passionnel*. And yet she had everything but the temperament; beauty, a gentle appeal about her, even youth – she was only forty, and older women have changed history in their time. Maybe this wasn't the first time *she* had met Lucien Galt.

No, it was crazy. He couldn't picture her in the role, however objectively he tried. Nevertheless, he found himself asking, with deliberate and crude abruptness: 'Have you seen any signs of a special relationship between Lucien Galt and Mrs. Arundale?'

Dominic was too startled to side-step, and too shaken to hide his discomfort. He stood staring in consternation, seeing again the ardent hands touch and clasp, seeing Arundale walk imperviously and majestically on his wife's left, while she gripped Lucien Galt's fingers on her right. The question was so unexpected, the incident had begun to seem so irrelevant, that the sudden attack took his breath away. After all, Arundale didn't enter into the affair they were investigating. He was the one person who was out of it, surely. The only person.

'I . . . what on earth has that got to do . . . I mean, nothing, really, nothing of any significance.'

'Come on,' said George quietly, 'tell it, and we'll see.' Tossa was looking from one to the other of them, lost, a small, hurt frown contorting her brows. Whatever Dominic had seen had certainly passed her by.

'Well, I don't know . . . It was just that on Friday night, when we left the drawing-room after coffee, and were walking along the gallery, we were behind the Arundales and Lucien Galt. Mrs. Arundale was in the middle. They were talking, just like anybody else, and Lucien's hand brushed . . .' Dominic's voice baulked at that half-willing distortion, and backed away from it. 'He touched her hand, and she opened it, and they clasped hands,' he said grudgingly. 'Only for a moment, though.'

'But . . . warmly?'

After a moment of silent debate Dominic admitted: 'Yes.' He went on rapidly: 'But it needn't mean much, you know. Just big-headedness on his part, and maybe she felt a bit irresponsible for once . . . an accidental touch . . .'

'Did it look accidental?' asked George quite gently.

Reluctantly but honestly again: 'No.'

'And they went on making conversation to cover it?' No need to answer that, it was in his mutely anxious face. 'Did anyone else see this?'

95

Almost to herself Tossa said: '*I* didn't.'

'Yes, I think . . . I'm almost sure Liri saw it. She was sitting in a dark alcove in the gallery, quite still. I think she saw.'

Add about fifty per cent to that, and you might have some approximation of the ardour of that episode. Dominic had a very natural and human reluctance to admit to having witnessed a show of affection between two people who thought themselves unobserved. And it was no more than a crumb of a connection, at that, though a very suggestive one.

'All right, don't worry, as you say, it probably means virtually nothing.'

But Liri had seen it, Liri of all people. Maybe the emerging pattern, after all, argued a man at the heart of it, not a woman. *Cherchez l'homme*! Women can be jealous, too, and dangerous.

'You'd better run,' said George, 'or you'll be late for your class. If you should want me later, I'll be in the warden's office.'

And they ran, Tossa looking back doubtfully at George for a moment with her chin on her shoulder. The lilac tree slapped a stray cone of blossom into her face as she turned, and she flung up her free hand – Dominic had taken possession of the other – and brushed it from her. The twig broke, leaving the spray of falling flowers in her hand. She allowed herself to be towed along the leafy ride still holding it.

'You never told me!'

'You wouldn't have told me, would you? I never *wanted* to see it.' He wasn't happy. 'What put it into Dad's mind, anyhow? I don't get it.'

'I don't know. Maybe he thinks *Liri* . . .'

'What, just because of that?'

'But it isn't *just* because of that. Liri was already mad with him about something, what could it be but another woman?'

'You mean she followed him here because she knew about him and . . .? I don't believe it! It wouldn't be like Liri, anyhow.' He had never realised until now how firm an idea he was forming of Liri Palmer's character. 'If she'd broken with him, she wouldn't follow him around to *watch* him perform . . . not to torment herself, not to hit him again, not for anything.' They had reached the foot-bridge; their hurrying footsteps clopped woodenly over it, and the flood below sent up a low, hollow echo.

'To get him back, she might,' said Tossa without thinking, and instantly drew back from a statement so revealing. She shook the loose blossoms from her spray of lilac with unnecessary care. 'This must be a very early kind, look, dropping already, and it's only late April. Did you ever see lilac quite such a pure blue?'

Even then she didn't realise what she had said, it was simply a pleasant, superficial observation, something blessedly remote from the ugly mystery that was bedevilling this weekend. They were skirting the open meadow when the truth hit her. She halted abruptly, pulling back hard on Dominic's hand; he turned in surprise to find her gazing at him in consternation.

'Dominic . . . *she was there*! Don't you remember? I said then, how blue, really blue, not purple at all . . .'

She thrust the tattered cone of blossom at him, brandishing it before his astonished eyes.

'Have you seen this kind anywhere else? There's lilac by the drive, and up by the pagoda, too, but it's all white or mauve, and it's only in bud yet. Nothing at all like this. But Felicity had some fallen flowers just like this in her hair yesterday! Don't you remember, she was combing them out with her fingers?'

'Good lord!' he said blankly. 'She had, too! *Just* like these!'

'I picked them up, afterwards. It was the *colour* . . .'

He remembered now with aching clarity how Tossa had turned her hand sadly, and let the small blue crosses float back into the grass.

'But she told Dad . . . she told *us* . . .'

'I know! She told us she parted from him where the paths cross. She said she left him there and came on over the stone bridge . . . She didn't know where he went afterwards, but *she* left him *there*. But she didn't,' said Tossa with absolute conviction, and very quietly. 'Because before she met us she was under

97

that lilac tree. She was there by the river with him. *She knows what happened*!'

They looked for her in the libraries, in the drawing-rooms, in the gallery, but she was nowhere to be found. In the end they were forced to go in to the afternoon session without having spoken to her; and at the last moment she slid in from nowhere and took a seat in a dim corner, and sat through the two hours of song and argument and speculation with a pale face and haunted eyes. But that meant that at least they could corner her when the session was over, before she could escape again into whatever lair she used for her private agonies.

The afternoon meeting ended with a tour-de-force by Liri Palmer, a thirty-five verse ballad without a dull line in it, all about a traitorous nobleman who killed his king and usurped his kingdom, but suffered the pregnant queen to live, on the understanding that if her child turned out to be a boy, he should be instantly killed, but if it was a girl she should be allowed to live. But the queen managed to elude her gaolers for a short time when her hour was near, and hid herself alone in the stables to bear her son. When the wife of one of the courtiers found her there, the queen begged her to exchange her girl baby for the royal boy.

> ' "And ye shall learn my gay goshawk
>   Right weel to breast a steed,
>   And I shall learn your turtle-dow
>   As weel to write and read.
>
> ' "At kirk and market, when we meet,
>   We'll dare make no avow
>   But: Dame, how does my gay goshawk?
>   Madam, how does my dow?" '

Thirty-five verses, all to one unchanging tune, and mounting excitement with every verse. Liri Palmer was an artist, no question of that. It was partly the pure, passionate drama of her voice, and the latent acting ability that enabled her to people her stage with so many living characters, without breaking the melody or distorting the tone; and partly the virtuosity of her accompaniment, which varied with every verse, and produced the rattle of duels and the muted agitation of women's plotting as fluently as the hammer of hooves or the ripple of rain. They reached the point where the gay goshawk had grown up, and was hunting with his foster-father:

> ' "Oh, dinna ye see yon bonny castell
>   With halls and towers so fair?
>   If every man had back his ain,
>   Of it ye should be heir."

> ' "The boy stared wild like a grey goshawk:
>   "Oh, what may all this mean?"
>   "My boy, ye are King Honour's son,
>   And your mother's our lawful queen." '

Tossa looked at Dominic, and her eyes signalled that they must be near the end of the story now. She was next to the wall, and in a quiet corner; she rose softly, and slipped back into the shadows, to circle the room unobtrusively to Felicity's hiding-place.

The goshawk had reached his apotheosis, leaping the castle wall and confronting False Foundrage in arms. Not all ballads have happy endings. This one did. The boy killed his enemy, delivered his mother, and took the turtle-dow as his bride. The entranced hush broke, the moment the last shuddering chord of Liri's strings had vibrated into silence. Under cover of the applause Felicity got up to slide out of the room; and Tossa's hand closed on her arm.

'Felicity, come into the little library. We want to talk to you.'

The tone was quiet and reasonable, but Felicity recognised its finality. Perhaps she had been waiting for someone to take the burden out of her hands, with even more longing than terror. She went with them, stiff and silent, not trying to escape now, except into the deeps of her own being, and even there hoping for little. They sat her down in a quiet corner of the small library; the cheerful pre-tea din told them where all the others were, and assured them that their solitude here was safe for a little while.

Tossa laid the spray of wilting lilac flowers in the girl's lap. 'We found these this afternoon. We were looking for you before the session, to show you. These are the same kind you had in your hair yesterday, when we met you. We know now where you'd been. Not just along the path to the bridge. You'd been by the grotto, with Lucien. Hadn't you?'

Felicity looked all round her in a last convulsion of protest and despair, and shrank into herself and sat still, her eyes on the flowers. She didn't try to deny anything.

'You'll have to tell us what you know, Felicity. You understand that, don't you? It isn't any use trying to pretend you know nothing now. We *know* you were there.'

Felicity melted suddenly from her frozen stillness and began to shake uncontrollably. She linked her small hands together before her, and gripped until the slight knuckles were blanched like almonds.

'Yes,' she whispered, the word jerking out of her like a gasp of pain. She looked up at Tossa in desperate appeal, and asked in a small level voice: 'What happens to people who're accessories before the fact? Of murder, I mean? Supposing someone caused someone else to kill a person, but without meaning to?' Her face shook, and as resolutely reassembled its shattered and disintegrating calm; she wasn't crying, and she wasn't going to cry. What was the use now? 'Or suppose they *did* mean to, but never really believed it could happen? What do they do to people like that? Do you know?'

They looked at each other over her head, shaken to the heart.
'I think,' said Dominic, with careful, appalled gentleness,
'we'd better go into the warden's office and wait for my father.
You'll have to tell him, you know. *We* don't matter, but we'll
stay with you, if you want us to. It's *him* you have to tell. You
go and sit in there with Tossa, and I'll go and find him.'

Chapter 6

'You tell it,' said George reasonably. 'You know what happened, and nobody's interested in tripping you up or trying to make you say something you don't want to say. Just tell us exactly what happened, and don't be afraid that we won't understand. Yes, Tossa'll stay with you. Don't worry! You'll feel better when you've told us all about it. Take your time. We won't interrupt you.'

They were all in the warden's office together, the door safely shut, the room quiet and confidential, nobody to worry them or interfere with the desperate sympathy of their communion. Felicity sat shrunken in the armchair, her hands tightly clasped; the pressure seemed to help her to concentrate a mind which otherwise might fly apart from pure over-strain. Tossa sat beside her with an arm laid round the back of the chair, ready to touch the child or let her alone as the need arose. Nobody would have suspected that Tossa had so much patience and forbearance in her, least of all Tossa herself; but then, it had never been called into use until now. Dominic sat withdrawn on a rear corner of the desk, willing to remain unseen and unnoticed as long as possible; he was hardly more than an extension of Tossa at this moment.

'Lucien went out alone into the grounds yesterday afternoon,' George prompted gently, 'and then you went out on your way to look at the swan's nest, and saw him ahead of you, and you ran and caught him up. Tossa and Dominic saw you go down towards the footbridge together. Go on from there.'

'It wasn't quite like that,' said Felicity, in a voice small, hard and clear. Now that she had reached the point of speech there were going to be no prevarications; there was even the faintest note of revulsion in her tone for this too fastidious consideration. She straightened her slender spine, and looked fairly and squarely at what confronted her, and didn't lower her eyes. 'I didn't care a damn about the swan's nest. There *is* one there, of course, but I wasn't going out to look at that, I was just following Lucien. I watched him go out, and then I went after him. I wanted to be with him. I wanted to get to know him really, properly, and for him to get to know me. Because I loved him. I *do* love him! I did, in a way, even before I ever saw him in the flesh, and as soon as I saw him I knew it *was* love. I knew I was the right person for him, and so I went straight for my objective, and I was sure he couldn't help but feel the same way.'

Carefully, nobly, they all sat without stirring a muscle or drawing a hastened breath, nothing to suggest amusement, censure, or surprise. But Felicity knew her grown-ups, even those who were only a few years ahead of her. Faint, proud colour rose in her cheeks. She looked George fiercely, if wretchedly, in the eyes, and said with dignity:

'People think that at fifteen one has no deep feelings. They forget about girls like Juliet. It just isn't a matter of age. And in any case women are always much more mature and formed than men of the same age, and *much* more likely to recognise the real thing when it happens to them. Look at Tatiana, in *Eugene Onegin*. She was the young one, and he patronised and talked down to her, and treated her like a child, and wouldn't take her seriously, but she was right, all the same, and he lived to find it out when it was too late. And this was . . . rather like "Onegin" over again. Lucien just didn't realise how important it was, what was happening to us. He didn't want anyone then, I suppose.

He surely didn't want me. He didn't try to send me away, he only walked on and took no notice of me. We went along the ride there, on the other side of the river, and then we came to that gate, and he pushed it open and went on down to the grotto. He sat on the bench in there, looking at the river, and I sat by him and tried ... I wanted him to *understand*, not to make a terrible mistake, but he didn't understand at all. He was like all the rest, he thought I was just a kid. It was "Onegin" all over again.'

All quite predictable, thought George sadly, but quite innocent. And yet something happened down there that wasn't innocent, and she knows it, and is forcing herself towards it inch by inch. But he didn't prompt her again. However she delayed, however deviously she approached what she had no intention now of softening, it couldn't be long in coming. Only a quarter of an hour or so later, Tossa and Dominic had met her coming back towards the house.

For the first time it occurred to him as a serious possibility that Felicity had killed Lucien Galt with her own hands. Her situation must have been disastrous enough, and her disillusionment bitter enough, and a moody and impatient young man, getting up to prowl along the water-side without a thought for the love-sick child who meant no more to him than a persistent mosquito, would have been a very easy victim indeed. All that talk, faithfully reported by Dominic, about accessories before the fact, about causing somebody else to commit murder, without meaning to, all that might be mere talk at random, fending off the horrid fact itself. Or so he would have been tempted to believe, if this had been any other girl but Felicity. Felicity didn't talk at random, didn't toss about terms like 'accessory before the fact' without knowing only too well what they meant. Her solitude had been peopled from books, and her vocabulary, at least, was an adult's. No, wait for the truth to emerge, don't anticipate. She didn't push him. Nothing so simple.

'I told him,' she said, moistening her lips, 'that I wasn't a child, and he couldn't solve anything by telling me to run away and play, I told him outright that I loved him, and he'd better think carefully before he threw away what he might never be offered again. And I said I'd prove it in any way he chose, because there wasn't anything he could ask me that I wouldn't do for him.'

She looked at her locked hands in faint surprise, suddenly aware for a moment that the tightness of their grip was hurting her. She relaxed them a little, and they remained steady at first, and then began to shake; the thin fingers clamped tight again and held fast.

'And then he turned on me,' she said in a precise, drained voice, 'quite suddenly and viciously, and said: "All right, then, prove it. If you're ready to do anything, then do *this* for me. Go and find Mrs. Arundale, tell her where I am, and tell her I've got to talk to her alone. *Got to*," he said. "Ask her to come to me as soon as she can," he said, "and I'll be waiting for her here. *And give her my love!*" '

The brief silence hung blankly expectant, shocked but still braced for greater shocks, waiting for what was to follow. This was brutal enough, but no more than they might have expected; and yet there was something in the air that warned them that here the path twisted, and the place of their arrival, when they reached it, would be very far from where they had reckoned on finding themselves. The faint click of the door-latch drawing back hardly seemed to break the stillness; only the distant babel from round the tea-trolleys, gushing in through the opening door, made them all turn their heads sharply.

Audrey Arundale stood in the doorway, her eyes large and startled in her pale face, looking from one to another of them without comprehension, but with a remote and immured intelligence as piteous in its way as Felicity's.

'I'm sorry,' she said. 'I didn't know you weren't alone. I'll come back later.' And she was actually withdrawing, her eyes fixed upon George, when he called her back. Of course she had heard her own name. What was the point of shutting her out now? In any case, she had a right to hear this, it might even be helpful to have her there, to watch the impact of her presence on Felicity, and of Felicity's words on her.

'Don't go, Mrs. Arundale! If you're free, please stay. I think you should be present at this.'

'If you think I ought to,' she said, her eyes opening wider; and she closed the door quietly, and sat down in the chair Dominic hurriedly drew out for her from behind the desk. Felicity had given her one long, unreadable look, and returned to the painful contemplation of her own rigid hands.

'But if you don't mind, I should be glad if you'd make no comment or interruption until Felicity has finished what she has to tell us.'

'Of course,' said Audrey, 'I won't say anything.' Her voice was light and plaintive, as though the weight of events was too much for her, and she had lost the thread; but her behaviour would always be gentle, coherent and dignified. If there was something tougher and shrewder, and altogether more passionate, beneath that bland, bewildered and charming exterior, she had it under absolute control.

'Go on, Felicity. I'm sorry if we've broken the thread for you.'

'It's all right,' she said bleakly, 'I can't lose my place. I wish I could. Well, that was what Lucien said to me. And it was so cruel and so wicked, and I was so terribly hurt, that I just looked right back at him and said all right, I would. And I walked away from him, and away from the grotto, and latched the gate after me, and came straight up to the house. That was when you met me.' She flashed one grey glance towards Tossa. 'And Uncle Edward and Aunt Audrey were still sitting over their coffee in their sitting-room. So I delivered Lucien's message.'

Something vengeful was still left in the thin voice of hopeless despair and regret. At first they didn't understand fully; she saw the faint, cloudy questioning in their eyes, and made full and patient explanation.

'Word for word, just like he'd given it to me, I recited it aloud in front of both of them. I said: "Aunt Audrey, Lucien's down at the grotto by the river, and he says he's got to talk to you alone, and will you please go down to him there as soon as you can, and he'll be waiting. And I was to give you his love".'

In the instant of horrified comprehension the silence was absolute. Then Audrey Arundale's long, elegant hands made a sudden abortive motion of protest and pain, groping forward along the arm of her chair; her fair head arched back, and speech came bubbling into her throat, but never reached her lips. George gave her a sharp glance and a warning frown, and she subsided into her old apparent calm, even sighed the worst of the passing tension out of her soundlessly, and continued watching her niece with nothing in her eyes but a grieved and helpless sympathy.

'I see,' said George, in the most impersonal of voices. Possibly Felicity had wanted to shock, not wantonly, but to ease the burden of her own horror, and to reassure herself that this crisis of hers was indeed something large and dreadful, even by adult standards, and not a triviality of childish spite of no significance to anyone but her. That would make her anguish even sharper by making it pointless. She needn't have worried on that score, he thought ruefully. What was done to her was a truly cruel and ferocious thing, and what she did in return was large enough even for a Shakespearian woman scorned, or one of those ballad heroines whose wrongs and revenges Liri Palmer sang.

'And then?' he said, in the same neutral tone.

'They sat there staring at me like stones, both of them. It was terribly quiet, you can't imagine how quiet. And then they both turned, ever so slowly, and stared at each other, and Uncle Edward got up, and put his coffee cup down on the table very carefully, as if it was full and might spill over, but it was empty. He thanked me, and told me I could go. You know? Just as if

I'd come to say tea was ready. So I did. I went out and closed
the door, and left them there.'

'And you knew then,' asked George, 'what you'd done?'

'I knew what I'd done. I'd even meant to do it, and yet in a
way I hadn't, but by then I couldn't undo it. You can't, you
know. The very next minute is too late. I wanted somewhere to
hide, so I went up into the turret and on to the roof, the side
where I couldn't see or hear anything from the river. I stayed
there until tea, hoping nothing would happen, hoping everybody'd appear as usual. But Lucien didn't come. And then I
knew I'd done something terrible, but I couldn't tell anyone.
I was afraid to.'

She raised her eyes to George's face, and from behind the
windows of her glass prison he saw her staring out at him in
awful panic, while her slight body sat demure and still.

'It's all through me,' she said with terrified certainty, 'that
Lucien's dead, and Uncle Edward's on the run.'

Audrey uttered something between a gasp and a cry, and put up
her hands to her face. Her eyes appealed wildly to George. How
could this child possibly know about Edward being missing?
Nobody had known but the three of them, George, Henry Marshall, and Audrey herself. And now Felicity brought out this
flat, fearful pronouncement as though its certainty was not in
question. George shook his head at her, just perceptibly, and she
clutched at the hint of reassurance with unexpected quickness
of apprehension. Of course, Felicity was merely drawing an
inference which seemed to her self-evident, not speaking from
knowledge at all. Audrey sat back wearily, one hand shading her
face, her long-drawn, aching breaths shaking her whole body.

'We don't yet know,' said George sensibly, 'that anyone has
died, or that anyone has any cause to run. It may very well turn
out that we're all worrying without cause, and that goes for you
as much as for any of us. Whatever you did, and whatever
you think may have followed from it, don't jump to any con-

clusions yet. Wait and see. Mr. Arundale isn't due back from Birmingham until this evening. It won't be time to conclude that he's on the run, as you put it, until he failed to do as I hear he always does, come back right on schedule. Give yourself and him the benefit of the doubt until tomorrow, and don't be in too big a hurry to think you've caused a tragedy. Who knows? You may find yourself sitting opposite Lucien at breakfast.'

He seemed, Dominic thought, to be choosing his words with some care, and he could not be sure if it was for Felicity's benefit, or for Audrey's; or, in some more complicated process, for both of them, and in different ways. Felicity looked at him doubtfully, afraid for a moment of disbelief or disparagement; but though his voice was dry, reasonable and quiet, his face was grave. He contemplated her without a trace of the indulgence she dreaded; she believed that she had let loose a death, and he acknowledged the validity and solemnity of her belief.

All he was doing now was reminding her that evil sometimes misses its target. So that was all right, in so far as anything so monstrous could ever again be made all right; and there was now nothing more she could do. Unexpectedly, Felicity began to cry; she had had neither time nor energy to spare for it until then. Between her sheltering hands she said indistinctly: 'Is there . . . anything else you want to ask me?'

'Not now. But later I would like to talk to you again. What I suggest is that you three skip the next lecture, and go and have some tea by yourselves, in the small library, perhaps. And you come to me here, before dinner, Felicity, say seven o'clock, and I may have one or two questions to ask you then. Thank you for telling me all this. In the meantime, don't think about it more than you can help. If you have no objection, you and I will think about it together, this evening.'

'I'll go and grab a tray,' said Dominic, picking up his cue, 'before they clear everything away. I'll see you in the library.'

Felicity reached the door in Tossa's arm, her brief tears already spent. She was not a crying girl. She turned a pale, drained face to look back at George, with fixed attention and a degree of wonder; the bleakest of smiles, like a ray of winter sunlight, pricked its way through her clouded despair.

'Thank you,' she said, 'for believing me.'

'But you don't believe her,' said Audrey Arundale tiredly, 'do you?'

'I keep an open mind.' George saw her look round vaguely for the cigarette-box on the desk, and leaned to offer his own case. 'I'm glad you came in when you did, it saves a lot of explanation. And thank you for letting her tell her own story in her own way. Now I should like to hear your version of the same episode.'

'You're quite satisfied, then, that it happened?' She stooped her fair head to the lighter he offered, and drew in smoke hungrily.

'It happened. She didn't in the least mind your being here while she told it. I'm quite satisfied that it happened just as she described it.'

'I'm afraid,' said Audrey sadly, leaning back in her chair, 'she rather enjoyed my being here. It can't have escaped you how much she hates me.'

'You think so? If you want to dispute anything she said, now's your chance. I should be very glad to listen to your account of what happened.'

She looked up at him in a way that reminded him for a moment of Felicity. There was no coquetry in her, he found himself thinking that she would not even know how to begin to use her prettiness and femininity to influence a man; and yet he could never encounter her directly. She, too, was immured within a self which was not of her own choice or creation, as difficult to reach as the child.

'It's strange,' she said, and it was probably her weariness speaking, 'not to be able to guess at all what you're thinking about me.'

What he was thinking at that moment was that she seemed twice as large and twice as real as she had seemed to him yesterday, perhaps because she was a day farther removed from the shadow and the support of Edward Arundale.

'*Do* you want to dispute the facts?' asked George, avoiding the pitfall.

'Not the facts. Only their implication. She did burst in on us just as she says, and came out with that . . . that rigmarole. I believe it was pretty well word for word as she reported it. And certainly Edward and I were utterly shattered by it. But it was by what we'd just learned about Felicity, not by anything else. If there was a message, it couldn't have been phrased like that, you may be certain. Maybe he did send to ask for me . . . after all, I was responsible for starting this course in the first place, and there could have been things any of the artists might want to bring up with me. But if he did, it was in very different terms. Much more probably, I'm afraid, Felicity was angry with him, and made the whole thing up out of malice.'

'Against Galt?' asked George. 'Or against you?'

'If you ask me to guess – what can it be but guesswork? – I think both. It seems that Mr. Galt was the occasion. If you'd seen her efforts to ingratiate herself with him on Friday night, and his rather strained tolerance, you'd understand. But occasion and cause are two things. Mr. Felse, this is entirely a private matter between us? I must tell you, then, that Felicity has been a problem for quite some time now, with a special animosity, I'm afraid, against me. That wasn't news to me. But this display yesterday was shocking. Edward showed great restraint in getting the child out of the room, because we simply had to discuss what was to be done with her. Sylvia sends her here every holiday, but with all our goodwill the experiment has been a disastrous failure. We never quite realised how disastrous, until yesterday. We were wondering if it would be any use suggesting to Sylvia that she send the child abroad *au pair* for a year or so, and see what quite fresh companions and surroundings can do for her. But we didn't have much time to talk about it, because Edward had to leave just before three, on his way . . .'

She wrenched her head aside in a gesture of pain and revolt from the futile mention of the place where Edward had never intended to go, and the thought of the innocent engagements he had deliberately cancelled before setting off only he knew where. 'I don't understand!' she said. 'I don't understand anything!'

'You can't tell me for certain,' said George, 'whether there actually was some quite innocent message behind Felicity's apple of discord? – intended apple of discord, at least, even if it didn't come off. You didn't, I suppose, feel enough interest to go down to the grotto and find out?'

'I didn't! I was too upset to do anything of the kind, and then, it would have been, in a way, a capitulation to her. Wouldn't it? Personally I think she made the whole thing up.'

'And your husband didn't go there, either?'

'Of course he didn't! We were together, talking anxiously about what on earth was to be done with her, until he had to leave. His car was already out in the courtyard at the back . . . I expect you've seen the lay-out of the house by now.'

'But you didn't actually see him drive away?' For their private rooms were at the front of the house, and did not overlook the drive.

'Well, no, I didn't, of course. But we know that he did leave . . .'

'We know he didn't leave for Birmingham. At least, not for the two meetings he was supposed to address.'

She put up her hands to her forehead in a gesture of hopeless bewilderment.

'But I don't believe, I don't believe for a moment that he went down to the river. I simply don't *believe* that he was attaching the slightest significance to what Felicity had tried to suggest. Wouldn't he have said so to me, wouldn't he have asked me about it, if he'd believed it? Even if he'd had the least doubt?

112

I don't believe he ever for a moment treated it seriously, or felt the least need to investigate.'

'I appreciate your confidence. But you can't,' he insisted delicately, 'testify of your own knowledge that he didn't?'

'I can't prove it, no. All I know is that it still seems to me quite impossible.'

'Yet he did change his plans, and call off his engagements, and he did it then, immediately after this incident.'

This was not a question, and she did not offer an answer, or even a protest.

'He may, of course, have had other and quite legitimate reasons for that. If he comes back this evening he'll answer such questions for himself, no doubt. You'll understand that there are certain obvious things I can't avoid asking you, however, in view of what has emerged.'

'Yes,' she said with weary distaste, 'I understand that you must.'

'How long have you known Lucien Galt?'

'About six weeks now.'

'How did you first meet him?'

'At a cocktail party given by his recording company. Peter Crewe was at the same party, that's where I got to know him, too.'

'Were you acquainted with any of the other artists who're here now? Prior to this course, I mean?'

'Yes, with all of them. I've been interested in the subject for a long time. I told you, I was the one who first suggested this weekend, and of course the ones we invited were the ones I knew slightly.'

'Has there ever been anything in the nature of a love affair between you and Lucien?'

She said: 'No!' so fiercely and disdainfully that it might have been a different woman replying, after the flat exchanges of a moment ago. He looked at her mildly and steadily, caught and deflected by the change.

'Nothing at all improper? Nothing to justify the interpretation Felicity obviously placed on what he said to her? An interpretation I think anyone would have placed on it, to be honest.'

'Nothing improper has ever taken place between us. And we have only Felicity's word for what he said to her, as of course you know.'

But Dominic's word, he thought but did not say, for one tiny incident of far from tiny significance, in the circumstances. A small straw, but swayed in a gale-force wind, and a detached, observant and deeply reluctant witness. Dominic couldn't have been greatly surprised by Felicity's story, after that glimpse of passion.

'And – forgive me! – just one more question. Why didn't you tell me about this incident, when you accounted to me for your afternoon, yesterday?'

'It was wrong of me,' she admitted wretchedly, 'but I couldn't. It didn't seem to me relevant, not then. And one doesn't advertise one's family problems if one can help it. It was for us to solve this matter of Felicity. She isn't our child, but she is our kin. I didn't want to expose her . . . or us. One just doesn't do that.'

And that was perfectly good sense, and fitted the known facts without a flaw. He sat thinking about it, and about her, long after she had left him to go to her duty. She would be some ten minutes late for the opening of Professor Penrose's five o'clock lecture, but she had the gift of materialising into some quiet corner without disturbing lecturer or audience. One of her allies in this exacting life was silence, and another was unobtrusiveness. Both useful in an illicit love affair, if she ever did undertake one. She couldn't, of course, have been expected to reckon with the possibility that some day her perverse partner would be exasperated into turning on a pathetic adolescent who pestered him too far, and striking her down with the naked truth, which she, given the necessary fury and valour, could carry straight to the oblivious husband. No, such things don't happen.

In any case, when he came to think back over the conversation he had just had with Audrey, he found it increasingly difficult to believe that she was the cool kind of woman who could produce such sound and simple parries on the spur of the moment. Whereas Felicity undoubtedly had the force, fervour and ingenuity to take circuitous revenges when bitterly wounded.

But as often as he came near to conviction, he was visited again by the vision of those two hands meeting and closing warmly in the folds of Audrey's skirt, while her husband walked in blissful ignorance on her other side. And from there it was so short a way to accepting Felicity's story. No want of motive then! Believe that, and you could not but believe that they did indeed meet and clash, there in that smug little artificial pleasance by the flooded river. Once visited by that relevation, nobody ever had a more immediate stimulus to murder in hot blood, almost in a state of shock. Put that evidence before almost any jury, and their instinct would be to find a verdict of manslaughter.

But for one significant fact, of course. Edward Arundale had telephoned to cancel his appointments at about three o'clock, immediately after Felicity's bombshell, *before* he went to meet Lucien in his wife's place. That one point alone made this, if it was a crime at all, a more calculated and less excusable crime. For why should he do such a thing, unless he was already consciously contemplating murder and flight?

Chapter 7

'After dinner, if you're not bored with the subject by now,' promised Professor Penrose, switching off the record-player, 'we'll go on considering this odd question of historical origins, and try to find out why some of the events celebrated found their way straight into folk song, and why others, some of the bitterest, too, on occasion, became "innocuous" nursery rhymes. It's a far cry from a feudal social tragedy like "The trees they do grow high" to "Ring a ring o' roses", you might think, but which of them came into being as catharsis for the more unbearable memory? Or didn't you know about "Ring a ring o' roses"? The ring of roses was the outcrop of bubonic ulcers, the pocket full of posies was the bunch of herbs you carried to try and ward off infection, the sneezes were one of the initial and ominous symptoms, and once you'd got that far you all fell down and stayed down until the cart came along to collect. And some inspired Tom Lehrer of the plague year turned it into a nursery game! Well, after all, you all know what happened to "Gulliver". It's a way we have with the unendurable, to give it to the children to play with.'

He could afford to invite them to suppose that they were bored, because he knew they were not. Professor Penrose was not a boring man. He slammed his notebook shut, not having glanced at it throughout, and waved his arms at them as at refractory chickens.

'Out! Shoo! Go and get a breath of fresh air before dinner.'

And out they went, vociferous, argumentative and contented, at least as far as the walled garden and the terraces, there to continue with even greater animation the discussion which would be resumed on its scholarly plane after dinner. On the terraces even the non-singers burst into song. At times they sounded like a choir tuning up on several different test pieces at the same moment.

'I always knew I'd be good as a filibuster,' remarked the professor complacently, finding himself shoulder to shoulder with Liri Palmer on their way out. 'Nobody's ever *encouraged* me to try how fast and how long I could talk, before.'

She gave him a clear look, and said unexpectedly: 'You're a wicked old man. I like you.' She looked, as always, in full possession of herself, her secrets and her thoughts, but the signs of strain were there, once you knew what to look for; her air of withdrawal, the austerity of the set of her lips, the sombreness of the steel-blue eyes that were not interested in illusory hopes. He liked her, too; he liked her very much, but there was nothing he could do for her, except talk fast enough to divert attention from her when she was not singing, and listen to her with gratitude when she was.

'Only one more day,' he said, 'and we can send them all home.'

She said: 'Yes,' with a brief and shadowy smile, and went away from him with her lithe, long walk, down the back stairs and along the stone corridor, and out into the evening light just beginning to turn misty and green. Once through the courtyard it was only a dozen yards into the fringes of the ornamental shrubbery, and thence into the trees. She looked round once to be sure that she was alone, and then dug her hands deep into the pockets of her jersey jacket, and set off rapidly towards the river. It was easier to keep close to the bank on the farther side, where the trees were thinner, and the paths followed the course of the Braide with reasonable faithfulness. She crossed the footbridge, and went striding along the leafy ride, past the young redwood, past the huge, scrolled iron gate behind which she knew there must be a policeman on guard, though he had not showed himself at noon, and did not show himself now. No use searching within that enclosure, in any case; they would have done that already, very thoroughly. There could be no further trace of him to be found there.

She had begun her hunt, therefore, in the brief interludes between today's sessions, where the enclosure ended, and in two such forays she had reached a point somewhat below the stone bridge. There were no more weirs now between her and the massive wall of the Follymead boundary, less than a quarter of a mile away.

Liri knew nothing at all about the behaviour of drowned bodies, and nothing about the currents of the Braide, and the places where anyone lost in these reaches of it would be likely to cast up. She could see that there was a strong and violent flow of water, and that it would carry anything committed to it with speed and force; but the only way she knew of searching it was by walking downstream from the point of entry, and watching for any sign in the water, along the banks, among the swamped alders, and the lodged debris of the flood. She did it, as she did everything, with all her might.

The police, of course, must also be looking for Lucien, but she had seen no sign of them in these reaches. Let them search in their way, with all the aids their specialist knowledge gave them; she would search in hers, with no aids at all but her ignorance, which would not allow her to miss a single yard of undercut bank or a single clump of sallows.

Here, so close to the boundary, the artificiality of Follymead relaxed into something like a natural woodland. Where the view from the windows ended nature was allowed in again, still somewhat subdued, and the river surged away from the planed curves of its man-made vistas in an unkempt flood. Here for a while it rolled through open meadow and in a straight, uncluttered bed; she looked at the brown, smooth water, quiet and fast, saw the shallow, whirling eddies swoop past her, and felt sure that nothing would ground here. Ahead of her trees and bushes closed in again, leaning together over the water. These tangles of willow and undergrowth must have gone untended for a long time. She left the path and clung to the bank, and clambering through bushes, shouldering her way through sliding, whistling, orange-coloured sallows, she found herself suddenly marooned on a soft and yielding headland, with water before her and water on either hand. On her right the main flow coursed along sullenly, little checked by the lush growth; but the flood-water had spilled over among the trees and drowned the low-lying ground as far as she could see ahead through the twilight of the woodland. Before her and on her left it swirled in frustrated pools, and lay still, dappled with grasses. When she moved a foot, the water which had gathered slowly about her shoe eased away again into the spongy turf. She could go no farther, as close to the river as this. She would have to turn back and skirt the sodden ground at a greater distance.

But before she retreated she made a careful survey of the flooded area as far as she could see. Lodged in the stream on her right, ripping the water into a dozen angry spurts of sound and fury, a fallen tree, or perhaps only a branch from a larger tree, lay anchored with its tattered trunk wedged fast in the soft ground, and its splayed branches clutching and clawing ineffectively at the fast current that slipped hissing through its fingers. She peered into the seething fistful of water, half dirty brownish foam, and among the hundred fleeting, shifting pallors she thought she saw one pallor that remained constant, only nodding and swaying a little while the Braide boiled past it and swirled away downstream.

She had thought she had seen something so often by then that she felt nothing, except the compulsion to know. She set foot testingly on the torn bole, and shoved hard, and it remained immovable, deep sunk in the mud and wedged into place with all the driftwood it had arrested. She straddled a stubborn cross-branch, and felt her way out on the rough bark, holding by the alder wands that sprang through the wreckage and held it secure. Two, three yards gained, and the support under her grew slender, and gave a little beneath her weight, but still held fast. The water was rushing under her feet now, she looked down into it with fascination, finding something in it of music, in the melting of eddy into eddy, and current into current, the flow endlessly unfolding, able to plait into itself every thread that came drifting down the stream. Only the small, lax pallor hung idle and unchanging in the heart of change, and shook the pattern of unity to pieces round it.

Another yard, and she would be nearly over it. The branch bowed under her, the water touched her shoes, arched icily over one toe in a hiss of protest, and poured back into the flood. She dared not go any farther. But this was far enough. She stooped carefully, holding by the thin, swaying extremity of a branch, and looked steadily and long at the trapped thing in the water.

She must have heard, though in her preoccupation she had not identified, the small sounds that did not belong to the rhythm of the river. Nevertheless, she was startled when she turned to draw back from her precarious outpost, and found herself staring at Dickie Meurice.

He was a yard out on the tree-trunk after her, clinging and reluctant, but grinning, too, pleased at having crept up on her so closely without being detected. He must have been following her right from the house. He must have frozen into stillness, somewhere there in the arch of the courtyard, when she had paused to look back from the rim of the trees. It didn't matter now. Nothing mattered. Let him come, let him see something, at least, if not all, enough to assure him he hadn't come out for nothing.

'Oh, you!' she said, her voice flat and neutral. 'I might have known.'

'You might have known! Who else would be so considerate? I thought you might need help . . . if you found anything.'

'You're so right,' she said, moving back upon him without haste, knowing he could not pass her, sure even that if she abandoned him here he wouldn't dare to venture out where she had been. For one thing, he was heavier than she was, he'd be ankle-deep in the Braide. For another, he was more careful of himself than she was, not having her stake at risk. 'I do need help. I need somebody to stay here with it, while I go and raise the alarm.'

He didn't believe it for a moment; he hung still, clutching precariously at the still green but dilapidated branches of the wrecked tree, and staring at her narrowly and doubtfully. She laughed on a hard, high note, moving steadily nearer, breast to breast with him, forcing him backwards. He looked over her shoulder, and he saw the floating, languid whiteness, articulated, apparently alive, drifting at the end of its dark sleeve. He uttered a small, strangled sound, and gave back before her gingerly, clawing his way towards the soggy, yielding ground under the trees.

'Yes,' she said hardly, 'that's a hand you're looking at. With fingers.' Saturated grass sagged under her foot as she stepped from the tree. Water seeped into her shoe, and she never even noticed, beyond shifting her stance brusquely to safer ground. 'What's the matter with you? Can't you understand? Are you afraid of a dead man? He's there. I *have* found him.'

Between the thrusting alders and the penning branches of the derelict tree, the pale, flaccid hand gestured and beckoned on a sudden surge of water, and flicked its fingers at them derisively, demonstrating beyond doubt its quenched but unquestionable humanity.

'Stay here with him,' she said peremptorarily, and thrust past

121

towards the drier ground, fending off alders with a wide sweep of her arm. He saw her face closely as she passed him, intent and fierce, incandescent with excitement. 'I'm going up to the house to tell Inspector Felse.'

He caught at her arm, but half-heartedly, almost confused into obeying her without protest. 'Stay here, nothing! I'm coming with you.'

'Don't be a fool!' Liri spat at him over her shoulder, tearing her sleeve out of his hand. 'Stay here and keep an eye open, and mark the place for us. We don't want to have to hunt for him again, there's a quarter of a mile of this wild part. And suppose the river dislodges him? At least you can tell us. And if anyone else comes near, get them away from here. I won't be long.'

She was away before he could stop her, weaving like a greyhound between the clinging sallows, stooping under branches, running like an athletic boy. And so positive and compelling was her authority that for some minutes he stayed where she had stationed him, his gaze fixed uneasily on that small, idling whiteness in the surge of brown. He could not forget the burning blue of her eyes, so intense as to sear out all expression, and the taut lines of her face, drawn so fine that the bones showed through in fiery pallor. He had never understood her, and he never would. Something unsuspected within him, something almost old-maidish in its respect for the proper forms, was scandalised by her composure. Hadn't she just found her black-haired true-love drowned in the Braide? Wasn't that his hand playing horribly with the dimpled currents there, snared in the branches of the tree? Only an hour ago she had been singing, with shattering effect, about another lost love slain by the braes of another river:

> 'O, Yarrow braes, may never, never rain
> Nor dew thy tender blossoms cover,
> For there was basely slain my love,
> My love, as he had not been a lover.'

122

Suddenly he wanted to understand her, he wanted to know, his normal inquisitiveness came to life again and shook off her influence. He always had to probe into everything that came his way, in case there might be something in it for Dickie. He cast one rather reluctant but still avid glance at the elusive thing he was supposed to be watching. It idled on the current like a skater, swayed in a slight, rhythmic movement. *He* wasn't going anywhere. Fixed as the Rock of Gibraltar.

Dickie Meurice could move very rapidly indeed when he chose. He made better time than Liri herself over the obstacle-strewn course to the stone bridge. By the time he reached it, and paused on the edge of the open parkland on the other side, Liri was well up the slope towards the house, and running strongly. He kept to the edge of the trees instead of following her by the direct route, until she came to the steps that led up to the south terrace. She didn't climb the steps. He saw that, and hugged himself. She was up to something, or she would have taken the direct and open way in. Instead, she was circling the wing of the house to enter by the courtyard, as she had left it. Dickie let her slip from sight, and then abandoned his shadowy shelter, and set off at his fastest run across the open ground, and in at the front doors. By the time she had threaded the passage into the house from the rear, he would be hanging over the rail of the back stairs, ready for her.

The gong for dinner had not yet sounded, but everyone was gathering into the public rooms in readiness for it; he could hear the babel of voices from the gallery and the libraries, high and merry, as he slid through the quiet corridors and leaned over the well of the back stairs. Any sounds from below would come up to him clearly here; he would know when she arrived, and whatever her intentions, she would have to cross that quiet lobby below him.

The staircase was old, solid and tightly wound, and made a wonderful funnel for rising sounds, especially as the lower corridor was of stone. He made his way down perhaps a third of the flight, to a point where he would still be well out of sight of anyone approaching from below, and have time to make his escape into the labyrinth of public rooms before she reached this upper landing. Follymead might have been designed for monstrous games of hide-and-seek. He leaned cautiously over the oak rail, and peered down the coiled, enclosed space, as into the whorls of a shell.

He could see beneath him the stone flags of what had once been the central lobby of the service floor and was now a cool, indoor spot for summer days with a fantasy of plant-stands, tapestry-draped walls, a few white-painted wrought-iron seats, and two pay-telephones discreetly tucked into the corner under the stairs, and walled round, but not roofed, with reeded wood shells just six feet high, painted ivory-white. They provided adequate insulation on their own level, and an excellent sounding-board to carry conversation up the well of the staircase. No one involved in the redesigning of Follymead as a college had thought of that; none of them had envisaged a future clientèle, addicted to listening in on other people's telephone conversations. Their mistake, thought Dickie Meurice, speculating pleasurably on one possibility.

The crisp, chill sound of Liri's footsteps, walking briskly, came along the stone passage ahead of her, and rang hollowly up the stairs. Low heels, but narrow and sharp, tipped with metal. Kitten heels, they called them; appropriate enough for that young tigress. Their rhythm didn't slacken or turn aside towards the staircase. He saw her foreshortened figure cross below him, the dark brown head so erect and beautifully balanced, the impetuous outline of brow and nose, the great braid of hair lashing like a tail for the tigress. Straight towards the telephones! He heard the soft clash of the swing door closing, reed to reed, snug as the seam of a dress.

He dropped one turn lower, sliding down the rail of the stairs eagerly. Almost above her head now, and though she was out of his sight he could hear and time every turn of the dial. Two

124

revolutions, one long, one short. For the operator, so what she wanted was not a local call; but he had never supposed that it would be. And blessedly, that meant she must ask for her number. Things could not have been going more smoothly his way.

'I'd like to call a London number, please. Valence 3581. This is Belwardine 640.'

Every word clear and unmistakable so far. Coins rattled into the slot, below him. They waited for what seemed a longer time than the two minutes it actually was, and in the interval the gong sounded for dinner. That was the signal for the whole hungry party to come milling along the gallery from the small drawing-room, from the terraces, from all the corners in which they were disporting themselves, and converge on the dining-hall. It was on the same main floor, situated above the special level of the great drawing-room, and those once-menial regions where the telephones had been installed. Meurice could maintain his place on the stairs brazenly, and nobody would bother him. But the cavalcade of joyous voices drowned out Liri's first words when the distant party, whoever he might be, answered her, and blotted into meaningless murmurs half of what passed afterwards. It is hard enough making sense of one half of a telephone conversation; trying to make something of half of that one half is a job for the cypher experts.

'Never mind that,' he heard her say clearly, her voice low and guarded, but sharp with impatience and strain, 'there's no time . . .' And again, after a maddening moment when nothing was audible but the Rossignol twins marching along the gallery to the loud, gay strains of 'Auprès de ma blonde': ' . . . just *get out, fast. The body's been found . . .*'

There was more, a hard silence on her part, the distant voice inaudibly pouring words at her, never a name to identify him. Why must they sing even when they weren't getting paid for it? There went Andrew Callum, leading half a dozen disciples in 'The Boy from Killane', and away went a burst of words from Liri, down the wind with the heroic lament for Douglas Kelly:

'Tell me, who is the giant with gold, curling hair,
  He who rides at the head of your band?
  Seven feet is his height, with some inches to spare,
  And he looks like a king in command . . .'

And on the diminishing echo, clearly: 'Damn you, I've *told* you, forget all that, and *go*. Good*bye*.'

The receiver clashed in the rest, and the door swung before her thrust, she was out, and at the foot of the staircase.

He turned and took the rest of the stairs three at a time, in long leaps. By the time Liri came out on the main landing, he was away along the gallery and out through the great front doors, and bounding down the steps from the terrace towards the dimming slopes that led to the Braide. He ran like a hare, in exuberant leaps, back to the duty Liri had laid on him. The vacant, wandering hand was still languid and easy on the thrusting current. Meurice found himself a dry place to stand, and waited; it was certain he wouldn't have long to wait.

'I wish I hadn't done it now,' said Felicity, as many another has said before her with as little effect, and many another will certainly say in the future. 'If I'd known . . .' She stopped there, jutted a dubious lip at what it had been in her mind to say, and rejected it ruthlessly. Whatever she lacked, she was beginning to discover in herself a rare and ferocious honesty. 'I should, though,' she said, 'the way I felt, even if I'd known how it would turn out.'

'None of us knows that yet,' George reminded her crisply. He had placed a chair considerately for her, so that no too acute light should touch her face, and no too direct glance put her off her stride. Oh, there was stuff in Felicity of which she knew nothing yet, even if she was finding out some things about herself the hard way, and too rapidly.

'No,' she conceded, 'but we know the probabilities. I did know them, even then, or I could have if I'd been willing.'

'I doubt,' said George, doing her the justice of showing a like honesty, 'if you anticipated that much success.'

She looked up quickly at that, a little startled, and considered it gingerly. The faintest and briefest glint of a smile showed in her eyes, and as feebly withdrew. 'You're not trying to make me think I haven't done something dreadful, are you?' You, of all people! her tone implied.

'No, I wouldn't do that. But I am telling you that something like that happens in most lives. Most of us, when it does happen, are lucky enough, clumsy enough, or scared enough to make a mess of our opportunity for malice. You were the unlucky one. You had the perfect explosive put into your hand, and the perfect fuse for it into your mouth. Even then, for some of us, it would have failed to go off. But we shouldn't have been less guilty. Having something to regret leaves you anything but unique or particular in this world, Felicity, rather confirms you one of the crowd.' He saw her braced to think that out, and resolute to kick the argument to pieces, and saw fit to divert the event. 'Look; suppose I ask you my questions first, and then we can talk.'

'All right,' she agreed. 'But I've told you everything I can think of now.'

'Yes, this is a matter of something you did tell me. You said you left Lucien there by the river, and came away, "and latched the gate after me". Did you mean that literally? Not just pulled the gate to after you, but latched it?'

She was staring at him now alertly and brightly, momentarily deflected from her own problems. 'Yes, latched it. Of course! Why, is that important?'

'It's a detail. They all help. The latch was still in position then?'

She nodded emphatically. 'You couldn't very well miss it, it's nearly as long as my arm.' An exaggeration of course, what she was really indicating with a small flourish was her forearm, from elbow to fingertips. 'It hasn't had any rivets, or whatever they

127

are, holding it for a long time, it just hangs there in the slots, you can pull it out if you want to.'

'Yes, I see. And Lucien didn't think better of it, and come after you? Try to stop you?'

'No,' she said sombrely, 'why should he? He didn't know what I was going to do. He didn't care about me one way or the other. I suppose there wasn't really any reason why he should. He never even looked round. He was sitting in the grotto, glad I was gone. I realise now that he must have been at the end of his patience, to do what he did to me.'

'I suspect,' said George, 'that his patience was always on the short side.'

'Maybe. I didn't really know much about him, did I?' she said bleakly. 'And neither did he about me.' She looked up earnestly into George's face, and asked simply: 'What am I going to do?'

Outside, the gong for dinner was bawling merrily, but they didn't notice it, or hear the noisy parade to the hall.

'Live with it,' said George with equal simplicity, 'and make the best of it. I can't absolve you, and you wouldn't be grateful to me if I tried. I can't charge you with anything, and there isn't any penance to be found anywhere, if that's what you're looking for. No, you'll just have to hump the memory along with you and go on carrying it, like the rest of us, and learn to live with yourself and your mistakes. It's the one way you find out how to avoid more and greater failures.'

'But if I've killed him?' she said in a whisper, her eyes frantic but trusting.

'Whatever happens, *you won't have killed him*. Not unless you'd been responsible for living their two lives as well as your own, for all the qualities in them and all the things they'd ever done or thought that eventually made it impossible for yesterday to end without a tragedy – only then would you have killed the one and made the other a murderer. Your contribution was bitter enough to you, but only the spark that set off a fire already laid.

Don't claim more than your share, Felicity, you'll find your fair share quite enough to carry.'

After a brief, deep silence she said in a low voice: 'Thank you! At least you haven't treated me like a child.'

'You're not a child. Let's face it, you're not grown-up yet, either, not quite. But I'll tell you this, you're a great deal nearer to being a woman than you were yesterday, when I first met you.'

Her lips tightened in a wry and painful smile that was very close indeed to being adult, and she said something no child could have said. 'That doesn't seem much for Lucien to die for,' said Felicity, and finding her own utterance more horrifying than she had expected, rose abruptly to leave him. 'There isn't anything . . . useful . . . I can be doing?'

'Living,' said George, 'and perhaps for the moment just living, without any thinking. And don't think that isn't useful. For a start you can go in to dinner with the rest of them, and help to tide Follymead over tonight.'

Faintly she said, the child creeping back into her voice and eyes uninvited: 'Do I have to? I'm not hungry.'

'You will be. The least useful thing you can do is make yourself ill. And you're needed, don't forget you're part of the household, a bigger part than ever before.'

'All right,' she said grimly, and took a step or two towards the door. The weight of the house came down on her appallingly for a moment. She looked back at him in sudden piteous appeal, she didn't know for what.

'Somehow it wouldn't be so bad,' she said in a muted wail, 'if only I wasn't so damned dull and *plain* . . .'

'Plain!' George echoed incredulously. '*Plain?*' he repeated in a growl of exasperation. 'Child, did you never look at yourself in a mirror? *Plain!* Come here!' He took her by the shoulders and turned her about, and trotted her sharply across the room to the high mantel and the Venetian mirror above it. It hung so high that at close range only her head came into view, with

129

George's impatient face above. He cupped a hand under her chin and tilted her face up to the glass. 'My dear little idiot, for goodness sake *look* at yourself. What do you want, in heaven's name? Do you have to be coloured like a peony to be worth looking at? What if you haven't got your aunt's milk-whiteness and roses, and a pile of fair hair? *This* . . . this pale brown, baby-fine stuff you have got was made to go with *this* face. You find me a more delicately-drawn hair-line than this, or a better-shaped head. And as for your face, I'd like to know who put you off it in the first place. Look at the form of these eye sockets, look at this line, this curve along your chin and neck. *Plain*! You haven't finished growing yet, and the peak's still to come, but if you can't see it coming you must be blind, my girl. Don't you realise you've got bones that are going to keep you beautiful until you're eighty? The prettiest colouring in the world won't stand by you like these will.'

Felicity stood transfixed with pure astonishment, her hands raised to touch the cheek-bones his fingers had just quitted. Her eyes, huge with wonder, stared unrecognisingly at the face in the glass. Her lips moved very faintly, shaping distantly and incredulously the word 'beautiful'.

The sudden rush of feet outside the door, the rap of knuckles on the wood, never penetrated her stunned senses. Even when the door opened upon Liri Palmer's roused face and glittering eyes, with Dominic close to her shoulder, Felicity only turned like a creature in a dream, still lost to every shock but one.

'Can you come?' Liri's blue stare fixed urgently upon George. 'There's something I want to show you.' She had bitten back, at sight of Felicity, the blunt announcement she would otherwise have made. 'I'm sorry if I'm interrupting you, but it's important.'

Her voice was mild, but her eyes were imperious. Liri's maturity extended to sparing the children; or perhaps she was merely concerned with keeping them from under her feet.

'Felicity was just on her way to dinner,' said George, and started her towards the door with a gentle push between the shoulder-blades. She went where he urged her, obediently, like a sleep-walker. They moved aside from the doorway to let her pass, and she looked back for a moment with eyes still blind to everything but the distant vision of her own beauty, incredible and yet constant. She trusted George. There had been very few adults in her young life whom she had been able to trust.

'Thank you! I'll try . . . I'll do what you said.'

'Good night!' said George.

'Good night!' said Felicity remotely, and wandered away with a fingertip drawing and re-drawing the line of her cheek-bone and jaw, which George had found beautiful. *Beautiful*! She followed the beckoning word towards the dining-hall and her duty. She was enlarged, she contained and accepted even her guilt, even her inability to erase it. She had something to live for, so unexpected that it loomed almost as large as the death she had precipitated.

As soon as she was gone they all three came into the room and closed the door carefully after them. He should have known that where Dominic was, Tossa also would be.

'Well?'

'I've found the body,' said Liri, point-blank.

It couldn't have been anything else, of course; he had seen it in her braced and motionless excitement. So there wasn't going to be any blessed anticlimax, any apologetic reappearance. They had a body, they had a crime. And Follymead had the prospect of ruin. George looked at the dusk leaning in at the window, at the clock that showed five minutes past the dinner hour, and reached into the desk drawer for his torch.

'Where is he?'

'Caught in a fallen tree in the river. Below the stone bridge, in the wild part. I'll take you there.'

'We ran into Liri at the top of the stairs,' said Dominic, 'and she told us. I hope that's all right. You're going to need somebody, if only to run the errands.'

'That's all right. Anybody keeping an eye on him now?'

'Dickie Meurice,' said Liri, her voice suddenly shaken out of its calm by the surrender of her responsibility, as her legs shook beneath her for a moment. 'He wasn't with me . . . he just showed up. I told him to stand by.'

'Good! Tossa, you run across by the footbridge, will you, and find Lockyer, and tell him to meet us down-stream. Tell him to bring some ropes down with him. And an axe or a hatchet, something we can use on the tree.'

'Right!' said Tossa, dry-mouthed with excitement, and whirled and ran.

'Come on, then,' said George. 'Lead the way, Liri.' And they followed her out across the terrace, and down the slope of turf towards the distant stone bridge.

It took them half an hour to get him ashore, and not a word was said in all that time but for the brief exchanges that were necessary to the job in hand. If they had tried to hack away the driftwood that held him before they had a line on him, he would have escaped them again, for once dislodged, the flood would have taken him headlong down-stream out of their hands. It was Dominic, as the lightest weight among the men present, who clambered out bare-foot on the swaying barrier of branches, and secured a rope round the shoulder that just broke surface, cased in sodden tweed that was now of no colour at all but the river's mud-brown. The driftwood under him dipped when he ventured too far; the ice-cold darkness rushed over his feet and tore at his balance. He thought of nothing as he worked; his mind had shrunk into his numbed hands.

'All right, come ashore.'

George reached a hand to retrieve his saturated son. Lockyer carefully took in the slack of the rope, and tested it with a gradual pull downstream; the arm that was all they could see of the dead man rose languidly along the surface, like the arm of a man turning in his sleep, but the body did not float free.

George looked along the tangled arms of the tree, and found the one that pinned the body in its clenched fist, half out of the

132

water. 'All right, we'll bring him in branch and all, it'll make a useful brake. Meurice, give me that hatchet.'

Dickie Meurice handed it eagerly. He would not for anything have forfeited his place here. He was only guessing, of course, but if his guess was right the pay-off would be worth a little discomfort.

'And the other rope.'

There was still a cloudy daylight out on the open sward, but here among the trees they had to peer to see even one another. The girls stood well back on drier ground, their faces two pale, still ovals in a green monochrome. Nobody had tried to send them away. What was the use of banishing Liri, who had been the one to find this pathetic thing they were trying to bring ashore? In any case, she would not have gone. She stood silent and intent, and her composure was impenetrable.

George climbed out himself this time. There was no need to go so far that his weight would be a handicap. He made the coil of rope fast round a fork in the branch, and passed the ends back to Dominic's waiting grasp.

'Give him a hand, Meurice. Everything may come loose with a rush when this gives.'

He hacked at the branch, below the fork where the rope was secured. The wood was still green and young, clinging to life; it took him a few minutes to chop his way through it.

'Dig your heels in, it's going.'

They had heard the first ominous cracking, and were braced and ready. The whole branch suddenly heaved and turned like a live thing, tossing the body momentarily out of the water, and dropping it again in a flurry of dirty foam; then the tangle of wood broke loose from its moorings, and would have surged out into midstream at once, but the two ropes, drawn in gradually hand over hand, coaxed it sidelong into the bank. Torn foam seethed through the lattice of sodden leaves. George scrambled back to the muddy ground, and helped them to draw him in, and disentangle him from the tree. Ankle-deep in cold spill-

133

water, they hoisted the dead weight clear, and laid him on the higher ground padded with last year's leaves and starred with this year's late anemones.

The sagging, shapeless shadow that had been a man lay flattened to the moist earth by his mud-heavy clothes. Lank hair of the universal river-colour plastered the pallor that was his forehead. George said in a voice suddenly sharp and intent, 'Give me the torch.'

The cone of light sprang out of the dimness and brought shapes to life again in this twilit world that had no shape. The long body sprawled awkwardly, so weighted down with water that it seemed to be dissolving away from them into the ground. A massive, large-featured face, smooth and austere and once impressive enough, gaped up at them through soiled trails of river-water.

The single muted whimper of a cry came from Tossa. Liri Palmer made never a sound. Dickie Meurice drew in breath with a long-drawn hiss that might have been pure horror and excitement, but sounded horribly like glee.

'But *that* isn't . . .' blurted Lockyer, amazed, and let the sentence trail away helplessly into silence. He had a teenage daughter; in her vicinity there was no possibility of avoiding acquaintance with the features of the current pop and folk idols.

'No,' agreed George grimly, staring into the pool of light at his feet, 'no, it isn't Lucien Galt. It looks as if we've got to hunt farther afield for him. No . . . *this* is Edward Arundale.'

Chapter 8

'Perhaps,' suggested Lockyer blankly, after a long moment of silence, 'they *both* went into the river.'

'You think so?' George switched off the torch, and the deepening dusk fell on them like a cloak. 'And who drove Arundale's car away? It was there, in the yard, with his overnight case and his books in it, at three. It was gone before four, and nobody else had gone missing. Oh, no, they didn't both go the same way.'

'They didn't both go down the river, anyhow,' said Dickie Meurice softly, and they heard and felt him stirring in the darkness, again with that curious suggestion of pleased malevolence. 'Because just before Liri came to tell you she'd found this one, *she was talking to the other one on the telephone.*'

He had his sensation, and it was everything he had hoped it would be. Only Liri herself let the revelation pass without a sound. She had made one sharp movement, however, that did just as well. However stolidly she sat out questioning, after that, he'd know that he'd hit her where it hurt. She'd had her chance to have his goodwill, and done rather more than turn up her nose at the offer. Now she could try it the other way.

'How do you know that?' demanded George, 'if you were here keeping an eye on the body?'

'I wasn't. I had a hunch she was up to something, so I let her

135

get a head start, and then followed her up. If she'd been on the level she'd have come straight in by the terrace, but she didn't. She went off round the back of the house, to the passage from the yard. So I came in by the front and beat her to the back stairs, and I was there to see exactly what she did. She went straight to the telephone call box under the stairs, and asked for a London number.'

'Dear Dickie,' said Liri quite gently, as if neither he nor anything he did could matter to her now, 'always so true to form. Where were you? Hiding in the next box?'

'In the presence of the police,' he retorted maliciously, 'I shouldn't be too witty about eavesdropping, if I were you. They have other names for it in the way of duty. I can demonstrate that I heard all right, and I can repeat every word I heard, too. Including the number!'

'And including a name?' asked George dryly.

'No, I didn't get a name. But the number was Valence 3581. You can check it easily enough, but I wouldn't mind betting you'll find it's the number of Lucien's London flat. That would be the first place she'd try, even if she didn't *know* where he'd be – and maybe she did, at that!'

'And why didn't you tell me about this at once, as soon as we arrived? Instead of behaving as if you'd been here all the time and had no information to offer?'

'Because I couldn't make out just what it was all about, not until I realised *whose* body we'd found. And what mattered first was to get him out. *She* wasn't going to run.'

'So in fact you didn't actually know whose number it was, or to whom she was talking?'

'No, not then. I don't know, for that matter, but listen to the text, and draw what conclusions you like. I didn't hear everything, people were just coming chattering along the gallery to dinner. When someone answered her she said: "Never mind that, there's no time." And the next I got was: " . . . just *get out, fast. The body's been found* . . ." Then whoever was at the other

136

end was doing the talking, until she cut him off. "Damn you,"
she said, "I've told you, forget all that, and *go*. Goodbye!" '

'That was all?'

'Isn't it enough? I didn't know whose body she'd found, but
she did. She was climbing out on the tree when I came on the
scene, she'd had a good look at him. But maybe she'd known all
along which of them went into the water. Maybe she even helped
in the job, or at least helped Lucien to get away afterwards. Stay
here, she says, and keep an eye on him, while I run and tell Mr.
Felse! You have to hand it to our Liri, she's quick on the draw.
She couldn't suppress the discovery, because I happened on her
just at the wrong moment. But she could and did run like a
hare to warn the murderer, before she gave the alarm. And she
found me a job to do that would keep me quiet while she did
it, or so she hoped. Only as luck would have it I'd already begun
to smell a rat by then.'

He smiled, the well-known smile that charmed the tele-view-
ers regularly on Thursday nights, his fair head cocked towards
Liri; and though the smile was now invisible, they felt its weighted sweetness probing her.

'But in any case, you don't have to take my word for it. Ask
her! Ask the operator who got her her London number.'

'All in good time,' said George impassively, 'we'll ask everything that needs to be asked, but not, I think, here. I should be
grateful if you would all keep this to yourselves, just as you have
done until now. Lockyer, stay with him, I must go and telephone.
The rest of you, come on, let's get back to the house.'

They made their way back in single file to the dry pathway
and the glow-worm twilight that was left in the park, George
lighting them until they were out of the trees. At the end of the
line, Dominic and Tossa linked hands and drew close, shivering
suddenly with the chill of the river, and the cold oppression of
darkness, malice and death. She whispered in his ear, anxiously,
that he must go straight up and change. The suggestion, mildly
maternal, pointedly possessive, seemed to be left over from

another world, but at least indicated the possibility of recovering that world, when all this was over. Dominic, the shivers warmed out of him by her solicitude, pressed her hand impulsively and wondered again at the terrifying diversity of man.

'Come up to the office with me,' George said to Liri as they climbed the steps to the terrace. 'I must talk to you.'

'Of course,' said Liri. Her voice was curiously easy now, aloof and contained still, but something more than that. The word that suggested itself was 'content'. George understand that. They had their body and their case, a pretty substantial case now, though still circumstantial; but she had done everything she could, and it was no longer up to her. 'But it *will* be you talking,' she said gently. '*I've* got nothing to say.'

In the yellow drawing-room, as they passed through the gallery, Andrew Callum was singing, in a voice achingly muted and raw and sad:

> 'The judge looked over his left shoulder,
> He said: "Fair maid, I'm sorry."
> He said: "Fair maid, you must be gone,
> For I cannot pardon Geordie." '

'So that's the way it is,' said Duckett heavily. 'Well, we can put out a general call immediately for the car, and turn on everything to find it. That's no problem. About the boy I'm not so happy. We'll get all the airports covered, and have a watch kept on his flat – though if the girl was lucky enough to catch him there, that's one place he'll have written off. We've nothing to lose by avoiding a public appeal. There still *could* be another answer.' But he sounded exceedingly dubious about it. 'I suppose it's practically certain he did take the car?'

'I'd say a hundred per cent certain,' said George. 'He knew, as everyone here knew, that Arundale wouldn't be expected back until tonight. He could give himself many hours grace by making off with that car.'

'Well, since she's tipped him off about the body being found . . . you say she hasn't admitted anything about that?'

'She won't say anything at all. She's done what she could for him, now she doesn't care what happens to her.'

'You don't think she actually *was* in it with Galt? After the fact, say?'

'I'm certain she wasn't. If she had been, the last thing she'd have done was to go looking for the body. She'd just have sat back and prayed for us not to find it. But she did go looking for it. According to Meurice, she's been hunting it at intervals all day. Oh, no, it wasn't Arundale she expected to find, it was Lucien. That's why she's so calm now, almost happy. He may be in trouble, but at least he's alive.'

'Then why won't she talk about any part of it?'

'Two reasons, I think. First, because she knows nothing herself, and isn't sure how much I know, so that even by opening her mouth on something that seems innocuous to her she may be handing me another little fact that makes damning sense to me. And second, by refusing to say anything at all, she may be able to leave us in some doubt about her, and divert a bit of our attention from him.'

'I thought she hated him?' said Duckett.

'She thought so, too. She knows better now, and so do we. One more point, he certainly has a valid passport, because in three weeks' time he's due to leave for a tour of Latin America. First destination Buenos Aires. And since she caught him successfully at his flat, he's undoubtedly pocketed his passport. Most likely that's what he went there for. And possibly to raise some quick cash.'

'You think he was heading out in any case?'

'I think so.'

'Right, airports, then. Ports, too, but less likely. For the car we'll put out a general call immediately. Where d'you want the wagon to come? That drive's too public by far.'

'We're lucky there. Have them go on along the main road,

past the lodge and over the river bridge beyond the edge of the estate. Just beyond the bridge there's a gate, and a cart-track crosses two fields – it's drivable, all right – and reaches Follymead ground at a third gate by the river-side. Lockyer's down there on the spot, and I'm going back there now. No point in viewing the place where we got him out, it's pure chance he got held up there. The doctor can have him right away.'

'*Did* he drown?'

'Unlikely. If so, the water won by a very short head. His skull isn't the right shape. I didn't do any close investigating, there were too many spectators, and the doctor will do it better. But something hit him.'

'It couldn't have been a fall?'

'Could have. Pending closer examination, of course. But in that case, why run for it? It looks as if Arundale went hopelessly wild when the ground reeled under him. It looks as if he was the aggressor. And lost. They've been married twenty years, and never anything, not a shadow.'

'It happens,' said Duckett, and drew in breath gustily through the moustache that would have done credit to a Corsican *maquisard*.

'It does, I only wish it hadn't.'

'You can say that again, George . . . they're due out tomorrow evening, this folk-music party?'

'There's a final concert after tea, five to half-past six, then they disperse. We can hold it that long, if we have to. I'd prefer it, too.'

'Keep it wrapped, then, and I'll manage this end. If the lid has to blow off, let it be when they've gone home. We may save something.' His hard breathing rattled in the receiver. 'But . . . *Arundale*! My God, George, he was impregnable. Do you reckon Buckingham Palace is safe?'

'Think of me,' said George bitterly. 'I've still got to break the news to the widow.'

Black is the Colour of My True Love's Heart

The class came chattering and singing from the after-dinner session at a quarter to ten, and headed for the small drawing-room to continue their discussions over coffee. Every evening the noise had grown, and the gaiety, and the exhilaration. Professor Penrose must have surpassed himself, in spite of being deprived of the services of Liri Palmer and Dickie Meurice. It was extraordinary how the two dramatic productions being staged at Follymead had run parallel all the way, even in their crises and accelerations, apparently unconnected and without communication. Only Liri linked them now, or rather, moved from one to the other freely, and had a part in both. Meurice, thought George, reluctantly but clearly, was largely irrelevant. He stirred up a little mischief in passing, but he was of no importance. In a sense he never had been. His malice frayed the edges of events, but never determined or even deflected them. He was the mouse gnawing at the exposed root of an oak tree already split by lightning.

When Audrey Arundale passed along the gallery – and he noted that she had so arranged matters as to move as long as possible alone – George was waiting for her. He saw her pause for a moment outside the open door of the small drawing-room, and brace herself to enter and put on her hostess face.

'Mrs. Arundale . . .'

She turned and saw him, and her look was almost glad. Whatever business he had with her would be preferable to going in there and making pleasant talk. But she didn't know, of course, what it was going to be.

'Can you spare me a few minutes? There's something I have to tell you.'

'Of course. Shall we go into the office?'

There is no easy way to tell anything as heavy as bereavement, and the spiral approaches are worse than the straight. The victim has so long to imagine and fend off belief. George was only just back from seeing the body removed from the Follymead grounds by the police ambulance, and was very tired. Everything he could do tonight was done, every inquiry he could set in motion was already on the move. By this time all the airports were alerted to look out for Lucien Galt, and the number and description of the stolen Volkswagen were being circulated on all the police transmissions. They had reached a dead point where there was nothing for them to do but pause and draw breath. George and Audrey looked at each other across the hearth of Arundale's office with a shared exhaustion, not enemies, not even opponents.

'Mrs. Arundale, I think you must know that ever since I was called in here we've been accepting it as a possibility that a death was involved, and in fact have been looking for a body. I'm afraid what I've got for you is not good news. This evening we've found it. We took him out of the river about an hour and a half ago.'

She set her hands to the arms of her chair, and rose. Her eyes, wide and fixed, held steady on his face. She said nothing at all, so plainly waiting that there was nothing to do but complete the half-arrested blow.

'It isn't Lucien Galt, as we'd expected. It's your husband. I'm very sorry.'

Her lips moved, saying automatically: 'I understand,' but there was hardly a sound, only a faint rustling of her breath. She turned her head questingly this way and that, and put out her hand with that remembered gesture, feeling for Edward, her prop and mentor; but Edward wasn't there, and would never again be there ready to her hand, and there was nobody now to tell her what to do. She was alone.

He saw the blood drain from her face, and her eyes roll upward in her head. As if she had indeed leaned on the arm that unaccountably failed to be there, her balance forsook her. She swayed, and then, like a shot bird, collapsed in broken, angular forms at his feet; and he lunged from his chair on one knee, and took her weight in his arms as she fell.

George drove home to Comerford through a sudden squall of

142

rain, and his eyes were full of Audrey Arundale's reviving face. When she came round she had apologised for her lapse, and resolutely refused to have anyone fetched to her, or to concede that she might be in need of help. 'I'm quite all right now!' How often he'd heard it, hurried and insistent and forbidding, from people who were anything but all right, but dreaded above anything else being the centre of a fuss. If you over-rode them, you sometimes precipitated the total collapse you most wanted to avoid. And besides, he had detected in Audrey a kind of relief, a kind of relaxation, that meant she wouldn't break. After you have been living with horrible uncertainties, even the definition and finality of death come as an almost welcome change.

Now at least she knew. And what was there he could do for her? Not bring the dead man back to life again, certainly; and not, in his present state, even attempt to assess her degree of guilt or innocence.

So George drove home, and Bunty fed him and asked him no questions. She never did, but he sometimes confided. It might not be exactly approved procedure, but given a discreet and intelligent wife and an appropriate case it would have seemed to him a waste, even a dereliction of duty, not to use *all* the means to hand.

She looked him over from head to feet with alert eyes the image of Dominic's, noted the river-slime coating his feet and ankles, and probably got as much out of this instantaneous physical examination as ever he did on looking over a witness. But all she said was:

'Our two all right?'

'Very much so. I'm afraid they may even be enjoying themselves.' It was clear to her that George was not. Lesson One, do not become involved. But the effective text of Lesson Two, *how* not to become involved, no one has ever yet supplied. Perhaps as well. The best policemen are those who walk rather more in other people's shoes than in their own, and never lose sight of the relevance of the grace of God. 'That place is a

Disneyland fantasy,' he said, looking back suddenly at the monstrous bulk of Follymead, and astonished at the impact it made when viewed from homelier fields.

'We ought to go and spend a weekend there, some time,' said Bunty, busy with whisky and water. In a single hazel glance she estimated the amount necessary, in his present state of tiredness, to knock him out for the nine hours of sleep he needed. 'They're having a course on Mozart's wind music next month, it could be good.'

'We will, some time,' agreed George without conviction. If it's still functioning, after this earthquake that's brewing, he added in his own mind. The whisky was hot and strong and very welcome; buds of warmth and sleepiness opened in him like accelerated shots in some botanical film. 'I'm going to bed, I'm bushed. Get me up early, won't you?'

'With what?' said Bunty disrespectfully. 'Dynamite?'

But she didn't need dynamite; the telephone did it for her, rather too early, to her mind. George had awakened once with the first light, and stayed awake just long enough to enjoy the realisation that he need not move yet, his wife's long, soft breathing beside him, and the sudden awareness that one thing of significance had certainly been said last night between them, though not by him.

'Our two all right?', indeed!

Here had he been treading cautiously and watching the weather in the house, wondering what it would be like for Bunty to awake to the fact that her son had brought home a remarkably positive and permanent-looking girl friend; and all the time Bunty had it weighed up accurately and fairly, and was giving him the nudge, in case he had missed the significance of what was going on. 'Our two' sounded large enough to set at rest more minds than his. He fell asleep again smiling. When he awoke again to the clamour of the telephone, it was half-past seven, and Bunty was downstairs preparing breakfast. He reached for the instrument beside the bed, before she could pounce on the one downstairs and silence it.

'Sorry to wake you,' said Duckett, 'but I wanted to make sure of getting you before you left. I've got an interim report from the doctor for you.'

'Already?' George sat up abruptly wide-awake. 'That's quick work.'

'He didn't drown. No water in the lungs. He was dead before he ever went in.'

'The head wound?'

'Fractured skull. It turns out he had rather a thin one, but not one of those extreme cases. Somebody hit him a lot too hard, from almost behind him, slightly to his left. He'd be dead in minutes.'

'And the weapon? Has he got anything on that? Kind, shape, material? He must have been up all night,' said George with compunction.

'He *was* up all night. He wants to know why you can't find 'em at a civilised hour. We can't give you proper details yet, but I asked him for a long shot. And here it is. Traces of rust in the wound. Iron, he says, and narrow, say half an inch thick at the most. Width might be as much as two inches or so. Squared-off edges to it. It penetrated so deeply that it must have been swung at him pretty desperately, edge-on. Doc argues a fairish length, eighteen inches to two feet, maybe even more. Something like a flat iron bar, or a very large file. Does it make any sense?'

'It makes a lot of sense. Now I've got a request for you. Can you borrow me a frogman, and get him to Follymead during the morning? The sooner the better.'

'I can try. Where d'you want him?'

'Have him brought in the same way the ambulance came last night, and I'll have Lockyer on the lookout for him at the boundary.'

'All right, you shall have him. And one more item of interest for you. Arundale's Volkswagen has been found. Abandoned at a parking meter in Mayfair, locked, unrifled, everything intact. He took it to London, George. He went to his flat, the girl's phone call proved that. But he can't have been there long, there's no word so far of anybody seeing him. In any case, he won't go back there now he's warned. Where d'you reckon he'll turn up next?'

'Rio, probably,' said George, and reached for his dressing-gown. 'I'll call you from Follymead.'

'Oh, and George . . .'

'Hullo?'

'Those blood-samples you brought in earlier, from the ground there. Arundale was an AB, a universal recipient. Your specimens are A. They may be Galt's, we don't know his group yet. They're certainly not Arundale's.'

Duckett's police frogman was a wiry Blackcountryman who had dived in these parts before. He barely made the minimum height requirement, and had a chronic cigarette-smoker's cough, but he was tougher than leather, all the same, and had a lung capacity abstemious athletes might well have envied. He stood at the edge of the bank where Edward Arundale had almost certainly entered the water, and looked down into the black pool above the third weir. The surface water whipped across its stillness so impetuously and smoothly that it appeared still itself, to break in a seethe of white foam over the fall. Beneath the surface it would be mercilessly cold; he was going to need his second skin. The colour of the pool was perhaps more truly olive-green than black, and opaque as the moss-grown flags that floored the grotto.

'Soup!' he said disapprovingly, and trod out his cigarette into the soft ground. 'How am I supposed to see through that?'

'That's your problem. We've tried fishing for it with hooks, but it's deep here, deeper than you'd think.'

'I should have thought anything going in here would be carried over the edge. You've got some force running there.'

'That's what we thought, too, and why we looked for him well downstream. Too far downstream, as it turned out. But what we're looking for now would go down like a stone, and stay down.'

'Yeah,' said the diver, dabbling a toe thoughtfully, 'What is it I'm supposed to be looking for? I might as well know, I suppose.'

George told him. Shrewd, deep eyes set in nets of fine wrinkles in the sharp face visualised it, measured, weighed. 'If that went in here, it's still here, all right. Any idea what the bed's like?'

'Mucky. Maintenance isn't what it once was. But there doesn't seem to be much weed.'

'All right, let's go.'

It was about half-past ten when he lowered himself into the pool, and submerged, plunging promptly beneath the rushing surface water. In the yellow drawing-room at the house the first session of the day was still in progress, and even when the students emerged for mid-morning coffee, at eleven, the interval wouldn't be long enough to allow them to stray. The operators by the river had the grounds to themselves. Given a less absorbing subject and a less expert persuader, there would have been truants by this time. George had half-expected two truants, as it was, but it seemed that Dominic and Tossa were doing their duty.

So there were none but official witnesses when the diver rose for the third time, breaking the surface tension in a surge of unexpected silver in the day's first watery gleam of sun. The Braide streamed down his black rubber head and shoulders, and pulled at him viciously. George had insisted on having a line on him, in case of accidents; small river though the Braide was, it could be dangerous even to an expert when it ran as high as this. But in the issue he had needed no help. He hoisted himself ashore, black and glistening, with a lizard's agility, and pushed up his mask.

'Got it! Half sunk in the muck down there. I hit something else, too, that I'd like to have another go at, but this is your prize.'

147

He unhitched it from the cord at his belt, and held it up to be seen.

Felicity hadn't been exaggerating, after all, it was a good three inches longer than the span of her forearm and stretched fingers. The laboratory guesses weren't far out: half an inch thick, roughly two inches wide at the business end, which still retained traces of its last coat of paint, and possibly traces of haemoglobin, too, in spite of the river water; somewhat thicker and wider where it had rested in the wards, and this central part of it was a dead ancient-iron colour, since paint couldn't reach it, and nobody had used oil on it for year. And at the other end, a huge, coiled handle to balance its weight, decorated with a flourish of leaves. An ideal handle for grasping to strike a blow edge-on. With a thing like that you could hit out and fell an ox. And there it had hung in the wards of the gate, where Felicity had been the last to drop it home when she walked away from Lucien on Saturday afternoon, and went to set light to the fuse and fire the charge that was to blow Follymead apart. Ready and waiting for the hand that would be next to raise it, the hand that drew it out of the wards to use as a weapon of vengeance. Trees were set round in a screen between the gate and the waterside, thirty yards away; the waiting victim would see nothing.

'That's it,' said George, 'just a gate-latch, right there on the spot, waiting to be used.' The weight of it was formidable, and yet not too great for even a scholar's arm to be able to swing it effectively. 'That fills the gap. Thanks!'

'I'm going down again. Maybe it's nothing, but I'd like to make sure while we're on the job.'

He slid down from the bank again, feet-first into the water, and dropped from view. They were left contemplating the length of wrought iron that lay on the slippery turf between them.

'It looks straightforward enough now,' said Lockyer. 'Arundale came down here pretty well in a state of shock, without thinking what he was going to do. And when he bore down on the handle, he felt the latch loose in the socket. And took it on the spur of the moment. You could say it was this thing put murder in his mind.'

'And then what?' asked George dispassionately. 'It was Arundale who got his head stove in and his body slung into the river.'

'He was up against a much younger and fitter man. There was a hand-to-hand struggle, and this thing changed hands in the fight, and the boy hit out at him with it, and found he'd killed him.'

'A case of self-defence. Could be. He might still panic, get rid of the body and run. People do do such things.'

'Especially as he might not get away with a manslaughter verdict, if his misconduct with Mrs. Arundale was taken into consideration.'

'In any case,' observed George, brooding, 'even if you're being attacked, there are limits to what you're entitled to do. Getting your enemy's weapon away from him is one thing, bashing his head in with it when you've disarmed him is another. Watch it, here he comes.'

A coil of wet roped surfaced like a languid snake, and Lockyer furled in the slack. The diver broke surface in a fountain of spray, and they eased him in to the bank and leaned to help him ashore. For this time he carried something in his hands. He uncovered his face and drew in air greedily, and held up his prize triumphantly.

'Look at that! Maybe it's nothing to do with your affair, but don't tell me its proper place is in the slime down there. Or that it's been there long, either.'

A black walking-cane, with a chased metal knob for a handle; the shaft an appropriate length for a fairly tall man, perhaps rather thicker than pure elegance would have decreed, but tapering away to a fine metal ferrule. The diver balanced it in his hand curiously. 'Not so heavy. I'd say if that was just tossed in and happened to fall flat, it would go downstream. It was speared deep into the mud, ferrule down. I kicked the knob, groping for the other thing. What's the wood – ebony?'

'It looks like it.' George took the stick from him and turned

149

it in his hands. He rubbed with an inquisitive thumb at the metal of the ferrule, and it brightened suggestively under the friction. 'I believe this is silver. Looks as if it must have come from the house.'

He took out his handkerchief, and wrapped it about the knob, which was traced all over with coiling leaves. Not much possibility of getting any prints off the thing, after it had been at the bottom of the pool, but the action was automatic. He had the knob lightly enclosed in one hand, and the other hand holding the shaft of the stick, when he felt a slight play between them, as if the handle had worked loose. Gingerly he closed his fingers and tried to move it; it would not turn, but it did shift uneasily in his hand, drawn out a fraction of an inch from its socket.

'Wait a minute! Look . . . look at this!'

He drew stem and knob apart, and they gave with a slightly gritty resistance. Inch by inch the long, fine blade slid into view, until he drew it completely from its sheath and held it out before them. A blue runnel of light, edged with the dulled rainbow colours of tarnish, ran down the steel like captured lightning and into the ground.

'Good lord,' said Lockyer, fascinated, 'what is it?'

'A sword-stick, I suppose they'd call it. Sort of city gimmick the members of the Hellfire Club would carry and use for kicks.'

'That's me all over,' said the diver, staring admiringly, 'always a whole-hogger. You ask me for one weapon, I find you two. All zeal, Mr. Easy!'

'Well, but,' blurted Lockyer, 'if Arundale brought *that* with him . . .'

They looked at each other over the thin blade, that gleamed sullenly in the sun, and down the wind went one plausible theory. The man who had had the forethought to cancel his engagements had also taken care to provide himself with a weapon. And not even a would-be murderer needs a bludgeon in his left hand when he has a sword in his right.

Chapter 9

'Why, that's the sword-stick from the collection in the gallery,' said Marshall, as soon as he saw it. 'It always hangs in a display pattern of curios on the wall there. The Cothercotts amassed quite a museum of these things. How could it have got into the river?' It was a silly question; he saw it as soon as he'd spoken, and wished it back again. Who knew better than the warden of Follymead where to find a killing weapon, if he wanted one?

The handsome, deadly thing lay between them on the desk, a bit of fashionable devilment from the eighteenth century, probably never meant to be used. The blade had been sheathed fully before it was thrown into the water, and its point was engraved with fine vertical grooves; it might very well preserve traces of haemoglobin still, if this was what had drawn that blood that was not Arundale's blood. Another job for the laboratory.

'Was it in its place on Friday evening, when the party assembled and was shown round the house?' George asked.

'I can't say I noticed particularly. Perhaps someone else may have done. I didn't comment on it to my group, there are so many things to be seen.'

'And of course, no stranger would have the slightest idea what it was, unless he was told.'

'No, I suppose not.' That brought it still more closely home to the few who were not strangers, and did know what it was.

Mr. Marshall went back to his duties a very unhappy man. He cared about this place, he cared about music, he cared passionately about the Cothercott collection of keyboard instruments. Who was going to maintain them properly, as living things for use and pleasure, if the college folded? For them a museum would be a coffin.

It was a quarter to twelve; still three quarters of an hour before the class would come bursting out from the yellow drawing-room, hungry and vociferous, heading for lunch. Better get this thing out of the house now, thought George, while everything was quiet, and let the lab men worry about it, while he got on with some of the inevitable and tedious routine work that waited for him here in Arundale's desk.

He rolled the sword-stick in soft paper, and took it down to Lockyer, who was smoking a cigarette in a quiet corner of the stableyard at the home farm, neatly screened from the house by a belt of trees. The tenant farmer was used to seeing overflow cars from the house parties parked here, and took no interest in them. Nor was it unusual for Midshire students, who knew the lie of the land, to go in and out by the back way, and so save themselves a mile or more on the way into Belwardine. Lockyer had his motorcycle tucked away under the stable arch. The sword-stick would be in headquarters at Comerbourne in twenty minutes.

George went back to the warden's office, and began to turn out the drawers of the desk one by one. In all probability for nothing, but he wouldn't be sure of that until he'd gone through everything. Extraordinary how one weapon too many could make nonsense of an otherwise perfectly sound theory. The thing could have happened exactly as Lockyer had outlined it, the wronged husband coming to confront his wife's lover, the heavy instrument presented almost accidentally to his hand, and then the struggle in which the younger and more athletic man wrested the weapon away from him, and struck him with it; the appalled realisation that he had killed him, the disposal of

152

the body and the latch in the river, the opportune recollection that the victim's car was waiting and ready, and he was due to leave at this very hour, the subsequent flight to London, the abandonment of the car there, everything fitted in. Except this one grotesque thing, this Georgian whimsy that yet was not a toy, this fop's gimmick that could kill. And this one thing threw everything out of gear.

He had still to find out whether it had been in its usual place on the wall on Friday evening; possibly Dominic could help, there. But whenever it had been taken from its place, one thing was certain, Lucien Galt had not taken it to the grotto. Felicity had been with him from the time he left the house until they parted by the riverside in exasperation and offence; if he had had any such bizarre thing with him then, she would certainly have mentioned it. Nor was there any suggestion that at that time he had been thinking in terms of danger or violence. No, it was not Lucien.

But if Arundale had taken it with him – and if he had, it was one more proof that he went with intent to kill, sanely if not calmly – then what did he want with a heavy iron latch? And if *he* did not take it from its place, who did? Lucien, to defend himself? Rather a clumsy defence against two and a half feet of steel, but better than nothing. But there were considerable objections to that theory. One weapon too many, and nothing fitted snugly any longer. Better, for the moment, concentrate on these personal papers. And nobody ever had them in more immaculate order.

The records of Follymead were here from its inception, press clippings, photographs, a full list of all its courses, concerts, recitals, lectures. And the total was impressive. Music is one of the fundamental beauties, consolations and inspirations of life, a world without it would be unthinkable. This crazy, perverse, slightly sinister house had never in its history served so useful and beneficent a purpose as now. And that was largely Arundale's work, and it ought to be remembered to him. He had certainly loved it; the proof was here to be seen. For the first time George felt an impulse of personal warmth and pity for that elusive figure, now never to be better known.

He had adored his wife, too, that was to be seen everywhere. Perhaps with the possessive fervour of a husband who looked upon his wife as an extension of himself, but he wasn't alone there, and the passion was no less real for that. The last drawer of the desk yielded a harvest of photographs of her. George worked backwards through them, and experienced the eerie phenomenon of watching Audrey grow younger and younger before his eyes, dwindling to the nervous young wife, the frozen bride, refrigerated among her trappings of ice, the blooming debutante, the schoolgirl . . . Here in his private drawer Edward had preserved the complete record, decently hidden from alien eyes, the entire history of a love affair, the passion of a man not given to passions.

Here she was in full evening splendour for some grand event, very beautiful, very austere. And here at some function at Bannerets, being gracious, adequate and charming with parents. Too handsome, perhaps, for a headmaster's wife, but that air she had of being always at one remove from the world stood her in good stead. It was impossible to suppose that Audrey did not know she was considered beautiful; it was equally impossible to believe that she realised what that meant, what power it gave her, or should have given her. She looked out from her many photographs, a creature manipulated by circumstances, always filling her role well, always withdrawn from it in the spirit. And defenceless. Why should the camera be the eye to discover that quality? If ever there was a sad woman, here she walked, successful, influential, well-off, envied and admired; and always lost, anxious and alone.

He had worked his way back to her younger days now, the twenty-year-old with her new engagement ring discreetly displayed, the fiancée photograph posed specially for her distinguished in-laws. Then an even younger girl, with Arundale in some restaurant booth, the kind where souvenir pictures are taken. Somehow not quite typical of either of them. And then, almost abruptly, the school-girl. Three pictures tied together with a pink tape, the last of the collection, evidently taken during the first year of his acquaintance with her.

The first showed her in school uniform. How old? Sixteen? Surely no more, and already a beauty, indeed perhaps she had never been so beautiful since. No puppy-fat here, a slender, ethereal, glowing girl, not at all awkward or immature, indeed with a lustre upon her like a woman already admired and coveted and glad of her femininity. She must have been a thorn in the flesh of the others at that exclusive school to which her shop-keeper parents had sent her at such cost. On her, adolescence, so often a torment and an affront, hung like an apple blossom splendour, fragrant and joyous.

None of the subsequent pictures of her had this look.

George turned the half-plate portrait, and found the imprint of the photographer in blurred mauve type:

Castle Studios
E. McLeod, A.R.P.S.
Auchterarne 356.

Yes, of course. Nineteen-forty-two or thereabouts, this must have been, and Pleydells had been exiled into Scotland, like so many British institutions disseminated into the wilds to avoid bombing.

The second of the three pictures was of Audrey in tennis clothes, laughing, with her racket in her hands. The same imprint was on the back, the girl was approximately the same age. Probably all these Scottish pictures were taken within a few months. And the third . . .

The third was of Audrey in a white, virginal party-dress, impeccably suitable for a school festival, with small puff sleeves and the Pleydells version of a décolletage, pretty liberal for its

155

time and circumstances. The same indefinable aura of bliss hung about her; it might have been merely youth and health, but it seemed to George to be more than that, a sort of radiant fulfilment rare enough at sixteen. Mr. McLeod had done well by her. A good photographer, not concerned with glossing the lines of a face and showing up in immaculate definition every detail of a costume, the focus faded at her sleeves and the neck of her dress, leaving the face brilliant and surely almost untouched as the centre of attention. So successfully that George had returned the picture to its fellows and was retying the pink tape before he realised what he had seen depending from the silver chain round her neck.

He uncovered it again in a hurry, and stared disbelievingly. The fading definition blurred the design, but that was probably what had nudged his memory. This had been taken twenty-four years ago; the armoured saint in the nutshell helmet had been sharper and newer then, the hazing of his outlines only brought him nearer to what he was to-day. The spread eagle on his shield was faint but recognisable. Saints have their hall-marks, exclusive for all time. Saint Wenceslas had his copyright in this princely armour and heraldry, and once noted, could not be mistaken for any other sanctity in the calendar. So Dominic had said, and the books bore him out.

There couldn't be two of these things circulating among these few people. This was the same medal Lucien had worn. It was from Audrey he had got it!

There had been altogether too much and too conflicting evidence about that small disc of worn silver. Audrey swore that she had known Lucien only six weeks, Liri, on the other hand, testified that he had worn this medal round his neck ever since she had known him, which was a matter of two years. Lucien had said, according to Liri, that he had got it from his father. And now this picture said clearly that the thing had belonged to Audrey, and Audrey must have given it to him. So how many of them were lying?

Or, wondered George, the premonitory quiver of intuition chilling his flesh, *were none of them lying?*

He had to hunt out a road atlas and gazetteer to find out where this Auchterarne place was. Stirlingshire. He'd never yet had any communication with the Stirling police, but they'd be the quickest way to what he wanted to know. Probably the school had been evacuated to one of those Gothic mansions that decorate the Scottish countryside, to remind one that while England is for ever England, Scotland is in many ways Europe. With upland wastes around it on all sides, and every kind of embattled refugee group deployed there, from Scandinavian timber-men to Polish pioneers. Maybe army, he thought, as he lifted the telephone and asked for a line to the police at Stirling; there were a lot of wild and mixed army units waiting their time up there. But more likely air force. That was where the young, the cultivated, the engaging, were, in those strange and wonderful days when life had an enormous simplicity and purpose, and everybody knew where he was going, even if the way there proved uncommonly short.

'I'm sorry,' said the operator, after a few minutes of waiting, 'there'll be a slight delay, but I'll get you through as soon as I can. Can I call you back?'

'Please do. I'll be right on hand.'

He heard the students emerge from their session, and the gong pealed for lunch. Marshall had taken to sending him in a tray as soon as the party were all accounted for and busy. Not long to go now; this evening they would disperse, he hoped with only pleasant memories of this extraordinary weekend at Follymead, and then the survivors could look round without secrecy, and see what could be salvaged.

George propped up before him the photograph of Audrey in her party dress, and sat waiting, eye to eye with all that youth and innocence and happiness. He wondered if she'd ever looked like that for Edward Arundale.

Ten minutes later the telephone shrilled, and he reached for it eagerly, expecting his Scottish connection. But the voice that grated amiably in his ears was that of Superintendent Duckett, in high feather.

'George? We made it in time, after all. You can relax. They picked up Lucien Galt at London Airport half an hour ago.'

'Nothing to it,' Duckett was elaborating happily a minute later. 'Came in by taxi and checked in as if nothing had happened. Best thing he could do, of course, only he didn't do it quickly enough. Yesterday morning he could have flown out like a V.I.P. and no questions asked.'

'Why in the world didn't he?' George wondered. 'Inexperience?'

'Money. It takes a little time to knock together about three thousand pounds in notes.'

'That's what he had on him?'

'In his case. As much as he could turn into cash in the time, obviously. He had a ticket for Buenos Aires. They're holding him at the airport for us, and I've started Price and Rapier off to fetch him back. On the car charge, of course – taking away without owner's permission. And even for a holding charge that must be the under-statement of the year.'

'How did he react when they invited him to step aside and talk things over?' asked George. He'd seen that moment walk up behind so many men and tap them on the shoulder, and he had a pretty clear picture of this young man he'd never yet seen, proud to arrogance, impetuous, used to respect and adulation, even if he thought he despised it.

'Quietly. From what I hear, he looked round smartly for a way out, and might have tried to make a break for it if he could, but he sized things up at once, and went along without any fuss. He hadn't a chance, and I fancy he'd hate to make an unsuccessful scene. Now the question is, how do we handle him. It's your case, George, you know the people and the set-up there, you're

158

up with all the new developments, if there are any since you fished up that queer affair the boys are working on. You suggest, I'll consider.'

So now it was up to George, and he had to make up his mind a shade too early, before he really had anything but a hunch to go on. It was a gamble, and he was no gambler, and yet all his instincts told him to trust the conviction in his blood.

'All right, I'll tell you what I'd like done. Have him brought straight back here to me, to Follymead. I'll be waiting for him, and I'll be responsible for him.'

Duckett digested that in hard silence for a moment, and then said: 'Right, I'll do that.' Duckett was an admirable chief even in his acts, George found himself thinking, but better still in his abstentions. Not everybody could leave a subordinate alone to do a thing his own way. 'How do you want the boys to handle him meantime? Press him, let him alone, what?'

'Don't discourage him, don't press him. Just let him stew, and if he wants to talk, caution him, but then let him talk. It might be very interesting.'

'You think he *will* talk, don't you?'

'It wouldn't surprise me.'

'Just a minute, George . . . hang on, here's Phillips in from the lab . . .'

'Yes?'

'There's a positive reaction on the blade of that sword–stick affair. It seems to be A, the same as your specimens from the ground.'

'Good, thanks! No prints, of course?'

'Not a ghost of one. What did you expect, after being in the water all that time? In any case that knob's so finely chased it breaks up all the lines,' said Duckett philosophically, 'and nobody's going to hold a sword by the blade . . . not while he's using it.'

The second time the telephone rang George pounced on it like a hunting leopard, assured that it must be Stirling this time. But it was Scott, reporting from London at last.

'Well, about time,' said George, round a mouthful of chicken sandwich. 'What's been keeping you?'

'Mobile people, mostly,' said Scott crisply, the light tenor voice buoyant and detached. 'I struck unlucky at that children's home of yours. The old house-parents – Stewart and his wife – they retired just about a month ago. There's a couple named Smith in possession now, brand new. Naturally they know some of the past kids as names, but no other way. The only people about the place who know young Galt know him only from his visits since he left. Nobody there knows a thing about this medal of his.'

'Did you follow up the Stewarts? They must have retired somewhere around London. Londoners don't go far away.'

'I did. They've got a little house in Esher, all very nice and accessible. But they've got time on their hands, too, for the first time in years, and they've gone off to Italy for an early holiday. Can't say I blame 'em. They'll be back next week, but next week doesn't help us now. Well, that took a fair amount of time without much result, I grant you. So I took off for that garage and service station where the kid started work. Purley and Sons, Highbury. Quite a nice chap, Purley, old-fashioned paternal style. Good little business, and still personal. Garages can be, even in London.'

'And they remember him?'

'They remember him. Give him quite a good name as a worker. Didn't mind how mucky he got, and loved cars nearly as much as guitars. And you know he was only a kid when he started with them? Well, this is the one pearl I've got for you with all this diving, George. Purley took a real interest in the kids he employed, and was a stickler for the regulations. And you know the birth certificate juveniles have to produce when they start work?'

'Of course, what about it?'

'Just that in his case it wasn't a birth certificate. It was an adoption certificate.'

So he had known, of course, he had known all along. It is, in any case, the modern policy to ensure that they know, and so avoid future shocks. He had always known; and this was the one fact he had always refrained from mentioning, if not suppressed. He talked freely to interviewers about his upbringing in public care, he went back to his old home regularly as a visitor. No sore places there.

But never, never did he tell anyone, even Liri Palmer, that John James and Esther Galt were only his adoptive parents. That was a spot he was careful never to touch.

For fear of pain?

A quarter of an hour later the telephone rang for the third time, and this time it really was Stirling. By that time the inquiries he had to make there seemed almost unnecessary, but he set them in motion, all the same. It would take a little time to get hold of details from so far back, names, dates of death, and so on, but the services kept everlasting records. He would get what he wanted, though perhaps not in time to affect or simplify the issue.

And now there was nothing left to be done, except sit back and wait for Lucien Galt to come back to Follymead under escort.

In the back of the police car, purling steadily along the M1 at seventy, Lucien Galt sat closed into himself like a locked house, but like a locked house with someone peering through the curtains, and possibly a gun braced across the sill of a just-open window. He had said hardly anything since the large, civil men closed in on him at the airport, and wafted him smoothly aside into a private room. If he had seen the slightest hope of giving them the slip, then or afterwards, he would have risked it, but they didn't take any chances, and they didn't give him any. No use looking back now and cursing the mistakes he had made. He had a situation to deal with here. Nothing else mattered now.

He was horribly tired, that was the worst thing about it. He needed to think clearly and carefully, and he was in no condition to do it, but he had to try. This perfectly decent and pleasant person beside him, and the other one, driving, they were human, they had treated him throughout with slightly constrained civility and consideration. It was an extraordinary feeling, being wound about with chains of forbearance and watchfulness, like a mental case, like a psychopath under observation. But it did mean that they would listen to him and report on him with all the detachment of which they were capable.

'I'd like to tell you how it happened,' he said abruptly, breaking the silence which had been largely of his own making. At first he hadn't known what to do, or how to conduct himself, and though he had despised the normal bluster and pretence with which the guilty cover up their guilt, it had seemed to him that a profession of non-understanding was the only course left to him, and after that, silence, and such dignity as he could find a way of keeping. I know nothing, I understand nothing, I am a citizen of substance and some importance, (*am I?*) but I am certainly not going to make a fuss in this public place. Since you apparently have a duty to do, by all means let's go back and sort out this misunderstanding in private. All very well, but it made this blunt and exhausted opening now seem very crude. He shrank from the sound of it, and yet he was aware that it made a credible beginning. The guilty first protest (at least he had done that only once, and briefly), then sit back and think, and begin to worry, and break into a sweat of anxiety, and finally come to the conclusion that a half-admission may get them something. What he had said must have that ring to this solid, quiet person beside him, who looked like a merchant skipper on leave, brown-faced and far-sighted, and at ease anywhere.

The eyes had shortened their focus upon him, along a broad tweed shoulder. The good-natured teak face gave nothing away.

162

'How you drove the car away, you mean?' asked Detective-Sergeant Rapier placidly.

'All right, I did drive the car away, if you want me to say so.'

'I don't want you to say anything you don't want to say. We're not asking you for any statements.'

'I know that. I'm offering you one. If you want to take it down, you can. But even if you don't want to, you can listen. I'm tired of running, anyhow, I want it straightened out.'

'If you want to talk,' said Rapier philosophically, 'who's to stop you? But I feel I ought to remind you that there are two witnesses present, whether there's a record or not, and that anything you say may be used in evidence. Maybe you should take another long, quiet think – about as long as from here to Comerbourne. There'll be time there to do all the talking you'll need to do.'

'I have thought,' said Lucien bleakly. 'I should have done better to think before I ran. What has it got me? I don't suppose I ever had much chance of getting out, but what chance I had I seem to have muffed. Talking can't make things worse now. It might even make them a shade better. Because I never meant to kill him, of course. If I hadn't had the most hellish luck he'd be alive now.'

In the small, pregnant silence, shatteringly apparent even while Price continued to direct the car calmly at the same smooth speed, Lucien observed his two escorts exchanging in the mirror a speaking glance that was yet very careful not to say too much.

'I didn't know,' said Rapier mildly, 'that anybody'd mentioned a death.'

'Oh, for God's sake,' said Lucien in a spurt of nervous fury that left him trembling, 'let's pack in this pretence that you're after me for running off with a car. People don't try to skip out to South America for that, and you fellows don't have the airports alerted to stop them. That's not what all this is about. You know as well as I do that Mr. Arundale's dead, and if you weren't as good as certain I killed him, you wouldn't be here

163

taking me back with you to Comerbourne. So why put on this act with me!'

'Have we asked you any questions about Mr. Arundale's death, sir? I don't recollect that we have.'

'You don't have to ask me, I'm telling you. I want to tell you. I'm sick of being the only one who knows.'

'It's a free country,' allowed Rapier considerately. 'But no charge has been made against you formally yet on any count. I shouldn't be in any hurry to make statements, if I were you.'

'But if I do, you'll keep a record of it? Not that I care, except that I'd rather get it over in one. I'm so damned tired.'

'Very well, sir, if that's what you want. But you will bear in mind that I've cautioned you.' And with the minimum of movement and fuss, suddenly the sergeant had his notebook on his knee, and his ball-pen in his hand. Probably wise to the fact that I'm one of those contra-suggestible types, thought Lucien bitterly. If they seem to be heading in the direction you want them to go, push like the devil the other way, and they'll persist. If you give them a hand, they'll turn back.

'Oh, I give you full credit for that. But it's all right, I want it finished now. It never should have begun. It was all unnecessary.'

He moistened his lips nervously. How much did they know? Better assume they knew most of it. How could Felicity keep her mouth shut for long, once she realised what she'd unleashed. And even if they hadn't yet recovered everything the river was supposed to conceal, they soon would when the level went down. No, better leave out nothing that was there to be found.

'I was down by the river,' he said, and shivered as if he'd plunged into its coldness, 'and the kid had followed me there, the warden's niece, the Cope girl. She'd been round my neck ever since I'd got to Follymead, I couldn't shake her. And I was in a miserable way because I'd quarrelled with my own girl, and she was around, too, and things were pretty bad with me. I wanted to get somewhere by myself, and think, and there was this silly little thing bleating about love, when she didn't know

164

she was born yet. I stood it a long time, and then I blew up. All I wanted was to get rid of her, and I wasn't particular how I did it. I'm not proud of it now. I suppose it was about the cruellest thing I've ever done. I gave her a message to take to her aunt . . . to Mrs. Arundale . . . as if there was something between us. There wasn't, of course, I only met the lady a couple of times before. It was just that Felicity was already mad jealous of her aunt, that's why I made it her. It cut deeper. And it worked, too. She took offence and walked off and left me there, and that was all I wanted. I never thought she'd go and deliver the damned message, right out in front of both of them . . . or just to him, I don't know . . . to him, anyhow, because he came. I'd said to tell Mrs. Arundale I was waiting for her there. But it was her husband who came.'

The sergeant's hand seemed to do no more than idle over the paper, spraying shorthand symbols like rain. But he wasn't missing anything. And he could still spare one eye, occasionally, for a quick glance at his prisoner's face.

'Must have been a bit of a shock, when you expected Mrs. Arundale,' he said sympathetically.

'I didn't expect anyone. I told you, all I meant to do was shoo the Cope girl away. I never thought she'd have the devilment – I don't know, though, I asked for it! – or the guts, either.' Lucien shivered, a nervous compulsion that ran through his bones in a sharp contraction of cold. 'He was there before I knew. I wasn't paying any attention to anything. I was just glad to be alone, and then there he was coming out of the trees, with this thing in his hand . . .' A compulsive yawn followed the chill; he smothered it in his hands, and shook himself violently. He wasn't through the wood yet, he had to keep his mind clear.

'This thing . . .?' said Rapier, patiently nudging.

'Maybe you don't know it. It hangs in the gallery there, among a lot of other exotic junk, Victorian, maybe older. The Cope kid showed it to us when we went round the house, the first evening. It's a black walking-stick with a silver handle, but really it's a sword inside an ebony sheath. I knew it as soon as I saw it, but I never thought . . . He just drew it out and came at me. Never said a word, simply ran at me with the blade. I tried to talk to him, but there was no time at all, and anyhow I doubt if he could even hear. He looked quite mad . . . stone-cold mad. I couldn't believe in it, I nearly let him get me because I couldn't take it in. But then I knew he meant killing, and I just put the rocks between us in time, and ducked aside into the trees, hoping to beat him to the gate and get away. But he saw what I was about, and cut back there as fast as I did. I got my hand to the latch, and then he was on top of me, and I jumped round and put up my other arm to fend him off, and the tip of the blade ripped my fingers . . .' He flexed them painfully, and there indeed was the sliced cut, imperfectly healed, crossing all four fingers diagonally between second joints and knuckles. 'And the latch had pulled half out of its place, so I knew it was free, and I pulled it out.'

He shut his face tightly between his palms, trying to suppress the sick yawns that were tearing at him now like bouts of pain. Queer the way you reacted when the time came, mentally calm but physically disrupted, a rash of nervous symptoms with a tensed and wary mind. This pause he prolonged in the hope of eliciting a question, anything that would make things easier for him, and give him a signpost, but Rapier waited politely with his ballpoint suggestively poised, and said not a word.

'But I had to spring away from the gate to get out of range. And then he was between me and it, and even if I had a weapon I couldn't match his reach. He drove me down towards the water again, and all I could do was try to parry his strokes. But then it was no good backing any more, I should have been in the river, so I had to try and jump him. I'm no more good at that than he was, and I was in a state by then, and . . . I don't even know exactly what happened. We were struggling together there, and I hit him . . . He went down. I didn't know I'd hurt him badly, the only thing I thought about was to grab the sword, while he was stunned. But after a few minutes, when he still didn't move, I got scared, and took a closer look at him. His head was like a ploughed field, and yet there was next to no blood. He wasn't breathing, and with a head that shape he wasn't going to breathe again. I knew I'd killed him. And all for nothing. I never wanted to, I hardly knew him . . . What was I supposed to do, with that on my hands?' he appealed passionately.

'The right thing,' said Rapier, accepting this literally, 'in a case like that, would be to leave everything as it is, call the police, and tell them the whole story.'

'And how many ever do the right thing, when they get into a jam like that? Try it, some day, and see if you don't do what I did – run. There wasn't a thing I could do for *him*. He was dead. I pulled him to the edge of the river, and threw him as far out as I could, into the current, and I saw it take him downstream over the weir. I threw the swordstick and the latch in the pool there. And I remembered that he was supposed to start for Birmingham, and his car was out in the yard ready. So I took it. Nobody'd look for him again until Sunday night. But you can't get money out of banks or turn other assets into cash on a Sunday, I had to wait over until today. If it hadn't been for that, you wouldn't have caught up with me.'

'And how,' asked the sergeant mildly, 'did you know that we were inquiring into this death, then? You say nobody'd be expecting him back until last night, and nobody'd panic at one extra night, would they? Or did somebody tip you off? Did you hear from somebody that his body'd been found?'

Lucien took his hands away from his drawn face, and stared him steadily in the eye. 'No, how could I? I thought I was still ahead of you until they dropped on me at the airport. After that, I couldn't help knowing you'd either found him, or found traces that were just as good. You wouldn't have known about the car being stolen, otherwise. And what you didn't know before,' he said wearily, 'you know now. Have you got it all down?'

'Yes, Mr. Galt, I've got it all down.'

'Good! I should hate to go through all that again.'

'I'm sure you would, sir,' agreed Rapier serenely.

'I don't want anybody else to be pestered,' said Lucien, leaning back in his corner with a drained sigh, 'when nobody but me had anything to do with it. I didn't have a thing against him, I hardly even knew him. But *I killed him*.'

'Yes, Mr. Galt,' agreed Rapier, accommodatingly, watching the stillness of the pure, dark profile against the streaming world outside, 'yes, you've made that quite clear.'

Chapter 10

Audrey Arundale emerged from her privacy to preside at the final gala tea. She wore black, but like many primrose-and-silver blondes, she very frequently did wear black, and there was nothing to remark on in that. She was pale, her eyes a little remote, and shadowed by bluish rings that made them look larger and more lustrous; but there was nothing in her appearance to give rise to comment or curiosity. Her manner was as it had always been, but at one remove more, and the wall of glass that separated her from the rest of the world, even while she touched and conversed and was patently present in the flesh, was so thin and clear that happy people never noticed it.

She was about again on Follymead's business, and had a couple of calls to make. On her way to the small drawing-room she looked in at the deputy warden's office. Henry Marshall looked up from his laden desk as she entered, and came to his feet in quick concern.

'Mrs. Arundale, I'd no idea . . . You're not going in to tea?'

'Yes, I must. I'm quite all right, I assure you, there's no need to worry about me. I just wondered if there was anything I could help *you* with. I'm so sorry to have left everything to you, like this.'

'You mustn't trouble about the running of the place at all, that's what I'm here for.'

'I know,' she said, 'and I know how well you can do it. I hope . . . I hope they'll give you the job, Harry.'

'Thank you!' he said uncomfortably. He hadn't thought of her bereavement, until then, as his opportunity. 'I think we've got everything in order. It's lucky that we had no special fixtures for the next few days. We're circulating all the people who've booked for the course next weekend, and cancelling the arrangements. I thought it would be impossible to go through with it. I have it from the police that no statement will be given to the press until tomorrow, and I very much hope it will only affect the local and regional press at the moment.'

'But there'll have to be an inquest, won't there?' she said, contemplating the complexities of death with eyes of stunned distaste.

'It's to open on Wednesday morning, I'm told. But Inspector Felse says it will be only a formal opening, and the police will be asking for an adjournment. At least that will allow time for the public to forget about us a little.'

'And find some newer sensations,' she said with the blanched ghost of a smile. 'Yes . . . And what about the subscription concert, on Monday evening of next week? So difficult to cancel a thing like that, when all the tickets have been sold, and then it's hardly fair to the artists . . .'

'I think we ought to go through with that. A whole week will have passed, and the public who do use Follymead will know by then what's happened here, and I think they'll be reassured to find that the work is to go on. I'm sure the governors will approve.'

'Good,' said Audrey. 'I'm glad you feel that way about it, too. I thought myself we ought to honour the arrangements. It's certainly what Edward would have wanted us to do. I'm so glad you're here to look after everything, Harry. I see you don't need me at all. Now I must go along and have a word with Inspector Felse before tea.'

He sprang to open the door for her, his anxious eyes searching her face, but there was nothing to be seen but a white calm. 'I don't think you should attempt too much. The social load is taking care of itself, you know, you've only to listen to them. And it'll soon be over now. You weren't thinking of attending this last concert, were you?'

'Yes, I feel I must. Edward would have wished it.'

She went along the corridor from the gallery to the warden's private office. George Felse was sitting behind the desk with his head propped in his hands, the telephone silent now, the photograph of Audrey in her party dress, Audrey at sixteen, leaning against a trough of Edward's books. George could look from the girl to the woman, and feel time whirl past over his head, and she, since the picture was hidden from her, would not even be able to guess at the reason for the look of wonder and compunction in his eyes.

'Mr. Felse, I hope I haven't done something I shouldn't have done, but it seemed to be my job. I've told Felicity, in confidence, that her uncle is dead; and I've telephoned her mother, and told her that I'm sending the child home by the half-past five train. Wilson will drive her to the station. If you have no objection? I know you'll probably need her, later on, but you'll find Mrs. Cope's address there in the book, and Felicity will be available whenever necessary.'

'I'm glad,' said George. 'It's the best thing you could have done. You may be sure we shall spare her as much as we can. It may not even be necessary to bring her into it at all. If we can avoid it, we will.'

'I know. She told me . . . she said you've been very kind to her. She . . . we have never understood each other, I know that. I feel guilty towards her.'

'So does she,' said George quietly, 'towards you.'

'Yes . . . we can hardly take a step, it seems, without infringing someone else's liberties. I've suggested to Mrs. Cope that she should try sending Felicity abroad for a time, perhaps even to school abroad. A completely new environment, new companions . . .'

'It would be the very best thing for her. And I believe she could make good use of it, now.'

'I believe she could. Thank you, I'm glad you think I've done right.'

She closed the door gently after her, and went towards the hubbub in the drawing-room. And there she dispensed tea, and made conversation, and was everything the hostess of Follymead should be, always with the invisible and impenetrable veil between her and reality.

'Such a delightful weekend, my dear,' said Miss Southern, balancing a china teacup as old and fragile as her own thin, bluish fingers. 'So wonderful to get away from this awful modern world and enjoy an island of such *peace*.'

'I'm so happy,' said Audrey, 'that it's been a success.'

'Oh, it has! Everyone's enjoyed it *so* much. That charming little girl with the harp . . . I do think the harp's such a *graceful* instrument for a woman, don't you?'

'Mrs. Arundale,' shrilled the girl with the butterfly glasses, bounding between the chattering groups with a cucumber sandwich in one hand and a teacup in the other, 'it's been *fab*! I can't *wait* for the next one.'

'I'm so glad you've enjoyed it. We must try to fit in another one as soon as we can.'

'I'm only sorry Arundale's missed most of it,' said a thin gentleman in a dog-collar. 'Do tell him, when he gets back, what an enormous success it's been.'

'I'll tell him,' said Audrey, and her glass smile never wavered.

Felicity came down the stairs from her room at a quarter to five, carrying a coat over her arm and a suitcase in her hand. She cocked an ear towards the small drawing-room, but on reflection did not go in. Instead, she looked round the recesses of the gallery for a secluded spot, and there in a cushioned corner of one of the built-in seats was Liri Palmer, sitting alone.

'Hullo!' said Felicity. 'I was just thinking of going to look for you, only I was a bit scared, too. Do you mind if I sit with you? I've got ten minutes, and then I've got to go.'

'You're leaving?'

'My aunt's sending me home.' Felicity put down her case, and dropped into the cushions. 'I think she thinks the children should be kept out of the way of crime and the law, and if there's going to be unpleasantness, Felicity must be shipped off to more sheltered places. Very correct, very conventional, is my Aunt Audrey.' She looked along her shoulder at the clear, still profile and the glorious, envied hair. 'You know my uncle's dead, don't you?' Her voice was low, level and determinedly unemotional, but her face was solemn and pale.

'I found him,' said Liri simply. 'How did you find out?'

'Aunt Audrey told me. She knew I was in it already, up to the neck, so she told me how it turned out. I was grateful to her for that. It's horrible to know bits ... too much, but not enough ... And to have to find out the rest maybe from a newspaper. Now at least I know where I am, even if I don't like it much.'

'Who does?' said Liri.

'No ... nobody, I suppose. But *you* haven't *done* anything.'

'And you have?'

'Yes, that's what I wanted to tell you. You see, the bits you know are different bits from mine. And I only found out today, from Dickie Meurice, that you and Lucien ... You were engaged, weren't you? Or as good as, what's the difference? I wanted to tell you, I didn't know that. If I'd known, I wouldn't have tried to make him interested in me, and none of this would have happened. Not that that makes it much better for you, I suppose, because in any case he was playing you false.' The phrase came strangely but without affectation; whatever was on her mind now, Felicity was not pretending, even to herself. 'He was Aunt Audrey's lover. I suppose you knew that?'

Liri stared straight before her. 'He broke three dates with me, always with a good excuse, always on the telephone. It's easier to lie to somebody on the telephone. Twice I swallowed it, the third time I was a shade low, so I took myself out to dinner at a little place we sometimes used. He was supposed to be at rehearsal for a recording session, but he wasn't. He was there with her. They were glowing like studio lights, and talking like bosom friends, as if they had a lifetime's talking to make up. He was holding her hand, right there on the table. They didn't see me. They weren't seeing anyone but each other. I didn't interrupt them. I waited until the next time he came for me, and then I threw it at him that he'd been standing me up for another woman. He said there was nothing in it, I was making a mistake. But I knew better. We both went mad, and that was the end of it.' She sat up abruptly and shook herself, between anger and amazement. 'Why am I telling you this?'

'I don't know,' said Felicity humbly, 'unless it's because I've grown up suddenly.'

'Afterwards I thought about it, and I thought, no, that was too big a thing to throw away like that, without even trying to straighten it out between us. So I came here to Follymead, because he had this engagement here. I came to make it up with him if I could. And the first person I saw when I got here – no, the second, actually, *you* were the first, through the lighted windows right here in this gallery – the second person I saw was this woman who'd been with him in the restaurant. So then I knew why Lucien had taken this engagement . . . maybe why the whole weekend course had been thought up. And that was the end of it as far as I was concerned. I *thought*! Actually it turns out things don't just end when it's appropriate, they go on whether you want them to or not. Is that what you wanted to know?'

'It isn't that I wanted to *know*. But thank you, all the same.

174

It makes it easier to understand. Me, I didn't know any of all that, or even about you. All I could see was Lucien. I was in love with him, or I thought I was. I went out after him last Saturday afternoon . . .' She told that story over again, softening nothing; Liri had a right to know.

'That was what he said. And I did it. I went straight back to the house, and Uncle Edward and Aunt Audrey were sitting there together, and I said just exactly what Lucien had told me to say, right out loud to both of them. And that's the part you didn't know. That's all. That's why Uncle Edward went down there to kill him, only he got killed himself, instead. But whichever way it went, somebody died, and I was the cause of it.'

'You did *that?*' Liri had turned to study the girl at her side with wide-eyed attention. 'Went and chucked his private invitation down on the table between them, "where they were sat at meat"?'

'Well, not exactly that,' said Felicity, puzzled. 'They were just finishing coffee, actually.'

'Don't mind me, it was just something that came into my head. It happens in one of the ballads, didn't you know? Just like that.' She stared sombrely at the story that now unrolled before her remorseless and complete. 'It's something I might have done, too, if he'd done a thing like that to me.'

'Oh, might you? Do you really mean that? But you didn't,' said Felicity, clouding over again. 'I was the one who did it, and I was the one who caused Uncle Edward to get killed.'

'You and all the rest of us who've had any part in this affair. And Mr. Arundale himself, that's certain. Don't claim more than belongs to you,' said Liri hardly.

'That's what Inspector Felse said,' admitted Felicity, encouraged.

'Inspector Felse is a pretty deep sort of man.'

'He is, isn't he? There; that's the station wagon for me.' The horn had blared cheerfully in the courtyard. Felicity picked up

175

her coat and her case. 'Good-bye! I wish things could turn out better than they look now. I'm sorry!'

She turned her slender, erect back, and marched away along the rear corridor towards the back stairs. At the warden's office she hesitated for a moment, and then tapped on the door. It would be only polite, wouldn't it, to say good-bye to Inspector Felse?

'Oh, hullo!' said George. 'I heard you were off home.'

'It's all right, isn't it, for me to go? Aunt Audrey said she'd tell you.'

'Yes, it's all right. If we need you, we shall know where to find you. Take care of yourself, and good luck. Better luck,' he said gently, 'than you've had so far.'

'Thank you. You've been very kind.' He saw her glance stray involuntarily towards the glass over the hearth. 'You did mean what you said, didn't you? You do really think I'm going to be . . . pretty?'

'No,' said George firmly, 'you're never going to be pretty, and that isn't what I said.'

'I was afraid to say the other word,' Felicity admitted simply. 'But you *did* mean it, didn't you?'

'I meant it. You'll see for yourself, before very long.'

'It's not that it makes any difference to what's happened,' she explained punctiliously. 'But it's something to start from – like having capital. You know!' She picked up her case sturdily. 'Goodbye, then, and thanks!'

'Goodbye, Felicity! You'll be all right?'

She understood that in its fullest meaning, and she said: 'I'll be all right.'

The station wagon taking Felicity away to catch her train left the courtyard and circled the house to the front drive just two minutes before Price drove in by the farm road. The tower clock, which was several minutes fast, was just chiming five. In one and a half hours the students would be dispersing, by car, by bus, by the house transport and the local trains, to homes scattered over the whole of the Midlands, and some even farther afield. Let them, at all costs, get off in peace. An extra car suddenly appearing at Follymead was nothing to wonder about at normal times, but better to take no chances now. Price parked carefully in the obscurity under the archway, where they could not be seen from the windows.

Lucien awoke from a wretched and uneasy doze with the exaggerated alarm of nightmare, and stared round wildly to find the familiar and unwelcome apparition of Follymead enclosing him. He could face what he had to face, but he shied at the idea of added ordeals.

'Why have you brought me here?' he demanded, roused and resentful. 'I thought we were going to the police station at Comerbourne.'

'I don't remember that we mentioned exactly where we were going. Inspector Felse has been working from here, and this is where we shall find him.' Rapier got out of the back seat, and locked the car upon the two who remained; not that he thought the boy would try to make a break for it now, but, there was no point in leaving him even the meagre opportunity. The sergeant climbed the back stairs, and let himself into the warden's office.

George looked up from the report he was compiling, short as yet of a few details, a date or two, a name, but by this time essentially complete. 'Well, how did it go?'

'No trouble,' said Rapier complacently. 'He's below in the car.' He laid his notebook on the desk, and flicked through the close pages of shorthand. 'There you are! He insisted on making a statement, didn't seem able to rest until he had it all in order. I'll send it up to you as soon as I can get it typed. He's made a full confession.'

'Ah,' said George, with a faint smile that Rapier found, in retrospect, more than a little puzzling. 'Yes, I thought he might.'

'He says Arundale attacked him, and he killed him in self-defence. You won't have any trouble, he's filled in all the details, and they all fit.'

'Oh, yes, I quite thought he'd make a good job of it.' The smile was still present, wry, private and sad, and yet understandably touched with the pride and satisfaction of a man whose judgement has been vindicated by events. 'And what about Mrs. Arundale?'

'She has nothing to do with it. I will say that for him, he went out of his way to make that clear. He hardly knew her. He says he used her name to shock the kid, because he knew she was jealous of her, anyhow, and the kid must have gone and told her uncle. Oh, he's made your case for you.'

'All right,' said George, 'bring him up.'

Rapier went back down the staircase and unlocked the car, dropping the keys into Price's hand. 'Ready for you now, Mr. Galt. Up the stairs, that's right.'

Lucien heard the distant, starling clamour from the great drawing-room, and reared his head in a wild gesture of mingled ardour and revulsion. 'But they . . . do *they* know about this?' He climbed the tight spiral flight, tensed and suspicious, his ears stretched. They surely couldn't know. The high-pitched din was eager and innocent, untouched by death.

'You'd better ask the inspector that. In here.'

Lucien entered the warden's office, and the door was closed quietly behind him.

George rose from behind the desk. 'Sit down, Mr. Galt. You must have made very good time. I was reckoning on this final concert being over, or nearly over, by the time you arrived.'

It was like coming into a familiar room which had been emptied of its furniture, and was no longer familiar. All the echoes were wrong, all the tones distorted so acutely that Lucien felt his balance affected, and spread his feet aggressively to grip reality more firmly. Even in the car he had this feeling of disorientation, but now it went over him as acutely as panic, and left him sick and frightened. He had made a detailed statement admitting his responsibility for the death of Arundale, why wasn't he under arrest? Even if his escorts from London had been instructed only to deliver him safely to the man in charge, here, presumably, *was* the man in charge, and still nothing seemed to be about to happen. He gripped the back of the chair that was offered him, and stood taut and distrustful, his eyes roving the room.

'I don't understand. Why did I have to come back here? Was that fair? I haven't made any trouble for your men, I've co-operated as well as I can, I'm not disputing anything I've done. So *why* . . .?'

'Sit down,' said George.

It wasn't worth arguing about; Lucien sat. George came round the desk and sat on the front corner, looking his capture over with interest. Black as a gypsy, string line as a violin, a slender, dark, wild creature, with arrogant eyes shadowed now by grief and fear, and a hypersensitive, proud mouth that was ready to curl even at this moment. Like his picture, but even more like the picture his friends and enemies had built up of him for the man who had never set eyes on him until now.

'I've made a statement,' said Lucien. 'It should clear up everything for you. I suppose he has to transcribe it, or whatever. I don't know what more you want.'

'Then I'll tell you. I want another hour and a half of apparent normality here. After that we can be as business-like as you please.' He saw the tired eyes question doubtfully, and smiled. 'Mr. Galt, I believe you'll have a certain sympathy with our concern for this place. It may not be perfect, what it does may not go very far, or be very profound. But with all that, it is a pretty remarkable institution. It brings music, and what's more, knowledge and desire of music, to people who've perhaps never really experienced it before. If its appeal fell off as the result of a scandal and a notorious case, or if its enemies – oh, yes, anything that can be called cultural has always more than enough enemies – if its enemies got an effective weapon to use against it, it might be killed for good, and that would be a real loss. There's going to be publicity, inquest and trial can't be avoided. There's going to be a bad period; but if we can minimise the effect as much as possible, Follymead may survive. That's why I want to take no action whatever until this course has dispersed. The next can be called off without too much backwash. So let's at least wait until the house is empty tonight, before we start talking in terms of guilt and arrests.'

After a brief and dubious silence Lucien said slowly: 'I'm not sure what it is you want of me.'

'I want you to give me your word not to try to get away, just to wait and behave normally until the party has left.'

Lucien moistened his lips. His eyes kindled suddenly into a slightly feverish glitter. 'This is a straightforward concert for the finish?'

'Yes. Until half-past six. Then they all go home.'

'Is Liri taking part?'

'Yes, Liri's taking part.'

He thought of her head bent over the guitar, the great braid of hair coiled on her neck, the suave curve of her cheek and the intent, burnished brow, and of the voice achingly pure and clear and passionate. He thought of a future blank with confinement and solitude, where the voice could not penetrate.

'If you'll let me sit in on this concert, all right, I give you my word I won't cause you any trouble.'

He didn't believe there would be any response to that offer, he was sure they'd never risk him among the crowd. But Inspector Felse had got to his feet briskly, and swept his papers into a drawer.

'Agreed, if you don't mind my company. And in that case we'd better go in, hadn't we? They'll be starting any minute.'

From her place among the artists, Liri saw them come in.

The lights were already dimmed, the hum of voices was becoming muted and expectant, and it was time. There at the back of the great room people moved about gently in obscurity, settling themselves, changing their places, finding comfortable leg-room. For once Professor Penrose came a little late to his place, and in haste, having taken too long a nap after tea; but for that the programme would have begun before the padded door at the back of the room opened again, and her attention would have been on the singers, and not on the two late-comers. As it was, she was gazing beyond the last rank of chairs in the shadow, beyond even the walls of the room, when the opening of the door caused her to shorten her sights, and return to here and now. And the person who came in was Lucien.

Her heart turned in her, even before she saw George Felse follow him into the room, and edge along after him behind the audience, to a seat against the wall. So they had him, after all. He wasn't used to running from things, and he hadn't run fast enough, and now they had him, back here where the thing had happened that never should have happened, the wasted, meaningless thing in which she still couldn't believe. She felt the walls closing in on her, too.

And yet if he was under arrest, what was he doing here? There seemed to be no constraint upon him, even if the inspector had come in with him, and taken a seat beside him on the elegant little gilt and velvet couch against the tapestried wall. They sat there like any other two members of the audience, she even saw them exchange a few words, with every appearance of normality. What was happening? There was something here that was not as it seemed to be, and she could not make out what it was, or whom it threatened.

She looked to the inspector for a clue, but his face was smooth and reserved and quite unreadable, there was no way of guessing what was going on in the mind behind it. If she had gone in terror of the obvious end, now she found herself equally afraid of some other eventuality beyond her grasp. Why bring a prisoner here into this room? She could understand that the police might prefer to get all these people out of here before they took decisive action, but even so, why bring Lucien to the gathering?

A hand jogged her arm. The professor's insinuating voice begged her winningly: 'Your legs are younger than mine, lass. Run and fetch my notebook for me, will you? I went and left it in the warden's office before tea, and forgot to collect it again.'

His notebook was a joke by that time. He couldn't talk without it open before him, and yet he had never been known to consult it for any detail, however abstruse.

'You've never needed it yet,' protested Liri, her eyes clinging to the distant pair at the back of the room, lost now in an even dimmer light. Someone had turned out the strip-lights over the pictures. 'You're not likely to start tonight.'

'There has to be a first time for everything. Go on, now, like a good girl.'

And she went, impatiently but obediently, flashing to the doorway and running along the corridor. Her heels rang on the polished wood with a solitary and frightening sound, for outside the great yellow room the house hung silent and deserted. Nothing now was quite real, so much of her mind laboured frenziedly with this crisis she could not comprehend. She pushed open the door of the warden's office, which for the past three days had become an extension of police headquarters, while the house went about its blithe business oblivious of all evil. The massive folder of the professor's notes lay on a walnut table near the window. She tucked it under her arm, and turned to the door again, and then as abruptly turned back, and crossed to the desk.

Would he leave anything, any unconsidered trifle, where she could find it and make sense of it? She had to know; there was a feverish pulse beating in her blood that insisted it was imperative for her to know.

She put down her portfolio on the desk, and began trying all the drawers one by one, but they were fast locked. She should have guessed that. There was nothing here for her.

But there was. Her eyes fell on it as she straightened up with a sigh from her useless search. There it was, propped against Arundale's rack of reference books, eye to eye with her, the half-plate photograph of a young girl in a white party dress. She had never seen the living face joyous like this, but she knew it at once, as she knew the little silver disc that hung round the girl's neck on a thin chain.

Lucien's medal, the one he had worn ever since she had known him, long before he met Audrey Arundale. The one thing that had been his father's. And yet here it hung round the neck of the sixteen-year-old Audrey, how many years ago, how many worlds away?

Now she did understand. Intuitively, without need of details or evidence, she understood everything. Yes, even why Lucien was sitting there among the audience in the dressing-room, under no restraint, though he surely expected arrest afterwards. Liri knew better. She knew what was going to happen afterwards; she knew what went on behind George Felse's unrevealing face.

She caught up the portfolio and slipped from the room, to run like a wild thing through the silent libraries, and along the corridors to the warden's private quarters. But there was no one there. The lights were out and the rooms deserted. And she must go back, she couldn't hunt any farther. Too late now to make any amends, too late to look for Audrey, too late to warn her. A minute more, and someone else would be out hunting for *her*.

She went back to the yellow drawing-room, back to her place on the dais. She gave the professor his notes, which of course he would not need or use. It was no use now; there was no way of reaching her. Liri raised her eyes and looked carefully over the array of attentive faces, little moons in a mild twilight. Those two at the back, side by side on their crazy little gilded perch, looked improbably at ease. The professor was talking about the summing-up of all that they had experienced together, the relationship of folk music to the wider and deeper field of music itself. Presently the Rossignol twins were singing, two angelic voices, eerie and sweet.

The long range of windows that led out on to the terrace brought the dim and cloudy day in upon them in tints of subdued violet and green. Not even dusk yet, not by a couple of hours, and yet the low and heavy cloud hung like a pall, turning this after-tea hour into night.

The most distant of the long windows, down there at the back of the room, stood ajar. A while ago they had all been closed. The last chair at the end of that row, certainly empty then, was occupied now. Someone had come in by the window, and moved the chair aside into the embrasure, drawing a fold of the heavy curtains round it to screen her from at least half the room. A dead black dress, the sheen of pale, piled hair.

Edward Arundale's widow, still chatelaine of Follymead, had come to the final concert. They were there in the same room together, there was only about fifteen yards of air between them, and yet they could not communicate.

Or was there still a way? That curious conversation with Felicity had started a tune running in Liri's head, and it would not be quieted. It plagued her with reminders of the rogue page who tossed just such an apple of discord in among Lord Barnard's household 'where they were sat at meat'. The verse ranged through her head, in the light of what she had just learned, with a new and terrifying aptness. If they talked to her, they could talk to another person, one, the only one except George Felse and Lucien Galt, who knew the whole story, and would recognise only too well the full implications. She might still misunderstand; but that had to be risked. Liri could not leave her to step over the edge of the pit without so much as reaching a hand to her. Whatever her own wrongs, she owed Audrey that and more. She was indebted to her for a world, and she could make so little repayment now.

Liri folded her hands on her guitar, and waited. She knew now what she had to do.

Chapter 11

Past six o'clock. The darkness was purplish, thundery, the air still as before a storm. It must be her turn soon. Why had the old man kept her until last?

'And now for Liri. She promised to sing us "The Queen's Maries" in the full text, which is by way of being a marathon performance, so I've reserved enough time for her to do herself justice. But now she's whispering in my ear that she'd like to change her choice. It's a woman's privilege. So I'll leave any introduction to Liri.'

'I thought,' she said, clearly and quietly, 'that everyone knows the story of Mary Hamilton, and there are so many fine stories that very few people know. I warn you, this is a marathon performance, too, but I hope you won't find it dull. I'd like to sing the ballad of "Gil Morrice". Anybody know it?'

Thank God, nobody did. She knew the proud, proprietary emanations of those who find themselves one up on the rest, and here there was nothing like that, only pleased expectancy. It's still true, people love to be read to, to listen to stories. Even those kids who are so with it that they've completely lost contact with most of it – 'it' being the total body of mental and spiritual fulfilment and delight, the mass of music, the body of books, the entire apparition of art – even they will shiver and thrill to this blood-stained tragedy, though they won't recognise their

185

excitement as something dating back into prehistory. They'll think it's because this is 'folk', of all the odd labels. This is human, which is more than being folk.

'Here goes then. "Gil Morrice".'

She curled over the guitar, felt along its strings with a sensuous gesture, and raised her face, filling her lungs deep. The guitar uttered one shuddering chord, and that was all. She began in the story-teller's level, lilting voice:

> 'Gil Morrice was an Erle's son,
> His name it waxed wide;
> It was not for his great riches
> Nor for his mickle pride,
> But it was for a lady gay
> That lived on Carron side.'

So much for the introduction, and straight into the story. The guitar took up a thin, fine line of melody, low beneath the clear voice, that had as yet no passion in it, but remained a story-teller, uninvolved, unwrung:

> ' "Where shall I find a bonny boy
> That will win hose and shoon,
> That will go to Lord Barnard's hall
> And bid his lady come?
>
> "And you must run my errand, Willie,
> And you may run with pride,
> When other boys gae on their feet
> On horseback ye shall ride."
>
> "Oh, no, oh, no, my master dear,
> I darena for my life.
> I'll not go to the bold baron's
> For to tryst forth his wife.

"But oh, my master dear," he cried,
"In greenwood ye're your lane,
  Give o'er such thoughts, I would you rede,
  For fear ye should be ta'en." '

The guitar had enlarged its low comment, the thick chords came in rising anger. A stillness began to bud in the centre of the audience, and opened monstrous petals in the gloom. A little more, and she would know she had them; but whether she had Audrey she had no way of knowing. The pulsing excitement of the telling took her like a trance. She heard her own voice deepen and grow harsh, and she had done nothing at all, issued no orders:

' "My bird Willie, my boy Willie,
  My dear Willie," he said,
"How can ye strive against the stream?
  For I shall be obeyed.

"Haste, haste, I say, go to the hall,
  Bid her come here with speed.
If ye refuse my high command
  I'll gar your body bleed."

"Yes, I will go your black errand,
  Though it be to your cost,
Since you by me will not be warned,
  In it ye shall find frost.

"And since I must your errand run
  So sore against my will,
I'll make a vow, and keep it true,
  It shall be done for ill." '

The guitar came crashing in now with the dark themes of the page's hate and love, and the rapid, rushing narrative of his ride to Lord Barnard's castle. He swam the river and leaped the wall, and burst in upon the household at table. She had them in her hand, and the instrument sang for her, passionate and enraged beneath the far-pitched thread of her voice stringing in the words like pearls. Oh, God, let her understand what's coming before *he* does, let her listen with every nerve. All I want is that she should have time to get her armour on, and be ready for him.

The page was in the hall now, striding in upon the assembled company. The voice sang full and clear, almost strident to ride over the meal-time talk:

> ' "Hail, hail, my gentle sire and dame,
>   My message will not wait.
>   Dame, ye maun to the good greenwood
>   Before that it be late.
>
> "See, there's your sign, a silken sark,
>   Your own hand sewed the sleeve.
>   You must go speak with Gil Morrice,
>   Ask no bold baron's leave.'
>
> The lady stamped with her foot
>   And winked with her ee,
>   But for all that she could say or do,
>   Forbidden he wouldna be.
>
> "It's surely to my bower woman,
>   It ne'er could be to me."
> "I brought it to Lord Barnard's lady,
>   I trow that you are she."
>
> Then up and spake the wily nurse,
>   The bairn upon her knee:
> "If it be come from Gil Morrice
>   It's dear welcome to me."

"Ye lied, ye lied, ye filthy nurse,
    So loud I heard ye lee.
I brought it to Lord Barnard's lady,
    I trow you are not she."

Then up and spake the bold baron,
    An angry man was he.
He's thrust the table with his foot,
    So has he with his knee,
Till silver cup and mazer dish
    In flinders he gar'd flee.

"Go bring a robe of your clothing
    That hangs upon the pin,
And I'll go to the good greenwood
    And speak with your lemman." '

Her mouth, as always when she attempted these appalling
feats, was sour and raw with the myriad voices that spoke through
it, and the bitterness that century upon century could not swee-
ten or abate. There was sweat running on her lips, and until
this moment she had not been able to raise her head and rest,
letting the guitar speak for her again. Now it sang softly,
unalarmed, waiting in serenity, and she cast one urgent glance
towards where Audrey sat beside the open window. There was
a tension there, something braced and ready and wild, to which
her own heart rose with answering passion; but whether it was
really more than the tension that held them all was more than
she could guess. There was so little time, because the thread of
this compulsion rested in her, and she must not let it flag. The
sylvan song had been prolonged enough, and here came the
ultimate test of her powers, the key verse that must reach Audrey
before the rest had time to aim at understanding:

'Gil Morrice sat in good greenwood,
    He whistled and he sang . . .

It had dawned upon George already that for some reason of her own Liri was re-telling the whole story of what had happened here. Perhaps not to the end, for how could any ballad encompass everything that had happened? And this was genuine, no doubt of that. The effort he had to make to tear himself out of its spell for an instant was like tearing the heart out of his body. This girl was marvellous. Listen to her now, the voice light and careless again, and yet with an indescribable overtone of premonition and doom disregarded:

> ' "Oh, what mean all these folk coming?
> My mother tarries lang."
> The baron came to the greenwood
> With mickle dule and care,
> And here he first spied Gil Morrice,
> Combing his yellow hair . . .'

The word, the unexpected, the impossible word, had passed George as it had been meant to do, drawn away before his mental vision in the tension of the story. But suddenly as it slipped away from him he caught it back, and the stab was like a knife-thrust into his consciousness. 'My mother . . .'

My mother!

What did she know, and what was she about? How *could* she know? This couldn't be accidental, it couldn't be purposeless, and it couldn't be wanton. What Liri Palmer did was considered and meant, and he doubted if she ever took anything back, or regretted much.

He cast a quick glance round into every corner of the room, but everywhere the tension held. She had them all in her hand.

> ' "No wonder, no wonder, Gil Morrice,
> My lady loved thee weel,
> The fairest part of my bodie
> Is blacker than thy heel.

190

> 'Yet ne'er the less now, Gil Morrice,
> For all thy great beautie,
> Ye'll rue the day ye e'er were born.
> That head shall go with me." '

The rage and grief of the accompaniment remained low and secret, hurrying bass chords suppressed and stifled. For a few moments she let her instrument brood and threaten, and looked down the room. Inspector Felse was sitting forward, braced and aware. Beside him Lucien was shadowed and still, very still; there was no way of knowing, with all her knowledge of him, what he was going through now. After all, it was not Lucien she was trying to reach.

But there was a movement now in the folds of the half-drawn curtain at the last window. Audrey's little solitude lay in comparative light, but the curtains were of heavy brocade, and lined, there would be no shadow to betray her. Softly she got up from her place, and softly, softly, with infinite caution, she slipped back step by silent step from her chair, towards the unlatched window. Audrey had understood.

Now cover her, whatever happens. Don't let any of them look round, don't loose their senses for an instant. Cry out and cover her with the steely shriek of murder and the savagery of mutilation:

> 'Now he has drawn his trusty brand
> And whatt it on a stone,
> And through Gil Morrice' fair bodie
> Has the cauld iron gone.
>
> And he has ta'en Gil Morrice' head
> And set it on a spear,
> The meanest man in all his train
> Has gotten that head to bear.

And he has ta'en Gil Morrice up,
Laid him across his steed,
And brought him to his painted bower
And laid him on a bed.

The lady sat on castle wall,
Beheld both dale and down,
And there she saw Gil Morrice' head
Come trailing to the town . . .'

The clamour of violence died into the lamentable threnody of death. The guitar keened, and the voice extended into the long, fatal declamation of that which can never be put right again. The tension, instead of relaxing, wound itself ever tighter until it was unendurable. The singer's face, sharpened in the concentrated light upon her, was raised to look over the heads of her audience. The lady was at the window, easing it silently open, melting into the outer air.

And this might well have been her voice, if things had gone differently, high, reckless and wild, as she came down from her tower to welcome her lover, her life laid waste about her for ever:

' "Far better I love that bloody head,
But and that golden hair,
Than Lord Barnard and all his lands,
As they lie here and there.'

And she has ta'en her Gil Morrice
And kissed him cheek and chin.
'I was once as full of Gil Morrice
As the hip is of the stane.

'I got ye in my father's house
With mickle sin and shame . . ." '

To the last moment Audrey kept her face turned towards the singer; and as she slipped back through the window the freer light found her face, and showed Liri its white and resolute tranquillity, and the already irrelevant tears on her cheeks. The two women who loved Lucien exchanged one first, last glance of full understanding and acceptance, that paid of all the debts between them.

The spell-binding voice soared in fearful agony to cover the moment of departure:

> ' "I brought thee up in good greenwood
> Under the frost and rain . . ." '

Audrey was gone, lost to sight at once, across the blind end of the terrace, and down the steps.

George felt the boy beside him strung tight to breaking point. He saw the bright lines of Liri's face drawn silver-white in the light of the lamp on the dais, the huge eyes fixed and frantic. Something was happening, and yet nothing was happening, not a movement anywhere in the room, she wouldn't let them move, that long, strong hand of hers that plucked the strings was manipulating them all like marionettes, the generous, wide-jointed fingers that drummed a funeral march on the body of her instrument held them nailed in their places.

> ' "Oft have I by thy cradle sat
> And fondly seen thee sleep,
> But now I go about thy bier
> The salt tears for to weep . . ." '

In the changing temperature of the evening the normal small dusk wind arose, as suddenly as was its habit here over the open sward. It took the unlatched window and swung it wide against the curtain, seized the folds and set them swinging. A chill draught coursed along the wall, and fluttered the skirts of gold brocade at every window embrasure.

George heard and felt the abrupt, cold whisper from the outer world. He came to his feet with a leap, lunged silently along the wall, and whisked round the curtain to the open window, now swinging fitfully in the fresh currents of air. Far down the slope of grass he saw the fair head receding. The curtain shook, and he, too, was gone, down the steps and after her in a soundless run. And Lucien, the thread of his passionate concentration broken by the sudden movement beside him, came out of his dream to the sharper and more personal pains of the real world. She saw him rise, and felt the belated shock of knowledge and realisation sear through him; but there was nothing she could do, as he groped his way blindly after George, except sing on to the end, prolong the postlude, cover the slight, the very slight disturbance, and make those few who had noticed it forget it had ever been.

> ' "And syne she kissed his bloody cheek
>   And syne his bloody chin:
> "Oh, better I love my Gil Morrice
>   Than all my kith and kin."
>
> "Away, away, ye ill woman,
>   And an ill death may ye dee.
> Had I but known he'd been your son,
>   He'd ne'er been slain for me." '

Five minutes more, to preserve the integrity of the course, and nobody, certainly not the professor, would dream of filling in with something smaller after this monstrous *tour-de-force*. Liri knew her worth. But don't let them go yet, hold them fast, keep them from looking out of the windows yet, tie their feet from following. She didn't know what she had done, but she knew there must be no interference with it now, no well-meaning unlookers, no witnesses to tell the story afterwards.

She raised the volume and passion of her instrument to a crisis of anguish, improvising in a galloping rhapsody that bore the fortunes of Lord Barnard and his lady and Gil Morrice racing to ruin together, away down the wind and into the distance of antiquity, where old hatreds and old agonies lay down together between the four lines of a ballad verse as in a bed, and slept, and dreamed. The threnody sobbed away beneath her fingers, diminuendo, and died on a mere breath, one muted quiver of a single string.

She felt the sweat cold on her forehead and lip, and the silence came down on her stunningly, like the fall of a roof. It seemed to last for a long time, while she could hardly breathe or stir for weakness; and then a sigh like a gust of wind went through the room, and they were all on their feet roaring and clapping together, and Professor Penrose had his old arm round her shoulders and was shaking her in a joyful embrace, while out of the contortion of her mouth that passed for a smile she was howling at him over and over, under cover of the din:

'Get them away, quickly! Get them out of here . . . get them out . . . *get* them out . . . *get them out!*'

After they were gone, with all that merry racket of cars and voices and horns, like a wild hunt of the twentieth century – and some of them still singing – the house was awesomely quiet. So quiet that it was hard to remember that somewhere downstairs some dozen or so resident staff still remained, few of them ever seen by visitors.

Celia Whitwood had tucked her harp lovingly into the back of the huge old car she drove, and set off westwards for home with Andrew Callum as a passenger. The Rossignol twins and Peter Crewe had clambered gaily into the station wagon, bound for the London train, and after them the professor, embracing his inevitable notes and leaving behind in his bedroom the same case of recording tapes he had forgotten at Comerbourne station on Friday evening. Even Dickie Meurice was gone with him, edged competently and civilly into the transport by the deputy warden, with his consuming curiosity still unsatisfied. From his front seat, for once in the audience, he had not seen Lucien appear or Audrey disappear. To him it was only a matter of time, of a little patience, and Lucien's arrest was a pleasurable certainty. Let him go, let him sit and gloat in town, waiting for the flare headlines he was never going to see. He had never been of much importance; now, in this immense calm after the whirlwind, he was of no importance at all.

Liri sat in a deep chair in the gallery, her eyes half-closed, exhaustion covering her like a second skin. She saw the growing dusk take away the small possessions of the Cothercotts one by one into shadow, the fan that concealed a dagger, the empty place where the sword-stick had hung, the silver-chased pistols, the miniatures on ivory; and then whole pieces of furniture, the love-seat with its twisted arms, the spinet, the inlaid cabinets, the entire end of the long room. Darkness crept in upon her, and was welcomed. She seemed to have been there alone for so long that it was strange to hear a movement in the room with her. It could have been Felicity's fictional ghost; but it was only Tossa Barber, sitting just as quietly on a high-backed chair by the library door.

'It's only me. It's all right,' said Tossa simply, 'I'll go away when they come.'

'I don't mind. I thought everybody'd gone.'

'We have to wait for Mr. Felse. We're driving back with him, if . . .' She let that fall. Nobody knew when George would be ready to go home. 'Dominic went down to see if he . . . to find them . . .' Every sentence flagged into silence. All they were really doing was waiting.

It must have been nearly eight o'clock when they heard the first footsteps crossing the terrace, the clash of the window-latch, a heel on the sill, stumbling, uncertain. Two people, the second closely following the first, but never touching him. A hand reached over an oblivious shoulder to the light-switches at the end of the gallery, hesitated, and chose the single lamp that made only a faint pool of radiance in a corner of the twilit room. Nobody said anything; but Dominic caught Tossa's eye, and Tossa rose softly and slipped past Lucien Galt, who neither saw nor heard her. Dominic took her hand, and drew her away with him, and Lucien and Liri were left together.

He saw her, and his eyes came to life in the shocked grey mask of his face. He pushed himself off from the doorway, and walked into her arms without a word, and without a word she opened them to him. He slid to his knees at her feet, and she held him on her heart, along with the chill and the dank smell of the river; and she knew where Audrey had gone. After a while he stopped shivering, and locked his arms tightly round her body, and heaved a huge sigh that convulsed them both; and neither he nor she would ever know whether it was of grief at his loss, or involuntary relief at this vast and terrible simplification of his problems, or both, and in what measure.

'I called to her,' he said presently, in a voice drained and weary. 'She was on the parapet. I wanted to tell her that we . . . that you and I . . . that we didn't care, that it didn't matter any more . . .'

'It wouldn't have been any good,' said Liri. 'It *did* matter to her.'

No, it wouldn't have been any good, even if she had listened to him. How can you convince a person like Audrey Arundale that she no longer has to sacrifice everything to respectability, to public reputation, to what the world will say? What's the good of arguing with her that her parents are dead now, and Edward's dead, and the people she has left simply don't look at values that way, simply won't care, that they would welcome her back even after years of prison, and damn the world's opinion? How do you set about convincing her of that, when she's been trained to subdue everything else to appearances all her life? She couldn't be expected to change now. This way there wouldn't be any murder trial, there needn't even be much publicity of any kind. The police are not obliged to make public the particulars of a case which is closed to their satisfaction, when the person who would otherwise have been charged is dead, and the public interest wouldn't be served by stirring up mud. They simply say the case is closed, no prosecutions will be instituted as a result of it, and that's the end of it. General curiosity only speculates for a very short time, till the next sensation crops up. This way everything would be smoothed away, everything hushed up, everything made the best of, just as it had always had to be. Maybe they'd even succeed in getting an open verdict on Edward's death, and the locals would evolve improbable theories about a poacher or a vagrant surprised in the park, and hitting out in panic with the nearest weapon that offered. Audrey wouldn't care. Audrey had observed her contract and her loyalties as best she could to the end. Edward would have wished it.

'I got her out,' Lucien's labouring mouth shaped against Liri's heart. 'They've been all this time trying . . . trying . . .'

Yes. Trying to revive her, of course; but Audrey, it seemed, had made quite sure.

'All I meant to do was warn her,' Liri said. 'I'd just found out that *he* knew . . . It was the only way I had . . .'

Her voice flagged, like his. They had no need of explanations, and speech was such an effort yet that they could afford to use it only for the ultimate essentials. With her cheek pressed against his wet black hair: 'I love you,' said Liri gently, and that was all.

'She was my mother,' he said, 'and I can't even bury her.'

The ambulance had come and gone. Henry Marshall had had a fire lit for them in the small library, and left the handful of them there together in the huge and silent house. Lucien had bathed and changed, and put on again with his fresh clothes a drained and languid calm. Liri sat across the hearth from him and watched him steadily, and often he looked up to reassure himself that she was there. Two dark, reticent, proud people; in the intensity of this unvoiced reconciliation their two young, formidable faces had grown strangely alike, as though mentally they stared upon each other with such passion that each had become a mirror image of the other.

'I've got to sit back and let Arundale's relatives do it for me, because I can't compromise what she wanted left alone. All her life keeping up appearances, doing the correct thing, and now she has to die the same way.'

'She chose it,' said George.

'She never had a choice, being the person she was. If my father hadn't been killed . . .'

'You do know about your father?'

'Do *you*?' challenged Lucien jealously.

And neither of them was speaking of John James Galt, though he had done his part well enough, no doubt, during the year or so he had been in the place of a father.

'I know the Galts re-registered you as theirs when you were only a few months old, presumably as soon as the adoption proceedings were completed. I'm reasonably sure that your real father must have been one of the Czech pilots who were stationed at Auchterarne during the war. I guess that he must have been killed in action in 1942. But adoption certificates carry only the Christian names given to the child, and the name of the adoptive parent. *His* name I don't know yet. I shall get it eventually either from Somerset House or from the service records. But that's unnecessary now,' said George gently. 'You tell me.'

'His name was Václav Havelka. I know, because *she* told me about him. Václav is the same name we call Wenceslas. That's why he gave her his Saint Wenceslas medal. He hadn't got anything else to give her. He hadn't even got a country, then, only a job and a uniform. He was twenty years old, and she was sixteen, nearly seventeen, and they met at some innocent local bunfight when her school was up there in Scotland. There wasn't a hope for them. Her people were set on her getting into society and marrying a lord, or something, not a refugee flyer with no money and no home. So she did the one thing really of her own that she ever did, she gave herself to him. Maybe she hoped to force her parents' hands, and maybe she might even have managed it, but it never came to that, because my father was shot down six months before I was born. After that, she didn't put up much of a fight for me.'

'How much chance did she have?' said Liri in a low voice.

'Not much, I know. With my father gone she hadn't got anybody to stand by her. She had to tell her folks, and they took her away from school quickly and quietly, and then set to work on her, for ever urging her to have it all hushed up, to spare them the shame, to think of her future, when she hadn't got any future. She gave way in the end. She'd have had to be a heroine not to. She let them hide her away somewhere to have me on the quiet, and then she let me go for adoption. But she insisted on meeting the Galts before she'd sign. They were decent, nice people who badly wanted a child, she knew I'd be all right with them. So she asked them to make sure that I kept my father's medal, and then she promised never to trouble them again, and she never did. And after the war they married her off to Arundale, a big wedding and a successful career, everything they'd wanted for her. You know how *he* first met her? He gave away the prizes at her school speech-day, the last year she was there. It must have been only a few weeks before my father was killed.'

A school speech-day, George thought, dazzled, why didn't I think of that? The white dress, the modest jewellery permitted for wear on a ceremonial occasion, the radiance in her face – Arundale must have had that vision on his mind for ever afterwards. And she without a thought of him, or of anything else but her lover, the bridal gift round her neck, and the child that was coming.

Liri was frowning over a puzzling memory. 'But you know, what I don't understand is that Mr. Arundale practically told me that his wife *couldn't have* any children. Not in so many words, but that was what he meant.'

'Felicity told me the same thing,' said George, unimpressed. 'That's not so strange. Can you imagine a man like Arundale being open to the idea that the fault might possibly be in him?'

'No,' she agreed bitterly, 'you're right, of course. Even in the Bible you notice it's always barren *wives*.'

'And how,' asked George, returning gently to the matter in hand, 'did you come to meet your mother again?'

'It was at a party the recording company gave, about six weeks ago.' Lucien turned his face aside for a moment, wrung by the realisation of how short a time they had had together. 'She'd lost sight of me all these years, but after I started singing she began to follow up all the notices about me. I kept my own name, you see, so she knew who I was. She began to edge her way into the folk world, to get to know people so that she could get to me. And I . . . it's hard to explain. I'd grown up happy enough. After the Galts were killed it was the orphanage, of course, but that was pretty good, too, I didn't have any complaints. They told me I'd been adopted, naturally, they always do that, because you're dead certain to find out one day, anyhow. We had one committee-woman who'd known the Galts slightly, and she told me how this medal I had had belonged to my father, who was dead, and my mother had let me go for adoption. I never had anything against my father, how could I? But there was always this thing I had about my mother, pulling two ways, wanting her because after all you're not complete without one, and hating her because she just gave me up when the going got rough. And then this one day, at this party, there I was suddenly alone in a corner with this beautiful, fashionable woman, and she said to me: 'I've been trying for ages to meet you. I'm your mother."'

He doubled his long hands into fists and wrung them in a momentary spasm of anguish, and then uncurled them carefully, and let them lie still and quiet on his knee.

'You can't imagine it. Not even you, who've seen her. She wasn't like she is . . . was . . . here. The way she said it, with a terrible kind of simplicity, sweeping everything that didn't matter out of the way. I thought I hated her, I even felt I ought to hate her, but when it happened it wasn't like that at all. It was like falling in love. The way she was, it wiped out everything. She wasn't courting me now because I was a lion, she'd just found her way back to me because she couldn't keep away any longer. All she wanted was to be with me. Edward – that was a contract, and she must keep it. You know? She was even very fond of him, in a way, and very loyal. But loving . . . I don't think she'd loved anyone or anything but me since my father died.'

'And you?' asked George with respectful gentleness.

'It was queer with me. If I'd always had her I should just have loved her casually, like anyone else with a mother, and that would have been it. But getting her back like that, quite strange, and beautiful, and still young . . . and so lost, and to be pitied! Sometimes I didn't know whether I was her son, or her brother, or her father. I knew I was her slave.'

Yes, of course, from the moment he saw that she was his. Her adoration might well have disarmed Lucifer, pride and all, grievance and all. She had loved her Gil Morrice better than all her kith and kin, how could he help returning her devotion?

'We had to meet sometimes, we couldn't help ourselves. We had so much time to make up. But then there was Liri . . . Liri broke it off with me, and I knew it was because of *her*, but I couldn't explain, you see, it wasn't my secret. We could never let it be known what the real connection was, my mother's whole life, and his, too, all this build-up, would go down the drain if we did. We must have been mad to start this weekend course, and bring the thing right here into the house. And it was awful here, always so many people, we never could talk at all. And I had to talk to her, I *had* to. Because when Liri followed me here I saw she wasn't absolutely finished with me, I was sure I could get her back, but only by telling her the truth. And I couldn't do that, even in confidence, without my mother's consent.'

'So the message you sent by Felicity,' said George, 'was a genuine message, after all?'

Lucien shook his head, wretchedly. 'It was a lot of things . . . I don't know . . . I'm not proud of that. It was a vicious thing to do, but there she was offering to do anything for me, and I wanted her out of my hair, I needed to think and she wouldn't let me think. And I did want my mother to come, while the whole place was nearly empty. I thought *he'd* be away by then, safely on his way to town. So I told Felicity what she could do for me, if she meant it. I knew what she'd think, I knew what she'd feel, I knew I'd hurt her. I meant to, though I wished afterwards I hadn't. But I did believe she'd give the message to my mother, and I was sure she'd come.

'And instead, it was Arundale who came, with that damned murderous toy. It was like an unbelievably bad film. It was even funny at first, because I couldn't believe in it seriously. I tried to talk to him, but I swear he never heard a word. I think in a way he was mad, then. All he wanted was to kill me, and he'd have done it, but then suddenly *she* was there . . . She must have heard us right from the gate, because she came running with the latch in her hand, and hit out at him like a fury, almost before I realised she was there. And then he was on the ground, and it was all over. Unbelievably quickly. He was dead in minutes.'

Lucien passed a tired hand over his face. 'She hit out in defence of me. She never thought of killing, only of stopping him from killing. But afterwards she knew she *had* killed him. She was totally dazed, but quite docile. It was up to me. She did whatever I told her. I taught her what to say when you questioned her. But it was partly true, you know, he did behave like she said, after Felicity left them. He did put it all aside as a piece of childish spite, and made out he was leaving for town, just as he'd planned. It was only after he'd gone that she got frightened, and came herself, to make sure . . .'

'You didn't know, of course,' said George, 'and neither did she, that he'd telephoned to both bodies he should have addressed in Birmingham, and called off the engagements. Yes,' he said, answering the quick, dark glance, 'he was going to make good use of those two days' grace, too. He intended murder.'

'My own fault, I snatched the world away from under his feet. But that was something *I* never intended. I told her to go back to the house, and to be sure not to be seen on the way. And she did whatever I told her. Ever since her heart broke, between my father and me, she's always done what people told her, what they expected of her. When she'd gone I tried to bring him round, but it was no good, and I knew he was dead. I threw him into the river, and the sword-stick and the latch after him. And I sneaked up to the yard and took his car and ran for it. I thought I was taking the whole load of guilt away with me, and she'd be all right. I should have known better, but I was in a pretty bad state myself. How could she ever be all right again?' He shook his head suddenly in a gesture of helpless pain. 'How did you know? Why were you sure it wasn't me? I thought I made out a pretty good case.'

George rose from his chair. It was late and it was over; and if these two could sleep, sleep was what they needed.

'I haven't even read your statement yet, but if it's any consolation, you convinced Rapier, all right. Don't worry, we shall never be asking you to sign it. I knew the latch was still in its place when Felicity left you. And what did Arundale want with it? Like Lord Barnard, he came with a sword. And he was between you and the gate, he and forty yards of ground. You'd never have had the slightest chance of getting to it. No, someone else, someone who followed him there, dragged that latch out of its wards.' He cast a summoning glance towards the corner where Tossa and Dominic had sat silent throughout this elegiac conversation. 'Come on, I'd better get you two home before I go in and report.' And to Lucien: 'You're staying here overnight?'

'Mr. Marshall was kind enough to suggest it. Then we can move into Comerbourne, if you still need us. I suppose we'll have to stay within call until after the inquests?'

'Probably, but we can talk about that tomorrow.'

'I realise,' Lucien said abruptly, 'that there must be a good case against me as an accessory after the fact.'

'Then so there is against me,' said Liri at once. 'I warned you, and I warned her.'

She would probably never realise, George thought, how grateful he was to her for that. 'What fact?' he said dryly. 'There isn't going to be any primary prosecution, why should I go out of my way to hunt up secondary charges? Much better just get on with the business of living. It may not always be easy, but it's still worth the effort.'

'Is it?' Lucien raised bruised eyes in a challenging stare. 'What did *she* ever get out of it? In her whole life she never had any real happiness.'

'You think not?' said George.

He walked suddenly to the door and out of the room, and they heard his footsteps receding along the passages now populous only with echoes. In a few moments he was back with a half-plate photograph in his hands. He dropped it in Lucien's lap.

'Here you are, a souvenir for you. And you can add me to the crime-sheet – petty theft from Arundale's estate. Incidentally, that makes you a receiver, too.' He watched the flooding colour rise in the boy's dark cheeks, and the warmth of wonder ease the tired lines of his mouth. 'Taken at that last prize-giving, unless I miss my guess. If I'm right, then *he* was still with her, and *you* were on your way. Maybe it didn't last long, but believe me, she had it.'

Lucien looked down in a daze at the Audrey he had never seen before, with the bloom and the radiance and the spontaneity still on her, and caught at their height. If ever he doubted that he had been the child of love, he had only to look at this, and be reassured. And it was, for some reason, almost inevitable that he should look up in suddenly enlarged understanding from Audrey to Liri, whose eyes had never left him.

George wafted Tossa and Dominic quietly out of the room before him, and they went away and left those two to come to terms with the past and and the future in their own way.

Nobody had bothered to draw the curtains. Dominic looked back from the courtyard, before he climbed into the car, and there were the last two guests left over from Follymead's folk music weekend, framed in the softly-lighted window of the small library on the first floor, locked in each other's arms. They must have sprung together and met in splendid collision as soon as they were alone. Their cheeks were pressed together as if they would fuse for all time, their eyes were closed, and their faces were timeless, as though love had fallen on them as a new and cosmic experience, original and unique in the history of man.

Dominic climbed hastily into the car and slammed the door, ashamed and exalted.

George Felse drove round the wing of the house, and out upon the great open levels of the drive, suddenly moon-washed and serene after the thunderous sulks of the evening. Follymead receded, the partial rear view of it grew and coalesced, became a harmonious, a symmetrical whole, making unity out of chaos. Gradually it withdrew, moonlit and magical, a joke and a threat, a dream and a nightmare, deploying its lesser shocks on either side of them as they retreated. Even those who escaped always came back; there was no need to set traps for them.

' "Black, black, black," ' sang Tossa softly to herself in the back seat, her chin on her shoulder, 'is the colour of my true-love's hair . . ." '

The Grass Widow's Tale

Chapter 1

The day before her birthday turned out to be a dead loss right from the start. It dawned reluctantly in murk, like a decrepit old man with a hangover half-opening one gummy eye, to glare sickly at the world and recoil into misanthropy. Morose commuters groped their way through a gloom that did not lift. Slimy black mud picked up by the set-back heels of the new season's shoes spattered mini-skirted legs to the thigh with miniature cow-pats, which dried greenish-grey and clung like glue. Desultory moisture in the air, balanced irritatingly between rain and mist, caused half of the hurrying morning tide to open their umbrellas, while leaving the other half unconvinced, and to walk the length of the street was to witness the formation of two inimical factions. There was no letter from Dominic in the post, nothing but a dismal circular for a furniture sale and a quarterly gas bill, first delayed and then wantonly inflated by a perverse computer. It was impossible to do the housework without switching on lights, and the spectral world outside the misted windows instantly sank deeper into the all-defiling ooze of dirt and darkness. There was no real daylight all that day.

When October turns traitor it can sometimes outdo the worst of the winter in nastiness. By the time George came home, late in the afternoon, it was raining with a restrained malice that wet people through before they realised it, and yet did nothing to rinse the spattered shop-windows and greasy pavements. All the lights were hazed with condensation and clinging filth; the day was a write-off, and the night already settling malevolently over Comerford.

Bunty heard the car slurp dejectedly along the kerb and slow to turn in at the gate; and her heart rose so violently that only then did she realise with a shock how low it had sunk. George was home, there would be a letter from Dominic in the morning. She examined with astonishment, and rejected with disdain, the feeling that she had been for some hours utterly alone.

And George came in, tall and tired, stained with the greyness of the day, and said, so abruptly that she knew he was hardly with her at all: 'Pitch a few things in a case for me, will you? I've got to go down to London.' Some sense of guilt touched him vaguely through the cloud of his abstraction. 'I'm sorry!' he said. 'Something's come up.'

Bunty had been a detective's wife for just over twenty years. Her responses were as nearly automatic as made no matter. You do not send your husband out on a job with a divided mind; least of all do you claim any part of his concentration for yourself when he needs it all intact for his own purposes. She closed her magazine briskly, crossed to him and kissed him with the brevity of old custom.

'Got time for tea? Ready in five minutes. What difference can that make?'

'You don't mind?' he said, tightening his arm round her for a moment. His voice was weary; so were his eyes. The Midshire C.I.D. were having no easy time this autumn, and there wasn't much Bunty didn't know, directly or indirectly, about their pre-occupations.

'I mind like hell!' Since when had they dealt in polite, accom-modating lies? 'But there it is. You get something good out of it, and I'll be satisfied. Anything promising?'

'Hard to say. It might be a breakthrough, it might just drop dead. You know how it is.'

She knew just how it was; usually it dropped dead. But they had to pursue it just the same, as long as there was breath in it. 'It's time you had a break. Is it the wage-snatch? Has something broken there?'

'No, the fur job. If we're lucky it might turn out to be something. They've picked up a small floating operator on another charge, one of the possibles we had listed. Specialises in driving jobs, anything on wheels, especially get-away cars. He answers to one of the two descriptions we got out of the driver of that van, but not any better than a dozen other professionals do. The thing is, he produced an alibi for the time of our job, but as soon as they probed it, it fell down. There may be nothing in it. Maybe his own gang want him shopped, for some reason of their own. Anyhow, they don't want to know about him, and he's left wide open. It may be the moment to get something out of him, or there may be nothing to get. But we've got to try it.'

'Of course! I hope it turns out right, I hope he's your man. You sit down,' she said, steering him backwards into his own chair by the fire, 'and I'll put the kettle on. By the time I've packed it'll be boiling. How long will you have to be away?'

'I don't know, maybe two or three days. If I do get a lead, it'll be down there I shall have to follow it up. I told Duckett, this is some metropolitan gang moving out. I'm sure of it. Distances have shrunk since we got the motorways, and town's getting too congested and too hot. The pickings are better out here. And we're beginners,' he said grimly. 'They know where the pastures are green, all right! And the police greener!'

'They think!' said Bunty from the kitchen. The gas hissed under the kettle, and the busy, contented purr of water heating began almost at once. 'You're taking the car?' she asked.

'It's quicker, and I need to be mobile. I shall have to fill up on the way out. Thank the lord, at least it isn't foggy.'

'I'd better reckon on three days or so, then? Keep an eye on this kettle, I'll be down in a few minutes.'

She had had plenty of practice, there had been a great many

211

abrupt departures during those twenty years. She packed the small black suitcase with brisk movements, and by the time she brought it down George had the tea made, and was shuffling papers together in his briefcase and locking his desk.

'Has the van driver seen a photograph of your man?' she asked, pouring tea.

'Yes, but he can't be too clear about anything but the general build and movements of the two he saw. It was night, and they had a powerful torch trained on him the moment he pulled up. We might get an identification when we can show him the man himself. But between you and me, I doubt it.'

Bunty doubted it, too. The van-load of furs bound from the London dealer to Comerbourne's leading dress-shop had been hi-jacked shortly after leaving the motorway, on a night in early September, nearly six weeks past, and the driver was still in hospital. The wonder was that he had been able to tell them anything at all. A quiet stretch of road, a red triangle conspicuously displayed, a car askew, half off the road, a man running along the verge and waving a torch towards the cab of the big van – add up the details, and who wouldn't have deduced an accident, and stopped to help? The driver had seen a second man dart out of the shadow of the car, and he had an eye for the characteristics of movement, and insisted he would know this one again if he could ever see him in motion. But no sooner had he pulled in to the side of the road and jumped down from his cab than he was hit on the head from behind, by someone he never saw at all, and that was the last thing he knew about it. Hit three times, as it turned out, to make sure of him. He had a tough constitution and a hard skull, and he survived, and even remembered. But for him they would never have known where the attack took place, for the empty van was picked up later on a road-house parking-ground twenty miles off its route, and the driver was found in the morning dumped in the remotest corner of a lay-by on a country road in the opposite direction. Every part of the van that might have carried prints had been polished as clean as bone. A thoroughly professional job. And nobody had seen hide or hair of the load of furs since then. Probably they had been delivered to an already waiting customer that same night.

If Midshire had had any doubts, after that, that crime on a big-business scale was moving in on its territory, the wage-snatch three weeks later would have settled the matter. But the driver who regularly conveyed Armitage Pressings' weekly pay-roll to the factory on Thursdays had not provided any information for the police, because he had been unconscious when the ambulance-men lifted him on to the stretcher, and dead before they got him to hospital. As for the van, someone had ditched it among the skeletons in a local scrap-yard within an hour of the crime.

And this time the weapon they had used on him had not been a cosh, but a gun. Guns had seldom featured in Midshire crime before, and then usually in the haphazard and amateur kind. This was professionalism on a highly organised scale. The planners were extending their territory, and it looked as if the march of progress had reached Comerbourne.

'I'd better get off,' said George, sighing, and rose to pick up his case.

'I'll come in with you.' Bunty got up very quickly, and whisked out into the hall for her coat. 'You can drop me off at the Betterbuy, and I'll get a bus back. I want to pick up a few things there.'

There was nothing she needed, but with his preoccupations he couldn't hope to read that in her face, which was bright, tranquil and sensible as always. The truth was that she had suddenly felt her very bones ache at the thought of seeing him go, and being alone in the house with the autumnal chill and silence after he was gone. Even a few minutes was worth buying; even the struggle on to a crowded bus on the way back might break the spell of her isolation, and restore her to the company of her neighbours. Tiresome, troublous and abrasive as one's fellow-men can be, only the friction of human contact keeps one man-alive.

'I thought you hated the supermarket,' said George obtusely, frowning over his own anxieties, and smiling through them abstractedly at his wife. He had loved her ever since he was twenty-two and she eighteen, and so whole-heartedly and firmly that talking to her was something as secret as confiding in his own conscience; which was why she seldom questioned him, and he never hesitated to tell her what troubled him. No betrayal was involved; it was a conversation with himself. Only occasionally, as now, did he stiffen suddenly to the devastating doubt whether she in return opened her own agonies to him, or whether there was something there denied to him for reasons which diminished him, and removed her to a distance he could not bear. The moments of doubt were appalling, pin-points of dismay, but unbelievably brief, vanished always before he could pursue them, and forgotten before they could undermine his certainty. But he never knew whether this was because they were delusions, inspired by some private devil, or whether she diagnosed them and herself plucked them out of his consciousness before they could sting. She was, after all, the antidote to all evils. How could he know whether the exorcism worked as efficiently the other way?

'I do hate the place,' said Bunty warmly, 'but what choice have I got? Haven't you noticed that all our four groceries in Comerford have switched over to self-service?'

'I thought it was supposed to make shopping quicker and easier,' he said vaguely. What he was thinking was how beautiful she was, his forty-year-old wife, how much more beautiful now with her few silvery hairs among the thick chestnut waves, and the deep lines of character and laughter and rueful affection in her face, than the unblemished ivory girl of twenty years ago. Those smooth, eager, glowing young things are so touching, when you know only too well what's waiting for them. They don't all weather and mature into such splendour as this.

'Hah! You try it! Getting round is all right, once you know where everything is, but getting out is the devil. Give me the old corner gossip-shop every time. You could hang around if you weren't holding anyone else up, and get out fast if you were. And no damned stamps!' said Bunty feelingly. 'But that's progress for you – all part of the same process. We've all got to get mechanised, like the criminals.'

They went out to the car together, the house darkened and locked behind them. Once in the car shoulder to shoulder, with the doors fast closed against the dull rain and the muddy remnant of the light, they recovered a certain security. The demons clawed at the glass impotently, tracing greasy runnels of water through devious channels down the panes, splitting the street lights into a dozen flat, refracted slivers of sulphur-yellow, smoky playing-cards shuffled in an invisible hand. The raw new bungalows on the other side of their own residential road perforated the darkness with eruptions of pink, featureless brick.

'Change and decay!' said Bunty bitterly. She hadn't meant to say it, it was all too plain. The population explosion must settle somewhere, but homes ought to have a certain reticence, as well as a degree of assurance, and these were hesitant, at once aggressive and apologetic, meant for units, not families.

'I know! You wouldn't think this was just a village when we settled here, would you? With about three service shops, and farms right on the through road, and a pet river like a tortoiseshell kitten chasing leaves all down the back-gardens.'

'Careful!' said Bunty. 'You're getting lyrical.'

'I'm getting homesick. For the past. It's a sign of age creeping on. By any standards, this is a town now. You don't notice it sneaking in, but suddenly there it is. Chain shops, supermarkets, bingo halls and all. Automatic-barrier parking-grounds, gift stamps, special offers, fourpence off – the lot! Bunty, let's move!'

'It used to be so lovely,' she said; and then, reasonably: 'We couldn't go anywhere that it wouldn't catch up with us. Why run?'

In the main street, which had once been the road through the village, neon lights peered shortsightedly through the murk, all their greens and blues and reds filmed over with sour grey gloom. The jostling cars of the affluent society glared shoulder to shoulder from the new car parks, their colours dimmed with thin, glutinous mud. The cinema frontage sustained with evident effort an almost-nude blonde twelve feet long, sprawled the length of its lights, three feet of flaxen hair extending her at the head, as though someone had dragged her there by those pale ropes. She wore a bikini, and she might have been merely sun-bathing, but she looked dead. There was no queue to find out the truth; no one was interested.

'Wait till you see what they're doing with old Pearce's place,' said George, between resignation and revulsion. 'Or didn't I tell you he's sold out? To some chain moving in from the south. He had too good a spot to survive long, once the urbanisation started.'

He turned the car left out of the High Street, and slowed as he approached the glittering frontage of what had once been Pearce's Garage, long inhabited by three generations of passionate motor-maniacs without a grain of commercial acumen between them, but able to do just about anything with an engine. All its capital had been in the background then, and the forecourt and petrol sales had been a somewhat tedious chore, very modestly lit and little regarded. No advertising was needed for a first-class service to which every well-run car in the county knew its own way.

Within ten days of the sale things had changed radically. A long festoon of lights in four colours stretched all along the frontage, which was being torn back into a great arc to accommodate nine new pumps of the latest type. They looked more like something from outer space than mere petrol pumps. A large neon sign over a repainted office flaunted the name of the chain in the single word: FLEET. Two large posters in fluorescent orange proclaimed apocryphally: 'Double stamps' week!'

216

'See?' said George, with bitter satisfaction.

'Oh, well,' sighed Bunty helplessly. 'He was pushing retiring age anyhow, and the offer must have been monumental.'

'Still, if Tony hadn't emigrated his dad would never have sold out,' observed George, drawing the Morris neatly into position by the nearest Super pump. He opened the door and slid out as a snub-nosed, shaggy-headed youngster came loping down from the office in answer to the bell. 'Fill her up, Bobby.'

'Sure, Mr. Felse!' The sombre young face brightened faintly at the sight of them. Bobby had been on probation, an apparently incurable driver-away of unlocked cars, when George had followed a hunch and talked old Pearce into taking him on and giving him a gloriously legitimate interest in the machines he couldn't resist. George found himself hoping that two years had been long enough to effect a cure, because he felt in his bones that this experiment wasn't going to survive the change of ownership. Commercial garage chains have very little interest in the salvation of local problem children. In such a county as Midshire, however, there are still plenty of family businesses in the remoter areas, and a two-year apprenticeship with Pearce's is a very sound recommendation.

'Well, how's it coming along?' said George, avoiding any appearance of actual concern.

'Not sure it is, Mr. Felse.' Bobby frowned darkly over the purling petrol, watching the level with dubious eyes. 'You know how it is, you get used to certain people's ways. I don't reckon this lot care all that much about cars.' He delivered this indictment of blasphemy with more sorrow than anger.

'Then you'll be all the more likely to score a personal hit,' said George reasonably, 'since you do.'

'Well, maybe – but they don't really want you to. It's the quick money they're interested in. *You* know! Make it *look* good, and that's it. The money's out here, really, not back in the workshops. Not unless you can pick up a nice juicy insurance job,' said Bobby disdainfully, and withdrew the pipe accurately

217

and dexterously at the crucial moment. He hung it up, and wiped the neck of the tank, though it was spotless. 'I don't reckon I shall be here long, Mr. Felse.'

'What's the pinch?' asked George easily. 'The new boss?'

Bobby shrugged and grinned. '*He* wouldn't matter so much, we shan't be seeing much of him, anyhow. Thirty-seven of these stations they say he's got now, most of 'em in London and the south. We're about the most northerly yet. No, *he* wouldn't matter. It's this new manager he's put in. Proper thruster he looks like being – you know, town style, all flash and everything on the surface.' Bobby counted change expertly, with one eye on the new, large window of the office, festooned with pot plants. 'That's him now, just coming out on the concrete – the one who looks like a bruiser.'

Two men had emerged from the glass doorway, and were pacing the length of the concreted arc, studying the renovations with critical approval. The one in the white overall was large-chested and thick of feature, and had a peeled-down, aggressive confidence in his manner that would not have been out of place in either a boxing ring or a sales ring. The other was several inches taller, a long-striding, elegant figure in a pearl-grey suit.

'*Mister* Mostyn,' said Bobby, eyeing the distant white figure with eloquent dislike. 'Don't you never let him sell you a used car, Mr. Felse, that's all!'

'Who's the other?' asked George, pocketing his change.

'Oh, that's the boss . . . that's Fleet himself. Been looking his buy over and viewing the development plans. Mostyn had me working on *his* car this afternoon . . . believe me, that was *one* he wanted done properly.' He closed the door firmly upon George, and waved a hand. 'See you, Mr. Felse!'

'So long, Bobby! Just give it a whirl before you make up your mind. But he'll go,' George prophesied the next moment, for Bunty's ear alone. 'That's not his kind of set-up now.'

The Morris wheeled back from the apron on to a dark, slimily gleaming street, and the long festoons of lights slithered away behind them. They re-entered the main street at the next corner, close to the southern edge of the town now, with the ordered glimmer of the new housing estate of Well Meadow terraced up the green slope in the darkness ahead. Across the street the six plate-glass windows of the Betterbuy supermarket glared steamily, plastered with bargain offers in poison green and electric orange.

'Not my kind, either,' Bunty sighed, and reached over into the back seat for her basket and handbag, as the car hissed to a standstill in the thin ooze alongside the kerb. 'But if you'll believe me, this is the only place in Comerford where I can buy whole black pepper!'

At this last moment it felt like tearing herself in two to get out of the car and leave him behind, but a kerbside stop affords no time for hesitation. She cast the usual quick glance behind, opened the door of the Morris, and slid her feet out to the greasy pavement, tilting her cheek back at the same moment for George's customary kiss.

'Good luck, then, mate! I'll expect you when I see you.'

'Just as soon as I can make it. 'Bye, darling, take care of yourself.'

'Listen who's talking,' said Bunty derisively. '*I'm* not the one who goes hobnobbing with gunmen and such.'

She was on her feet in a light leap, the door slammed, the car gathered way and was gone, its rear lights dwindling to cigarette-ends just visible in the soiled, wet darkness, as it rounded the curve by the White Hart. And that, thought Bunty, is how it should be done, when it has to be done at all. She furled in the frayed cords of her personality that had been torn loose with George's departure, but this time the ache did not dull, and the bleeding did not stop.

Any one of those separations in the past twenty years might have been the final one; even before the armed professionals arrived on the scene, a policeman's hadn't been the safest of careers. Is it only on the edge of middle age, she wondered, that you begin admitting the possibility? Or, more simply, do you never even notice it until then?

Overheated air closed round her like warm treacle as she pushed her way into the supermarket, and made for the dry goods' shelves. Even husbands who take their cars out in the morning to drive tranquilly to work in banks and shops may be heading unawares for a pile-up at the first corner, or a hold-up and a shot over the counter. But life would be impossible if their wives spent every separated moment thinking so.

She sat in the empty, silent house, brushing her hair before the glass and watching her mirrored face as if the secret of this unforeseen and inescapable dismay lay there behind her own eyes. She had avoided the bus, after all, and walked all the way home through the thin, unclean rain, in the dim, amorphous colourings of evening and autumn, inexpressibly elegiac and sad. And where there should have been shelter, under her own roof, the other darkness had closed down appallingly on her spirit, the darkness you see when you look over your shoulder half-way through life.

How was it that she had turned forty without a chilling thought, and now at forty-one must run head-on into the skeleton in the way?

It happens to everyone, sooner or later, even the best balanced and happiest, that sudden hesitation and the long first look behind, the first qualm of wondering whether all has been well done, whether there is really anything there at all to record the course of a life suddenly seen to be half-over. October is a searching time even for the young, but for them it is only a seasonal disquiet, they have the renewal of Spring within them, they have good cause to believe in it. Bunty's heart ached inconsolably for the beauty that was gone, for the youth that would not renew itself. She looked into her own eyes, and they were no longer unaware of passing time, and no longer innocent of the implications, age, infirmity and death.

She had turned out the main light in the room. Her brush crackled and sparkled through her thick brown hair in the dimness, and her eyes stared back at her unwaveringly from the glass, sometimes obscured by the swaying strands of hair, but always constant and naked in their questioning when the curtain parted again. What is the matter with you? she asked the image that fronted her. They were two, not one, there might even be an answer. You're a lucky woman, a happy woman. You've always been aware of it. You have a husband you love, and a son you adore, you are equable and outgoing by temperament; in a modest way, which has always satisfied you up to now, you have every possible blessing. Even a sense of humour! Or have you? Or has it only been mislaid for a short testing time?

And that's all? wondered the eyes confronting her. And that's enough?

The clouds were breaking outside the window, but only in tormented shapes of scudding flight and bitter pursuit, driven by a sudden wailing wind. All the too static air was abruptly in motion. She felt time rushing away from under her feet, leaving her falling through space in a howling greyness. There had once been a certain Bunty Elliott who had known beyond question that she was going to be a great singer, and leave a treasury of recorded music that would make her immortal. But she had never put her gifts to any serious test, because she had met and married George Felse, and turned into a mere wife, a policeman's wife. And what was she now but George's wife – no, George's grass widow at this moment, and this moment was her whole life in microcosm – and Dominic's mother? Did she exist, except as a reflection of them? Was she condemned only to act, only to be anything at all through her husband and her son?

What had become of Bunty herself? Somewhere she had got lost between George and Dominic, and rediscovery would not be easy. George's face looked up at her from the photograph on her dressing-table, ten years younger than now but essentially the same, grave, thin, thoughtful, with dark, steady eyes, and sensitive lines about his mouth. She could paint in for herself the new furrows that had grown deep into his flesh since the picture was taken, and they added to his worth and significance, which were not and never would be in question. She loved him so naturally that she had never had cause to stop and assess how much she loved him. He, nevertheless, had an identity of his own, and was in no danger of losing it. And she?

If you were here now, she thought, you would be enough to restore the balance; I should be over the crest and on my way home. Why aren't you here? Why did you have to be somewhere else on this night of all nights?

And her son? Dominic was complicated, fascinating and absorbing, because he was half George and half herself. They had been devoted friends all his short life. She could even laugh at him, and not be excommunicated. But they grow up, and grow away. Dominic was at Oxford, with exams hanging over him, and Dominic had chosen a girl, and chosen her for life, for better or worse, for richer or poorer, for all time and with all his heart. Maybe he himself didn't yet know it, maybe he was too close to Tossa Barber to take in her full significance. But Bunty knew it. And approved it. He might have made so many mistakes, but in the event his instinct was true enough, and his choice sharp and sure. And she was glad. But where, now, was Bunty?

She had been prepared, insofar as any woman can be prepared, to be sloughed like an outworn skin. It presented no problem in her relationship with him, or even with his Tossa. But she was confronting the shell of Bunty Felse, and coming to terms with that gutted presence was not so easy.

What am I now? she thought. Am I anything? Yes, to George, certainly. I have a reason for going on being, I have a hollow to fill, maybe a bigger hollow than before. But whether I have enough substance to supply the vacuum, that's another matter. And whether anything exists which is truly me, and not reflections of these two, God only knows!

The bed was smooth, sterile and cold. She lay in the panting, unquiet darkness, and did not sleep. And in the morning, which was her forty-first birthday, there was no letter from Dominic and no telephone call from George. The early light of Saturday was grey, chill and calm, and she was utterly alone for perhaps the first time in her life. In a life which was half over, and shrinking in upon her even as she dressed to face it.

Chapter 2

She could have called up her friends, of course; she had plenty of friends. But with them she would simply have worn her normal face and manner, and kept her own counsel. You do not burden your friends with a sudden stranger half-way to the grave. You hide yourself while the darkness lasts – being, even at this crisis, reasonably secure that it will not last long – and emerge when you are yourself as they know you, and fit for their society again. No, at this moment what you need is a stranger in an express train, someone you need never see again, one of those accidental priests in the fleeting confessionals of this life where souls are often saved against the odds.

That was why she took herself for a long, solitary walk that Saturday evening in October, avoiding the places most familiar to her, and the haunts where her friends might be. The air was dove-coloured and still since noon, chilling by dusk to the edge of frost, but never quite touching it. The cloud was low and grey, but the atmosphere beneath it was clear. If it froze by morning, the crests of the roads, at least, would dry, and the film of slime would corrode away in pale dust.

The silence at home had helped to drive her out, but the silence here on the country roads two miles from Comerford was vaster and even more oppressive. She had never been afraid to walk alone in the night, not here; in a city she might have been warier. She met shadows, and, occasionally responsive to some alchemy of recognition in anonymity, exchanged good nights with shadows. She kept aloof from the roads that carried traffic, and the few cars she met passed mysteriously, absorbed in their own missions. And where she came at length to the main road again, she found herself before the broad car park and polished frontage of a modern roadhouse, the sort of place where none of her acquaintance could possibly be encountered.

'The Constellation Orion'; a beautifully imaginative name, at least. She remembered the place being opened, though she had never been inside it. Well, why not now? The building, twentieth-century metal box crossed with by-pass Georgian, didn't live up to its name, but surely promised strangers as transitory as any to be met with in express trains. And she had plenty of time to walk home, all night if need be; she had nobody at home waiting for her.

Warmth and noise met her in the doorway. The saloon bar was so aggressively modern that it had almost reverted to the jazz-age angularity of the twenties, and its décor reminded her of fairground vases from her childhood. It was almost uncomfortably full. For some reason the same degree of actual discomfort in the bar itself seemed more acceptable. The lighting was mellower and milder there, and it was clearly the only room the locals, if they used this place at all, would dream of frequenting. Bunty edged her way to the bar-counter, bought herself a modest half of bitter, and carried it to a remote corner where a young couple had just vacated two chairs at a spindly table. Over the rim of her glass she surveyed the company, and let the confused roar of their many conversations drum in her ear without any effort to disentangle words. There was no one whom she knew, and no one who knew her. Nobody was interested, either; in twos, in threes, in shifting groups, they pursued their own preoccupations, and left her to hers.

She had been sitting there in her corner for ten minutes or so before she noticed the only other person who seemed to be alone. She saw him first over the shoulders of two sporty types in mohair car coats, and from his position he might easily have been a part of their circle; but emphatically his face denied it. He looked at them out of another world, a world as private and closed as hers. Quite a young man, maybe somewhere in his late twenties, maybe even turned thirty. Tall, a light-weight but well enough made, rather brittle and nervous in his movements, his straight dark hair disordered. What she noticed first was the greyish pallor of his face, and its tight stillness, like a clay mask, so apparently rigid that the sudden nervous quiver of one cheek was shocking, as though the whole face might be shattered. The taut surfaces quaked and recomposed themselves into the same stony tension. Deep within this defensive earthwork dark eyes, alert and bright to fever point, kept watch from ambush, glaring from bruised, blue-rimmed sockets. He looked as if he had been on the tiles for two or three nights in succession; but she noted that the hand that held his glass was large, capable and perfectly steady.

He was getting too tightly hemmed in by the group at the bar. She saw him leave himself clear of them, edge back into the open, and look round for a more peaceful place. His ranging glance lit upon the single chair still vacant in her corner, and he started towards it.

Then he saw her. Really saw her, not as any unknown woman sitting there, but as this one particular woman, taken in entire in one flash of genuine concentration. It was the first time he had been fully aware of anyone in that room except himself and the personal devil with which he was surely at grips. He halted for a moment, poised quite still in the middle of the shifting, chattering, smoky bar, his eyes fixed on her. She thought that he almost drew back and turned away, that if she had lowered her eyes or looked through him he would have done it; but she looked back at him steadily and thoughtfully, neither inviting nor repulsing him, unless it was an invitation to show interest in him at all. One person under stress recognises another.

226

The moment of hesitation was gone; he came on with a quickened step. He had a whisky glass in one hand and a small bottle of ginger ale in the other. A long little finger touched tentatively at the back of the vacant chair.

'Do you mind if I sit here?' The voice was low-pitched but abrupt, as though he had to measure it out with care and constraint.

'Of course not, help yourself!'

She moved her glass to make room for his on the tiny table. It had a tray top of beaten brass that had never been nearer Benares than Birmingham. He looked at it for the fraction of an instant with disbelief, and then sat down carefully, and looked up at her.

'I agree,' said Bunty with detachment. 'It's rather nasty, but it's somewhere to put things down.'

Something kindled in his face, no more than a momentary easing and warming of the haggard lines of his mouth, and a brisk spark that was burned out instantly in the intensity of his eyes.

'You didn't *look* as if you belonged here,' he said. 'Why *are* you here?'

Conversation came out of him without premeditation, and indeed with a famished urgency that ruled out premeditation, but in brief, jerky sentences, spurting from the muted violence that filled him. Violence was the word that first occurred to her, but she found it unacceptable on reflection; agitation might have been nearer the mark, or simply excitement. There was nothing impertinent in his manner, and whatever he was looking for, it wasn't a pick-up.

'Because I was alone,' she said, with a directness equal to his own. 'Why are you?'

'The same reason, I suppose. And I needed a drink.'

It appeared that this was no more than the truth. The whisky had brought a faint warmth of colour into his clay mask, its frozen lines were at least growing pliable now.

227

'You don't mind my talking to you? I'll shut up if you say so.'

She did not say so. What she did say, after a moment of deliberation, was: 'I came out because it was too silent at home, and I came in here because it was even more silent outside.'

He uttered a short, harsh sound that might, if he had been less tense, have emerged as a laugh. 'That won't be our trouble here, anyhow. Or would you say this was a kind of silence, too? A howling silence?' The babel was reaching its climax, it was only half an hour to closing-time. The young man cast one brief glance round the room, and turned back to her, his eyes for a moment wide and dark with awareness of her, and strangely innocent of curiosity. 'We've got something in common, then,' he said, emptying his glass without taking his eyes from Bunty's face. 'You weren't expecting to be alone, either.'

'No,' she agreed, thinking how different a celebration this forty-first birthday might have been, 'I wasn't expecting to be alone.'

'Nor was I. I'm heading north,' he said jerkily, revolving the empty glass dangerously between his fingers, 'for a long week-end. Not much to look forward to now, though. There should have been two of us, if everything hadn't come to pieces.' The glass was suddenly still between his long hands; he stared at it blackly. 'I suppose I ought to lay off, but I've got to have one more of these, I'm still twenty per cent short of human. May I get you the other half? Or would you prefer a short?'

'Thanks, the other half would be fine.'

She watched him worm his way to the bar with the empty glasses, and knew that she had done that deliberately. Why? Because if she had refused he would have taken it as a rebuff and been turned in again upon his own arid company? Or because she would have lost touch with him and been driven back upon hers? What she was courting was the loss of herself in another human creature, and that was what he wanted, too. Not that it would ever be much more than two parallel mono-logues, the passing of two trains on a double track, somewhere in the dark. But at least the sight of a human face at one of the flying windows would assure the watcher of companionship in his wakefulness. Their need was mutual, why pass up the opportunity of filling it?

So she waited for him, and watched him come back to her, balancing full glasses carefully as he wound his way between the jostling backs of the Saturday-night crowd.

'I'm sorry about your spoiled weekend,' she said. And with carefully measured detachment, since clearly this was no light matter to him at the moment: 'Of course, there *are* other girls.'

He was just setting down his glass on the table, and for the first time his hand shook. She looked up in surprise, and met his eyes at close range, suddenly fallen blank in a frozen face, as grey and opaque as unlighted glass. He sat down slowly, every line of his body drawn so taut that the air between them quivered.

'Who mentioned a girl?'

'There are only two sorts,' she said patiently. 'There was at least a fifty-fifty chance of guessing right first time about the companion who let you down.'

He drew in a long, cautious breath and relaxed a little. The slow fires came back distrustfully into his eyes. 'Yes . . . I suppose it wasn't difficult.' His voice groped through the words syllable by syllable, like feet in the dark feeling their way. 'We fell out,' he said. 'It's finished. I can't say I wasn't warned, at least half a dozen of my friends must have told me she was playing me for a sucker, but I never believed it.'

'You could still be right about her,' said Bunty reasonably, 'and they could still be wrong.'

'Not a chance! It all blew up in my face today. For good.'

'There may be more to be said for her than you think now. You may not always feel like this. You and she may make it up again, given a little goodwill.'

'No!' he said with quiet violence. 'That's out! She'll never have the chance to let me down again.'

'Then – at the risk of repeating myself – there *are* other girls.'

He wasn't listening. No doubt he heard the sound of her voice quite clearly, just as those blue-circled, burning eyes of his were memorising her face, but all he saw and all he heard had to do with his own private pain. Bunty was merely a vessel set to receive the overflow of his distress.

'We only got engaged ten days ago,' he said. 'God knows why she ever said yes, she had this other fellow on the string all along. Whatever she wanted out of it, it wasn't me.'

'It happens,' said Bunty. 'When you commit yourself to another person you take that risk. There isn't any way of hedging your bet.'

'She hedged hers pretty successfully,' he said bitterly.

'She wasn't committed. And you're better off without her.'

So softly that she hardly heard him, more to himself than to her, he said, 'Oh, my God, what is there in it, either way?' His hands clenched into white-knuckled fists on his knees. She thought for a moment that he was going to faint, and instinctively put out a hand and took him by the arm, no hesitant touch, but a firm grip, tethering him fast to the world it seemed he would gladly have shaken off in favour of darkness. It brought his head up with a jerk, his eyes dazed and dark in that blanched face. They stared steadily at each other for a moment, devouring line and substance and form so intensely that neither of them would ever be able to hide from the other again, under any name or in any disguise.

'Look,' said Bunty quietly, 'you're not fit to drive any distance tonight. Go home, fall into bed, sleep her off, drink her off if you have to, get another girl, anything, only give yourself a chance. It isn't the end of the world . . . it had damned well better not be! You've got a life before you, and it isn't owed to her, it's owed in part to the rest of us, but mostly to yourself. You go under and we've all lost.'

She wondered if he even knew that she was at least twelve years older than he was. She had begun by feeling something

230

like twenty years older, and now she was no longer sure that there was even a year between them. This was no adolescent agony, but a mature passion that shook the whole room, even though the babel went on round it, oblivious and superficial, a backcloth of triviality.

'It *is* the end of the world,' said the young man, quite softly and simply. 'That's what you don't understand.'

The clock behind the bar began to chime with an unexpected, silvery sound.

'Time!' called the barman, pitching his voice on the same mellifluous note. 'Time, gentlemen, please!'

She spent an unnecessary few minutes in the cloakroom, tidying her hair and repairing her lipstick, not so much to escape from him as to give him every chance to escape from her if he wanted to. Men are much more likely than women to repent of having said too much and stripped themselves too naked, and it might well be that now, having unloaded the worst of his burden, he would prefer to make off into the darkness and never see or think of her again. But when she stepped out from the lighted doorway, under the silver stars of the sign, he was there waiting for her, a slender, tense shadow beside the low chain fence of the car park. She felt no surprise and no uneasiness.

'Have you got transport? Then may I give you a lift home?'

'It's out of your way,' she said equably. 'I live in Comerford, and I imagine you're heading for the M.6.'

'It won't add more than three miles to the distance. And there's nobody waiting for me,' he said tightly. She was growing used to that tone, but it still puzzled her, because for all its muted desperation it was strangely innocent of self-pity.

'Then if you don't mind going round that way, I should be glad to ride with you.' Why not? All he wanted was to warm his hands at this tiny fire for a few minutes longer. And she could take care of herself. She was a mature woman, self-reliant and well-balanced, she was not afraid to venture nearer to another person, not afraid that she would not be able to control

231

the relationship, even extricate herself from it if the need arose. She was old enough to be able to offer him the companionship he needed, and not have it mistaken for something else.

His hand touched her arm punctiliously as they walked across to the car, but he kept the touch light and tentative, as if mortally afraid of damaging the grain of comfort he had got out of her. The broad space of tarmac was emptying fast, the last few cars peeling off in turn between the white posts of the exit. Soon they would have the night to themselves on the dark country road into Comerford.

'Here we are!'

He leaned to open the door for her, and closed it upon her as soon as she was settled. She was incorrigibly ignorant about cars, and worse, in the view of her family, she was completely incurious. Cars were a convenient means of getting from here to there, and sometimes they were beautiful in themselves, but they made no other impression upon her. This one was large but not new, and by no means showy, short on chrome but long on power under the bonnet, and he handled it as though he knew what do with all the power he could get, and probably considerably more than he could afford. Bunty might have no mechanical sense at all, but she had an instinctive appreciation of competence.

'Have you very far to go?' she asked, watching the drawn profile beside her appearing and disappearing fitfully as they passed the last lights of the frontage and took the Comerford road.

'About three hundred miles. It won't take me long. It's a quicker run by night.'

'Maybe . . . but all the same I wish you'd go home to bed. I don't feel happy about you setting off on a run like that, in the state you're in.'

'There's nothing the matter with my state. I'm not drunk,' he said defensively.

'I know you're not. I didn't mean that. But in any case, it

isn't going to be a very long weekend, is it, to be worth such a journey? It's nearly Sunday already. And you did say there was no one waiting for you.' The silence beside her ached, but was not inimical. 'Am I trespassing?' she asked simply.

'*No*!' It was the first time she had heard warmth in his voice. 'You're very kind. But I've got to go. I can't stay here now. It won't be such a short stay as all that, you see, I'm not due back till Wednesday. Don't worry about me, I shall be all right.'

Abruptly she asked: 'When did you last eat?'

Astonished, he peered back into the recesses of his memory, and admitted blankly: 'I don't even know! Yes, wait . . . I did have a lunch . . . of sorts, anyhow. Opened a tin . . . one of those repulsive dinky grills.'

'Nothing since then?'

'No . . . I suppose not! I haven't wanted anything.'

'No wonder you look sick,' she said practically. 'You'd be wanting something before you got to the end of your journey, believe me. And those two whiskys will settle better with some food inside you. If Lennie hasn't closed up his stall we'll stop there and pick up some sandwiches or hot dogs for you, and a coffee.'

'I suppose,' he admitted, 'it might be an idea.'

The lights of Comerford winked ahead of them, orange stars against a moist black sky. Old Lennie's coffee-stall always spent Saturday evening on the narrow forecourt before the old market cross, handy for the late crowds emerging from the Bingo hall and the billiard club. All the new estates and the commercial development lay at the other end of the town, and this approach across the little river might still have been leading them into the old, sprawling village the place had once been. A foursquare Baptist chapel, built a hundred years ago of pale grey brick, looked out across the water between pollarded trees. Once over the slight hump of the bridge, they could see the white van of the coffee-stall gilded by the street lamp above it, and with its own interior light still burning. The small, lame proprietor, hurt in a pit accident twenty-five years ago, was just clearing his counter.

'Pull in for a minute and drop me,' ordered Bunty, 'and I'll see what he's got left. We can't park here, but we can turn down by the riverside and find a place there for you to eat in peace.'

She was back in a minute or two with two paper bags and a waxed carton of coffee.

'It's a good thing Lennie knows me so well, he wouldn't have opened up again for everybody, not after he's cashed up.'

The old man had come limping out from his stall to close the shutter, and stood looking after his customer now with candid curiosity, watching her tuck her long legs into a strange car, beside a strange young man. He stood stolidly gazing, with no pretence at other preoccupations, as the car took the right-hand turn that would bring it down towards the park and the riverside gardens.

'This is all right, anywhere here. This is only a loop road, it brings us back to the main one just before the lights. We shan't be in anyone's way here, there won't be much traffic at this time of night.'

There were no houses along here, and hence no homeless cars parked overnight outside them, an inevitable phenomenon in every urbanisation. He halted the car with its hub-caps brushing the overgrown grass under the trees. A narrow path and a box hedge separated them from the park on this near side, and across the road, beyond fifty yards of ornamental shrubbery and trees, the Comer gleamed faintly. After he had stopped the engine it was very quiet, and unaccountably still, as if every necessity for measuring time had stopped. Nobody was waiting for either of them at the end of their journey.

Suddenly she felt him shaking beside her, the only shaken thing in all that stillness. It happened as soon as he took his hands from the wheel and let his concentration relax, and for a full minute of struggle he could not suppress the shudders that pulsed through him. Bunty tore open the waxed carton of coffee and put it into his hand, closing her own fingers over his to guide the cup to his lips. He drank submissively, and presently drew a long, cautious breath, and let it out again in a great, relaxing sigh, and she felt his tensed flesh soften again into ease.

'I'm sorry . . . I'm all right, just more tired than I realised.'

'At least get some food inside you and rest for a bit.' She dumped the paper bags of sausage rolls and ham sandwiches on his knees, and watched him eat, at first with weary obedience and little interest, then with sudden astonished greed, as though he had just discovered food. 'You see, you were hungry.' She sat nursing the half-empty coffee carton, studying the shadowy form beside her with a frown.

'Look, you simply can't go on with this, it would be crazy.'

'Maybe I am crazy,' he said perversely. 'Did you ever think of that? You were right about the food, though. Look, I owe you for all this, you must let me . . .'

'My round,' said Bunty. 'A return for the other half.'

He didn't argue. He stretched himself with a huge sigh that racked and then released him from head to foot, and lay back in the driving seat, turning his forehead to rest against the glass. A large hand crumpled the empty paper bags and held them loosely on his knee.

'Better?'

'Much better!'

'Then listen! You shouldn't go on tonight. It isn't fair to other road-users to drive when you're as exhausted as this. You might pass out on the motorway, what then?'

'I shan't pass out on the motorway,' he said through a shivering yawn, 'I can't afford to.' The note of grim certainty sank into a mumble; he yawned again. 'No choice,' he said distantly, 'no choice at all . . .'

She sat silent for a while, though she had had much more to urge upon him; for after all, she told herself, he was not hers. And the moment that thought was formulated she knew that he was, that he had been hers since the moment she had accepted him. Now she didn't know what to do about him. People to whom you have once opened your doors can't afterwards be thrown out, but neither can they be kept against their will. If he would go on, he would, and she had no right to prevent him even if she could. Only then did it occur to her how completely, during this last hour and a half, she had forgotten about herself.

What drew her out of her brooding speculation was the rhythm of his breathing, long and easy and regular, misting the glass against his cheek. He was asleep. The hand that lay open on his knee still cradled the crumpled paper-bags; she lifted them delicately out of his hold and dropped them into the empty carton, and he never moved.

So it seemed that she had nothing left to do here, after all. She didn't even consider waking him; sleep was probably the thing he most needed, and perhaps if he had his rest out he would wake up ready to see sense and go home. And you, she told herself, might just as well do the same. It was no distance from here, she could walk it in ten minutes. A pity, in a way, to slip away without a good-bye, but these encounters are sometimes better ended without ceremony, and the partners in them don't need any formulæ in order to understand and remember them.

She waited a little while, but he was deeply asleep, she could easily depart without disturbing him. The sky had cleared overhead, there were stars, and the moisture in the air would be rime by morning. Not a good night to be sleeping out in a car. Maybe he had a rug tucked away somewhere, old cars without modern heaters often carry them as a matter of course. She looked round on the back seat, but there was nothing there but his suitcase. If there was a rug that lived permanently in the car, it might be in the boot; and there were his keys, dangling in the ignition close to her hand. Would he regard it as a breach of their delicate, unformulated agreement if she made use of them to look for something to cover him?

She hesitated for a few moments over that question, but when it came to the point she knew she could not leave him to wake up half-frozen in a rimy dawn. She raised her hand to the keys, and carefully drew them out, and her companion slept on peacefully. Quietly she opened the door, and quietly closed it after her.

The black butt-end of the car was as broad as a cab. There was enough light for her to find the lock easily, and the key was the second she tried. The large lid of the boot gave with a faint creak, and lifted readily. Faint starlight spilled over the rim into the dark interior, but called into being only vague shapes under the shadow of the lid. She felt forward into the dimness, and her hand found something woolly and soft, but with a hard stiffness inside it that rocked gently to her touch. She felt her way along it, and her fingers slipped from its edge and grasped something cold, articulated and rigid.

For one instant she was still, not recognising what she held; then she snatched back her hand with a hissing intake of breath, so sharply that the chill thing she touched was plucked momentarily towards her. With minute, terrible sounds the folded shapes within the boot shifted and rocked, leaning towards the open air as if they would rise and climb out to confront her. The marble hand she had grasped hung poised at the end of its sleeve. Something pale and silken and fine swung forward and flowed over Bunty's hand, encircling her frozen fingers in the curled ends of long, straight blonde hair.

The girl coiled up between the tool-box and the spare wheel was dead and stiffening. Until that blind touch disturbed her, she must have been lying like a child asleep. Her dark coat was unbuttoned over a cream-coloured sweater, and in the breast of the sweater, even by this curious, lambent half-light, a small round dot of darkness could be seen, crusted and rough-edged like a seal, the only indication of the manner in which she had died.

Bunty crouched, staring, her hands at her mouth, numbed and cold with shock.

So this was why that girl of his was never going to have the chance to let him down again, this was why he had to get out of here tonight at all costs. This was how their quarrel had ended.

Chapter 3

A hand reached past her shoulder and slammed the boot shut. And if there had ever been a moment when she could have turned and run, with a hope of eluding pursuit in the trees, it was already over, had passed unrecognised while she stood there incapable of utterance or movement, all her senses stunned with horror.

She had heard nothing, had seen nothing but the slight, contorted body before her; but something had roused him, the cold air as the car door opened, the cautious sound of the latch closing again, maybe even some subconscious instinct of self-preservation that needed no help from the physical senses. For there he was at her back, recoiling now to evade her touch, in case shock gave her the reckless courage to attempt any move against him, edging silently along the side of the car to show to her, and hide from anyone else who might choose this of all moments to come by, the small black gun levelled at her heart. His hand was still steady. And the evidence was there between them, hidden now but unforgettably present, that the gun was loaded, and that he knew how to use it.

'Keep quiet,' he said, in a thread of a voice that had the tension of hysteria. 'If you make a sound or a move, I shall kill you.'

She was deathly quiet, and frenziedly still. Numbness clogged all her senses, but somewhere within her burned a core of intelligence frantically alert to all the possibilities, and quick to guard itself from any mistakes.

'My God, my God,' he said in a howling whisper, to himself rather than to her, 'why did you? . . . *why did you?*'

Yes, why, she thought, her mind lost in this drugged body, groping like a sleepwalker, why did I? Because I felt responsible for you! See what it gets you, feeling responsible! This is involvement gone too far. But there wasn't any turning back; none for him, and none for her. She said nothing. As yet she had no voice, she couldn't have screamed for help even if the round black muzzle of the gun hadn't been trained on her with its one hypnotic eye. Screaming is, in any case, harder than you might suppose. It takes an experience of this kind to teach you how tough a resistance your sensible flesh, mind and spirit put up to believing in danger and death. Such things happen at a dream-distance, to others; never to you. When they do crop up in your way, like some skeleton apparition in a medieval legend, you don't believe in them. Not until you've had time to acclimatise. By which time it is too late to take avoiding action.

But this was reality. She wasn't at home in bed, dreaming it. There he was, in the soft, diffused light, rigid and quivering, but a hundred per cent awake and alert and dangerous, staring at her with bruised eyes now wide-open and impersonal as fate in a shadowless, porcelain face, over the gun which had become a third – no, a fourth – character in this impossible scene.

She looked down at the closed lid of the boot, and there was a tress of pale hair glimmering over the rim.

'Lock it,' he said. And when she stooped mechanically to turn the key: 'No . . . that hair . . . push it out of sight, all of it . . .' The voice was thin, harsh and piercing, like broken glass.

She fumbled at the silvery tendrils, which seemed still to have such innocent, sparkling life in them. She tucked the last strand out of sight, and her fingertips touched the cold, ice-cold face. The chill passed out of the dead flesh into the living without revulsion; all she felt was a dreadful, quickening pity over so much waste. She let down the lid gently, like the lid of a coffin, and turned the key upon the body. Slowly she straightened up and looked round blindly at the man with the gun, the bunch of keys outstretched in her hand.

'Put them on the wing between us,' he said, and drew back a step out of her reach, with infinite care to be silent and restrained even in this movement. He didn't want to startle her into some panicky reaction that would make the shot necessary.

She laid down the keys where he indicated, releasing them softly, with the same exaggerated caution against any sound. And he reached out his free hand without taking his eyes from her, and gathered them up and pocketed them.

'Let's have it clear.' His voice was more assured now, and deader, if there are degrees in death. 'If you make a single false move, even by mistake, I'll kill you. What choice have you left me? You see I've nothing to lose now.'

Her mind was beginning to work, clearly enough, but like the logical threading of a dream. She saw, and acted in accordance with what she saw. He had indeed nothing to lose. His back was against a wall, and he was proof against fears and scruples; and she was not going to make any false move. She looked back at him, motionless and attentive, and said nothing.

'Get back in the car. I shall be close behind you.'

She turned stiffly, obeying the motion of the hand that held the gun, and slowly circled the back of the car and walked to the passenger door. Slowly, in case he suspected her of an attempt at escape. She might, indeed, have risked it if the car had been drawn up on the other side of the road, but here there was only the narrow path and then the thick hedge, nowhere at all for her to take cover. He followed her step for step, she could feel the muzzle of the gun not six inches from her back. The transit of those four or five yards seemed to last a lifetime; at least it gave her a sudden dazzlingly clear distant view of her own situation. Only a few hours ago she had been laboriously extending her powers to cope with the realisation that half her life had slipped away almost unnoticed, and now she saw the other half bridged in one monstrous leap, and death within touch of her hand.

No car came along. No one walked home by this way. No belated lovers dawdled in the dark. In summer there might have been a hope, there was none now. She was on her own, and there was nothing she could possibly do except obey him. Except, perhaps, leave some sign here to be found?

Her handbag was on her wrist, and there was no chance of opening it without being detected. But her purse was in her left-hand coat pocket, and it contained a perspex window in the flap, with her name and address in it. Goodbye to seven pounds and some loose change, but what did she need with money now? At least it would show where she had been. She drew it out carefully but quickly, the swinging handbag hiding the movements of her hand, and tossed it slightly aside into the overgrown autumnal grass that separated the footpath from the road. It fell with very little sound, but she risked letting her foot slip from the edge of the kerb in a noisy stumble to cover the moment, and spread her right hand against the car to steady herself. The man behind her drew in his breath with a hiss of warning, alarm and pain, and the muzzle of the gun prodded her back and sent an icy chill down the marrow of her spine.

'*Be careful!*'

But he meant the stumble, not the purse she had thrown away. All his attention was focused on her, he didn't look aside into the grass. And now it was up to fate. If an honest person found what she had left behind, he would try to return it, and failing to find her at the address given, take it to the police, who would most surely wonder at her absence. If a dishonest person – or even a humanly fallible one – found it . . . well, so much the worse.

He stepped past her at the appropriate moment, and held the door open for her. As soon as she was inside he slammed the door upon her and darted round to the driver's door; and as soon as he took his hand from her own door, she reached for it again, wrenched at the handle and flung her weight against it in a sudden passion of realisation that it was now or never. Leap out and run for it, back towards the cross . . . The car's bulk would cover her for the first few moments, he would have to take aim afresh and in a hurry, she might get clean away.

The door held fast, the handle moved only part-way, and the thrust of her body was spent vainly. There was a safety catch with which she wasn't familiar, and she hadn't seen him set it before he slammed the door. By the time she had found it and was clawing at it frantically, he was in the driving seat beside her, and the car was in motion.

The door catch gave, the safety catch held. He reached a long arm across her and slammed the door to again, and she had lost her only chance, if it had ever been a chance. The impetus of their take-off flung her back in the seat, hard against his shoulder. The trees hissed by on either side at speed. To attempt to jump out now would be as good a way as any of committing suicide.

She sat with her hands clenched together in her lap, confronting the truth fully for the first time, and so closely that she saw nothing else. What difference could it possibly make who found her purse, or whether it was ever found at all, or how many police they turned out to look for her tomorrow? Nobody could get to her in time to be of any use; she was absolutely on her own, and her time must be short.

What could this man do now, except get rid of the witness?

He took the turn into the main street fast and expertly, and at such an angle that her mind, working with frosty clarity somewhere within the shell of shock, registered the certainty that he knew this town very well. Then she remembered the traffic lights. There was no way of evading that crossing in the middle of Comerford; and she knew, if he did not, that on Saturday nights there was usually a police constable keeping an eye unobtrusively on affairs there, at least until all the Espresso bar and

243

motorbike brigade had gone home to bed, which they seldom did until after midnight. Now if the lights should be against them there . . .

There were still several groups of young people conducting their leisurely and noisy farewells along the pavement when the car drew near to the crossroads. The dance at the Regal wasn't over yet, and there was P.C. Peter Hillard standing by the window of the jeweller's shop looking at nothing and watching everything, with his hands linked behind him, and the usual deceptive expression of benign idiocy on his face. Now if the lights were at red, surely she dared . . . He wouldn't shoot here, he'd run. Remember the safety gadget on the door this time . . .

The amber changed to red before them. A convulsion of hope ran through her, she sat forward very slightly, bracing herself, as the car slowed and rolled up to the lights. And suddenly there was the stab in her side, the blunt black barrel reminding her, and the blue-ringed eyes more chilling than the gun.

'*Don't!*' he said, his right hand still gently manipulating the wheel. 'You might do for me, but I should do for you first.'

He had known exactly what was in her mind. Either he had foreseen it all the time, or else the slight tension of joy had communicated itself to him as clearly as if she had declared her intent aloud. And all she had out of it was one more odd fact about him: he was ambidextrous, he could shoot her as readily with the left hand as the right. Now she had the option of inviting her own death at once, or waiting for a better chance, with conviction that there would ever be one.

What she actually did emerged not as the consequence of thought at all, but blindly, on an impulse she had no time to assess. The car was still very slowly in motion, about to brake to a halt, and Hillard was looking their way, though from across the street he had no chance of seeing and recognising her. He could, however, read off a registration number without difficulty from there, if there should be a blatant offence . . .

She turned her head and peered back through the rear

244

window, and in a sharp cry of vengeful delight she crowed: 'There's a police car pulling up behind us! *He's getting out . . .!*'

She might have killed herself one way, but she had as nearly risked doing it in another. The driver's foot went down on the accelerator so violently that she was jerked back stunningly in her seat, wrenching her neck and setting fireworks scintillating before her eyes. Light and darkness flickered wildly past her, as the car shot across the intersection at high speed. A large Austin, crossing sedately with the lights in its favour, braked hard, a van's tyres smoked and squealed on the tarmac dry with frost. But they were through, untouched, and boring along the modestly-lit tunnel of Hawkworth Road at an illegal sixty-five. Bunty clung to the edge of the seat, gasping for the breath that had been knocked out of her, and recovered it only to break into weak, involuntary laughter, rather from relief at finding herself still alive than from any sense of achievement.

No more of that sort of thing! If she had stopped to think she would never have taken such a chance. The wonder was that the gun had not gone off in his hand when she sprang the trap; the violence of his reaction showed her how near she had come to that ending. Hair-trigger nerves might be expected in a murderer on the run. And if only he'd kept his head and looked in his mirror, instead of tramping on the accelerator the instant she had sounded the alarm, he might have got through Comerford and away without question.

'Damn you!' moaned the bitter voice beside her, shaky with fury. '*Damn you!* There wasn't any damned police car!'

'There soon will be,' she said, 'now.'

If Hillard had missed getting their number, someone in the Austin or the van would surely have noted it. Was that anything gained? It might be, if Hillard was quick to act on it. If the fugitive was heading for the M.6 he could hardly avoid going through Hawkworth, and there would be time to alert the police there by telephone, and even to set up a road-block. There was a strong campaign on against dangerous driving, and their exit from Comerford had certainly been spectacular.

If she could work out all that, so could he. He knew the odds now, he was concentrating on getting past Hawkworth in the least possible time, but if her luck held he wouldn't be quick enough, even at this lawless speed.

At this moment she would have been certain of her own imminent death, if he had dared take a hand from the wheel or divert a thought from his driving to kill her. That was her only security, after what she had just done to him: nothing could happen to her while he was driving at this intensity. Better pray that the police would stop him at Hawkworth. If they did not, only one encouraging consideration remained, that he would surely prefer to remove her as far as possible from home before killing and disposing of her, in order to gain more time to make his own escape. Given a few hours' grace you can hide a body, even two bodies, competently enough to delay inquiries for weeks, by which time he undoubtedly meant to be far away.

Now she was nothing but a passenger, quiescent from self-interest. He still had the gun ready in his left hand, even as he held the wheel. At the next threat he could use it instantly. She sat tensed and silent, waiting for the first glimmer of the sodium lighting of Hawkworth.

They reached the well-lit approach road, and he didn't slow down. Now she could see his face by fits and starts as they passed the lamp standards, fixed like marble, in brittle, nervous lines of strain, with sweat glistening on his forehead and lip. And suddenly he was braking, but with a deliberation that promised nothing, and positioning the car well out into the centre of the road. He had seen the barrier before she had. Hillard hadn't failed her, the police had closed half the road here at the approach to the town. But only half! And he was going through, she felt it in her blood.

From behind the white trestle on the left of the road a young police constable stepped out full into their path, with his hand extended to wave them down. Bunty heard the man beside her gulp in air in a huge sob, and felt his foot go down on the accelerator.

The boy in uniform was standing confidently in the centre of the free way; his confidence in the law he represented drew a warning scream up into her throat, but she choked on it silently and could not utter a sound. She would have closed her eyes, but it was impossible, the young figure held them fixed in fascination. She saw his face leap towards her, saw it dissolve from tolerant serenity into incredulous doubt, and then into terror, as the car drove straight at him.

At the last instant the wheel swung dizzily, and was hurled impetuously back again. The constable leaped backwards, late but alive, as the car swerved round him and surged away. They missed the boy by inches, and the lamp standard on the other side by the thickness of the old car's well-maintained paint. Bunty uttered a cry, and clawed her way round to kneel on the seat and look back through the rear window; the young policeman was just getting up from the ground, and the police car that had been standing by, not expecting any trouble, was charging off the mark after them, too late to hold them in sight for long, unless it could better the crazy seventy-five they were exceeding through the sleeping town.

She slid down into her seat weakly, and lay limp beside her enemy. His eyes were dividing their attention now about equally between the road ahead and his rear-view mirror. He didn't ask her anything; she might not have been there. He was nothing but a machine for driving, and what a machine, precise, confident, daemonic. Well, they knew now what they had to contend with. That attempted murder was notice enough. It was more than a case of dangerous driving and jumping the lights now. This pursuit would be serious. To be honest, she was more sure that they would chase him to the ends of the earth for trying to kill a police constable than for murdering an anonymous girl.

As for her, she had lost her chance. Unless that pursuing car, just about holding its distance, managed to stop them short of the motorway, she was as good as dead.

But between them – shouldn't he share the credit? – they had ensured that the hunt should be up in full cry after them.

He shook off the police car in the country roads between Hawkworth and the M.6. No doubt of it now, he was a local man, or at least he'd lived here long enough to know these roads like the palm of his hand, better than the police driver knew them. They hit the motorway at the quietest entrance, well away from the town, and after that he took the fast lane and drove like an inspired devil. Who was there to enforce the limit? It was an unreal limit, in any case, on a clear, starlit night with visibility equal almost to that in daylight, and little traffic on the road. And whatever this man might or might not be, he was a driver of exceptional gifts. They would take some catching now.

The marvellous road unrolled, broad, generous, splendidly surfaced, unwinding before them in a hypnotic rhythm. Service areas sprang up beside them in a galaxy of lights, and passed, committing them again to the dark. Her tired eyes began to dazzle, and then to ache inconsolably. She closed them, and instantly could see more clearly. The ride was so calm that with closed eyes it was possible to rest, and think, and even understand.

Almost certainly, she was going to die. It was essential to grasp that, and to come to terms with it. She must not expect anything better. If better was to be had, somehow she would fight her way to it; if not, she had to deal with what was possible. Inordinately clearly she saw what was happening to her, and it was no longer a dream, and no longer fantastic.

After all, this sort of thing happens to other women, too, in slightly different circumstances, but to the same ultimate effect. Doctors tell them suddenly, after what should have been a routine examination, that they have been carrying malignant growths round with them unknown, perhaps for months, perhaps for years. Symptoms come late in the day. Or, worse, the doctors don't tell them, but subscribe to the convention that cancer is unmentionable, and coax them into hospital with soothing pretences that minor treatment is necessary, and only slowly, with infinite anguish, do the victims penetrate to the knowledge that they have been carrying the balance of life and death within them, with all the betting on death. A mistake, to make death the enemy. Death is the ultimate destination of every one of us, and what's beyond remains to be seen. But fear, doubt, delusion are the real enemies. If you know, you have at least the chance to effect a reconciliation.

She had that chance. If he had killed her at once it might have seemed to be a mercy, but now she knew that it would have been nothing of the kind. There was always the last moment of realisation, the horror of knowing too late, without time to come to terms, without one instant to muster the last dignity. It is not death which is the violation, it is fear.

It was there within her eyelids, death, within touch of her hand, smiling at her. Already it was becoming better-known, almost familiar. It was waiting for everyone, somewhere along the line, often when least expected. What's the use of claiming immunity? Of yelling at fate: Why *me*? In effect, why not me? Those who go out innocently to do their regular shopping, and inadvertently step under buses, seemed to her, strangely enough, infinitely more to be pitied.

They were off the motorway, unchallenged, and striking north still for Kendal, Penrith and Carlisle. She knew this road, she had travelled it before, and could recognise landmarks, even in the dark. There had been a long, hallucinatory interlude of half-sleep, drugged with speed and darkness and isolation. Nothing could happen to her, as long as he drove. No succour could relieve her, as long as he drove.

It was somewhere between Penrith and Carlisle that she spoke to him, softly and reasonably as to a backward and capricious child. Her own senses were dazzled with this rush through the night, she heard her voice as a stranger's, a calm, rational stranger's, arguing with unreason.

'Murder isn't a capital crime any more, you know that? They don't hang you now.'

He didn't say anything, he merely drove like a machine; she might as well not have been there.

'What you've done may not even be considered murder. If there was great provocation on her part, and loss of control on yours, they might reduce the charge. You think you're forced to kill again, now that I know, but that's an illusion. Your life isn't threatened.'

He took no notice at all. Everything in him, every sense, every force, was concentrated on just one purpose, to get to wherever it was he was going, and get rid of his burden. He heard her, though, she was sure of that; he knew exactly what she was saying. He had nothing to say in reply because nothing she had said made any difference to his resolution. And she herself felt exasperatedly how futile it was to tell a young man he could keep his life and spare hers, at the cost of a mere fourteen years or so in prison! No, he wasn't interested in that prospect. He meant to get clear away, to escape undetected, and there was only one way he could hope to do that. She knew too much to be left alive. None the less, she went on trying. She had to. Acknowledging that you may have to die doesn't absolve you from putting up the devil of a fight for your life.

'And supposing they do catch up with you? They know which way you were heading, and they won't give up, you know that. There's a policeman involved now. Why make it worse for yourself if they do get you? You might get by with a plea of manslaughter for her – you won't for me!'

Her eyes had grown accustomed to the night by now, she could see clearly the outlines of the sharp profile beside her, and they remained as fixed as stone. It was like talking to a reanimated corpse that could function mechanically, but could never be reached by any human contact.

'It would be simpler to ditch me here. I don't know where you're going, I don't know who you are, I don't know anything about you. By the time I got to anyone, you could be miles away. And,' she said reasonably, 'you wouldn't have the delay and trouble of disposing of me. That might make all the difference between getting clean away and getting caught. Because you don't think I'm going to make it quick and easy for you, do you?'

Maybe she had been wrong in thinking he couldn't be reached, for the knuckles of the capable hands that lay so knowledgeably on the wheel had sharpened into pale points of tension, white as china, and his cheek-bone strained at the stretched silvery skin as if it would break through.

'And there's hardly room for two in the boot,' she said viciously.

'Shut up!' he gasped in a muted howl of pain and despair. 'Shut up, *damn you, shut up!*'

The last thing she remembered recognising was the smithy at Gretna, journey's-end for so many runaway couples pursued north by this road. The irony roused her to a faint spurt of laughter. She was so drugged and lightheaded with exhaustion by then that nothing was quite real. Even fear could not keep her awake any longer. Uneasily, stiffly, she slept against her enemy's shoulder.

She awoke with a violent start, flung forward against the dashboard, fending herself off feverishly with her hands, still half-dazed and jangled between truth and illusion. He had braked violently, and for the moment that was the only reality she could grasp. Then it was like a curious dance, the car swinging first left and then right in a frustrated measure, like a man in a hurry trying to get past a slower walker on a narrow pavement. She heard the man beside her swearing furiously through his teeth as he wove this way and that. And then she saw the hare, bounding along in front of them in the middle of the road, as hares will, frantic with fear but still trusting in his speed to get him out of trouble. The car, driven with patience and precision, tried to edge him aside into the hedge-bank, and always he resisted the suggestion and raced straight ahead.

'Go on, curse you, get *out* of it!'

She looked at the light and the land outside the windows of her moving prison, and saw that it was almost morning, the air grey and still before dawn, and they were on an upland road between rolling wastes of heath, with the shadowy shapes of hills beyond, like gauzy folds of sky. If he slowed much more, she might almost dare to claw open the door and run. . . . He had pocketed the gun long ago, on the side away from her, and his eyes were on the stupid creature that loped ahead of him, he would be slow to react at this moment. But run where? There were no houses here, and little cover.

And it was too late now in any case. He had dropped back and ambled to give the hare a long enough start to feel safe, to forget the impulse to flight, and return to the heather. And there went the long ears and lolloping hind-quarters, off into the bracken under the low hedge, and out of sight. The car shot forward again in a smooth acceleration, and sailed past the spot where the creature had vanished. The needle of the speedometer crept back energetically to seventy. Since the moment when they had driven at the policeman on the edge of Hawkworth, only that hare had kept them for a few minutes within the legal speed limit.

She had no idea where they were, or how long they had now been on the road. In the chill of the dawn her sense of fear seemed to have reached a dead level where her predicament was at once disbelieved-in and accepted. She was finding out a great deal about the human mind under stress, the odd detachment and accuracy of observation of which it is capable even in terror, and the rapidity with which terror itself can became familiar, and cease to impress. You even reach, she thought, the point of contemplating without panic that there really may not be any way out; and you reach it unbelievably quickly.

The car swung sharply to the right, hardly slowing for the turn, and entered a narrow, winding, sunken lane. The air had a cold tang that made Bunty's nostrils quiver, and the trees along the ridge on their right all leaned towards them in a way there was no mistaking. Somewhere just out of sight before them lay the sea.

The miniature valley, trees leaning over it on either side on the sheltered slopes, opened in a few minutes into a broad circle of gravel before a small cottage, pink-washed over walls of stone below and brick above, with a low-pitched, overhanging roof. It had a bright, polished, cared-for look which meant that someone with money and leisure had taken it over. There was a brand-new garage to the left, tucked under the slope of grass and trees, there were modern windows, obviously installed since the take-over, and decorative shrubs had been deployed artfully among the grass to make the most manageable of gardens. Someone's pleasure place, there's no mistaking the signs. And this man knew his way about here; she recognised it from the manner in which he had taken the sharp bend into the lane, and she saw it again in the dexterity with which he swept the car round and stopped it right in front of the cottage, in such a way that on her side there was just room to open the door, and she would be stepping out practically into the porch.

The moment the engine stopped he had the gun in his hand again, ready, and in one swing he was out of the car.

'Get out. And don't try to run, you wouldn't get far.'

As she straightened up stiffly after the long ride, the round black eye of the gun stared at her steadily across the roof of the car. She didn't try to run. Against the ten yards of pale wall on either side she would have been an easy mark. He came round to join her at his leisure, and taking her by the arm, put her before him into the porch, where his own bulk securely hemmed her in. He reached above him under the low roof, and swung aside a corner of the wooden beading. The key had its regular hiding-place, and he was in the secret.

'Go in, please.'

The growing daylight showed her a tiny hall in spectral pastel colours, a staircase on one side, two white doors on the other, the minimum of holiday-cottage furniture, but of an elegant kind. The outer door closed behind them with a solid, final sound, and they were shut in together. She heard the key turned again in the lock, and watched him withdraw it and pocket it. And now at last he was no longer occupied with driving; his hands were free.

'Upstairs! You'll find the bathroom on the left. I'm sorry there'll be only cold water until I see to the main switch. Take your time.'

It was fantastic. The automatic politeness of his upbringing still clung to him, glaringly odd in this relationship. He might have been apologising to a guest for the lack of amenities, except that his voice was too dull and drained of feeling to match the words. She looked back from the door of the bathroom, and saw that he had seated himself on the stairs below, and had the gun ready in his hand still. No chances were going to be offered to her, no chances of any kind.

The back view of him was strangely desolate, the head drooping with its lank black hair dishevelled, the shoulders sagging. If she was sick with weariness, what must his exhaustion be? In the end there might be the chance he could not deny her; even he must succumb to sleep sooner or later.

She shot the bolt of the bathroom door after her, and groped for the cord of the light-switch, but nothing happened. Of course, the main switch was off, somewhere down there in the back premises, and there'd be no lights until he turned it on. The window was small, and the light from outside seemed to have dwindled almost into night again, now that she saw it from withindoors. It was barely half-past five, after all that nightmare journey.

The cold water was bracing and welcome, and simply to be alone there, with a door and a bolt dividing her from him, was in itself a new lease of life. Evidently this place was used frequently and always kept ready for occupation, for there was soap on the wash-basin, and towels in the small white cupboard. Neat, small guest tablets of soap that fitted admirably into the palm. She considered for a moment, and then rolled the one she had used in her handkerchief, and slipped it into her handbag. There was nothing else she could see that might be useful to her; she took her time, as he had suggested, about looking round for a weapon to use against him. She had hoped there might be a razor, at least of the safety variety, in the cabinet, and therefore blades; but of course, the owner used an electric, there was the socket for it beside the mirror. Nothing there for her. The bolt on the door was a fragile thing, if she refused to come out it wouldn't preserve her for long. There remained that window, discouragingly small and high though it was.

She carried the stool over to it, climbed up, snapped back the latch and hoisted the sash. Empty air surged away before her face. Craning over the sill to look down, she saw that on the rear side of the house the ground fell away sharply in a tumble of stones, almost a cliff, and instead of being one modest storey from safe ground, she found herself peering down fifty feet of broken rock. No hope of climbing out from there.

So in the end she would have to open the door again, and go back to him. She did it very softly and cautiously, easing back the bolt without a sound, for she had left him sitting on the stairs a long time, and sleep might have caught up with him while he waited. But the moment she set foot on the landing he was on his feet, too, and turning to mount the remaining steps of the flight.

'Into the next room, please.' He reached past her to open the middle door of the three. 'Yes,' he said, following the rapid glance she gave to the curving latch and the key-hole below it, 'there's a lock. I can't afford any slips now, can I? You didn't leave me much choice.'

Just over the threshold of the little bedroom, primrose and white, a charming place to house a guest, Bunty halted. With her back turned to him she said softly and deliberately:

'Do you know why I opened the boot?'

She didn't look round, but she felt, almost she scented the effusion of his desolation, bewilderment and despair, and the ache of his amputation from the harmless creature he must once have been.

The dull voice behind her said, dragging with weariness:

'What difference does it make?'

'I was looking for a rug,' she said, 'to put over you.'

There was one instant of absolute silence, then the door closed as abruptly as a cry, and she heard the key turned hastily, clumsily in the lock. For a long minute she caught the deep, harsh, strained accent of his breathing, close there against the door, so that almost she could see his damp forehead pressed against the cold white panelling, and the veined eyelids heavy as marble over the burned-out grey eyes. Only slowly and with infinite effort did he drag himself away; she heard his steps slur along the carpeted landing, and stumble down the stairs.

Chapter 4

The first thing she did was to cross to the window and hoist the sash, to have a second look at the lie of the land seawards. The bedroom looked out, like the bathroom, to the rear of the house, but not directly towards the water. To the left lay the outline of the coast above the cliffs, undulating between tree-lined hollows and blanched grassy brows, but beneath the walls of the cottage the land crumbled away towards the sea. By craning out to extend her view to the right she could see the cliffs broken by a small, tight inlet, where the tide came in to a tiny jetty and a boat-house. Many a small house like this must have been snapped up by boating enthusiasts as desirable weekend accommodation, all round the Scottish coast. Did it belong to this man's family? Surely to someone who knew him well, or he wouldn't have been admitted to all its secrets. There seemed to be a rocky path leading down from the house to the inlet, but only here and there could she glimpse a level, slated spot that formed a part of it.

The drop from the window she abandoned as impossible. Even if she had had sheets enough to knot into a rope, and confidence enough in the finished article to trust herself to it – after all, what had she to lose? – she didn't believe she could climb round the corner of the house to level ground. Forget that, and consider the contents of the room.

She was closing the window again when she heard the car below start up, and gently roll the few yards into the garage, and in a moment the double doors closed hollowly over it. Naturally he wouldn't risk leaving that where it could be seen, and draw attention to itself and him.

Well, if she couldn't get out of here, could she keep him from getting in? The trouble with modernised holiday cottages is that everything tends to be either light-weight or built-in. Wardrobe and dressing-table here were neatly contrived with white-wood shelving built on to the wall, there was nothing of any solidity that was movable, not even the bed. A child could have shoved that across the floor on its admirable and infuriating ball castors. There were no bolts inside the door to supplement the lock, and she couldn't barricade herself in.

There remained only the lock itself, new and presumably efficient, but surely also a light-weight, a token seal on privacy. She emptied the contents of her handbag on the bed, and fingered them over for anything that might provide a tool or a weapon. The obvious lock-picker was her nailfile, a giant from the lavish manicure case George had once given her, long and strong and with a formidable point. She had another use for that, however. It was the only thing she had that even suggested a weapon, all it lacked was a comfortable handle that would give her more control and force in using it, and she supplied that by embedding the unpointed end firmly in the cake of soap she had stolen from the bathroom. It wasn't much as defence against a gun, but if she got a chance she intended to forestall that direct confrontation. If she had had this in her hand half an hour ago, when he had sat there in broken exhaustion on the stairs, with his back turned to her . . .

So this, she thought, pushing back the tangled hair from her forehead, this is how killers are made. No, I can't! Not unless . . . not until . . . All the same, she fingered the point of the file, and remembering that there were bricks outside the window, went and flung up the sash again, and began carefully whetting the

258

improvised dagger, first one end, then the other, watching the scored surfaces grow bright.

The light was growing brighter, too. She was facing to the right, towards the sea, and the layer of mist that floated above the water thinned before her face into diaphanous wisps, and dissolved in light. She looked down towards the inlet, her eyes drawn by a tiny point of colour and movement. Out of the boat-house a graceful blond shape slipped demurely, all pale, smooth woodwork and gleaming brass and bright blue paint, stealing along like a cat to rub itself delicately against the jetty. Of course, how lucky for him that he knew somebody with a secluded cottage on the coast, and a boat that could make it, in the right hands, over to the Low Countries. Somewhere at any rate, on the way to a much more distant place where a man could vanish.

He was there in the boat, she saw the thin dark figure step ashore and make the boat fast. He was bringing something in his arms from the foot of the path. What it was she could not see at first, though she saw him stoop to hoist it, and could easily recognise that it was heavy, and filled his arms. Only when he stowed it aft, and went to drag up a tarpaulin cover over it, did she realise how simple and significant a thing it was. A large, jagged stone. That was all.

She stood at the window, the file arrested in her hand. Of course, that was one of the simpler essentials. He would need a weight.

No, she corrected herself, two weights. And here he came with the second one, placing it carefully, to avoid disturbing the trim of the boat. There would be two bodies, a double burial at sea. No use hiding the first without at the same time disposing of the second, and rendering it silent for ever.

She was looking on at the final preparations for her own death and burial.

She was probing desperately at the lock with a straightened hair-grip, two of her nails broken and a fingertip bleeding and raw, when she heard her enemy enter the house and begin to climb the stairs. The key turned in the lock; the door opened.

'Come down, when you're ready.'

His voice was level and dull. His eyes, though they did not avoid her, hardly seemed to see her, but she had no doubt that they would give him notice sharply enough if she made a false move. Nor could she see the gun, but it must be ready in his pocket in case of need. The dimness on the landing sheltered him a little, turned him into a mere lay figure, a cardboard cut-out in shades of grey. She picked up her handbag from the bed, walked steadily past him to the bathroom, and bolted the door; and after a moment she heard him go slowly down the stairs, step by heavy step like a lame man.

All the time that she was in there, making up her face with almost superstitious care to get everything right, and with a flat, dream-like sense of saying good-bye, she could feel his eyes down below, never swerving from the staircase, penning her in. When she had done her extended best for her appearance she would have to go down and face him. You can't just crouch in a corner and close your eyes, and wait for a miracle. She made sure that her make-shift dagger was disposed at the right angle at the top of the jumbled possessions in her bag, with a fold of her handkerchief covering it. If you have to go down, you go down fighting.

Sunday morning breakfast she thought numbly, on a brief weekend jaunt before the winter sets in! Where was I yesterday? Safe at home in all that autumnal oppression, with nothing to do but wait for everything to be all right again. If it had been a clear, sunny morning like this, nothing need ever have happened, all those cobwebs would have melted from me like mist. She counted the years now, and they were nothing, a triviality, dropped petals, with illimitable wealth still to fall. She took her sights from the past resolutely, and set them on the shrunken future.

With a step as slow and drugged as his, she went down the

stairs; and he was there, as she had known he would be, waiting for her. He held open the second white door in the hall. The living-room of this spectacular little house would obviously be designed to overlook the sea. A remnant of curiosity remained to her. She looked round the room with remote, unreal interest. There was a picture window, with the dawn sun framed in it in impossible beauty, for they were looking almost due east. There was a narrow white door beside it, no doubt leading into a tiny, built-in kitchenette. Everything was white wicker and orange corded silk, bright, inexpensive and gay, cushioned chairs, a light settee, a small dining-table with an orange-coloured cloth.

Her sense of unreality grew extreme. There must be a store of non-perishable and tinned foods left in the cottage. He had made tea, and produced tinned ham, cheese and crispbread. For himself, no doubt, and he must have needed it, but he had laid two places. Either he was gone beyond the boundary of reason, or the cottage exerted on him the compulsions to which he was accustomed within its walls, and the first of them was hospitality, even to his victim.

She lost touch with her own destiny then, the unreality of that room was too much for her. She knew the facts, she knew what they predicted, but she could no longer behave in accordance with what she knew. Beyond a certain point you abandon carefulness, because it is so patently of no more use, and silence, because it makes no difference any more, and because caprice may by some freakish chance hit the jackpot you'll never get by taking aim. She began to range the room, paying no attention to him, examining everything that bore witness to the absent owners. And there on the small white bookcase, stocked with Penguins and other paperbacks for their guests, was their double photograph, a studio portrait of man and wife in their comfortable fifties, he in white open-necked shirt and silk scarf, with a round, amiable face and receding hair, she in the ageless Paisley silk shift, with a modish new shingle and a good-humoured middle-aged smile.

'Your parents?' she asked with deliberate malice; for she was quite sure that they were not his parents.

'Friends,' said the heavy voice behind her. 'Louise is my godmother,' he added, with shattering calm.

'Ah, so that's why you're so at home here,' she said. 'What's their name?'

'Alport. Reggie and Louise Alport.' Why care enough now to make secrets of these details? He answered her because it would have taken more energy and effort to keep silence than to speak. 'If you want some tea,' he said remotely, 'help yourself.'

She turned to look at him then, and even came to the table and sat down, suddenly aware how desperately she wanted some tea. The suggestion of the laid table was too strong to be resisted, even though all this was a pointless interlude on the way to something else, something final.

'Do they live in Comerbourne, too?'

'No, in Hereford.' A dreary and desperate wonder sat upon him; and now that she saw him in the full light from the eastern window he was pale and insubstantial as paper, perished paper, so brittle that it might crumble to dust at any moment. 'That's where my family come from.'

'Then you work in Comerbourne.' She could not have explained why it was so important to keep talking, to keep drinking tea, and swallowing mouthfuls of sawdust food that stuck in her throat; to maintain, not a pretence, but a hypnotic suggestion, that everything here was normal, and had to be preserved, so that scoring through its normality with an act of violence should be increasingly difficult. Nor could she have said why a grain of information added to her knowledge of him should seem to add to her meagre resources. The nail-file was surely a better bet. Yet she persisted. Of course, who else enjoys even one October weekend lasting until Wednesday morning? It was the half-term break; she ought to have known. 'You teach,' she said, feeling her way, 'at one of the schools in Comerbourne.'

'I did,' he said distantly.

'What did you teach?'

'Art . . . if it matters now.'

I wonder, she thought, feeling the shuddering undertones beneath these exchanges, whether he knows what I'm thinking as clearly as I know what's going on inside him? Kill me here and now, and he'll have the trouble of carrying or dragging me down to the boat, and the risk of being seen at it. Make me walk there to be killed on board, and he takes the chance that I may try breaking away, even at the last moment. Why not, with nothing to lose? The whole thing *could* go wrong then, even if it's an outside chance. I *might* survive to talk. No, he'll want to make sure. It will be here!

He's just made up his mind!

'How odd,' she said, her eyes holding his across the table, her right hand in the open handbag on her lap, 'to think that I don't even know your name.'

'Why should you?' he said. And suddenly he set both hands against the edge of the table, and pushed back his chair. His face was more dead than alive, blue-stained at lips and eyes, cemetery clay, but he moved with method and certainty, like a machine.

'Yes, what are you waiting for?' she blazed abruptly, on her feet with the nail-file in her hand. Her handbag went one way, her handkerchief another. 'Do you think I don't know you've got everything ready? Even the stone for my feet?'

He got up slowly and started round the corner of the table after her, hooking a hand under the edge to hoist it aside from between them. She caught the brief reflection of light from eyes opaque and dead as grey glass.

'I'm sorry!' said the distant voice, from somewhere far beyond sorrow. 'What can I do? You shouldn't have looked in there. What choice have you left me? I *liked* you,' he said, wrenching at his own unavailing pain, 'you were *kind* to me! But what can I do about it now?'

'You could let me walk to my grave,' she said, backing from

263

him inch by inch, 'and save yourself trouble.' Anything to spin out five more minutes, three, even one, to give time one more chance. And still, at this extremity, she had a corner of her mind free to wonder where the gun was, why it wasn't in his hand. He couldn't be afraid of the shot being heard, not here, there was no other dwelling in sight. If he'd had the sense to use the gun he needn't even have come within her reach, she would have had no chance at all.

His hand swung the table round, shedding the teapot from its tilted edge, and drove it hard against the wicker armchair beside the wall. She dared not turn her head to look, but her hip rammed hard into the arm of the chair, and she could retreat no farther.

'Not you,' she heard his voice saying hopelessly, 'you'd run, you'd swim for it, *I know you*. Why did it have to be *you*?'

Bracing her fingers round the hilt of her dagger, she had just time to feel one angry stab of amusement, involuntary and painful, at his appropriation of what should surely have been her question. And then the moment and he were on her together.

He took the last yard in one fast, light step, and reached for her with long hands crooked; and she stooped under his grasp instead of leaning back from him, and slashed upwards at his throat with all her weight, uncoiling towards him like a spring. She felt the impact, and sudden heat licked her fingers, but in the same instant he had her by the wrist, and had wrenched hand and weapon away from his grazed neck, forcing her arm back until her grip relaxed. Distantly, through the roaring in her ears, she heard the nail-file tinkle on the wood blocks of the floor, a light, derisory sound. Then his groping hands found their hold on her throat, and chaotic eruption of light and darkness blinded her eyes.

She put up her hands and clawed at her murderer's face, until the pressure on her throat grew to an irresistible terror, and then an agony, and she could only fight feebly to drag his hands away. Her eyes burned, quite darkened now, there was nothing left in existence but a panic struggle for breath. A sound like sobbing thudded in her ears, the great breaths she could no longer drag into her lungs seemed to pulse through her failing flesh from some other source. Someone else was dying with her, she heard him in extremity, moaning and whining with pain, and long after she had no voice left to complain with, that lamentable sound followed her down into darkness and silence.

Consciousness began again in an explosion of fiery pain; the red-hot band of steel round her neck expanded, burst, disintegrated. She was dead, she must be dead. Or why the delirious cool rush of air into her body again at will, the abrupt withdrawal of pressure and fear, the sudden wild awareness of relief and ease? Nothing was holding her any more, nothing confined her, her own limp hands wandered freely to touch her bruised throat. Her knees gave way under her slowly, she slid down against the arm of the wicker chair, and collapsed into the cushions like a disjointed doll, and lay gulping in air greedily, tasting it as never before, experiencing it as a sensuous delight. The darkness lifted slowly. She opened her eyes, and colours and shapes danced dazzlingly before them. She saw sunlight reflected on the ceiling, and a shimmer that was the refractions of broken light from the motion of the sea.

Her eyes and her mind cleared together, into an unbelievable, unprecedented clarity. She lay still for a long moment, seeing the outlines of things round her with a brilliant intensity that was painful to her eyes after the darkness. The same room, the same signs of struggle, the fallen handbag on the floor, the broken tea-pot, the tablecloth dragged into disorderly folds. She was alive, she was intact. Not because of any miraculous intervention, but for solid reasons, in pursuit of which her mind stalked in silence within her recovering body. The clarity within there was as blinding and sharp as the clarity without.

She sat up slowly, clinging to the edge of the table, and looked round for her murderer.

Head-down in a dark huddle on the wicker settee, he lay clutching the orange-coloured cushions to his face with frantic energy, fingers, wrists, forearms corded with strain, as if he willed never to show himself to the light again. He had withdrawn from her the full width of the room when he snatched his hands away. Shuddering convulsions shook through him from head to foot; a touch, and he would fly apart and bleed to death. He was bleeding now, she saw the oblique graze on his neck oozing crimson, and staining the orange silk. Who had come nearer to killing?

It was at that moment that the black dolphin knocker on the front door banged peremptorily three times on its curling cast-iron wave.

Chapter 5

The man huddled on the settee lay utterly still, the tremors
suppressed by force, his breath held. He did not raise his head;
he wanted never to raise it again. It was Bunty who dragged
herself up out of her chair and went into action. She could
move, she was in command of herself. And she knew what she
was doing, now. Hurriedly she stooped for her handbag, and ran
a comb through her hair. Would there be marks on her throat?
Not yet, probably, but she shook out her chiffon scarf and tucked
it in around her neck to make certain of being unremarkable.
There was blood on her fingers; she dipped her handkerchief
into the nearest liquid, which was the spilled tea on the table,
and wiped the stains away.

'Give me the key!'

Speech hardly hurt at all. She had time to realise, even in that
moment, how little she was damaged. He must have snatched his
hands away from her as soon as he felt her pain.

He lifted his head at the sharp sound of her voice, and turned
upon her a blind, mute face.

'The key, quickly! Give it to me!'

He sat up and felt through his pockets for it numbly, and held
it out to her without a word. From his last safe place at the end
of despair, where there is nothing left to lose or gain, he watched
her walk out of the room, leaving the door open behind her. He

heard the bolts of the front door drawn back, heard the key turned in the lock.

In those few yards Bunty lived through a total reassessment of everything that had happened to her. Her senses were abnormally acute, her mind moved with rapidity and certainty. She remembered things observed at the time without comprehension, and made sense of them. Her legs might be shaky under her, but mentally she was on her feet again.

She opened the door of the cottage with the accurately measured reserve of a woman alone, knocked up at an unusually early hour on a Sunday morning. Not too wide at first, ready to close it and slip the bolt again quickly if she didn't like the look of her visitor; then surprised and relieved, setting it wide and coming confidently into the doorway.

The two uniformed policemen on the step of the porch gazed back at her in silence for a moment, more surprised to see her than she was to see them.

'Good morning!' said Bunty, and waited with the polite, questioning curiosity of the innocent to hear what they wanted of her.

'Good morning, ma'am!' The elder of the two shoved up his flat cap civilly on the furze-bush of his pepper-and-salt hair, and eyed her with circumspection, plainly finding her of a reassuring respectability. 'Sorry if we startled you, but we saw a light in one of the windows here a while since, from up the coast road a piece, and knowing that the lady and gentleman who summer here have left, we wondered . . . You never know, just as well to check up, when a house is empty.'

'Oh, I *see*! Yes, of course, and how very good of you! Reggie and Louise will be so grateful,' said Bunty warmly, 'to know that you keep such a good watch on their place. I'm a friend of the Alports, they've lent me their cottage for a long weekend. I drove up last night.'

'Ah, that accounts for the light, then.' He seemed to be perfectly satisfied, and why shouldn't he, when she produced the owners' names so readily? An Englishwoman of forty, dressed in a smart and rather expensive grey jersey suit, must seem probable enough as an acquaintance of the Alports; indeed, it was unlikely that such a person would ever find her way to this spot unless directed by the owners. 'And you found everything in order here, ma'am? No signs of anyone prowling around in the night? No trouble at all?'

The younger policeman, tall and raw-boned, and surely a local boy, had drawn back out of the porch, and was using his eyes to good purpose without seeming to probe. The front window, through which he had already taken a sharp look, would show him only a room where everything must be as the Alports had left it. He was eyeing the hard gravel, too, but all it would tell him was that a car had arrived here, stood a little while before the door, and then been put sensibly away in the garage, which is exactly what one would expect the English lady to do with her car on arrival. Now he was turning his blue and innocent regard upon Bunty, and taking her in from head to foot, without apparent question of her genuineness, rather with a degree of critical pleasure on his own account.

'Trouble?' said Bunty, wide-eyed. Her smile faded into faint anxiety, nicely tempered with curiosity. 'No, nobody's been here. Everything was all right when I arrived. Why, is something wrong?'

'Och, nothing for you to worry about, ma'am,' said the sergeant comfortably. 'You're no' likely to be troubled here. Most like he's gone on northwards.'

'*He?*' she echoed. 'You mean there's somebody you're looking for? A *criminal?*'

'We've had warning to look out for a car, ma'am, a large old car, black, thought to be a Rover, registration NAQ 788. It's known to have driven north out of England during the night. Constable at Muirdrum believes he saw the same car go past about three hours ago, heading for Arbroath, but he's no' sure of the number. We're checking up and down all these roads, just in case. But there's no call for you to worry, ma'am, you'll be fine here.'

So no one, it seemed, was looking for her just yet. No one had mentioned that there'd been a woman aboard, most likely no one knew. Obviously they knew it hadn't been a woman driving.

'NAQ 788,' she repeated thoughtfully. 'A black Rover. I could get in touch with you if I do see anything of it, of course.'

'Ay, you could do that, ma'am. But I don't think you're likely to catch sight of him, I doubt he's as far north as he can get by now.'

'What do you want him for?' Bunty asked inquisitively. A woman without curiosity would be suspect anywhere. 'Has he run somebody down, or something?'

'Well, no' just that!' She hadn't expected a direct answer, and clearly she wasn't going to get one, but his business-like, unalarmed attitude told her most of what she needed to know. 'Constable somewhere down south had a narrow squeak, though,' he vouchsafed, after due consideration. And that was all she was going to get out of him; but it seemed that he had given a second thought to getting something out of her in exchange.

'We'll be on our way then. Sorry if we disturbed you. And by the way, maybe I should have your name and home address, ma'am, just for information.'

She hadn't been expecting that, but she was equal to it. Startled by her own readiness, she responded without hesitation: 'I'm Rosamund Chartley – that's *Mrs.* Chartley, of course . . .' The young one, if not the other, had long since assimilated the significance of her ring. 'And I live at 17 Hampton Close, Hereford.' She couldn't be sure how much he would know in advance about the Alports, but her use of their name had registered immediately, she might as well play for safety and assume that he knew their home town, too. She watched him write down her instant fiction, and smiled at him as he put his note-book away; not too encouragingly, on the contrary, with a slight intimation

that if that was all she could do for him she would like to go
back to her interrupted breakfast.

'Thank you, ma'am, we won't keep you any longer now.
And I'm sure ye needna be at all uneasy. Good morning, Mrs.
Chartley!'

He readjusted his cap on the grizzled heather he wore for
hair, summoned his subordinate with a flick of a finger, and they
departed. She closed the door, and leaned back against it for a
moment, listening. They had a car, they must have turned it on
the gravel and withdrawn it into the shelter of the trees before
knocking at the door. She heard it start up and wind away into
the convolutions of the lane. Only then did she re-bolt and
lock the door, and go back into the living-room.

The young man was sitting bolt upright on the settee, dark
against the brilliance and shimmer of the sea, every nerve at
stretch, his eyes fixed wildly on the empty doorway, waiting for
her to reappear there. The gun was in the clenched right hand
that lay on his knee, and his finger was crooked on the trigger.

She saw it instantly, and instantly understood. He must have
lowered his hand in sheer stupefaction when the meaning of that
astonishing performance of hers penetrated his mind, with his
death only the tightening of a nerve away.

Oh, God, she thought, suppose he hadn't waited to hear?
Why didn't I take it from him before I went to the door? But
there'd been no time to consider everything. And thank God,
he *had* waited, and confusion and bewilderment had kept him
from dying. Or curiosity, perhaps, curiosity can be a valid reason
for going on living, when no other is left.

So the first thing she had to do, without delay but without
any hasty gesture that could startle him back into despair, was
to cross the room to him, and gently take the thing out of his
hand. He didn't resist; his cramped fingers opened at her touch,
and gave it up without protest. Enormous eyes, cloudy with
wonder, devoured her face and had no attention for anything
else.

'*Why?*' he asked, in a rustling whisper.

'You won't need it now,' she said. But she knew that was not what he meant.

'Why didn't you bring them in and give me up? *Why didn't you tell them I tried to kill you?*'

Without a word in answer, she opened a drawer of the little writing-desk on the other side of the room, and thrust the gun far back out of sight. Then she came back to the settee and sat down beside him.

'Look,' she said urgently, 'you and I have got to talk. We've got a little time now, and the car's safest where it is. They won't come looking for it here now – not yet!'

'But *why did you send them away?*'

'Never mind that. There are things I've got to know, and we may not have all that long. That girl in the car – *who is she?*'

'Her name's Pippa Gallier,' he said, with the docility of despair, shock and hopeless bewilderment, but with some positive motion of faith, too, as though she had surprised him into drawing back the first of the bolts that sealed his terrible solitude from the world. 'We were going to be married. *I thought* we were . . .'

'She's a Comerbourne girl? That *is* where you teach, isn't it? What was she? What did she do?'

'She worked at the big fashion shop, Pope Halsey's, and did a bit of modelling for them when they had dress shows. She was an assistant buyer. She wasn't a Comerbourne girl, though, her family belong to Birmingham. She had a little flat over one of the shops in Queen Street. Why?' he asked dully, but at least there was a grain of life in his voice now, and in his eyes, that never wavered from searching her face. He had some kind of stunned trust in her now that told him she must have a reason for probing these irremediable things. Nothing she did was wanton; it didn't follow that she could change anything.

'And how did she come to die?'

272

'I shot her,' he said, staring through her and seeing the girl's dead face.

'All right, you shot her! But that's not what I want. I want to know how it happened, every detail, everything you remember. Tell me about it.'

He drew breath as if the effort cost him infinite labour, and told her, fumbling out the sequence of events with many pauses. He was terribly tired, and completely lost, but he was still coherent.

'I wanted to marry her. We were running about together steadily, until about a couple of months ago, and we were as good as engaged. And then she got very off-hand with me, for some reason, and started pulling away. She turned down dates, or she rang up to make excuses, and if I objected she flared up and walked out. They'd always tried to tell me she had other men on a string, too . . . I never believed it. I was daft about her . . .'

'They?' said Bunty, pouncing on this lack of definition. 'Who were *they*?'

'The chap who shares – shared – my cottage, Bill Reynolds, he teaches at the same school. Other friends of ours, too.'

'And some of them knew her well? Could they have been on her string themselves?'

'I don't know. I don't think so. They knew her, but not that well. I never believed it. And then just over a week ago it seemed as if we'd got past the bad patch. You know how it can be, everything straightens out and starts running on wheels. She was the sweetest I've ever known her, and things were back as they used to be. I bought her a ring. She'd never let me get that far before. I was *happy*! You know what I mean? I'd never believed there was anything wrong about her, but I'd never felt sure of her before, and now I did, she'd promised, and we were engaged. And then she suggested that we should go to London together this half-term . . .'

'To London?' said Bunty sharply. '*Not* up here, then?'

273

'No, to London. She had a few days of her holiday left to use, she suggested we should drive down on Friday evening. So when it came to Friday evening I was ready well ahead of the time we'd fixed, and I ran the car round into town, to her flat, to pick her up. It was a good half-hour earlier than she'd be expecting me. And I was just parking the car, a bit away from the house – you know what it's like trying to find anywhere to park in Comerbourne – when I saw her come out of the private door of her flat. Not alone, with a fellow I'd never seen before. And she was hanging on his arm and chattering away to him and looking up into his face, like . . . like a cut-price call-girl! You can't mistake it when you do see it.'

'Did they see you?' asked Bunty intently.

'No, I told you, I could only find a place farther along the street. No, they didn't see me . . .'

'And you didn't go after them? You didn't challenge them?'

'I never had time. I'd just got out of the car when they came out, and they turned the other way. He had a car parked there just in front of the shop, and they got into it and drove off in the other direction. By the time I was across the road they were turning the corner out of Queen Street.'

'What sort of car was it? Would you know it again?'

'I didn't get the number, I never thought of it, but it was a light-grey Jag. Does it matter?'

'It matters,' she said sharply. 'Every detail matters. What about the man?'

'I'd know him again,' he said bitterly. 'A big chap, well-dressed, over-dressed for Comerbourne, you don't see many dinner jackets around in Queen Street. But he made everything he had on look like slightly sporty wear, this type. You could imagine him rally-driving in a special one-off, instead of rolling round in a Jag. He had this he-man touch, and yet everything about him was smooth, his clothes, his movements . . . everything except his face. That had some pretty crude, craggy lines,

274

a knubby forehead, auburn hair growing low, cleft chin, eyes buried in a lot of bone. Yes, I'd know *him* again!'

'And she went with him willingly? You're sure?'

'Willingly? Gladly! You should have seen her!'

'And what did you do?'

'What could I do? They were gone, and I didn't know where. But it was pretty safe betting she wasn't going to be hurrying back within the next half-hour to meet me. I went back home, trying to kid myself there must be another answer, persuading myself there'd be a message for me. And there was! Bill was just rushing off for his own half-term, to his parents' place in Essex, when I got back. He told me there'd been a phone call for me from Pippa, he'd left me a note. She was terribly sorry, but she'd had to put off leaving for our jaunt until tomorrow evening. Her mother'd turned up unexpectedly, meaning to stay overnight, and she hadn't the heart to run out on her, and couldn't even tell her she'd had a trip planned, because Mother would be so upset at having spoiled it for her! So would I mind keeping away until tomorrow evening, and she'd come along and join me as soon as she'd seen her visitor off home! And it could all have been true,' he said bleakly, staring into the past with the sick fascination of one contemplating disasters about which nothing can now be done, 'if I hadn't known beforehand that her visitor wore a dinner jacket and stood about six feet three in his shoes. Because we'd only just got engaged, and her mother knew nothing about me yet, and we wouldn't have wanted to spring it on her in circumstances like that, without any preparation. It could all have been true, only I knew that there wasn't a word of truth in it.

'So I went out and got horribly drunk. Black, vicious, murderous drunk. I don't usually drink much, but I seem to have an abnormally high tolerance, it takes a lot to fill me up. But I wasn't too tight to walk round by her flat after the pubs closed, and I wasn't too far gone to know what I was seeing, either. The grey Jaguar was parked discreetly round the corner in the mews. Mother stayed the night, all right!'

'And this was Friday? But if she'd ditched you, and if you'd written her off as a dead loss, how did you come to tangle with her again on Saturday?' demanded Bunty.

'You forget, *she* didn't know I'd written her off. She thought she only had to drop me a message, and I'd swallow it whole and sit back until she wanted me again.'

'Of course,' she said, enlightened, 'she turned up on Saturday evening according to programme!'

'According to *her* programme. And if you'll believe me, that possibility had simply never occurred to me. I was so full up with what had happened, the thing was so completely finished for me, that I'd clean forgotten she didn't know I knew! She thought everything was serene, and she only had to stroll in at my place and say: Darling, here I am, all ready! and I'd run to fetch the car, and we could start. So that's what she did, around seven o'clock on Saturday evening, came rolling up in a taxi with her biggest suitcase, and started on another apology for Friday's hold-up as soon as she came in at the door. And I'd been howling like a dog all morning with the hangover of a lifetime, and topping it up again in self-defence most of the afternoon, and I was fit for murder.'

'You do realise,' said Bunty, frowning with concentration, 'that so far you haven't so much as mentioned that you owned a gun? Legally or illegally!'

'I didn't own a gun. Legally or illegally. I'd never had one in my hands, as far as I can remember. I know damn-all about the things. When I do mention it you're not going to believe me. I wouldn't believe myself.'

'I might, though,' said Bunty. 'All right, get to it your own way. She came breezing in, expecting to be taken to London. And you told her that she'd had it, that it was over, and she might as well go home.'

'What I told her was meaner than that, but let it go, it added up to much the same. I asked if her mother had slept well, and whether I could have the name of her tailor. She was always quick on the uptake, Pippa, not as clever as she thought she was, perhaps, but pretty sharp, all the same. She got it in a moment that I'd seen them, and she came up with a good story faster than you'd ever credit. That was her mother's cousin, that man with the Jaguar, it was because he'd turned up for a visit that her mother'd been able to make the trip, and that's why she had no warning. And she was all set to put me in the wrong and herself in the right, as usual, and *I* was the one who was supposed to apologise. Only this time it didn't work. Damn it, I'd *seen* them! I asked her whether they'd locked Mother in the flat while they went out to dinner, because I'd seen her just slipping her keys in her bag. You're a liar, I told her, and a cheat, and what else you are you know best, but as far as I'm concerned, I've done with you, you can go to London, or the devil, or wherever you please, *but not with me.* She couldn't believe it. I'd been so easy up to them, it took a little while to sink in. But as soon as she did manage to get it into her head that I meant it, things got even crazier than they already were. She started persuading, threatening, even fawning . . . you've no idea how fantastic a performance that was, from Pippa. You'd have thought getting to London that night was a matter of life and death to her. She'd expected the car to be waiting in the road for her, and instead, it was locked in the garage Bill and I rent – rented – down at Floods', at the end of the street. When she realised nothing was going to get her her own way any more, she suddenly dived her hand into her bag and pulled out a gun. *That* gun.'

He glanced across at the drawer where Bunty had hidden it, and then at her attentive face, and said wryly: 'I told you you wouldn't believe me.'

She gave him no reassurances, and made him no promises. Not yet. 'Go on,' she said.

'Well, I still can't believe in it myself. These things don't happen, not in connection with people like Pippa. Where would she get a gun? Why should she want one? And why, for God's sake, should she care enough about going to London with me to grab it out of her bag and point it at me, and tell me I'd better keep my promise to drive her down, or else! Why? It mattered to her just getting her own way, I know, but surely not *that* much? And she meant it, I know she did, now. But then . . .'

'Then,' said Bunty, 'you were too furious to be cautious.'

'Too drunk,' he said hardly. 'She waved this thing at me, and threatened, and as far as I was concerned that was the last straw. I *wanted* to kill her . . . or, at least, I was ready to. Oh, I know that, all right! When it happens to you, you know it. I just went for her. No holds barred. I got her by the wrist and we had a wild, untidy sort of struggle for the gun. About the rest I'm not sure. But I *know* I ripped it out of her hand. I *know* that. I know *I* was holding it when we both fell over together, and went down with a crash. I'm not sure what I hit. The edge of the table, I think. I hit something, all right, I've still got the hell of a headache and a bump like a hen's egg to prove it. All I know for certain is that I went out cold for a time. I don't know how long, exactly, but not long, not more than twenty or twenty-five minutes, I'd say. When I came round, I was lying over Pippa on the floor. And I still had the gun in my hand. And Pippa . . . she was dead. It took me a few minutes to understand that. I was shaking her, talking to her, telling her playing the fool wouldn't get her anything . . . Oh, my God! You wouldn't believe how little different she looked . . . not different at all. There was no blood, nothing to show for it, only that small hole in her sweater. She looked just as if she was pretending, to frighten me. And that would have been like her, too. But she didn't move, and she didn't breathe . . . and there was that hole, and just the ooze of blood round it, that her sweater absorbed. And in the end I knew she was dead, really dead, and I'd killed her. You,' he said abruptly, turning the full devastating stare of his haggard eyes on Bunty, 'you change things. But not even you can change that.'

She leaned forward and laid her hand possessively on his arm, holding him eye to eye with her. 'The shot . . . There's just one bullet-hole. Did you hear the shot?'

He thought that over with agonised care. 'Not that I can remember. I'd expect the moment when we fell to be the moment when the gun went off. When I fired it,' he corrected himself grimly. 'I told you, I meant murder. But I don't actually remember hearing the shot. All I know beyond doubt is that I came round, and she was dead.

'And I panicked. I can't blame the drink for that. I wasn't in very good shape when I came round, but I tell you, I was stone cold sober. I tidied up the room, and locked the house, and ran for the car. You can get it round to the back gate, and it's quite private there. I packed up girl and luggage and all in the boot, and picked up the spent cartridge case – it was there on the floor right beside her – and locked the place up again, as if we'd set off according to plan, and got out of there. It didn't take long, there was no mess, no blood . . . She was lying on her back, you see, and I reckon the bullet must be still in her, I couldn't find any exit wound. I threw the spent case in a field as soon as I was out of town. All I thought of was getting away. At first I didn't know where, I was driving round and round on the country roads in a state of shock, trying to think, and I had to have a drink to help me. I *had* to. And that was when I met you.'

He looked up, and for a moment studied her with wonder and care, forgetting himself. 'It's funny, how you've changed. You had the black dog on you then, too. It was because you were sad that I wanted to talk to you. I wish I'd left you alone. I'm sorry!'

'What were you going to do?' asked Bunty.

'I thought of this place. I've been here several times with Reggie and Louise, and they gave me an open invitation to use it even after they'd packed it in for the year and gone home.

They're like that, they probably invited other people, too. That's why they leave a key. And I thought of Reggie's boat.'

'You were going to drop her overboard,' said Bunty, 'and head for Denmark, or somewhere . . .'

'Norway, actually. It must be possible to land unobserved somewhere on all that tremendous coastline, and I know my way around there a little. I've even got friends there . . . though I don't suppose,' he owned drearily, 'that I could have dragged them into this mess.'

'And I,' she said practically, almost cheerfully, 'was to go overboard, too, in mid-passage.'

He stared back at her mutely, out of the extremes of exhaustion, unable any longer to be ashamed or afraid. Even the tension which had held him upright was broken now, after the slow blood-letting of this confession. He was close to total collapse.

'Why didn't you take your chance when it came?' he asked in a thread of a voice. 'Why did you send the police away?'

She got up slowly, and moved away from him to pick up the shards of the teapot. 'I'd better get this mess cleaned up,' she said, momentarily side-tracked, and lost that thread again on the instant. The housewife was there, somewhere inside, but fighting against the odds. She straightened up with the fragments in her hands, and stood frowning down at them thoughtfully.

'I didn't need them,' she said, and turned to face the boy on the settee, whose eyes had never ceased their faithful study of her through the cloud of their guilt and sorrow and resignation.

'I'd only just realised it,' she said deliberately, 'but I knew I didn't need them. In the night I wasn't thinking or noticing very clearly, or I might have known before. Things are distorted as soon as you're afraid. Maybe I did know, subconsciously. I think I may have done. I had all the evidence, if I'd been able to recognise it. When you drove at that constable in Hawkworth . . . did he jump back first, or did you swerve first? I didn't work it out then, I know now. And what a lot of trouble you went to, to avoid running down a hare, even when *you* were on the run. No wonder you couldn't go through with it when it came to my turn.'

Half of that, she realised, was lost upon him. He was in no condition to follow her through such a maze; but he clung to his own question, and it bore a slightly different inflection now, tinted with the living wonder of genuine curiosity, and – was it possible? – hope!

'Why did you send them away? Why didn't you hand me over to them, and be safe?'

'Because,' said Bunty, now with something very like certainty, 'I *was* safe. Because I don't believe you are a murderer. I don't believe you ever killed anyone, *not even Pippa!*'

Chapter 6

For a long moment he stared up at her in absolute stupefaction, hardly able to grasp what she had said, and even when his battered mind had got hold of the words, the sense was too slippery and elusive to be mastered without a struggle. She saw his lips moving automatically over the incredible syllables, and understanding came in a late, disruptive agony, and set him shaking again.

'My God, I wish that was even possible,' he said, panting, 'but it's crazy. Look, there were only two characters in all this lousy scene, Pippa and me. Nobody else! Don't *you* start kidding me along at this stage. It's nice of you even to pretend to believe I might be human, after all I've done to you, but . . .'

'I'm not pretending,' she said strongly. 'That's what I do believe. Time's short, I can't spare any for kidding you along, and you can't spare any for having doubts about me, if we're going to make anything of this mess.'

'*Make* anything of it?' he echoed incredulously. 'For God's sake, what is there left to make, except restitution?'

'We could begin by making sense of what we know. *Know*, not assume.'

He clutched helplessly at his head, squeezed his thin grey cheeks hard between his hands, and shook himself till the lank dark hair flopped on his forehead; but when he opened his eyes again and stared up at her dizzily until her image cleared, she was still confronting him with the same fixed and resolute face.

'Don't!' he said piteously. 'Not unless you mean it! I was just coming to terms with what I am. If you start me hoping now it only means I've got to go through this hell twice over. I couldn't stand it! *What we know!* I know I was lying on top of her, and she was dead with a bullet in her, and I was clutching the gun. I know I got it out of her hand, I know I was holding it when we fell. I know I wanted to kill her . . .'

'You wanted to kill me,' said Bunty bluntly. 'What does that prove?'

'No,' he said passionately, 'I never *wanted* to kill *you*. I *meant* to . . .'

'Meant to or wanted to, I'm still here.'

'But there was no one else there, only the two of us . . .'

'*How do you know that? You were out for twenty minutes.*'

'You *do* mean it,' he said, staring, and quaked with his sudden devouring hope and fear. He dared not believe that there was anything in this intuition of hers, but it was an impossibility to doubt the genuineness of her conviction. He began to want his innocence with an agonising intensity.

'But if I didn't kill her, who did? Who else had my motive? Who else had a motive at all?'

'How can we know that, when we know next to nothing about her? If she was betraying you she could have been betraying others as well. And if it was a sound motive for you, so it was for them.'

'But how could any of them even know where she was? She came in a taxi. *I was there*, motive and all. The most I could squeeze out of it,' he said wretchedly, 'was that it might have been almost an accident, when it came to the point . . . that the gun might have gone off when we fell. Even that I couldn't make myself believe. So if that's what you're trying to prove . . .'

'No,' she said at once, 'not that. Because I think murder *was* done that evening. *But not by you.*'

'I wish to God,' he said, trembling, 'you could convince me.'

'Give me a chance to try. Let me look at that bump of yours, where you hit the table – if you did hit the table.'

He sat charmed into obedient stillness as she took his head in her hands and turned him a little to get the full light from the window on the place. She felt his lean cheeks, cold with his long weariness, flush into warmth and grow taut with awareness of her touch. His eyes, which he had closed at her approach, as a measure of his devoted docility, opened suddenly and looked up at her, moved and dazzled. For the first time she realised how young he was, surely three or four years short of thirty. She was looking at an over-wrought boy, who had delivered himself into her hands, now absolutely defenceless. And she had promised him a miracle! Miracles are not easy to deliver; she trembled with him as she thought of her responsibility.

'It's crazy,' he said, shivering. 'After all this, I don't even know what to call you.'

'Most people call me Bunty. Bend your head forward . . . that's it.'

The mark of the blow he had taken was there to be found without difficulty, a swollen, tender pear-shape, above and if anything slightly behind his right ear. The forward end of it was higher, and only there was the skin slightly broken in one spot. She parted the thick dark hair to examine the mark carefully.

'I'm not a doctor, or even a nurse. But unless you've got a table with padded edges, it certainly wasn't the table that did this. If you'd hit any sharp edge you'd have had a considerable cut.'

'There's an old wooden-framed chair with leather upholstery,' he said indistinctly from under the fall of tangled hair. 'It was close by the table, on my right. Not the overstuffed kind, you'd feel the wood underneath, all right, if you fell on it. It could have been the back of that.'

'It could . . . but you'd have had to fall sideways . . . or else to turn your head sharply as you fell. You've got a diagonal welt, like this . . .' She drew her fingers along it, and their course ended decidedly behind his ear. 'It looks to me much more the kind of mark you'd have if someone had come up behind you and hit you one nice, scientific tap to put you out for the count. And somebody who knew how to go about it, and had the right sort of tool for the job.' She smoothed back his hair over the tender place, and came round the arm of the couch to face him. 'Maybe a piece of lead piping inside a sock,' she said. She was smiling, faintly but positively. 'Or more likely the simplest thing of all, a rubber cosh.'

He fingered his bruise and gaped at her dazedly. 'But it's mad! If you're thinking of a common burglary, there wasn't a thing in the place worth a man's while. Nobody'd be bothered burgling a cottage belonging to the likes of Bill and me, why should they? They always seem to know where the right stuff is. And if you mean something less accidental . . . if you're thinking I might have some sort of connection with crooks . . . I swear I haven't. I've never had anything to do with anybody like that. Not out of virtue, or anything, they just never came my way.'

'You've got something there,' she agreed. 'The people who carry coshes are much the same sort of people who carry guns.' She added pointedly: 'Pippa had a gun. *You* hadn't any acquaintance among the pros., but how do you know *she* hadn't?'

After a long moment of hurried calculation, swinging hurtfully between his anxiety to grasp at this life-line and his terror of finding it gossamer, he asked very quietly, his eyes clinging desperately to her face: 'Bunty . . . do you really believe what you're saying? You wouldn't try to . . . soothe me, would you? Just out of kindness?'

'No,' she said sturdily, 'I wouldn't. I'm only saying what I mean.'

'Then . . . what *do* you think happened?'

'I think someone else walked into that room – and I'll back my judgment by betting you what you like that you had your

back to the door and Pippa was facing it – laid you out economi-
cally with a knock on the head, and then dealt with Pippa. For
some reason of his own, which we don't know. As evidence for
her having got involved in something in which she was out of her
depth, there's the gun. As you say, what would such a girl as
Pippa want with a gun? Where would she get one? It's the pros.
and the would-be pros. who carry them. So there was Pippa
dead, and you beautifully set up to take the blame. So beautifully
that you yourself believed you'd killed her. That's the lines on
which I'm thinking at this moment. But as yet we've hardly
begun.'

'Then in any case it looks as if I've cut my own throat, doesn't
it?' he said with a lopsided grin. 'I've run out and pointed the
finger at myself. What do I do now? Who's ever going to believe
I can possibly be innocent?'

'They might,' said Bunty. '*I* believe it.'

'Ah, *you!*'

She saw it in his eyes then, though she was too intent on the
matter in hand to pay much attention, that for him she had
become a creature immeasurably marvellous and unforeseen. But
he didn't expect to find more than one of her.

'Bunty, what am I to do now? Go to the police and give myself
up?'

'No,' said the law-abiding police wife without hesitation. 'Not
yet! I've burned my boats, too, remember? I bought a few hours
for consideration by lying to the police and sending them away.
I gave a false name. To them I'm an accessory after the fact.
What we do now is make use of the short time we've got in
hand. Before we go to the police, let's see exactly what we have
got, and have a go at making sense of it. The more evidence we
can hand to them, the better prospects we've got.'

'We?' he said softly, and one black eyebrow went up unexpectedly in sympathy with the corner of his mouth. A slightly
wry, slightly careworn smile, but nevertheless a smile, the first
she had seen on this haggard face.

'*We!*' she repeated with emphasis. 'And the very first thing *you* do is get a few hours' sleep . . . and a bath, if it'll help. You've had no sleep for two nights, and I haven't had much, and we're going to need our wits about us. I'll tidy up this mess, and then I'll snatch a sleep, too.'

'A bath!' His face brightened childishly. 'I never thought I should be looking forward to anything again!'

'Go and get it, then. You'll be more use when you've had a rest, and can think straight again.'

He rose and made for the door like a bidden child, dropping with sleep, but in the doorway he turned once again to look at her long and earnestly. His eyes had cleared into a pure, tired greyness, young and vulnerable and still heavy with trouble, but hesitant now on the edge of hope.

'Bunty . . .'

She was already gathering up the scattered dishes from the tea-stained cloth, and piling them on the tray. She looked up at him inquiringly across the table.

' . . . what's the Bunty short for?'

She smiled. 'Bernarda. But I don't tell everybody that. They took to calling me Bunny, and I wasn't having that, cuddly was the last thing I intended to be. So I twisted it into Bunty myself. At least that's got one sharp angle to it. What can I call you?'

'Luke. My name's Luke Tennant. *All* sharp angles. Bunty . . . Bernarda . . .' His voice touched the names with timid delicacy, like stepping-stones to what he wanted to say. '*I'm sorry!*' he blurted painfully. 'Did I . . . hurt you very much . . .?'

'No!' she said quickly. 'Hardly at all. It's all right!' She had scarcely noticed the stiffness and soreness of her throat, and touched the bruises now with surprise.

'I'm sorry! How could I? I must have been clean out of my mind . . .'

'Think nothing of it!' Bunty was beginning to experience a lightheadedness that could all too easily be mistaken for lightness of heart. She looked ruefully at the long scratch on his neck, on

287

which a few beads of dried blood stood darkly. 'I'm sorry I tried to kill you, too, for that matter. Neither of us was much good at it. Let's just say we both failed our practical, and call it quits!'

The turmoil of hope had finally overwhelmed and wrecked him. He rolled himself in the quilt on the Alports' bed, and drowned in the vast sea of sleep that had been waiting for his first unguarded moment. And Bunty, having restored order in the living-room, lay down on the cushions of the settee and tried to think. It was the first time she had had a moment for thinking since this fantastic affair began, and it was the last such moment she would have until this affair ended. At least she was sure now of herself and him. But who could be sure of the ending?

She had meant to go carefully over his story, to try to extract from his halting account some significant point which had meant nothing to him. But as soon as she closed her eyes George's thin, middle-aged, scrupulous face was there within her eyelids, and she could see nothing else. If she had wanted something of her own to do, as proof that she had been in the world in her own right, she had it now, and for her soul's sake she must succeed in it; and George was far away and knew nothing about it, and could not help her. Be careful what you pray for, she thought wryly, you may get it. And to the beloved face within her closed eyes she said: You concentrate on your own case, chum, this one's mine – whether I like it or not. I got myself into it, and now I've got to get two of us out of it. You know how it is, there's no other way home. So go away, like a good boy, and let me think.

But he wouldn't go away; and in a few moments she let go of her anxieties and embraced the thought of him instead, with a still and grateful passion, and the instant she let her mind lie at rest in him she fell asleep.

It was nearly noon when she awoke, the sun was high, the light harder, more than half the room now out of the direct sunlight. She got up stiffly, sticky with sleep, and the sense of time pressing fell upon her like fear. She washed and made up her face, and then went to explore the contents of the kitchen cupboard. A canned Sunday luncheon was something of which her family would have disapproved, but it was better than nothing. There were no potatoes, of course, but there was rice, and ham, and some exotic canned vegetables. And blessedly, there was coffee. The kitchen was tiny, built out to the extremity of the level ground, with a broom-cupboard and a store under the same roof. She opened the back door, and the shimmering reflected light from the sea flooded in; and beyond a tiny, flagged terrace, the slatey stairs began to plunge downhill towards the inlet and the jetty, and the moored boat below.

She knew then, busy in the sunlit kitchen with can-opener and pans, that the silence and the brightness were an illusion, and nothing was going to be easily salvaged, neither Luke Tennant's liberty nor her own peace of mind.

He came down the stairs with a brisk, self-conscious tread that told her plainly he meant to resume responsibility for his own fate. He was a new if slightly battered man, polished, shaven, combed into aggressive neatness; he was the lucky one in one respect, at least, he had his luggage with him on this trip. He had even changed his clothes, perhaps as a symbolical gesture of hope and renewal. The sleep he had had, too short and too drunkenly deep, had left him a little sick and unsteady, but very determined. His face was still pale, but the terrible tension was eased once and for all. He could even smile properly. He smiled when he opened the door of the living-room, and looked for Bunty, and found her. It was as if his eyes had been waiting with the smile in readiness, and she was the spark that set light to it.

'I hope you're hungry,' she said, rising. 'You've probably got to be, to eat this concoction I've knocked up. It was the best I could do. If you don't mind, I'll dish it up in the kitchen and bring it in on the plates.'

'Bunty, I've been . . .' His eyes took in the order she had restored to the room, the laid table, the signs of activity in the kitchen; he was side-tracked by sheer amazement, and then abashed by a devastating sense of his own uselessness by comparison. 'Good lord, you can't have slept at *all*!'

'Oh, yes, I did,' she called back from the kitchen. 'This is one of those five-minute meals. The only thing that isn't instant, I'm glad to say, is the coffee.' She appeared in the kitchen doorway with the piled plates in her hands, and closed the door behind her with one foot. 'Look out, these are hot!'

She had found Louise Alport's hostess apron, gaily printed crash linen with pockets shaped like tulips, and her nursery towelling oven gloves. The cottage had a fantasy quality, unreal, inexhaustible, and in such dreamlike experiences you take anything you can get, to balance the everything you have lost, your normal world. Also, perhaps, for a better reason, to dazzle your companion, and keep the machinery of his life ticking over until the normal world is recovered.

If, of course, it ever is recovered.

'Bunty, I've been thinking . . .'

'Good!' she said heartily. 'Maybe you can infect me. After lunch we've got a lot of hard thinking to do.'

'Not we,' he said gently. '*I*.'

She looked up sharply at that, eyeing him doubtfully across the table. He had regained his balance, at least; whether he yet believed seriously in his own innocence or not, he wasn't going to be shaken into induced behaviour again. No more doing his worst to act like a killer because he believed that he had reduced himself to that role, and had no right to any other.

'Bunty, I'm more grateful to you than I can ever tell you. But now I've got to go on with this by myself. It's my problem, not yours. I've let you do too much for me, and without you I should never have come to my senses. But now I *am* in my right mind, and I want you out of this mess, clean out of it. I want you home, untouched, as if you'd never known anything about me

290

and my sordid affairs. After lunch I'm going to drive you into Forfar, and put you on a train for Edinburgh, on the way home. I'd make it all the way to Edinburgh, and see you safe on the express, only I doubt if I could get the car that far without being picked up.'

'I doubt,' said Bunty, laying down her fork with careful quietness, 'whether you'll get it as far as Forfar, either.'

'I think I shall. I know these roads. And you know what they said . . . they're looking for a car that jumped a red light and scared a policeman out of a year's growth, but not for a murderer. So they'll be hunting me, all right, but they won't have turned out the whole force after me. I'll make it safely to Forfar with you. And I shall feel a little less guilty if I know you're clear away. I can't let you go on carrying my load for me.'

'Aren't you forgetting,' she said dryly, 'that they know I'm here? That I gave them a false name and address, which they may very well be checking up on at this moment? You think that young constable won't know me again?'

His eyes, devouring her with an unwavering stare of anxiety, compunction and reverence, said clearly that any man who had talked with her even for a moment would know her again among thousands. His voice, quietly reasonable, said only: 'What does that matter? He's never going to see you again. All they've got is a false name. They may find out that your Rosamund doesn't exist, but that still won't help them to find Bunty. By tomorrow you'll be home again, and nobody'll know where you've been, and nobody here will know who the woman was who answered the door to the police this morning.'

'It's impossible,' said Bunty firmly. 'In any case, I've got no money, not a penny.'

'*We* have,' he said, and smiled at her.

What surprised her most was the violence of the temptation that tugged at her mind and heart, to accept the offer and escape now, back into her old prosaic life, to close this secret interlude and lock the door on it for ever. She thought with an astonishing

surge of joy and longing of her unexciting household in Comerford, and the half of her life that was over seemed to her in
retrospect, and from this pinnacle of strangeness, full, satisfying
and utterly desirable. Luke was not talking of impossibilities at
all. By morning she could be home. No one would ever know
where she'd been in the interval. Probably no one need ever
know she had been away at all. *Not even George*!

The very mention, the very thought of George turned her in
her tracks, and brought everything into focus for her. Of course
she couldn't consider it. She had never seriously believed that
she could.

'And what,' she asked deliberately, 'are *you* proposing to do?'

'As soon as I've seen you safely out of here I'm going to tidy
up this place and leave it as nearly as possible the way we found
it. Maybe I shan't succeed, but at least I can try to keep the
Alports out of the deal. And then I'm going to take the car and
everything that's in it, and somehow get myself to a police station
without being picked up on the way. I can manage that much,
if I put my mind to it. And I'll tell them everything I know
about how Pippa got killed. Everything,' he said, his grey gaze
wide and steady on her face, 'except about you. And then it will
be up to them.'

And I will remember you for ever, the grey eyes said, but not
for her to hear; whether I ever see you again or not, and whatever
becomes of me.

The moment of silence between them was brief and hypnotic;
she couldn't let it go on, there were those urgent realities all the
while drumming in her brain, and she knew, and it was time he
knew, too, that she had no intention of going anywhere.

'Eat your lunch,' she said practically, 'it'll be even more revolt-
ing cold. You're wasting your time, in any case. I won't leave
you. We're in this together, and we stand or fall together. I'm
not going home to Comerbourne until I can take you with me,
a free man.'

In a sudden harsh gasp he burst out: 'I meant to kill you!' and shuddered at the memory.

'I know you did. I know you meant to, but you couldn't. There was never any possibility that you'd be able to do it, when it came to the point. And neither can I go away and leave you now. Maybe I *meant to*, for a moment, but I can't. We mean to do things, out of some misconception of what we are, but what we really are always goes its own way when it comes to the point.'

'I owe you everything I've got in the world now,' he said carefully, 'and everything I am, for whatever it's worth. You don't owe me anything, except a great deal of fear and pain.' But he didn't say that he wanted her to go; it wouldn't have been true.

'That isn't how I see it. You chose me for a companion in your extremity. But it happened to be my extremity, too, and I chose to accept your companionship for my own salvation. That's a bond, and I'm not going back on it. You didn't make it alone, I helped to make it. *We* made it,' she said, 'and now *we've* got to resolve it.' And abruptly she rose from the table, and marched away into the kitchen for the coffee.

When she came back, he was staring out of the window with his chin on his fist, his face turned away from her; and she would never know whether he abandoned argument because he knew it would not be effective, or because he was only too afraid that it might, and he didn't want to lose her. For what he said, after a long pause, was only:

'Then I'd better bring in her things from the car, and see if there's anything there that means anything, to begin with.'

'We should have a look at the gun, too,' Bunty agreed, relieved.

'I suppose,' he said, 'I ought to bring *her* in, too.' Bunty, watching his profile narrowly, noting its determined calm, and impersonality brittle as glass, saw sweat break in beads on his lip. 'In any case I shall have to, to get at her suitcase.'

She almost offered to help him, and realised in time that she must not. Where death was concerned she was stronger and better rehearsed than he was – hadn't she, in a sense, passed clean through a death of her own to this uncanny understanding of him? But there were now almost more ways of hurting and affronting him than there were of helping him, and most of them had to do with his wish to protect and spare her. She knew him now as well as she knew her own son, she was sensitive to everything that happened within him. It wouldn't cost her much to humour him. So she refrained from offering him the obvious comfort that would have shocked him deeply; for she had been on the point of reassuring him that by this time rigor mortis would most probably be passing, and he wouldn't have to struggle with a twisted marble girl.

He laid her down carefully on the bed, and turned back the folds of the blanket from her. She was limp and pliant in his hands. He settled her head on the pillow, and straightened her legs and arms, trying to remember whether there had been any expression of fear in her face, where now there was nothing but indifference, and sadly conscious that he would have been unable to see it for the fear in himself. The dead never look as if they are alive and sleeping, whatever people may say. They always look dead. There is an absolute quality about death.

So there she was, young and slender and lovely, the sum of three years of his life, and the focal point of everything he knew about suffering. And maybe he had killed her, but in his heart he felt an increasing conviction that he had not. If he could have been quite sure of his innocence he might have felt the last convulsion of love for her at this moment; but because he was not quite sure, all he dared feel was a terrible, aching pity at such cruel waste. He smoothed her long, fair hair on either side of her face, trying to make something orderly out of disorder.

Then he locked the door, and went down to bring in her suitcase and handbag from the car.

Chapter 7

The gun lay between them on the table, a tiny, compact shape of bluish steel, hardly more than four inches long, to the outward view of so simple and innocent a construction that it looked more like a theatrical property or a toy than a machine for killing. It had a tiny cameo head engraved on the side of the grip, and the lettering along the barrel clearly announced its name and status:

LILIPUT KAL. 6.35
Modell 1925.

'I suppose there's no point in handling it carefully,' said Bunty, eyeing it dubiously. 'We've already plastered the outside of it with our prints, and in any case we can be certain they haven't left any others there to be found.'

Nevertheless, neither of them was in any hurry to touch it again. This trifle, hardly too big to have fallen out of a child's lucky-bag, had bound them together and held them rigidly apart the whole night long, but it had no place in their relationship now. For a moment Bunty had an impulse to ask him why, when he had dragged himself to the very brink of murder against his nature, he had not, after all, used the gun. But that was only one of the many things she could never ask him, and in any case he would not have known the answer. On reflection, she felt that she might be better able to explain it to him. The Luke who had approached that moment in such sickness and despair had believed himself – no, had *known* himself – to be a murderer; but his own blood and sinews had felt no conviction of any such identity, and had done everything possible to avoid making it true. The gun might have made success only too certain, and his hands had shirked it at the last moment, and come to the decision naked, and still fighting hard against what he was trying to make them do. So she was alive, and he . . .

He picked up the Liliput suddenly, and thumbed over the small, grooved catch at the left side of the grip. 'It's all right,' he said, holding it out to her with a faint smile, 'I've only put it on safety. That won't foul up any evidence there may be, and if we're going to handle it we may as well take no chances.' He caught the sudden kindling flare of her eyes, and made haste to answer before she asked. 'No, really, it hasn't been like that all the time. I put the safety on after I came round, as soon as I made up my mind I had to get out and take everything with me. I don't even know why. I suppose I was afraid to handle it without, not being used to such things. Pippa was no good with it, either,' he said wryly, 'she had to shove it over with her free hand instead of just using her thumb. She always had to wrestle with anything manual, even bottle-openers.'

Bunty turned the little thing incredulously in her hand. It couldn't have weighed much more than half a pound. 'You mean it was on safety all that time . . .' She let it go there, sparing a brief smile for the memory of her night's ordeal. His subconscious rebellion against death had certainly been doing its best for him and for her.

'I think so. I *hope* so! I don't actually know which way is which, and I haven't fired it, to find out. But you can't help picking up the general principles if you see enough telly serials. And she certainly wasn't in any mood to be switching it on to safety when she started waving it at me. And it wasn't muzzled

296

when it killed her, either, that's for sure. I only pushed the catch off again,' he said, paling, 'when the police . . . when you went to the door . . .'

She knew exactly when he must have given this little snake its teeth back, and for what purpose, and the less he thought about that now, the better. 'I suppose we can take it for granted,' she said briskly, 'that this *is* the gun that killed her? It's the only way it makes sense. They wouldn't leave you there holding a different one, what would be the use? As soon as the police had recovered the bullet you'd have been in the clear. We could at least have a look how many shots have been fired from it, couldn't we? How do you open this thing, do you know?'

He took it from her. 'Most of them seem to have a little catch at the bottom of the butt, and the magazine slots in there. This must be it . . .' His finger was on the little clip when she suddenly caught him by the wrist, her eyes flaring.

'No, wait . . . don't! I've just thought of something! What's it like, this magazine thing?'

'A sort of little oblong steel box with one side open. You slot the bullets in, and a spring moves them up singly into the chamber. I *think*! But we can have a look,' he said reasonably.

'No, don't open it! If there are good hard surfaces, like that, it would hold prints, wouldn't it? Whoever loaded it would have to handle it . . . and I know we've completely wrecked any chances there might have been of getting anything off the out-side, and in any case there wouldn't be any traces there but ours. But we haven't touched the inside! And I bet nobody thought of wiping that part off before they planted it on you.'

'But it isn't going to tell us anything, is it?' he objected ruefully. 'Whoever shot Pippa didn't have to touch the magazine. *She* was the one who loaded it. . .'

'Ah, but *was* she? How do we know that? She got that gun from somebody else, probably somebody shady. And you said yourself, she was hopeless with her hands, she had to wrestle with things. If she got somebody to give her a gun, *wouldn't she get him to load it for her, too?*'

'You could be right, at that!' he agreed, reflecting the cautious glow of her excitement back to her; and he took his finger from the clip in haste. 'You don't think, do you, that the chap who gave it to her may be the same as the chap who killed her?'

'Why not? Pippa got into something that was too deep for her, if you ask me, and where the guns are the motives for murder often are, too. But even if we only find out who gave it to her, that'll be something. You know,' said Bunty intently, 'what really puzzles me about Pippa? Not so much why she dropped you – most likely that was when she picked up with this other man – but why she picked you up again. Not out of any affection, you soon found that out. She wasn't changing back, not on the level. No, she came running after you and made herself charming again because she wanted something out of you.'

'It would make sense,' he agreed painfully, remembering Pippa alive, ambitious and energetic. 'Only she never actually asked me for much, did she? A trip to London in my company. Oh, yes, and the loan of the car on Thursday, because she was going shopping for clothes. It's a bind, getting on buses with dress-boxes. She brought it back in the evening, and we went to a cinema. But that's all she asked from me. And what is there in that?'

'But that drive to London with you she wanted very, very badly. She showed you that when you held out on her. What could possibly have been so urgent about it? I mean, she could as easily have got herself there by train, if she wanted to go as badly as all that. But that wouldn't do. *It had to be with you.*'

'But why? Why should it matter to her how she ran out, even if for some reason she had to run?'

'I don't know. But Pippa knew. She knew of a very strong reason indeed, or why should she still go on persisting, even when she found out that you knew about her visitor, and weren't going to be taken in any more? When she couldn't get her own way by charm, she was even desperate enough to use the gun. And now I've thought of something else about this gun. You were meant to be found right there on the spot, a sitting duck, ready to be charged. Either still out, or half-dizzy and half-drunk, dithering over the body and not knowing which way to run. Caught red-handed with a murder you couldn't even begin to deny . . . even believing yourself guilty . . .'

'Yes,' he said, 'that's the way it would have been.'

'Then,' she said, closing her eyes tightly in concentration, 'whoever planted you would have to take steps to ensure that you *should* be found like that. He *couldn't* leave it to chance. I'd stake my life that the police got an anonymous telephone call to go to your house, just as soon as the other fellow had made sure he was out of range. From a public call box. Not too near. He'd have liked to keep a watch and make sure everything went according to plan, but he wouldn't risk it. Professionals don't take chances, he'd get well away. And you said you were only out about twenty-five minutes . . . Whoever he was, he was relying on having much longer than that.'

She opened her eyes, wide, brilliant, greenish-hazel, and stared at him. 'You know what? I reckon you slid from under simply by having a good hard head, and coming round more quickly than anyone could have expected. Your part was to be discovered groggy and helpless with drink, if not still out, with the girl dead on the floor and the gun still in your hand, caught in the very act. Instead, you came round too early and scared sober, cleaned up the place, ran for the car, and got out with all the evidence. And you know, I begin to think it may have been the best thing you could do.'

'Maybe I had one more small stroke of luck,' he said, taking fire almost reluctantly from her sparks. 'I'm sure about one thing, we were wrestling for the gun, and somehow we lost our balance and started to fall. Supposing someone coming in behind me had just let loose with a cosh – just *supposing* it's true – then if I was already falling with the blow I should partially ride it. And he might not even know.'

'And that *is* how you were placed? I was right? You had your back to the door?'

'More or less, yes. If you'd known Pippa . . . She owned whatever she made part of her outfit, like me. She owned whatever was mine. When she walked in, she walked right in. You always ended up with your back to the door.'

'So if either of you saw a third person enter, it would be Pippa. Did her face change? Did she cry out?'

'Oh, God, do I know?' he said, groaning with the effort to remember clearly. 'We were so tangled, neither of us knew about anyone else but the two of us. I don't know . . . I don't remember . . . She was yelling at me all the time, what would one yell more mean?'

'No, I see that. No, don't worry, it wouldn't prove anything, anyhow. Let it go.'

'Bunty,' he said suddenly, reaching across the table to touch her hand, 'I don't want you to hope too much, and find yourself badly let down in the end. God knows you've made me begin to believe I couldn't have done it, but everything we've got is only conjecture. There isn't one blind bit of evidence to show that there was ever anyone else there but the two of us. Not one! Not that I'm giving up so easily, I don't mean that . . . I don't *want* to believe I'm a killer. But if it should turn out . . . I don't want *you* hurt!' he concluded with abrupt passion, and plucked his hand away.

There could hardly, Bunty thought, be a better demonstration of her contention that he had nothing of the killer about him, and not even his own despairing conviction had been able to instil the makings into his nature. Here was he struggling to extend himself to accept the possibility of his guilt, and his chief worry was to save her from becoming so involved that she might be seriously damaged by the disillusionment.

'Give me time,' she said, wisely sticking to the practical point he had raised, 'and I'll find the sign you want. I'll *prove* there was someone else there. There wasn't, for instance, anything missing from the body? Or from the house?'

He shook his head with a wry smile. 'That's just what I was thinking of, as a matter of fact. Pippa's still wearing her engagement ring! It isn't such a valuable job, I know, but surely if some sort of crook acquaintance had followed her to my place and killed her, he'd have gone to the trouble to take a solitaire diamond from her finger before he left? It wouldn't delay him long.'

She thought that over rapidly, her lip caught in her teeth. 'That could also mean something that seems to me much more likely. After all, you don't just kill over a slight difference of opinion, or a few shillings in crooked money. The mere fact that it was worth murder suggests to me that whoever it was wasn't interested in one ring, not even on the side. What was at stake was bigger than that. The ring was worth more to him right there on Pippa's finger when the police came, to make them say just what you're saying: If there'd been an intruder here, he'd have made off with this. Everything *had* to be left intact, or there was a hole in the case against you.'

'Then how,' he asked with a perverse smile, 'are you ever going to produce that sign for me?'

'You want to bet?' said Bunty. 'Don't side-track me, and we'll get there yet. Where were we? Yes . . . with you set up as the fall guy, and the murderer telephoning the police from a suitably distant call box. Now you can take it as read that the police would *have* to check on such a call, whether they took it seriously or not, simply because it always *might* be true. In this case they found only an empty house, locked and innocent, no body, no criminal, no gun, nothing – just a bachelor cottage with the two tenants gone off for their half-term breaks, as probably some neighbour would confirm. Or the school caretaker, if there isn't a neighbour who occasionally swops gossip with you. All in order. So what would they do next? Shrug it off as a false alarm?

They *do* happen, all too often, out of spite, or boredom, or just a perverted sense of humour. Or would they put in the squad and go over the place thoroughly? In their present state, short-handed and over-worked, and taking into account the surface improbability of two respectable young men like you getting involved in murder, I'd say they wouldn't spare the time. On the other hand, they'd still be a little bit curious, just as to what was behind that call.'

'Do you think the caller would mention names?' Luke asked alertly.

'A good point! No, I don't think he would. The more anony-mous your anonymous call is, so to speak, the less likely ever to tie up with you. No, he wouldn't mention Pippa's name, certainly not if he had some traceable connection with her himself. He'd just say, you boys want to get along to such-and-such an address, fast, there's a girl been killed in there.'

'Then when the police drew a blank at my place, they'd have no way of following up by checking on Pippa's flat and move-ments. So what more *could* they do?'

'I'll tell you. They could pass out to the papers a little news item about the police being called to an apparently false alarm of the murder of a girl at a Comerbourne address. And then they'd sit back and wait to see if somebody comes forward with word of a daughter, or a sister, or a friend, going missing. No details, of course, just the general bait.'

'But today,' he said, 'is Sunday.'

'Exactly. And the Sunday papers go to press before Saturday evening, and couldn't even get this para. into the stop-press. So nothing can result until at least tomorrow. For my money, the police don't yet know, *nobody* yet knows but you and I and the murderer, that Pippa is dead. Which matches with what the police here said. All they were following up was a case of dangerous driving.'

'That does give us a little time, anyhow,' he acknowledged.

'And a hypothetical good mark if we're the ones who come

302

forward voluntarily to report her death and tell all we know about it.'

He had turned away to pick up Pippa's suitcase, but he swung on his heel then to take a long, considering look at her. Her face was intent, candid and utterly serious.

'You really have a lot of faith in the police, haven't you?' he said, studying her curiously.

'Yes. They're human, and not all of them what they ought to be, but by and large, yes, I've got a lot of faith in them. Bring that over here on the settee, where the light's good.'

Pippa Gallier's suitcase was of the air-travel persuasion, large but light, in oatmeal-coloured fibreglass with a rigid frame, and secured, in addition to its twin locks, with a broad external strap. Luke laid it on the couch, unbuckled the strap, and tried one of the locks with his thumb. The flap sprang back at once, a success he had not expected. He released the other one, and opened the case on as tempting a collection of feminine fashion as Bunty had ever seen under one lid. Pippa had loved clothes, and cared for them tenderly. Everything was delicately folded and cunningly assembled, protected in plastic and held in place by pink corded ribbon. Luke shrank from touching these relics, almost as much from awe of their perfection as from remembrance of their owner. It was Bunty who loosed the ribbon tethers, and began to lift out the upper layers carefully, surveying each before she removed it.

'She did herself well. Doesn't it seem to you that a lot of this is brand-new?'

'I told you, she took the car shopping on Thursday. I said she'd have time to shop in London, but she couldn't wait. She loved clothes,' he said helplessly, watching delicate feminine colours lifted one by one from Pippa's treasury.

'I see she did. Too well,' said Bunty sharply, 'to have let *this* pass when she was packing.'

He had noticed nothing wrong, and indeed there was little to notice, just a corner of a folded skirt in its plastic envelope crumpled together like a buckled wing after a collision, stubbed into creases. And directly below that, the lace edge of a slip folded back on itself. Bunty slid her hand into the corner and felt down past layer after layer, turning them back to examine each as she came to it. Then she readjusted them, a glint of excitement in her eye, and treated all the other corners in the same way.

'You see?'

He didn't see; his own packing would have looked so different that this still appeared perfection, but it is on perfection that tiny blemishes show most clearly.

'He was very neat, he hardly disturbed anything, but he left his traces, all the same. She'd never have left those corners crumpled like that, not even by one fold. Even if she had to disturb her case again to put in something else, she'd do the job properly. Somebody has been through this case, hunting for something. Something big enough to be easily found, because he didn't lift out the things, he just ran his hands down in the corners and here, at the front, and felt for it. And what's more,' she said with certainty, '*he didn't find it*!'

'Oh, now, hold it! How can you possibly know that?'

'Because if he had, something big enough to be located that way, he would have to lift things out to get at it, or else pull it out by force from under, and in either case we'd be able to tell. If anything sizable had been yanked from under these pretties, not only would they have been disarranged a good deal more, but also the hole where the thing had been would be there to be seen and felt. You try it, some time. And even if he'd lifted things out, I think I'd be able to tell the difference. Besides, I doubt if he had time.'

'He certainly didn't have too much, but . . .' He was afraid to believe too readily in her conclusions. She might consider this as proof positive that some third person had been present in the cottage that night, but he was still waiting for the unmistakable sign, something that didn't depend on opinion, something as positive as a fingerprint.

'I wonder,' said Bunty, 'what he was looking for?' She closed the lid again over the delicate remains of Pippa's human vanity, and turned to their last card, the large handbag of cream-coloured glove-leather, soft as velvet and almost as expensive as mink. 'This is new, too? She was really intending to start afresh, wasn't she?'

He said sombrely: 'Yes'; thinking, but not with me.

Bunty unclasped the opulent bag, and turned it upside-down over the table, letting its contents slide out gently through her fingers to be spread out on the polished surface and examined almost in one glance. She moved the items aside one by one, innocuous things like comb, handkerchief, purse-cum-wallet, stamp-case, compact, lipstick, tissues in a clear plastic holder, Quickies . . .

' . . . ball-pen, manicure, Kwells . . . Was she a bad traveller in a car?'

'Not that I know of. But we hadn't made any long trips together before. Maybe she was. When you come down to it, I didn't really know much about her.'

' . . . a folder about what's on in London, a small wallet of hair-grips. That's all. Well?'

'Well?' he repeated, without understanding. 'Yes, that's all. Nothing remarkable there.' His voice was discouraged, though he tried to keep it level and reasonable. What, after all, had he been expecting? 'Nothing there to tell us anything new.'

'Oh, no?' said Bunty. '*Then where are her keys?*'

'Keys?' he echoed, shaken, blinded, transfigured with realisation. '*Keys!*'

He began to shake uncontrollably, and she put her arm round him and held him strongly, watching his face. In similar circumstances she might even have ventured to put her arms round Dominic, yes, even at his ripe, daunting age of twenty, rising twenty-one, though with Dominic she would have had to go very much more carefully, simply because he was her son, and still a little in love with her, and terribly in love with someone else, and jealous of his own manhood. Luke was an easier case, their relationship, complex as it might be, had not that ultimate complexity.

'Yes, her keys. Didn't you think of them? Her suitcase wasn't locked, was it? Would Pippa go anywhere with her suitcase unlocked? Of course she locked it! Of course she had her keys with her, here, in this handbag. She was locking up her flat, wasn't she? She was locking her luggage. He – whoever he was – he took her keys to look through her case, and he didn't find what he was looking for, so he kept the keys. Why? To look for it in her flat . . . don't you think so?'

She led him in her arm to the nearest of the white wicker chairs and persuaded him into it, and sat on the arm and held him against her shoulder, talking to him in a soft, reasonable, detached voice, coaxing and reassuring without directly doing either.

'He wanted something she had, or something he believed she had. He thought it would be in her case, but it wasn't. So he went to her flat to hunt for it there. Now you know,' she said, and had no need, and felt none, to explain what it was that he knew.

'There *was* someone there,' he said, suddenly laughing, shaking with laughter like a lunatic. 'I *didn't* . . .' And he put his head down in her lap and laughed and wept, with relief, with rapture, because he wasn't a murderer.

'She always carried them,' he said, clearly, almost gaily, staring out over a sea now deep-blue and shadow-green in the late afternoon light. His face was warm, human, mobile, with fluctuating colour and live, ardent eyes. His age, which went up and down on the yo-yo of circumstances, had steadied at twenty-seven, and now he was well able to hold it there. 'She was a

306

person who took care to lock things. She had a little leather case shaped like a climbing boot, she'd bought it somewhere in the Tyrol, one holiday. A little kid climbing boot with a key-ring. You fitted your keys on the ring, and it went inside the boot, and the boot zipped up. She wouldn't go away without that! And it isn't here. And I didn't take it. So somebody else did. So I believe – I *believe* now! – that I didn't kill her. Someone *did* come in on us. I *was* set up purposely to take the blame. Can you credit it?' he said, lost in wonder. 'Now I don't even care so much if they convict me. Just so I know I didn't do it.'

'They're not going to convict you,' said Bunty quietly. She had taken her arm from him, even withdrawn herself from the arm of the chair and left him unsupported, as soon as he reared himself up intact and joyful, with that fresh, live face she had never seen before, but which she liked on first sight. 'They can reason, too. And they'll listen, I'll see to that. And there's her flat in Comerbourne, that ought to furnish some evidence, too. The gun . . . her suitcase searched . . . her keys missing . . . We've got something to offer, now.'

He looked at the light, and he looked at the poor little relics disposed about the table. Then he looked again over the sea, and calculated chances, and wondered.

'Maybe we ought to wait a little, just until it's dusk? I should hate to be picked up now. I want to drive up to the police station and report in without any question of compulsion.'

'We could wait a little longer,' said Bunty. 'Why don't you put the boat away, while we're waiting?'

He had forgotten about the boat, riding gently beside the jetty, nuzzling its fenders like a kitten as the water rocked under it. It must be nearly full tide now, the deck swaying high, and the inlet full to its limit. It seemed a life-time since he had hoisted those two stones aboard, and covered them guiltily from sight. He could hardly believe, now, in the person he had been during those morning hours, so short a time ago. Bunty had peeled that incubus off from his flesh and spirit, and brought

307

him to this intoxicating freedom, which was proof against any charge others might bring.

He looked at her across the white and orange room, and tried to assess the quality she had for him, and the physical aspects of her that expressed, so inadequately, her essence. So beautiful, with that chestnut hair like a ripe brown cap moving suavely round her head, and those few grey strands so alive and silvery that they set light to every movement she made, like attendant spirits embracing and guarding her. Powdered freckles golden over the bridge of a straight nose. And those eyes for which his experience had no measure, so blazingly honest and gallant and clear, at once green and golden and brown, the eyes that had first drawn him to her. They were looking at him now with a direct, contented regard in which he found undoubted affection, but did not dare find more.

But I love you, he thought, I shall love you for ever and ever and ever, as long as I live, and with everything there is left of me that knows how to love, even after I'm dead. I had no conception that there could be a kind of love like this, or a kind of person like you. Utterly without deceit, or meanness, or the very shadow of anything second-rate. I thought one always had to compromise, to make allowances, to be ready to come to terms with love. Nobody ever told me you were possible, or I would never have settled for anything less.

'Yes, of course,' he said, fumbling after ordinary words through the golden haze of a revelation for which no expression was possible, 'I'd better get Reggie's treasure under cover.'

And he took off his coat and slung it on the back of a chair, putting on instead an old duffle jacket that Reggie Alport left permanently hanging in the hall cupboard, as working gear for when the east coast proved blustery and unkind. In a few moments Bunty, putting away crockery and tools in the kitchen, heard his footsteps, unbelievably light and young now, leaping down the slatey stairs towards the water.

Chapter 8

By the time Bunty had washed out the stained table-cloth and hung it to dry, and sat down to wait for Luke's return, she was no longer entirely easy in her mind about those keys. Supposing she had read too much into their absence, and built him up on insufficient evidence to another shattering fall? What if they were upstairs all the time, for instance, in Pippa's coat pocket? No, that was hard to believe. Someone who loved clothes so much wouldn't spoil the set of them by carrying things of any bulk or weight in the pockets. Which is why the handbags of today have grown bigger than shopping bags.

I don't know, though, thought Bunty on reflection. This year's coats have at least got flared skirts again, not straight, so that even a loose threepenny-bit shows through in a duodecagonal bump. Why not slip up and make sure, now, while Luke's out of the house?

He would have locked the bedroom, of course, she quite understood that. She was to be protected from touching or seeing again the sad wreckage of his first love. But there was his coat on the back of the chair by the desk, and there was a good chance that the key was in his pocket. He need never know that she had circumvented his concern for her feelings, if she made her search at once.

The bedroom key was there, she found it in the left-hand

outside pocket. She ran up the stairs, and let herself into the pastel-coloured room; and there on the bed lay the youth and beauty for whose passing she had been startled into grieving only two days ago. Wasted and spoiled, and withdrawn now into supreme indifference, Pippa was never going to look into her mirror at forty-one, and wonder if everything had been well done, and whether this was all. Just being alive again would have been prize enough for Pippa. Bunty stood beside the bed and looked down at her with wonder and pity. Touching her started no other feelings, no repugnance at all; Bunty had seen death before.

The charcoal-coloured coat had fine silver threads running through the weave, a flared skirt, and two large slant pockets. There was nothing in them, but the trouble was that they were cut so wide and shallow that they might easily shed their contents when the wearer was recumbent. Better look in the boot of the car, too, and make quite sure. The matching skirt had no pockets. Slenderly cut for an almost hipless figure, it could not possibly have accommodated one. There was nowhere else to look. Bunty passed her hands all down the still, chill body, avoiding the encrusted brown hole in the fine cream sweater. No, Pippa had no keys. And no more use for keys.

The large, delicate eyelids, blue-veined like pale hare-bells, were imperfectly closed. A faint gleam of reflected light from the hooded eyes followed Bunty to the door. She looked back once, and the stillness of the slight figure had the quality of tomb sculpture, monumental not so much in the absence of movement as in the total renunciation of movement. The infection of silence and stealth that possesses the living in the presence of death is not awe but sympathetic magic, used as a protection. Do your best not to seem alien and alive here, and death won't recognise another victim and turn on you.

Bunty tiptoed out of the room, and closed and locked the door. She was still moving soundlessly when she slipped the bedroom key back into Luke's pocket. Poor girl! How old could she have been? Twenty-three or twenty-four? She didn't look so much, but apparently she was senior enough to be a deputy buyer at a first-class store like Pope Halsey's. Probably very good at her job; a pity, a thousand pities, she hadn't been content to stick to it, but had meddled with something out of her scope.

The garage key was hanging on its own proper hook in the kitchen; Luke had made no attempt to hide it, once he had brought Pippa and her belongings into the house. Bunty took it, let herself out by the front door, and crossed the gravel to the creosoted timber building, large enough for two cars. She unlocked the door and went in. There was the big old Rover, a hulking black shape in the light from the dusty window, unfashionable, powerful and solid, built when cars were meant to last, and to run remorselessly until every part dropped dead together. At the last moment she wondered if Luke would have locked the boot again, and whether she would have to go back and hunt for more keys; but the huge lid gave easily to her hand, and bounced open to its fullest. There was nothing to hide in there now.

Pippa had travelled a great many miles in this dark coffin, and there had been some pretty rough riding on the way. The Tyrolean climbing boot could very easily have rolled out of those shallow pockets and into a dark corner here, and escaped notice. But no, there was nothing to be found but a gallon can for petrol, the spare wheel braced to one side, and a wooden tool-box and a jack shoved well to the back. Bunty moved those items which were movable, and felt all round the dusty floor until she was satisfied. Nothing. And the thing could hardly have found its way into the petrol can or the tool box.

Nevertheless, for no good reason, she opened the lid of the box. A roughish affair, but solid, maybe as old as the car. There was a top tray full of small tools and a good deal of accumulated rubbish, of the kind one keeps because it may come in useful some day, and finally throws out in a grand clearance about two days before the occasion for its usefulness does arise. She lifted the tray. It sat upon two stout wooden supports, and below was a larger compartment.

The clean, new, flat package that lay there, almost as large as the inside dimensions of the box, and wrapped neatly in decorative bookshop paper, startled her by its sheer incongruity. It was about fifteen inches by ten, and could easily have been one of the lavish gift-books currently fashionable for leaving negligently around on coffee-tables. Only it wasn't. She prodded it, and it had no bound hardness, but a thick, yielding, heavy, papery quality. It might have been unremarkable enough almost anywhere else; but here it arrested her attention like the eruption of a Roman candle.

She lifted it out, and on impulse pulled at the end of the pink tape that tied it, and unwrapped it at one end. It felt like paper, and it was paper. Neat bundles of thin, limp oblongs printed in sepia browns and muted greens on white, and held together in regular order by girdles of narrow brown gumstrip. Six bundles in one layer, four of them ranged side by side, and two lengthways alongside them; and several layers.

She riffled the ends through her fingers unbelievingly, and stared, and stared again. She had never seen so many ten-pound notes in her life. At a lightning estimate, she was holding in her hands something over twelve thousand pounds.

For just one moment her mind recoiled with horror and revulsion, suddenly seeing a Luke who had been lying to her throughout, who had been in some shady deal with the girl, and killed her over the proceeds. Here was this bundle hidden in his tool box, in his car, and here was he on the coast, ready and equipped with a boat for his escape, and funds to keep him afloat wherever he went.

It shook her to the heart, but it was gone as suddenly as it had come. It blew through her mind like a gust of wind, and died into invulnerable calm. No, she had the best possible reason to know better than that. If he had killed Pippa, then Bunty

Felse, too, would have been dead by now, there would have been
no recoil from the act. He wasn't a killer, and he would be the
least effective of partners in anything criminal. Moreover, her
instinct told her that he could not possibly have been acting all
this time. For what purpose, even if he had the ability? No, she
had not really been shaken. She knew she was right about him.
She would stake her life on it. She *was* staking her life on it.

Not Luke. Pippa.

Hadn't he mentioned twice that she had borrowed his car to
carry home her shopping on Thursday?

So that was why she had been frantic when Luke had told
her in no uncertain terms that they weren't going anywhere,
when she had found him disillusioned, and the car still in the
garage, and out of her reach for ever. She couldn't tell him about
the money, and she couldn't get access to her hiding-place to
recover it. She had put it clean out of her own reach. No
wonder she raved, no wonder she committed the final folly and
threatened him with the gun.

Yes, someone had been involved in crooked business, but it
wasn't Luke. Pippa was running out in a hurry with hot money,
but it wasn't from Luke she was running. On the contrary, she
had run back to him and ingratiated herself with him afresh in
order to make use of him for her get away. That was what she
had wanted of him. That was what she had had in mind when
she came back and couldn't have been sweeter. And his engagement ring? Well, a little bonus like that is always welcome. Why
say no? He was more likely to do what she wanted if she accepted
him. And a solitaire diamond, even a little one, is not to be
sneezed at.

There were more and more implications crowding in beyond
these. Bunty was dizzy with the flashing of chaotic particles
falling into place, as though a jigsaw puzzle had abruptly decided
to solve itself.

Any minute now Luke would be coming up from the sea. Let
him find this parcel as she had found it, let him demonstrate to

himself as well as to her what the find meant in terms of his own integrity. And let him destroy for ever, in the finding, whatever grain of doubt had remained to suggest to her, even for an instant, what she had just found herself momentarily believing. He had a right to know that she had doubted, provided he understood that the doubt was the last.

She smoothed the end of the package hastily back into order, re-tied it exactly as before, and replaced it in the tool box. She closed the boot, locked the garage and went back to put the key in its place.

Presently Luke came up from the inlet, with the salt smell of the coast eddying from the shoulders of Reggie Alport's jacket. She let him hang it up in the hall cupboard, and put on his own coat again, before she leaned out from the kitchen and said: 'You don't think she could have had her keys in her pocket, after all, do you?'

He shook his head emphatically. He had had that slight figure in his arms, and composed it into order on the bed, he knew there was nothing in her pockets. She wasn't a pocket girl, anyhow, she was an outsize-handbag girl.

'And they couldn't have slipped out while she was in the boot? I only want,' she said, 'to make *certain* that someone took them.'

'I don't think so for a moment,' said Luke, 'but it won't take a minute to have a look.' And he reached for the key of the garage, and led the way blithely.

He found it. She didn't even have to prompt him. He groped all round with buoyant thoroughness in the huge boot, shoved the petrol can aside, scooped a hand round the spare wheel, and hoisted the lid of the tool box.

'Nothing,' he said; and then, arrested by a capricious memory: 'Do you know, this is the only thing I ever made in woodwork class at school? Not much finesse, but you must admit the zeal.'

He was happy, he hoped for grace, and believed in justice, and he knew, *knew* he was not a murderer. She wondered how there could have remained to her even one scruple of insecurity. After all, few people in the world could know him as well as she now knew him; not even his mother, if he still had a mother, knew him better.

'A tour-de-force,' she said. 'What do you keep underneath, Black and Decker's total output? It's nearly big enough.'

'Junk, mostly,' he said. 'I'm a jackdaw.' And he hoisted the tray in one hand, himself fleetingly curious.

'Hey!' he said sharply, his voice losing its reminiscent ease. 'What's this? I've never . . . Father Christmas has been!' But there was no recapturing the note of innocence. Wary, mystified and calm, he lifted out the book that was no book, and studied the gay wrapping paper, dotted with variegated bookworms of all ages, with their noses appropriately buried. 'I don't understand. *I* didn't put this in here.'

'What is it?' asked Bunty at his shoulder. 'Open it!'

And he opened it, on the lid of the boot, sweeping the folds of paper aside with a large vigour which it seemed belonged to him when he was in possession of himself. She watched the sudden rigidity of his face, the dropped jaw, the bewildered eyes, the wonderfully quick apprehension. All genuine. What she was less prepared for was the instant understanding, the blazing intelligence with which he turned his face upon her.

'You knew, didn't you? You'd already found it?'

No bitterness, no accusation, only that quick, alert, brittle tone of someone who feels ice cracking under him. She had every right in the world to put him to the test; the ache in him was only the longing to be found intact after the test was over.

'Yes,' she said, 'I found it while you were down at the boat.'

'I give you my word, I didn't know.'

'I know you didn't. I wondered for about five seconds,' she said steadily, 'but that was all. No, Pippa put it there, of course. It was why she had to go to London with you. No other car would do. And it was why she died.'

He had paled afresh at the revelation of how difficult and new

315

and vulnerable was his relationship with her. You had to work at this as hard as at a marriage. What was more surprising was the clarity with which they both suddenly saw that there would never be any need for a second such assay. From that moment they knew each other through and through.

They locked the garage again, and took their find into the house and there opened it upon the living-room table. All that money, they couldn't believe in it. Neither of them had ever seen so much.

'So *that*'s why she was in such a state when I told her to get out,' said Luke, looking down at it with a shadowed face, almost afraid to touch. 'And that's what *he* was looking for. He searched her case, and then took the keys away to search her flat, and all the time it was where she'd hidden it, in my car. Where do you suppose she got it?'

'It's stolen money. What other possibility is there? I can't believe she was up to anything on her own. Somebody deposited this with her until it cooled enough to be distributed or moved out of the area. And before the heat was off she'd had it in her possession so long she'd come to think of it as hers – so much in clothes and clubs and parties and travel and fun. Everything she wanted. She'd begun to question whether it ever need be distributed at all. Who could make better use of it than she could?'

'You really think it may be that? I know she was extravagant and spoiled . . . But she'd never . . . Oh, I don't know!' he said helplessly, winding the pink tape nervously round his fingers.

'What else could it be? How could she come by this much money in cash, otherwise? And if she had, honestly, why *keep* it in cash and have it hanging around? And why did she acquire a gun, unless it was because she had something to protect, and somebody willing and able to find her a gun to protect it with? Who carries this kind of money in a parcel? Not honest people.' Bunty sat down and stared at the uncovered notes, brooding with her head in her hands. 'How long has Pippa worked in Comerbourne?'

'Nearly three years. I met her soon after I started work there.'

'Then this comes from some local coup,' she said with authority, and closed her eyes the better to think back over recent history. The sight of all those miniature queens, so demure and complacent in whatever hands, was distracting. 'You said she started getting off-hand with you about two months ago. That was probably when she first picked up with these people. And just over a week ago she came back and began to make up to you. And she worked at Pope Halsey's, as an assistant buyer . . .'

Her voice snapped off abruptly. She opened her eyes wide, bright-green in this slanting pre-evening light, dazzled eyes. 'Oh, no! That *must* be it! Tell me again, Luke, what department did she work in?'

'I don't think I did tell you. But it was furs,' he said, puzzled, forgetting the money in her intensity. 'Why?'

'And she was assistant to the buyer?'

'Yes . . . she used to model furs for their advertisements. She looked marvellous . . . I've seen the stills . . .' He caught Bunty's bright stare, fixed as a fortune-teller's crystal-hypnotised gaze, and trembled with a premonition of final truth. '*Why?*'

'There was a big van-load of furs,' she said like a clairvoyant, 'coming from London for Pope Halsey, just about six weeks ago. It was hi-jacked soon after it left the M.1, flagged down near a lay-by, by somebody pretending there'd been an accident. The driver was picked up with bad concussion next day, the van was ditched on a minor road. The furs were gone, clean trade. Probably turned into cash that very night. Somebody had advance notice of that consignment. How if Pippa gave them the tip-off?'

'Oh, *no!*' he said, with the last anguish on her account, and drew back his hands from the banknotes on the table. 'You think this could be that money? After all this time?'

'No,' said Bunty positively, 'not that money. The last place

317

they'd be likely to unload the goods and pick up the cash would be Comerbourne, where the stuff was consigned. No, not that. But supposing she'd been the contact for that. And supposing the same gang needed a safe deposit in Comerbourne on a later job, and thought they had a reliable little girl there – respectable, above suspicion, and already implicated in one affair. Because there *was* another gang job in Comerbourne, just three weeks ago. Didn't you hear about it? The pay-roll of Armitage Pressings was snatched on its way from the bank. The gang vanished, and so did the money. There were road-blocks up almost at once, but the money vanished, all the same. I reckon it vanished inside Comerbourne. Don't you? They found the van in a scrap-yard afterwards, right there in the town. The money had to lie some-where until the heat was off. Deposited with some confederate inside the town, somebody they could trust. Somebody they *thought* they could trust. Armitage's pay-roll per week is around fifteen thousand. How much do you make this lot?'

He had been counting the number of notes in one bundle, and the number of bundles, but he couldn't believe the answer. 'I figure it as something over fourteen thousand, anyhow. There'd be change, too, of course, if it was wages money, but that wouldn't be so portable, maybe she ditched that. Even the notes . . . but banks don't keep the numbers of the used notes they hand out, do they?'

The timing was right and the amount was right, and where else would a shop assistant get fifteen thousand pounds in notes? Bunty watched him fingering through the neat, banded bundles, still dazed. She saw his hand halt upon one of them, and his face grew sharply intent as he turned its edges towards him.

Black, rigid card – or was it a blue so dark as to be nearly black? – jutted on either side of the banknotes by a fraction of an inch. Luke had felt the alien stiffness even before he had seen the slivers of darkness. He thrust his thumb under the brown paper band and ripped it open, tumbling out upon the table a small black book, its cover printed in gilt lettering and heraldry between two white windows.

'A passport!'

Fire-new, virgin, its stiff cover opened a little as soon as the constriction was removed.

'Pippa's. Of course!' said Luke in a low voice, and opened it where the blue-tinted pages yielded of their own tension. Something folded double inside began to unfold in sympathy. 'Aaaah!' he said in a long sigh. 'Now I see!'

It was a B.E.A. ticket. He unfolded it and studied the details with a closed and unrevealing face.

'Dated for today. A single from Heathrow to Le Bourget. The eight o'clock Trident flight. So that's why she needed the Kwells! She'd have had to be at West London Air Terminal by seven o'clock. I don't suppose I should even have been awake by the time she took off for Paris. There wouldn't have been any difficulty. We . . . hadn't planned on sharing . . . The only trick would have been getting this out of the tool-box while I wasn't around to see, and that wouldn't have bothered her. She'd only have to say she'd left something in the car, some time when I was shaving, or something, and couldn't run her errand myself. She could do harder things than that by far. And I don't suppose I was much of a problem to manage.'

'No,' agreed Bunty, 'I don't suppose you were. But things didn't work out so easily. They came back for their money, just when she had everything planned for her run-out. What else could it be? They followed her to your house. Maybe they had someone watching her moves all along, those people don't trust anyone far. They saw her leaving with a suitcase, and followed her, and it would be simple enough getting into your place, even if the door was locked, but I don't suppose it was . . .'

'It almost never was,' he owned, fingering the airline ticket sombrely on the table. 'Sometimes not even when we went to bed. We hadn't anything worth stealing, we didn't think in terms of locking things up.'

'So they just walked in. Just like Pippa. And they heard part – I'd say not very much – of what passed between you, and saw the struggle for the gun. How very easy, to knock you on the head, and then they could get rid of a liability and leave you to take the blame. When even you were convinced of your own guilt, why should the police look any farther? But you see where they went wrong. They were sure the money would be in Pippa's case. But it wasn't! And now it was too late to try and make her tell what she'd done with it. *They'd killed her!* She wasn't going to answer any questions any more. Probably they searched your cottage, but they can't have known about the car, waiting in the garage a whole street away, with this money packed inside it. They couldn't begin to guess where the loot really was. No! But they took her keys with them, and went back to make a thorough search of her flat. My guess is they'd take it for granted she'd moved the actual money, but they'd be looking for a left-luggage ticket, or a safe-deposit key, something that would show them where she'd hidden it.'

He looked up at her, and his face warmed into a faint smile. 'That's quite a lot of supposing.'

'I know it is, but it adds up. And in that case we can be certain of one thing, the anonymous caller who alerted the police to come and fetch you *didn't* identify the corpse. They'd want the police busy round your place with everything they had. They wouldn't want any premature clue to send the investigation over to Pippa's flat, because they had a longish job of searching to do there themselves. And did you notice, none of these things in her bag has her name on it – not even in the purse, now I come to think of it.'

'And now *I* come to think of it,' he said, suddenly rearing his head like a hound pricking his ears at the distant sounds of the hunt, 'they'd be expecting sensational news by this morning, a broadcast item about the murder at the least, police activity all round our quarter. And there wouldn't be any! They'd know it had gone wrong. They'd know I'd somehow managed to dispose of the body and get clean away.'

Bunty made a soft, smothered sound of dismay. She got up quickly, beginning to thrust the bundles of notes together and fold the paper round them. 'Yes . . . Luke, I hadn't thought . . . I didn't realise . . .'

'And as they wouldn't find anything at Pippa's place,' he said, 'not even a left-luggage ticket, the next thought that would occur to them would be that I must have got away not only with Pippa and all the evidence, but also *with their fifteen thousand pounds.*'

Chapter 9

They stared at each other across the table, across those absurd trivialities for which murder had been done, and the small, vicious personal treasons that make love unlovely; and each of them was furiously reckoning the risk to the other, and beginning to erect barricades.

'They'd be on the alert today,' said Bunty, 'for *any* police news from yesterday. There'll be nothing about murder, but they won't miss the significance of a car that went through a red light, and then nearly ran down a constable, because it was in such a guilty hurry to get away from Comerbourne.'

'No,' he agreed grimly, 'they surely won't. The police up here were alerted, so there'll be something to give the tip down there, even if it isn't exactly public yet. They'll know which way the police hunt has come. Within limits, they'll know where to look for me . . .'

'For us,' she said instantly.

'For *me*! Oh, Bunty . . . Oh, God, I ought to have sent you home!'

'You did try. Don't think of it, it isn't your fault that I wouldn't go. I wouldn't go even now,' she said stubbornly.

'Then let's take all this stuff and get out of here, while the going's good. I want to get you to the police. I've never wanted the police so much,' he said, and laughed rather breathlessly, tying the pink tape hurriedly round the parcel of notes. 'Put your coat on,' he said. 'Never mind anything else, we'll bring them back here. *I'll* bring them back here. You'll stay where you're safe.'

Yes, she thought, just get yourself and me into police hands, and I might even sit back and leave the rest to them, and to you.

'But we still have to avoid notice. The car . . .'

'It doesn't matter now,' he said with decision. 'If the police are on the look-out for me, so much the better, I'll gladly pull in and hand over to them. The others won't know details like our registration . . . or will they?' he wondered blankly, pulled up short at the thought of their complete isolation all day from the bulletins of the B.B.C. 'Oh, lord, why doesn't Reggie put a proper radio in here? They bring the transistor, of course, damn the thing! We haven't a clue what they've been putting out all day, but I'll bet the gang have had a constant radio watch operating. You can pick up the police broadcasts, too, if you hunt round the wave bands. Many a time I've listened in to their two-way conversations about stolen cars. Ours is just the sort of item they'd be batting back and forth all day long.'

'Those people may not be all that efficient,' said Bunty scornfully, shrugging into her coat. She stooped to unplug the electric fire. 'Don't forget the main switch, you know where it is, I don't. Look what a bad blunder they made, killing her . . .'

He said: 'Yes . . .' in so low and bitter a voice that she was suddenly visited by a private revelation of the love he had felt for that wretched girl upstairs, and the hooks it still had in his deepest sensitivities.

'Here, you have this!' He thrust the parcel of money upon her. 'I'd rather . . . You found it. And you wouldn't believe,' he said, 'what a bad moment it gives you to have several thousand pounds of someone else's money in your hands, when you're broke every month–end without fail.'

'It sticks to my fingers, too,' she said, shaken by the knowledge that she was uttering no more than the truth. 'Poor Pippa!' she added, and the connection was clear enough. 'But we're luckier. It's better than fifteen thousand pounds to us, it's evidence for you.'

The room looked as they had found it. When he threw the main switch there would be nothing but the tins and the broken china in the bin to show they had ever been here. Luke looked round him alertly, approved what he saw, and thrust the gun carefully into his right coat pocket, barrel foremost, a dormant devil. There remained, of course, out of sight but not out of mind, that pale blonde girl upstairs, impenetrably asleep in the pale blond room.

Outside the windows the world already looked dark; in reality it was no more than dusk. When they put out the lights within, the light without would revive and blossom almost into day.

Luke leaned into the broom cupboard. 'Ready? I should get out to the front door, it'll seem dark at first. I'll bring a torch, there's one they keep in the store here.'

She didn't move. She knew the geography of this house now rather better than that of her own. And she was going nowhere without him. Her honour was involved. What you pick up of your own will you can't in decency lay down. You must carry it as long as there's need, until it can stand alone, and walk alone, and not be challenged by anyone.

The light went out, and the window bloomed gradually into greenish, bluish pallor, lambent and enchanted, casting a faint gleam upon shapes inside the room. She waited with the flat packet under her arm, clutched tightly against her heart; and in a moment light, assured steps brought him to her side. A hand felt delicately in the gloom after her free hand, and found and clasped it.

And in that moment they heard it, the engine of the car that was winding its way cautiously along the sunken lane towards the house. A slow, sly, casing note, moving in methodically and without haste by the only approach, sure of closing the box on whatever was within. They heard it stop, somewhere round the curve of the grassland, beyond the trees. They stretched taller in the brief silence, waiting for it to start up again; and faithfully it throbbed into life and came on, with the deliberation of fate itself. Nearer now, but still with swelling ground between. But for the twilight silence it might have passed for traffic somewhere on the road, innocent and absorbed, not touching them.

Bunty thought hopefully, the police coming back. And as though she had spoken aloud, he said in a whisper: 'No!' And after a moment of listening with held breath: 'Not the same car.'

He drew her out into the hall, and loosed her hand gently, and she heard him climbing the stairs in long, ranging, silent steps, three at a time. She groped her way after him, and found him in the large front bedroom, crouched at the window. Her eyes were already adjusting to the half-light, she could see clearly.

She saw the car creep very gently round the curve of the drive, shy in the shelter of the trees. She saw it halt to breathe, to observe the house in darkness, and then to accelerate and slide onward, reassured, into the gateway. Reassured? Or galvanised into more open action by fear that the place was indeed empty, that the birds were flown? It came on without concealment now, but quietly, hissed on to the edge of the gravel, rolled round before the door.

The doors of the car opened before it was still. Silently and purposefully two men slid out of it, one on either side, and then the motor cut out as suavely as a held sigh, and the driver slithered just as noiselessly from behind the wheel. Three figures, mute, shapeless and anonymous, deployed across the width of the gravel court, and looked up contemplatively under shading hat-brims at the blind frontage of the house. And two of the figures, quite suddenly and smoothly and naturally, as though these were the inevitable fruit you would expect to see ripening there, had guns in their hands.

Luke drew back from the window, caught Bunty in his arm, and swept her away through the doorway to the landing, closing the door of the bedroom silently behind them. Silence was everything now. Neither of them risked a word, even in a whisper. Thank God they'd switched off all lights before the car came within sight of the house. But they were both remembering what the police sergeant had said in the morning. He and his companion had seen a light in one of the windows here 'from up the coast road a piece'. So might these men have seen one, a quarter of an hour ago. Bunty and Luke hadn't thought to be cautious about showing lights. Mrs. Chartley had reported her presence to the police, so why disguise it? And now it was too late to worry. Simply get out of here by the only remaining way, and pray that the searchers were merely following up one possibility, and would come to the conclusion that the house was empty, and go away to hunt somewhere else.

But the guns, flowering miraculously in hands that had seemed to conjure them out of empty air, hadn't looked at all tentative, or in the very slightest doubt of their premises.

Neither of them stumbled on the stairs, even in that quietly frantic rush they made; neither of them fouled any of the gay, impermanent fixings of the hall. They could hear the faint, deliberate crunch of gravel under cautious feet as the invaders cased the windows; but the darkness inside was sufficient to swallow all movement, and the glass in the panel of the front door was pebbled and opaque without light to bring it to life. Luke felt his way through the living-room door, and closed it gingerly after them just as a hand eased up the latch of the front door, with the faintest of metallic sounds, and tested it and found it locked. After that they had more freedom to move, more insulation between themselves and their enemies, and they could concentrate on saving time, which was the most vital factor of all. They had to be well down the slate staircase to the inlet before the hunters found their way round the corner of the house to the rear terrace and the faint, lambent plane of the seascape beyond.

The boat was the only card they had left. Why, oh, why had she listened to her tidy, housekeeper's mind, and sent him to lock it away in the boat-house again? If it had still been riding at the jetty it would have saved them minutes now.

Out through the kitchen, out past the store, and Luke spared a moment to turn the key of the back door behind them. It slowed their retreat, but it completed the picture of an empty cottage, if only they could be far enough down the path to be out of earshot. There was no moon yet, but a faint starlight that brushed the flags of the tiny terrace, and gleamed on the level places in the pathway down the cliff. Thank God for the twists and turns in that erratic descent, that would take them out of sight within seconds. Sound would be a more dangerous betrayer.

Luke plunged to the edge of the terrace and led the way down in the dusk. He was on a path he knew, and could make good speed on the descent, but out of that complex of rocks the smallest rattle of a stone displaced would start a volley of rising echoes; and those characters out on the gravel weren't going to waste much time getting into the house. A shot will open a lock, if there's no other means at hand.

Luke put all thoughts out of his head for the moment, and concentrated on keeping his footing at a crazy speed, and bracing his left arm steadily to give Bunty a safety barrier from falling as she leaped and slid and bounded after him, and a grab handle whenever her foot stepped askew on the slates. The way was narrow as well as steep, his body would prevent her from crashing down towards the sea, even if she lost her footing. Whenever they reached one of the more level stretches he took her hand, but on the patches of broken shingle, laid with loose slate slabs for steps, she pressed close at his back and held by his shoulder. And at every step he quivered to the touch of her fingers with delight and agony, and wished her away, miles away in safety out of this mess in which he had involved her. But even then wishing her away was almost more than he could manage.

They were half-way down when he heard the back door of

the cottage crash open above them, and at the same time the sound of running feet on the paved path that led round the house to the seaward side. One man had come round; two, probably, had gone through. Round the other end of the house it was impossible to go, it was built out to the edge of the drop. You could climb below safely enough if you had a fairish head for it, but not in the dark. Luke gripped the key of the boat-house in his pocket, his knuckles pressed for comfort against the gun. A finger of light from a torch fumbled down into the crevices of the rocks. They were sheltered from it by the tortuous turns, and close to the jetty now, but the pursuers could not fail to see the path, and the roof of the boat-house a sheen of grey in the sudden beam. With a light they could cover that descent only too quickly.

He was so intent on the movements of the men above that the movement below took him by surprise, bringing him up shocked and short like a blow to the heart.

A fourth man rose out of the shadows and bulked in their path darkly, blocking the way. The large, square-shouldered shape, neckless and muscular, closed the passage between the rocks solidly. A flat grey voice like the flat grey slates said: 'Hold it right there, mate! Stay put, and get your hands up!'

Luke, arrested in mid-flight on steps steeper than average, pulled up with a suddenness that jarred him from heels to head, and cost Bunty her balance. Her foot slipped on a shifting stone, an unstable slate tilted forward as she stepped on it, and she was down on hands and knees, clinging to the rock, the displaced slab hard and heavy against her side. Some of the stones that supported its forward edge had rolled out of position and made it treacherous. She shoved her shoulder under it and heaved it back to its proper level to free herself of its weight, and the moment of confusion and alarm dissolved in understanding at that instant, and she knew they were not going to get away. They'd underestimated their opponents. The lay-out had been surveyed from the seaward side before ever the car drove up to the house. And this way, too, was closed to them.

She scrambled to her feet again, covered by Luke's body. She heard the hard voice below say impatiently: 'You heard me, chum. Let's see your hands.'

Luke fired from the pocket of his coat on the last word. He hadn't known he was going to do it, he hadn't even realised that his thumb had already shoved off the safety catch. Still less consciously had he calculated the angle of the drop before him, and tilted the thing well down in his pocket, to startle and cripple, perhaps, but not to kill. At this distance even he couldn't miss, the whole crevice between the rocks seemed to be full of the bulky body, with the lambent native silver of the sea outlining it clearly. He and Bunty had the dark and solid rock behind them; but even so, he reached for her with his left hand as he fired with the right, and drew her close to his back, covered from sight by his body.

The report was sharp and loud between the rocks, and followed closely by a gasping grunt and a curious, waspish whine. The dark shape before him buckled suddenly sideways, clutching at its knee, and went down in a toppling fall on to the stones, sliding downhill a yard with scrambling feet before it found a stable resting-place. What astonished Luke most was that the other gun didn't go off, but he had no time to speculate on the reason. Without a word he launched himself forward down the path, swung Bunty before him past the grovelling, groaning, cursing man on the ground, and charged after her.

The threshing shape heaved suddenly, as if the rock had risen under him; an arm came up and reached for him. He hurdled the body blindly, felt the fingers claw at his ankle and miss their hold. Then he came down by ill luck on shifting stones that rolled away from under his foot and flung him on his back, knocking the breath out of him, and half the sense with it. The hand that had missed his ankle scrabbled after him hungrily, and found a grip on his hair. A solid weight rolled over on top of him, holding him down; the hand shifted to his mouth. Not to his throat, his mouth! That was it, that was why no shot, either, he realised, struggling to free his arms from the weight that pinned them. They wanted no sound carrying for miles up-coast and down over the sounding-board of this placid sea. This back-gate guard had been told to threaten, not to fire. In that case Luke had good reason to be glad of his own single shot; someone, somewhere, might have heard. Bunty, he thought desperately, wrenching one arm clear and jabbing upwards viciously under a thick jaw, scream, *now*, while you've got the chance, and keep on screaming. They might cut and run yet. But what was the use, she wasn't a screamer. Not a sound from her!

An arm swung at his head, and he rolled aside from the blow and felt something hard graze his temple and clang like metal on the rock. Whalebone fingers ground deep into his cheeks, clamping his lips against his teeth. He fought for breath, and heard his opponent pumping in sobbing gasps of air and spending them in incoherent, monotonous curses, hissing with pain between the words that were hardly words. When the weight on top of him shifted for another attempt at clubbing him with the gun, he heaved up one knee and tried to throw his incubus from him, but it was too heavy to be lifted or unbalanced so easily. And from somewhere above, a crazy accompaniment to this disordered scene, came the busy, absorbed sound of feet descending endlessly towards them, like the Goons padding along some impossibly long radio corridor to open the door to one more visitor to Bedlam.

It was Bunty, however, who reached them first, Bunty with a sizable stone in her two hands, and some furious atavism stirring in her that made fear of secondary importance. It was not a particularly well-chosen stone, but she had had to grope for it in the dark. Nor was she very deft at using it; perhaps she was right, and they both of them had some built-in prohibition against killing that handicapped them badly in a situation like this. But she did her best. The stone thudded against the back of a classically Alpine skull, low towards where the neck should have been if there had been any neck, and rolled down hunched shoulders to bounce away down the slope. The throttling hand slackened, the weight slumped with a grunt over Luke's threshing body. Bunty, taking what she could find, reached over the wide shoulders to seize the lapels of the man's raincoat, and drag it back with all her strength to pinion his upper arms. Luke heaved himself clear with a convulsion that sent them all three slipping and staggering downhill; and Bunty caught at his hand and helped to pull him to his feet.

They were at the edge of the jetty, hand in hand, the injured man dragging himself along after them half-stunned and moaning, when the three men from above overtook and fell upon them. Luke, swinging to fight them off a shade too late, went down heavily beneath two of them, and stayed down. Bunty, turning at the edge of the water, watched the small, murderous black eye of a revolver advance at leisure until it touched her breast.

'All right, sweetheart,' said the small, murderous, black-a-vised man behind the gun, in just the mild, metallic, indifferent voice the gun might have used, 'upstairs again, and see and be a lady on the way. Your boy-friend here can't afford no slips on your part. He's got enough troubles as it is. Walk!'

Bunty walked, at an even and sedate pace, leading that procession up the cliff-path and back to the house, with the gun not a yard from her back, and a torch pricking her consciousness occasionally to remind her that every step was watched. She walked with the same erect stride she always had, stretching her long legs to the steeper steps without slackening speed. There was nothing she could do, except make it clear that she had no tricks to play. Luke was only a few yards behind her, and the enemy, though reduced to three against two, had now four guns at their disposal, and none ranged against them. There was no sense in provoking death.

Far behind them among the rocks, the wounded man hoisted himself painfully from stair to stair, dragging one leg and leaving a long smear of blood behind him. When the prisoners were safely in the house and under guard, perhaps one of his fellows would help him to finish the journey. Now it seemed that he was of no importance. His thin, quiet cursing followed them up to the terrace, and behind it like a backcloth rolled the soft, absorbed night-singing of a calm sea.

How queer, thought Bunty involuntarily, I still don't know where we are. Somewhere on the east coast of Scotland. North of Muirdrum, I remember the policeman there thought he'd recognised Luke's car passing through. Luke mentioned going into Forfar. Her mind sketched in, with lightheaded clarity, a map of the Angus coastline. Somewhere between Arbroath and Montrose? Up the coast there must be Lunan Bay, and farther north are the Bullars of Buchan, where Doctor Johnson insisted on sailing into the rock cauldron in a small boat. You can only do it when it's calm. *Calm*! Like tonight. You could do it to-night.

Luke came up the path after her between two guns. The key of the boat-house had been taken from him along with the gun from the same pocket. All their evidence lost. He was bruised, sore and sick with chagrin; but most of all he raged that he had not sent Bunty home or taken her to the safety of the nearest police station in the morning, while there'd been time, time they'd frittered away in supposing that they had only the police to contend with. Now they knew better, and now was too late.

But at every step he felt that there was something wrong, that something about Bunty was not as he had expected it to be, and his battered and confused mind could not run the discrepancy to earth. Not until they were hustled and prodded through the back door into the kitchen, and there penned in a corner until someone found the fuse-box. The wounded man, out in the darkness, laboriously groaned and fumbled his way up towards the terrace, and no one seemed to care. If you're incapacitated, you're finished with. Throw the broken one away and get a new one. The modern trend even with human beings, it seemed. Luke shivered, but even in the middle of this horror there was a grain of comfort that glowed securely, so clear was the division between himself and these people with whom, for a while, he had been confusing himself.

It was worth finding out, even if it was the last thing he did.

'Draw the curtains,' ordered the irresponsibly cheerful voice from inside the broom-cupboard. 'Don't want to embarrass the visitors, do we? Neighbours are nosy enough without encouraging 'em.' A curious, high-pitched giggle echoed brassily out of the enclosed space.

'They're drawn,' said the small, dark, deadly one. 'Get on with it.'

'All right, the current's on.'

The third man flipped down the light-switch, the round fluorescent fixture blinked its daylight eye once, and then glowed steadily. And there they were, all five of them, two prisoners and three captors. No, six altogether, the lame man was just fumbling his way through the doorway, holding by the latch with all his weight. They hauled him inside not out of any concern for him, but so that they could close the door and keep the light within.

It was then that Luke realised at last what had been wrong with Bunty. How could she have used both hands to heave up that rock and crack this wretch on the head with it? She'd been carrying something when they set out. She wasn't carrying anything now, except the handbag that swung from her wrist. She had both hands in the pockets of her light grey coat, and was looking round at them all measuringly and warily, her face stonily calm. She met even his eyes, and her expression didn't change, was significantly careful not to change.

Somewhere, at some moment which he could not locate in his frantic recapitulation, Bunty had disposed of the better part of fifteen thousand pounds. The package of banknotes and Pippa Gallier's passport and air ticket had vanished without trace.

Chapter 10

'Nothing else on either of 'em,' reported the giggler, shoving Luke back into the corner of the wicker settee with a careless vigour that made the white frame creak indignantly. 'Never thought there would be. I told you these babes are sharper than he reckoned.'

So there was another he, not so far present. They had been gradually coming to some such conclusion. Why should all hands have kept off them so indifferently, otherwise? The one who called the tune wasn't here yet. These four were merely waiting, and filling in time with the necessary preliminaries while they waited.

Bunty and Luke sat side by side in the two-seater settee, pushed well back into the window embrasure, as far as possible from the door of the living-room. It was easy for one man to control them there. The third man, the youngest, the dimmest, but perhaps the most vicious, too, sat on a chair placed carefully before them, far enough away to be out of their reach, close enough to have them both infallibly covered. He held his gun as though he loved it, as a call-girl might hold diamonds, and his eyes above it were like chips of bluish stone, flat and impervious, a little mad, the cunningly inlaid eyes of a stone scribe from later Egypt, built up with slivers of lapis lazuli and onyx and mother-of-pearl to give a lifelike semblance of humanity. He was dressed in what his kind and generation would certainly classify as sharpish gear, and he couldn't have been more than twenty-one. Bunty, watching him, sat very still indeed. The little dark man would kill for what seemed to him sufficient reason, and without any qualms except for his own safety afterwards. The other two would probably kill if they were ordered to. But this young one was the kind that might go off without warning, like a faulty grenade, and kill to ease his tension, or relieve his boredom, or simply because it occurred to him momentarily as something it would be fun to do, and no consideration of his own safety would keep him back, because thought had nothing to do with his processes.

The giggler could have passed for normal any time he liked. He was big and rosy, and looked like a country butcher, well-fleshed but not yet run to fat. There was nothing at all suspect about him, except the slightly hysterical pitch of his laughter.

And the other man, the one who had been posted well down the rock path to intercept them, sat hunched in one of the big chairs now, with his left trouser-leg rolled up above the knee, painfully sponging at his calf, where Luke's shot had torn its way straight through to ricochet from the rock behind. He had bled a lot, the water in the bowl at his feet was red. He pawed self-pityingly at the thick white flesh, and took no notice of what the others were doing. The giggler had fetched down gauze and wool and a bandage for him from the bathroom cupboard, and the victim was totally absorbed in nursing his wound. And indeed, thought Bunty, eyeing the damage, he must have been in a good deal of pain. When he had finished his bandaging, and got up gingerly to try his weight on the injured leg, all he could manage was a slow hobble, clinging to the furniture for support.

He was the biggest of them, and the oldest, a massive, muscular person with a white, sad, fleshy face. His hair was receding, and his expression was anxious and defensive. The small dark one had called him Quilley. There was something odd in the attitude of the younger ones to him, the way they left him out of their calculations, or included him only as an afterthought. Or perhaps it was not so odd, in such a world as theirs, that a man's stock should crash when he's disabled, or has got the worst of an encounter. He was a doubtful asset now, and a potential liability. Some wild animals, the kind that hunt in packs, kill off their injured or infirm members, as some sort of measure of social hygiene.

'It's here, though,' said the small dark man with certainty. 'It's here somewhere. Either we find it, or he tells us where. The place ain't that big. You sure about the car, then, Skinner?'

'I'm sure,' said the giggler cheerfully, spinning the garage key round his finger with absent-minded dexterity. 'Clean as a whistle.'

'You didn't miss out on anywhere? Under the back seat? Down the upholstery?'

'I didn't miss out on anything. There's nothing there.'

'What you wasting time for?' the boy with the levelled gun demanded querulously, without removing his unwinking stone gaze from his charges. 'I could get it out of him easy. Or *her*!' The flick of excitement on the last word indicated that he would rather prefer that alternative. Bunty supposed that in its obscene fashion it was a compliment, but if so, it was one she could well have done without. She could feel Luke's muscles stiffening beside her, his whole body rigid with anxiety. She cast one glance at him, and found his fixed profile almost too still. The cheek nearer to her was bruised and soiled. His mouth was drawn and stiff with fear for her.

'Yeah, I know!' said the dark man sardonically. 'And all at once we got no clues and no witness. If anybody shuts *this* one's mouth for good, it ain't going to be while *I'm* in charge. Think the boss'd wear that from anybody but himself? Sooner you than me, mate! But till he gets here, you take orders from me, and my orders are, *lay off*. OK?'

'Well, OK, Blackie, it's all one to me. I'm only saying . . .'

'You always are. Quit saying, and just keep your eye on 'em,

337

that's all, while we take this room apart.' He cast a long look round the airy living-room, and ended eye-to-eye with Luke. He wasn't expecting anything to come easily, but he went through the motions of asking. 'You could make it easy on yourself and us, kid. In the end you may have to, you know that? What *did* you do with the money?'

'What money?' said Luke.

Skinner, dismantling the drawers of the writing-desk one by one, giggled on his unnerving high note. 'Get that! He knows nothing about any money. *What money!*'

'All right,' said Blackie, sighing. 'You want it the hard way, you can have it. We've got time. But don't say I didn't ask you nicely. If you think better of it, just say, any time. We're going to find it in the end.'

And they set to work to find it, emptying books from the shelves, letters from the bureau, rolling back the rugs for loose blocks in the parquet, but discovering none. They took the living-room to pieces and put it together again, neatly and rapidly but without haste, with the thoroughness of long practice. But they found nothing of interest. And Bunty and Luke, so close to each other that their arms brushed at every slight movement, sat and watched the search with narrow attention, and kept silent. They had nothing to say in these circumstances, even to each other. They hardly ventured to look at each other, for fear even that exchange should give something away. Yet something had passed between them, tacitly and finally. Neither of them would dream of giving in, unless or until the case was beyond hope. Perhaps not even then; they were both stubborn people. He didn't know what Bunty had done with the parcel of notes, but if she'd had the presence of mind to hide it even out there in the dark, pursued and ambushed as they'd been, then she certainly wasn't going to give away its whereabouts now without the toughest of struggles. And Luke couldn't because he didn't know.

'Clean as wax-polish in here,' concluded Blackie, looking round the room. 'Let's have a go at the kitchen.'

The kitchen, compact though it was, was full of fitments that would keep them busy for quite a while. Blackie sized up the job in one frowning stare, and jerked his head at the youth guarding the prisoners.

'Hey, you, Con . . . hand over to Quilley and come and give us a hand here.'

'What, and leave nobody but him between this lot and the front door?' Con said disrespectfully. 'With the lock broke? Or did you forget?'

With impassive faces and strained senses Bunty and Luke filed away for reference one more scrap of information that might, just might, with a lot of luck, be relevant and useful. They'd had to break the lock to get in. The bolts hadn't been shot, so there might still be those to contend with, supposing a chance ever offered; but on the whole it was unlikely that they would have bothered to shoot them home now. They were expecting the boss; and the boss sounded the sort of man who would expect all doors to open before him without delay.

'Watch it!' said Blackie, without personal animosity. 'You're nearly too fly to live with, these days, you are. So if he can't sprint, he'll still have a gun, won't he?'

'Yes, and instructions not to do any real damage with it!'

Con talked too much for his own good. That little weakness might have been there to be discovered in any case, but there'd been no need to spell it out and underline it. For the sake of the information they – or one of them – held, Bunty and Luke must at all costs be preserved alive until they had confided it. Once the secret had been prised out of them, of course, they were expendable enough.

'What if they jump him? So he plugs one of 'em in the leg, and the other's out of the room and out the front door, and us all back there in the kitchen. And that'll sound good when you make your report, Blackie, me old Crowe.'

339

'All right, then, we'll make dead sure. Bring 'em in here with you, and lock 'em in the store. There's no window in there, and only one door, and that's into the kitchen. That'll make four of us between them and any way out. Satisfied?'

'Whatever you say.' Con rose, unfolding his long legs and arms with the stiffly articulated movements of a grasshopper. He made a brisk upward gesture with the gun. 'Come on, then, let's have the pair of you. You heard the gentleman. You want showing the way to the store? Hey, Blackie, there's nothing useful in there, is there? Garden shears or sécateurs, or like that?'

'Nah, nothing, we done in there. Bring 'em along!'

'After *you*, lady!' said Con with a whinnying laugh, and ground the barrel of his revolver hard into Luke's ribs out of sheer exuberance. From his chair Quilley watched them go with harassed, apathetic eyes, as if he had resigned perforce from the whole business, and was waiting with apprehension for someone to decide what was to be done with him now.

All Mrs. Alport's primrose-coloured kitchen fitments stood open, and the giggler was grubbing among the taps under the sink. The store measured only three feet by two, and some of that was taken up by shallow shelves at the back, where Reggie Alport kept his electrical spares, bulbs, fuse-wire, plugs and adaptor. Luke had to stoop to enter it; even Bunty's hair brushed the roof.

Con watched them fold themselves uncomfortably and closely together in this upright coffin, and shrilled with horse-laughter as he closed and locked the door on them.

'Nice and cosy for two . . . I call that just the job. Hey, Blackie, I hope you know what you're doing. I can't see 'em wanting to come out o' there.' He thumped the locked door just once with the flat of his hand. 'Have fun!' he called, and went off to sack Louise Alport's cupboards.

In the darkness, smelling of timber and fine dust, Luke shifted

340

gently to make more room for her, and drew her closely into his arms; there was no other way of finding adequate space. Her head fitted into the hollow of his shoulder and neck; she felt his cheek pressed against her hair, and his lips close to her ear.

'Bunty . . .' The finest ardent thread of a whisper. 'Did you understand? They can't lock the front door, they had to break the lock. Bunty, I'm going to try to start something . . . the first chance I get, when they fetch us out of here . . .'

'No,' she breathed into his ear as softly and as urgently, 'you mustn't. They'll shoot you . . .'

'Not until they've found out what they want. They don't want to go to extremes until *he* gets here. You heard them. They as good as said *he*'s already rubbed out one person too soon, before he got his questions answered. Bunty, I'm going to try it. What else is there for us? I'll try to give you the item, but when I cut loose, *you run* . . .'

'No!' she said, an almost soundless protest.

'*Yes.* I'll cover you . . . somehow I will. You go straight for the front door and out. And, Bunty . . . don't stay on the road, *get into the trees.* . . . This lot are car men, cross-country you can leave them standing. . . .'

'I'm not going,' she said.

'*Yes* . . . you've *got* to go. You can go to the police, then, you can tell them. I'll stick it out here till they come.'

'In what sort of shape?' she whispered bitterly.

'Alive . . . and not a murderer. Better shape than I was in this time last night.'

'But Luke, listen . . . the police have had time by now to check up on that name and address I gave them. Suppose they do? Suppose they find out your friends have never heard of me, and the address I gave doesn't exist? They'll be back to find out what I'm up to, what's going on here. This is the one place they'll make for – *they'll* come to *us*. They could be back any moment,' she said, and her breath was warm on his cheek, turning his heart faint and crazed with love.

'Yes, they could,' he said, and his whispering voice trembled with the effort it put into being convincing; but she knew he didn't believe in it.

Neither did she, altogether, but it was at least a possibility. Especially if, by any remote chance, someone had brought in that purse with Bunty Felse's name on it, and tried to return it, and so set the Midshire police hunting for a missing woman, whose description would fit the totally unexpected woman in the Alports' cottage here in Angus. Such a long and complicated 'if'; but no one is more likely to fit diverse pieces of a puzzle patiently together than the police, whose job it is. And no one has better communications.

'But I want you out,' he said, 'before it comes to shooting. Even if they do come, it might be touch and go. I'd rather get you away. If I can make that chance, promise to try . . . promise me, Bunty . . .'

She lifted a hand and touched his cheek gently, let her palm lie there for a long moment holding him, partly in apology, partly as a distraction, because she had no intention of making any promises. When the time came she would play it as seemed best, weighing the chances for him as well as she could in the split second she would have for consideration. But she could not conceive of any combination of circumstances that was likely to induce her to leave him now.

He wanted to turn his head the few necessary inches, and press his lips into her palm, but he didn't do it, because he had no rights in her at all but those she had given him freely, and they were not that kind of rights. Until they were out of here – if they ever got out of here alive – there was nothing he could say to her, though his heart might be bursting. Afterwards, if they could clear up this affair with all its debts and start afresh, things might go very differently. But the darkness in which they stood seemed to him a symbolic as well as an actual darkness, and he couldn't see anything ahead. And there might not be any more time for talking, tonight or ever.

'Bunty, I'm sorry!' he breathed, and that seemed to be it. He had never been so short of words, and in any case, what good were they?

'For what? For getting into a mess through no real fault of your own?'

'For everything I've done to you. For involving you. I wish I could undo it,' he said. 'Forgive me!'

'There's nothing to forgive. You couldn't have involved me if I hadn't involved myself. No debts either way. Simply, it happened.'

'No ... I began as your ... murderer ...' The word was almost inaudible, lost in the tangle of her hair. 'Don't let me end like that now. I'll make the chance and you must go. That's why you *must* ... I can bear it if *you* get back safely ... I'll be satisfied then.'

And he meant it. If she had come out like a pilgrim, looking for something uniquely her own, some justification of her whole life to show to the gate-keepers and the gods when her time came, she had it. For every journey, even the last one, you need a ticket.

The dulled accompaniment of voices and movements from the kitchen had halted, recommenced, changed, and the two of them in their narrow prison had never noticed. Nor could they hear the approach of the car through so many layers of insulation. The first they knew of the boss's arrival was when the door of the store-cupboard was suddenly flung open, and Skinner beckoned them out into the light. They came, dazzled for a while after such a darkness, eyes wide and dazed from staring into a different kind of light. Luke kept his arm about Bunty as they were herded through the kitchen and into the living-room.

And the living-room was full of a large, restless, top-heavy man in a light overcoat and a deeper grey suit, standing astride the orange-coloured rug. It was a still night, but he seemed somewhere to have found a reserve of tempestuous wind, and

343

brought it into the house in the folds of his well-tailored but untamed clothes, so that the room seemed suddenly gusty and tremulous, convulsed with the excess of his energy. He was nearly half a head taller than Luke, and twice as wide, massive shoulders and barrel chest tapering away to long, narrow flanks. For all that bulk, he moved with a violent elegance that was half exuberant health and half almost psychotic self-confidence and self-love. He straddled the floor and looked them all over with the eye of a proprietor, viewing a new acquisition which didn't look like much now, but of which he could make something in double-quick time, and something profitable, too.

His head was big, to match his shoulders, and startlingly rough-hewn after the disguise of his immaculate clothes ended at the collar; a head of crude, bold lines, and a face in which the bone strained glossy beneath the tanned skin, not because there was so little flesh there, but because there was so much bone. He had a forehead ornamented with knobbly projections like incipient horns, and above it bright auburn hair grew low to a widow's peak. An upright cleft marked his massy chin. The deepset eyes – boxers should have eyes like that, invulnerable, lids and all, in cages of concrete skull, cased with hide like polished horn – twinkled with restless, reddish lights, good-humoured without being in the least reassuring.

. . . auburn hair growing low, cleft chin, eyes buried in a lot of bone . . .

Luke's fingers closed meaningly on Bunty's arm. He couldn't say anything to her, but there was no need, he had described this man to her so well that even she knew him on sight. This was the man on whose arm Pippa Callier had leaned devotedly as they left her flat together on Friday night, the man whose car had stood all night in the mews round the corner, waiting to take a mythical mother and her mythical cousin home again to Birmingham. How strange that she should have thought she could get away with such a pretence, even for a moment. And how innocent and unpractised it suddenly made her in Bunty's

344

sight. This was nobody's cousin, and one could almost believe, nobody's son. He could have burst out of a rock somewhere of his own elemental force, self-generated and dangerous.

She pressed her elbow into Luke's side in acknowledgment. But there was no way of telling him that she suddenly found herself better informed even than he was, that she, too, had seen this man before, just once and briefly, too distantly to have known all those details of his appearance, but clearly enough to know his movements again wherever she saw them, the long, arching stride of a man with vigour to spare, the appraising tilt of the big head, the swinging use of the high shoulders. On Friday evening, when he had meant nothing to her, before he changed into the dinner jacket that Luke had found so conspicuous in Queen Street.

Luke knew the boss's face again, as he had said he would. But Bunty knew more, his trade, his provenance, even his name, that last magic that every elemental being should guard as he guards his life, for in a sense it *is* his life.

This one hadn't guarded his. He had had it printed on windscreen stickers, blazoned on fluorescent posters, strung along thirty-seven be-flagged frontages in neon lights for all the world to see and memorise.

His name was Fleet.

Chapter 11

The huge newcomer revolved on the heel of a hand-made shoe, taking in all the inhabitants of this minor kingdom of his, and dealing in turn with them all.

'Hah!' he said, a bark of satisfaction and amusement, as he surveyed Luke from head to foot with one flash of his coarse-cut-marmalade eyes. 'I see you got the right party, anyhow. That's something!'

The snapping gaze swept over Bunty with interest, sized her up with casual appreciation, and flicked another glance at Luke. 'Well, get that! He finds new ones fast. Who'd have thought it!'

He tossed the key he was swinging across to Skinner. 'Turn the Jag round, will you, and wheel it up to the gate ready for off. You never know, we might have to leave on the hop.'

The skirt of his pearl-grey Terylene overcoat whirled, and another spin brought him to Quilley. 'What's the matter with *you*?' There was no sympathy in the inquiry, rather a note of outrage, even of immediate reserve. His employees had no business to get hurt on duty.

'I stopped one, boss. He had a gun.'

'Couldn't you bet on him having a gun?' Bunty had the impression for one instant that he had almost said '*The* gun', and thought better of it in time. 'What's up, then? How bad is it?' The top span, and he confronted Blackie. 'If he's a write-off for anything active, we can use him upstairs. Why haven't you got someone up there keeping a watch out? I tell you, half the constabulary could be walking in on us, and you sitting here playing hide and seek.'

'Somebody'd have been up there any minute now,' said Blackie, without noticeable chagrin; and indeed, the big man's voice, vibrant, full and pleasantly pitched, had no displeasure in it, he flashed and fulminated from excess of energy, and took delight in it as a kind of self-expression.

'Yeah, I know, because you cleaned up down here! All right, then, Quilley, get up there and keep a watch out front and back both. You can take it easy up there, just so you don't miss any movements around this place.'

'He can start looking around inside, too,' said Blackie. 'Because it ain't in here, it ain't in the kitchen or back there. And these two are playing dumb and daft.'

'It has to be somewhere here. Stands to sense. Go take that little front room apart, Skinner, and then go up and join Quilley. If he's there by then.' He cast a thoughtful eye at Quilley's painful and laborious progress across the room and out to the stairs. 'They get old and slow,' said Fleet with tolerant regret, like a practical farmer contemplating putting down a worn-out horse. And he peeled off his smart driving gloves, dove grey and tan, and dropped them on the table, beside the scattered belongings they had taken from Luke's pockets.

'These what were on him?' He pawed them over thoughtfully. 'Keys . . . several. His own bunch . . . house . . . car . . . suitcase? That'll be upstairs . . . or had he got it away somewhere?'

'It's upstairs. They never had time to take anything with 'em, they just ran when they heard us. There's a way down to the water, and a boat-house down there. Locked. I reckon this would be the key to that. He had it in his coat pocket, along with the gun. This one's the back door. We sprung that, it was an easy touch. The front we had to bust.'

'And what's this other one?'

Echoing hollowly down the wall of the stairs dead on cue, Quilley's voice, dutifully anxious to please, reported: 'Boss, there's one of these bedrooms locked up.' He was hopeful of a discovery. A locked door was promising.

'That'll be it,' said Fleet, pleased. 'There's a key here could belong to it,' he called. 'Skinner, come and take it up to him, see what he's got there. And better have a quick look through the suitcase.'

Skinner came at leisure, cheerful as ever; it began to seem a lunatic cheerfulness.

'And now,' said Fleet, dusting his hands, 'suppose you two sit down prettily over there, where we can keep an eye on you, and we'll have our little talk.'

He caught a dining-chair by the back, and swung it into a reversed position in front of the wicker settee, to which Con had again herded his prisoners. The light skirts of the pearl-grey coat whisked out like wings. Fleet sat down astride the chair, and leaned his folded arms comfortably on the back.

'Straight to the point, that's me. *Where's the money?*'

'What money?' said Luke woodenly. 'I know nothing about any money.'

'I'm a reasonable man, I'll try to help you remember.'

'Pippa Gallier didn't bring any money over to my place Saturday evening,' said Luke. 'You're barking up the wrong tree.'

'Kiddo, she sure as fate didn't bring it Friday evening, but who's arguing about dates? She brought it. She was shinning out, and you were the ferryman. You may as well tell me now what you've done with it, because I'm going to find out in the end.'

'She never brought any money to me, I'm telling you.'

'You're telling me fairy-tales, kid, but go ahead. I've got time.'

Uninvited, Bunty said in a hard, detached voice: 'That's what you think. But what you don't know is that the police have been here before you. This morning. I got rid of them then, but what I told them isn't going to last them long. My bet is they could be back any moment now. I expected them before this. You don't think this place *belongs* to him, do you?'

Fleet turned his head the little way that was necessary, and gave her his full attention for the first time. She sat with fixed, motionless face, smoothing a chipped nail on one hand, but at Fleet's persistent stare she raised to him the full hazel glance of her eyes, wide and unwavering.

'You know,' said Fleet, 'you're not at all hard to look at, now I come to notice, but girl, you're no hand at lying.'

'That makes it even funnier,' said Bunty, unmoved, 'because I'm not lying. But you know it all. Don't say I didn't warn you.'

It was essential that none of these men should suspect how easy it would be to wring concessions from her by tormenting Luke, or from Luke by tormenting her. She had even toyed momentarily with the idea of trying to act the part of a disillusioned pick-up with cheapened accent and roughened voice, but she knew she couldn't make a job of it. And it occurred to her now that that might not have confused Fleet in the slightest, while this more unexpected female companion put him slightly off his immaculate stride. And all the while she was straining her ears after what was happening upstairs. Maybe they were turning out Luke's suitcase first, as the best bet. But the discovery couldn't be long now. Her nerves tightened, waiting for it.

'And where,' inquired Fleet curiously, 'did he find you? It sure didn't take him long. I wouldn't have thought he was that quick off the mark.'

'I picked her up in a pub,' Luke said harshly. 'I should have left her there.'

The words were acknowledgment enough of the lead she had given him, and fitted the image of indifference now turning to resentment. It was lucky that they were also true, Bunty thought, for up to then she had no great opinion of Luke's potentialities as a liar.

And it was at that moment that the pair upstairs unlocked

the door of the guest bedroom, and walked in upon the treasure secreted there.

The cry that came hollowly down the stairs was almost a scream, brief, horrified and unreasonably alarming. Fleet came to his feet in a cat's alert, hair-triggered leap, whirling the chair away from him across the room. Blackie span round to face the doorway, gun in hand. Con kept his weapon levelled, but even his stony eyes wandered. It was the first moment of disarray, and it was useless. Three here between the prisoners and the door, two more scuttling in haste down the stairs to add to the odds. Luke's braced muscles ached with longing, but he knew it was no good. He would only succeed in killing them both.

'For Pete's sake . . .!' exploded Fleet exasperatedly. 'What's with you two?'

Skinner appeared in the doorway, mouth and eyes wide open, with Quilley limping and shivering at his back.

'In that room, the locked one . . . You know what's in there, boss? *She* is . . . the Gallier girl! He brought her up here with him! She's there lying on the bed!'

Fleet struck his large, well-kept hands together with a clap like a gun going off and uttered a brief crow of amusement, astonishment and triumph.

'And her things? Is her case here?'

'It's there.' Blackie indicated the corner where it stood against the wall. 'Her bag, too, it's there on the bookcase. We started with them, but there's nothing . . . Well, we *knew* . . .' He swallowed that admission in time. 'But I never thought he'd bring *her* all the way up here. I thought he'd ditched her somewhere . . .'

Fleet came strolling back across the room like a contented cat, long-stepping, disdainful, spread his feet wide before his prisoners, and leaned over them with a benign smile.

'So you don't know anything about my money, eh? And I take it you know nothing about the girl up there, either? She just

350

flew here! As for the police, they kindly called in this morning, I suppose, and helped you carry her upstairs? Now we know where we stand.'

He plucked back the chair, span it about in one hand, and resumed his place astride it in high good-humour; and the trouble was that Bunty could not for the life of her see how his mind was working. Something obscure and complicated was going on in that formidable skull, something of no advantage to anyone but himself, something that involved and made sense of the body upstairs, and still left him free. He'd admitted nothing, except that he was looking for the money; and such indiscretions as the others had let fall didn't amount to much, and in any case, she realised with a small leap of her heart, he didn't know about them, and was planning whatever he was planning without taking them into account. He was *pleased* about Pippa being here in the house, it had suggested something to him, something neat and workmanlike that afforded for him an effective exit. Bunty wished she knew what it was.

'So you brought her body up here, and all her things, and left the deck clean. Nobody could blame you for that, either, kid, nor for bringing the money along, too. Where was it? Not in her case, I know that . . . I was looking for it, while you were still out cold . . . *right after you shot her . . .*'

His voice moved like a cat, too, suavely and softly and bonelessly along the insinuating sentences, and pounced suddenly, a fishing cat. But the flashing paw clawed up more than he had bargained for. Until that moment it had not dawned on either of his listeners that he might well be in doubt as to how much Luke knew about the events of Saturday night, and how guilty he believed himself to be. A little push in the right direction might get him the information he needed. But it was a chance two could take; and the right reaction might even provide them with a slender and precarious advantage.

Luke closed his eyes and sank his head in his hands. He made

351

no attempt to deny anything. Bunty held her breath, feeling her way after him blindly.

'So I reckon the money was in the one place I couldn't get at. *In the car . . .*'

'The car's clean,' said Blackie. 'Skinner took it apart.'

'*Now* it's clean. But that's where the stuff was. Must have been. We looked everywhere else. So you found it, kiddo, and you were all set to make a clean get-away with it, is that it? After all, you had to run, they'd soon be after you for murder. Better run with a nice little nest-egg like that than without it. You know what, I've got a lot of sympathy for you! She was a crooked little bitch, if ever there was one. Crossed you up for me, and crossed me up for the money I trusted her with. She asked for what you gave her. If it hadn't been you it would have been someone else. The way I felt when I found she'd cut and run with my money, I tell you straight, it might have been *me* if you hadn't got in first.'

'I was drunk,' protested Luke from behind his sheltering hands, and the dark hair shook forward over his brow and helped to hide his face. His voice was high and unsteady, it would do well enough for an ordinary, harmless young man who had been running all day from the nightmare knowledge that he was a murderer. 'I didn't even *know*,' he said, writhing. 'She waved the damn gun at me . . . she made me mad . . .'

'I know! She asked for it. I'm not planning on turning you in for that.'

Not this time, thought Bunty; because you've thought of something better. I wish I knew what it is! I wish I knew, I wish Luke knew, exactly how much of that quarrel you did overhear.

Luke looked up mistrustfully under his disordered hair. The big man loomed over him mountainous and daunting, his face in shadow.

'What were you planning on doing? . . . you and the lady? I hear there's a boat . . . was that it? You reckon you could make it across to the Continent from here?'

352

'Yes, I could make it . . . I *could* have made it,' Luke corrected himself bitterly, 'if you hadn't sent this lot after us.'

'And Pippa? She was going half-way, I suppose?'

The dark head drooped again, the thin hands came up and scrubbed wearily at the thin cheeks. An almost inaudible voice said: 'Yes . . .'

'Look,' said Fleet reasonably, 'I'm not a cop. I've got nothing against you. Why should I have? She did the dirty on both of us, I've got a fellow feeling for you. There's no reason in the world why you and I shouldn't do a deal.'

He was, in his way, a marvellous performer. To look at him sitting there, his rocky face placid and benevolent, was almost to believe in his genuineness. He could create a kind of hallucination even when you knew he was lying, by the sheer force of his energy. Yet at the same time he had produced on Bunty an effect for which not even she was prepared. Up to now she had merely reasoned that this man had killed Pippa with his own hands; now, perversely, she knew it. Not these others, not even Con with his cold, impervious eyes – Fleet.

Luke lifted his head and studied the face before him with eyes narrowed in calculation; and somewhere deep in those wary pupils a spark of hope and encouragement came to life.

'What are you getting at?' he asked cautiously.

'What I say, if you like to take the lady and light out for Holland, or wherever, what's that to me? I'm saying nothing. *Just so you don't take my money with you*! You can have your freedom and welcome, but my dough you can't have. You tell us where you've put it, and as soon as I've got it in my hands we'll all clear out of here, and leave you to put out to sea as fast as you like.' He leaned a little nearer, with a wolfish smile on his lips, which were thrust out aggressively by the massive teeth within. 'But if you don't act like a sensible lad, and hand over, I *will* turn you in. Better freedom without the lolly than neither a one of 'em. You think it over!'

'How do I know,' demanded Luke with growing confidence,

but still with some reserve, 'that you'll keep your bargain? How do I know you won't take the money and then call the police on us?'

'Why should I? What have I got to gain? I came for the money, and that's all I want. And I don't need to tell you, I'm sure, that I'm not anxious to call attention to myself among the cops unless I have to. I've got to be feeling very mean to take that risk. Once I've got my money back, what have I got to feel mean about? But make no mistake, you cross me now and I can be mean as all get-out.'

He got up suddenly, airily, light on his feet like so many bulky men, swung his chair back to the table, and strolled away across the room.

'Take your pick, kiddo. It's up to you.'

In the momentary silence Skinner came down the stairs again, his researches completed. He spread empty hands and raised his shoulders. 'Nothing up there. I left Quilley on look-out, but it's as quiet as the grave, and black as your hat on the land side. What cooks here?'

He looked from Fleet to Blackie, who was frowning in frantic thought, many coils behind in following his boss's complex proceedings; and from Blackie to Con, who had shut off what mind he had and given up the struggle some minutes ago, and was now no more than a machine for pointing a gun to order. They were all of them confounded that the hard questioning had not begun long ago. There must be a reason.

There *must* be a reason, and the reason was not any squeamishness or compunction on Fleet's part. It was just barely possible that he really meant to withdraw once he got his hands on the money, exactly as he had said, and that he found it preferable and less messy to trade on Luke's conviction of his own guilt rather than to beat the required information out of him. But still Bunty couldn't believe it. He was more devious than that, he enjoyed being devious. There was something buried deeper, beneath this apparent reasonableness. Did he, for some obscure

354

purpose of his own, want a Luke completely unmarked by violence? *And for what?*

'Hush!' said Fleet. 'Our young friend's making up his mind. To be sensible, I hope.'

'I haven't got a lot of choice, have I?' said Luke loudly; and his manner became, in some way Bunty could recognise but not define, a direct response to Fleet's, a nice balance of nervousness, doubt, and growing assurance. He had not looked at her throughout, and she understood that he dared not, that if he did his eyes would betray him, and the enemy would no longer believe in this guilt-ridden, squirming fugitive.

'It's an alternative,' said Fleet, smiling at him with the first careless glint of contempt. 'You can hand over and go free, or rot in gaol for fourteen years or so thinking about the money you can't get at. For a million it might be worth it – not for this little lot, not by my measure. You please yourself.'

'It isn't worth it by my measure, either.' He licked his dry lips and swallowed hard, reluctant but driven. 'All right!' he said in a gulping breath. 'You can have the damned money!'

'That's better,' said Fleet warmly. 'I knew you'd see sense. Where is it?'

Bunty had not the least idea what Luke was going to say. She was lost, like Fleet's henchmen, she could only wait, and be ready to follow whatever lead events and Luke offered her.

'You ought to have known, if you'd given any thought to it,' said Luke, with the feeble spleen of a defeated man scrabbling for what crumbs of dignity he can salvage. 'You think we were going without it, or something, when we lit out of here down to the sea? We had the stuff down there already, of course, waiting till it was dark and we could slip away without being seen.'

'Aaaah!' breathed Fleet, and pondered in silence for a moment, his eyes narrowed upon Luke's face. It was apt, it was reasonable, it would certainly have to be tested. 'Go on, tell us more. Why didn't you take off as soon as you got here?'

355

'Because it was nearly daylight. Anybody round here would know the boat. Even if they didn't start investigating us, they might very well take it for granted the Alports were up here, and the local shop might send in, even on a Sunday, to see if they wanted supplies. There's no telephone here, people *come*. The Alports are good customers, and well known. We didn't want anyone poking around here and finding us instead, and that car in the garage. It seemed better to risk lying low today, and setting out after dark.'

'But you put the cash aboard in advance! Then why not your luggage, too?' demanded Fleet shrewdly.

'We wanted it. Damn it, we'd been up all night, we needed a bath . . . I had to shave . . . We weren't *expecting* any trouble. I've been here before with the owners, I could account for being here if I *had* to – for everything except Pippa and the money.' He wiped his forehead feverishly; there was no need to act, sweat stood on him in globules, bitter as gall on his lips. 'Pippa – it was too light to risk being seen carrying her down to the boat, and anyhow, there was no way of hiding her there any better than here. No use trying to sink her here, inshore. She *had* to wait for dark. But the money, just a flat parcel, that was only a minute's job, so we made sure of it.'

'It occurs to me,' said Fleet thoughtfully, 'that with all this talk of "our" luggage your lady friend here doesn't seem to have any belongings, beyond a handbag – I take it that grey one belongs to her? That was going to be a bit awkward, wasn't it, girl? Are you always so improvident?'

'I've got nothing but a handbag,' Bunty said with hard deliberation, 'because I walked out with nothing but a handbag. Why, is my business. *He* doesn't know the reason, and you're not interested, either. He told you, he picked me up in a pub. What's the odds? If you know anything about that kid upstairs, you know that king-size case of hers is full of brand-new stuff. I carry a few extra pounds, but we're much the same size. I could get by.'

Amazed, she watched the image she was projecting emerge and parade before him, no predictable bar-fly, but a woman on the dangerous verge of middle-age, a woman who had suddenly rebelled, looked over her shoulder and cut her losses. And how far from the truth was that picture? There had been a time, only twenty-four hours ago, when it would have seemed to her as close as a mirror-image. Now it was clear that she and this imaginary creature were at opposite poles, and never could, by any miracle, have touched fingertips. Fleet's eyes went over her with mild curiosity, and looked away again. To him it was a reasonably convincing portrait she had drawn, or perhaps he didn't care enough to probe any further.

'So you hid the money ready,' he said, eyeing Luke, 'in the boat.'

'I didn't say it was in the boat.' That would have been too easy, one man could go over the whole craft in ten minutes, and Luke wanted at least two of them out of the way. 'It was getting light, we couldn't hang around to unlock the boat-house. We had the stuff all proofed up for sea, in oiled silk and plastic, we just fastened a nylon line on the parcel and let it down over the edge of the jetty, into the water. There's an old mooring ring down there, right at the seaward end, well down the stone facing, it'll be under water now. But you can reach it, all right, if you lie on your stomach and reach over. The end of the line's made fast to that.'

Blackie Crowe had paled with shock at the thought of fifteen thousand pounds bubbling about beneath the tide on the end of a nylon line. Even Fleet's thick eyebrows arched as high as the Neanderthal bone-structure within would let them.

'I hope for your sake you *did* make it fast,' he said grimly. 'How come, is it weighted, then?'

Luke nodded. 'Enough to keep it down out of sight.' He came to his feet, slowly and cautiously, in order not to provoke Con's jumpy trigger-finger, but readily enough to show his willingness to oblige. 'I'll go down with your man and show him,' he said, in a soft voice that did its best not to seem too eager.

'Ah, now, just a minute, not too fast.' Fleet waved him down again, but Luke, though he stayed where he was, remained standing. 'How do I know you're not in Channel class in the water? You might make a break for it with a nice clean dive while one of the boys was fishing off the end of the jetty. You might even stick a toe under him and help *him* into the water. And we might still be whistling for that money. Oh, no, laddie, you won't do any showing, only on paper. We might never see you again.'

Luke jerked his head at Bunty. 'You'd have her, wouldn't you?' he said, aggrieved; but the very faint, opportunist glint in his eye was not quite concealed. 'Think I'd do a thing like that to her?'

'Since you ask me, yes, I think you would. I'm not so sure you put the right value on the lady. No, you'll stay here.'

'One man alone won't have an easy job finding it,' Luke urged earnestly. 'It's pitch dark down there now, he'll need somebody to give him a light, and hang on to him while he leans over. The ring must be eighteen inches under by now, and there's a tidy drag below those rocks. You could lose him and the money.'

Fleet hesitated. 'Know what, kid? I think you're trying to pull something. You didn't have much trouble putting it there, seemingly.'

'I didn't have *any*! It was nearly daylight, and low tide, and I know the place. It's a different cup of tea now, for somebody who doesn't. Better let me go. I'll do the fishing, if that'll satisfy you.'

He made the offer with a tight, strained urgency and fevered eyes, sure now that it would be refused, and sure that he could get two of the enemy out of the house on this fools' errand. He ventured one brief flicker of his eyes in Bunty's direction; she knew, she was on his heels now, close and eager.

Fleet made up his mind. It might be true, and it would take no more than a quarter of an hour or so to put it to the test.

'Here, come to the desk. Draw me a map, and make it good. Direction and distance from the foot of this path you talk about – the lot.' He watched Luke stoop to rummage in the top drawer of the desk for pen and writing-pad, tear off the top sheet of the pad, and without hesitation begin to sketch in the jetty and the approach angle of the cliff path. Satisfied, Fleet turned to Skinner, who was lounging against the wall by the door, one shoulder hunched as a prop. 'You go down and fish up this parcel. Take Con with you. And give me that Colt, just in case.'

For one moment his back was turned squarely on Luke, and his bulk partly hid the desk from the eyes of the others. For once Luke could move a hand in the shelter of his own body, and not be observed. The large, smooth granite pebble, veined and beautiful, that his friends used as a paperweight, lay close to his right sleeve. He closed his hand over it and drew it towards him, sliding it quickly into the pocket of his coat. By the time Fleet swung round on him again he was scribbling measurements on his sketch map, and turned to show his hands otherwise empty and innocent as he handed it over.

'There you are. X marks the spot where the treasure's buried.'

He stayed where he was as they examined it, his back to the desk. It was a good place, if they'd let him keep it. It meant that when the moment came he could draw the two remaining armed men to this side of the room to deal with him, and leave Bunty a clear run to the doorway. The lame man upstairs, edging anxiously and audibly from front window to rear window and back again, would never get down the stairs in time to intercept her.

'Seems straightforward enough,' said Skinner, memorising the lay-out. 'Better get that big torch out of the Riley, Con, this one here's giving out.'

Without a gun in them, Con's hands were discontented and at a loss what to do with themselves. Only the weight and solidity of the Colt had held them still. They had the twitches now. Maybe Con was already hooked on one of the hard drugs, maybe he was only half-way there on LSD. Fleet himself was watching him, as the boy left the room, with a considering coldness, a practical speculation. Con might not last very long in Fleet's employ; but he hadn't become a liability yet.

Luke strained his ears for the sound of the front door opening and closing on Con's exit, opening and closing again as he came back with a large, rubber-cased torch. The latch clicked into place lightly on his return, and he came on without any delay into the living-room. The bolts were not shot, the lock no longer functioned; the way out was open.

'And who,' Fleet asked suddenly, settling back in his chair, 'has got the other gun – *his* gun?'

Skinner turned in the kitchen doorway. 'I have. Want it?'

'Yes, hand it over.' Fleet laid down the Colt close beside him on the edge of the table, and took Pippa's Liliput in his hands. No doubt he had supplied it in the first place, while he still half-trusted her. 'That's all. Go on, get on with it.'

Then there were four of them left in the room. They heard the receding footsteps cross the kitchen, heard the outer door open and close, and for a moment or two faint sounds still reached them, dropping away down the first steps of the path. Bunty sat erect and rigid, her eyes fixed on Fleet. Luke quietly turned the chair round from the desk and sat down there; and no one ordered him back to join Bunty in the window embrasure. So much gained. Two ways to aim and shoot now, instead of one.

Fleet had pulled a handful of paper tissues from his pocket, and was polishing idly at the Liliput, his hands at work almost absent-mindedly, filling in time by getting on with the next job while he waited. His eyes studied Luke thoughtfully across the room, with the detached assurance of a practised mathematician solving a routine problem.

The Grass Widow's Tale

Or an experienced undertaker measuring a potential client for his coffin?

Bunty had been watching the active fingers for several seconds before their movements abruptly clicked into focus for her, and made blinding sense. Her heart lurched and turned in her with the shock of realisation. Suddenly she knew what had been lying there all the while beneath the surface manœuvrings of that tortuous mind, she knew what kind of bargain it was that Fleet had struck with his prisoners, and why he wanted Luke unbruised and unbattered. Once he got his hands on the money the whole gang would pack up and get out of here, yes; but not until they'd staged a second and less fallible tableau for the police to discover when they finally caught up. A murdered girl upstairs, a girl who would eventually be traced back to Comerbourne; in the garage the car for which the Midshire police had been putting out calls all day; and down here in the living-room another victim, some woman the fugitive had picked up in his flight, perhaps intending to escape abroad with her, only to despair and put an end to her here, before – last act of all – putting a bullet through his own head and dying beside her. The experts would easily demonstrate that the same gun had killed all three, the gun the police would find in dead Luke Tennant's grip when they came. There would be no other prints on it but his; those softly polishing fingers were busy making sure of that now. She watched them in fascination. They had already finished with the barrel, wiped the grip clean, taken care of the trigger-guard, and now they were twisting another tissue neatly about the butt.

There remained only the trigger. There was no point in wiping that, of course; not until afterwards.

Chapter 12

So now she knew the score, whether Luke knew it or not, and they had nothing left to lose. She had perhaps two minutes or so to make up her mind. When he starts something, she asked herself, do I run or don't I? Things are changed now, this is a life and death matter whatever I do. Have we a chance of getting out of here together? She considered that with the searching eye of one who has been through death once already, and is no longer flustered by its proximity, and told herself with detachment that the answer must be no. And if I run, have I a sporting chance of getting clear alone? Yes, I believe I might have. But have I any chance at all of reaching the police, or any other reliable help, and bringing them back here in time to save Luke? Over that she hesitated, but in the end the answer was that it might be betting against the odds, but it still might come off. With one of the victims lost, with a witness at large who could identify them, they might scrap the whole plan and think it wisest to get out, leave Luke alive, and cut their losses.

Do I run, then? Yes, she told herself, I run. On balance it seems the sanest thing to do, for both of us.

There were snags, of course, in Fleet's design, but he couldn't be expected to know about all of them, and in any case he would take the small risk involved as a natural gamble. There was the broken lock on the front door. Presumably his plan envisaged that break-in as being attributed to Luke on the run; he didn't know that the key had its hiding-place right there on the spot, and that Luke was admitted to the secret, and had no need to break locks. The Alports would testify to that, and the point might stick in some Scots policeman's craw, like a husk in porridge, and refuse to be dislodged. She knew it would have stuck in George's. The shadow of the unknown other person would be there to be found, once the possibility was acknowledged. It is very difficult to erase yourself completely from the scene where you have once been, the imprint of your presence and your acts remains as a faint outline still, an indentation, never entirely smoothed out.

She wondered, for one broken instant, whether it was worthwhile calling Fleet's attention to all the discrepancies he couldn't possibly trim into his pattern. But that was no use; he didn't expect a hundred per cent perfection, perhaps he wouldn't even be happy without the residue of risk. Certainly he wouldn't be deterred by it. No, there was nothing to be done here. What she had to do was be ready to seize the moment if it came, and make sure of getting through the doorway and into the trees.

It couldn't be long now. She had done all the thinking she could do in approximately twenty seconds, though it had seemed an age. Now she rebelled at the silence. Nothing had a chance of happening successfully in this still, charged air; with a wind blowing through it there might be more hope.

'Do you mind if I have my handbag?' she said acidly, her bright stare hard and steady on Fleet's face. 'You guessed right, the grey one is mine. Your fellows have had everything out of it but the lining, so don't be afraid I've got a bomb in it.'

It frees the tongue, knowing that what you say will make no difference, that buttering up the devil isn't going to get you anywhere, and damning him to his face can't do more than destroy you. Something else was stirring in the unexplored depths of her being, something never yet exercised in the serenity of family life, a pure personal fury that this man and his hangers-on should take it so insultingly for granted that no one could do anything against them, that guns called tunes, that lives were expendable like draughts in a game, and their proprietors would go quietly as lambs to the slaughter, just because the odds were against them. She cast one glance at Luke, and he was waiting for it with eyes flaring wide and aware. They conversed briefly, and were at one. Neither of them knew who was going to precipitate what was coming; both of them were playing by ear. But they understood the one weapon they had, their absolute unanimity. Whichever called, the other would respond; and they had no reservations, they trusted each other through and through. It was almost worth dying for that.

'*Did* you vet it?' asked Fleet lazily, without condescending to glance either at Bunty, who had addressed him, or at Blackie, whom he was now addressing.

'Yeah, there's nothing, just women's stuff.'

'I need a handkerchief,' said Bunty. 'Not to weep into, in case that's what you're thinking. To blow my nose. There's a smell in here. Queer, that, it was all right until you people arrived.'

'Give her her bag,' said Fleet, half-bored and half-amused.

It was on the bookcase, cheek by jowl with the sumptuous cream-coloured concoction Pippa had affected; and Blackie was sitting sprawled all over a high-backed chair close beside the bookcase, with Bunty diagonally to his left, and Luke diagonally to his right. He had his gun braced ready in his right hand, but his left was free to reach for the bag and toss it to Bunty. He did so, lazily and inefficiently, as if under protest.

It was a disdainful cast, an insult in itself, designed to fall short and make her stoop for her belongings. She could have caught the bag if she had cared to lean forward and stretch out her arms. Instead she sat with a straight back and a scornful face, her lips curled in detestation, and never moved a finger, but let it fall, with a dull plop and a rattle of small feminine arms within, just a yard from her feet. It lay innocently on one end of Louise Alport's most beautiful rug, a Scandinavian piece in broken forms and muted colours. A long rug, it was; the other end reposed under Fleet's hand-made shoe and Fleet's wicker chair, tilted back lazily on its rear legs beside the table.

She looked down at the bag with a fine, considering smile, and her eyes travelled the length of the rug slowly, and measured the distance to the door, and the half-way mark in that five-yard journey, the console record player with the single brass candlestick and the Benares ashtray on top of it. Her eyebrows signalled amused disdain.

'I perceive,' she said, 'that I am in the company of gentlemen. That's always so satisfying.' And she leaned forward without haste, and stretched out a languid hand towards her property.

She moved slowly, because their eyes were too intently fixed upon her movements, she had to give Luke time for his own diversion; and as though she had whispered in his ear, he provided her with what she needed. He rose abruptly from his chair, whirled it about under the knee-hole of the desk, and took two rapid steps forward towards the bag, as if to pick it up and hand it to her, exasperated by his own impotence and their boorishness.

Attention swung upon him in an instant. Fleet dropped Pippa's gun upon the table at his elbow, and picked up the Colt with the smoothness of a snake uncoiling. Blackie's thin, sharp profile swung towards Bunty, the gun in his hand levelled and pointed, freezing upon Luke's middle. Bunty said in a high, clear voice: 'Don't bother! I can stoop to conquer!'

She leaned from her place, both hands reaching for the hand-bag; but what she grasped, fingers clenched deep into the blessed long woollen pile, was the edge of the Scandinavian rug.

She tugged with all her heart and soul and venom and love. The rug surged across Louise Alport's polished wood-block floor like a live thing, plucking the rear legs of Fleet's chair irresistibly after it, an enthusiastic Sealyham tangling its boss in its lead and bringing him down with a shattering crash on his back.

The wicker chair screeched like a parrot, Fleet went over in a backward dive on his heavy shoulders, and his head hit the parquet with a most satisfying crunch. Attention swung back to Bunty like mad magic, and Blackie came out of his chair in a frantic leap, hesitant whether to pounce upon her, fire at her, or rush to salvage his boss. For one instant no one had time to spare for Luke, and though it was only an instant, it was enough. He plucked the granite paperweight out of his pocket, and hurled it into the light fixture with all his might – he had played cricket for his school and college as a fast bowler of erratic speed but deadly accuracy.

To Bunty, swept suddenly away out of reach of fear on a wave of exultant battle-madness that stemmed from somewhere very far back in her ancestry, the sequence of events was for ever crystal clear, though they all followed one another so rapidly as to be virtually simultaneous. The first thing was that Fleet was on his back, but still with the Colt in his hand, and all his resilient faculties gathering in his trigger-finger. The next was that she was on her feet, hands stretched up to the extreme of her reach, flourishing the rug. It was interposed between her body and the gunmen for an instant too brief to measure, but in its shelter she flung herself to one side, expecting the shot that would surely come. It came from Blackie, though she would have bet on Fleet. Fleet was always to surprise her. Even on his back, balance gone and senses momentarily disorientated, he made an instant decision, and it was at Luke he fired. The two shots stuttered like a double report, but between the two Bunty, hardly aware whether she was intact or not, had done the beautifully simple thing, and hurled the rug from her, to descend with all its woolly suffocation over the sprawling figure on the floor. Fleet's shot, blanketed by Swedish blues and greens, foils to all that orange and white, burned a hole in the rug and went wild, plunking harmlessly into the wall.

And only then did Luke's pebble hit the glowing fluorescent ring in the middle of the ceiling, hard and accurately at the point where the glass fitted into its plastic seal. A loud note of song, almost too high to be within human range, vibrated above their heads. There was a spitting explosion of brilliant, bluish radiance, like close lightning, and then a darkness like midnight and heavy rain, absolute darkness coruscating with piercing, infinitesimal points of sound, a rain of bitter ice. Fine particles of glass whispered down into hair and eyelids and folds of clothing. And on the instant all the lights in the house went out.

In a darkness which he could navigate only from memory, Luke took a flying leap, and came down heavily with both feet on the threshing canvas backing of the Scandinavian rug. He had aimed for where he hoped Fleet's solar plexus would be, but no part of Fleet was ever going to be where one expected to find it. Nothing else so big could ever have been so elusive. He had foreseen the line of attack, and rolled himself under the table, swinging clear of the mouthfuls of exquisitely-dyed long-pile wool that had threatened to smother him. From under the table he lunged in a round swipe, found Luke's left foot, and gripped like an octopus. Luke lifted his right foot, and stamped it down with all his weight on the wrist of the hand that held him. There were no rules. He hadn't even known, until he began, whether he could fight or not. He had never fought since he was about ten years old. He wanted to cry out to Bunty to run, but he dared not, for fear one of the enemy should divert his attention to her in time. Surely, surely she would take her chance now, as he had begged her.

And Bunty had meant to; but it must have been out of some misconception of what she was, for things turned out quite differently. She launched herself towards the doorway, made a long controlled sweep of her left hand along the wall, and found the brass candlestick on top of the record player. The rounded candle-holder fitted snugly into her hand. She gripped it firmly, even took time to settle it comfortably. There seemed to be no haste, the gale that carried her accommodated itself to the speed of events, and made everything seem easy and leisurely, as though these happenings took their time from her, and not she from them. She paced out without hindrance the remaining yards to the door, seized the handle and hurled the door wide open, so that the wooden panels shuddered against the rubber door-stop. But when she ran, it was because the darkness was already beginning to pale for her, and the direction in which she ran was back into the room, towards the shapeless mêlée in the twilight there. She did not think at all, except with her blood and her bones. Bunty had lost herself in the gale-force wind of her own instincts, which had never been loose like this before, and probably never would be again.

Fleet's long arm heaved convulsively under Luke's foot, and a grunting curse jerked from under the uncurling edge of the rug. Then the right hand that held the Colt hooked itself round Luke's knees and brought him down in a crashing fall on top of his adversary. The moment of alarm was already over, and Fleet still wanted him alive, and if possible undamaged. A suicide should not have the grazes and bruises of a stand-up fight all over him, it tends to complicate the proceedings of the coroner's court. Bunty, one hand extended to catch at Luke's sleeve and guide him to the doorway, had a precarious hold on him when he fell, but the fall dragged him out of her grasp. She circled the two threshing bodies on the floor, and could not distinguish friend from enemy. But the third presence, still erect, was now visible as her eyes grew accustomed to the darkness. Blackie, too, was circling the wrestlers, and probing forward into the untidy struggle with his gun hand. And Blackie was not in his master's secrets, and by the shape and the movement and the long, steady, hissing breath of him he meant to shoot the instant the chance offered.

A head and shoulders reared out of the tangle on the floor. Someone got a foot to the ground and laboured to pull clear and spring erect, and by the slightness and shape of the shadow emerging from shadows Bunty knew him for Luke. So did Blackie, and took a rapid step to one side to have his target well clear of Fleet's bulk when he fired. The movement took him nearer to Bunty, who had hung for one appalled instant torn between grabbing at Luke's arm to pull him clear, and hurling herself at the weaving manikin who threatened him.

She chose Blackie. The brass candlestick, swung underhand with all her strength and fury behind it, took him fairly and squarely on the point of the right elbow. The blow had been designed only to sweep his gun hand upwards, but by luck it did much more. It hit his funnybone with a tingling shock that paralysed him to the fingertips. The gun was jerked out of his hand, and flew jarring across the parquet floor. He uttered a weird, sharp yelp of pain that trailed off into incoherent curses, and went groping lamely after his weapon across the floor, like a crippled spider, one arm dangling.

Bunty swung the candlestick back, startled and exhilarated by success, and struck blindly at Fleet. The blow was smothered in a thick shoulder that rolled aside and rode it almost casually, and then a hand grasped the base of her weapon and pulled dexterously and sharply to jerk her off her feet. Instinctively she released her grip and let the thing go, springing back from too close contact. And then Luke had scrambled clear and was on his feet, and had her by the hand.

'Quick . . . *run!*'

Neither of them had heard, or could possibly have heard in that chaotic interlude, the labouring footsteps dragging their way down the stairs. They had forgotten Quilley. Fleet fired after them towards the door as he came to his knees, but the bullet plugged harmlessly into the lintel. It was the other shot that stopped them cold as they hurled themselves out into the hall, a shot that spat accurately into the wood blocks of the floor just before their feet, and flung them back in a frantic recoil against the balustrade of the staircase. It came from the corner just within the front door, out of absolute darkness, whereas they had one faint light upon them from the glass panel of the door, and another behind them from the open doorway of the living-room.

'Hold it right there!' said Quilley's voice, faintly stirred this time with earnest zeal, for who was the useful one now? 'I can see you, and you can't see me. One step this way and I plug you.'

Luke recovered from the check in a moment, but a moment was too long. If they could not both get away, he could still break a way through for Bunty, and this time she would have to go, because there would be nothing left for her to do here, no one to salvage. He put her aside by the shoulder, flattening her into the shelter of the newel-post, and sprang for the armed darkness, diving low.

His arms found and circled Quilley's knees, Quilley's gun hand swung towards the ceiling, and down they went in an ugly, heavy fall in the corner beside the door, both heads jarred against the wall.

'*Run*, Bunty!' Luke panted, clawing his way along Quilley's right arm towards the gun, and forcing the struggling wrist to point the barrel away into the wall.

The way was clear for her to reach the door, but time had already run out. The narrow hall was suddenly full of people. Blackie had an arm locked round Bunty's neck, and his gun pressed left-handed into her back. And was lunging past them to reach Luke and Quilley and drag them apart. A faint, flickering pencil of light suddenly sprang up, scurrying through the living-room to shed queasy pallor on the struggle, and after it a cone of steady light from Con's long, rubber-cased torch came surging eagerly in. They were back from the jetty far too soon, and empty-handed, just in time to put the quietus on all hope of escape.

The beam of yellow light swung upwards and bounded along the ceiling, swung downwards again and danced over the glass panel of the door. The thick rubber case hit Luke low in the back of the head with a solid, sickening sound. His shoulders hunched oddly, he hung still for an instant, and then collapsed

370

over Quilley like a discarded rag-doll, and lay in a motionless sprawl of arms and legs and lolling head, dead to the world.

'All right,' said Fleet's voice out of the dark, soft, savage and frightening, 'bring them back inside. All right! There are other ways.'

He was out of breath, ruffled, bruised. He looked from Luke's huddled body to his own awed and silent lieutenants; he looked at Bunty, and the ray of the torch showed her his face outlined in abrupt lights and shadows, planes of steep pallor and obliques of dusty black. All the debonair, easy, vigorous bonhomie had cracked and fallen away from those razor-edged surfaces. This was basic Fleet, the bedrock fact of what he had made of himself, for in every aspect of him Fleet was a selfmade man. Neither her life nor Luke's was worth half a crown now, but for one thing. Fleet still didn't know where the money was. And Luke was past questioning. A respite for him, at least; he'd had more than enough. Now she was left. Fleet's marmalade eyes, orange-flecked, glowed almost to red as he stared at her.

Without turning his head he addressed Quilley, who had clambered painfully to his feet again, and was holding himself up by the wall. 'Get back upstairs, and keep a sharp eye out. Somebody could have heard the shots.'

'Yes, sure, boss, I'm going. I had to come down . . . the front door . . . they'd have made it if I hadn't . . .' He edged away along the wall, eager and anxious, hooked an arm heavily over the bannister rail, and began to drag himself back to his guard duty. The torch caught the whites of his eyes, turned back hopefully and fearfully upon Fleet.

'All right, you had to come down! *Now get back*!'

Quilley went in fear, groaning as he climbed.

'Well, what happened to you two?' But he knew already. 'There was nothing there, of course.'

'Nothing. No ring, even. A lot of lies,' Con said indignantly.

'We had to get out of sight fast, too,' Skinner supplemented.

'There's a boat making up-coast, not far offshore. We didn't want to be seen. But we'd already made sure. He was lying, all right.'

'Bring him in,' said Fleet, and stalked ahead of them into the living-room.

Blackie prodded Bunty before him into the ravaged room, and pushed her down into the settee. The other two dragged in Luke by his arms and tumbled him on the floor in front of her feet, a thin, long, disjointed puppet. They had only the two torches for light, the small, guttering candle that belonged to the Alports, and the illuminated club that had battered Luke into unconsciousness. Fine slivers of glass crunched under their feet, and drew thin silver-point lines the length of Luke's dangling hand.

By this curiously stagey lighting Bunty looked round the chaos of the room, from the shattered light-fixture to the door-lintel where Fleet's second bullet had buried itself. There was no passing this off as a murder and suicide from despair now. Did that make bargaining possible? No, not a hope. There was a lot of room in the sea, and such witnesses as Fleet had at his mercy were better out of the way.

'You'll need a new script, won't you?' she heard herself saying with unbelievable calm. 'Four bullet-holes to account for, and all this wreckage. And after you'd polished all the prints off the business gun, too! I can't wait to see you tidy this lot up.'

'Too true,' said Fleet, in a voice as soft as it was vicious. 'You couldn't have put it better – *you can't wait*! You're too sharp, my dear, too sharp altogether. A lot too sharp for your own good. Wouldn't you do better to co-operate, and tell me where the money's hidden?'

'No,' she said with a tight, tired smile, 'I shouldn't. That's the last thing I'd be likely to do, even if I knew. You're so sure I've got no time left. But I have! I've got until you know the answer to that, either from him or from me. That long, and not many minutes longer. You think I don't know a killer when I see one? If I told you what you want to know, that *would* be the last thing I should do. So wouldn't I be a fool to tell you? *Even if I knew?*'

Fleet hit her then, with his open hand, deliberately and yet not too hard. He took pleasure in weighing and measuring the blow nicely, to jerk back her head and send a jarring shock down her spine without, as yet, doing her any damage. And Bunty laughed.

'You think you can open my mouth that way? I should have to find living more uncomfortable than dying before I'd be driven to talk. And I like living. I'll put up with a lot for it. By the time you'd got me to the amenable stage, I should be incapable of telling you anything at all. I'm not the kind that dies easily. Either way, you'll never know.'

Luke, crumpled at her feet, heaved a deeper breath into him, and moaned. Ignoring the guns, Bunty slid from her place and crouched upon the parquet beside him. She lifted his head into her lap, and stroked back his lank hair. A spasm dragged his face awry for a moment, and smoothed out again into the indifference of unconsciousness.

'Boss,' said Blackie in a low voice, 'I reckon you'd be wasting time on her. I don't believe she knows. He'd never trust her that far. Damn it, he only picked her up last night, on the run. It's *him* we want.'

She gathered the limp body more closely into her lap, arched over him jealously. Let them think that, by all means, until Luke showed signs of coming round. Until then, he was safe. There was nothing they could do to him, and nothing effective they could do to her. To keep silence might be a slow sentence of death, but to speak was instant death, and between the two there was not much doubt of her preference. Time, if it took sides at all, was on her side, hers and Luke's. Things become very simple when you have no choice, when there's nothing left for you but to endure as long as you can, and survive if you can.

'Get him round, then,' Fleet spat viciously. 'Pour cold water on him, anything, only bring him round, quick.'

Bunty laid her hand on Luke's forehead, holding him at rest, willing him to remain absent.

'*Damn you!*' hissed Fleet through his teeth, in sudden fury, and kicked out ferociously at the limp body before him.

Bunty uttered a brief, furious cry, and flung herself across Luke's helpless form, spreading her own arm and shoulder to ward off the blow. The face that glared up at Fleet, with bared teeth and flashing eyes, was the face of the antique woman that Cæsar respected, the red-haired Celtic Amazon who emerged at need to fight shoulder to shoulder with her menfolk, huge, noble and daunting. Bunty's Welsh ancestry went back beyond the small dark men. She saw Fleet start back from her in astonishment, almost in dread, so unused was he to people who forget to be afraid. She saw the gun in his hand prick up like a live snake, its cold eye fending her off; and she laughed, staring it down defiantly, with Luke gathered close into her arms from harm.

'Go ahead, then, shoot! Shoot, and then hunt for your money till your heart bursts, and much good may it do you, *Mister Fleet!*'

His mouth fell slack, he drew back from her a step in almost superstitious recoil; and in the moment of stricken silence they all heard Quilley's voice calling down the well of the stairs in agitation, and trailing a hollow echo after it:

'Boss . . . boss! There's a boat-load of men coming in towards the inlet. They've put out their lights . . . they're coming in to land . . .!'

Fleet turned and rushed to the window, dragging the curtains aside and craning to see down into the inlet, to the faint phosphorescent glow that was the sea, palpitating and shimmering with almost imperceptible movement. Skinner, who was nearest to the door, made for the stairs and went up them three at a time. Crouched on the floor with Luke inert in her arms, Bunty heard their footsteps crossing the boards overhead, Skinner rapid and blunt, Quilley dragging like a crippled beast, crossing and re-crossing from front windows to rear, and back again. Con and Blackie crowded to the window behind Fleet's hulking shoulders, peering, straining their eyes, holding their breath.

They had forgotten her. In a moment of time everything had gone into reverse. She could have risen and walked out at the front door, and she felt that no one would ever have noticed. Fear, anger and stress withdrew and stood at gaze, distant in the dark corners of the room, still present but now almost dreamlike, unable to touch the island where she knelt with Luke's heavy head in her arms. She made no move, she said nothing, she had no conscious thoughts; there was no longer any need for her to think or act, and because there was no more need, suddenly she had no more power.

Distantly, like something remembered, she heard Skinner's voice calling urgently down the well of the stairs:

'Boss, they're over the other side, too . . . among the trees, five or six of 'em . . .'

There had been no sound of a car, no glimpse of headlights. They had drawn in as silently as the night itself; so they knew what kind of hunt this was, and what to expect when they sprang the trap. Could this be all on account of Rosamund Chartley and her mythical address in Hereford?

There was a hoarse, muted shout overhead, a rush for the stairs. Skinner came bounding down in three stumbling leaps, fending himself off from walls and furniture with flailing arms.

'Boss, it's the police! We better get out of here fast . . . they're all round us . . .'

A sudden pale eye of light stroked its way down the wall, dimmed and diffused by the drawn curtains, probing at the window and passing in absolute silence. In a moment they saw it through the open door of the living-room, spilled in a lace of pallor on the floor of the hall, patterned by the frosted glass in the front door. When it passed from there, there would be darkness across the stretch of gravel to where the Jaguar stood in the shelter of the trees, turned and ready to run.

'That's it, then,' Fleet said in a clipped whisper, meant for no ears but his own, though Bunty heard it with the exaggerated clarity of voices in dreams. He knew the game was up. He knew when to throw in his hand.

The light passed on from the hall, and left the front door in darkness again.

'Now!' hissed Fleet. '*Out! Run for the Jag!*'

And out they went, tumbling, jostling, thrusting, all in something so like silence that their flight became more dreamlike than their lingering. Fleet was first out of the door, fast and light on his feet, a man well named; and after him Blackie, hurtling like a terrier, Con, outlined for a moment in the doorway all arms and legs, Skinner pounding along heavily in the rear and rolling like a half-filled barrel. All the darkling crew streamed out across the open court before the cottage, night-birds startled from their carrion. Bunty sat dazed with all the accumulated weariness of a night and a day, and listened to their flight.

There was a postscript. Leaning heavily on the bannisters, Quilley came stumbling and groaning after, down the stairs and through the hall.

'Boss, wait for me . . . don't go without me . . . !'

She heard the moaning complaint ebb along the wall, and reach the front door. And then the two of them were alone. Stiffly she got up from the floor, laying Luke gently down out of her arms, and went out into the porch.

The sound of all those running feet on the gravel had roused the whole garden. It was like Birnam Wood coming to Dunsinane. Pencils of light sprang up from three points, two among the trees on one side of the gate, one from the rough grass on the other, and converged upon the racing figures; and suddenly the copse began to spawn men, they came swarming out on the run, and streamed from all directions towards the Jaguar. They were already between the fugitives and the Riley. A little spurt of flame stabbed the darkness, a shot fired at the tyres, not at the men. Fleet didn't retaliate, didn't swerve or halt or hesitate, he charged straight for the grey car, darted round in its shelter to the driving seat, and in a moment the engine soared into life, and the car began to move, gathering speed like a greyhound out of a trap. With three of its four doors wide open and vibrating like wings, it surged across the gravel towards the open gate, while the rest of the crew scrambled and clawed their way aboard. He kept it idling for them a matter of seconds only. The nearest policeman was not ten yards away.

Quilley, last of the queue, came hobbling agonisingly after, appealing aloud in a high wail of outrage:

'Boss, wait for me . . . wait for me . . . you can't . . .'

He was hopping frantically alongside as they gathered speed; he got a grip on the front passenger door and clung in desperation.

'Give me a hand . . . Con, give me a hand . . .'

But it was Fleet who gave him a hand. They were four aboard, and wanted all the speed they could make, and no overloading. Fleet leaned across Con to the open door, spread his large palm against Quilley's chest and shoved him off, neatly catching the door as it swung loosely back, and slamming it shut. The car leaped clear of the pursuers by a matter of feet, and Quilley, hurled from his hold, fell sprawling under it.

The rear wheel heaved and lurched over his foot, the Jaguar slewed round insecurely for an instant, and then shot away through the gate and roared round the curve of the drive. Quilley's scream and the exultant tiger-purr of the acceleration died away together, diminuendo along the calm air of the night. A cluster of dark figures surrounded the rumpled heap on the ground. The light grey Jaguar was gone along the sunken lane, hell-bent for the main road.

Suddenly it was abnormally quiet, and everything was over.

Chapter 13

Luke came round with a skull full of hammers and a mouth full of old cobwebs, springing into instant, jangling awareness of Bunty's arm under his head and Bunty's palm cupping his cheek, and a bolt of hurtful light probing over them both out of the darkness. The edge of the falling beam showed him the end of a man's dark sleeve, and a hand holding a gun.

There was no end to it, and no escape. He set a palm to the floor in frantic haste and levered himself up groggily to his knees, leaning between Bunty and the threat, trying to put her behind him, though the sudden movement set his head ringing like a cracked bell, and the torch burned a hole through his eyes and into his brain. And Bunty drew him back gently into her arms and held him there, her cheek pressed against his forehead.

'It's all right, my dear, it's all right! The police are here . . . It's all over, we're safe . . .'

'Safe . . .?' he repeated dazedly. He lifted a shaky hand and touched her cheek. 'They didn't hurt you . . .? Where are they?'

'They got away in the Jaguar . . . all but the lame one . . .'

'They'll no' get far.' The darkness spoke in the voice of the sergeant with the pepper-and-salt hair, in tones of ripe satisfaction. The gun vanished into a jacket pocket. The torch settled briefly upon Bunty's pale, soiled face, and considerately turned

378

its beam aside. 'We've got a road-block up in the cutting. They'll no' get through that. You're all right, ma'am?'

She nodded: now that the tension was broken she was almost too tired to speak.

'And your right name, now,' he asked cautiously. 'It wouldn't be Felse, would it?'

'Yes,' she said, 'I'm Bunty Felse.'

'Thank God for that!' said the sergeant with profound satisfaction, and in all innocence kicked away the newly-recovered world from under Luke's feet. 'Your husband's been going daft, worrying about you.'

How strange, how very strange, that it had never even occurred to him to think that she might belong to someone else! As if such a woman as she was could ever have come so far through life without being recognised, desired, loved. She had seemed to belong so surely to him, to be a miracle created specially for his salvation, without any existence previous to their meeting. But of course she was flesh and blood, like ordinary women. For him she had no age, no class, no kin, there had been nothing before he found her. But of course she had known all those years of her life without him, before ever he existed for her. She had known a marriage, and a husband who was going daft, worrying about her.

Luke lay very still, overwhelmed with the magnitude of his desolation and loss. And what confounded him most was the paradox of being in her arms, linked with her in an alliance such as surely she had never in her life experienced with any man before, or ever would with any man after. He both possessed and had lost her.

Three men came in from the seaward side, and one more from the landward, and this last was an inspector, no less. They found candles in one of the kitchen cupboards, and the young constable of the morning, taciturn as ever, rummaged among Reggie

Alport's electrical spares and did some minor miracles with fuse-wire. Soon he had the current working in the kitchen, at least, so that they could do a little preliminary first-aid on Quilley before the ambulance came. The door stood open between the kitchen and the living-room, to share the benefit of the light.

'No,' admitted the inspector ruefully, 'I'm afraid we didn't check up on your fictional Mrs. Chartley at first. I only wish we had, we should have been here earlier. But you seemed all above-board to McCabe, and we had no reason then to be looking out for a woman. No, what put us on to you was further information from your home county. You can thank your son for it, indirectly. It seems he came home without notice late on Saturday evening, and found nobody there to welcome him. When nobody came back by eleven he called your husband's chief, and found that Mr. Felse had gone down south on a job, so he naturally took it for granted you might have decided to travel with him for the ride. It wasn't until some child turned up next morning, saying she'd found your purse, that he began to wonder.'

All the threads were beginning to tie in neatly into the pattern, even some of which the police would never know anything. So that was why there'd been no letter from Dominic, because he intended to rush home in person for her birthday, and surprise her. And if he'd been a couple of hours earlier, perhaps she would never have gone out walking to shake off her demon, never entered 'The Constellation Orion', never met Luke Tennant. And perhaps, when he was at the end of his tether, Luke Tennant would have given up thinking of Norway, and pointed that little gun at his temple and pulled the trigger, as he had so nearly done when the police came knocking at the door.

'So he told your C.I.D. chief, and they got in touch with your husband, and nobody knew where you were, or why you should be missing. Then they really began hunting. And it seems there's an old chap who saw you late on Saturday night with a young man he didn't know, and was sufficiently nosy to take note of the car and its number.'

'Old Lennie,' she said, and smiled. 'We bought some coffee at his stall. Thank God for nosy people! I see! So then they added my description to the information about NAQ 788, and circulated it. And Mrs. Chartley filled the bill well enough to be worth investigating. And you found the Alports had never heard of her, and her address didn't exist.'

'That's about it. So we thought it best to move in on you here pretty cautiously. We felt you must have been under duress this morning when you answered the door. A loaded gun a yard or so from your back can turn anybody into a first-class dissembler. It was the only way we could account for your behaviour.'

'I know,' she admitted, 'my behaviour throughout has been far from what you'd expect of a policeman's wife. But there's more to this than a couple of traffic offences. They haven't said anything to you about a murder?'

They hadn't. Nor, it seemed, about the snatching of Armitage Pressings' weekly pay-roll. Apparently nobody had missed Pippa Gallier yet, and no one suspected the connection between these events scattered through two months of time and three hundred miles or so of country. Bunty and Luke had still quite a lot to account for. The dead girl upstairs was going to come as a shock. And the money . . .

Bunty had almost forgotten about the money, but it was high time to retrieve it now. It was, after all, the chief evidence they had to offer for their own integrity, and the stake for which they had defied Fleet and all his private army.

'Before we start,' she said, 'could you send one of your men down to the jetty to fetch something? Something I hid there. A flat parcel in gift-wrapping paper.' She turned her head and looked at Luke, sitting drained and pale and sad beside her. 'It's under one of the slabs of slate that form the steps, only about three yards up from the jetty,' she said, for Luke rather than for anyone else. 'I pushed it under there when I slipped and fell. If you hadn't been solidly between Quilley and me I could never have got away with it, even in the dark.'

The inspector looked at the raw-boned young constable who was good with fuses, and the constable, whose ears, like his eyes, missed nothing, took one of the torches without a word, and went off through the kitchen to the cliff path.

'And exactly what,' asked the inspector curiously, 'is in this gift parcel? What has it got to do with this business?'

'Everything,' she said simply. 'It's what those men were after, it's what they killed the girl for – the girl upstairs – not to speak of the man who was driving the van when they snatched it in the first place. It's a week's pay-roll from a big firm outside Comerbourne. Getting on for fifteen thousand pounds in notes.'

'I think,' said the inspector carefully, after a pause to regain his breath, 'you'd better tell me the whole story.'

Between the two of them they told him. By the time they were half-way through, the recital was punctuated by Quilley's first half-conscious moans from the kitchen, and the inspector was unrolling the parcel of notes on the table before him. The sound of police cars halting before the door of the cottage put in the final full-stop. Fleet and his lieutenants were back under guard.

A hefty red-headed sergeant came in first from the night, his arms full of guns and his face one broad, freckled beam of fulfilment.

'Regular arsenal, sir . . . four of 'em!' He laid them out proudly on the table before his chief, and for an instant his jaw dropped at sight of the treasure already deployed there. 'Two revolvers, nice brand-new Colt Agent and a German Pickert .32. A Webley and Scott .25 automatic . . . and this little squib . . . that's another German job, a Menz Liliput. Wouldn't think that could do any damage, would you?'

The inspector viewed them without noticeable enthusiasm. Guns had never figured in the crimes that came within his ordinary range, and to him, as to George in Comerbourne, they were an omen of times changing for the worse. He looked up at Luke over the array of armaments.

'Which one?'

'The one you're holding.' The Webley was almost as tiny, but he would have known that Liliput again among thousands, by the associations that clung to it, by Bunty's confiding presence at his side, by the memory of that ride in which he could hardly believe now, when this little ugly shape had bound her into stillness and submission, who now sat beside him as an ally of her own will, held by nothing but her own generosity and loyalty. At every mention of her husband and son, those two who had genuine rights in her, the pain in his heart had tightened and intensified by one more turn. But still, every now and again, she spoke for both of them, and said 'we', and all that tension was released each time she said it, and he knew that she was not lost to him, that she was indeed, in some measure, his, and his for life.

'You realise, of course,' said the inspector gently, for he was a man of intuition as well as intelligence, and had already placed his own stake, 'that he's sure to have alibis for everything?'

'Yes, I know. I don't care now. If you want to hold me, that's all right. I'm satisfied now.'

'What happened?' asked the inspector, folding the gay paper over the indecent display of wealth, and looking up at the sergeant.

'They tried to crash the barrier. Bent that nice grey paint job badly, stove her nose right in. They poured out in all directions when she stalled, but we got 'em all fielded in quick time. They didn't fire. Soon as we laid hands on 'em they started acting legal. They hadn't done anything, they were on their lawful occasions. Only the big chap talks.'

'Yes,' said the inspector resignedly, 'only he would. Still, better bring 'em in until the wagon arrives.'

Fleet came in with rock-like assurance, his hands in his pockets, his henchmen mute and stolid behind him. And of course they would all have a dozen witnesses to testify that they had been somewhere miles away when the Armitage pay-roll was snatched, and at least outside the house when Pippa Gallier was shot; and of course they would even have licences for all those guns, except Pippa's, of which they would deny all knowledge prior to yesterday. And of course, regarding the money and their presence here, and their flight when the police came, Fleet would tell the same old story of being robbed by Pippa, of actually breaking in on Luke's house to find Pippa dead and Luke drunk and unconscious, of pursuing Luke here into Scotland after the money – with some mildly illegal origin for the money, something almost innocuous, but enough to account for a certain shyness of the police . . .

Yes, it was all implicit in his bearing as he came in.

'Keys?' said Fleet, smiling, always smiling, with deep-sunk marmalade eyes mildly indignant, but no more, with salient bones grown bland with tolerance under the tanned and gleaming skin, a benevolent, misjudged man. 'What should I know about her keys? I expect he threw 'em away. *I* never saw any such little leather boot. You can search me.' Which of course they could, and any residence of his into the bargain; he wasn't such a fool as to keep a thing so easily identifiable.

'Look, I've told you that money was ours, and it's got nothing to do with any pay-roll, it's racing winnings. We had a syndicate. And a system. You fellows wouldn't approve, but you'd have a job to pick us up on it, all the same, I'm telling you that. Naturally we came after it. What would you have done, written it off? More fool me, for ever letting that little bitch hold the kitty, but she had a way with her . . . Ask *him*, *he* knows! She double-crossed him, too, and he paid her her dues, and good luck to him. But don't look at *me*! I can prove where I was all the early part of Saturday evening. By the time I got there it was all over.

384

'And that's all I am saying,' said Fleet, still beneficently smiling. 'I want to see my lawyer before I say another word.'

'And you've got licences for all these cannon, I suppose?' said the inspector, mildly shuffling Pippa's passport and air ticket in his hands. The bone-cased eyes lingered on them hungrily, but gave nothing away. There was something else there, too, sandwiched between the two documents, something Bunty and Luke hadn't discovered because it was slim enough and small enough to hide among the notes: a sealed white envelope, stamped, ready for the post.

'One of 'em's nothing to do with me, ask *him* about that. For mine I have. All but the Pickert, maybe. I picked that up during the war. It's damned hard to keep within the law *all* the time,' said Fleet tolerantly.

'But you deny playing any part in Pippa Gallier's death? Or in the wage-snatch from Armitage Pressings?' The inspector slipped the point of his ball-pen almost absent-mindedly inside the flap of the envelope, and began to slide it along. It was noticeable that he did not touch the envelope itself, but held it between passport and ticket; and the address had appeared for a moment to engage more of his attention than he was actually giving to Fleet.

'That I don't mind repeating. I followed her to this chap's place, I got kind of restless waiting for her to come out, and I went in to find out what was happening. She was on the floor, dead, and this young fellow was out cold on the top of her, with the gun in his hand. And if he didn't shoot her, then get on with finding out who did, because you won't get anywhere looking at me. Two of my lads were with me, they know she was dead when we went in. That's it!' said Fleet, with a snap of his formidable jaws like a shark bisecting an unlucky bather. 'I've finished talking.'

'*But I haven't!*' snarled a sudden ferocious voice from the kitchen. '*I'm just set to begin.*'

*

As one man they swung to face the doorway. The voice was one they had none of them heard before, though several of them had heard the same man speak. Fleet knew this voice muted, anxious and willing to please, Luke knew it injured, whining and doomed, aware of its narrowing destiny. The police had heard it only in one wild scream as the car went over its protests, and flattened them into the gravel.

Propped on a policeman's arm, Quilley leaned from the kitchen rug, his left leg stripped from the knee down, his foot crushed and leaning disjointedly sidewise from the ankle. By straining to the limit of his strength he could just get his eyes upon Fleet, and they aimed there like gun-barrels, as deadly and as fixed. He was not afraid now, he had nothing to lose, he could close the doors on the man who had tyrannised over him, and if he closed them on himself, too, that would still be liberation. Fleet had tossed him to the police like a bone to hounds, to delay the pursuit. There was a price for that.

'Here's one,' said Quilley stridently, 'who wants to talk, and he's got plenty to tell, too. Of course that's the Armitage money, and I was there when we snatched it, and what you want to know about that I can tell you, *even who fired the shot*. But it wasn't *him*, not that time. He hasn't got the guts to go out and do a job, he just directs from a safe place. It was the girl he killed . . . with his own hands . . . and I was there to see it . . .'

For one moment it seemed that Fleet would hurl himself, out of his chair, clean through all opposition, and clamp his hands round Quilley's throat. But he did not. He sat back by a cautious inch or two in his seat, to demonstrate how little this attack meant to him; and his face with all its death's-head boniness continued to smile.

'It was after she asked for the gun,' Quilley pursued loudly and firmly, 'that he got uneasy. She was getting above herself, and his women don't do that. But he still fancied her, then, so he gave her a gun of sorts to keep her happy – that rubbishing little

386

thing you've got there, the one he's trying to kid you is nothing to do with him . . .'

'That?' said Fleet blankly, wide-eyed in innocence. 'I never saw the thing in my life until yesterday.'

'Like hell he never saw it! He gave it to her. He was never too sure about her after that, but when he slept with her Friday night he took a peep at the case with the money in it, and it looked all right. But still his thumbs pricked about her, so he had us watch her, see what she'd do. And Saturday night, after she thought he'd gone back to town, she came bustling out with a suitcase, and locked her flat, and went off in a taxi, so we had to notify him. Con and Blackie followed her in the Riley, while I waited for *him*, and he let us into her flat to make sure about the money. He didn't need her keys for that, he'd had one made for himself long ago, but she didn't know that. You think he'd leave any money of his behind a door he couldn't get through when he liked? And what do you know? She'd filled the case up with bundles of newspaper cuttings, only the top note in each clip was real. So then he knew she was off with the dough. They had orders to pick her up and bring her back if she tried to run out by train, or anything, but she never, she went to this little house, and walked right in, so they called him at her flat, and we went over there fast. The door wasn't locked, it was easy. We walked in, and there she was waving this gun at this kid, and raving how he'd got to keep his promise to her, and he went for her as if he thought it was a pop-gun, he was so tight, and there they were fighting for it, and *him* in the doorway weighing it all up, like he always does everything, *what's in it for Fleet*! And *I*,' said Quilley vengefully, '*I* was the one who was right there beside him. I saw him club this kid cold. Nobody knows how to do it better. I saw him take the gun out of his hand. And she, she was all over him suddenly, she says, darling, she says, thank heaven you came, she says, he'd have killed me! And there she is hanging round Fleet's neck, hoping he's only just busted in, and he puts that gun to her chest and shoots her dead. Just like that!'

'Poor devil!' said Fleet, with hardly a pretence at sincerity. 'Hysterical. He's got it in for me, I always knew he hated my guts. He'll say anything.'

'Not anything, just the facts, Fleet. Nobody needs more. I tell you, he shot her. And then he wiped the gun and put it back in the kid's hand, and arranged the two of 'em there, all ready to be found, so the kid could take the rap. We called the cops from a call box to come and get him, only he must have come round too soon and cleared out. And there's one thing I can tell you, too. She'd been getting ready to put the finger on the lot of us, and especially Fleet. In her flat we found some trial runs for a letter she was putting together for the police, all cut out of newspapers, half a dozen different types. She was headed out, and she was going to make good and sure we wouldn't be at large to hunt for her. Oh, yes, we went back to her flat . . . just as soon as we found there was no money in her suitcase and nothing in her bag, no left-luggage ticket, or anything like that. We took her keys and went back to turn the whole place out, but all we found was these bits of paper, where she'd been experimenting with this letter. About the Armitage job, and about Pope Halsey's furs, too. She knew all about that, she was the one who tipped us off about the shipment. We had a proper hunt, but we never found anything else, and he burned those bits of paper. Anything you want to know,' said Quilley, incandescent with vengeance, 'you ask me. I was there every time, there's nothing I can't tell you.'

'Nothing,' said Fleet, crossing one grey-worsted leg negligently over the other, and grinned towards the kitchen doorway, round which the frantic eyes glared and gloated on him. 'And nothing he won't, either, true or false. You can see he'd do anything to knife me in the back. But I've got witnesses will prove the opposite . . . witnesses with nothing to gain.'

'*Except money!*' said Quilley. 'Alibis he gets wholesale.'

'You see?' said Fleet, sighing. 'Poor chap! Psychopathic, really!'

'Then you didn't go back to her flat?' asked the inspector mildly.

'Who said we didn't? She'd run out with my money . . . *our* money . . . we didn't know what she'd done with it . . .'

'And he couldn't ask her,' said Quilley viciously. 'He was too sure it would be there in her suitcase, he'd fired first and looked afterwards.'

'Of course we went back to look in her flat, where else was it likely to be? But we didn't find any trial shots at synthetic letters to the police . . . that cheap little judy didn't know anything about any crimes except running out with our winnings, you can bet on that.'

'He's making the whole thing up, then?'

'Of course he is. I came after my money, yes, that's fair enough, and I wasn't particular how I went about recovering it, either, if it comes to that. But he'll have a hell of a job connecting me with that girl's death, or that gun he's raving about.'

'Will I?' shrilled the vengeful voice from the kitchen, whinnying with triumph and whimpering with pain. 'You think you're in the clear because you wiped off the grip nicely? Who loaded it in the first place, mate, think about that! Wait until they get their little insufflators on that magazine before you crow too loud.'

Bunty closed her fingers excitedly on Luke's arm. And Fleet laughed. A little too loudly, perhaps; there seemed suddenly to be a bleak, small hollow inside the laughter, that echoed like a bare cell.

'Come off it, man! You know as well as I do I opened the thing up here tonight, here in this room, to see how many rounds were in it. You watched me do it! Like all the rest of the boys, and they'll all swear to it.'

'You think so? This time you don't own all the witnesses, Fleet. At the best it'll be a draw, three-three. And by the time

389

they've got it through their thick heads that you're going down for twenty years, you think you'll even be owning three of 'em? They won't be able to shift over to our side fast enough.'

'You talk too much to be feeling sure of yourself,' Fleet said tolerantly, and beamed at the inspector with a face of brass. But was there a very faint flare of uneasiness far down in the wells of his eyes? 'You won't get far on his uncorroborated word,' he said virtuously, 'he's got a record as long as your arm. I don't know why I ever risked taking him on, but somebody has to give the lags a chance.'

'A bit of corroboration would certainly be helpful,' agreed the inspector reasonably. 'Even on one specific point . . . say these trial letters she was supposed to be compiling, now. But of course, you deny there ever were any, and he says you burned them. In either case, nobody else is going to be able to give us any fresh information now.' He was gently unfolding the sheet of thick white paper he had withdrawn from the envelope. He took his time about it, and its texture, or some quality he found in it, seemed to be affording him a certain obscure amusement. They observed that he handled it only by the edges, with considerable care. 'Of course, if we could have called the girl herself as a witness . . .'

He looked up, smiling. 'Now isn't that a coincidence! She had it among her papers, all ready stamped and addressed for posting, I suppose she was going to slip it into the box at London Airport at the last moment. No point in taking risks until she was actually on her way out. It's a good surface, it should hold prints well.'

He turned it for them to see the sliced-out words and phrases of print from which it had been compiled.

'You want to know how the text reads? It's addressed to Superintendent Duckett, Chief of the Midshire C.I.D. It runs:

'The man you want for the Armitage hold-up is Jerome Fleet, who has the chain of garages that just opened a branch in Comerford. He uses his business for cover and transport. He has a man named Blackie Crowe working for him, also one called Skinner, and Sam Quilley, and a young one they call Con. They were all in the wage-snatch, and they did the fur job, too. I am not sure about his new manager, but think all his men except the locals are crooks. *But Fleet is the boss.*'

'Underlined, that last bit. And she signed herself, not too originally: "A Well-Wisher".'

He looked up across the paper as he refolded it, and smiled into the amber eyes of a caged tiger. 'Isn't it lucky, Mr. Fleet, that the fair copy survived?'

The moment of flat silence was broken abruptly by an outburst of loud, rattling, jarring sound from the kitchen, fed by gulping indrawn breaths of pain. It took them a few shocked seconds to realise that it was only Quilley, laughing.

Chapter 14

In the back of the police car, speeding south down the A.73 south of Cumbernauld New Town, Bunty and Luke sat all but silent, shoulder to shoulder as on the white wicker settee in Louise Alport's devastated living-room.

'How am I ever going to face the Alports?' Luke had said, looking round his battle-field despairingly from the weary vantage-point of victory. 'Louise will kill me!' So soon do words resume their normal easy and unthinking meaning. And Bunty had consoled him. 'They'll forgive you! On this story they can dine out for life!'

'Your husband's on the line, Mrs. Felse,' said the driver. 'He's through Kendal now, it won't be long. We'll run off and rendezvous with him at Lockerbie.' And to the radio he said cheerfully: 'You know the King's Arms, in High Street? They've got no parking space, but at this hour there'll be room in the street.'

'He'll find it,' said Bunty.

'You want to speak to him, Mrs. Felse?'

'Just give him my love,' she said.

'Your boy's coming on now, ma'am. He says you cost him twenty-two bob for flowers, and they'll be dead before you see them.'

'Tell him half a bottle of Cognac would have kept better.'

'He says no Cognac, but there's a bottle of Riccadonna Bianca, though you don't deserve it.'

She laughed, and her eyes gushed tears suddenly and briefly. Luke had never seen her in tears. There was always a new snare, a fresh, impossible attraction. Of course, they were crazy for her, those two men of hers rushing north to meet her because waiting was impossible. There would never be anyone like her, never, never, never. And now there wasn't much time left for him, he could feel the minutes slipping through his fingers like sand, and there was so much to say, so much that he wanted to say properly before he lost her for ever, so much he knew would never be said. There was the police driver, sitting there in front of them impersonal and incurious, but human. And nothing must ever be said of love, however love crowded his thoughts and made his heart faint.

It was enough, in a way, that she had invited him to go south with her. Naturally she was free to go, and naturally she wanted to reach her family as soon as possible, and return home with them; but he had still certain charges hanging over him, and he could have been held, had not she expressly asked to have him with her, and even punctiliously invited him to go with her, as if he could deny her anything, as if he would willingly have parted with her a moment sooner than he needed. It was enough because it meant that what had happened between them had a validity of its own, present and eternal, for her as well as for him. And in the car, between their few exchanges, she had slept confidingly against his shoulder, even nestled into the shelter of his diffident arm, and settled her cheek against his breast. The journey north, with death on his back and a gun in his hand ready for her, was only twenty-four hours past.

'I could stay,' he said haltingly. 'In Lockerbie, I mean. There'd surely be a room for me, this time of year. I mean, you'll want . . . your family . . . they'll want you to themselves . . .'

'Don't be silly!' said Bunty warmly. 'You're coming with us. Didn't I say I wasn't going home till I could take you with me?'

'I'm not much of a trophy,' he said, and could not keep all the bitterness out of his tone.

'You're *not* a trophy. You're my co–victor. Without you there's no triumph, and I need a triumph. My family are very critical.'

'I can imagine,' he said, racked with unwilling laughter. And in a moment, very seriously indeed: 'You know there are still several counts against me.'

'I don't think anybody's going to be interested in throwing the book at you now,' she said, yawning into his sleeve like a sleepy child. 'Not after what we're bringing them.' It still turned his heart over in a transport of joy and humility when she said 'we'.

'I don't mind. I shan't complain. Bunty,' he said shyly, 'you're happy, you've got everything. Why were you sad? When you came into the "Orion", why were you so sad?'

She looked back at that moment with some astonishment, it seemed now so alien and so far away.

'Sometimes being happy doesn't seem enough. I was alone, and I'd stopped being young, and suddenly I didn't know where I was going or what I was for. It was you,' she said, without calculation, 'who cured me.'

'I did? But I . . . I don't see,' he said, trembling, 'how *I* can have been much comfort or reassurance to you!'

'I didn't *want* to be comforted or reassured! I wanted to be *used*! You had a use for me. *Me*! Not my husband's wife or my son's mother. Me, Bunty!'

She felt his helpless adoration in the devoted stillness of his body and the agonised tenderness of the arm that held her, and she thought: Poor Luke! No, lucky Luke! Everything rounded off firmly and finally for him, no letdowns afterwards, no waking up gradually to the fact that I'm nearly old enough to be his mother, and it's beginning to show more grossly every year. No rejections, and no disillusionments. Here he has me for ever. And for ever – no, not young, perhaps, but never more than forty-one! And brave and loyal and good, everything he wants to believe me. When I need that reference to forward to the gods, I shall know where to apply.

'All my life,' she said, inspired, 'I shall remember you and be grateful to you.'

And he, who had all this time been crying in his heart how he would remember her always, and with eternal gratitude and love, was so disarmed and so perfectly fulfilled by her taking the words out of his heart that he never missed the word she had omitted. So that it did not matter, in the end, that she should wonder whether she had done well to avoid the mention of love. It was not the only word in the language; and as one of the most misused, it was thankful, now and again, for reticence and silence.

She was asleep in his arm when the car ran off the dual carriageway and wound its way into the small, handsome town, half asleep at the end of Sunday. The car from the south was there before them, Luke saw the two men standing beside it, heads up, eyes alertly roving, waiting for them to arrive. In the beam of headlights the two faces burned out of the darkness eager, intent, impatient, as was only proper when they were waiting for Bunty; and as the car that brought her to them slipped smartly into a vacant parking spot beside the kerb, Luke saw them both smooth away the residue of wild anxiety out of their eyes, and the tension of longing out of their faces. There is a certain duty to take old love easily, even when it scalds.

Luke put a finger under Bunty's chin and gently raised her face, and she awoke with eyes wide open, and smiled at him as if he had always been there, and then, remembering, grew grave, because she knew he wasn't going to be there much longer. She had too much sense to try to turn him into a family friend, or even offer him a bed for the night in the house where she belonged to someone else. No, he would go, and not look back; he was wise, too. And even for her it was going to be a kind of amputation, another little death.

'Wake up,' said Luke, 'we're here in Lockerbie. And look who's waiting for you.'

She looked, and there was George already leaning to open the door of the car for her, and his smile was muted, indulgent and a shade superior, the smile every married man keeps for the unpredictable idiot who lives somewhere within his sensible wife. Marriage is a round-dance as well as a sacrament.

Bunty slid her feet out to the pavement, and stepped into her husband's arms, as simply as if he had been meeting her train after a shopping expedition to London. This is how it's done, Luke thought, watching. If you're clever, this is how it's done. The panic being over, and the fear gone, why exclaim? Why startle and shake the assured equilibrium of a relationship on which the foundations of three lives rest? And why express what is already known, valued, impregnable? Not to say inexpressible! No affectation, no fuss, no explanations. If they ever talked about the fearful truths of that weekend it would be afterwards, in tranquillity, walking softly to shake no hearts. But it did not mean that the hearts had not been shaken. Luke saw George's face over his wife's shoulder, as he held her briefly in his arms, and there was no question after that of Bunty being under-valued. George knew what he'd got, all right.

'You're a fine one,' he said, kissing her roundly. 'So you don't mix with dangerous types who carry guns! Talk about famous last words!'

She kissed him back joyfully. 'Did you have a nice trip, dear?' she said wickedly.

'No, I did not!' He took his hands from her slowly. Their delight in her wholeness cried aloud, and their reluctance to relinquish her even to Dominic, who stood waiting his turn. 'My man was a dead loss. A perfectly respectable person who didn't know him has put him miles away from our job. And the next thing I knew, Dom was on the line demanding to know what I'd done with *you*.'

'It's all in the family,' said Bunty largely. 'You don't have to go on north to pick up the pieces, do you?'

'No. This one Duckett's finishing off himself. My only orders are to take you two safely home.'

Bunty turned to offer her cheek for Dominic's dutiful kiss. The boy – he was absurdly like her – was less practised in carrying the burden. He hugged her fiercely all the time he was saying, in his best throw-away manner: 'Many happy returns of yesterday, Mummy! How was the fishing?' The hazel eyes, the image of her own, were devouring her hungrily and jealously with every word, but the voice was all right.

'You mean it's *still* Sunday? It seems to have lasted for ever.'

Luke had got out of the car, and was standing well back from a ceremony in which he conceived he had no part. But it seemed that Bunty thought differently, for she turned back to him, smiling, holding George by the hand.

'And here's Luke. He's heading home for Comerbourne, too, the police had to hang on to his car for the time being.'

Luke never wanted to see that car again, though he had loved it in its time. When it was released he would get some dealer to remove it, and get rid of it, perhaps even forget it some day.

'You won't mind if Luke and I collar the back seat, will you?' said Bunty, looking appreciatively at the large black police car George had borrowed for the sake of its radio. 'We haven't had much rest over the weekend, we're probably going to sleep all the way home.'

We! God bless her for that 'we' that bound him to her even now, for the little while they had left before normality set in.

'Hallo, Luke!' said George gravely. 'You seem to have been doing my job for me . . . even to bringing my wife back safely. Thank you!'

Luke looked from the smiling dark face to the two linked hands, that fitted together with so much passion and so deep a calm, and he suddenly saw in them the whole essence of this marriage, no, of marriage entire. He thought it would be worth waiting and hunting through half a lifetime to find another hand that would fit into his like that.

When he shook hands with George, it was like touching Bunty again, they were so deeply one. What Bunty had given to Luke he couldn't begin to appraise. What they gave him now between them was a dazzling promise. It seemed this union was possible. If it had happened once, it could happen again. Even in this measure. Even, some day, to him?

Bunty awoke towards morning with a soft, alarmed cry of: 'Luke!' stretching out her arm protectively over George's wakeful body. All night he had lain beside her and watched her exhausted sleep, and learned by heart, even in moderate moonlight, the shadows that marked her face, the memories of things lived through and still not put away. He could wait; he must wait. She had told no more than the half, the rest she would tell when the right time came. He cupped her cheek in his hand and soothed her fully awake, to end her distress.

She folded her arm over him more closely, caressing his neck, and even in the darkness of his shoulder he felt her smile.

'I love you!' she said in a deep sigh. There are times to mention love, as there are times to take it for granted, and keep silent.

'Did you love *him*?' said George gently, stroking back the tangled brown hair from her forehead.

'It depends,' said Bunty after due thought, 'on what you mean by love.'

This is an acid test, if ever there was one. Forget the narrow, deep confines of marriage, so exclusive and so profound, and what *do* you mean by love?

'I mean,' said George, moistening his lips in awe, 'whatever it is that makes it possible to achieve a complete human contact with another person, maybe only for three minutes on a crowded bus. I mean the thing, whatever it is, that suddenly makes you move in on somebody else's need, and strike clean through conventions into their hearts, so that there'll always be a link between you, even if you never meet or even think of each other again. I mean the communicated warmth that keeps people alive, the most universal and generous thing there is, not the narrowest. Not sexual love, not married love, not platonic love, not filial love, nothing that has to be qualified – the absolute. I mean *love*, love!'

She lay beside him for a long while in stillness and silence, he began to think she had fallen asleep again, and this time without dreams. But presently she turned to him impulsively, and wound her arm about him with a sharp, sweet sigh of fulfilment, and embraced him with all her might.

'Then, yes,' said Bunty, 'I loved him.'

The House of Green Turf

Chapter 1

But for a five-minute shower of rain, and a spattering of penny-stone clay dropped from the tailboard of a lorry, Maggie Tressider would have driven on safely to her destination, that day in August, and there would never have been anything to cause her to look back over her shoulder and out of her ivory tower, nothing to make the mirror crack from side to side, nothing to bring any unforeseen and incomprehensible curse down upon her. She would have been in Liverpool by tea-time, relaxing before her concert; and then she would have dressed carefully and driven with her accompanist to the Philharmonic Hall, to give her usual meticulous performance in Brahms's 'Alto Rhapsody', which was one of the things she did best, and Schumann's '*Frauenliebe und Leben*', which in her opinion was not. And the next day she would have shared the driving with Tom Lowell again on the way home, and then settled down to consider her next engagement, which was a recording session in London for a new and expensive *Fidelio*. And everything would have gone on hopefully and auspiciously, just as it had during all the past ten years, every new undertaking adding a further burnish to her reputation and fresh laurels to her crown.

But the clay fell, shaken loose from a careless load just where the road leaned the wrong way on the long curve by the brick-works; and a following lorry squashed the glutinous lump into a long, murderous slide, unobtrusive on the pale surface. And then the thin little shower came and passed, too feeble to wet the road thoroughly, but enough to leave sweaty globules all along the slide of clay, and give it a more treacherous sliminess. The trap was now all ready for the prey.

Maggie, new to the road but a good driver, estimated the angle of the curve as she reached it. It uncoiled right-handed in a sharp descent, one of those hazards due to be ironed out some day, when county funds permitted. It went on and on until it seemed they must be spiralling back beneath their own tracks, but Maggie continued to drive confidently round its convolutions, and checked her speed only slightly. At the most acute point of the curve the slide of clay waited for them, just where the gradient sagged away outwards instead of giving them support.

They hit it at forty, and everything went mad. Away went their wheels sidelong in a long glissade, while Maggie did all the correct things to adjust to the skid and get control again, and nothing responded. She fought the car with every sense and every nerve she had, and still inexorably, greasily, derisively, it went its own pig-headed way, outwards towards the white kerbing and the fall of tousled grass beyond. They hit the kerb and leaped shuddering into the air, and she dragged frantically at the wheel to get them back on to the road before they touched again, but then they were over, lurching in crazy, lunging bumps like an elephant amuck, down the tufted grass towards the quick-set hedge below, and the stumps of three long-felled trees.

Earth and sky flickered and changed places, and sizzled and blinked out like broken film. She heard Tom cry out, and felt his hand beside hers on the wheel, which was no help at all. Doggedly she clung and swung, correcting head-long lurches as best she could, struggling to hold the car upright and bring it to a halt, but the gradient was against her. You might as well try to pat a bullet out of its course with your palm. But she never let go, and she never stopped crying.

She remembered yelling at Tom to loose his safety belt and jump, while they were still on the grass. But because of course he wouldn't, she remembered leaning across him and trying to open his door. A mistake, she had to take one hand from the wheel. Cool air blew in on her. The weight of the door swinging brought the car round and almost broadsided it short of the hedge, but its own impetus rolled it against the weight and sent it hurtling over in a slow somersault. The door flapped, like a wing trying to lift them clear, but as helpless as she was to save them. Then the seat beside her was empty, and the spiky shapes of the hedge surged upwards one moment, downward the next, to spear her, and the squat, solid, moss-grown stump of a tree launched itself from the sky to stamp her into the ground.

The world exploded in her face, and a fragmentation bomb in her lap. And then there was darkness, aeon upon aeon of darkness, and the last thing she knew, extended diminuendo long after everything else was gone, was her own voice, or perhaps only the silent phantom of her own voice, lamenting inconsolably: My God, what have I done! I've killed poor Tom! My God, what have I done, I've killed Tom, I've killed him . . . killed him . . . killed him . . .

Two voices were discussing her over her head. They didn't know that dead people can hear. Quite dispassionate voices, cool, leisurely, and low. Either they had no bodies, or dead people can't see. She was dangling just below the level of consciousness, clinging to the surface like the air-breathing nymph of some water creature.

'Beautiful, too!' said the first voice critically.

'Nobody's beautiful on the operating table,' said the second voice cynically.

'Beautiful, gifted and famous. It seems some people *can* have everything.'

'Except immortality.'

'What *are* her chances?'

'Oh, pretty good now. Nothing's ever certain, but . . . pretty good. She had us on the run, though! Set on dying, you'd have said.'

'Scale tipped the right way in the end. Pity if she'd slipped through our fingers. Maggie Tressider . . . what a loss!'

' "*Maggie is dead. And music dies!*" '

'Pardon?' said the first voice blankly, not recognising Byrd's despairing tribute to Tallis, his master and idol. But Maggie recognised it, and was enchanted, disarmed, humbled.

'Never mind,' said the second voice. 'She'll do now. That's one of us with the chance to begin again. I could almost envy her.'

Something pricked her thigh. She went down again gratefully, fathoms deep into the dark.

Faces loomed, receded and vanished like puffs of smoke. Voices, some of them real and some illusory, whispered, barked, shouted, fired themselves like pistol shots from every corner of unreality, in the crazy round-dance of disorientation. Hands lifted her, trickles of water fed themselves into her mouth. There were periods of light and sense, but she always lost them again before she could orientate herself or make anyone understand her. Pain, never acute but never absent, ebbed and flowed in a capricious tide. Through a shadowy underworld spiky with quickset hedges and shattering glass she pursued and was pursued, at every lucid moment reaching out feverishly after whoever was nearest: 'Tom . . . please, find Tom! Never mind me, look for Tom . . . he's hurt . . .' And all the while the dead man pressed hard on her heels, tapping at her shoulder; but the voice that panted in her ear was always her own voice, thinly wailing: My God, what have I done? I've killed him . . . killed him . . .

Later she hurt all over, and that meant that there were senses there, nerves that were working, muscles that didn't want to work; and she tried to move, and did move, and that hurt more, but nevertheless was not discouraging.

The House of Green Turf

A face hovered, impressed: 'My, you're mobile!'

'Tom . . .' she said urgently. 'Please, I've got to know about Tom . . .'

'Tom? Who's Tom?'

'Tom Lowell. He was with me in the car . . .'

'Oh, *he's* all right. Don't worry about him. He was the lucky one, he got off with only a few bramble scratches and mild concussion. He was discharged yesterday.'

She couldn't believe it. 'You mean he isn't dead? Really he isn't? You're not just trying to keep me quiet by telling me that?'

'Not a bit of it! He's far from dead. If you're fit for visits to-morrow he's coming in, so you can see for yourself. Got his face scratched, but that's all the damage you'll see. He was thrown out just short of the hedge. *You're* the one who took the brunt, and you're going to be all right, too. Drink?'

'We were going to Liverpool,' said Maggie, groping after departed urgencies that might have validity again any moment. 'We should have been at a concert . . .'

'Mr. Lowell fixed that as soon as he came round. We tele-phoned them, and they got somebody else. Everything's taken care of.'

So there seemed nothing more to ask about, and nothing more to say. She sank back into a chaos now less frightening because almost meaningless. Everything was taken care of. Tom wasn't dead. After all, she would never have to face his wife and try to excuse herself for the crash that killed him. He was alive, not even badly hurt.

Then if it wasn't Tom, who was it, tapping her on the shoulder, treading on her heels, dunning her for his life?

It wasn't any delusion, he was still there; even in the instant of absolute relief over Tom he had still been there, close and faceless, making use of her voice because he had no voice of his own, being dead: My God, what have I done? He's dead, and I killed him! *My God, what have you done to me? Killed me . . . killed me . . . killed me . . .*

How could she have mistaken him for Tom? Only out of the remote past, where so much was forgotten, could something so ominous and shapeless surface again to haunt and accuse. When the waters are troubled, dead people rise. But all her dead were decently buried, and she had never done them any wrong.

'Nurse! There wasn't anyone else, was there? We didn't hit somebody else, when we crashed . . .?'

'There was nobody else around. Just the two of you, as if that wasn't enough! What are you worrying about? You're both going to be all right.'

No answer there, either. Much longer ago, much farther away, than the badly-engineered curve by the brickworks. Somewhere, at some time, she had done something terrible to someone, something that destroyed him. Oh God, what was it? How could she know she had done it, and not know what it was? The silence that had covered it could only be her silence. She must have known at some time, and held her tongue in the hope of universal silence. And gradually drawn breath easily again, because there'd been no sound, nobody to rise up and accuse her, nobody to dig up what was dead, nobody she need fear, after all. Only herself, lulled, bemused, bribed, persuaded, subdued into acquiescence, but never convinced. Only herself and this roused ghost clawing at her shoulder, and this now constant and inconsolable ache inside her of a debt unpaid and unpayable.

'Well, how are you feeling this morning?' asked the ward sister, coming in on her daily round.

'Much better, thank you.' The patient was pale, lucid and astonished among her pillows, staring great-eyed at a recovered world in which she seemed to find nothing familiar. 'I'm afraid I've been causing you all a great deal of trouble.'

'You haven't done so badly, considering. You did give them rather a run for their money in the theatre – very naughty reactions to the anaesthetic. But that's all over now. Your temperature's been down to normal since last night, and Nurse tells me you're eating well this morning. Keep it up, and we'll be getting you out of bed in a couple of days.'

'I seem to have been lucky,' said Maggie, flexing her legs experimentally under the bedclothes. 'Everything works. What exactly did I do to myself?'

'It wasn't half as bad as it looked when they brought you in. A lot of blood, but no breakages. But you were pretty badly cut about, down below, you're going to look like a Victorian sampler when you get all that plaster off. Never mind, the scars won't be where they show, and if you usually heal well you may not have much to show for it in a year or so. There've been any amount of callers enquiring after you. Your sister telephoned, and your brother . . . your agent . . . In a few days we'll let you have a telephone in here, but not just yet. But I think we could allow you visitors this afternoon. Mr. Lowell sent you the roses, and said he'd be in to see you the minute we let him.'

'Wasn't I in a ward? I thought . . . I seem to remember more beds . . . a big room and a lot of people sleeping . . .'

'Your agent asked us to move you into a private room, as soon as he knew what had happened.'

'Oh,' said Maggie, 'I see!' He would, of course, to him it would be a matter of first importance. 'It sounds silly, but I don't even know what hospital this is. I'd never driven that road before.'

'You're in the Royal, in Comerbourne. We're the nearest general to that nasty bend where you crashed. You're not the first we've had brought in from there, and I doubt you won't be the last. Take things easily, and don't worry about anything now, you're doing very nicely.'

'Everybody's being very kind. I'm sorry to be a nuisance.'

'It's what we're here for.' The ward sister looked back from the doorway, and saw the dilated blue-black eyes following her steadily from the pillow, but without any real awareness of her. They gave her the curious impression that they were staring inward rather than outward. 'There isn't anything troubling you, is there? If there's anything you want, anything we can do for you, you've got a bell there by your bed.'

'Thank you, really there's nothing more you can do for me.'

There was nothing more any of them could do for her. Not the ward sister, not the wiry little staff nurse with a bibful of pins, not the tall, splay-footed Jamaican beginner from Port Royal, who herring-boned up the ward like a skier climbing back up a slope, and warmed the air with her split-melon smile and huge, gay, innocent eyes; not the young houseman who made the daily rounds, nor the consultant surgeon who had sewn her torn thighs back into shape, not the anaesthetist who had kept her breathing on the table when it seemed she had been set on giving up the struggle. Nor her visitors, who came with flowers and chocolates as soon as they were allowed in: Tom Lowell, tongue-tied with unwary joy at seeing her on her way back to life, and half-inclined to blame himself, though heaven knew why, for what had happened; her agent, swooping in from London laden with roses and reassurances; a young conductor passing through Comerbourne on his way to an engagement in Chester; a famous tenor who had recorded with her a few months ago; a concert violonist, and others who had shared platforms with her. They sat by her bed for an hour or so, happy and relieved to find her recognisable for the same Maggie, with a steady pulse, a satisfactory blood pressure, and a voice unimpaired. They went away with the comfortable feeling of having visited and consoled the not-too-sick. There was nothing more she could do for them, or they for her.

The unidentified visitor, the one without a face, did not so much return after their going as sit with her silently throughout their stay, patient and apart, and move into her heart's centre when they went away. Often, then, she turned her whole attention upon him suddenly, in the effort to startle him into revealing some feature by which he could be recognised, before the concealing mists swirled over him and hid everything; but he was always too quick for her. She would not give up the search, and he would not be found.

But the visitors went away content, finding her as they had always known her, even though she would never be the same again. True, she had survived, physically she was intact, now that she was over the unexpected hazard of the anaesthetic. We shall not all die, but we shall all be changed, she thought, left alone in the relaxed hour before supper. In a moment, in the twinkling of an eye. About as long as it takes for a somersaulting car to smash itself against a tree-stump, and spill you out among the broken glass and twisted metal on to the grass. And probably about as long as it takes to launch the decisive word or act that looks almost excusable at the moment, and only afterwards, long, long afterwards, turns out to have been your damnation.

She awoke from an uneasy sleep in mid-afternoon, to find a small, elderly, shaggy man in a white coat sitting beside her bed. She had seen him making his official rounds twice since her admission, and she knew he was the consultant surgeon who had perseveringly stitched Humpty-Dumpty together again; but until this moment she had never seen him still, and never without his retinue.

'Good!' he said. 'I've been waiting for the chance to talk to you. You worry me.'

'Do I? I'm sorry!' she said, startled, and her memory fitted one detail, at least, into its true place. 'I know you now,' she said obscurely, 'you're the one who said I had a chance to begin again.'

'Did I? I don't remember that. But you have, that's true enough. What are you going to do with it?'

'Use it, I hope.'

'I hope so, too, but I'm not so sure of it as I was three days ago. You're my investment, I want to see you thriving. After a tricky start you got over your physical troubles marvellously, and believe me, you can think yourself lucky to have a constitution

411

like yours. Your pulse is steady, your blood pressure's satisfactory, and your body's functioning like a first-class machine. But Sister tells me you've lost some weight and are losing your appetite. Why? Why have you less energy than you had two or three days ago? Why do you have nothing to say to anyone unless you're obliged by politeness? And never use that telephone we gave you?'

Her eyes, which were the darkest, deepest blue he had ever seen, and in any but this lofty light might have seemed black, widened in alarm, astonishment and compunction. 'I didn't realise that,' she said. 'I'm sorry!'

'And for all this, let me tell you, there isn't the slightest physiological reason. Your body's doing its job. Doing everything it can to get well. So since there has to be a reason why you've come to a halt, and even begun to lose ground, the reason must be in your mind. Now probably you'll tell me that what's in your mind is no concern of mine,' he said dryly, 'but at least don't tell me there's nothing damaging there, because I shan't believe you.'

'No,' said Maggie, and raised herself strenuously on her pillow to be eye to eye with him. 'No, I do realise . . . It was you who put me together again.' He understood what she meant; it gave him rights in her. Every artist, every craftsman, has the right to demand that his work shall not be wasted by somebody else's wanton irresponsibility. 'I do want to get well,' she said. 'I want to go on singing – what's the good of me, otherwise? And I want to do you credit, too. It's a priority bill that I must pay before I can get any peace. But, my God, don't you think I've been trying?'

'I know you have. Even successfully, until something else distracted your attention. Something with a higher priority?'

She let her head fall back on the pillow. Her eyes closed for a moment, but opened unwaveringly to hold him off. There were defences there only an old man with privileges could hope to breach, and even he only when the wind and the hour and

412

the mood were favourable. She was a strong, fit woman, thirty-one years old and one of the treasures of the world, even if she herself didn't know it, and he was disposed to believe that she did; and unless somebody managed to goad her back into living, she would draw in upon herself and die of absent-mindedness. Literally absent-mindedness, for all her energy and will-power and passion were engaged elsewhere, and her body, however robust and heroic, could not survive unaided.

'No, don't say anything yet. Listen to me. I know you love what you do. I know you realise what you possess, a voice in a million. You couldn't use it as you do, if you didn't know its value. I'm your surgeon, it's in my own interests to ensure that what I do isn't erased by some other force, whether outside or inside my own province. But I'm a man, too, dependent upon music to a degree you maybe don't suspect. Would you be surprised to hear that I have every recording Maggie Tressider has ever made? You live by my grace, I live by yours. And I need you, I need you whole and effective, I need you because you excel, and your excellence belongs to me, as it does to everyone who feels and understands it. If you can use me, use me. I'm here to be used. It may not be surgery, but it comes somewhere within the bounds of healing, and that's my business. And this is a kind of confessional, too. I'm here to forget and be forgotten, afterwards.'

She lay silent and motionless for a long time, her blue, unblinking stare wide and wary upon his face.

'You'd have to have faith in me, too,' she said warningly, 'or you'll take the easy way out and think I'm a mental case.' Her voice, used now like a weapon, had recovered much of its resplendent viola tone; he had never heard anyone sound saner.

'*I'm being haunted*,' she said, '*by somebody I've killed*. A higher priority . . . that's what you said, isn't it? That's exactly my case. I'm possessed. I owe you and everyone here a return on your investment, I owe the world whatever it is I contribute. But I owe this ghost of mine a life. You can't get ahead of that, can you? I'm very much afraid my debts to you are going to be difficult to pay. By the time he's paid I shall be bankrupt.'

The dark-blue gaze speared him suddenly, and found him appalled and pitying, exactly as she had suspected.

'I told you you'd think I was mad. It's all right, I quite understand. Sometimes I think so, too. That's when I lose ground. But if you really want me,' she said, 'you'd better believe me sane and go on listening. You did say this was a confessional, remember?'

'I remember. What you say now remains unsaid. Absolutely and eternally. And I believe it.'

'I've done something terrible,' said Maggie. 'I don't even know what it is, or when it happened, but I drove somebody to his death. I knew it when I came round in the night, after the accident. He was there breathing down my neck, whispering to me that I'd killed him. Not at all vague or distant, absolutely real and present, but when I turn round to look for the details there's nothing to be found. Just this sense of guilt. What I feel is that somewhere, at some time, I failed somebody, or betrayed somebody ... something unforgivable ... Criminal? I don't know, I think it may have been, if only in keeping silent about something I knew. Somebody relied on me, and I turned my back and let him fall. What matters,' she said, her eyes straining upwards into the quivering blue and white radiance of reflected light on the ceiling over her head, 'is that he's dead, and I killed him.'

She waited, almost disdainfully prepared for the soft, humouring tones that medical men keep for the mentally unstable.

'And have you managed,' he asked, very soberly and thoughtfully, 'to find anything in your memory that lends colour to this belief?'

'No. I've tried and tried, and I can't trace any such incident. But it's still there. He never stops treading on my heels.'

'But there's no known ground for this obsession. Don't forget, you've been through fairly drastic surgery, and a considerable degree of shock. It isn't at all unusual for the kind of experience you've lived through to leave a nightmare residue, that may surface at the least expected moment. Details submerge, and a sense of horror remains, something you can't pin down. Something that passes gradually, if you concentrate on the live world and let it pass.'

'No,' she said instantly and chillingly. 'You forget, it's almost a week now, and I've waited and held my breath, and it doesn't pass. Because it's real, not a dream at all, not a floating residue left to surface by chance. *It's there!* In the corner of my eye always, and when I turn to look at it, it's everywhere but where I'm looking. I don't know when, I don't know how, but it's something I did, and I can't get away from it.'

'You do realise, don't you, that even if there is some factual basis for it, it may turn out to be in some incident grotesquely out of proportion to the feeling you have about it?'

'It may,' she agreed; but he knew by the set of her face that she did not believe in that possibility.

'But even so, if it does exist in your past, however inadequately, then it must be possible to run it to earth.'

'That's what I've been trying to do for days. I've been forwards and backwards through my life, poking under all the stones I can find. At first I took it for granted it was Tom, you see . . . that I'd killed him when I crashed the car. But they told me at once that he was safe. Then I thought that there might have been somebody else involved in the accident, but there wasn't. It isn't as simple as that, and it isn't as recent. The knowledge seemed to come from very deep, as if an earthquake had split the ground and thrown up something from miles down. There are no levels any more, everything's torn up and thrown about, and everything has to settle all over again afterwards, and make a new surface to walk on. The first steps are liable to be pretty shaky. And buried things may break out and meet you in the way.'

He saw the quickened breathing heaving her breast, and the

415

hectic flush of exertion flicking her cheekbones. 'I'm tiring you,' he said.

'No, don't go! No, you're helping me. After I'd dredged up every recollection I could, right back to school, I did try, you see, to put it out of my mind. I told myself it was one of those freaks, the shock and the fright and the pain choosing to hit me after the event in this way. Nothing behind it. But I couldn't satisfy myself, and I'm afraid you won't be able to satisfy me, either. I'm not running a temperature, I'm not in shock, I haven't any worries, my career will wait for me the short time it has to wait, and all I have to do is lie around and enjoy myself while I get well. There simply is no reason at all – is there? – why this terrible conviction of guilt should stay with me still. Only one possible reason. That it's true, that it's justified.'

'But if there existed any real source for it, you would have found it.' It did not convince him, and he knew as soon as it was out that it would not convince her.

'No, because I'm the wrong person to do the searching. Oh, I *believe* I want to find it, but how can I be *sure*? Isn't it possible that there's at least as much of me trying to stamp it back into the ground, quickly, before I ever get a good look at it? Isn't that the most likely reason why I always see it out of the corner of my eye?'

'But did you never stop to consider that you have relatives, associates, friends, people who have been intimately involved in your life for years, and none of them accuses you of anything? Do you really believe you've committed some mortal fault against another person, without a single one of your acquaintances knowing anything about it? Is there an empty place anywhere in your life where you even *could* have done this hypothetical thing, in absolute isolation from any witness? That would rule out anything but the cruder possibilities, like flat, planned murder, that *has* to be kept secret. And that would involve more complications, like skills I very much doubt if you possess.' He span

416

out his theme to its ultimate absurdity. 'And a body. And there never was a body featuring in your affairs, I take it?'

'No . . . no body.' She shivered, and passed the heel of her hand over her eyelids. 'It wouldn't be like that. There are more oblique ways of killing. Even without meaning to. But you see, it's just because I've been dead in a way myself that I *must know.* After coming back to life again as I have, I've got to make this a new beginning, otherwise it will be unbearable. If I have something shameful buried somewhere in my past, then I want to know what it is. I want to settle the account, if it can be settled. I want to be out of debt.'

'And you've said nothing of all this to anyone else? To your agent, or your family?'

The look she gave him, beginning with blank incomprehension and burning up into horrified recoil, more than answered that question. Clearly it would have been unthinkable to confide in any one of those circling satellites. She had dealt openly with him only because of his reassuring distance from her, and because he was a professional with a legitimate and impersonal interest in her recovery. And only a moment ago he had come very close to touching her hand, by way of establishing a closer contact! If he had done it he would have lost her irrecoverably.

'Well, supposing now,' he said carefully, 'that someone else, someone completely detached, took over this search for you?'

He grudged her to the psychiatrists, but they might well be the obvious answer, if she could be persuaded to co-operate. And Harlingford was a good man, and old enough to see her with a disenchanted eye. If, he hedged wryly, any man still living is old enough for that. To love her would be to be powerless to help her, that was clear, for at the first touch, no more than the meeting of eyes, she would draw back out of reach, retreat into the castle and bar the doors. Now I wonder, he thought, I really wonder why?

'Supposing someone else, someone who makes a job of that kind of thing, took over the stone-turning for you? If he found some lost detail – most probably perfectly innocent – to account for the setting up of this cancer in your mind, would that satisfy you? You would have to have faith in your man, of course. But there are people, you know, who are trained in these techniques, highly skilled professionals who take this sort of thing as their special field.'

If he had only known it, he had gone about this oblique approach all too gently; they were on different wave-lengths, and communication as he understood it had ceased, though to her mind he had just begun to make sharp and practical sense. She sat up alertly. The word professional had a reassuring sound in her ears. Why not? He was right, what she needed was someone who knew how to set about unearthing lost incidents, someone who put his talents on the market at a fair price, and could be hired to do a specific job on a business footing. In a relationship like that, mutually agreed, there would be no violation of privacy.

'Would you like me to put your case in the hands of somebody like that, and leave it to him to do your searching for you? And if the expert fails to turn up anything discreditable, then will you be satisfied?'

'Yes,' she said eagerly, 'oh, *yes*! That's what I need, somebody completely objective. But I shouldn't know where to look for the right person, and I don't want to ask anyone else to . . . to be an intermediary for me. Find me a good private detective, and I'll turn the whole nightmare over to him, and abide by whatever he finds.'

Chapter 2

His name was Francis Killian, and he was forty-one years old. Strictly speaking, he was not what is usually thought of as a private detective at all, and he never called himself one. The small plate on his office door above the book-shop in Market Street, Comerbourne, said only: 'Confidential Enquiries', and that was precisely what he dealt in. He didn't touch divorce business or commercial spying; sometimes he wondered why, since he had no very inflated opinion of his own holiness, and there was more money in these lines than in the cold, retired researches he did undertake. An eventful life, which had begun its adulthood with national service in Korea, could hardly leave him many illusions; and even after that unspeakably horrible trap had opened and released him, scarred for life, he had half-chosen and half-drifted into situations and callings which were not for the squeamish. Trying, perhaps, to rediscover disgust as the clean feel it, a luxury out of reach of those already soiled.

So he couldn't congratulate himself that it was any particular moral purity that had won him a recommendation from one of Comerbourne's most respectable solicitors to one of Comerbourne's most eminent surgeons, improbably in quest of a private enquiry agent 'for a friend', of course! All that had kept Francis acceptable to such clients was a fastidious sense of cleanliness, a cold dislike of the feel of dirt. If he still had moral scruples, it was from old habit, and they were by no means clearly defined.

He was unmarried and alone. He hadn't always been alone. He remembered women he had known, too many of them and too intimately, but all past. He expected now to continue alone. You can stand only so much self-exposure and so much self-division; in his case very little, the godhead in him was a jealous god. It had been clear to him now for five years that there must be no more women gnawing away at the edges of his integrity. Such as it was! Not the world's treasure, that was certain; but all the treasure he had and he valued it.

So Francis Killian was a lonely man, in the large sense that precludes any feeling of grievance in being alone. And he worked hard, as men alone do, in dry, precise, painstaking ways that commended him chiefly to the legal profession. Most of his work was done for solicitors, tracing witnesses to accidents, combing ancient church registers, making abstracts of tedious documents; and for scholars and writers, running to earth elusive authorities, compiling précis of acts and regulations, searching records for lost details Sometimes he traced lost persons, too, and even lost ancestries, some of them better lost for good. Occasionally he consented to undertake a shadowing job, where a witness was liable to abscond, or worried parents wished to keep a wary eye on a young son's questionable associates.

Dealing with documents was clean, sterile, congenial business that neither moved nor disturbed him, and that was what counted. It brought him in a modest living, and in money for its own sake he had no great interest. Indeed he had reached a midway breathing-space in his life when he had only a detached interest in anything, and what mattered most to him was to have the ground about him cleared of all encumbering passions and all human entanglements, like a man who finds it necessary to throw away all his possessions in order to feel free.

There were still things in the world, however, that gave him positive, profound, irresistible pleasure, burdening him with a kind of obligation to look again at a human race which could occasionally produce perfection. The first and greatest of these unwilling relationships he had was with music. Against the grain he conceded that there must still be hope for a species which had produced Mozart.

So against his instincts he agreed to consider stepping out of character to oblige Maggie Tressider. He thought of her as a voice rather than a woman, but the voice needed a human vehicle, and according to the old man the vehicle, the superb mechanism that produced that inimitable sound, was seriously threatened. Her recovery, he said, was being impeded by an obsession.

Any other name, and Francis Killian would have astonished and affronted his visitor by saying no. Obsessions were not in his line.

The old man wasn't enjoying his errand. He would much rather have handed her over to the head-shrinkers, of course, and kept it, as it were, in the family. He had entered the office stepping with the delicacy of a duchess slumming, and been curiously disarmed, even reassured, by the pale, austere, orderly room, as clinical in its way as his own consulting-room. He too could appreciate professionalism. But the man behind the desk had cancelled out the soothing effect of his own environment. There would always be something ambivalent about Francis, however gravely he comported himself, a faint aura of self-caricature, as if in despising mankind he could never completely conceal his despite against himself.

If Gilbert Rice could have retreated then, he would have done it; but Rattray, Rattray, Bell and Rattray – all four of them – had testified that this man was secret, reliable and conscientious, and to open the case to yet another operative was unthinkable. And Francis redeemed himself. At the mention of Maggie's name he froze, abandoning whatever he had been about to say, and sat thinking for a long minute, honestly eye to eye with his visitor. Then he said: 'Tell me about it. If I can help Miss Tressider, I will.'

'You understand, it is she who insists on employing a private detective. I . . . it was a misunderstanding. I would have preferred to recommend a psychiatrist. But Miss Tressider is a strong-willed woman, and very clear about her own state of mind. Whether it is a psychiatrist or a detective she needs, the fact remains that she can only be helped with her own co-operation, and she absolutely refuses a psychiatrist.'

Francis readjusted his image of her at once; she might, indeed, be rejecting what she most needed, but a woman who knew her own mind so firmly might well be a reliable witness. His own instinct, had anyone proposed to meddle with his mind, would have been to defend his flawed privacy to the death. The unknown woman who was Orpheus, who was Eboli, who was disembodied beauty shut in a body by some cosmic paradox, moved a step nearer to him.

'And you think,' said Francis shrewdly, 'that the first step in curing her is to act as if you're taking her preoccupation seriously. In short, I shall be fulfilling my only useful function by going through the motions of trying to trace the thing that's worrying her. In that case, the answer is no. If I enter her employ I shall do my best for her, and it's from her I shall take my orders. If she wants me to look for a skeleton in her cupboard, I shall look for it. I may even find it But I can't be hired to jolly her along towards recovery by *pretending* to look for it. *You* don't believe,' he said curiously, 'that there's really anything to be found, do you?'

After a struggle with his distaste and distrust, Gilbert Rice surprised him. 'Yes,' he said flatly, 'there is something. Almost certainly something. I'll be quite open with you, Mr. Killian. In my judgment Miss Tressider is a person of quite exceptional generosity and integrity, who has fared rather badly in her personal relationships. She comes from a very ordinary lower-middle-class family – you understand, I am using current terms simply because they are useful in establishing a picture – whose other members have sponged on her from the beginning of her celebrity without shame and without gratitude, and privately resent her pre-eminence as much as they publicly rejoice in it. I believe she has behaved towards all her relatives and associates with great loyalty, which in her heart she knows very well is cast on stony ground. I think it is entirely possible that once, just once, she rebelled and recoiled, that just once she turned and tore somebody, in a protest which was overdue. I suppose it's even possible that there was a disastrous result, for someone who surely deserves little sympathy. She is incapable of real malice or meanness. But her standards are high. I think from her point of view there may well be something to regret. I believe it would be better if she knew what it was, and could be forced to accept it. You need not be afraid of the result, if you do run the thing to earth. She has a sense of responsibility to the rest of us, too. Whatever you find, you won't destroy her, you can only liberate her. She knows of what a marvel she is the custodian.'

Fantastic, Francis thought, shaken clean out of his objectivity. This antique pillar of society, thirty years established, father and grandfather, suddenly wrenching his heart open over a neurotic young woman he never saw before, because some accident of nature gave her the voice of an archangel. And how if he's right? How if she really needs to be rid of an incubus that might kill her? No more immortal Orpheus, only that lament on a gramophone record, slowly paling for want of new, living breath. Stiff little, grey little stuffed shirt as he might be, Maggie Tressider's surgeon had the courage of his convictions.

'I take it,' said Francis carefully, drawing the classic profile of Orpheus on the half-filled page of notes before him, 'that the best thing I can do is come and talk to Miss Tressider during ordinary visiting hours. . . This evening?'

He went home and played the Gluck records. She was better even than he remembered her. It was not a dark, weighty, velvet

423

contralto, but agile, thrilling and true, a quality in it that sheared through the heart like pure pain, like love itself, excising everything of lesser urgency. It was the voice the old man was in love with, of course. No face could live up to it, much less the heart and the being that went with the face.

She had a crooked mouth in photographs, and a wide, defensive glance, like a child's, and a more than usually asymmetrical face, larger on the right side.

Well, there was the voice to be saved.

She was sitting up in bed when he came, looking exactly like all those other women in the long ward next door, polished and brushed and neatly tucked in for visiting-time. She had even the same half-apprehensive, half-expectant look as they had, and her eyes, like theirs, enlarged in a face blanched and honed to transparency by the experience of suffering, turned towards the doorway of her room as soon as his hand touched the handle, and transfixed him as he entered with their blue intensity. She looked glad, and eager, and afraid; exactly as if he had really been a personal visitor, and one to whom she had long looked forward.

'Miss Tressider? My name is Killian.'

'It's very good of you,' she said, 'to come so promptly.' Her speaking voice was low-pitched, warm and vibrant. 'Please sit down. I believe Mr. Rice has explained to you what's worrying me? . . . what I want you to find out for me?'

It seemed that everything was to be conducted with despatch, practically, as between business associates, without any suggestion of anguish. Unless, he thought a moment later, you looked too closely at the fine-drawn lines of her face, which had still something of the chill of shock about them, the faint, reflected image of death as it missed its hold on her; or deeply enough into the wide, wild stare of the eyes to discover the fixed, silvery gleam of panic behind their honest, well-mannered blueness.

424

She shopped for the commodity she needed with the directness of a child, but there was nothing childish about her need.

It was illuminating, too, that the paperbacks he had brought with him came as a shock to her, and an embarrassment. When he laid them on the bed convenient to her hand she touched them blankly, and didn't know what to do or say. The thanks came mechanically, and what was really on her mind couldn't find words. How right he had been to pass up roses! Unless, of course, he wanted her to withdraw the offer of this job? He still wasn't clear about that, but if he had wanted it, roses would have been as good a way as any of making sure. He wasn't here to have any personal relationship with her, she mustn't be touched. All that he must inevitably discover about her she would countenance and assist as case-notes necessary to the job, but never as the impalpable web of a man's understanding. This would have to be strictly clinical. So much the better; that suited Francis.

'It seemed advisable to be as convincing a visitor as possible,' he said dryly, 'and you'll have observed that they never come empty-handed. The women in the ward might not notice. The staff certainly would. I take it I'm right in thinking that *only* Mr. Rice is in your confidence?'

'Oh,' she said, flushing, 'I see! Yes, of course, that was thoughtful of you. I thought . . . I was rather afraid that you might be too well known to pass unnoticed, in any case.'

'I'm hardly the celebrity type of detective,' he assured her, amused and disarmed. 'Few of us are, if the truth be told. Nobody here is likely to know who I am or what I do, and your privacy needn't be compromised.'

'That's what I should prefer, if it's possible. But of course you must include the books and everything in your expenses.'

The tone was perhaps a little arrogant, but so, in all probability, had his been.

'We can come to an agreement about all that later,' he said. 'Since our time's limited, what I think you should be doing now is lying back and relaxing, while you tell me yourself about this experience that made you send for me. By this time I take it you've found a way of surrendering yourself into the hands of doctors when you have to? Consider me one more in the same category. Close your eyes and shut me out if it makes it any easier. Most of us do that with doctors, when the handling begins.'

'And dentists,' said Maggie unexpectedly, and smiled.

'And dentists.' It might, he conceded ruefully, be a better analogy. 'I shall have to take notes. You won't mind that? They'll all be destroyed, afterwards.'

'Yes, I understand.' She let her head fall back on the pillow. 'I want to do everything that may help you to find out . . . what it is that's haunting me. You understand, I must know. There'll be no peace for me, no possibility of living normally, unless I know. *He* wanted me to put it out of my mind, but I can't do that. If I've done somebody a terrible wrong, and now for the first time I *feel* what I've done how can I just push it away and pretend I know nothing about it? Then he wanted me to put myself in the hands of a psychiatrist. Why should I do that? I don't want it rationalised out of existence, if it really does exist, *I want it put right!* I'm sorry,' she said, suddenly fixing those disturbing eyes upon his attentive face, 'if you find all this a little unbalanced. All that got through to me was the fact of my guilt. It's because I can't give a rational account of the thing that I need you. Do *you* think I'm out of my wits?'

'No,' he said, 'I think you are very much in command of them. Tell me!'

She told him, slowly, carefully, picking her words with concentration and precision, like a party to a case in court who must make the right impression now or never. And after a few moments she closed her eyes and put him out of her recognition except as a disembodied confessor, the better to feel her way towards objectivity. It seemed that her passion for truth and justice was large enough to compel absolute candour, as if she

426

felt herself to be addressing God. In his experience women could be devious even in their prayers, but he would have staked his reputation that this one was not.

Maggie talked and Francis listened, made notes, and watched her face, a pure oval, its irregularities hardly discoverable here in the flesh. Photographs always exaggerate any disproportion in the features; but her photographs were almost caricatures, so far were they from doing her justice. It was largely a matter of colouring. Those dark, dark eyes of hers you would have expected to be softly purple-black like a pansy, but instead they were the startling, piercing blue of high-altitude gentians, as vivid as noon in their midnight darkness. And now he came to think of it, that was exactly the colouring of her dark, dark voice, too. And her hair, refined English mouse-brown in pictures, who could have guessed it would be this unbelievable tint between dark gold and orange-russet, even subtly greenish in the shadows, the colour of the budding foliage of an oak tree in spring? She was much thinner than in any photograph he had ever seen of her; but then, she was probably much thinner now than she'd been a few weeks ago, after extensive surgery, and with this obsession eating her alive.

He made the same discovery as the anaesthetist had made, paying his midmight visit to her in the ward to make sure she had really decided to take up the business of breathing again. She was beautiful. Very beautiful. It seems some people *can* have everything. Except, of course, peace of mind and a quiet conscience.

It was at about this point that he observed the first interesting peculiarity about her narrative. He didn't make a note of it, it wasn't necessary.

'Thank you,' he said when she fell silent. 'That was very comprehensive, and I doubt if I have many questions to ask. If you'd had any clue to time and place you would have included it. But I gather we can't limit the possibilities at all, apart from ruling out the last few years. Forgetting is mortally easy, easier than remembering, but it does take a little time. Assuming this haunting has a foundation in fact, if it had been recent it would have surfaced more completely, with more detail.'

'But is it genuinely possible,' she asked, opening her eyes wide, 'to forget something so important? Even after years?'

'It's possible, all right. What we retain over a lifetime is only an infinitesimally small proportion of the whole. Think how many impressions are run through in an hour, and how many brief acquaintances in a year. The most phenomenal memory can't contain a tenth of the total.'

'But something like that . . . a matter of life and death . . . *that* would surely be retained, whatever was thrown out.'

'We don't know that it was a matter of life and death, or that it seemed so important then. Maybe this is hindsight. I don't suggest your condition conjured up a totally illusory bogy, but I do think it possible that it magnified and distorted a comparatively innocuous incident. Wait,' he said reasonably, 'until you know.'

'You forget,' said Maggie mildly, 'that I'd just slipped through death's fingers. When you find yourself staring at close range into judgment day, you get your values right.'

'Not necessarily. Not unless you believe fear to be the best introduction to truth. Even the just aren't going to feel too sure of themselves on judgment day.'

'Oh, no,' said Maggie oddly, 'I wasn't afraid. You go clean through that, you know. It doesn't apply any more. Even now it isn't like being afraid, it's just that it's impossible to live without *knowing*. Like Oedipus. There isn't any possibility of turning back and letting well alone. There wouldn't be any solid ground to stand on. And you can't sing without truth!'

No, *she* couldn't, he quite saw that. It took a bit of believing, in such a bogus world, but this woman had never severed her infant relationship with reality, and while she felt truth to be impaired everything would be devalued for her, even her art. He

428

knew then that he was committed, not simply to accepting her commission, but to bringing it to a successful conclusion.

'We still have half an hour. If you're not too tired, I should like you to begin talking to me about yourself. Right from the beginning, your family, your childhood, things you remember. Names you remember. Don't worry about looking for the seeds of this present trouble. Forget about it now. It may come to light of itself, it won't if you try to trace it. Tell me who played with you, who were your friends, your fellow-students . . .' Though the name that mattered she might not even recognise; she was almost sure by now that she had excised it from her memory for good reason, and eternally, unless some act of God or of Francis Killian raised it again to confront her. Between the conflicting needs and wants of the divided halves of her, what was a man in her employ supposed to do?

But she couldn't sing without truth; she had said it, not he. And she couldn't live without singing.

'Just talk to yourself,' he said, 'and I'll be quiet.'

And she talked, and he was very quiet. Her lips moved slowly and thoughtfully, unrolling before him a cartoon of that ordinary family of hers, odd little vignettes of her schooldays, without sentimentality, without nostalgia, almost without interest. She had had to leave her kin to find her kind, like many another. Not a matter of class at all, but of quality, which is a different and a mysterious thing. She mentioned names faithfully. Most he did not bother to note down, but some were still quick in her memory. He was sensitive to the intonations now. And then her first singing days, the little local successes, the audition that took her into Doctor Paul Fredericks' classes, the serious study beginning. No doubt of the urgency now, his pen was busy writing down names that mattered to her almost as gravely as her own.

She was still twelve years back in time when the bell rang for the end of visiting-hour. She opened dazed eyes. Her forehead was moist, but the lines of her face were relaxed and tranquil.

'I'll come the day after tomorrow,' he said, putting away his notebook, 'in the evening, if you can manage to deflect all your other visitors. I've tired you out too much . . . I'm sorry!'

'Oh, no!' she said quickly. 'I'm glad! Just to be doing something about it is worth anything. I feel happier now. I trust you.'

Now that, he thought bitterly, winding his way across the car park to his third-hand Riley, is about the most unfair and terrifying thing one human being can say to another. She trusts me! To come up with miracles, to get her out of her little private hell. What sort of spot does that put me in? But of course, she'll be paying my daily rate and all expenses . . . even the paperbacks! That puts it on quite a different footing for her, all she's asking is fair work for fair pay. But what does it do for me? It may take more than a little patient research, more than leg work, more than you can buy for any daily retainer, to turn up X for her and get the thorn out of her flesh.

Still, he reflected, driving home to his flat in Market Street, bare as a hermitage, he had got one positive thing out of this first session. All the female names he had written down were recorded only as possible sources of information; apart from that he might as well cross them off at once. Maggie Tressider was quite certainly honest in claiming that she could not recapture a single limiting fact about the identity of X. But every time she spoke of her victim and persecutor she said 'he'.

He went to the trouble to check on her family, though he felt and found that they were of no interest. Her parents were dead, the father long ago, while Maggie was still at school, the mother four years ago of heart disease. There remained a sister and a brother, Alec, both older than Maggie. The brother played the horn in a Midland orchestra, well enough to hold his place but not well enough ever to get any farther. A little probing produced a picture not at all unexpected; he had been trading on his sister's reputation and his relationship to her ever since she emerged into celebrity. He had made one flying visit to see her in the hospital, since it wasn't far out of his way. Rice was of the opinion that he had come for money, and hadn't gone away empty-handed, but he did at least make himself pleasant, affectionate and cheerful while he was there.

The married sister, eldest of the three, lived in Hertfordshire with an insurance-agent husband and two children. She hadn't visited. There was a record of telephone enquiries from her, beginning with an agitated lament on the first evening, before Maggie was up from the theatre, expressing endless devotion and the fixed intention of leaving everything and rushing to her bedside; but the tone had cooled off after it became clear that the bed was not going to be a death-bed. Mrs. Chalmers still called in with loving messages, but she didn't suggest coming. These details Francis also gleaned from Rice, who had them from the ward sister, through whom all those earlier phone calls had been channelled.

It began to seem as if all those who professed affection for her also harboured in secret a corrosive resentment. Yet everything went to show that she had remained loyal and generous to her family and early associates. Maybe that was her really unforgivable virtue. If she had shaken them off and gone her own way unimpeded, they could at least have felt that she was down on their human level, and taken pleasure in her flaws for their own comfort. People who have everything stir in ordinary mortals a venomous ambition to take everything from them, or if that's impossible, at least to spoil what is spoilable. No, Maggie had never caused any of her tribe to lament at her shoulder in the night. They were much more likely, given the chance, to ruin and despoil her.

Then there were the others, colleagues, fellow singers, accompanists, conductors, admirers. Would-be lovers, most of them, whether they knew it or not, though a few had the integrity and detachment to be disinterested friends to her into the bargain. God knew she had need of those, they seemed to have been few and far between in her life. The music teacher at

431

her local school, perhaps, who had first realised what a glorious instrument she possessed, and done his best to help her develop its possibilities. And afterwards, Paul Fredericks, that eccentric and wealthy old genius who had spent the last years of his life squandering the profits of his own musical career on the musicians of the future. But how many more?

Plenty of would-be lovers, though, from the modest admirers of her girlhood, through the teeming procession of her fellow-students, to the celebrities who surrounded her now. And wasn't there, somewhere in the sweet chorus of their devotion, a slightly sour note, too? The courting male knows his worth, and expects to make an impression, but Maggie Tressider had always stayed unattainable. They still praise and they still pursue, when the object of the pursuit is such a valuable cult image and status symbol; but after a while a slight acidity sets in, the heart goes out of the charade, and something alien comes to birth in its place. Spite?

He didn't realise, until he tapped at the door of her room for the second time, and saw her propped on her pillows with delicately made-up face and burnished hair to receive him, exactly what it was about her that disturbed him most. He entered with his memory marking off like spent beads the names of her adorers, who were legion; and there in the white bed in the white room, tense and still, sat this one slender, solitary creature, the cobalt mirrors of her eyes waiting for a human image to reflect, so that she could be peopled. He had never known anyone round whom such numbers of worshippers revolved; and he had never known anyone so intensely and disastrously alone.

She was a good client, patient and humble. She was ready to pick up her autobiography where she had left it two days before, and even paid him the compliment of following his recipe for relaxation while she recollected, as if he had indeed been one more doctor with authority over her, if only a temporary author-

432

ity. Slack in her pillows, with closed eyes, she recorded her testimony; and in the pauses, which were frequent but brief, long enough for thought but not for concealment, he watched her marble stillness, even her breath held, and thought, what would happen if one kissed this Sleeping Beauty? Would she wake up? On the contrary, she would withdraw into the hundred-year-long death-sleep at the first touch. You'd be lucky if you didn't impale yourself on the thorns before you ever reached her mouth.

'Dr. Fredericks used to pick out a small group of his pupils every spring and autumn, and take them on a tour of the Continent. He had good connections everywhere there, and it was his way of giving us proper concert experience before we tackled the big things. Freddy's Circus, we all called it. We used to attend some of the smaller festivals, and fill in with concerts all through Switzerland and Austria, and part of Germany too. There'd be two or three solo singers, and maybe a couple of instrumentalists, usually a pianist – one of the accompanists was always good for a concerto or two – and maybe a violinist, and a small orchestra. It cost him the earth to keep it all up, but now and again he even made a profit. I went three times. Once in 1954, in the autumn. I was eighteen. And then both the tours in 1955. After that I had my first big break, I was asked to sing Cherubino. He let me take it, so I knew I was ready. I never went abroad with him again, there were concerts, engagements, recordings ... things began to go very fast. Two years later, Freddy died. In Bregenz, at the festival. There weren't any more Circuses.'

'And who was with you on those tours? Can you remember?'

She mentioned several names. Two of them had followed her aloft, though less rapidly. One had died in a plane crash. Some were still, and presumably for ever, lost in obscurity.

'I don't remember any others. Oh, yes, the last time there was a change, because Freddy's sister, who always used to tour with us and act as chaperone for the girls, had to go into hospital just before we left, and one of his old pupils came along with us instead. Bernarda Elliot was her concert name. I think it was her maiden name. She was a contralto . . . a good one, but she'd been married for quite a time then, to somebody named Felse. She was living somewhere in the West Midlands, I remember. She came along with us just to oblige Freddy, and only that once. It was the only tour Miss Fredericks missed. She died, too, only a few months after Freddy. Voluntarily, I think. You know what I mean? They'd always worked together, without him the world wasn't worth hanging on to.'

'I know,' said Francis. 'This Cherubino . . . that was at Covent Garden, wasn't it?'

'Yes, I was lucky. We recorded with the same cast, afterwards. It wasn't the best "Figaro" ever, but it got a lot of notice.'

From then on it had been simply a climb from one eminence to another, steadily extending her range, always waiting for a few additional years to bring new works and maturer parts within her grasp. She told him about it just as she had experienced it, without either arrogance or modesty, and it dawned on him suddenly that she was not quite the gifted child he had begun to believe her, that this headlong simplicity and directness of hers was not a property of innocence, but the deliberate choice of an adult mind, the weapon of a woman with a great deal to do and only one lifetime in which to do it. Maggie Tressider had no time to waste on circumlocutions. There was, it seemed, at least one quality in her which might well destroy either her or anyone who got in her way. Generous, scrupulous, loyal, all these she might be, but ambitious she certainly was. Not for herself so much as for the voice of which she was the high priestess. If ever there was a clash of interests, she would sacrifice everything and everybody to that deity, including Maggie Tressider.

By the time the bell rang to send him away, she had arrived at the present. Iris-circled, with half-transparent lids veined like snowdrops, her eyes remained closed for a moment after she was

434

silent. The long lashes that lay on her cheeks were coloured like her hair, green-bronze-gold. When they rolled back from the wide stare that fastened unerringly on his face, the unveiled blue of her eyes was blinding.

It was then that it happened to him, sharp and clean as a knife-thrust, so that for an hour afterwards he never felt the pain.

'I'll contact you,' he said, 'as soon as I have anything to report. It may be a few days, but I'll ring you.'

'Yes . . .' She wanted to ask what was in his mind, whether he had got anything at all out of her self-examinings; but she refrained. She had said that she trusted him, and now it was in his hands. 'I feel better,' she said, offering him the one encouragement and commendation she had to give. 'Since you came I haven't lost any more weight. And I *sleep* now. I'm going to get well.'

'Of course!' he said.

'And to put this right . . .' She smiled at him, a grave, grateful, impersonal smile. The burden of her confidence sagged heavily on his heart, and deep within him, secretly and slowly, the mortal wound began to bleed.

It was half-way through the evening before the numbness thawed away, and the injustice and indignity and rage and pain, the reasoned hopelessness and irrational hope, all hit him together.

He was sitting over his notebook with a full ashtray at his elbow, methodically compiling lists of names and considering the significance of the periods into which her life fell. There was always more to be gained by sitting and thinking, and evaluating what was given, than by rushing about questioning people, and he had his starting point.

'I've done something awful to *him* . . . killed *him* . . .' '*He's* here with me all the time, *he* never leaves me . . .' 'It wouldn't be so bad if I could ever see *him* clearly . . .' Where there's no precise identification the masculine pronoun can embrace the feminine, too, of course. Maybe! But that was by no means the effect of the repeated 'he' in her mouth. She didn't know even the sex of her enemy; no, but some spark of her subconscious knew, all right. All Lombard Street to a china orange, X was a man.

What sort of man? Not a member of her family; those she bore with, visited occasionally, subsidised as a matter of course. Rice had suggested that there might have been some such hanger-on who chose the wrong moment, or the wrong approach, and started in her a spurt of distaste that caused her for once to lash out in rebellion against her rôle. But did any of them matter to her enough to make that probable? Francis thought not. And whoever provoked her into cruelty would have to matter to her pretty fundamentally.

The more he thought about it, the more clearly did X put on the likeness of the one person who was so conspicuously absent from Maggie's life. A face so rigidly excised from memory might well belong to the one man who wasn't there.

Plenty of men had loved Maggie, but not one of them, by her own account and the world's, had Maggie ever loved. Never once had she mentioned the word 'love'. And that in itself was remarkable enough to arrest attention. Here was a gifted, beautiful woman, still defensively alone at approaching thirty-two. On the face of it that was the most mysterious thing about her. Why did she never marry? Because she was married to her art? Even so, why did she never, apparently, even consider taking husband or lover, never let any of the candidates get within arm's-length of her? Take a step too near her, and she would take three away from you, and then keep retreating until she was out of sight. He had seen it for himself, and so, if he wasn't mistaken, had Gilbert Rice. So what was wrong with her? What was the block that shut men out? The same that blotted out the face of X?

And if the hunt for X was the hunt for the invisible, the non-existent lover, the only one who got past her guard, where was he most likely to be found? Somewhere fairly far back, or she

436

could not have expunged him so completely and for so long. In the world's eye not, perhaps, a very great figure in her life, or, again, she could not have forgotten him so successfully; yet great enough in retrospect to turn her whole life barren afterwards. *What was it she had done to him?*

No need to look back as far as childhood or early adolescence, either, because this was a thing that had fixed its claws into her adult being, and pierced deep. Somewhere at the emergence of the woman, say at eighteen or nineteen, when her career suddenly opened before her and she knew she was going to be great, when she was intoxicated and dazzled by music, and men, perhaps, faded into the background just when they should have been growing clear and important. Twelve or thirteen years ago. In twelve years she had had time to suppress a lot of regrets, to forget genuinely a lot of once-important people.

He performed, almost idly, the small exercise of looking back twelve years in his own life. Where had he been then? More to the point, with whom? He found a narrow boat on a Midland canal, a summer frittered away on an antique business that had folded under him because he didn't work at it, and a woman who had been the reason for his lack of application; but when it came to recalling the woman, she was only a small, blank, woman-shaped space without face or name. Nothing but an empty shape and a bitter taste, and no guilt except the guilt he felt for the squandering of whatever promise he'd ever had, and that held no mystery.

And then, abruptly, like a flower bud opening marvellously under the camera, the pale non-recollection put on colour and form and life, the head flushed into the incredible colour of oak foliage in spring, the burning blue eyes pierced him as they had pierced him an hour ago, and the searing realisation of his position broke out like blood at last, and he knew he was lost. Who had he thought he was, writing off women so confidently? Who did she think she was, writing off men?

For the first time in his life he hadn't seen it coming, hadn't side-stepped and dictated the ground on which it should approach him, and the terms on which he would entertain it. Now it was too late to do anything but stop the bleeding by force of will, and somehow claw his way back to the job in hand. Because he had just established to his full satisfaction that no man alive had a dog's chance of getting within Maggie Tressider's guard. Want her as he might, want would have to be his master, as it had been many another's.

Or would it? If he played his cards intelligently, hadn't he certain advantages?

She trusted him! She'd said so, and meant it. Who else had her ear as he had? Who else had access to her as he had? The hunt for X could be prolonged until his position was secured, and the uncovering of X could be so handled – assuming he was found, and in whatever circumstances – as to serve the interests of Francis Killian no less than those of Maggie Tressider. Yes, he had unique advantages . . .

And unique disadvantages, his own saner self warned him tartly. You're taking her money to do a job for her, the only trust she has in you is the trust intelligent people place in competent professionals bound to them by contract. Take one step out of line, tomorrow, next week, ever, and she'll be gone. And you'll be a bigger heel even than you've ever been before. At least until now you've kept your business clean.

I shall still be doing that, he persisted strenuously, fighting off his better judgment. I'm not proposing to cheat her. The job I've taken on for her I'll finish, if it can be done at all. But while it lasts I've got her ear, I've got a measure of her confidence, and I'll earn more. I'm wronging nobody if I conduct my own campaign alongside hers.

And you think you've got so much as a dog's chance? asked his *doppelgänger* venomously. You know what that woman is, a world figure, a beauty, a towering artist. Do I need to tell you? And you know what you are, don't you? Or maybe you've forgotten. It's a long time since you looked in a glass!

The House of Green Turf

There wasn't a mirror in the room, or in the flat apart from the one in the bathroom. But he didn't need a glass, he knew what he looked like, and what he was. A man of forty-one, average height, light weight, not bad to look at as average men go, if he hadn't spent all his adult life being knocked about by circumstances, and knocking himself about when circumstances let up. All that kept him from looking and being seedy was the odd vein of austerity that persisted from his Nonconformist upbringing, still unsubdued after a life-long battle with chaos and self-indulgence, and that basic dislike of dirt that would have been glad to believe itself a virtue, but sadly realised it was no more than a foible.

Yes, agreed his demon, reading his thoughts, you've had things cleaned up for the past five years, from artistic squalor into monastic order, and it cost you plenty to do it, and you know damned well the value you put on it. There was going to be no more of that! How much of your soul will you still own, if you let love break in here now? Don't you recognise a disaster when you see one? Take a look round this cell of yours. It's more than it looks, it represents the only safety you've got, because it's the only order, it's what's left of your morality, it's your identity. Open the door and let love into that, and it'll kick the whole structure apart before you can say: Maggie!

And he knew it was true. Only a fool could welcome in the invader of his painfully-won privacy, and run to meet the power that humiliated and outraged what he had made of himself at so much cost. And for such an impossible hope! He knew, none better, that he would never reach her. If he regrouped his defences now, while there was time . . .

But there was no time left. It was already too late.

All right, he said defiantly to his double, sit back and watch. A little patience, a little craft, a nice mixture of blackmail and gratitude, and you'll be surprised what I can do, when I want something enough. What will you bet me I don't get her in the end?

439

And if you do, said the demon, with the finality of ultimate, unquestionable truth, what you get won't be what you want. It will be only to possess and enjoy, you know that, don't you? And spoil! Never to unite with her.

All right, damn you! said Francis, setting his teeth, *then I'll settle for that!*

Chapter 3

So from then he had two people's interests to serve, Maggie's and his own; and for the time being they were identical. If ever the two interests should diverge, God only knew what he would do, or which of them he would put first. There was no sense in trying to anticipate the event, and no comfort, either.

Back to the business in hand, then. If X was an injured lover, he belonged somewhere at the threshold of success. Ever since she was twenty years old she had lived in the sun, known exactly where she was going, and needed no claws. The more he thought about it, the more he was left with two formative years, the last two she had spent under Paul Fredericks.

What wouldn't he have given to be able to question the old man, or even his sister who had worked with him? Perhaps especially his sister, for an elderly woman sees more of what goes on inside ambitious girls of genius than does a doting old man whose protégées they are. But they were both dead long ago. Francis had, however, the lists of names of those who had accompanied Maggie on her three tours with Freddy's Circus. He began with the last, in the autumn of 1955. The last for an excellent reason, because after it she had been invited to sing Cherubini at Covent Garden, and Freddy had acknowledged that she was ready. That was also reason enough why Francis should consider it first.

And there in the list, if he couldn't have Esther Fredericks, was the woman who had taken her place on the trip. Bernarda Elliot. Now Bernarda Felse. If Freddy had turned to her in a crisis, she must have a good head on her shoulders, as well as a contralto voice in her throat. And hadn't Maggie said that she lived – or had then been living – somewhere here in the Midlands? Felse is not a very common name.

He looked in the regional telephone directory. Felse is not a common name at all, he found. There was just one of them in the whole of two border English counties and a large slice of mid-Wales. George Felse, of 19 Prior's Lane, Comerford. In the circumstances it wouldn't be much of a trick to find out whether his wife's name was Bernarda.

It was; though most people, he discovered, seemed to know her as Bunty. And her husband – well, well, who would have thought it? – turned out to be a detective-inspector in the Midshire C.I.D. A far cry from Freddy's Circus to a modest modernised cottage in the village of Comerford, only a few miles out of the county town, and just in sad process of becoming a town itself. Thirteen years is a long time; George Felse must have been a bobby on the beat when this girl – and Maggie had said she was good – decided he was what she wanted most.

So it can happen!

Don't build on it, Francis, he warned himself grimly, it couldn't happen to Maggie. A little interlude of a few months – even a year or so – you might get if you're lucky and clever, but not a lifetime, don't look for it.

He called the number in the book. The voice that answered was lighter than Maggie's, and more veiled. 'Yes, I'm Bernarda Felse. But how did you know?'

A good question, but for some reason a daunting one. He might have to be on his guard with a woman like that, in case he gave away more than he got from her.

'My name's Francis Killian. I got your name from Maggie Tressider. You know she's in hospital in Comerbourne, after an

442

accident? I do private research for anyone who needs it, in connection with books, indexing, that sort of thing. While she's laid up, Miss Tressider is compiling material for a possible monograph on Doctor Paul Fredericks. She's using me to do some of the donkey work for her. I believe you knew him well?'

'I studied under him,' said the distant voice, with pride, with affection, with gaiety; entirely without regret. 'He was one of the world's darlings. But irascible as the devil! No, come to think of it, the devil wouldn't be, would he? Somebody ought to put Freddy on record, that's a fact.'

'It would be a great help if I could talk to you about him. May I come over and see you, some time?'

'Any afternoon that suits you,' said Bunty Felse. 'Today, if you like?'

The moment he set eyes on her he stopped wondering if she had any lingering doubts about her bargain. She was one of the few people he'd ever seen who looked as if they had never regretted anything in their lives. She was about his own age, a slender person of medium height, with a shining cap of glossy hair the colour of ripe conkers, and a few engaging silvery strands coiled in the red here and there. Her eyes, large and brightly hazel, looked straight into his over the coffee cups and declared her curiosity quite openly, and the effect their candour had upon him was of a compliment.

'Will she really ever do anything about it? . . . this book on Freddy?'

'Ah, that's another question,' admitted Francis. 'Not for me to ask. *You* could, if you went to visit her. I think she'd be pleased.'

'That,' said Bunty, reaching for an ashtray from the bookcase, 'one doesn't do. I have just about as much claim on Miss Tressider as I have on half the big names in music today – I once studied for three years under a man they all knew and valued. So did dozens, maybe hundreds of others, most of them

443

as obscure as I am. No, I contracted out, and you can't have it both ways, and personally I've never even wanted to. Well . . . hardly ever, and then only for a day or so. I never really knew the girl, in any case. I was married some years before she even came to Freddy. It was only the accident of Esther's illness that made us acquainted at all.'

'But you remember her? As she was then?'

'You wouldn't,' said Bunty with the slow smile that made the freckles dance across the bridge of her short, straight nose, 'be likely to forget her. I assure you she was already glorious. I may have contracted out myself, but I haven't lost interest. I knew what we had with us on that trip abroad. Freddy told me, for that matter, but I'd already noticed for myself. In a way I think that particular tour was the turning point for her. She suddenly realised her full possibilities. As if everything in her had discovered its pole and fixed on it for good. She turned her back on everything except music.'

The phrase arrested his mind and his pen together; he had a couple of pages of notes on Dr. Fredericks by then, since that was where his interest ostensibly lay. By this time he could surely afford to manifest some curiosity of his own about Maggie.

'She had her first big successes on that tour?' he asked.

'She did, that's true enough. But it was more than that, something that happened inside her own mind. I should guess she had plenty of faith in herself when we set out. After all, it was her third trip with Freddy. But somewhere along the line she seemed to wake up fully, and after that she set her sights on the top of the mountain and started walking. And she's never looked back.'

She had, though, in the end; but Francis kept that to himself. When death put its hand on her and stopped the breath in her throat on the operating table, and then changed its mind and withdrew from her after all, somewhere a forgotten window had opened and Maggie had looked back.

He closed his notebook on his knee, and sat looking at Bunty

Felse over it for a moment of silence. Then he said: 'Tell me about that particular tour. Where did you go? Where were the concerts held? Did anything out of the ordinary happen? Tell me everything you can remember about it.'

The hazel eyes, dappled with points of brilliant green in the sunlight, studied him thoughtfully. Now was the time for her to say: 'I thought it was about Freddy you were collecting material!' but she didn't say it. Whatever she saw in him seemed to her logical enough reason for the change of emphasis. She didn't even find it necessary to comment.

'I've still got the whole itinerary and my working notes somewhere. It was the only time I had the job to do, so I had to get it right. I did all the secretarial work, you see, bookings, bills, the lot, as well as keeping an eye on the girls.' She got up, and went to rummage in the drawers of the bureau. She hadn't kept these papers as treasured souvenirs, apparently, or if she had they had long outlived her reverence for them, and found their way somewhere to the most remote corner.

'Did you have much trouble?' asked Francis.

She laughed. 'Very little with the girls. There were only three of them, and they were all completely serious about their careers. Freddy's students usually were, or they didn't last long. There was more trouble with Freddy himself, actually, that trip. He was always excitable before concerts, and we had one rather turbulent member among the boys who was just beginning to get in his hair.' She found what she wanted, somewhat crumpled at the back of a loose-leaf book, and came back to the coffee-table smoothing it out in her hands; a dozen or so sheets of quarto paper stapled together, a handful of hotel bills and a sketch-map of their route across half of Europe and back to Calais. She dropped the little file before him, and sat down again. 'Take it if it's any help to you.' Her eyes met his levelly, and still she refrained from comment. She had her own ideas about the nature of his interest in Maggie Tressider, and who was to say she was wrong?

'I'd like to, if you're sure you don't mind? I'll return it . . .'

'Don't!' she said, and smiled. 'It was a nice thing to do, just once, more interesting in a way than when I went with him as a soloist myself. But I've finished with it now. I did just one Circus when I was nineteen, and then opted for marriage, and that was it. My son was seven years old, going on eight, that summer when Esther went to hospital. To tell the truth, I felt more flattered being asked to stand in for her than if he'd asked me to go back to singing. And my mother took over the family for me while I was away. Everything went off nicely, and it's something to remember. But it's a long time ago now.'

'You were saying,' prompted Francis, his eyes on the map, 'that Dr. Fredericks was having a certain amount of trouble during the trip. Did something happen to upset him?'

'Nothing very surprising. There'd been friction for some time in that quarter. We came home to England one member short, that's all. One of the orchestra walked out on us in Austria. Well, one of the orchestra . . . he was our occasional 'cello soloist, too, we had to rearrange some of the programmes after he defected.'

'I take it this was the turbulent one who was getting in the doctor's hair? Do you remember his name?'

She leaned over to take the crumpled papers out of his hand and flick through them for the typed concert programmes she had compiled so long ago. 'Yes, here we are . . . Robert Aylwin. That's right, they called him Robin. He was quite a brilliant player, if he'd ever worked at it, but it was becoming pretty clear that he never intended to. He'd been with Freddy for two years, but that trip he was putting all his deficiencies on show, and it was plain he wasn't going to last much longer. I doubt if he'd have lasted that long, if he hadn't been such a charmer. That was probably his trouble, he was used to smiling at things and having them fall into his hands, not having to work for them. Music was too much like hard labour. He was getting bored with the whole thing, and treating it with distressing levity. With

Freddy that was naturally heresy. They'd had words two or three times, and we all knew it. Nobody was very surprised when the boy just took himself off, one night between dinner and bedtime, and never showed his face again. There were rumours that he'd been misusing his respectability as Freddy's protégé for a little smuggling, and Freddy's conscience was such – not to mention his natural sense of outrage – that he really might have turned the boy in. If true, of course! But one could believe it. Probably not much wrong with him except this incurable light-mindedness, but that was enough for Freddy.'

'You mean he just packed and slipped away without saying a word to anyone? Not even to one of the other boys?'

'Well, supposing there was anything in the smuggling rumour, and he'd come to the conclusion he'd better disappear, then he wouldn't take anyone in the Circus into his confidence, would he? He probably wouldn't in any case, he was a very self-sufficient young man, he ran his own show.'

'And you've no idea what happened to him afterwards?'

'Not the slightest. He was never going to hit the headlines as an instrumentalist, he couldn't be bothered. We just went on with our schedule without him. Freddy made no attempt to trace him, after all he was over twenty-one and his own master. He probably drifted back home when he felt like it, or signed up with some small orchestra over there. He was the kind to fall on his feet, and he spoke both German and French, he'd get along all right. We weren't worried about him.'

But the strange, the unnerving thing was that suddenly Francis was worried about him. For no reason, except that the boy had been near to Maggie, and had walked away into a long-past evening and left no trace behind him.

'Didn't his family want to know what you'd done with him?'

'He had no close family, as far as I know. He'd been knocking about on his own for two or three years already.'

'What was this boy like? You haven't a photograph?'

She shook her head. 'No photographs. I had loads of publicity pictures at the time, of course, but obviously I didn't file them. It's a long time ago. I remember him as a very attractive young man, and well aware of it. Girls liked him.' She added after a moment's thought: 'He laughed a lot.'

'And where did this happen . . . this walking out?'

'We were staying in a little resort in the Vorarlberg, a place called Scheidenau. You'll find it all in the papers there. Freddy always used the Goldener Hirsch as a convenient base for all our concerts round there – Bregenz, Bludenz, Vaduz, St. Gallen, Lindau, all those places. It's very near to the German border, and quiet, and rather cheap.'

'And he walked out between dinner and bedtime? Just like that? Did you notice anything different about him at dinner? Nothing to show what he had in mind?'

By this time, he realised, she ought to have been asking questions herself, and the very fact that she was not had drawn him into deeper water than he had intended venturing. He smiled at her, shaking away the betraying tension of his own concentration. 'It seems such an odd time to cut his moorings.'

'All he seemed to have in mind at dinner,' said Bunty, disconcertingly remaining grave, 'was ingratiating himself with Maggie. He'd been paying her special attention for several days, that I do remember. Not that there's anything remarkable in that. She was . . . she *is* a most beautiful person. All our boys were a little in love with her.'

He kept his eyes steady and faintly amused on hers, his hands placid on the papers they held, with an effort of will that left him no energy for speech for a moment. And he wondered if she could have hit him so hard and so accurately without knowing exactly what she was doing. Not out of malice, perhaps, just by way of experiment; there are other ways of satisfying one's curiosity, besides asking direct questions.

'I'm sure they must have been,' he said evenly, when he had his voice under control again. Let her wonder, too, by how much

she had missed her target. 'And what about Miss Tressider?
Did she respond?'

'Maggie had other things on her mind by then. She knew
what she wanted. She was nineteen,' said Bunty, 'she liked being
liked, and she was a very nice, patient, quiet girl who would in
any case have been kind to him. But she never took her eyes
from her objective, for him or anyone.'

Her voice was gentle, deliberate and detached. It was more
than time to work his way back unobtrusively to Paul Fredericks
for ten minutes or so, and then take himself off, before he gave
her more than he was getting out of her. She was altogether too
perceptive. He managed his retreat with finesse, but finesse
was not enough. Never mind, she had made it clear that she
sympathised, and also held it to be no personal business of hers;
and he was never going to see her again closer than across a
Comerboune street.

'Of course,' said Bunty Felse disconcertingly, seeing him out
at the door, 'after all this time she may have changed.'

It did not occur to her that there was anything to disturb her in
this interview, for fully an hour after it was over. Her visitor was
presumably what he purported to be, and it was only his misfor-
tune that an aching preoccupation of his own had side-tracked
him from the master to the pupil. If there hadn't been something
she had liked about him she might not even have noticed, much
less felt obliged to warn him that she had. But after he was gone
her mind began to nag at the curious implications of their
conversation. Surely everything he had learned from her about
autumn, 1955, Maggie already knew at least as well, and he must
have known she would need no help in recalling details, supposing that she was serious about this book. No, that probe had
been for his own satisfaction. And granted he had his own
unhappy reason for wanting to talk about Maggie rather than
her teacher, why just that incident, and why with so much
controlled intensity? Why dwell so insistently on Robin Aylwin,

who was of no significance whatever? Why want a photograph of him? The more she thought of it, the more it seemed to her that their conversation had gathered and fixed upon that enigmatic young man with quite unjustified interest.

She had not been asked to treat the interview as confidential. So she told George about it over tea, as she did about most things that stirred or puzzled her. George, who had had a fairly boring day, listened to her with pleasure and affection, but with only one ear, until a single harmless word unexpectedly caused all his senses to prick into life together. He came erect out of a faint blue cloud of cigarette smoke.

'*Scheidenau?*' he repeated sharply.

'Scheidenau,' agreed Bunty, opening her eyes wide. 'Why? Ring a bell, or something? I must have mentioned it *ad nauseam* at the time, but of course it's a long time ago. Anyway, it's only a tiny little resort, nothing special about it. What made you sit up and take notice suddenly?'

'Who did you say this fellow was? The one who came to see you?'

'Name of Francis Killian, a sort of private enquiry agent from Comerbourne. I told you, he's working for Maggie Tressider, collating all this stuff about Freddy, she's thinking of doing a book about him.'

'Oh, Killian, yes, I know the name. Never met him, but as far as I know he's all right. But how did you get on to Scheidenau? I'd clean forgotten you'd ever been near the place.'

'So had I, until I got the records out to show him. Was that just a jab from your subconscious, when you sat up and barked Scheidenau?'

'That's it,' agreed George amiably, blinking at her through dissolving smoke. 'It reminds me of a recurrent nightmare – Dom eight years old and in temper tantrums, and you twenty-nine and as pretty as new paint, shaking a loose leg in the Vorarlberg. I had the horrors all the time you were away.'

'There wasn't a soul around you need have worried about,'

Bunty assured him scornfully, 'even if I hadn't been up to the neck in bills and transport arrangements. Just Freddy, and all those callow young men years younger than me. Not to mention the competition! Only three girls, but two of them were presentable, and the third was a beauty. Still is,' she said, abruptly recalled to the serious consideration of her afternoon's entertainment. 'He's in love with her.'

'Killian? With Maggie Tressider? How do you know?'

'Killian. With Maggie Tressider. And I know, all right. Oh, he wasn't obvious in any way, but there it was. I liked him,' said Bunty, who always knew her own mind, and added, relevantly enough: 'Poor boy!' That he was her own age, within a year one way or the other, did not invalidate the sentiment. 'I knew you weren't listening,' she said, 'I told you all this.'

'I'm listening now. Tell me again.'

She told him, well aware that this was not a game. She had touched some recollection which had nothing at all to do with her own stay in that remote Austrian village.

'And he never showed up again, this Aylwin chap?' said George, when she had reached the end of the story.

'You know, I never once thought of it in those terms. He wasn't any greenhorn, he spoke three languages, he knew his way around. I would bet he made his own erratic way wherever he was going, and is playing that 'cello of his somewhere around Europe now. But no, I suppose he didn't show up again anywhere *we* went, at any rate. Why? What makes him suddenly so interesting to everybody?'

'Just that he disappeared in Scheidenau. That would be how long ago? Twelve years? . . . thirteen. Because it so happens,' said George, handing over his cup for a refill, 'that another young man failed to come home from a continental holiday just a couple of years ago. A Comerbourne young man, which made him our case. An art student named Peter Bromwich. Stepfather works at the power station, mother has a job at the ordnance depot out at Newfield. Twenty-three years old, off on his own with a rucksack. He knew the answers, too, it wasn't his first trip by several, and he was a bit of a know-all by inclination. But he didn't come home, and nobody's heard of him since.'

'In Scheidenau?' asked Bunty, now very grave indeed.

'Not quite, not this time. Bromwich was last seen on the German side of that border, trying to thumb a lift towards Immenstadt. From then on he just vanished. We made pretty wide enquiries at the time, and more police forces than you can imagine got into the act, since so many borders meet around those parts. German, Swiss, Austrian, even Italian. Nobody found Peter Bromwich. What we did find, when we all got our heads together, was that an awful lot of major and minor mysteries had dwindled away into dead ends just where all those frontiers tangle, over the past ten years or so. Some were currency cases, some were drugs, some were stolen valuables, mainly small but first-class stuff, jewellery, antiques, art pieces. Two escaped convicts from an Austrian gaol disappeared off the face of the earth in 1960 after being chased as far as Langen – not the Arlberg one, a little place up there near the border. A suspect wanted for murder in Munich was traced to Opfenbach, and then completely lost. Quite a remarkable collection of loose ends, as if they'd originally tied up neatly into a skein at the eastern end of Lake Constance, and somebody had sheared the knot clean out and got rid of it. And not a thing there to think much about until we got the lot together, because a case or two in one country's records, that's not so impressive, but a dozen together begin to look like something above lifesize. But nothing ever led anywhere, and Bromwich never reappeared.'

'And the case is still officially open?'

'Very much so. And I'd still be more than interested in closing it. It did emerge that Bromwich was on cannabis, and may have graduated to the hard drugs, and there were indications that he might have brought the stuff through Customs with him at least a couple of times before when coming back from holidays. It looked rather as if he'd got himself tangled into the fringes of some sizeable organisation. Maybe this time he got a little too cocky? Or too curious about his employers? Now I suppose there wouldn't be any such indications in the case of your young Aylwin, would there?'

'In a small way,' admitted Bunty, 'there would. Not drugs, though, I'm sure. If Freddy'd had any such suspicion he'd have turned him over to the police like a shot, and my impression is that he just intended to get rid of him and leave it at that. There were *rumours* that Freddy had accused him of taking advantage of his position as one of the Circus – so respectable as we were, you see! – to get away with some petty smuggling. I took it to be simply the little personal luxury things everybody's tempted to try and sneak in once in a while. His real crime – or disability, rather – was that he simply couldn't take life, or music, or even Freddy seriously.'

She sat back to consider, with a dubious frown, the picture she had just painted, and it did seem to her, on reflection, that there might be a basic similarity between these two troublesome young men.

'You think *he* may have stumbled into waters too deep for him, too? Chanced his arm with somebody dangerous, and come off worst?'

'Or blundered into something dangerous by accident, and failed to get clear? There are, of course, other possibilities. Maybe he's still hitch-hiking his way round the world somewhere at this moment.'

'That,' said Bunty, though without conviction, 'is the ending I prefer.'

'It's the ending Peter Bromwich would have preferred, I don't doubt. But I very much doubt if it's the end he came to.'

They sat silent for a moment, eye to eye. They could see deeper into each other than most people, and it was often like looking into a glass, their minds moved with such unanimity.

'But why,' asked Bunty then, 'was it the name Scheidenau

453

that brought all this back to you now? Peter Bromwich was some miles away in Germany when he was last seen.'

'He was. A good point! I told you we turned up, between us, any amount of other queer cases that ended in blanks, all roughly round that eastern end of Lake Constance. It occurred to Duckett once, when he had nothing better to do, to link them all up into a squashy sort of circle and see what he got. And then, just for the hell of it, he plotted the centre. And whether it means anything or not, where do you think it fell?'

'Scheidenau,' said Bunty.

'Scheidenau. A tiny little dot on the map that nobody'd ever heard of, but that's what he got. Maybe if we plotted the exact centre of the figure described by linking up all last year's bank raids, it would drop on Windsor Castle. But still my thumbs prick. Scheidenau once may well be a freak, and I might even have had a lurking suspicion that my dear chief didn't do his sums right. I never checked! But Scheidenau twice, and do you wonder I have the feeling that fate is nudging me?'

'But this man Killian *is* working for Maggie Tressider,' Bunty said positively. 'That's true enough. He suggested I should go and visit her, he isn't afraid of his credentials being investigated.'

'Oh, I don't doubt that. But he may be working for her on something rather different from what he gave you to understand. He seems to have spent more time asking you about the lady herself than about her teacher.'

'Yes, I know. Though we'd already been talking about Freddy for some time. But it's natural he should want to talk about Maggie. I told you, he's in love with her. Even this fixation about Robin Aylwin . . . I had a feeling even that was a personal thing with him. As if jealousy was eating him alive, and he had to find somebody to bear the burden, somebody round whom he could crystallise it and get rid of it. And when I talked about Robin, good-looking and close to her, and her own age, for the first time – and I'm sure it *was* the first time he'd so much as heard of him – he felt he'd found a possibility. Somebody to resent. Not that it helps,' said Bunty wryly, 'but they always think it will.'

'God forbid, love,' said George piously, 'that you should ever feel the urge to psychoanalyse me. I hate to think what you might come up with. No, I'm not suggesting there's anything wrong with Killian or with Miss Tressider, I should say it's very long odds against it. But if her commission, whatever it may be, is turning his attention to the disappearance of a young man in Scheidenau, then I'm very, very interested. It might be well worth while keeping an eye on his moves. Even if he doesn't find what he's looking for, he may accidentally turn up something interesting to us. I'll try to get a look at him myself as soon as I can. What's he like?'

She told him. It appeared that she had been weighing up Francis Killian's physical attributes as acutely as his state of mind, and the odds were that she was pretty accurate about both.

'Fortyish, middle height, on the thin side but I think he's solider than he looks. Dark brown hair and eyes, thick brows, hair a bit grey just at the temples. Quite a good face, clean-shaven, a lot of bone and not much meat, a long, straight nose and a rather high forehead. Daunting way of looking at you, guarded and aloof but critical, too, as if he held you at arms'-length to get a stranger's view, and didn't want to get any closer to anyone. Slumps his shoulders a bit, but when he's on his feet he moves well, so it may be an affectation. Or pure discourage-ment! He did look rather as if he'd nearly given up, and then suddenly got kicked back into the race. Not quite seedy – he's physically too trim for that – not so much a shabby elegance as an elegant shabbiness.'

She had closed her eyes, the better to see the man who was not there. When she opened them they were bright, thoughtful and clear. 'How's that?'

'Strictly for the fiction shelves,' said George rudely, and tucked away mentally every word of it. 'Now supposing – just

455

supposing – you wanted to get to Scheidenau quickly, and money was no object. How would you go? Air to Munich . . . Zurich . . .?'

'Zurich,' said Bunty promptly. 'Could do it either way, but Zurich would be quicker and easier.' She sat looking at him wide-eyed, a shining mirror reflecting his thoughts back to him. 'I happen,' she said cautiously, 'to be on rather good terms with Laura Howard in the B.E.A. office in Comerbourne. I could have a word with her. Very discreetly, of course. What did you mean about money being no object? He didn't look as if it would be no object to him.'

'If she's retained him to do a job for her,' said George, 'Miss Tressider will be paying the expenses. And *if* he takes off for Austria after your long-lost 'cellist, the quick, expensive way, that should clinch one thing, at least: he'll be following up this line on *her* business, not his own.'

'But we,' said Bunty, now with unmistakable regret, 'shan't be able to follow him there.'

'Too true we shan't. But we just might, with a lot of luck, get an inkling of what, if anything, he brings back with him.'

The violinist who had shared Robert Aylwin's room at the Goldener Hirsch in Scheidenau, thirteen years ago, lived now in Birmingham, and played in the City of Birmingham Orchestra. Bunty's working papers of the tour had proved very useful indeed, supplying the names Maggie had forgotten, and even such day-to-day details as room accommodation. Charles Pincher and Robert Aylwin had been room mates throughout, so they must, if not friends, have been reasonably congenial companions. Why should Maggie remember the one, apparently the less memorable, and forget the other?

Mrs. Felse had said clearly and kindly that Maggie had not been interested in Aylwin or in any man, and probably never would be. But Mrs. Felse might be mistaken. And still Francis saw, or thought he saw, the shadowy outline of a person round whom his bitterness could gather corrosively, a man who must have meant something to her, probably much, perhaps everything, if she hadn't disastrously mistaken her own heart, and kicked away love too hastily from trammelling her feet on the climb to the heights. Why else should she fasten so suddenly and hungrily on fame, why come back changed, unless she had not merely turned her back on the alternative, but herself destroyed it?

So he went to see Charles Pincher. And Charles Pincher, tall, stooped, balding and cheerful, remembered the Scheidenau affair very well.

'There was one rather odd thing about it, you know. He didn't take anything with him when he lit out.'

Slowly Francis closed his notebook on his knee. 'He didn't . . .? You mean he just walked out empty-handed? But Mrs. Felse said nothing about that . . .'

'No, well, I don't suppose she ever realised. But his suitcase and his 'cello were there in the room still, after he'd gone. Freddy left them in old Waldmeister's charge when we left, he said he'd be sure to come back and collect them as soon as he knew we'd gone, and the bill was paid.'

'*And did he?*'

'I suppose so, old boy, but I was never there again. I had the chance of a good job, so I quit the Circus. I expect he did, you know. We all knew he'd fallen out with Freddy. He'd just keep out of sight until we were on the move, and then stroll back and pick up his traps at leisure.'

The sensible thing to believe, of course. The only question left was whether it had actually happened like that. Whether, in fact, there had been some sound reason why it couldn't happen like that. And there was only one infallible way to find out, and find out quickly.

'We were right,' said Bunty over the telephone to George. 'Zurich! Laura booked him in on the two o'clock Trident flight

457

from Heathrow tomorrow. Open return. Took him a day and a half to make up his mind.'

'Now I wonder,' said George at the other end of the line, 'I do wonder to whom he talked yesterday, and what they told him, to make his journey really necessary?'

Chapter 4

The little Scheidenauersee, a silver-blue pear-shape three-quar-
ters of a mile long, lay in green folded hills under a late summer
sky, smooth as a looking-glass and brushed clean with feather
dusters of cloud. Its narrow end, where the tiny Rulenbach
flowed into it, pointed south into the foothills of the Vorarlberg,
and round this southern tip the village of Scheidenau lay, three
short streets arranged in a Y shape, the cup of the Y filled with
the water of the lake as with silver-blue wine. The northern end
of the lake widened and overflowed from the cup, mirroring two
or three tiny islands, and at the north-eastern corner the Rulenbach flowed gaily out again, twice its former size and bouncing
down a crumpled, stony bed, to make an unexpected six-mile
detour through Germany, owing to the complicated contours of
the land, before returning into Austria in a series of right-handed
twists, to empty itself into the Bregenzer Ach, and eventually
into Lake Constance south of Bregenz.

Where the three streets met there was the usual village square,
with a well-head and a modest Trinity column in the middle,
and on all three sides – for in fact the square was an irregular
triangle, dwindling towards the south into the stem of the Y –
the beautiful, exuberant housefronts and shopfronts, the overhanging eaves, the mellow dark wood and virtuoso wrought iron
that makes almost any small Austrian settlement look like a stage

set for operetta. There was a baroque church, of no particular merit but of pleasing appearance, one restaurant that was not also an inn and two that were, and a confectioner's noted for its rum babas. All the down-to-earth shops like the butcher's and the baker's and the ironmonger's, lined the landward street. The two roads that embraced the end of the lake, and dwindled later into footpaths along its undulating shores, found room for the villas and gardens of the better-off, for a small public park nestling in the base of the Y like the dregs of the wine, and for the two larger of Scheidenau's three hotels, which peered into each other's windows across the placid surface, just where the arrow-straight clay-blue line of the Rulenbach's inflow, coloured by mountain water, foundered and became invisible in the deeper, calmer blue. The third and smallest hotel, the Weisses Kreuz, faced the church across the broader end of the square.

Outside the village the farms and fields began, rolling, heaving, foothill fields white with the shaven stubble from which the harvest had been taken, and upland pastures scalloped like fish-scales from the marks of the scythe. The highest point visible from the square was the abrupt hummock of the castle hill just to the west of the lake, with its snaggle-toothed ruin on top, meanly reduced now to its last few feet of broken wall and a tangle of overgrown rubble, useless as a tourist attraction. Outcrops of bedrock and outcrops of masonry spattered the sides of the hill over an area of a square mile or so, and because of the rich rooting of trees and bushes it was sometimes difficult to tell which was which. In parts of the forlorn shell the practical natives had dumped rubbish, and there were rats as the only inhabitants; but still that scattered rash of worked stone erupting everywhere among the grass bore witness to the formidable extent of the place in its hey-day. The Waldmeisters, who owned the Goldener Hirsch, and had been there now for seven generations, took their name from an ancestor who had once been head forester to the Lords of Scheidenau.

The Goldener Hirsch, sprawled along the lake-shore on the

western arm of the Y, with its shoulder turned solidly to
the remnant of old splendours on the castle mound, was in a
curious state of suspension between village *gasthaus* and tourist
hotel. To the huge traditional house, with its beetling eaves,
strongly battered walls, built-on cattle-byres and carved wood
verandahs, had been added a new wing in brick and stone, in
an austere modern style that did not offend. Two Waldmeister
daughters, still unmarried, and the wives of the three Waldmeister sons, continued to run the place with a couple of poor
relations and almost no outside staff; but there was a smart little
reception desk in the hall, with a smart little Austrian blonde in
a mini-skirt seated behind it, darting like a humming-bird
between her typewriter and adding machine on one side, and
the telephone switchboard on the other.

It was already September, and the high season dwindles away
very rapidly when August ends. Yes, she had a room and a smile
for the unexpected Englishman who had made no reservation.
But the woman who showed Francis up to his room wore the
full, flowered skirt, embroidered apron and laced bodice of old
custom, and had her mane of black hair coiled on her head in
the old heavy bun, and to judge by the waft of warm milk and
cattle-flesh that drifted from her skirt as she walked ahead of
him up the scrubbed wooden stairs, she had just come in from
the cows.

The first-floor corridor was wide enough for a carriage and
pair, the door she flung open for him broad enough to admit
them two abreast. All-white, high ceiling, spacious walls, huge
billow of medium-weight autumn feather-bed on the creamy-
white natural wood bedstead. He was in the old part of the
house; so much the better. The window looked sidelong on a
large, ebullient, untidy garden, and only a sliver of the lake
winked in at him. No room in the world could have been more
at peace.

'The gentleman is English?' His German had been hesitant,

and in any case the unmistakable stamp is always there, for some reason. He owned to his Englishness; he might as well.

'The room will do?' Her voice was low, abrupt and vibrant, curiously personal in uttering impersonal things.

'The room will do beautifully, thank you.' He dropped his bag on the luggage-stand, and felt for the keys of the hired car in his pocket, and the loose change under them.

'A moment! I will open the window.' The scent of her as she passed near to him was like the wild air from outside, part beast, part garden, part earth, part late summer foliage ripening towards its decline. She turned her head suddenly as she passed, so close that her sleeve brushed his, and he saw her face full, olive-dark and olive-smooth, and the great, bold, sullen, inviting eyes for once wide-open and glowing. But the next moment she was looking round the room with the glow veiled, and the faint, dutiful frown back on her brow.

'No towels. I will bring.'

She was, he realised, a very striking woman, her tall figure as lithe as an Amazon, her features good, her hair splendid. Until he had looked at her so closely he had failed to notice that there was a flaw, for her articulation was so clear that there seemed to be no malformation in her palate. Only that small, vicious botch put in to spoil the pattern and embitter her life; her upper lip was split like a hare's. The effect was not even ugly, prejudice aside; but prejudice is never very far aside from the hare-lip in an otherwise handsome woman.

She came with the towels, and he took them from her at the door. Her fingers touched his in the act. He was sure then that it had not been by accident that her breast, braced high by the black bodice, had brushed his sleeve as he had stepped past her into the room on entering.

'If you should need anything, please call for Friedl. I shall be working below. I shall hear.'

'Thank you, Fräulein Friedl. I'll remember.'

Her eyelids rolled back for an instant, and again uncovered, so briefly that he could believe in it or not, as he chose, the buried volcano. Probably she had not much hope, but as a gesture of defiance against the world she persevered and deployed what little she had.

'You are Herr Waldmeister's daughter?'

The hare-lip quivered in what was not quite a smile. 'His niece,' she said, and walked away along the great, scrubbed corridor with her long stride, and left him there. But the slow, swaying walk, the erect back, the beautifully balanced head with its sheaf of black hair, all were still quiveringly aware of him until the moment when she passed from sight.

So that was one of the amenities, and one that wouldn't be in the brochure, nor, he thought, available to everyone. Some special kind of chemistry had elected him. One cast-away hailing another, perhaps, for company in a huge and trackless sea. One insomniac welcoming another in the long, lonely, sleepless night.

He washed, and went down into the bar. There were voices in the garden and boats on the lake. Across the shining water the windows of the Alte Post blinked languidly in the sun. There were still plenty of visitors to keep the natives looking like deliberate bits of folklore – which emphatically they were not – but in a couple of months the stone-weighted roofs, the beetling eaves, the logs stacked beneath the overhang ends-outwards, all up the courtyard walls, would no longer look like window-dressing, but a very practical part of the seriousness of living. Soon the stocky, old-gold cattle with their smoky faces would come clanging down from the high pastures to their home fields for the winter.

The scrubbed boards of the floors were almost white in the guest-rooms. It was early afternoon, the quietest hour of the day in the bar, but there were a couple of obvious French guests sipping coffee and *kümmel* in one corner, and a bearded mountain man with a litre pot before him was conducting a conversation with the woman behind the bar, clear across the width of the room in the booming bass-baritone of the uplands. The woman

463

was middle-aged, grey-haired and solid as a wall, and could be no one but Frau Waldmeister.

Francis ordered an *enzian*, and went straight to the point. She heard him broach his business, smiling at him a benevolent, gold-toothed smile, but as soon as legal matters were mentioned she did exactly what he had expected her to do, and referred him to her man. That saved him from having to go through the whole mixture of fact and fiction twice, and got him installed in a quiet corner of the empty dining-room, across a table from the master of the house. Old Waldmeister was something over six feet tall, with shoulders on him like a cattle-yoke, and a wind-roughened leather face decorated with a long, drooping, brigand's moustache. Courteous and impassive, he listened with no sign of surprise or suspicion at being suddenly asked to think back thirteen years.

'Herr Waldmeister, my name is Killian. I am representing a firm of solicitors in England, who are looking for a certain young man. A relative of his family resident in New Zealand has left the residue of his small property to him. The dead man had been out of touch with his cousins in England for some years, and we find now that the legatee parted company with his parents some time ago, and they have no idea where he is at the moment. We have advertised for him without result, at least so far. We therefore began to make enquiries in the hope of tracing him. The last record we have of him, strangely enough, terminates here, in your hotel, thirteen years ago.'

He waited to elicit some sort of acknowledgment, and what he got was illuminating. The first thing old Waldmeister had to say was not: 'What was his name?' but: 'How much is it, this legacy?'

'When cleared, it should be in the region of fifteen hundred pounds.' Not so great as to turn out the guard in a full-scale hunt for him, but great enough to pay the expenses of a solicitor's clerk as far as Scheidenau, in these days of off-peak tourist

464

bargain travel. The old man nodded weightily. Property is property, and the law is there to serve it.

'How is he called, this young man?'

'His name is Robert Aylwin.'

'I do not remember such a name. *The last record* of him, you say? It is a long time ago. To remember one visitor is impossible.'

'You will remember this one, when I recall the circumstances.' And he recalled them, very succinctly and clearly. There were names enough to bolster everything he had to say. Fredericks had regularly used this inn on those tours of his; neither he nor his students would be so easily forgotten. 'I understand from a man called Charles Pincher, who shared a room here with him, that Aylwin left his suitcase and his 'cello in the room when he went away, and that Dr. Fredericks gave them into your charge, expecting the owner to come back to collect them. Is that so?'

'It is so,' said the old man without hesitation. 'The name I had forgotten, but this of the cases and the Herr Doktor, that I remember.'

'In that case I'm hoping that you can help me to the next link in the chain, that he gave you at any rate a forwarding address, when he came back for them.'

'He did not come back for them,' said Waldmeister, and volunteered nothing more.

'He didn't? Then in all these years you've had no word from him?' The chill at the back of his neck, like icy fingers closing there, made Francis aware that he had never believed in this. Considered it, yes; believed in it, no.

'No word. That is right.'

'Did you . . . expect to?' What he meant was, did you know of any reason why it would be no use expecting it.

'I expected, yes. People do not just go away and leave their belongings. You understand, it is a very long time since I have thought of this matter. No, he did not come, and I knew no way to find him. I kept the things for him, that was all I could do. But he did not fetch them.'

'Then . . . you still have them?'

'Come with me!' said the old man, and rose and led him from the room, out to the broad stone passage-way with its homespun rugs and its home-carved antique chairs and spinning-wheels and boot-jacks, over which a London dealer would have foamed at the mouth. Up the uncarpeted, scrubbed, monumental back stairs, spiralling aloft with treads wide enough at the wall end for a horseman to negotiate. One flight, a second, a third, and they were up among the vast dark rafters, in a series of open attics that hoarded rubbish and treasure together in the roof.

'Here,' said Waldmeister simply, and pointed.

The 'cello-case, leaning sadly against a scratched wooden box, might have been covered in grey felt, but when Francis drew a dubious finger along its surface the blanket of dust came away clean from a finely-grained black leather. Of good quality, expensive, and surely almost new when the owner abandoned it here. A medium-sized black suitcase, its upright surfaces still almost black because it was of glossy, plastic-finished fibre-glass, stood beside the 'cello.

'This is his? May I look? Under your supervision, of course. All I want is to see if there is anything there to suggest a further line of enquiry. Are they locked?'

'They are not locked.'

Of course, they would be as he had left them in his room, and in a hotel room which is itself normally locked, not everyone bothers to make doubly sure with individual keys. And the keys themselves he must have taken away with him, in his pocket.

The contents of Robin Aylwin's luggage had little enough to say about him. He travelled light. The slacks, lambswool sweater, shirts, were good but not expensive, and kept about as carefully as most young men of twenty or so keep their clothes. Black dress shoes for concerts, a dinner jacket, shaving tackle, handker-chiefs, a Paisley dressing-gown, pyjamas, a Terylene raincoat, all folded and packed so carefully that Francis detected the hand of some female member of the Waldmeister family.

'Had he packed these? Or were they simply lying about in his room?'

'They were in his room, as in use. We packed everything as you see it, to wait for him.'

No passport, no documents, no wallet, no keys, no letters. All those he would most probably keep on him, whatever clothes he was wearing. The dinner jacket being here meant nothing; he almost certainly wouldn't wear it for the evening here, when resting between engagements. Probably it was only there for the concerts. There were writing materials, a folder of stamps both English and Austrian, two local postcards, unwritten; but not one written word, to him or from him, to help to establish that he had ever really existed at all.

Francis got what he could from the remnants. The shirts were size fifteen and a half, the shoes nine, the slacks were long-legged and small-waisted and made to measure, but from a firm of mass tailors with shops everywhere. The wearer must have been nearly six feet in height, if not an inch or two over, and on the slim side, though by the evidence of the sweater, which was a forty-two inch chest, he had needed accommodation for good wide shoulders. And that was all there was to be discovered about him here. The 'cello, silent in its case, was just a 'cello, and the pockets that filled in its curves contained only resin, strings and a spare bridge in case of damage.

Francis closed the lid again and restored the case to its corner. He dusted his hands and looked at Waldmeister.

'No, nothing. When he didn't turn up, I expect you looked through them, too.'

'I also told it to the Herr Doktor, when he came again. He knew nothing of the young man, either. He said keep them still, so we kept them.'

'Herr Waldmeister, there is always the possibility that some member of your household may have talked with Aylwin while he was here, and may be in possession of some detail that might help me to find him. It's a long time ago, and your staff may have changed, of course, but still there may be someone who remembers, and may be able to add to what we know. Will you be kind enough to tell them, all those who were here at that time, that I am trying to trace this man, and for a reason which makes it to his advantage that I should find him?'

The old man's heavy shoulders lifted eloquently. 'I will do so. But I do not think, after all this time, they will have anything to tell.'

'I'm afraid you may be right. But please ask them to come to me if they do remember anything. I shall be here for two or three days.'

'I will ask them,' said Waldmeister.

He had reckoned on the force of curiosity to bring them to him even if they had nothing to tell, and would have bet on the women being in the lead. But the eldest Waldmeister son was the first to bring his stein over and join the new-comer in the bar, after dinner that evening. He could surely have nothing to tell about a chance guest in the hotel, since he spent all his time well outside it, running a timber business which was merely one of the multifarious Waldmeister activities. What he wanted was to have a closer look at the English solicitor, and at least offer his desire to be helpful, if he could do no better. Frau Waldmeister and two of her daughters-in-law made roundabout approaches during the next day, to the same effect. None of them knew where Aylwin might have gone, none of them knew why. Francis doubted if they really remembered anything about him at all, beyond that he had left in the attic tangible evidence of his stay. The third daughter-in-law hadn't then been married to her Johann, and the two youngest Waldmeister girls must have been still at school.

The one person for whom he had trailed the bait held aloof. Friedl, somewhere in her mid-thirties now by his estimate, must have been turned twenty at the time, and not the girl to miss a personable young man. Aylwin had been, by Mrs. Felse's testimony, of striking and engaging appearance, and even at twenty Friedl, the dowryless niece with the hare-lip, must have been half-way to the hungry, embittered woman she was now. Deprived enough to reach out for whatever man she could, and not yet crushed into acceptance of her lot, and schooled to limiting her reach to waifs like herself. If anyone here knew anything about the good-looking and light-minded young man who laughed a lot, the odds were it would be Friedl.

He knew she would come. She was only biding her time. He had caught her dark, sullen glance upon him several times in passing, but she had made no sign. He understood. Where the Waldmeister family was within earshot or sight, no one would get anything out of Friedl. They were perhaps hardly more the enemy to her than was the rest of the world, but she would make no move where they might get wind of it. It was not a matter of the importance of anything she might have to say, but rather of preserving the integrity of her own secret life, which had nothing to do with them. She might have nothing to tell, but she would come, all the same, given the chance, because he had, and deliberately, offered her a reason for approaching him.

There was no real difficulty. After dinner was cleared away he sat with a *kirsch* on the verandah that overlooked the tip of the lake, until she came out, off duty at last, to enjoy the luminous air of the evening. He had seen her emerge the previous night at this hour, and he felt reasonably sure that it would be the same tonight. All she had done was to stroll in the garden and talk a little with such guests as were solitary, but she had done it in a smart black wool dress, with a gold chain and cross round her neck, and her great mane of hair coiled in a glossy chignon on her nape; a manifestation at least that she did exist as a human being, like them.

She was a little later in appearing tonight, but she came. As soon as he saw her in the doorway, Francis moved away to the rail of the terrace, where the steps led down into the long slope of trees between the inn and the lake-shore. It was already dusk, but the afterglow had turned the western sky to a pale, glowing green, and its reflection from the lake, calm as a looking-glass laid down among the hills, cast a subtle radiance up through the trees. Without haste and without looking back, Francis went down the path.

The Goldener Hirsch stood on a bluff, higher than the Alte Post on the other side of the lake, but equally close to the thin yellow line of gravel that bordered the water. Sixty yards wide and gradually broadening as he penetrated deeper into it, the belt of trees wound along beneath the balconies and windows of the new wing, and the path, narrowing, wandered diagonally down it to the water. Not there, it would be too light there. Somewhere here in this curious woodland world quivering and swimming in greenish gleams, like a weedy aquarium. He had already left the evening strollers behind. There might be a pair of lovers holed up somewhere in the twilight, but there was room for them. He let the path slip right-handed away from him, towards the dappled, moon-pale water, and took to the grass beyond, moving at leisure among the trees. He didn't know how far behind she might be, but he knew she would find him.

He lit a cigarette to simplify the process for her, and the act shook him for a moment into full consciousness of what he was doing. He was on Maggie's business, and if there was anything here to be found he must find it. He needed Friedl's testimony for Maggie's sake and for his own. But Friedl had her own needs, and as good a right to make use of him as he had to make use of her. Whichever way you look at it, he told himself derisively, you're not going to find anything to be proud of, and since when have you started breaking your heart over a bit of necessary, ambiguous disloyalty? Get what you have to get, and pay whatever you have to pay for it. That's what Friedl will be doing. Maggie will never know. *You* will, of course, but what sort of drop will this be in the ocean of what you know already about yourself?

He felt her close to him before ever he heard or saw her. His senses homed on the awareness he had that she was there, and then he found the tall, motionless darkness, the two pale flowers of hands quiet at her sides.

'Herr Killian . . .' A muted breath hardly as loud as a whisper; and not a question, she knew who was there.

'Fräulein Friedl . . .' he said as softly.

She crossed the few yards that still separated them, and as she came the greenish, reflected light flickered over her face twice, tremulous and faint; it was like seeing a drowned face float through clear, shallow water. Thus delicately touched, Friedl achieved beauty. The flaw did not show at all, the enchanted light brushed her weatherbeaten skin with its own liquid jade.

'Herr Killian,' said the dream-like murmur, 'I can tell you about the man called Aylwin . . . if you want to know . . .'

'Yes . . . yes, Friedl, I want to know . . .'

He went the necessary, the imperative step to meet her. She walked into his arms.

'The last time I sat here with a man,' she said, drawing fiercely on the cigarette Francis had just lit for her, 'it was with him. With Robert Aylwin.'

They were sitting on a felled tree in a half-circle of bushes some distance along the lake-side, looking out through a filigree of branches over the water. She had brought him there by the hand, moving like a hunting cat, silent and certain in the dark.

'They were here three, four days. He was nice to me. We came to this place together. He was not like me, he was gay, always gay.'

No one, thought Francis, could accuse us of that particular indiscretion. Something was there with them, heavy and fatal, something of warmth and tenderness and bitterness and pity that left an indescribable, rank flavour on the night. But most surely no gaiety.

'Aylwin had been here two or three times with Dr. Fredericks,' he said. 'Hadn't you met him before?'

'I was not here until that summer. I came when my father died. I had nothing, you understand? Not even a human face. Who would want me? But he was lively, and funny, and kind. On that last evening I was late finishing the dishes, and I saw him go out, across the terrace, down the path . . . as you did to-night. And when I was finished I followed him.'

'You had an arrangement?' asked Francis, lifting the heavy sheaves of her unbound hair in his hands.

'No, we had no arrangement. Simply, I hoped he might come here and wait. But before I reached this place, a little way back there among the trees, I heard his voice. And another voice. A girl's . . . So I drew back a little, not to break in on them, but it was quiet there, and I was among the bushes. I didn't want them to know, and I could not get away quickly because of the branches . . . they would have heard me . . .'

His throat was dry. 'Could you see them?'

'No. It was also September, and a little later in the evening. No . . . but both voices I knew. His, of course. And hers . . . you could not mistake it, even speaking. She was the one from his own party, the one they said was going to be a great singer.'

He heard his own voice saying with careful concentration, for fear he should frighten her away from the issue by too great an intensity: 'Could you hear what they were saying?'

'No, most of the time not. All was in undertones, and it was he who talked, and she who listened, only now and again she said some few words, and with her it was impatience and disbelief . . . you know? He was arguing and pleading. And she did not want him, she was sending him away, but he would not go. At the end he forgot to be quiet, he cried out loudly at her: ' . . . if *you* don't want me!' And she said, 'Hush, don't be a fool!' And he said: 'No, I won't be fool enough to endure it. *There's always an alternative!*' That is what he said, and like that. Do you think I could imagine that?'

'No,' he said. His voice felt and sounded thick and muffled in his throat. 'No, I don't think you could.' Carefully, carefully

472

now, or she would catch the spark of passion and take fire, and he would get nothing more. 'And what did *she* say?'

He never knew what it was that betrayed him. Not the voice, that was level and light, interested but detached, under complete control now. Not even the mere fact that he should ask after *her* reactions, when it was in Robin Aylwin's movements he was supposed to be interested. Something deeper and more fundamental than any such details, something she felt through the almost indistinguishably altered tension of the arm that circled her, a dark lightning striking from his blood into hers. This was a creature who felt with her blood and thought with her bones and flesh, and saw with some intuitive third eye under her heart like a child. For suddenly all the air was still about them, with something more than mere silence, and very slightly and stealthily all her sinews drew together, contracting into her closed being, lifting the confiding shade of her weight from his shoulder. She did not move away from him; she did not even lift her head. It would have been less frightening if she had. But all the essence of herself that she had spilled so prodigally about her on the night air, as securely as if she had been alone, drew back like ectoplasm and coiled itself defensively within her. There was a third person there, almost palpable between them.

'She laughed,' said Friedl in a clear hard voice.

'No . . .!' he said involuntarily. There seemed to be two Friedls there now, one of them warm against his shoulder with the black waterfall of her hair streaming across his chest, one of them standing off at the edge of the clearing, watching him narrowly, waiting to see him react in anger or pain. There was not much she did not know now, in that dark blood-knowledge of hers, about his relationship with the absent woman who had laughed.

'*Yes!* You wished to know about him, I am telling you what happened. Nobody else can tell you, nobody else knows. She laughed at him, that girl. And then I heard the bushes crashing as he turned and ran away from her, down towards the lake. Only for a few moments, because the ground drops there, and

473

this hillock where we are cuts off sound. There was this thrashing among the bushes, and sometimes his feet stumbling against a tree-root, and then it was quiet because he was down there close to the water, under the curve of the ground. But if there are voices in a boat on the lake, then you hear them. That night there were no boats, no voices, it was already dark. It was another kind of sound we heard, that girl and I, coming up from the water. A splash. Not so great a sound, clean, not broken, not repeated . . . but all the same, it was not a fish rising, even though there are very big fish in the lake. It was too late, too dark, and besides, one gets to know all such sounds. No, this was something, something heavy, plunging into the water and going down . . .'

She had turned in his arm, tensed and brittle against him, and he felt her eyes searching his face even in the dark, experimental, inimical and savage. Suddenly the night had engendered, seemingly out of her very flesh, a small, murderous wind that chilled him to the bone.

'I don't believe you,' he said, 'you're making it up.'

'You think I am lying? Ask *her*! When you go back to her, ask her!'

'You're crazy! What have I got to do with a woman like that? If this had been true you'd have told somebody about it then. Did you? Did you go down to the water to look for him? Did you tell what you knew when he failed to come back?'

'What did I know? What did I *know*? That there were voices, that I heard a splash, nothing more. No, I never told anyone I was here in the trees that night. No, I did not wait to see, I did not try to find out anything. I ran back to the house, and I held my tongue. *And so did she*! Why should I speak? I wanted no part in it. What did I owe to any of them? Better to be quiet and keep out of trouble. So they never dragged the lake, they never even looked for him, he was simply the one who was out of favour and ran away. But *something* went into the lake that night. And she heard, as I did, and wanted not to hear, as I did,

474

but with better reason. And he never came back for his baggage, did he? *And he never will*!'

She drew herself out of his arm suddenly and roughly. 'I've told you everything I know. I must go back.'

'I still think you're lying,' he said, but without anger, and without conviction, only with an almost insupportable weariness and sadness.

'Then ask her, when you go back to her. You will see.'

He could have denied Maggie a second time, but what was the use? Friedl was as sensitive as a dog to the presence of ghosts.

'Help me do up my hair. They will be looking for me.'

He stood behind her and drew back the great fall of her hair, smoothing the sheaf between his hands; and then for a moment her hands were on his, guiding them, her body leaned back against him warm and yielding, and she turned her head and laid her cheek against his. Without movement and without sound she was weeping.

'Friedl . . .'

'No . . .' she said. 'You cannot help . . .' Silenced under his kiss, her marred mouth uttered one lamentable moan, and clung for an instant before she pulled herself away. She thrust the comb into her heavy coil of hair. 'Don't come with me!' she spat back at him, and was gone, abrupt and silent between the trees.

Chapter 5

So now he knew what lay at the bottom of Maggie's memory like truth at the bottom of a well. She, too, dazed and enchanted with her vision of fame, impatient with the importunate boy who blundered into her dream in defence of his own, had heard that muted splash round the curve of the lake-shore. And she had chosen to bury it, not to understand, not to remember. Not because she didn't know what she had done, but because she did!

Surely she must have loved him!

All the way across Switzerland in his hired car, Francis was eaten alive by the knowledge. What else could explain the obsession that rode her now? Nothing less than love, recognised too late, could have made this disaster so terrible to her. And yet there was some excuse for her. There had never been any proof, never any body, everyone else had taken it for granted that Aylwin had simply decamped, and their acceptance had made it the most reasonable course for her to accept that probability, too.

Only in her heart she knew that he hadn't!

Every time the knowledge surfaced she must have thrust it under again, until at last it drowned, and stayed down. Her conscious mind had succeeded in sloughing the memory utterly; but deep below the surface something in her had relentlessly

476

remembered and reproached and grieved, and at the point of death had bestirred itself again to struggle into the light and challenge her with her debt.

He lingered a day in Zurich because he didn't know what he was going to do, what he wanted to do, what he could bear to do. And about Friedl he thought only once during that time, with a violent tearing at his own conscience, and the shock of realising that the suppression of what galls and accuses is not so difficult or rare. That we all do it. That life would be impossible if we did not.

On the second day he asked for a passage home, but had to wait one more night before getting one. He was glad of the respite. Because what *was* he going to do about Maggie? No use trying to shield her by lying to her, she was utterly sincere, when she said she wanted the truth, that he couldn't live without truth. Did he even want to spare her? There were times during the flight when he realised that he wanted rather to rend her, to make her pay not only for Robin Aylwin, but for his own self-torment, too, and even for poor Friedl, with the tiny blemish on her flesh and the great cancer in her spirit, and the men who had slipped through her fingers because Maggie was innocent and dedicated.

He telephoned the hospital in Comerbourne as soon as he landed. He still had no idea what he wanted to say. It was almost a relief to get the ward sister, brisk and cheerful and immune, explaining that Miss Tressider had made rapid progress and was now discharged. Yes, she was still in Comerbourne, she could be contacted at the Lion Hotel, where she had taken a suite for a period of convalescence under supervision. She had wanted to have a grand piano, an amenity the hospital naturally couldn't provide.

That was no great surprise. The voice that used her as a means of communication was restless and fretful, aching for an outlet again. Had she, after all, had any choice when she kicked

love away from her? Wasn't she, from the moment she realised
the incubus that rode her, a woman possessed?

He telephoned the Lion Hotel.

'Yes . . . Oh, *yes!*' she said. The voice, full, clear and eager,
drew her upon the air in front of his eyes. 'Yes, much better,
thank you! Do come! I wondered about you. I shall be looking
forward . . .'

'I've been following,' he said, with the even delivery of a machine,
'the course of that last tour you made with Dr. Fredericks.' He
dared look at her only briefly and occasionally, because the blue
of her eyes blinded him, so vivid and wondering and hopeful
they were upon his face. 'I stayed at a small resort called Scheidenau, near the German border. Do you remember it?'

'Yes, vaguely. There was a lake . . . and a castle . . .'

'And a small hotel called the Goldener Hirsch.'

'You mean the one Freddy used to take us to? I'd forgotten
the name, but I remember how it looked.'

The Lion Hotel was by the Comer bridge, and her suite was
above the waterside. The tremulous light, reflected from a high
ceiling and white walls, shimmered over her face, which was
clear and pure as crystal, without shadows. She looked marvellously more substantial than when he had seen her in her hospital
bed, but still fine-drawn and great of eye, and the tension that
held her seemed more of hope than fear, as if the very act of
sending him out to probe her disease had somehow absolved her
and set her well on the way to a cure. Perhaps for a few days,
in his absence, she had even begun to feel that setting out to
look for the answer was the same thing as finding it, that now
she could take up her life again, that the crisis was over.

He approached her not with clear statements, but with
promptings, for what seemed to him a good reason. For Friedl,
in spite of her reckless challenge to him to go back to his Maggie
and ask her outright, might still have been lying. And supposing
he confronted Maggie with this story, and still her memory

478

failed or refused to fill in the blank spaces, so that she could never positively know whether the thing had happened like that or not? The last thing he wanted was to burden her with a grief she had not deserved. So he came towards his point by inches, waiting for a spark of understanding and enlightenment to kindle in the blue, attentive eyes; and the name he held back to the end. If she spoke it first, then they would both be sure.

'That was a very important tour for you, wasn't it? You had your first great successes, and you knew what they were worth. You began to see a really great future ahead of you, quite rightly. Do you recall anything else of importance that happened to you on that trip?'

'In Scheidenau?' She was watching him closely, her lips parted. The faint hint of an eager smile quivered and died, two pale flames of anxiety burned up in her eyes. He saw her fine brows draw together, painfully frowning. 'I can't think . . .'

'In Scheidenau. On the last evening before you left. No? In the woods along the shore of the lake, below the hotel. There is a maid at the hotel named Friedl, a niece of the family. You remember her?'

She was harrowing all the recesses of her mind for anything that could account for his gravity. Every line of her, from the long fingers tightly clasped in her lap to the pearly curve of the skin over her cheekbone, strained thinner and whiter with mounting tension. 'Please!' she said. 'If you know something, tell me!'

'Are you sure,' he said harshly, 'that you want to know?' He had meant to be gentle, but the rage and pain came up into his throat like gall. And now not only was she afraid, but also there was something deep within her stirring in response to his passion, tearing her in its frenzied attempts to get out, the deep-buried knowledge heaving into wakefulness at last. It was on its way to the light, and nothing could keep it imprisoned now.

'Yes, I want to know.'

'Friedl says that she was in that strip of woodland that night,

479

the night before the Circus was due to leave. She says that she heard two people talking there, and that one of them was you. The other was one of the boys who toured with you. She says that he was arguing and pleading his cause with you, and that you were trying to get rid of him. She says he cried out at you that *something* would happen "if you didn't want him!" He said – she remembers the words – : "I won't be fool enough to endure it. *There's always an alternative*!" . . .'

Maggie's lips moved, but there was no cry. She clutched the edges of the stool and leaned forward, trying to rise. He would never forget the sudden blind, blank stare of her eyes, lancing clean through him after another face, another accuser.

' . . . and then he ran away from you down the slope towards the lake, and she heard – and *you* heard, didn't you? – the splash of something falling into the water. And he never came back, that night or ever . . .'

She was torn suddenly erect before him, the convulsion of knowledge passed shudderingly through every nerve of her body and flamed into her eyes. She clutched her cheeks hard between her palms, and a wailing cry came out of her, thin and lamentable:

'*Robin!*'

He would not have believed that she could ever utter such a sound, or he provoke such a sound from her. Sick and mute, he stood and stared at his work. Whether she wanted the truth or not, they both had it now, and there was no shovelling it back into its grave.

'*Robin!*' she said in a rustling whisper. 'So he never came . . . But how could I have known? He wasn't any responsibility of mine . . . was he? *Was he?*'

She had appealed to Francis, and therefore she became aware of him again, no longer as an apocalyptic voice ripping away the layers of her forgetfulness one by one, but as a man, a live human creature shut in there with her, and one who knew more about her than any man should know. All that long-buried

480

burden of her guilt lay there in full view between them. They looked at each other across the wreckage with horror, anger and hatred. Each of them knew what the other was seeing, and each recoiled in outrage from the violation of privacy involved. Nothing was hidden any longer, everything assaulted Maggie's lacerated senses at once, his love, his resentment of love, his humiliation and rage at the invasion of his bleak solitude. Both his love and his antagonism were unbearable, and there was nowhere to hide.

Her body, newly schooled in the use of weakness where there remains no other weapon, found the only way of escape. Francis saw her deliberately, resolutely withdraw from him into the dark, and sprang across the room towards her a second too late. She let her hands fall, and dropped like a crumpled bird.

She came round in his arms, on his heart, aware of his agony before ever she heard his voice panting and whispering her name. Fingers light and agitated and gentle smoothed back the tumbled hair from her eyes. A broken and contrite murmur entreated her:

'Maggie, forgive me . . . forgive me! Oh, my God, what have I done?'

She lay like a dead woman, and made no sign. It was the only way to keep any part of her integrity free of his touch, of his love which she did not want, of his nearness which affronted her, of his pain, of which she was mortally afraid. No one must come this close to her, no one touch her with this wounding fervour. She must get rid of him. He must know no more of her, he already knew too much. So she kept her eyes fast closed and her spirit tightly withdrawn from him, even when the shadow of his face stooped between her and the light, and he kissed her on the mouth. The touch shook her to the heart with pity and panic and distress. She held her breath and remained apart.

'Maggie, speak to me . . . look at me . . .'

Suddenly he was up from his knees and plunging away from her across the room. She heard the faint single ring as he lifted the telephone.

'No!' She opened her eyes and raised herself unsteadily among the cushions of the couch, where he had carried her. 'No, please don't! I'm all right . . .'

He spun on his heel, and for an instant she saw such abject hope, relief and solicitude in his eyes that her head swam again. Then she felt as a convulsion in her own flesh the effort with which he drew down over his face the austere mask of professional detachment he normally showed to the world, and hid his nakedness from her. She thought wretchedly, we've destroyed each other. This proud man will never forgive me for frightening him so far off-course into humility and self-betrayal, any more than I can forgive him for penetrating so far into my jungle, and caring too much about what he found. What affair am I of his, outside the terms of the agreement? And what right had I to find my way under his skin and reduce him to this?

'I was going to call your doctor. I think I should.'

'No, please hang up. I don't need anyone. I don't want anyone.' She sat up, smoothing her dove-grey skirt. 'I'm sorry I alarmed you,' she said. 'It was only a momentary weakness. I shall be all right now.'

'I'm afraid I've upset you too much. I wish you'd let me call someone.'

'Please, no, it's quite unnecessary. Now, if you'll be kind enough to hand me my bag . . . It's there on the piano . . .'

He brought it, handing it to her with fastidious carefulness, not to touch, not to make any claim upon her, now that she was awake and aware. Her pallor was less extreme now, her face was calm, almost cold. The fear was gone and the hope was gone; she was past the moment of impact, it seemed, and beyond there was an emptiness, an area of shock, where as yet nothing hurt and nothing comforted.

'Don't worry about me, I shall be quite all right now. I'll lie down and have a rest, after you leave. Thank you for all the work you've put in on my case, you've been most efficient, and I'm very grateful.' She was riffling through the contents of her handbag, her head bent; and in a moment she looked up at him, holding out a sheaf of notes. 'I hope I've reckoned up right. This is only the fee for the actual number of days, of course, including today. Please let me have the amount of your expenses, they must have been considerable. Don't trouble to itemise, I shall be quite satisfied with a round figure. And again, thank you!' Very courteous, very low, very final, that wild-silk voice of hers, dismissing him; but so gentle that at first he hardly understood, and when he did, he could not believe.

'You mean you're dispensing with my services?' His face was whiter than hers.

'But surely, you're completed your assignment very successfully. I asked you to find out for me what it was I'd done . . . to feel that I had a death on my hands. And you've done it. There's nothing else I need.'

'You're accepting this without examination? I should have thought we needed to go into it in detail, to satisfy you that it's authentic. I was too brutal, I beg your pardon! I wanted to avoid mentioning names, to see if there was any genuine memory of this incident . . .'

'You have seen,' she said, 'that there is. It needed only to be uncovered. There is no mistake. And I am quite satisfied.'

He stood gazing down at her, and felt time and the world grinding to a stop, and only a blank before him. She continued to sit there, pale, resolutely withdrawn into herself, holding out the sheaf of notes patiently in a hand that trembled a little from weakness; and her eyes had become the heavy, opaque blue of Willow Pattern china. There was nothing he could do. He was not going to plead with her for a small corner somewhere in her life, and he could not force his way where she did not want him to go. He had not even the right to turn on his heel and walk out, and leave her holding the money she felt she owed him. He was a hired employee, commissioned, paid off and dismissed. What could he do but take his fee, and go?

'I ought to point out,' he said, in a voice almost as dry as the desert he saw ahead of him without her, 'that what I've reported and what you may have remembered is not enough to prove what actually became of this man Aylwin. You yourself know that there were completely logical reasons for believing, as Dr. Fredericks certainly did, that he had simply walked out. Granted that you have additional knowledge, you still have no proof that Dr. Fredericks' version is not the correct one. For all the real evidence anyone possesses, Aylwin may be very much alive and perfectly well. If you won't allow me to follow up the possibilities for you, at least remember that.'

Did he for one moment believe what he had said? Certainly she did not. Perhaps now she knew more than he did. She remained marble-still, the notes extended gravely in her hand.

'Thank you, you're very kind. Please believe that I appreciate what you've done for me, but there's no need to follow it up any farther. And now, I'm a little tired . . .'

He could not keep her waiting any longer. He took the money without a glance, and thrust it into his pocket.

'May I know . . . what you intend to do?'

'I have no plans,' she said.

'If there should be anything further to tell you, can I rely on finding you here?'

'For a while, yes. I don't know how long.'

'If you should need me, you know where to reach me.' She did not offer him her hand, and he did not expect it. He walked to the door without looking back. 'Good-bye, Miss Tressider!'

'Good-bye, Mr. Killian!'

The trouble was that he didn't mean it, and she did. Wherever she looked for help, out of friendship or for hire, never in this world would she turn to Francis Killian again. She had crossed him out of her experience, buried him as deep as the body he'd dug up for her. After the compromising intimacy of what they'd just done to each other, he thought grimly as he walked down the stairs, it was either that or marriage.

He had taken her money, because he had had no right to refuse it, but now that he had it, it was his business what he did with it. He walked into the church opposite the hotel, and cast a sullen eye over all the almsboxes, but the combating of dry-rot and death-watch beetle and the financing of overseas missions in countries arguably more moral and likeable if not more Christian than England did not appeal to him as a job for Maggie's money. He went down to the Salvation Army shelter by the embankment, where they had a permanent collecting-box on the wall outside, in the form of a giant tambourine, with his favourite appeal written across it in large, cheerful characters: help up the down-but-not-outs. He pulled out the untidy wad of notes from his pocket, and stuffed them anyhow through the slot.

A disinterested-looking man sauntering past with his eyes apparently on the river took in this surprising act, and loitered to lean on the rail and the embankment and think it over, as Francis stalked away.

George Felse had been following him ever since he had shouldered his way through the revolving doors of the Lion Hotel and butted savagely through the traffic into the church opposite. It was a chance meeting only, in fact George was on his way to the car-park where he had left his car. But the apparition of Bunty's visitor, back from Austria and striding stony-faced and hot-eyed away from an encounter with his principal, had lured him out of his course. Everybody knew from the local evening paper that Maggie Tressider had taken a suite at the Lion; and by this time George had studied Francis Killian's photograph too thoughtfully to miss that face when he saw it cross the pavement in front of him. First the almsboxes in the church, and now this startling treatment of a fistful of money. And the desolation and rage in the worn, illusionless face. It takes a lot to wound a man without illusions. It takes a touch of madness to make most people throw money away.

George walked to his car slowly and thoughtfully. Whatever Maggie Tressider's commission had been, it looked as if it was over. And there at the Salvation Army shelter her agent had jettisoned his pay, in anger and offence. Was it possible that Bunty had been right about him? Had he a far larger stake at risk?

And might it not be well worth while, so far as other duties allowed, continuing this unofficial watch upon him? In fact, upon both of them?

It was on Saturday, the fourteenth of September, that Laura Howard telephoned from the B.E.A. office.

'Bunty? Something rather intriguing – if you're still interested in your party? He looked in yesterday afternoon, and asked me to do exactly what *you* asked me to do! He wants to know if *Maggie Tressider* books a passage anywhere. He knows I shouldn't do it but he was in dead earnest. And of course, I didn't promise, not exactly, but remembering what you said last time . . . Well, I didn't say I wouldn't, either. I thought I'd better consult you, and see what was on. Because, you see, *she has*! This morning! She rang up and wanted a passage to Zurich next Wednesday and I've got one for her on the 16.10 from Heathrow.'

Bunty had waved George over long before this point, and his head was inclined intently beside her own, listening to the distant clacking with ears stretched.

'Well, I mean, *Maggie Tressider*! But he seems on the level, and he says he's been working for her. Has he?'

'Yes,' said Bunty, 'that's right, he has.'

'Then what do I do? Should I let him know?'

'Ask her,' hissed George, 'if there's another flight to Zurich the same day.'

'Hallo . . . Laura? Is there another flight that same day?'

486

'Lots . . . 10.10, 10.50, 14.10 . . . and tourist night flights, of course . . .'

'Tell him,' breathed George, 'and a thousand to one he'll be on one of 'em if there's a vacancy.'

'Yes, Laura, tell him. He's O.K. And Laura . . . let me know if he books a crossing for himself, will you?'

'Oh, well,' said Laura philosophically, 'in for a penny, in for a pound. O.K., I'll call him. And I'll call *you*, double-quick, if there's any trouble.' She rang off.

Bunty cradled the 'phone, and gazed round-eyed at George over it. '*Now* what's going on? It doesn't make sense for him to be peering round corners and suborning B.E.A. employees to find out what his own client's up to. He can't have been lying about working for her, because he wasn't at all worried about the possibility that I might pop out and buy some flowers and go round to the Royal to visit her. In fact he suggested it. And plenty of people would have, especially after being told she'd remembered them. Now it seems he's expecting her to go running out there herself, and not to say anything to him about it. So what *is* going on?'

'I rather think,' said George, 'that they've parted brassrags.' He recounted the incident of the Salvation Army shelter. 'It looks as if he brought *something* back with him, and something that got him paid off and sent about his business. And somehow I don't think it was book material about Paul Fredericks, do you? Anyhow, he wasn't a bit happy about the result, you should have seen his face! And he certainly got rid of her money so fast it might have been scalding him. But now it does seem that he hasn't exactly accepted his dismissal, doesn't it? Far from it, he's still going to be bloodhounding along after her wherever she goes, unless I miss my guess. Only this time unknown to her, and unpaid.'

'I told you,' said Bunty, 'he's in love with her. If she's going to walk head-on into trouble, he's going to be on the spot to pull her out of it.'

'And you think she *is* going to be walking into trouble?' demanded George, of himself at least as much as of his wife.

'It looks as if *he* thinks so. And after all, he's the only one who knows what he found there, isn't he?'

'You're so right,' agreed George ruefully. 'I only wish he wasn't. I'd give a good deal to be in the know myself.' He sat mute for a few moments, his eyes fixed on Bunty in bright speculation; she knew him so well that she could almost see him making up his mind. 'Bunty, how would you like a few days in the Vorarlberg?'

'Us?' she said, startled. 'You and me? You mean follow them over and keep an eye on them?'

'*If* he decides to go after her. Yes, you and me – why not? I've still got a week of leave to take, some time, why not now and why not in Scheidenau? If nothing comes of it, we've lost nothing and had a holiday. And if something does come of it, if he's turned up something about the disappearance of your young Aylwin . . . Well, who knows? If we roll one more stone over we may find Peter Bromwich, too. I'd give a good deal to close that case.'

'We couldn't travel on the same flight with either of them,' pointed out Bunty. '*He*'d know me, for certain. And *she* just might.'

'I was thinking rather of hopping over with one of the tourist night flights, ahead of them. They won't all be fully booked, not in September. And it would give us time to lay on a car from Zurich, ready to trail those two as soon as they land. Train or road, we can tag along once we've got them in our sights. What do you say?'

Bunty reviewed her responsibilities, and could find nothing against it. Dominic and his Tossa wouldn't be home from their student trek in Yugoslavia for a fortnight yet, just in time to head back to Oxford.

'I say yes, let's!' said Bunty with enthusiasm. '*If* he follows her, of course,' she conceded with a sigh.

The House of Green Turf

It was late afternoon when the telephone rang again.

'Bunty? Laura here! How did you know? He's booked on the 14.10, two hours ahead of her!'

Chapter 6

Second cousin Gisela, of the mini-skirt, the blonde ponytail and the white wool knee-stockings, heard the car drive through into the courtyard of the Goldener Hirsch, and whirled her stool round to see who was arriving. The French couple from the second floor had left this morning, and most of the currency-starved English were already gone. The slight chill of approaching autumn fingered thoughtfully at the roofs of Scheidenau. A new arrival was not only profit, but entertainment, too.

The driver, a frequent visitor here during the season, brought in two cases of modest size but excellent quality, and his manner indicated that he had been more than adequately tipped. Gisela reviewed the accommodation she had to offer, and looked up with hopeful brightness as the new arrival came into the hall. English, a lady alone, very beautiful, very pale, very fragile. She wore a fashionably simple little tube of a dress in fine wool jersey, printed in rich warm tones of rust and amber and peach that did their best to reflect some colour into her face, but Gisela could see that without that reflected glow she would have been ashen, with lavender hollows in her cheeks and deeper violet shadows under her eyes. Her clothes, from the narrow black shoes to the small, gold-rimmed halo of a black hat, spoke of money. Her face, white, remote and abstracted, seemed not to belong to the picture, even though everything she wore had been carefully chosen to set it off at its best. Gisela had the feeling that she had seen that face before in magazines, and that it was famous and ought to be recognized, but the firmament of opera and the concert platform was not her world, and she had no memory for the stars that revolved in it.

The voice which asked for a room was very quiet and a little husky with fatigue, yet it was the most vital, vigorous and live thing about the visitor, as if it used and drove everything else. A voice that would make you prick up your ears and turn round to see if the face matched it, even if you heard it simply ordering beer in the bar.

'How long will the lady be staying?'

'I don't know . . . several days. If I'm not asking for impossibilities, I should like to have a piano to myself somewhere. I have to practise,' she explained with the shadow of a smile, 'and I don't want to disturb anyone.'

Gisela was eager. 'If you would like it, there is a suite on the first floor which has a large sitting-room. Tomorrow they could bring up a piano for you from the dining-room, there are two there. Only an upright, but it is a good tone, and in tune.' The suite was the dearest apartment in the house, and someone who wanted a piano as part of the amenities could well afford to pay for it.

'Upstairs?' said Maggie doubtfully. 'I shouldn't like to put them to so much trouble. Won't it be very heavy and difficult?'

'The stairs are so wide and so shallow, there is no difficulty. Like a castle, you will see. And the suite is very nice, it looks over the lake, and has a verandah with steps down to the grounds. I will show you.' And she whisked open the flap of her desk, picked up the two suitcases like handfuls of feathers, and started sturdily up the length of the vaulted hall.

Maggie followed the straight young back and twinkling white wool legs to the vast rear stairs, and along a broad, echoing corridor on the first floor. She had no conscious memory of anything here, yet she knew where something was changed. It was like revisiting the place of a dream, or perhaps even more like dreaming of a place so uncannily familiar as to convince her she had dreamed it before. On those long-past visits with Freddy she had slept far up on the third floor, in rooms appropriately cheap for aspiring young performers. This large blue and white room, with its verandah blazing with geraniums, the airy bedroom opening from it, the bright hand-made cover on the old, carved bed, these she had never seen before. She went out into the open air and leaned over the flowering rail, and the scent of the trees came up to her, and the glimmer of the lake refracting light to her invisible, in small, broken darts of paler green launched through the deep green dusk.

'Dinner is over,' said Gisela, 'but if you would like something to eat I will tell them. You are very tired, shall we not bring you something here?'

Maggie sat down on the edge of the bed, and its firm softness drew her like a magnet. 'I am tired. Yes, if you would be so kind, it would be very nice to eat here.'

'And you like the room? It will do?'

'It will do very well. But I haven't signed, or filled in a card for you.'

'Tomorrow,' said Gisela cheerfully. 'And in the morning they will bring up your piano. Everything tomorrow!' And she went darting along the corridor, in small, light thumps like a terrier running on the naked boards, and skittered down the stairs back to her switchboard.

Maggie undressed, her movements clumsy with exhaustion, wrapped herself in a housecoat, and lay down on the bed. The feather coverlet billowed round her, cool and grateful, closing her in from the world. There were no thoughts left in her at all, only this terrible weariness suddenly eased and cradled, and sleep leaning heavily on her eyelids the moment she lay down.

Only this morning she had left Comerbourne for London, picked up fresh clothes at her flat, and taken a taxi out to Heathrow in time for her flight. Then the train journey on to Bregenz, and the car to bring her up here to the border. And ever since Zurich, places and scenes familiar to her throughout the years of her fame had taken on a different, a remote familiarity, as though the nineteen-year-old Maggie had come back to savour them with another palate. A bitter taste, perhaps of poison. I am not yet well, she told herself, I see, hear, feel with distorted senses. But in her heart she knew that it was because all these places were populated now by one more person, many years forgotten.

It was five days now since she had remembered Robin living, and been brought face to face with Robin dead. Five days in which he had kept her company every step of the way.

She was discharged to her own care, she could go where she chose and take the responsibility for herself. None the less, she had gone gently and gradually about this pilgrimage, concentrating her forces to satisfy her doctors that she was fit to travel, and assuring them that her intention was to take a leisurely, convalescent holiday at a resort she already knew well, where she would be comfortable and well-cared-for, a complete rest that would set her up to tackle life again. Turning her head on the pillow and catching sight of her own drawn face in the glass, she felt certain she had not looked like this when they agreed to let her go. She must remember to send Mr. Rice a card full of reassurances tomorrow. Everything tomorrow!

She had done certain other things during those five days: cancelled a few more forward engagements, answered all her letters, arranged a transfer of money to the accounts of Alec and Dione, in case they found themselves in difficulties while she was absent.

'While she was absent' was how she phrased it in her own mind; but before she left England she had also made her will.

Across the water, in a room on the second floor of the Alte Post, Bunty Felse lowered the field-glasses from her eyes with a crow of satisfaction, and turned to meet George as he came into the doorway behind her.

'She's here, all right,' he reported. 'Came up in a car from Bregenz not a quarter of an hour ago, and turned up towards the Goldener Hirsch.'

'I know,' said Bunty, 'I've just seen her. Those are her windows, almost opposite to us, see? With the flowers and the balcony. The curtains are drawn now, but when the girl brought her up and put the lights on they were open. It was the lights that made me look there. I might have mistaken the face at this distance, even with glasses, but I couldn't mistake that hat.'

She had never been quite easy in her mind since they had taken their eyes off that hat, a thin gold halo in the back window of the taxi, on the road from Zurich airport, and allowed Maggie to be carried away towards the town without them. George had had to make a snap decision which of the two to follow, for the middle-aged hired Dodge with Francis Killian at the wheel had swung unhesitatingly north-east on the fast road to Winterthur.

'He knew where she was heading, all right,' said George, focusing the glasses on the pattern of lights over the water. 'And which hotel she'd make for when she got here. Lucky we followed him in by road, or we wouldn't have known which one he'd picked for himself. As it is, you'll be able to keep out of his sight here without any trouble.'

'I wonder why he did choose the Weisses Kreuz, when this one is so well-placed for keeping an eye on her?'

'He couldn't know she'd have that room, could he? And the Weisses Kreuz is on the corner where all the roads meet, all traffic going up to the Goldener Hirsch has to pass it. He was there on the terrace,' said George, 'waiting for her to arrive. When the car went by, he paid and strolled off in the same direction.'

'You think he'll try to see her?'

'No, I think he'll want to see without being seen himself. He won't want her to know he's spying on her, not if you're right about his feelings for her.'

'So we wait for him to move,' said Bunty, 'and *he* waits for *her*. And *she*, I shouldn't be surprised, waits for somebody else, I wonder who?'

Maggie, on her way down to breakfast, met a woman on the broad white spiral of the back stairs, a tall woman in traditional dress, with black hair plaited into two great, shining braids and coiled high on her head. She was carrying two heavy cases as she climbed, so that her head was bent, and that tower of glistening hair was the first thing about her to catch Maggie's attention. She drew aside to where the steps were narrowest, to let the burdened woman by, and because she was still a little shaky and hesitant from the fatigue of the previous day, she halted and held by the wall rather than risk proceeding on the tapering treads. The woman's eyes travelled upwards steadily from the narrow, elegant black shoes to the smooth russet-amber hair. Her head came up like the head of a deer scenting man. For a moment she halted, motionless and silent, and the sidelong light from a window accentuated the cleft in her lip, scoring the shadow there cruelly deep.

Maggie and Friedl stood mute and intent, gazing at each other. Thirteen years is a long time, but a hare-lip on an otherwise good-looking girl is bitterly memorable, and to be world-famous is to have one's photograph penetrate everywhere, if any reminder was needed. And even more surely, there stood between them the shadow of an absent third, at once a link between them and an impassable barrier.

'You are the lady from Number One?' said Friedl, with a gaunt smile in which her eyes played no part. 'Franz and Joachim will bring up the piano for you this morning.'

'Thank you!' Maggie hesitated for a moment only. 'You are Fräulein Friedl?'

'How kind of the gracious lady,' said Friedl, 'to remember

me.' The smile, returning, hollowed her brown cheeks and raised a hungry gleam in her eye that was neither gracious nor kind. 'It is a long time ago.'

'I must speak to you,' said Maggie.

'Not here. Not now.' Friedl watched the colour ebb and flow on the too-prominent cheekbones, and slow, burning resentment gathered about her heart and ached insatiably. This was the woman who had and did not value the devotion of every man who set eyes on her, while she, Friedl, beautiful of body but marred of face, provided a passing interest for such men as had nothing better to do, but was never noticed, never regarded, as a woman in her own right. Wait, she thought, there is always a price on everything, and you've had so much and paid so little yet! 'I have my work to do,' she said. 'I am not a daughter of the house.'

The tone was mild and even servile, but the eyes were inimical, and even the note of self-abasement had its implicit reverse of smouldering arrogance. Maggie shrank. If she could have turned back now she would have done it, but there was no way of turning back. It was even possible that this woman knew no more than she had told Francis; but if she did, Maggie had to know it. There might be no comfort in knowing, but not to know was to be balked of her own identity. She had come here, tidying up her affairs behind her, and leaving no dependent of hers unprovided, simply in the determination to know; there was no other thought or ambition left in her mind.

'When may I have a talk with you?' she asked patiently.

'I am not free until after dinner. And even then, if we wish to be undisturbed, better it should not be in the house.'

'I will come wherever you choose.'

'This evening, when I am free, I will go along the path to the wood, under your verandah. Come out by that way, please, after me. They do not like it if I mix too much with the guests.' It was a lie, but so well did it fit into the picture she was composing of an oppressed poor relation that she almost felt it to be true.

I will make you follow me, she thought, as I followed him. I will take you where I took him, and make use of you as he made use of me. And I'll hurt you as he hurt me, and with interest. When I'm done with you, you shall have one man round your neck for life, and go the rest of your way ringing him like a leper's bell to keep every other man off, for fear of bringing him to the same end. I know your kind!

'Very well,' said Maggie. 'I shall be watching for you. I'll come.'

'What more do you want?' said Friedl harshly. '*He* told you all this, didn't he? That man you sent here. Here in this very place he asked me what you have asked me, and I told him. And what did you need with either of us to tell you? Who knew better than you what sent Robin rushing down the slope there and into the lake? Yes, you had the right to refuse him, if you didn't want him, yes, you could tell him to go away – am I blaming you? What was it to you if somebody else loved him, and wanted what you didn't want? But you cannot have it both ways. If you think you did him no wrong, why do you come weeping back like a penitent, asking to be forgiven for killing him? If you did nothing shameful to him, why are you ashamed?'

In the half-circle of bushes, with the night deepening round them, all colours on the landward side had become an opaque wash of olive green. Against the faintly luminous shimmer of lake and sky, thinly veiled by a lace of branches, Friedl in her black dress prowled restlessly. The slight rustle of her feet in the grass frayed at the silence when her voice ceased. Somewhere a twig cracked. She reared her head to listen, frozen in mid-stride. The moment she was still the ultimate silence flooded in and possessed the world.

'No . . . Nothing! No, nobody else ever comes here at night.'

She came a step nearer, turning her back on the lake, and stood black and tense against the pallor of the sky.

'I loved him. You understand? For two days, just two days, I was his mistress. But he never thought seriously of me. What man ever did? You were there, you with everything. How could he even see me for long? You don't believe me?'

'I believe you,' said Maggie. 'I am sorry!'

The sense she had had on the staircase of something rank and bitter and unprovoked assaulting her had become here an emanation of horror, unrelieved by the breeze or the cool of the air. For the first time in her life she knew it for hate, and was helpless in face of it. The tall darkness seemed to grow taller, hanging over her malignant and assured. It was not fear that held her paralysed, but a sick revulsion from the proximity of such hatred, an intuition that if it touched her she would never feel clean again.

'It is late to be sorry. Why did you not call him back then? Why did you never tell what you knew?'

'Why didn't you?' said Maggie. 'After we were gone, when they waited for him to come back for his things, and still he didn't come?'

'Why should I? What would have been the good? What did I care about his things? Could I have brought him back from the dead by telling?'

'You are quite sure, then – you were quite sure all the time – that he *is* dead?'

It was the only question that remained, whether she asked it of herself or Friedl.

'His body,' she said, 'never came ashore. I don't say that is proof of anything, I only say it is so. If there is anything more that you know, anything final, please tell me.'

There was a soundless movement in the dark, and Friedl's face was close to hers, pale and fierce beneath the black hair.

'Dead?' she said softly. 'Yes, he's dead. You are right, I didn't tell your Herr Killian everything I know. The body never came ashore here in Austria, no – *but in Germany it did*! That same winter they sent me over to help at the hotel in Felsenbach. Marianne is married to the innkeeper there, and they have a good ski season while we are quiet here. You do not know this place? Our river runs through it after it leaves the lake, before it comes back into Austria. That year there was a sudden thaw early in February, and the Rulenbach came down out of the lake in flood and brought a man ashore. What was left of a man! No, I still did not speak! Why speak? What could it do for him or for me? And after so long one would not say he was recognisable, no, not easily recognisable. He had no papers on him . . . how could he? Almost he had no clothes. They buried him out of charity, and put a stone over him, too, but without a name. But *I* knew!' she cried, her voice rising dangerously. '*I* knew who he was! You want proof? He still had a signet ring on his finger, after all that time. I saw it, and I knew it. And so will you know it! Don't take my word, look for yourself! Do you remember *this*?'

The pale claw of her hand plunged suddenly into the pocket of her dress, and plucked out a slip of white card, and something else that she fumbled wildly for a moment before her shaking fingers could control it. She had come prepared with everything she needed for the *coup de grâce*. The torch was a tiny thing that nestled in her palm, but it produced a thin bright beam, enough for her purpose.

'Look! *Look!* You wished to know – *know*, then, be certain! Do you remember this face?'

She thrust it before Maggie's eyes, and held the torchbeam close. A postcard photograph, half-length, of a young man playing the 'cello. It was taken somewhat from his right side; his head was inclined in delighted concentration over his instrument, so that the eyes were veiled beneath rounded lids, and the highlight picked out the line of a smooth boyish forehead and a well-shaped jaw and chin. The lips, full and firm, curled slightly in an absorbed smile, the hair, wavy and thick, was shaken forward out of its concert-platform neatness by his exertions. He looked young, carefree, and as single-minded as a child. And the photographer, like every photographer who ever made studies of a string-player, had lavished his most loving care on the braced and sensitive hands. The bow hand, beautiful in its taut grace and power, occupied the forefront of the picture; and on the third finger was a heavy seal-ring with a black, oval stone. Even by this light Maggie could distinguish the curling flourishes of the letter R in reverse.

'Can you see clearly enough? Here, take it, hold it . . . It was you he wanted . . . you who killed him. Yes, killed him! Is it the right man? Is it the right ring? You know him?'

'Yes,' said Maggie in a broken whisper. 'Yes, I know him.'

Friedl snatched away her hand, and left the photograph quivering in Maggie's hold. She had reached the end of the journey, there was nowhere beyond to go. The darkness and the watery shimmer, the pencil of torch-light, the pale glare of Friedl's vengeful face, lurched and swirled round her in a moment of faintness, and suddenly the burden of this corrosive hate was more than she could bear. Her last refuge was gone, she could no longer hold on to any shred of doubt or hope. The photograph fluttered from her nerveless fingers. She turned and stumbled away through the bushes, blind and desperate, fending herself off from trees, tripping over roots, wild to escape from contact with this malice that pursued her with a defilement worse than guilt. Behind her she heard Friedl break into hard, breathless laughter, and swoop through the bushes to follow her victim still.

'Run . . . faster, faster . . . He is on your heels!'

Tearlessly sobbing, half-demented, Maggie clawed her way out to the open path at last, and began to run unsteadily along it, her course wavering from one grassy edge to the other, her hands spread to ward off the leaning trees. Once she fell, and picked herself up with wincing haste and blundered on. The voice had fallen far behind now, abandoning her to her own torments. No sound pursued her. She halted for a moment, clinging to the resinous trunk of a fir tree in the fragrant darkness, her chest labouring, her ears straining, awed and soothed by the night's huge silence.

It was then that she heard the sound. Not loud, if the measure of the preceding silence had not newly alerted her spirit, not even significant, if it had been the first time she had heard it. But this was time returning, experience rounding on itself to celebrate her destruction. This she had heard before, a long time ago, and pushed away from her strenuously into the limbo of disbelief because it must not be true. Some way behind her, distantly but clearly, echoed the mute, remembered splash of a body into water. She was mad, or damned, or both, she was the quarry of a specific retribution. History had dragged back a September night of many years ago, so that she should not be able to forget, or find it possible to mistake her hour.

When she could breathe again she crept on, mindless, exhausted, sunk now into the indifference of despair. The comfortable brown bulk of the hotel rose before her out of the trees. She dragged herself up the wooden steps to her own verandah, and let herself in by the curtained door. The furies were hard on her heels, but she could not run any more, and it was not from them she was in flight. Without putting on the light she fell face-upwards on her bed, and lay with spread arms, staring up at the high ceiling, waiting to embrace the judgment.

She knew, she acknowledged, her mortal guilt. A fellow-creature had leaned upon her in his extreme need, and she had shrugged him off and let him fall. She admitted to her consciousness at last the truth of what she was. She was Robin Aylwin's murderess.

She was roused from her timeless, aimless waiting before the first light of dawn had turned the sky from velvet black to smoke-grey. Something was pecking irritably at her senses, a small, insistent, nagging thing that hurt, and meant to hurt. With infinite labour her mind gathered its abandoned powers to locate and understand. Someone was tapping, tapping, softly

501

and tirelessly at the glass of the door in her sitting-room, the door that led to the verandah and the lake.

She rose like a sleepwalker, and felt her way across the bed-room. All the shapes within the room were defined in shades of grey. The sky framed in the window was metallic and bluish, like steel, and the outline of the figure pressed into the angle of the door-frame was black, sexless, without identity, one edge of it merged into the wall. Only the hand that tapped and tapped at the glass with some small hard object had a perceptible shape and size. A man's hand, tapping out that minute but penetrating sound with his keys to wake her.

She had no thoughts, no curiosity, and no fear. She drew back the bolt. The cool of the outer air gushed in before him as he slid into the room quickly and silently, and closed the door behind him. Her hand had gone up automatically to the light switch, but he caught her by the wrist before she could reach it.

'No, don't! No lights! They'd see them.'

She passed a hand confusedly over her eyes, for she was surely seeing and hearing things that could have no reality. The voice she knew, and the face, so close to her own in the dimness. Even the hard grip of the hand holding her was familiar. If he had not been many miles away in England, she would have said this was Francis Killian in the flesh, so solid did the apparition seem. She stood passive, not trying to free herself, not even recoiling from being handled, from having her haunted solitude trampled, from having to experience at close quarters his love and rage and fear for her. The force that frowned off the world to a respectful distance had deserted her and left her a shell.

He stood from between her and the paling light from outside, and turned her about in his hands, saw the grass-stains on her skirt, the torn stockings, the deep bruises under her eyes. He took her by the chin and turned her face up to him with a groan of exasperation.

'My God, my God, what have you done?' he said, hardly audibly, but that was to himself, not to her. 'Oh, God, why did

I ever take my eyes off you? Even at night! I thought you were safe in your bed . . .'

'It *is* you!' she said, with distant wonder. 'How did you get here?'

'I followed you. Did you think I could just wash my hands of you and let you go to hell alone? Why, for God's sake,' he demanded, his enforced whisper shaken and thick with fury, 'did you have to do this crazy thing? Couldn't you trust me and take my word for it? Why did you have to come here and expose yourself to *this*? And what were your damned fools of doctors doing to let you?'

She had nothing to say. He held her by the shoulders and she stood silent and submissive, looking at him, looking through him, with eyes huge and dulled, as though she still dreamed of him and had no interest in waking. Her passivity terrified him. He shook her between his hands, too frightened to be gentle.

'Don't you understand? Don't you realise your position? Don't you know that Friedl never came in last night? *That they've just fished her body out of the lake?*'

Chapter 7

Something came to life again in the dull depths of her eyes, a quivering intelligence that proved she was still within reach of argument and persuasion, if only he had had time for either. But it was growing lighter every moment, and he had to get out of there quickly, or she would have no chance at all. There was no time to question her. He made one attempt, and she said nothing, merely stood withdrawn into some remote dream of horror. There was nothing he could do but take charge of her, and hope to God she would do what he told her, and be too numbed to realise what a tightrope she was walking until she was safely over.

He drew her across the room in his arm, and thrust her into her bedroom.

'Get those clothes off, quickly! Give me the stockings and the dress . . . Hurry, I'll get them out of here.'

She went where he urged her and did what she was told like an automaton. In a few moments she emerged in her housecoat, the torn stockings and stained dress in her hands. He bundled them into his pockets, and drew her to the bed, and sitting her down there, held her by the shoulders eye to eye with him.

'Listen to me! The police will be here all day, asking questions of everybody. You, too! You've got to be ready for them. *You know nothing about Friedl*, you understand? You didn't see her last night, you weren't with her . . .'

It was then that her face awoke suddenly, stirred into agitation and pain, for it was then that it dawned on her that he half-believed she had killed Friedl. And in a sense so she had. There was a doom on her. People who came too near her died, without any motion of her will. And so might he, if she did not send him away from her.

'I must tell you,' she said, raising upon him eyes no longer blind, but brilliant with apprehension and resolve. 'I did see her . . . I was with her . . .'

'I've asked you nothing,' he said roughly. 'I don't want to know.'

'*I want to tell you*. There was more, something she didn't tell you . . .'

'Quickly, then!' He eyed the paling light, and shook with anxiety for her.

She had caught the sting of his urgency at last. She told him what she had to tell in a few words. He held fast to her all the while, afraid that she might relapse into her border world of despair if he took his hands from her.

'Felsenbach! That's over in the Allgäu. And this photograph . . . you're in no doubt that it is Aylwin?'

She shook her head. 'It's Robin. There isn't any doubt.'

'You went out by the verandah here . . . No one saw you? No one was about, when you left or when you returned?'

'No, no one.'

'Good, that makes it easier. If people saw you come upstairs after dinner, so much the better. Understand, you went to bed, and you've been here ever since. You've been ill, you're under orders to get plenty of rest.' They'll believe that, he thought, his heart aching over the pale spectre he held between his hands. 'You understand? You went early to bed, and slept, and you know nothing about any happenings in the night. That's what you have to tell the police, when they ask, and for God's sake get it right and stick to it.'

'I won't forget,' she said submissively.

'And listen, stay close to the hotel all today. Maybe they'll insist on that, but do it in any case. But tomorrow come to the restaurant in the village, for lunch, and I'll meet you there. The one next to the church, The Bear. Make it about noon. By then we may be able to see how the land lies. We're acquaintances in England, running into each other here by chance. Have you got that clear?'

In a whisper she said: 'Yes,' and let it be taken for a promise, though she had promised nothing. All she wanted now was for him to go away quickly, before the shadow fell upon him as it had fallen on Robin and on Friedl.

'I must get out of here, it'll be broad daylight soon. When I've gone, go to bed, sleep if you can, but go to bed anyhow, and when it's time, get up and go down to breakfast as if nothing had happened. As far as you're concerned, *nothing has happened*! That's all you have to remember.'

He left her there sitting on the edge of her bed, looking after him. Soundlessly he turned the latch of the door, and silently let it relax into its place again under his hand. The pre-dawn light was now dove-grey, but the woodland below, the invisible shore, the gardens, still drowsed in obscurity and silence. Quicksilver, dully shining, the lake lay in its bowl asleep; when the sun rose there would be faint curls of mist drifting across its surface on the south-west wind. Towards the north-east, and the dwindling corner where the Rulenbach flowed out on its detour across the German border. Towards Felsenbach, where, if Friedl had been telling the truth, Robin Aylwin was buried in a grave without a name.

When he was gone, she did as he had told her to do. She went to bed, and by some curious process of subconscious obedience she even fell asleep. She slept until the sun was high, and the usual morning noises had come to life all round her, the normal echoes of an old, spacious house with bare wooden floors. She rose and dressed herself with care, and made up her face as scrupulously as for a stage performance, which in a way this day was going to be.

She went down the stairs slowly, straining her ears at every step. There was a changed quality in the bustle of sound within the house, a high, soft, hysterical note on tension. From the staircase windows that looked into the courtyard she saw a police car and an ambulance standing on the cobbles. Within the broad double doorway of the hall Herr Waldmeister stood conversing earnestly and in low tones with a middle-aged police officer. Frau Waldmeister, in the doorway of the office, talked volubly to someone within, in a cataract of excited dialect supplemented with a frenzy of shoulder-heaving and head-wagging, and when Maggie passed by she could see another, younger policeman busy clearing the office desk for his own use. Two or three guests hovered just within the doorway of the dining-room, peering and whispering in delighted horror.

Gisela, hunched over her adding machine, punched out figures blindly with one hand, and held a handkerchief to her nose with the other. Not to question or comment would in itself be ground for comment. Maggie turned towards the reception desk.

'Whatever's the matter? What is it? Has something happened?'

Gisela looked up with brimming eyes. 'Oh, Miss Tressider, isn't it terrible? The police are here, they want to talk to everybody. Friedl . . . she's dead! She drowned herself in the lake!'

It was late in the afternoon before the police got round to Maggie. By then it was quite simply a relief to be called into the office, and it seemed to her that in closing the door behind her on entering she shut herself into a quiet island, immune to all the agitation and gossip and rumours that were convulsing the household. There was excitement, disquiet and awe abroad in the Goldener Hirsch; but there was no grief. Only Gisela, in love with living and genuinely sorry that anyone should have to surrender it, much less feel wretched enough to want to opt out of it, had shed tears.

In the office it was very quiet. The young man behind the desk, thickset, solid and tanned, looked up from the list he had before him, and smiled briefly and perfunctorily in tribute to a good-looking woman. Off-duty, he would have had more time to appreciate her.

'Sit down, please. You are Miss Maggie Tressider?'

'Yes,' she said, 'that's my name.'

'And you occupy room Number One. You know what our business is here?'

'Gisela told me, this morning. One of the maids has been drowned in the lake.'

'Friedl Schiffer . . . yes. We took her body from the water very early this morning.' He did not say what had brought them looking for her there at such an hour, but the rumours were already circulating, and by this time there were not many people in Scheidenau who did not know that a celebrated local poacher, out before daylight after his night-lines, had sighted the body in the water and given the alarm. 'Did you know her well?'

'I've been here only two days,' said Maggie simply. 'I knew her by name and by sight, of course, I've talked to her once or twice, but that's all.'

'We are anxious to find out when she was last seen alive. Can you help us? When was the last time that you saw her?'

'She helped to serve dinner. After that I didn't see her again. I went up to bed very shortly afterwards.' She caught his shrewd brown eye on her, and smiled faintly. 'I am not exactly on holiday. About a month ago I was involved in a car crash, and had some rather troublesome but not dangerous injuries, which required surgery. I came here for a complete change and rest during convalescence.'

He nodded sympathy; it had already dawned on her that he knew quite well who Maggie Tressider was, and in spite of all

508

his professional impartiality he would find it very easy to treat her as a privileged person. It made her almost ashamed of pleading illness, however truthfully. 'I am almost well,' she said quickly, 'only not yet quite strong again.'

'May I say that I hope this tragedy will not upset you too much? You must try to put it out of your mind once this enquiry is over, and I trust the air of Scheidenau will restore you to health. We are hoping to have the pleasure of hearing you at Salzburg again next year.' He turned back to the business in hand without hesitation and without embarrassment. 'Your room is on the lake side of the house. Did you hear or see anything out of the way? During the evening or in the night?'

'No. I have sleeping tablets,' she said apologetically. It was not even a lie; she had them, though she never took them. They were the doctors' idea, not hers. 'When I came down this morning you were already here, and Gisela told me what had happened.'

It seemed that he was satisfied; he was marking off her name in his list. 'One more thing. I would like you to look at this.'

He took it from under the papers on the desk; she knew it as soon as her eyes lit upon it, and it went to her heart like an invisible arrow, reminding her that she was herself the instrument not of one death only, but of two. She put out a hand that astonished her by not trembling – perhaps there was nothing left to make her tremble, if she accepted that sentence of damnation – to take the photograph he was offering her. She bent her head over it dutifully, and the passion with which she studied it was no lie.

It was the one thing for which she had not been prepared, and for a moment she did not know what to do. The boy in the photograph, head bent like hers, brow furrowed like hers, braced hands fleetingly happy in making music, bowed away at his 'cello and ignored her. No one could have cared less what she did about him; that was her affair. A stain of damp from the dewy grass had dried across one corner, a smear of green marked the neck of the 'cello. Suddenly she wanted with all her heart to acknowledge this boy, to declare her interest in him and her grief for him, and above all her endless and inescapable responsibility for his death. But she could not do it. If she dealt herself in, how long would it be before Francis Killian was dragged in beside her?

She shook her head helplessly, and looked up at the man behind the desk. 'Who is he? Is it something to do with Friedl?'

'We should be interested to have him identified. Do you know him?'

So all the Waldmeister family had either genuinely not remembered Robin Aylwin, or else preferred not to know him, not to be drawn in any deeper. She wondered which? 'No,' she said, 'I don't know him.'

'You never saw this before?'

'I'm sorry!' That at least was no lie; she was sorry that she could not lay down the load that was again crushing her, but if she did, someone else would find himself carrying it.

'Thank you, Miss Tressider, that is all. Don't worry, we shall try not to disturb you any more. Rest and relax, and think about other things.'

'You're very kind,' she said, and meant it. At the door she hesitated, looking back. It was without premeditation that she asked: 'Did Friedl fall in? Or . . . do you think she did it herself?'

She was never quite sure, afterwards, why he answered her, and apparently so unguardedly. Perhaps the directness of the question had surprised an answer out of him before he was aware; but that she could hardly believe. Or perhaps it was a deliberate concession on his part to a person he held to be above suspicion. She hoped it was not that. Or perhaps, and most probably of all, he chose her to fly a little kite for him, to put a small and deceptively innocent cat among the pigeons, in order to see what birds, if any, took flight, and what feathers flew.

'Hardly either,' he said with a hollow smile, 'if the fingermarks round her throat mean anything. Goodday, Miss Tressider!'

She walked out of the office and up the staircase like a creature in a dream. She saw no one, she heard nothing but that matter-of-fact voice repeating its calculated, its miraculous indiscretion. A huge, clean, boisterous wind was blowing through her mind and spirit, blowing the sickness from her soul and the corruption from her will. She closed the door of her room, and sat down before the mirror to stare into her own face, and saw it marvellously changed. She felt cold and pure, scoured into her ultimate clarity, like a Himalayan peak honed diamond-clear and diamond-hard by the withering winds of the heights. She saw herself bright and positive and brave in the mirror, and wondered where this self of hers had been hiding so long.

He would never know what he had done for her!

Friedl had died in the lake, but with the marks of hands round her throat. That meant murder! Not the obscure, malign influence of a woman who was accursed and carried death around with her against her will, but simple, physical, brutal murder, ordered by a human brain and carried out by two human hands. Not her hands, and not her brain. She was absolved; this at least she *knew* she had not done, nor caused to be done. Someone else had been prowling the woods at midnight, spying on them. A dead twig had cracked underfoot, and Friedl had shrugged it away as of no significance. And if this was plain, workaday murder, then surely so had Robin's death been, long ago.

Not hers at all, never hers, neither the act nor the guilt. All she had been was the diversion, the instrument, the fool of God blundering about helplessly in the path of some other force not troubled with a conscience.

There was someone else, then, who had wanted Friedl dead. There was someone else who had wanted Robin dead. What a fool she had been, what an inflated fool, thinking herself so important that heaven would put itself out to spread its light-

511

nings round her! Humility came to her aid now, she saw herself small and accidental, ridiculously irrelevant. Some other more urgent, more practical reason must account for these deaths. Someone else's advantage, or profit, or threatened security.

So *why*? Why kill Robin? Why kill Friedl? These two deaths, however far divided in time, could not be separate. There was no possibility of mere coincidence. Friedl had lived safely enough here all those years, but she had not long survived once she began to answer questions on this one subject. Questions which it seemed had never been asked by anyone before. She was malevolent and talkative, and she died. Someone had reason to fear her tongue. Someone who knew all about Robin Aylwin's death. Someone who flourished in anonymity and did not wish to be investigated, someone who could not permit curiosity, who could not *afford* curiosity!

The more she considered what knowledge she had, the more certain did it seem to her that the murderer of Robin and the murderer of Friedl Schiffer were one and the same. Why else should it be necessary to stop Friedl's mouth?

It seems, she told the bright, transfigured self in her glass, that these things began happening because I began to probe Robin's disappearance. His death, though I didn't know that at the time, not for certain. So that gives us all the more reason for continuing to probe, but also all the more reason for doing it very, very carefully, and thinking out and covering up every move before we make it. Above all, for going over every single word either of us got out of Friedl. Because she must have told us more than we've realised yet, if only we can find out which bits are really significant.

Tomorrow, she promised herself, I shall have help. Over lunch I'll tell him all this, he'll know how to go on from there, what we ought to do. Go straight to the police and tell them all we know and all we guess, or hold back until we have more to offer? I've already lied, I can bear to stay a liar until then, because he's implicated, too, once I admit what I know about last night. I can make no move until I've seen him.

So that was settled, and she was left staring in delight and disbelief at that shining image before her, with gentian eyes dilated and radiant, and a soft flush of excitement like summer bloom on her pale cheeks. She thought, astonished: He's never really seen me, and I've never really seen him. We shall be meeting for the first time!

At about the same hour of the afternoon when Maggie celebrated her miraculous restoration to sanity and health by washing her hair and giving her favourite dress to a chambermaid to be pressed, Francis Killian was standing beside a grave in the small cemetery of Felsenbach, five miles inside the German frontier.

A little excursion over the border into the Allgäu, itself a very charming district and on terms of intimate exchange with its southern neighbours, is a normal enough way of spending a day if you happen to be a tourist in the northern Vorarlberg or the north-western Tirol. And since English tourists habitually visit churches, even those tourists who hardly ever enter a church at home, Francis had felt it to be natural enough to make for the churchyard and do his own hunting, rather than risk asking leading questions in any of the inns of Felsenbach, let alone the one which belonged to the husband of Marianne Waldmeister. Buried, Friedl had said, as a charity, and with a stone over him, but without a name. That should be data enough to identify what Francis was looking for. If there was a stone there would be some inscription on it, if only to call attention to the piety of the donor.

Felsenbach lay in a shallow bowl among the hills, with the river circling round it, one bank deeply undercut. In the spring thaw this insignificant little stream would come down fast and bring a great deal of the débris of the higher lands with it. Now in the moist, mild September weather the Rulenbach ran lamblike round the northern edge of the village, and threatened no one.

The church lay on the southern fringe of the village, on rising ground, and the cemetery spread over a gentle plateau behind it. An old church, squat, whitewashed, with an onion cupola weathered to a beautiful Indian red. Its thick walls had a heavy batter, its windows were small and sunk far into the masonry like deep-set eyes. The burial ground, too, was old and thickly populated. Francis saw confronting him a miniature forest of close-planted, rigid little trees, wooden-shafted trees with complicated foliage of iron filigree and paper blossoms, and violet mourning ribbons turning a uniform dun-colour with age and weather.

He made several exposures of the church, in case anyone was interested in his activities, though it seemed unlikely, and one of the valley from over the tiled crest of the boundary wall; and then he began to move among the graves, taking a picture here and there. The display of iron-work was fantastic enough to turn any addict camera-happy. Most of the older memorials, the carved wooden crosses and pale stone kerbs, bore framed photographs of the dead, some of them so worn and faded that only a feature or two survived, a vast moustache from early in the century, a pair of unwavering, sad eyes, a piled nest of frizzy hair. Some of the newer granite headstones had their frontal surfaces glazed black, to carry more permanent and more startling reminders of the people they commemorated, portraits engraved into the glaze to last as long as the stone. These were never going to mellow into anonymity, every rain washed them clean, even if every All Souls' Day had not turned out the survivors with detergent and chamois leather to make sure not a line was lost.

It took him an hour or more to find the one he was looking for, but once found there was no mistaking it. It was tucked into a far corner of the cemetery, close to the waste plot where old flowers and garlands were piled together to await destruction, and it was the only stone he saw which was both modern and neglected. The charity which had buried Robin Aylwin could not be expected to visit him annually and clean him up for the festival of the dead; and even if the church took care of this task, the grave had had almost a year now to get overgrown. The grass was roughly trimmed back from it, there was still one faded wreath, but the black mirror of the squat headstone was filmed here and there with a thin layer of grey lichen. Nevertheless, its most startling aspect was immediately apparent; above the inscription there was an engraving of what was certainly a human head.

Francis found himself a fine sliver of shale, and began to pare away the growth of lichen, and then with a handful of moist paper flowers from the waste heap scrubbed the surface clean. The thing sprang out at him unnervingly clear and improbable. It was a human head, certainly, and with enough individuality in the face to suggest a portrait; but it differed from all the rest in being recumbent and seen in half-face, as you might have seen it if you had been called to identify it on a slab in the morgue. The eyelids were closed, the young features frozen into the lofty detachment of death. The thick hair, streaming back from the bland forehead as if still heavy with the water of the Scheidenauersee, had yet a suggestion of waves in it. The lips, full and firm, curled a little at the corners with a suggestion of the self-confidence of life. In its way it was an impressive piece, a pious generalisation for drowned youth, and yet with a markedly individual personality of its own.

Which, of course, was absurd! *Or was it?* Granted the corpse must have been at least four months in the water before it came ashore, they had been the winter months of almost total frost. Even if the clothes had been a complete loss, as Friedl had said, the body might still have retained some indications of its living appearance, enough to guide a skilled man. The doctor who conducted the post-mortem might even have advised on a reconstruction from the bones of the face. Given the interest, it could be done. But would the result look like this? Or perhaps it was entirely fanciful; the romantic and morbid German temperament, Francis reflected, had done stranger things than this in its time. And perhaps some rich man not far from the end of his span was concerned rather with making his own soul than salvaging Robin Aylwin's. The elaboration of his offering was what mattered.

Beneath the portrait – for reconstructed or imaginary, it was a portrait – was an inscription in German. Francis translated it loosely, and wondered:

'Pray for the repose of an unknown young man, drowned in the Rulenbach, and for those who erected this memorial over him.

February 1956.'

A modest donor, he had left his own name out of it along with the necessary omission of the victim's. Francis used up the rest of his film on the grave. The light was still good, and the definition in the engraving excellent. Developing the results would not be so easy, but at this time of year the backlog of work in the local studio would not be great, and a little persuasion and a discreet bribe might get him his pictures by tomorrow morning if he hurried back and handed over the film now. He would have preferred to spend a little time in making friends with the photographer and getting him to lend his darkroom, but with a police investigation going on in Scheidenau even so small a departure from the norm would invite attention. No, better just be a tourist in a hurry, there was nothing abnormal about that.

He went to the trouble, before he departed, to inspect every face of the stone. There was something about it that made him uneasy, something small and prosaic in which it differed from its kind, quite apart from the macabre quality of the work involved; but for the life of him he could not put his finger on it.

516

The House of Green Turf

He picked up his car in the square, and drove back through the valley towards Austria. For two or three miles the road was a gentle rise with open meadow views. Then, in the belt of country near the frontier, there were broken woodlands and outcrop rocks, and more than one short but dramatic defile between high walls of forest and cliff. In this complex countryside echoes played strange tricks. Occasionally he would have sworn that he was about to meet another car, yet nothing appeared, and it seemed that the sound of his own engine was being flung back to him from some oblique face of rock ahead. Twice he thought he caught the note of a car following him, and once went so far as to cut his engine and slide in among the trees to see if anything passed by; but nothing did, and as soon as the note of his own motor ceased he was surrounded by a profound silence. It was a dark, enclosed road, little frequented at this time of year. He completed the ascent, and emerged into the comparative daylight of the westward side, winding down among rolling meadows to the Customs' barrier. A bored official urged him through. In twenty minutes he was passing the Alte Post and entering Scheidenau.

In the darkness under the trees he stood and watched her windows, but he went no nearer than the water's edge, where the public path in the little park ended; for she was there, safe, he need not wonder about her tonight.

She was singing. The notes of the piano prelude drifted across the lambent silver of the water, refined into unearthly purity and clarity. And then the voice, molten gold, pouring out on the air a passion of hope and longing.

> '*Die Welt wird schöner mit jedem Tag,*
> *Man weiss nicht, was noch werden mag,*
> *Das Blühen will nicht enden . . .*'

Walled in and overshadowed with autumn, murder and sorrow,

she sang about spring and hope and certainty, proclaimed that the world grew more beautiful every day, that no one could guess what miracle would happen next, what prodigy of blossom burst before a man's eyes. And you would have thought, he reflected with an aching heart, that she truly believed it, she in her sickness and loneliness and undefined danger. Such a demon she had in her, and so little did it consider her. If he had not known in what extremity he had unwillingly left her that morning, he would have said, yes, this is the acme of joy.

'*Es blüht das fernste, tiefste Tal.*
Nun, armes Herz, vergiss der Qual!
Nun müss sich alles, alles wenden,
Nun müss sich alles, alles wenden.'

Now, poor heart, forget your pain; Now everything, everything must change!

I wish, he thought, following the last droplet of the postlude to its silvery resolution far over the lake, I wish I believed it. For you it may yet, my beautiful, my darling, for you it shall if I can make it. But not for me.

Chapter 8

Maggie pushed open the door of the restaurant Zum Bären just ten minutes after noon. He was there before her, credibly installed alone at one of the smaller tables for two. He saw her come, and his face, after the first blank glance, lit up with what she took for a creditable impersonation of a rather bored tourist spotting a totally unexpected acquaintance, though in fact the bravery of her appearance and the bloom that awakening had cast over her pallor and frailty had dazzled him out of all pretence. Maggie had been right, he was seeing her for the first time; the trouble was that he did not realise it. What he believed he was seeing, blessedly reassuring and agonisingly lovely though he found it, was what she could do by way of putting on a show when her life and future were at stake. Even so, he marvelled and adored her for it; but he would have been very chary indeed of taking it as genuine.

She walked across the room between the tables with her head up and her eyes roving, and her stride was young and elastic and easy, it would have done for the self-confident débutante she had never been. She made to pass him, and then looked straight at him, and halted, swinging upon him with delighted face and eagerly outstretched hand.

'Mr. Killian! Well, what are *you* doing here? How nice to see you!'

Not overdone, either, he thought with rueful approval; the voice still subdued, meant only for him, even the gesture preserving a thoroughly English restraint. She was, after all, an experienced opera singer, and no one needs acting skill more.

It was at that moment that he observed the man who had entered so unobtrusively after her. A tall man in a grey suit, who was just hanging up his hat and taking a seat at a table not too close to them, but strategically placed beside a pillar faced on its six sides with mirrors. He had his back to them, and the table was so aligned that Francis could not even see his face in the mirrors, but the stranger had only to turn his head a little to keep a close eye on them.

On his feet, beaming painfully at the apparition of beauty that was not and never could be his, going through the motions of inviting her to join him, seating her devotedly, Francis said into her ear, with no change of expression or intonation: 'You've picked up a shadow. No, don't look round! He's several yards away, he can't hear us if we're careful, but he has us under observation. Keep acting, and slip in what you want to say among the chatter.'

He felt her stiffen for an instant, but when he sat down opposite her she was smiling at him. 'How wonderful to meet somebody to whom I can talk in English. My German has been strained to the limit. Police, do you mean?'

'Yes, plain clothes. Very discreet. But for the hat I'd have said English.' He handed her the menu. 'Tell me what you're doing here?'

Frowning over a plethora of dishes, she said, 'Convalescing. But it seems I may have picked the wrong place. You'll have heard about our excitement? They were easily satisfied, it went all right. I got something, too, something definite.' She looked up at him over the long card with its border of vine-leaves. 'You think the venison would be a good idea?'

'I think it might. Beer or wine?'

'Wine. You choose.' She leaned her elbows on the table and

cupped her chin in her hands. It brought her a little nearer to him, and made it possible to use her fingers to screen the movement of her lips. '*Friedl was murdered. He told me there were fingermarks round her throat.*'

Francis kept the easy social smile fixed on his face; he had to, the man by the mirrors had just shifted his chair very slightly to have them more favourably in view.

'There's an open red wine, a local, shall we try it? *The police told you that?*'

'*Yes.* All right, let's.' She sat back as the waiter approached to take their order. This was not the interview to which she had looked forward. The very smile she was obliged to wear was becoming cramped and painful. Between trivialities they might manage to convey the bare bones of what they had to say to each other, but she would be no nearer knowing whether he believed her, nor could this kind of exchange ever communicate what she felt, the extraordinary sense of deliverance, the revealing quality of the light now that the shadow of guilt had dissolved from over her. This was the first meeting with him to which she had ever come with an open heart, willing to let him in to her, and because of the stranger watching them they must still remain apart. But she tried. As soon as the soup was served and the waiter had left them she lifted to his face one clear, unsmiling glance. '*I'm cured,*' she said.

If he had understood, he made no sign. To talk under these circumstances, in the sense of using language in order to effect a communion between two people, was impossible, and he was not going to attempt it. All they could do was exchange information. Some day there would be a time for doing more than that, but not now. 'She was strangled?'

'He didn't say that. Just that there were fingermarks on her throat. Apart from that there's been nothing. I'm just staying in and having a thoroughly lazy time. How about you? Have you got a car here?'

'I hired one in Zurich. Had it waiting for me at the airport.'

521

He busied himself with refilling her glass until the waiter had served their venison and left them to enjoy it.

'And have you found anywhere interesting to visit round here?'

'I was over in Germany yesterday,' he said. 'I went over to look up an old acquaintance, as a matter of fact. In Felsenbach.' Obliquely he told her the bare facts of his find, scattered along the way on a verbal conducted tour of one corner of the Allgäu.

'You must show me your pictures some time,' she said.

'You may not like them. It could be said I choose rather offbeat targets.' He had the sharpest and best of the prints already folded into the menu. 'Would you like something to follow?' He held out the card to her across the table, open, the blown-up photograph carefully secured by a forefinger. 'See what you think.'

Her eyes lit upon the starkly outlined face just before her fingers touched, and for an instant the colour was shocked out of her cheeks. Her mask shook, and was resolutely clamped back into place. She took the menu from him, and sat steadily gazing at the print.

'Yes, I think so. *Yes . . .*'

'An idealised guess?'

'*A likeness.* The way the eyes are set . . . *and the mouth . . .*' But for Friedl's thirteen-year-old treasure it might have been hard for her to recall that exact curl of the lips. 'Formalised, but really a likeness.' In Friedl's picture the full lids had also covered and hidden the eyes, whose colour she could not remember, and the lips had borne this same shadow of a smile. Maggie handed the menu back with composure. 'I'll just have fruit, I think. And coffee.'

Francis palmed the print and slipped it back into his pocket under the table. The setting of the eyes she had remarked on first; well, that could be guessed at even after months, better than a guess, in fact. There is nothing much more durable than bone. But the mouth . . . That was another matter. The soft tissue of the lips, even if it survived through the frost, surely would not retain much of its normal shape after being buffeted downstream in the thaw.

Maggie peeled a pear with rather strained attention, and asked brightly, without looking up: 'Have you any plans for this afternoon?'

'I thought I might have another drive in the same direction. There are some rather good woodcarvers over there, I might have a look what's to be found. Other artists, too.'

'*Take me with you!*' she said.

The first time she had ever asked him for anything except in return for a fee, and it was the one thing he would not and could not do for her. He wanted her safe in the Goldener Hirsch, with the police on the premises and a good lock on the door.

'If I were you I should stay in and get plenty of rest. With all this disturbance you must have been under a good deal of strain. Stay in, let them see you're there on call, not anxious, not involved.'

'I suppose it might be a good idea,' she admitted.

'Wait for me tonight. I'll come to you as soon as I can. By the verandah. Then we can talk.'

'*Yes!*' she said eagerly. She set down her empty coffee cup, and looked at him for a moment helplessly and hopefully across the table. '*You will come?*'

'I'll come.'

'What do we do about getting out of here? You think it's me he wants, or you? Shall we leave together?'

'No, you go first, I want to see if he follows.'

'At least we gave him time to eat his lunch,' said Maggie, and her fixed and tortured brightness dissolved for a moment into a real, youthful, entrancing smile. What might she not be, he thought, if only he could get her safe out of this with her recovered innocence unspotted?

'All right, you say when!'

He wanted her to sit there for a long time, smiling at him like that, but he had a lot to do before he could come to her room at night by the verandah staircase, and he wanted her watched and guarded while he did it. 'When!' he said, and groaned inwardly at seeing her rise. He came to his feet with her, hurried to draw out her chair and help her into her light grey coat. 'Don't go out at all,' he said into her ear, 'not anywhere!'

She marshalled coat and gloves and handbag, made feminine gesture in the direction of her hair without actually touching it, and held out her hand to him.

'Thank you, Francis, it was a lovely lunch. *I shall look forward to seeing you.*'

She was gone, weaving between the tables with her long, free, recovered stride. He stood for a few moments to watch her go, and then sat down again slowly, and lit a cigarette over the dregs of his coffee. His ears were full of her voice speaking his name for the first time, a stunning music, but full of cruel overtones. Gratitude and kindness can do terrible injuries, with the best intentions. It ought to be enough to be of service to her. It had to be enough, there wasn't going to be anything else for him.

The tall man in the grey suit was paying his bill, and rising at leisure to collect his hat from the stand. It was nice to have been right about something, at least. He kept his head negligently turned away as he walked to the door, but one mirror picked up his image in passing and gave Francis a glimpse of a thin, faintly whimsical, pensive face, of deep and generous lines and little flesh, with hair greying at the temples, and deep-set, quiet eyes.

Not, by any stretch of imagination, an Austrian face. Hat or no hat, that was an English sportscoat, and an English countenance.

Now what were the English police doing here in the Vorarlberg, tramping hard on Maggie Tressider's heels?

He fretted about her all the way to Felsenbach. But when all was considered, she was best and safest in the Goldener Hirsch, with the Austrian police deployed round her on a murder hunt. He had no doubt at all of the accuracy of what she had managed to tell him. Friedl had been, if not strangled, half-strangled and thrown into the lake. Whatever the eccentricity of Maggie's behaviour, they would not suspect her of an act like that. A woman may perhaps push another woman into a lake, but by and large, it is only men who strangle women. By and large, it is only men who have the necessary hand-span and the necessary force. No, he could leave her for a few hours. And after that, their best course might well be to go together and tell their entire story to the investigators, and leave the rest to them. For the more complex this business became, the more certain did he feel that Maggie was entirely and tragically innocent, a helpless victim caught into somebody else's schemes only by her hyper-sensitive conscience, and by the accident of a car smash which had shaken her off-balance and put all her defence mechanisms out of gear.

What was ironical was that only after talking to her had he had been able to put his finger on the thing that was most wrong with Robin Aylwin's gravestone. All that gratuitous anonymity! The victim, of course, couldn't be named, no one knew, or admitted to knowing, his name. But not only was the donor also anonymous; most improbable of all, there was not a name, not an initial, not even a mason's mark, anywhere on that stone to identify the memorial artist who made it! Unheard-of, for the craftsman in death not to avow his work! A monumental mason is a businessman, a tradesman like other tradesmen, he wants his excellence known.

This one didn't. Why?

There was only one monumental mason in Felsenbach, indeed only one mason of any kind, a builder of long establishment who employed none but his own family, the ramifications of which ran into three generations. Gravestones, kerbs, vaults he took in his patriarchal stride. He remembered the corpse from the Rulenbach, he remembered the funeral; but he had had no part in the business of burial or monument. Some wealthy resident of Regenheim, he recalled, had paid for the interment out of goodness of heart, and the small municipality of Felsenbach had naturally raised no objection. No doubt some mason from Regenheim had been employed to make the memorial, afterwards. The donor would obviously look on his own doorstep.

It was another fifteen miles to Regenheim, an undulating, busy road this time, clear of the mountain slopes. The place, when he arrived there, was no bigger than Felsenbach, but unmistakably more a town. There was a square almost large enough for aircraft landings, a waste of cobbles populated by a handful of cars. There were four or five cramped streets eddying out of it, overhung by black and white houses, tottering archways and jutting upper stories. There was a sprawl of modern villa-buildings beyond. And it was raining. The place had not got its name for nothing.

He parked the Dodge in the square and set about locating whatever monumental masons the town might hold. It was already evening, he had lost more time than he had bargained for in reaching this place. He bought some cigarettes at a solid family shop which was still open, and probably would continue so until ten o'clock provided one of the family happened to be spending the evening at home. The woman who served him was elderly and at leisure, and looked as if she and her forebears had been there since Regenheim's free-city days. If anyone knew where to put a finger on every tradesman in the town, she would.

She was very willing to talk, and showed no surprise at being asked for the local furbishers of graves. There were, she said, only two of any substance. One of them, the oldest established, had his mason's yard behind his own house, and he or one of his sons could always be found there. The other had built himself a new villa out on the edge of the town. She gave copious directions for finding it. Then there was, of course, the Klostermann outfit, still in business, though they had few clients now, that side of the family's trade had been neglected since they went in for road haulage. Indifferently she gave him instructions for finding even this unlikely firm, though her large shrug said that she herself wouldn't consider taking them any of her business.

The head of the old-established house happened to be putting away his pick-up in the corner of the yard. He took out a pair of gold-rimmed glasses to inspect the photographs Francis offered him. No, he had never seen this stone before. If he was curious he did not show it; he had been in the world something like seventy years, and learned to concentrate on his own business, and the discipline had paid him well.

The second one, the dweller in the new villa, was a younger man, a go-ahead type with social ambitions and a look of the townsman about him. The villa was aggressively modern and ostentatious, the wife who opened the door was decorative and well-padded. Francis apologised for calling on them out of the blue and at such an hour, and made it clear at once that he wanted only five minutes of their time. He needed, as it turned out, even less than that.

'Thirteen years ago!' said the man of the house, and shook his head decisively. 'That is before we came here to open our business. We are from München, we have been here only seven years. I am sorry!'

Which left only the family Klostermann, of whom the old woman in the tobacconist's had thought so poorly. It was getting dark by then, so Francis was torn two ways; but he was not going back without having a look at even so dim a possibility. He threaded the outer edge of the town, and turned back towards the square by side streets that lacked both the black and white fascination of the town centre and the green spaciousness of the suburbs, but were merely utilitarian early-twentieth-century, without squalor or distinction. And there, sure enough, was a dark and almost empty window, once designed for display, with nothing left in it now but a dusty imitation-marble urn, and a shelf of granite vases with perforated aluminium flower-holders. Beside it the high wall of a yard ran for some distance, double

527

doors set in it. The upper windows were dark, the house was not lived in. But the paint on the gates was new.

The whole place appeared deserted, and Francis might have gone away and left it at that; but as he was turning back to the car a man came briskly along the pavement from the direction of the square, fitted a key into the lock of the yard doors, and let himself in. A thickset, youngish man in a belted leather jacket and a black beret, with a battered briefcase under his arm. Francis gave him a minute or two, and then followed him in. He had left the heavy door ajar, and his lively footfalls clashed diagonally ahead over the cobbles. In the far corner of the yard, in a one-storey building obviously added to the original house, a light sprang up.

All one side of the yard was garage doors, and several lorries and vans stood ranged along another wall. Behind the frosted window of what seemed to be the office the dark shape of the leather-coated young man moved vaguely. In a corner of the yard some relics of the expiring monumental business mouldered gently, synthetic granite kerbing, a half-shaped headstone, a small, drooping angel leaning on a cross.

Francis rapped at the office door and pushed it open before him. The man in the leather jacket swung round from the desk under the window, his briefcase open in one hand, a folder of papers in the other. The movement was silent, alert and surprised, but by no means alarmed. He had a smooth, well-fleshed face, high-coloured and bland, with round-set eyes of a bright and yet opaque black, like coal.

'*Was wünschen Sie?*' His voice was gravelly and deep, with no implications of either welcome or animosity.

'Herr Klostermann?'

No, he was not a Klostermann, it seemed. He relaxed, however, on finding that the late caller was looking for his boss. Francis went through his brief explanation for the third time, and produced his photographs. The young man bent his large head over them, breathing stertorously, and considered them for a few moments with respectful attention. Then he shook his head regretfully.

'I am sorry! I am with Herr Klostermann myself only two years. I drive for him. I came to pick up my delivery schedule for tomorrow. With the memorial business I have nothing to do. I do not know if he made this or not. If you could come tomorrow, he will be here.'

'I should like to get in touch with him now,' said Francis, 'if it's possible. I have to drive back to Scheidenau tonight, and I'd rather not have the same journey again if I can help it.'

'I am sorry!' He handed back the pictures, and closed his briefcase with deliberation, his round eyes still black and steady on Francis.

'Would there be records here for 1956?'

'No, no records. It is now chiefly a haulage business, everything else he has at his own house.'

'Could I go round there to see him now? It would be a great help to me.'

'I think he is not there,' said the gravelly voice gently. 'Wait, I will call the house for you, and see.'

He walked away into the dark corner of the room, and opened a narrow door there. His fingers touched the light switch within, and Francis caught a glimpse of a larger, less austere office, with filing cabinets from floor to ceiling along the visible wall, and some pleasant panelling beyond. Then the door was closed firmly between, and he was alone, free to move noiselessly after, and apply his eye to the minute keyhole, and then his ear to the thin panel of the door. It got him very little. There was a long table just within his vision, and the young man was leaning over it, telephone receiver at his ear, dialling a number; but the room within was larger than it seemed, and nothing more than an indistinguishable murmur reached the listener's ear. There was nothing whatever to make his thumbs prick. The young man had said he would telephone, and he was telephoning. A local number, too, or at least somewhere he could dial and get without delay. And he was already cradling the receiver, better get well away from the door before he reached it.

The door opened peacefully, the young man stood shaking his head sadly on the threshold. Behind him the light went out.

'I am sorry, Mr. Klostermann is at his married daughter's house for the evening. I can tell you how to reach him there, if you care to go? It is a farm, about five kilometres from here. You take the road from the square towards Kempten, then two kilometres on you come to a right-hand fork, the signpost says Maienbach. Follow that road for two kilometres, and on the left is a cart road to the farm. It is not hard to find. I should go and speak with Herr Klostermann there. He will not need records to know his own work.'

'No,' said Francis, 'I don't suppose he will. Thank you! If it's only five kilometres I might as well reach him now, and get it settled.'

'If you should have to ask, the name at the farm is Haimhofer.'

'Thank you very much!'

'*Bitte!*'

Francis walked purposefully across the yard, pulled the unlocked gates to behind him, got into his car and drove up towards the square with aplomb. Arrived there, he circled right-handed about the central parking space, and passed without a second glance the sign marked: Kempten. Reasonable or not, his thumbs were pricking almost painfully. He took the road for Felsenbach, and stepped hard on the accelerator as soon as he emerged from the narrow confines of the streets. He was heading back towards Scheidenau as fast as he could go.

He was past Felsenbach, half-way to the frontier and immured between encroaching plantations of conifers, before he could be quite certain that he was being followed. There were all yesterday's prickings of uneasiness, all yesterday's minute outward signs, but magnified by the extreme, washed clarity of the air. The rain had scrubbed the atmosphere clean as bone, sounds carried as in an echo-chamber. When he stopped his engine for a moment under the trees on a sharp bend, there was not so much a perceptible sound of an engine following, as the vibration of a motor just cut out, by some hypersensitive perception, to match his. Then the superhuman silence. They were there, not too far behind, not too close on his tail; they knew where he was, and were not anxious to overhaul him, as long as they could hold him at this convenient distance, and be sure of not losing him. He wondered what spot they would choose, where they would elect to close the gap. He wished he carried a gun, but knew it was not his weapon and not his style, and that he would have been useless with it even if he had had one. There are killers and non-killers. Guns don't make them.

He was on the climbing sector now, bend after sharp bend, the margins unfenced and with only shallow ditches, the trees crowding close. Silence all round, apart from his own re-echoing sounds, and darkness but for his own head-lights glazing and gilding the embossed trunks of the trees, the inset panels of mirror, the scoured faces of rock. If he craned to look upwards he could not distinguish a line where earth and sky met. It had rained fitfully all the way, and was raining still. The sky was shrouded, there were no stars, and no moon.

There must have been someone watching for him, to make sure that he took the Kempten road and drove into the trap. Maybe they had lost time in setting out after him when he swung past it and turned towards Austria, but he had been fool enough to mention Scheidenau, and they were on his heels now, he was sure of that. The young man in the leather jacket had loosed the hunt after him with a vengeance, and if he was going to shake it, it would have to be now, on this complex stretch where the echoes would play on both sides, and confuse every issue. He put his foot down hard, and gave the car its head. The bends were well engineered, a joy to drive round, but also blind and deaf, at every swing light and sound cut off together, sharp as the descent of a guillotine.

All his senses were so trained on the threat behind that he was, in any case, curiously vulnerable to any hazards ahead. Anything approaching from Austria was his friend and ally, he had no need to be wary of it. Where there was company on the road there was safety. Who could close on him and attack while neutral headlights were bearing down on the scene?

He swung at speed round a right-handed bend, sharp as a shrew's elbow, and straight into the glare of headlights cut off sharp by the curtain of dark trees. Someone was running along the road towards him, a torch in an extended hand waving him down. He braked sharply and drew in to the right, and the face and the torch plunged to a halt and turned back, running alongside him. On the left of the road headlights leaned drunkenly into the ditch. A panting voice alongside implored him:

'*Bitte . . . bitte, halt! Unfall . . .*'

Somebody else's accident was due to be Francis Killian's salvation. Why not buttonhole the pursuers, too, from safe ambush among the victims, flag them down and send them back to call an ambulance, if necessary, or the police? What an irony! Francis pulled in obediently to the side of the road, half on the bald grass verge, swung open the door and piled out of the car, turning to meet the young man who came panting towards him with the torch. He saw a young, frightened, boyish face, wild with relief, blazing at him wide-open welcome.

Something hit him hard on the back of the head. The lights and darks exploded before him, changed places, merged, blinked out into single and absolute darkness. The ground came up and struck him in the face, scoring his cheek and lips raw. He groped along the grass, and the grains of loam were large as boulders. Dimly his mind pursued logic, argued, reproached him. The enemy were in front, not behind. *Then who was behind?* Someone else, assiduous on his heels, but not the enemy. The enemy were these shadows who had struck him down. *Enemies of the enemy, perhaps?* Leave them a sign! Not far behind, he had wondered when they would close the gap. The fingers of his right hand,

The House of Green Turf

hooked deep into his left inside pockets, gouged out the wallet that held his photographs, and spilled it into the lush, overgrown autumn grass in the ditch below him. He prised himself up arduously from the ground, the lighter by that load, his head spinning, and levered himself upright on wavering legs, one arm flailing to ward off the first assault.

They were three, he saw them clearly, even photographed them on some emulsion in his mind, his eyes recording nothing. The image sank in, and left his eyes blind.

Two of the three rushed him, one from either side. The third, the boy with the torch, swerved round him as he swayed to his feet, and plunged on. Francis stiff-armed the first of his attackers half across the road, but the second one was on his back in the same moment, one arm crooked round his neck, dragging him over backwards into the shallow ditch. They rolled confusedly together, the wet grass stinging and cold against their faces.

Francis heard a car door slam and a motor thrum into life, and knew it for the note of his hired Dodge from Zurich. Its lights swung impetuously forward and back, forward and back in the road, cutting yellow swathes out of the darkness as it turned, and then it surged past them and roared away at speed in the direction of Felsenbach. That was the last thing Francis knew. His assailant enveloped him suddenly in both arms, and rolled over beneath him, holding him helpless and exposed for the second blow. This time the man with the cosh made no mistake.

The world exploded in a flash of light, and collapsed into chaotic darkness. Francis slid slowly into the ditch, and lay still.

Chapter 9

The blanket of cloud on the heights had ripped into tatters and begun to dissolve away just before the smooth sound of the car ahead, steadily climbing, braked into a protesting whine, and the minor confusion of voices, barely audible, nevertheless made itself felt against the surrounding silence.

'*Now* what?' grunted George, who was driving. He put his foot down, willing to narrow the gap a little; nobody was going to hear them approaching, not until they reached that right-hand bend. They were making too much noise themselves, up there. *They*! Somebody had been waiting for Francis Killian, somebody for whom he wasn't prepared, by all the signs. George wanted to know who. 'I'm tired of this,' he said aloud, 'I'm closing up. Hang on, here we go!'

But there they didn't go, or no farther than the twenty yards or so it took him to brake sharply, swing the wheel, wallow across the ditch where a rough logging track crossed it, and burrow an abrupt and hazardous way in among trees on their right. For at that instant both he and his passenger had caught the sudden rocketing plunge of the Dodge into gear, the sawing alternations of its lunges fore and aft as it turned, and the triumphant roar as it launched into high speed. Its headlights were slicing round the fringe of the trees as the little black police Volkswagen rocked and waddled to a standstill deep among the

534

firs, and George cut motor and lights and prayed that they had been neither seen nor heard.

The young Austrian detective had the passenger door open before the car was still, and was groping and stumbling his way back the few yards to the road. George, afraid to leave the wheel, clawed his way round to peer intently over the back of the driving seat. The car from Zurich shot by at speed, hurtling back the way it had come a few minutes ago, with enough aggression and bravura in the driving to demonstrate blind that it was driven now by another hand. Somebody crude, young and violent. They had followed Francis Killian yesterday, they knew his touch. George never saw the face behind the wheel, but he knew it was not Francis Killian's face. He began to back his way out, tickling the wheel this way and that, grateful that he had grazed nothing in getting in, and fastidiously sensitive to the hazards in getting out. The Austrian detective came running, clambering back into his place and slamming the door just short of the last tree.

'Not your man . . . young fellow driving . . . Couldn't see any passenger. Which way now?'

'Ahead!' said George, and didn't wait to have his judgment endorsed. They swayed drunkenly out on to the road. George cut the lights to sidelights, and nosed uphill, swinging the wheel for the turn.

There were other headlights, somewhere a hundred yards or so round that hairpin, manœuvring rapidly but gently back and forth in a turn, just as the Dodge had done, but this time in the other direction. Their beams lurched upwards and levelled out, as though the car was just heaving itself clear of the ditch, and then danced forward and back and forward again, and the dwindling arc of their light wheeled, threaded the edge of the trees for an instant, and recoiled as the car came round, leaving the bend in the road darkened. But only for a moment. The moon sailed out from rags of cloud, pouring a wash of pallor down the tall faces of rock ahead, and bleaching the hunched shoulder of the bend to the white of bone. George accepted the omen with aplomb, and switched off his lights altogether. He went round the curve on faith and moonlight, hugging the dark side.

The car that had just heaved itself out of the ditch opposite and turned was drawn up now, somewhat farther ahead than George had estimated, engine running, wheels barely turning, close to the grass verge. On the verge itself, faintly outlined by the roof-light through the open door, one man was stooping with his arms about the end of a long, unwieldy bundle, which he was thrusting into the rear seat of the car. Someone else was already in there ahead of it, hauling it in. A limp, dead weight, all too recognisable as the feet were dragged aboard and the door slammed on them. The inside light blinked off, blinked on again as the front passenger door opened to let the last man leap aboard, blinked out once again as the car, broad and powerful, soared into speed and shot away.

Three to one, counting the man at the wheel; four, taking into account the young one whose job it was to whip away the hired Dodge somewhere into Germany, and no doubt get it a new paint job and a changed registration before daylight tomorrow. Much chance Francis Killian had had, George thought grimly, drawing a bead on the receding rear lights, with his foot flat to the floor and his lights still off. If they were, as he hoped, still undetected, they might as well stay that way as long as possible. The road surface, thank God, wasn't bad at all, and the fitful moonlight made the edge of the grass show up like a kerb; and there was nothing meeting them, and at this hour of the night, with luck, there might be nothing all the way to the crest and the frontier. The lights ahead would indicate the bends, and give him a chance to use his sidelights without being spotted. With luck! With, in fact, a lot more luck than Francis Killian had had.

At the moment the chief trouble was that the big car in front was gaining rapidly.

'Mercedes, I think!' yelled the young Austrian in his ear, peering excitedly after the shape ahead. His name was Werner Frankel, and he had been assigned to George as escort and assistant because he had received the whole of his primary education and most of his advanced education in English, as a refugee with his family during and after the war. 'We shan't overhaul *him!*'

There was no arguing with that; they would be lucky if they could even keep those diminishing tail-lights in view.

'Any hope of a telephone up here?' asked George, keeping his foot down hard, and his eye on the distant spark.

'Yes, an inn, half a mile ahead. You won't see it, but I'll tell you.' They were both thinking on the same lines, and it was pleasing to find that they both knew it, without any waste of words. 'Drop me off there, and try to hang on to him.'

'Sure? You know these roads better than I do.'

'You don't speak German,' said Werner unanswerably.

George would have managed to make himself understood somehow, but Werner wouldn't even have to try, and delay was what they could least afford.

'You'll call the German police, too? They might pick up the Dodge before they get it into hiding.' Nobody was going to be able to identify it afterwards, that was plain. 'And the frontier, in case. Though I doubt if they'll risk the frontier . . . not on the road.'

'At night it could be a very nominal check . . . they might. If they try some other way over, it has to be a rough one. You'll have a better chance of staying with him.'

'And the other side? What choice of roads?'

'After Scheidenau, it has to be Bregenz or Langen. I'll call both. Pity we weren't near enough to get a number, but a Mercedes in a hurry . . . black or dark blue? . . . I'd say black.'

'And the Dodge you know.' A cigarette-end in the dark, the sole trace of the Mercedes, vanished round one more bend ahead. George switched on dipped headlights, and made up a

537

little of the lost ground while there was a ridge of rock between them.

'The Dodge I know. Slow round this bend, my inn's on the right. You'll see a track going off uphill.'

George saw the pole first, the telephone wire sliding away from the road. He braked to a halt where the climbing path began, and Werner was out like a greyhound. 'Good luck!' He waved and darted away into the dark; and George ranged through the Volkswagen's willing gears and set off doggedly after the vanished Mercedes.

And now he was on his own, and any communing he was going to do would be done strictly with himself. But give Werner ten minutes with that telephone, and there would be large numbers of invisible allies turning out to his aid. He could use as many as he could get. The outfit that could plant four men and that kind of car to pick off Francis Killian had plenty of resources at its disposal. The thing began to look promisingly big. Big, thorough, and highly sensitive to any display of curiosity. Now which of those calls Killian had made today in Regenheim could have caused Them – whoever *They* were! – to set up this efficient ambush?

No doubt about now Werner would be reeling off the whole list to the German police, and leaving them to do the rest. If he was fast enough they might be able to stop the Dodge in Felsenbach, before some discreet garage doors closed on it somewhere – those double doors in Regenheim, perhaps? – and three or four waiting experts fell on it and transformed everything on it or in it that was transformable, and sent it out again to be palmed off on some innocent sucker the other side of the country. George had known the whole job done inside four hours, even in England, and in comparison with these big boys with the whole of Europe open to them the English were mere amateurs.

And if the car was meant to vanish without trace, ten thousand to one so was Francis Killian. Like anybody else who got too nosy about this complicated corner of Central Europe, about anonymous graves and mysterious disappearances. Like Robin Aylwin himself? Like Peter Bromwich? Hang on tightly enough to this one, thought George, picking up the distant spark and breathing again, and you may find out what happened to the others.

He wished he knew whether the men in that car knew he was there on their tail. His impression was that they did not, for though they were moving briskly, and had left him well behind, the fact remained that with their power they could have been much farther ahead of him had they wished. It looked as if speed, though important and desirable, was not the first consideration. They wouldn't wish to storm the frontier post as if they were in flight from the law; and if, on the other hand, they intended to evade Customs altogether, perhaps they had to look for a way not familiar to them. The crossing between Scheidenau and Felsenbach was a quiet one at any time, surely practically dead at night; but that might be a mixed blessing. Bored Customs men might take more interest in a car passing through than would those who had a constant stream of traffic. No, George's best bet was that they wouldn't go near the post. There are more ways over any hill frontier than are covered by the authorities.

About a mile to go now to the crest. If they were going to leave the road it must be soon, for the descent on the other side was through much more open country. It seemed that suddenly he was gaining on them a little; he could see the spark of red, obviously round another bend from his stretch of road, proceeding in a diagonal incline to the right, and now decidedly at a more sedate speed. He eased up slowly to hold his distance. Arrival at the point where he had seen the quarry change course gave him a shock, for he had been relying on the Mercedes as a guide, and travelling by mere unreliable moonlight or sidelights, or into the sharp cut-off of dipped headlights, which made progress hazardous and the angles of the road deceptive. So far from swinging to the right here, it turned somewhat to the left. He braked with his nose on the grass verge, and risked switching his lights on full beam for an instant. He had slightly overshot the opening of a narrow, stony track that branched off sharply to the right.

Where they could go, he could go, with room to spare. He backed a few yards, and turned into the track after them. His guess had been accurate, they had no intention of entering Austria by the road.

Now he had to use his lights, he would not have survived long without them. Luckily the driver of the Mercedes must also be having to concentrate hard, and the noise they were making up there would effectively drown out the noise he was making down here. Once launched on this track there was only one way to go, for trees and rocks encroached on it irregularly on either side. The surface was beaten earth, like any ramblers' path in the mountains, liberally toothed with outcrop rock and loose stones. In places it was more like a dried watercourse than a track, and in other places more like a bog than either, and reinforced with half-peeled logs laid as a causeway. It climbed steeply, twice negotiating narrow wooden bridges which George took at a crawl, forewarned by the earthquake rumblings his quarry had set up in crossing. Most of the time he lost sight of the Mercedes altogether, but from time to time he caught a glimpse of the rear lights, and knew he was holding his own. Caution, not haste, was what mattered to them here. He could even have closed up on them, at some risk, but he was unarmed, and there were three of them, almost certainly provided with guns. Much better hang back and remain undetected, as rather surprisingly he still seemed to be, until he could make contact with the reinforcements called out by Werner.

He had not the least idea at what point they re-entered Austria; there was never anything to mark the change. Nor had he any notion of how far they had come on this travesty of a road; three miles of strained attention can seem more like thirty. But it occurred to him suddenly that they had ceased to climb, and on either side of the belt of trees that shrouded them he could see the faintly lambent sky, still frayed with broken cloud. Then the descent, which was mercifully more gradual than the ascent had been, but still testing enough. The track, doubling like a coursed hare, tipped them abruptly into a lane enclosed between stone walls, no wider than the way they had come, but at once smoother, an ordinary dirt road that might have led to some isolated farm, and probably did. This in turn brought them at length to a metalled road, fields opening out on either side. George rolled the Volkswagen cautiously up to the turn, and cut his lights.

Now he knew where he was. They were back on the main road, a good mile on the Austrian side of the frontier; and well away to the right, solitary on the open sweep of road, the rear lights of the Mercedes were receding rapidly in the direction of Scheidenau.

On this highway no driver had the right to conclude that he was being followed, however many cars he observed behind him. George switched on his headlights, and set off at full speed in pursuit.

They circled Scheidenau by a ring road, and beyond the last lights of the village emerged again on to the steel-dark road that headed towards Bregenz. George had hung back at the turn, and let the Mercedes go ahead far enough to convince the driver he was unmarked. Perhaps he allowed him a little too much rope. It couldn't be long now. There should be either a road-block and a police check, or a patrol cruising this way to meet them, on the look-out for a dark-coloured Mercedes. So George idled contentedly his minute too long.

When he drove out on to the straight stretch along the floor of the valley there were no rear lights anywhere to be seen. He put on a spurt to reassure himself that the quarry was still around, but the night remained vacant, calm and clear. The moon was high, the wind had dropped, the rags of cloud had been fretted away into scattered threads. The road ahead was

541

utterly innocent of traffic going his way; and the first thing he encountered was one more black police Volkswagen, cruising gently along to meet him.

Somewhere between the edge of Scheidenau and this point rather less than a mile along the road, the Mercedes and its crew of three and their kidnapped man had all vanished without trace.

Chapter 10

Ever since midday the Alte Post had been taken over by a wedding party. Maggie could hear across the water the sound of their fiddles and guitars, and the blown drifts of singing that grew beerier and gayer as the evening drew in. Several times during the dusk the guests had made brief exploratory sallies down to the water, the women like bright, blown petals swept along in a gale, but each time the showers had driven them in again to their dancing and drinking. The array of lights winked across the lake; the windows had been closed against the rain, and only wisps of music emerged now when some door was opened. Every time that happened, the night seemed to be shaken and convulsed with a distant burst of gigantic laughter.

Maggie went in from the verandah with a few drops of rain sparkling in her hair, and a half-hearted ray of moonlight, the first to break through the clouds, following at her heels. It looked as though they meant to keep up the party all night over there, surely she could have another half-hour of practice before she closed the piano.

The old authentic delight had come back, the intoxication that had been missing for so long. She was alive again, she could sing, she hated to stop singing. When this was over she must get into form quickly, and go back to pick up the wonderful burden. When this was over!

She had not looked ahead at all yet; her vision stopped short, charmed and exalted, at the recognition of her own deliverance. What if that lunch at The Bear had proved only a torment and a frustration? It would not always be so. Francis had promised to come to her here, and he would come; and this time they would be able to talk freely. There had to be respect between them, and an honourable understanding, everything circumstances had made impossible before. It was still true, for all their efforts at noon, that they had never met. Maggie looked forward to their meeting now with passion and impatience; she wanted to know him, and she wanted to be known. The world is too full of impaired and partial contacts that achieve nothing, satisfy no need, do justice to no one. Their relationship should at least close on a better footing than that.

She had the Mahler song settings from 'Des Knaben Wunderhorn' on the piano. Contraltos are liable – Tom in one of his sourer moods had once remarked that there was no doubt about it being a liability! – to find themselves expected to include a good deal of Mahler in their recital programmes. Maggie, for her part, had no reservations at all. These full-dress romantic settings of folk-ballads four centuries old might stick in Tom's gullet, but they were strong wine to her.

> *Ich ging mit Lust durch einem grünen Wald,*
> *Ich hört die Völein singen.*

She sang that opening line, and as always it seemed to her a complete song in miniature, with a logical development, a single climax and a perfect resolution.

Many years ago, when she was first learning these songs, she had written in beneath the German words her own attempt at an English singing version. Her unfamiliarity with the original language had worried her, as though it stood between her and the depth of interpretation she wanted. It was easy enough to get someone to provide a literal translation into English, but the meaning divorced from the rhythm and feel of the German had been no help at all. She had wanted a true image, and the only way had been to make one for herself. She never thought of the songs now in her version, she no longer needed these stepping-stones into a world she knew better than her own heart. But in their time they had served their purpose.

> *As forth I went, all in the gay greenwood,*
> *To hear the birds a-singing . . .*

She sang it through in the English, with care and wonder, because now it was the English that seemed alien.

Curiously she turned the pages to see what she had made of some of the grander songs. 'Wo die schönen Trompeten blasen' belonged to the later set, originally conceived with orchestral accompaniment, and the piano was a poor substitute for those distant, haunting trumpet calls and drum rolls that hung like ominous storm-clouds over the illusion of happy reunion. The soft, brooding introduction came to hesitant life under her fingers, and her voice took up the doubtful, hopeful question with which the song opened:

> *Wer ist denn draussen, und wer klopfet an,*
> *Der mich so leise, so leise wecken kann?*

> *Who's that without there, who knocks at my door,*
> *Imploring so softly, so softly: Sleep no more?*

She had no intention of being asleep when Francis came . . .

> *Das ist der Herzallerliebste dein,*
> *Steh' auf und lass mich zu dir ein . . .*

> *Your love, your own true love is here,*
> *Rise up and let me in, my dear!*

545

And must I longer wait and mourn?
I see the red of dawn return . . .

. . . nor of keeping him waiting outside the door, patiently tapping, like the last time. This meeting had to pay a lot of debts.

. . . The red of dawn, two stars so bright.
O that I were with my delight,
With mine own heart's beloved!

. . . The maiden arose and let him in.
Most welcome home, my more than kin,
Most welcome home, my own true love . . .

She could not help remembering a moment in another hotel room, arms holding her, lips on hers, a voice whispering brokenly: Maggie, forgive me, forgive me! Whether she liked it or not, there was love also to be taken into account. You cannot demand truth, and then select half and throw the inconvenient remainder away. Something would have to be done even about love, if they were to be honest with each other.

Ah, do not weep, love, do not pine,
Within the year you shall be mine,
Ere long you shall be one with me
As never bride on earth shall be,
No, none but you on earth, love!

Across the heath to war I fare,
The great green heath so broad and bare . . .

She sang it through to the end, to the last hair-raising diminuendo among the distant fanfares.

For there, where the splendid trumpets blare and thunder,
There is my house, my house the green turf under.

The House of Green Turf

She would really have to stop this. When the last note of the postlude died away it was so silent that it was borne in upon her guiltily how late it was. Most of the guests must be trying to sleep. Much better, too, if she put out all the lights and seemed to be joining the sleepers; he would find it more difficult to approach if there was light spilling down the staircase into the trees.

She stood for a moment listening, after the lights were out, but everything was quiet and still, not even a thread of song drifted to her across the water. She lay down on the bed in her grey and white housecoat to wait patiently for Francis.

She was close to sleep, for all her resolution and eagerness, when the expected tapping came at the glass door on to the verandah. She leaped up gladly, switched on the small bedside lamp, and ran through the sitting-room to whisk aside the curtain and fling the door wide.

The maiden arose, and let him in . . .

The faint light from outside gilded a wet, glistening outline, the shape of a man tall against the sky. The little gleam from the bedroom lit upon the pallid hand that rapped at the glass, and the black stone in the remembered ring on his finger.

The breath congealed in Maggie's throat and the blood in her veins.

This was not Francis, this pale, tense face and shimmering wet body slipping silently into her room, with slow drops coursing down his temples and hair plastered like weed against his forehead. Not Francis, but a drowned man come back out of his grave, out of the lake, out of the past, just when she had allowed herself to be tricked into believing herself rid of him for ever. The rank scent of lake-water and death came over the sill with him, drifting over her in a wave of faintness and nausea. She gave back before him a few steps, and then was stone, unable to move or speak. She was cold, cold, cold as death.

Then everything began to slip away from her, like flesh peeling from her bones, all her delusions of hope, all her belief in the future, any future, even her passion for her own gift. All illusory, all drifting away like dispersed smoke, leaving her naked and lost and damned after all. The world and time came toppling upon her, closing in until there was nothing left but this moment, which was her death.

He came towards her slowly, smiling his pale, drowned smile, his hands held out to her. For what had he come up out of his grave if not to claim her? The hands touched her breast, and cold as she was, she felt their icy chill sear her to the bone. Cold, wet arms went round her and drew her down, down into green depths . . .

Her lips moved, saying: 'Robin!' but made no sound. There was a voice whispering in her ear, soft and distant through the darkness that was beginning to wind itself about her:

> *Auf's Jahr sollst du mein Eigen sein,*
> *Mein Eigen sollst du werden gewiss*
> *Wie's Keine sonst auf Erden ist,*
> *O Lieb . . . auf grüner Erden . . .*

Within the year you shall be mine . . . mine as never bride on earth can be . . . No, none on this green earth . . . How could she have disregarded the end? *Mine in my house across the heath, the last dwelling of the drowned . . . the house of green turf . . .*

His face drew near to her, floating through the gathering dark, smiling. When it swam out of focus his lips touched hers, and cold and dark burned into one absolute and overwhelmed her. She sagged in the arms that held her. She experienced death, the death that gave her back to him.

Stooping, the dead man hoisted her slight weight to his shoulder, and carried her away . . .

Chapter 11

Bunty Felse sat in the gallery at the Alte Post until past eleven o'clock, watching the fun and waiting for George to come home.

For two days, ever since the poacher and the police had fished Friedl Schiffer's body out of the lake, Bunty had been on her own. It was all very well for George to conduct his mild investigations in private, so long as he was merely keeping an eye on two English people apparently involved in something mysterious and possibly dangerous, but not known to be in any way criminal; but murder was quite another matter. So George had gone to the local police with his part of the story, and Bunty had been left to take care of herself from that moment on. What they had made between them out of their pooled information was more than she could guess, but its result had been to provide George with an English-speaking plainclothes-man and a car, with *carte blanche* to shadow Francis Killian's movements as he thought fit. As for the girl, she was safe enough at the Goldener Hirsch; the hotel was under police surveillance, and she had showed no inclination to try to go anywhere, except for a walk into the town to have lunch, surprisingly enough, with her compatriot at The Bear, a meeting which could hardly have been as unplanned as it appeared. And even there they had been directly under George's eye, whether they knew it or not. Bunty hadn't seen him since he walked into the restaurant on Maggie's heels, and

549

left his wife to slip back alone to the Alte Post, before either of those two caught a glimpse of her.

She arrived just in time to relieve the lunch-time loneliness of the elderly Englishwoman who had accidentally got herself included in a predominantly young party, at this tag-end of the holiday season, and found herself ruthlessly shaken from their every activity. To be honest, she was a bore, and Bunty had a certain amount of sympathy with the young people; but since there was no chance of being useful to George for the rest of the day, she resigned herself cheerfully enough to filling a gap for someone else.

The elderly Englishwoman was fascinated and repelled by the wedding party, which was a great deal more rumbustious and well-lubricated than any at which she had ever been a guest. The enormous energy of those young men and their strapping girls seemed to her slightly indecent, and even the lustiness of the music had a strongly earthy flavour about it. The boys might all be in their best dark suits and dazzlingly white shirts, but they still looked as ebulliently fleshy and muscular as in their everyday leathers, and the pointed town shoes pounded the wooden floor as solidly as local handmade mountain boots. And that awful man who seemed to be cheer-leader and master of ceremonies, the one with the beery paunch and the brick-red face who had always a girl in one hand and a two-litre stein in the other, such a man as that, totally uninhibited, simply could not happen in England. The elderly Englishwoman had, Bunty had discovered, run through two husbands, and one of them had been a butcher and the other a brewer, which made her views rather more surprising. Either the quality of English butchers and brewers was in decline, or she was remembering them rather as she would have had them than as they had been.

The master of ceremonies was, in fact, rather a splendid figure, over six feet high and nearly as wide, with a roaring laugh and the true mountain bass voice, straight out of a square mile of cavern. He was the one who kept leading little forays out into the mild evening, to see if it had yet stopped raining. If it cleared, he would have them all tumbling out to the hotel boat-house, with arms full of food and hands full of bottles, to embark with their musicians and their instruments and their inexhaustible energy on the pewter surface of the Scheid-enauersee.

The bride and groom had long departed, seen off with the maximum of noise and every traditional joke. The elderly Eng-lishwoman said good night and went off to bed, but the party showed no sign of ending as long as food, drink and breath held out. Now Helmut was charging out by the garden door for the fiftieth time, and out there one of the girls was hallooing that it had stopped raining and the moon was out. There was loud and hilarious conference, and the musicians began to pack up their music and stands. Might as well see the aquacade set off, Bunty thought, and went up to her room over the lake.

They would be a little time yet, they were hunting for lanterns to take with them, to turn the night into a carnival. Bunty took her hair brush to the open window, and looked at the long, comfortable bulk of the Goldener Hirsch, high above the trees. Several lights were still burning there, and several windows uncurtained, so that an ethereal golden haze brooded over the crest of the hill, as though a swarm of fireflies had clustered there. As she watched, one or two of the lights blinked out. Maggie's two windows were already dark. No, not quite, in the inner one there was a glow-worm spark that must be the bedside lamp. A convalescent like Maggie should sleep early and long.

Down beneath Bunty's window three wedding guests, the vanguard of the flotilla, were opening the boat-house. On impulse Bunty turned back into the room, and went to look for George's binoculars. She was not sleepy, and this promised to be quite a night. If only she had happened to catch Helmut's hospitable eye, down there in the hall, she could probably have got herself an invitation to join the party; everyone who was willing was welcome. Free transport across the lake to that lovely

551

and sinister shore where Friedl had died, two nights ago. Not that there would be anything relevant to find there, after the police had combed the whole stretch of woodland thoroughly. They had found merely several trampled places, hardly very informative where tourists were accustomed to walk, sit and picnic even thus late in the year, and one photograph, half-buried in long grass among the trees. It had not been there longer than a day or two, or the previous rains would have reduced it to a pulp; and the implications were too obvious to resist. Robin Aylwin, George had guessed, on being shown the thing, though he could not positively know whether he was right or not. And at his request they had showed it to Bunty; and Bunty did know. It was a long time ago, but Bunty, after all, had handled not only the bookings but also the publicity on that tour. It was not merely a matter of knowing the faces; she knew the photograph.

The glasses were powerful, and seemed to find light where the naked eye could find none, though she realised as soon as she looked again without them that the moon had emerged again, and was pouring a pale wash of silver across the surface towards the farther shore. Below her several boats were rocking gently on the water, and a shouting, laughing company was piling aboard food, drink, lanterns, guitars, game girls and husky boys. Oars rattled hollowly into rowlocks, there was a good deal of scuffling and scrambling for places. Bunty heard a motor sputtering experimentally; that would surely be Helmut, whose ambition knew no bounds. She lengthened the focus of the glasses again, and made a thoughtful sweep along the shore opposite, just as the wave of moonlight reached it. It looked almost close enough to touch. She fixed on the forward wash of the tide of light, and let her sweep keep pace with it; and for a moment she felt like a surf-rider. Round towards the bowl of darkness below the Goldener Hirsch, stroking the advancing light across the close-set trunks of the trees like fingers over the strings of a harp.

Thus she saw by pure chance, and was the only one to see, the figure that suddenly lunged forward out of the trees beneath the hotel. A man, tall, curiously top-heavy, bursting straight out of the shadow towards the water. The licking tongue of light found pallor about his shoulders, darkness below, a head bent somewhat forward. It had no time to find features or inform her of details, though her eyes in that instant had photographed more than she realised; for at that same moment Helmut got his motor-boat rocketing into life, and with a huge bass-baritone bellow of triumph shot out across the lake, a torch spearing the air before him and a lantern glowing bravely at the stern, three blonde girls trailing scarves in the slip-stream, and the first three or four rowing boats labouring valiantly after.

The figure at the edge of the trees recoiled on the instant, and vanished into cover. Appearing and disappearing were almost one movement, so abruptly was he come and gone. There had been a lift of the head, alert to record the gaily-coloured invasion of his solitude, a glimpse of a regular oval of pallor that told her nothing about his face except that he was clean-shaven. But the vehement movements said young and the aplomb of his responses said he was as quick on the uptake as a wild beast. Bunty ranged the whole rim of the lake there, and tried to penetrate the belt of trees, but she saw no more of him, and no movement to indicate where he passed.

There was, however, nothing about him that could possibly be imaginary, not even in retrospect. Bunty lowered the glasses, and watched the hilarious progress of Helmut's aquacade towards the very curve of shore where the apparition had emerged and vanished. She was unreasonably disturbed. Who recoils like that from being observed by good-natured, harmless souls bent on nothing but fun? Poachers? Where poachers had the sympathy of most people, barring officials, it seemed far-fetched.

True, now she came to think of it, that top-heavy appearance of his, and the slight stoop, the bending of the head, these were all consistent with the fact that he had been carrying something.

Something pale. Why else that pallor there at his shoulder? It wasn't warm enough to be running around at night in shirt-sleeves. That was it, he had been hurrying head-forward, bent under something he carried . . . And as soon as she had thought of it in those terms, she was almost certain it could not have been a net, even if night-poachers here used a net. No, something heavier than that. Nets are nylon now, they weigh almost nothing. This man had been carrying a considerable weight. Not too much for him, he had moved freely and forcefully under it. Nevertheless, something heavier than a net.

Heavy and pale, and turning him into an asymmetrical shape. The bulk poised on one shoulder.

A small core of ice seemed to spring to life in Bunty's heart. For the more she thought about that shape draped upon the stranger's shoulder, the more did it put on a positive and elo-quent form, and confront her, in spite of all her sound, sensible scepticism, with the idea of a girl's limp body in a light-coloured garment, something long and wide-skirted, a housecoat or a negligee. Her weight nicely balanced on the man's shoulder, one arm and hand dangling. Nets don't have hands, whatever they have! Was she imagining it now, after the event?

But why should he start back and hide himself so promptly, so instinctively, if his movements were innocent? And where, come to that, was he heading in such a hurry before Helmut scared him away? For he had started out of the trees at speed, straight towards the water. And there was no boat in all that sweep of shore, no landing stage below the hotel, nothing but the strip of gravel and then dark water.

She reached this point, and the short hairs rose on her neck. What business could he have had with the lake at this hour? What, except the business someone had had with Friedl? Maybe he was still there, somewhere among the trees in hiding, waiting for the revellers to get tired at last, and go home to bed.

And then?

She had a feeling that she was imagining things, probably

554

making the world's fool of herself. But one girl had been drowned, only two nights ago. And that had been murder.

Bunty made up her mind. There was another girl at the heart of this affair, and where could be the harm in making sure that she was safe in her bed? Midnight or not, there was no sense in waiting; and after all, they had known each other once, however briefly and however long ago. She dropped George's glasses on the bed, and went straight downstairs to the telephone booth in the hall.

Gisela, startled out of her beauty sleep by the extension 'phone beside her bed, was scandalised at the very suggestion.

'But Miss Tressider went to her room at nine o'clock, she will have been asleep for a long time. I cannot disturb her. Can it not wait until tomorrow, if you are staying in Scheidenau?'

'No,' said Bunty crisply, 'it can't. Or at least, that's exactly what I want to find out, whether it can or not. I tell you what, you have keys, you slip up and have a look if she's all right, and if she is, I'll call her tomorrow.'

Though even so, she thought doubtfully, there were other girls who might equally be in danger, supposing Friedl's killer was a random defective just breaking out after long harmlessness. What mattered was whether she had really seen what she supposed. But always her mind came back to Maggie. Who else stood so hapless and so alone in the storm-centre of all these happenings?

'I am sorry,' said Gisela indignantly, 'I cannot do such a thing.'

'All right, then,' said Bunty. 'I can! I'm coming over.'

Gisela was waiting for her in the vast vaulted lobby of the Goldener Hirsch when she arrived, out of breath, a quarter of an hour later. It would have been quicker to get Helmut to ferry her over, but Helmut was weaving inspired circles round the grouped rowing boats in the centre of the lake, and his massed choir was singing, pleasantly enough but very loudly:

> *Heute blau und Morgen blau*
> *Und übermorgen wieder,*
> *Ich bin dein, und du bist mein,*
> *Und froh sind uns're Lieder.*

Gisela, huddled in a red dressing-gown, was by this time rather less indignant and considerably more uneasy. What was the use of pretending no harm could come to anyone in this house, after Friedl?

'I have been up to her room. Everything is in order there, her door is locked and her light out. I am sure she is asleep. I tapped gently, but she didn't answer, and I do not like to disturb her rest.'

But her eyes were round and anxious, even afraid. Bunty understood. Somebody had to take the matter farther, now, but Gisela didn't want the responsibility. What Miss Tressider's friend insisted on doing was her own affair.

'The small light in her bedroom is still burning,' she said gently. 'She has a door on the verandah, hasn't she? Is there a way up from outside?'

'Oh, yes!' Gisela jumped at the idea. 'I will show you. We can go through the house.' And with luck, if they found the guest in Number One fast asleep, then they could all lock up and go to bed, and no one but themselves would ever be any the wiser about this night alarm.

They passed through the long corridor to the rear of the house, and out by a short passage on to the path from the terrace, and came to the fringe of the trees. A little way along in the darkness was the wooden staircase that led up to the verandah. Bunty felt her way up it by the rough wooden handrail, and half-way up her fingers, sliding along the wood, encountered a jagged knot, and a fragment of something silken soft and fine, like long strands of mohairs, that clung to her skin with the live persistence of synthetic fibres convulsed with static. She pulled the strands loose from the rough place where they had caught, and shut them in her palm as they went on up the stairs.

Gisela hung back, quivering. 'The door . . . it is open!'

The glass door stood wide on the darkness of Maggie's sitting-room. Through the half-open door that led to the bedroom beyond, the small gleam of the bedside lamp illuminated for them a pillow still covered by a hand-crocheted bedspread. The pillow was dented by the pressure of a head; so, when they put on the light to look round the room, was the bed itself by a light body. But no one was there now. The verandah door must have been open for some time, for rain had blown in . . . No, that was impossible. The verandah was not completely roofed in, but the jut of the eaves above covered a good half of it, and there had been almost no wind to drive the showers. Yet there was a damp patch just inside the doorway, slightly darkening the scrubbed boards. Everything was tidy, everything was normal, but nothing remained of Maggie Tressider except the score of Mahler's 'Wo die schönen Trompeten blasen' on the piano, and in Bunty's palm a small triangle of material woven from one of the more expensive synthetics, printed in a delicate feather pattern of grey and white, like fine lace, with a few long strands of silky nylon fringe trailing from it.

Gisela looked at it and moistened her lips. 'It is from girdle of her housecoat. I have seen her wearing it.'

'Yes,' said Bunty, 'I thought it might be. We've got no choice now. You can see that, can't you? Don't worry, it isn't your fault, I'll do the talking. You go down and call the police. And better tell Herr Waldmeister, he'll have to know. I'll wait here. Tell them the message is from the wife of Detective-Inspector Felse. They'll understand.'

They understood and they came, with all the more alacrity because they had already received, some ten minutes previously,

Werner Frankel's call from a mountain inn over the border in Germany. By the time they reached Bunty, waiting for them in Maggie's sitting-room, there were police patrols out in Germany checking all cars between the border and Felsenbach for a middle-aged light-brown Dodge with a Swiss registration, and Austrian police patrols converging from Langen and Bregenz on Scheidenau, watching for a dark-blue or black Mercedes in a hurry.

It sounded complicated enough without any new complications; but it was becoming quite clear that it was all one case, and too large for taking any chances. First an associate of Miss Tressider was ambushed and abducted on the highroad; and now the girl herself, it seemed, had vanished from her hotel room without warning or explanation.

Not, however, without trace. There were traces enough. A shred torn from her girdle by a knot in the handrail of the staircase. An unimpressive and rapidly drying patch of damp inside her verandah door. And down the slope towards the water, under her windows, search produced a silver chiffon ribbon, still loosely knotted, with one or two dusky gold hairs twined in the knot. It had caught in the fir branches where the half-grown trees grew close, and just at the height of a woman's shoulders. As if she had run from her room, leaving the door open, and straight down the slope in a frenzy of resolution and despair into the lake.

'Yes,' said Bunty, bolt upright on the piano stool, 'that what we were meant to think.' She stabbed a finger emphatically at the music on the stand. 'Even this could be part of the picture. She has a recent history of illness, and has been investigating the disappearance of a man who toured with her here when she was just beginning. That's what it looks like, anyhow. The man in the photograph, yes. And now it seems he's dead. And here is she running through a song like this, all about the demon lover coming back from the grave to claim his bride. If she drowned herself, people might be shocked, but I don't suppose anyone would find it incredible.' She added after a moment's thought: 'Except, perhaps, this man Killian. He seems to have got nearer to her than anyone.'

'And he,' said the man in charge dryly, 'has been taken care of at the same time, eh?'

She never got the police ranks of Austria clear in her mind, but his name, it seemed, was Oberkofler. He was probably in the sixties, a tall, rangy, mountain man with a wrinkled leather face and shaggy grey hair. He wore whatever had come to hand first when his subordinates got him out of bed, and most of it was non-uniform, but he still had no difficulty in looking like the holder of authority. He was Scheidenau born and bred, and looked the part. Bunty found him impressive. She was glad he was the one among them who spoke English, it gave her an excuse for staying in his vicinity.

'Four of them to take care of the man,' he mused, eyeing the damp patch now barely visible on the floorboards, 'and one to account for the woman. You are sure he did not come back to the lake later?'

Bunty glanced towards the window. The strains of 'Du kannst nicht treu sein' were borne bravely across the water. 'How could he?' she said simply.

'Yes . . . I think first we must make contact with our friends there, and make sure that they remain effective, all night if need be. That will make any drowning "accident" impossible, and any retreat by water, also. From what you tell me it seems that this man must be still somewhere close, perhaps still in the woods. Also, we hope, the lady . . . now, Frau Felse, if you would wish to get some sleep . . .'

'I'd rather stay,' said Bunty. 'At least until we get word from my husband.' But she meant rather, until we recover those two alive, and find out what this thing is all about. She had begun this hunt, she wanted to see it ended. There were police converging on Scheidenau from all directions, methodically threading the woodland along the lake-shore, a small army mustering because of what George and she had loosed in this quiet village. She intended to see finished what they had begun.

'Then of course you may stay. Where should we have been without you? You can rest here in your friend's room, why not?'

But he showed neither surprise nor disapproval when she followed him down to the office where he had set up his head-quarters.

The telephone was busy almost every moment for the next hour, but they found no further trace of Maggie Tressider. The revellers on the lake sang and rowed on unflagging, which in its way was as astonishing as it was admirable. It would have been only human to tire and long for sleep as soon as they were officially requested to go on celebrating. Outside among the trees the search proceeded, inside here Oberkofler directed and co-ordinated. The Waldmeister parents, philosophical and phleg-matic, not to say faced with their usual working day in a few hours' time, accounted for themselves and went back to bed, the sons volunteered their services and went to join in the hunt. And Bunty watched and listened and waited, and harried her memory for any submerged detail or any hopeful idea; and worried now not only about those two hapless people lost, but also about George, from whom there had been no word.

A call from Werner Frankel, over in Felsenbach. The Dodge must have got through before they had an effective block-up. They were getting out a general call on it, and hoped to pick it up somewhere near Regenheim.

Another call from Werner, half an hour later. They had returned now to the scene of the abduction, and found in the ditch where the attack took place a wallet containing the papers of Francis Killian, together with several photographs of a certain gravestone in the cemetery at Felsenbach.

'Of which,' said Oberkofler, 'perhaps you have heard from the Herr Inspektor?'

'He told me about it yesterday,' said Bunty. 'The day before yesterday, I mean.' She was a little lightheaded with so much waiting and thinking, and so little sleep. 'But I haven't seen it. George didn't have a camera. Our mistake!'

And at last, just before one o'clock, another telephone call which Oberkofler answered in voluble German, to switch suddenly and wonderfully into English.

'Yes . . . yes, good, I will send you every man I can, and more as they come in. Yes, your wife is here. Please, only a word . . .' He held out the receiver to Bunty with a smile as wide and deep as the sea. 'Your husband, Frau Felse.'

'George?' said Bunty, heaving a deep sigh. 'Did he tell you? We've lost Maggie as well.'

'Yes, I know. That makes us quits, love, I lost the car they had Killian in. Ran head-on into a patrol from Bregenz coming to meet us. We had a mile of road to comb for whatever hole they dived into, but it turned out there's only one, apart from farm-tracks. This one's blind, too, it goes to the lake and stops, so they tell me. Doesn't even pass anything, except that rubble that used to be Scheidenau Castle. But somewhere up there is where they must be. There isn't anywhere else. We're off to hunt for the car now.'

'George, isn't there anything I can do to help?'

'From all I hear you've done it,' said George, 'They also serve . . .! If we find him, the odds are we find her, too. This is all one set-up. Keep hoping! Sorry, got to clear this line, it may be wanted.'

'Yes, of course. See you, then!'

She held out the receiver to Oberkofler, but he shook his head at her and smiled. She hung up. She was suddenly shaking with reaction, and dared not try to guess how the night would end.

Distantly, inexhaustibly, across the lake and in at the window came the thunder of the guns of Helmut's navy:

The Second George Felse Omnibus

Es war einmal ein treuer Hussar,
Der liebt sein Mädchen ein ganzes Jahr,
Ein ganzes Jahr, und noch viel mehr . . .

Chapter 12

Two voices were discussing her above her head. They didn't know that dead people can hear. Quite dispassionate voices, cool, leisurely and low, discussing her in terms of life and death. Either they had no bodies, or dead people can't see. She was dangling just below the level of consciousness, clinging to the surface tension like the air-breathing nymph of some water creature.

'*So schön auch*,' said the first voice critically.

'Nobody's beautiful who gets in my way,' said the second voice in plain English and without overtones; a light, pleasant, untroubled tenor voice without a care in the world.

'*Aber schön*,' the first voice insisted with detached approval. 'She has everything!'

'Except immortality.'

'What are you going to do with her?'

The second voice was silent long enough to indicate a shrug of the shoulders. 'Did I make her wade in here so far out of her depth? She had a death wish.'

'Waste of a girl!' said the first voice with impersonal regret.

'There are others. Even some with perfect pitch.' And in a blithe half-tone the second voice began to sing to itself dreamily:

Mein Eigen sollst du werden gewiss,
Wie's Keine sonst auf Erden ist,
O Lieb . . . auf grüner Erden . . .

Any moment now she would feel the prick of the needle in her thigh, and submerge again. So this must be hell. What could be more absolute hell than to have to go on living and reliving these few weeks to eternity, trying to escape from the net, believing she had escaped, only to find herself back at the beginning and trapped as fast as ever? Everything to do again, everything to suffer again, everything to lose again. No, not quite a duplication, this time the dialogue had changed. The decision last time had been for life. This time it was for death.

Then, in the moment that she broke surface and knew herself conscious, miraculously the burden was gone. Last time she had awakened alone, oppressed and appalled by the horror of guilt without a source. Now that the verdict was for death she awoke to the calm and lightness of deliverance. She had not been deceived, after all, her guilt had been only a delusion, a sickness of which she was healed at last. Even if she died now, it would be as a whole, a sane person.

For this second voice she knew very well, and it belonged firmly in this world and no other. It was no poor injured ghost that had come to fetch her away, but a living and dangerous man, and he had come not because she owed him a death, but because she was a threat to him alive. Her probing had begun to uncover him of the carefully cultivated invisibility of years, he could not afford to let her go on with it. Grave or no grave, memorial or no memorial, Robert Aylwin was alive. She had neither killed him nor done him any wrong; and even if he killed her, she would never again be truly in his power, never his victim as she had been all these years. Neither living nor dead would Robin ever stand between her and love again.

She opened her eyes upon low stone vaulting that had a worn

564

and monumental grandeur, like a feudal hall before luxury came
into fashion. She was lying on a rough grey blanket spread upon
a stone settle built all along one wall, and in the wall itself she
saw the round fretted grooves left by the ends of barrels. The
flagged floor was sifted with fine sand, the accumulated dust of
wind erosion and time. The air felt moist and cool. There was
a dim light from one heavily shaded electric bulb, that showed
her only the side of the room where she lay, and a glimpse of a
door in the corner, a door not worn at all, but surely almost new
and very solid.

'*Achtung*!' said the first voice very softly. 'She's coming round.
Shall I . . .?'

'No, let her! Company will help to pass the time until those
fools go home to bed.'

She could see the pair of them only up to the shoulders, for
the dark shade over the light obscured their faces. One of them
stepped back accommodatingly into the shadows, the other came
forward and sat down on one hip on the edge of the settle beside
her feet. He saw that her eyes were wide-open and fixed upon
his face, and turned the lamp deliberately to let it illuminate
him fully.

'Allow me! Is that better?'

He no longer glistened and streamed, the fall of wavy hair
was nearly dry, only the unruly way it curled round his forehead
showed that he had recently been out in the rain. He must have
stood outside her room under the dripping trees all the while
she was singing, waiting for the appropriate moment. He must,
she thought, have been amused by the Mahler; a little Gothic
horror would appeal to his sense of humour. He was dressed to
go invisibly in the dark, in clerical grey slacks and a thick black
sweater with a polo neck; the same, perhaps, in which he had
prowled the woods that night he throttled and drowned Friedl.

Looking at him now, she found nothing surprising in that.
He sat smiling at her, a cigarette held delicately between forefinger and thumb, narrowing his eyes slightly against the smoke

that drifted towards his face in a light draught. The same boyish, regular features, the same full, mobile, strongly curling lips for ever on the edge of laughter. He laughed a great deal, always, at everything. For years she had forgotten the colour of his eyes, lowered in Friedl's photograph, closed in that dead faun's face over his grave. Perhaps it had cost her an extra effort to forget them, and she had managed it only because it was essential. They watched her now steadily, curiously, pale greenish-gold eyes, round and bold, a goat's eyes, intelligent, inscrutable, malicious. The eyes laughed, too, almost without cease, but at some private joke that was not for ordinary humans. He was hardly older than he had been thirteen years ago, when she had last seen him. Why should he be, when he lived – it was to be seen in the debonair face and the cool, bright eyes – immune from all feeling and all responsibility?

She drew herself up with an effort to sit upright, her back – how appropriately! – against the wall. Never for a moment did her eyes leave his face.

'It *is* you,' she said at last, 'it was *you* behind everything!' She braced her hands against the cold stone to take fast hold of reality. She knew her situation now, and her enemy. She had marvellously recovered the fullness of life only just in time to lose it again, and feel the loss double. But also she had now a double stake for which to put up a fight. 'So you *are* alive,' she said.

'Dear Maggie,' he said, lazily smiling, 'I believe so.'

'Then what *was* it I heard, that night? *What was it that went into the lake?*'

She thought for a moment that he was not going to answer her, but with a captive audience, and all the cards and all the strings in his own hands, and time to kill – *but how did it happen that he had time to kill?* – why not talk? After all, she wasn't going anywhere, was she, to repeat anything he might let fall? He could indulge his fancy with no risk to himself.

'Just one of old Waldmeister's stacked logs,' he said serenely.

'The whole clearing down by the water was full of them, he surely couldn't grudge me one in a good cause.'

'But *why?*' she said almost inaudibly, wrenching at the wanton shaft that had broken off short in her spirit as in wounded flesh, and festered ever afterwards. 'Why play me such a trick? Why did you have to *die* at all? And even if you had your reasons for wanting to vanish, why stage a scene like that with me first? Why pretend you loved me? Why ask me . . .' She drew breath slowly, and flattened her shoulders warily against the wall; the chill pierced her like a gust of cold air, and every such minute shock of reality helped to calm her senses and clear her mind. She, too, could talk; words were there to be used for her purposes as well as his. The more attention he gave to her, to impressing and subduing her, even to amusing himself with her, the less he would have left for imagining any counter-attack. 'Just think,' she said, eyeing him narrowly from under the fall of her loosened hair, 'I might even have accepted you! What would you have done then?'

He found the recollection of that night rather flattering, she thought; maybe his memory even embroidered it. But be careful of believing that. Conceit is only a discardable toy to a man without feelings.

'I should have married you, of course,' he said sunnily. 'It wouldn't have been too great a hardship. You'd have turned out quite a profitable investment, the way things have gone. And as my wife, you wouldn't have been asked to give evidence against me, either – would you?'

So that was one more piece of the puzzle falling into place. He had flicked it into her lap deliberately, she knew that. Nevertheless, record it, Maggie! He's quite sure of his security, but there are things even he doesn't know. He may yet live to regret dropping these small golden apples to distract you into running about at his will.

'I see,' she said thoughtfully. 'But what was I supposed to be able to tell? I never knew there *was* anything to be told against you.'

He leaned back to prop himself against the wall by one wide, lean shoulder, and grinned at her amiably through the smoke of his cigarette.

'Do you remember the spring trip we made that year with the Circus?'

'Well, well!' she said. 'You've still got the terms pat, after all this time.'

'Dear Maggie, I have as near as damn it total recall. I remember the whole ramshackle set-up, and you so dedicated and earnest, and such an easy touch. You remember carrying some expensive cosmetics through Customs for me, that spring? A girl could get by with declaring those jars, when a man would automatically get charged on them. And it turned out that way, didn't it? And a friend of mine met us at the boat-train, and I handed the whole works over as a present for his sister. Dear Maggie, you can't have forgotten that kind deed? After all, what did you ever have to declare, except sheet music and gramophone records?'

What money had she ever had, in those days, to buy any but the most vital necessities, all of which were comprehended in music? But all she said was: 'I remember.'

'Well, they picked up my anonymous friend later that year with rather a lot of heroin on him. Yes, that's what was in the jars, sealed below about an eighth of an inch of cream and stuff. We were in Basel on the autumn tour when I got word, so I had to make up my mind quickly what to do. There was no knowing for sure that he'd keep his mouth shut about me, and even if he did, there might still be something they could hook up to me. And if ever they had found their way to the Circus, you'd soon have told them how those cosmetics came into England, wouldn't you? It all boiled down to a choice between marrying you to close your mouth, and going home and chancing my luck, or staying here and turning professional. They'd been inviting me to do that for a year or more.'

'*They?*' said Maggie gently.

'What good would it do you if I named names, my dear? The whole set-up has changed since then. Just one organisation among many, until I made it over to my taste. Call it what you like. *Cosa mia . . .*'

Yes, clearly anything into which he entered would soon have to become '*his thing*'; he wasn't interested in being a subordinate. Perhaps that was why he'd never bothered to work at music, because even the disciplined approach necessary was only going to get him into the third, or at best the second, rank. 'So you'd been smuggling for them for some time,' she said, 'under cover of Freddy's respected name.'

'Every trip. You'd helped me once before. Oh, not always hard drugs, in fact, very seldom. Anything light and profitable, precious stones, lenses, passports, medicines, even watches when other fields were dull. Once I went into England with two medieval manuscripts among my sheet music. We had a customer waiting for those, of course. Miniatures, rare coins, stamps, small art items – anything portable enough and expensive enough. We provide a worldwide service, moving the goods to where the demand is. Even before the crunch came I'd been thinking of throwing up the Circus before it threw me up, and going into the business full-time. It looked as if my career with Freddy was nearly up in any case. I let *you* make up my mind for me. *You* turned me down, *they* got me. You even provided me with a reason for suicide, if people got too nosy, though I admit the log was an afterthought. I remember taking off down the hillside, and there were these stacks of wood ready for carting, and it was too good to miss. You were so damned confident and secure, it seemed an appropriate gesture to give you something else to think about besides your great future.'

'It must have been a disappointment to you,' she said dryly, 'when I didn't tell anybody the story you'd so thoughtfully set up for me to tell.'

He leaned his head back against the wall and laughed aloud.

'I was shocked to find you capable of such duplicity. You didn't want any scandals or other little stumbling-blocks in the way of your career, did you? But after all, it worked out very well. Friedl kept me informed. If everyone had accepted Freddy's dark hints, and come to the conclusion that I'd simply run out to avoid minor unpleasantness, that was fine with me. Just so long as nobody started a serious search for me *alive*.'

'Friedl was your creature? One of the organisation?'

'Hardly that. Let's say Friedl became a useful camp follower. One of our ears on the world. One of our tongues, too, though,' he added candidly, 'I ought to have known better.'

'Then it was you who put her up to telling all those lies to Francis and to me, to prove that you were dead?'

'To Killian, yes. But to you? There she exceeded her orders, she had her own bone to pick with you. Friedl . . .' He hoisted one shoulder in a smooth and eloquent gesture. 'She always preferred to lie rather than tell truth, if not for policy, then for pleasure. Her facility has been useful on occasions, but when she was mad with jealousy – oh, yes, hadn't you realised that? – she was a menace. She talked altogether too much. When she put you on to the grave, that was the end. She had to go. Probably the grave was a mistake from the beginning, I should have let well alone. But at the time it seemed a heaven-sent opportunity to have a second line of defence ready, in case of need. And then *you* had to get too interested in it, of all people, and of all people *you* would never have swallowed it. Anybody else she might have told, but *you* . . .'

'I've seen the photographs,' said Maggie. 'How did you even manage that affair? Was it you who provided the body? *Is* there really a body there?'

'Oh, yes, there's a body, just as she told you. He came down with the snow water in the thaw. No, that wasn't any master-stroke of mine, he was pure luck. I don't suppose anyone will ever know who he really was. No, all I did was take the chance when it offered. Then there'd always be a grave to which I could misdirect enquiries if ever I needed to suggest my own death. It was a body, male, near enough my height and build and age, and past being identified. All I needed to do was make the anonymous offer to pay for his burial, as an act of piety, and make sure the death of an unknown young man was recorded and dated. Nothing crude as a false identification or a name, of course. The portrait was an afterthought, a *jeu d'esprit*. Maybe too impudent, but it amused me.'

'So you have a monumental mason in your pocket, too,' said Maggie admiringly.

'We have one of everything we need,' he agreed calmly.

'You must have risen rapidly in the organisation.'

'To the top. Some years ago now. Class tells,' he said demurely, and his lips curled in the very same private laughter he had allowed the mason to engrave on the tombstone, giving the lie to the depersonalised brow and marble eyelids, turning the dead mask into a living demon.

'And then,' he said reproachfully, '*you* had to come along and start looking for me – you, who weren't going to swallow that grave without gagging. If you hadn't turned so curious, after all this time, none of this need have happened. For God's sake, *why did you?*'

She stared back at him wordlessly for a long minute, herself marvelling to find the landscape of her mind so miraculously changed. 'I had you on my conscience,' she said with deliberation. 'I believed I owed you a life.'

Very softly, and with the most beguiling of smiles, he agreed: '*And so you do.*'

It could hardly be a surprise. She had known all along that she had gone too far to be left alive. Would he be talking to her like this, otherwise? From the beginning she had known at the back of her mind that she was talking chiefly to engage his attention, to make him forget time, to gain minutes as best she could. Because of the one thing he did not know about that Mahler performance of hers tonight, the fact that she had been waiting for the arrival of another visitor.

What if Francis was late in coming? He would come. And whatever others might think at finding her bedroom empty – that she had gone off of her own will, to some appointment in the woods, to somebody else's bed, to the bottom of the lake – Francis would know better. Francis would know that she had been waiting for him, and that nothing would have induced her to leave the appointed place until he came. And whether he called in the police or not, he would begin a search for her on his own account until he found her.

On that one chance she pinned her hope, and saw that it was still a substantial hope. No point in over-estimating it, though. For Robin wouldn't be killing time with her in this idle way, however enjoyably, if he himself were not waiting for something.

At least go on talking, she thought. At least keep him from deciding not to wait, after all.

'How do you intend to dispose of me?' she asked conversationally.

His bright, probing, inscrutable yellow stare was fixed and blinding upon her face, and for once he was not smiling.

'My dear girl, you set the whole scene yourself. Here are you with a recent record of illness and odd behaviour, and apparently with some sort of obsession about me, a small, sad episode in your distant past. And then your rest-home is invaded by a tragedy – a girl drowned in the lake. Suicide is infectious. Now they're going to find your verandah door open, and a nice little trail laid down to the shore. I've seen to that. And on your piano, just as you left it, that wonderfully appropriate Mahler song about the dead lover returning by night to visit his beloved . . . Oh, yes, someone will be able to make the connection. With that sort of background, who's going to be surprised

that you finally ran off the rails altogether, and did away with
yourself?'

'Then why didn't you slip me into the water right away, while
you had the chance?'

He laughed gaily. 'Because there's a plague of drunken wedding guests holding a regatta all round the lake. And a damned
inconvenient moment they chose to embark.'

'That's a matter of opinion,' said Maggie tartly.

'Granted. But they'll get sick of it just now, and go home to
bed. Don't worry, tomorrow the police will be dragging for your
body.'

'And of course,' she said, 'they'll find it?'

'Oh, yes, they'll find it. Quite definitely death by drowning,
there'll be no injuries to spoil the picture, not even a bruise. A
pity I let Friedl make me angry, but what can you do? No, my
dear, for a Maggie Tressider they might go on searching too
long and too well, if I didn't make them a present of you. They
might find other things, one never knows. No, they shall have
you gratis.'

To make a suicide like that convincing, she reasoned with
furious coldness, and to ensure that she was found with satisfying
promptness, she would have to be put into the water near to the
hotel. So they must be somewhere quite close now. Why not go
on doing the direct thing, and ask? He had answered some
curious questions already, being quite certain of his security
here. But if this waiting continued long enough, and every
moment counted, what she had gleaned from him might come
in useful yet to convict him.

'Where have you brought me?' She looked round the dim
room as though she had just discovered it. There was a second
door in the distant wall, directly opposite the first one, as though
this was only one in a series of rooms. Cellars? Not in the hotel,
surely? Yet he could not have brought her far. The other man
sat silent on the far side of the single lamp, decapitated by the
sharp edge of the black shade, unconcernedly breaking, cleaning

573

and loading a gun, a pair of large, dexterous hands with no head to direct them, but remarkably agile and competent on their own.

'We're in the wine-cellars of the old castle. There was a whole labyrinth of them originally, but most are blocked up with rubble. We sealed off the safest part of the network as a repository. One of several. With three frontiers so close, we need a safe place handy in each country, where men and things can be got out of sight quickly until the heat is off. No,' he said grinning, 'don't look round for treasure, we've cleared everything out. After to-night we shan't be using this place again, it's likely to be a little too precarious for our purposes.'

'And you, where do you pass the – shall we say "unburied"? – part of your life? I suppose you've still got an identity somewhere among the living?'

'Oh, several,' he assured her merrily. 'Most respectable ones, and in more than one country. As one frontier closes, another opens. To a new man, of course. You know, Maggie . . .' She waited, watching him steadily. He was eyeing her with calculating thoughtfulness, like a sharp trader contemplating an inspired deal. 'In a way, it's a pity I couldn't have both, you *and* this. Who'd have thought you'd stay in mourning for me all this time?'

She remembered the anguish he had cost her, the obsessive hold he had had upon her, and suddenly it dawned upon her that Francis had made the same mistake about her that this man was making now. Because she had all but wrecked her life on him, they believed she must have loved him, if only in retrospect after he was gone. She opened her eyes wide, and laughed in Robin's face. It was perhaps the only luxury she had left, and not one that did her any credit, but she could not resist it.

'*In mourning* for you? Do you know what you've been to me? A nightmare, a curse, and that's all . . .'

The man with the gun said: '*Achtung!*' sharply and clearly, and came to his feet.

Maggie's laughter broke off in her throat. She crouched

against the wall with head reared, ears straining after those small, stony sounds approaching somewhere outside the door. Robin watched the little sparks of hope come to life softly in her eyes, and the smile shattered by her laughter came back to his lips like a reflection in a pool reshaping itself after the dropping of a stone. He slid from the settle and stretched himself contentedly.

'Too bad, my dear, it isn't what you think.'

She had already grasped that it could not be. This was someone who knew the way in here, and approached quietly but without stealth. Not what she had been hoping for; merely what Robin had been waiting for.

The man with the gun crossed to the door and drew back the bolts. Maggie lowered her feet quickly over the edge of the stone shelf and stood up, drawing the folds of her soiled housecoat about her, for it seemed that time had run out.

Into the room walked four men, bringing in with them gusts of the chill night air and the green smell of the wet woods. Two of them were big, raw-boned mountaineers, from which side of the border there was no knowing. The third was slim and lightweight and young, and belted into a wasp-waisted raincoat. The fourth, who was thrust in limping heavily, with blood on his face and a gun in his back, was Francis.

Maggie made not a sound, but as if she had cried out to him his gaze flew to her, and fastened on her with such dismay and despair that her heart turned in her; and what he saw in her face was the mirror image of his own anguish. The only grain of consolation he had had left was that she was safe in her bed; the only hope she had been able to keep was that he would launch the hunt for her in time. Both bubbles burst and vanished.

Maggie hardly noticed the dwindling of her own small chance of life in the sudden rush of rage and pain she felt for him. She had bought this fairly, but what had he done? She had brought him into this, unarmed and alone against a highly-organised and ruthless gang, and it was because of her actions that they were both going to die. She was to drown, because they wanted her found and accounted for. But Francis . . . No, better for them if he vanished altogether. What was the good of shutting her eyes? Since they had taken him prisoner somewhere on the road, perhaps well away from Scheidenau, why bring him back to this place if he was ever to leave it again?

Robin and his men were speaking rapid and colloquial German, Robin questioning, the others answering. She was soon lost in the language, but the implications were clear enough. Any trouble? No, no trouble, everything in hand, everything to numbers. There was something about a car – Francis's car? – that should be in Klostermann's yard by now. They were all easy and content, not elated but extracting a certain workmanlike satisfaction out of their efficiency. Maggie stood almost forgotten, trying to understand, straining her senses in case there should be something, anything, at which hope could claw as it went by, and find a hold. For one of them, at least. For Francis! But she knew there would be nothing now. Just a few hours of deferment, and they had lost their chance for ever.

His captors had loosed their hold of him as soon as they had him inside, and the door firmly locked and bolted. Why not? He was battered and unarmed, and they had several guns between them. Even Robin had a gun in his hand now, a tiny, snub-nosed black thing that he dangled on his forefinger like a toy.

Something had been said about her, a question in the other direction. All three of Robin's men were eyeing her with some concern; no doubt they had expected her to be in the lake by this time.

'Oh, Maggie!' said Robin carelessly, giving her a light glance over his shoulder. 'There was a slight hitch there.' He had slipped back into English, she thought, not by chance, but so that she should understand. 'We shall have to keep her now until the Volga boatmen go home to sleep it off. They're sure to tire sooner or later. Roker's keeping an eye on them upstairs, he'll give us the tip when they quit.' He looked back at Francis, and spun the little gun in his hand, and the butt nestled into his palm like a bird homing. 'But we may as well get this one underground,' he said.

Francis had taken out a handkerchief, and was quietly wiping the blood from his cheek. His face, grey and drawn, kept a total, contained silence. Even when he raised his eyes for an instant to take one more look at Maggie, they gave nothing away beyond a kind of distant, regretful salutation. In the presence of these people he had nothing to say to her, not even with his eyes. The burden of longing and self-blame and love was not something he wanted to display for them or pile upon her at this last moment. As long as he had a card to play – and he had one, the last – he might as well play it, and speak to the point. The rest could stay unsaid; she wouldn't be any the poorer or more unfortunate for ending her life without any declaration from Francis Killian.

'There's one thing you don't know . . . Aylwin,' he said, his voice emerging hoarse and clumsy from a bruised throat. 'I take it you *are* Aylwin? Who else? Your boys don't know it, either, but all the way up that mountain section there was a car following me tonight. It was on my trail yesterday, too, I couldn't be sure of it then, but I know it now. I thought it was your pack on my heels, till I hit your ambush ahead. There's only one other thing it could be, you know that, don't you? A police car keeping an eye on me. They weren't far behind when this bunch flagged me down. You think they're blind and deaf? Or do you suppose they'd drop their assignment just when it got interesting? They'll be hard after us right now, and there'll be reinforcements on the way. Do you think you're ever going to get out of here unobserved?'

'I think,' said Robin, smiling at him lazily, eyes narrowed and golden, 'that you are a gallant but hopeless liar, trying the only bluff you've got left. But just to be obliging . . .' He turned to the three who stood watching and listening, and snapped back

briskly into German. They shook their heads in vigorous rebut-
tal, laughing the story away with absolute confidence. 'You see?
No shadow, no police, no fairy tales. If you had a tail, it got
lopped off *en route*. But I think you never had one.'

'Your trouble,' said Francis levelly, 'is that you have to have
too much faith in your understrappers. The usual trouble with
businesses that get too big. That Dodge will never get as far as
Klostermann's. If they miss it in Felsenbach, they'll pick it up
before it reaches Regenheim. And in case there's any doubt
about the place where I was waylaid, and about *your* tie-in with
the affair, let me tell you I've left them my wallet and papers
there on the spot. With the whole set of photographs of *your*
grave.'

The first faint shadow of doubt touched but could not deface
Robin's smiling certainty. He turned his head again to shoot
orders at his underlings; and they laid hands ungently on Francis
and began to turn out his pockets, though they still poured
voluble scorn on his story. He raised his hands out of their way,
flinching as they handled him.

'No wallet, no passport, no driving licence. You think I came
out without those, Aylwin? Don't bother to send a man back to
pick them out of the ditch, the police did that long ago. And
did you know that there's an English detective in Scheidenau,
co-operating with the locals? He followed me from England.
Maybe he's the one who's been on my trail all day. He certainly
was when we had lunch at The Bear.'

'All right, so you left your wallet in the ditch. What good is
it going to do you? Someone will spend your money and throw
the rest away. I'll believe in your English detective when I see
him. And as for your police tail, Max with your hired job would
have run head-on into it round the bend, and got word to me
long ago.'

'Maybe he did run into it, and they picked him up on the
spot. Ever think of that? Better not write them off so easily,
Aylwin, they were there, all right.' It was his only anchor now,

a frail one, but not an illusion. They had been there. God knew what had become of them now, but they might yet find their way where they were needed. 'You haven't a hope of getting out of here unseen. Why add more murders to the score? It's long enough already. You might get away with Friedl. Touch Maggie Tressider, and they'll hunt you to the end of the world.'

It was breath wasted. Even if he had been subject to intimidation, even if he had believed, Aylwin had gone too far now to turn back. He yawned elaborately in Francis's face, and smiled, reaching up one hand to turn the shade of the lamp, and direct the light towards the darkest corner of the cellar. The circle of pallor flowed across the flagstones like a silent tide. Against the wall a heap of dark earth reared into view, and the rims of two of the stones showed black and thin as pen-strokes.

'Get them up!'

They had crowbars and spades propped in the corner. The slanting light cast monstrous shadows from the stooped shoulders and heads of the two mountain men, as they leaned their weight almost languidly on the crowbars, and the thin black line at one end of the nearer stone broadened into a gash, a gaping rectangle of darkness.

For me, thought Francis, not for Maggie; he said they'd have to keep her until the Volga boatmen went home . . . Boatmen! Yes . . . so someone's balking them from going near the lake. *At this hour?* A grain of hope clung obstinately to life within him, for the police might justify him yet, and come in time for Maggie, though not for him. Bargaining was out of the question, what had he to bargain with? Certainly not his own life, that was already forfeit. No means even of buying time. If he set out to sell his life as high as he could, there would be bullets flying here, and Aylwin might opt to cut his losses and change his plans, and hurry both his prisoners out of the world and into the ground together. No, nothing left to do but count on the Volga boatmen – whoever they were, thank God for them! – and submit without provocation, and pray that they might be police patrols who would never go home until she was found alive.

Robin Aylwin swung one long leg negligently from the edge of the settle, played with his little pistol, and watched his men at work. A job like any other. He paid no more attention to Francis, and Francis, arrived at the bleak conclusion that there was nothing he could do for Maggie but die submissively, had fallen mute. It was Maggie who broke the silence.

'Francis!'

Never in his life had he heard his name spoken like that. A small, fine-spun, golden, intimate sound, like the marvellous *mezza voce* she could float clean to the back row of the remotest gallery of any opera house in the world, to pierce the last listener's heart as if no one existed but himself and the singer. Out of the centre of one being, and aimed with certainty to reach the centre of another. For no one was present here now but Francis and Maggie. She had excised the others from her own consciousness and she banished them from his. There was only one thing left that she could do for Francis, and she was doing it as well as she knew how.

'Francis, I'm sorry I ever got you into this. Forgive me! But I want to tell you that for my part I'm glad to have known you, even on these conditions. Thank you for everything you've done for me. I don't have to say goodbye. I shan't be long after you.'

Robin had turned his head to stare at her. The men leaning hard over the half-open grave froze, and hung watching and listening. And then Robin's head went back with a toss like an angry horse balking, and he uttered a shout of brief and violent laughter. Something in the sound sent his men scurrying back to work on the second stone in haste. Never had Maggie looked at *him* like that, never spoken his name with that particular awareness that suddenly bestowed a greatly enlarged identity. Never had she turned on him this starry face, with blazing, recognising eyes wide-open to love. He had gone to the trouble to stage a beautiful declaration of love for her once, and she had not even heard him. A phoney love, of course! Still, by all the rules she ought to have succumbed.

The flagstones were propped back gently against the wall, uncovering the greyish, hard-packed earth, and the long, narrow hole from which the heap of soil had been dug out already in preparation for a new incumbent. Harsh darkness and a sinister bony light, distorted figures stooped over an open grave. Maggie's mind drifted, recoiling from a present that was unbearable and a future that was non-existent. This was the dungeon scene from *Fidelio*. But Leonora had at least had a pistol, and here all the pistols were on the other side. She had nothing to fight with, nothing with which to defend her own or attack her enemy. '*Ich bin sein Weib!*' No, this would be a *Fidelio* without any ecstatic love duet, without any final triumph for justice . . .

Robin slid from the settle and spread his feet firmly. She saw his thumb slide back the safety catch of the gun. He had forgotten her again; his attention was fixed on the open grave. Business as usual, he had his own affairs to look after, and no emotion had any part in them, not even offended vanity.

'You won't be lonely,' he said pleasantly, his amber eyes measuring Francis, 'you'll be joining the sitting tenant. A fellow-countryman of yours who also got too nosy. The errand-boy always thinks he can run the business better than the managing director.'

He raised his hand without haste, and levelled the gun. The grave-diggers and their colleagues drew off from Francis and stood clear, waiting phlegmatically to fill in the hole again and replace the stones. The long finger on the trigger contracted gently.

Maggie awoke before it tightened to the firing-point. Nothing to fight with? But she *had*! She had one weapon, the ultimate weapon, not effective to stand off death, but a grenade exploding in Robin Aylwin's orderly plans. She had a body he needed unmarked for his own purposes, with lungs that could still breathe in lake-water. She gathered it in a convulsion of vengeful energy, and flung it between Francis and the gun.

Chapter 13

The gun went off, a sharp, spiteful waspish sound, lost in Robin's startled cry. Maggie hung poised in front of Francis with spread arms, and felt him lurch and recover at her back, fending himself off from the wall. There was no pain, no impact, nothing. She had under-estimated the jungle speed of Robin's reactions. In the instant that she moved he had divined her purpose, and methodical in everything he did, had adhered stubbornly to his own intent. The bullet must have been in motion when he flung up his wrist to let it whine in ricochet from the vault above, and bury itself in the wall. He could not avoid her without avoiding Francis, too. Frantically she reached back a hand to feel for Francis, to assure herself that he was there intact, if only for one instant of communion, and to fasten herself to him indivisibly so that he could not be killed without killing her. His arm groped its way about her waist and lifted her. She felt the hardness of his body, and heard him breathing in heavy, painful groans.

But all she saw was Robin's face, and that she would never forget, however long she had for remembering. In the very moment that he had deflected his shot, to keep his prize suicide presentable for an autopsy surgeon and an inquest jury, everything in him had suddenly curdled and changed. Intelligence he had, it worked at the speed of light. The whine of the ricochet was still flittering about the vault like a disturbed bat when the true horror hit him, the thing that undid him utterly. He saw in a blinding vision the full significance of what she had done, and for once in a cold life he reacted without calculation, in a frenzy of irrational jealousy. He had never cared a damn for her, nor did he now, nor would he ever, for her or any woman. And yet it was an intolerable outrage to him that she, who felt nothing for him, should toss her life away willingly for another man. How could it matter to him? He had lived very successfully without need or respect or regard for love, and yet all that impressive erection suddenly crumbled to a mouthful of bitter ashes. It mattered, all right! It mattered to the heart, to the bone, to the marrow of the bone. She had tricked him, cheated him out of his whole achievement. She had done what no one else had ever done, made him feel.

He uttered a shriek of grief and rage, incredible from that composed and imperturbable throat of his, and the comely mask before her broke and crumpled horribly into ugliness. Two round, glaring, golden eyes in a grimacing chaos of hate levelled upon their target for once not coldly but in boiling fury. The bomb that had shattered him had shattered his plans with him. The only thing that mattered now was to kill Maggie Tressider. The little black pistol came up fast and accurately. He fired pointblank at her.

She had clamped her arm over the arm Francis had thrown round her, her hand gripping his hand, he could not throw her clear, she would not let go of him. All he could do was hold her fast and turn with her in his arms, putting her between him and the wall.

The bullet took him in the back of the left shoulder, a little high for where Maggie's heart should have been. The impact drove them both forward against the wall. They slid down it, still linked, still clasping each other, and on the chill, soiled flagstones Maggie drew herself clear, half-stunned by the fall and his weight upon her, and gathered him jealously into her arms. The heat of his blood jetted into the folds of her sleeve.

584

His head lay in the crook of her elbow, his face half-smiling up at her for one astonished instant, before all its precision of line dissolved into faintness, into a dream.

There were no more shots, and yet the vault above them was suddenly alive with discordant noises, none of them understood, none of them relevant. Francis and Maggie were alone in the centre of a whirlwind, in a cone of calm that was half shock and half the peace beyond exhaustion. For a moment she did not even realise that he was hit, she only held him like a trophy, like the palm after a long, hard race.

Then her senses cleared a little, enough to distinguish the hammering at the door, hysterical with alarm, and the clash of the bolts as the man in the raincoat opened. The man who burst in and slammed the door at his back she saw clearly. She saw him clawing at the bolts, turning the key again. Robin had called him Roker, and he spoke English, most likely he *was* English. Why not? They flourish everywhere. If ever they wanted a description of this one, she could give it, one that would find him wherever he ran. Her vision seemed to be inordinately clear, as in one kind of dream. He was a little, fast-moving, quiet man, who even screamed in a whisper; balding, nondescript, fortyish, tough as nylon rope and almost as synthetic, a product of his age. He was rattling out destructive sentences in a low, venomous monotone; and because of him, she and the man she held in her arms were forgotten.

'Police . . . hordes, I tell you! You knew I had the trap open, God damn it, I *had* to! Any minute I might have had to drop in here fast. It wasn't the shot so much . . . somebody screamed like a blasted woman. How could I know they were that close? Don't *ask* me what brought them snooping round here . . . They *are* here! They homed on that squeal like on a radar fix. Don't hope for it, they saw me drop, all right, they know where the stone is. Nothing's going to keep them out of here now. *Sure* I locked and bolted the door up there. You think two doors will hold them long?'

Robin's voice, riding high and authoritative above this hail of
disaster, said clearly: 'Out, the back way!' All his disintegrated
atoms had welded again into one efficient being at the first
pressure from outside. He dropped his victims without hesitation, without another thought. If he stayed to silence them he
would lose precious time, and leave the police two identifiable
bodies and two all-too-provable murders, should he ever be taken
to answer for them. If the police here were on to him, then the
game in these parts was up for good. Take the gains, cut
the losses, and get out clean. There were other continents besides
Europe, and there was money already carefully distributed there.

'They must have found the car in the coppice, they came up
from that way . . . No, I tell you there wasn't a sign . . . not until
that fool yelled like a banshee. Who the hell *was* it? You *knew* I
should leave the trap open! They came from everywhere, like
greyhounds on a hare . . .'

'All right, we've got the message. Open that door and get
going. Scatter and make for Dornbirn.'

A crisp, cool, commanding voice, not at all the scream of a
banshee now. And they were obeying him in something more
than haste. The other door was open, Maggie felt the chill of
outer air like a fine spray over her cheek and shoulder. Of course,
a rear exit would be an elementary precaution, and simple here
in a labyrinth of castle cellars. They were all slipping away like
flickering ghosts, the taciturn man who had cleaned the gun,
the two big, raw-boned Austrians, the slender young one in the
raincoat, the distraught sentry, all vanishing, all receding into
tiny, rapid footfalls swallowed up by the rock.

Give him this at least, Robin was the last to go. He saw all
his men away before he extracted the key from the rear door by
which they had withdrawn, and passed through it in his turn,
closing it briskly after him. His foot, as he crossed the room,
stepped in the slowly-gathering rivulet of blood that seeped
along between the stones. Maggie heard the key turn in the lock,
and then his long, light steps receding rapidly.

The House of Green Turf

It was very quiet in the wine cellar for a few blank moments, during which she drifted towards collapse, and dragged herself back desperately to press her hand against the hole in Francis's shoulder, where the blood pumped steadily out of him, sending thin, bright-red jets welling between her fingers. She hardly noticed when the new noises began, the shots that broke the lock of the outer door, the rush of feet advancing. Only when the battering at the nearer door began did she realise that the police were through one obstacle, and divided from her now only by that last barrier. She laid Francis down out of her arms gently, and went stumbling across the room to drag back the bolts. There were voices calling out to her from the other side, offering and demanding reassurance. She was almost too tired to understand or answer, but if she did not, Francis would die. She knew nothing about first-aid, but she knew arterial bleeding when she saw it.

'They've gone . . . another entrance somewhere . . .' Every word required an effort like shouldering the world. 'He took the keys away . . .'

'Miss Tressider, are you all right?' That was an English voice, not just someone local speaking English. It made its way to the centres of energy in her exhausted mind, and she drew reviving breath. 'Yes, I'm all right, but Francis . . . he's badly hurt . . . shot . . . Hurry, I'm afraid he'll bleed to death . . .'

'We're coming. We'll get through to you as fast as we can. Maggie . . . is he well away from the door? We may have to shoot a way through.'

'Yes, near the other end of the room . . . ten yards . . . to your left . . .'

'Stay there with him, and keep down. Maggie . . . Maggie, can you hear me? *Where is he hit?*' George Felse was one knee with his mouth as near to the keyhole as he could get it, yelling through to her over the probing and grating and cursing of an experienced professional struggling with the lock.

587

'In the left shoulder . . . an artery, I think . . . he's bleeding terribly . . .'

'Do you know where the pressure point is in the shoulder?' He told her in the fewest words possible how to locate and compress the subclavian artery. 'You'll have to keep pressing . . . you'll tire . . .'

'I won't tire.' No, not when she knew what to do. Her voice called back to him this time from farther away, she was already on her knees, raising Francis in her arms against the wall to strip away collar and shirt from his neck and feel for the pump that was emptying him of blood before her eyes. *'But hurry . . .!'*

'Good girl, we'll be through soon to help you . . .'

But the door was the door of a fortress.

From the moment that they found the Mercedes, tucked away in a hollow coppice on the Bregenz side of the castle hill, Oberkofler had taken no chances. He had a cordon of armed men strung round the hill on every side, methodically narrowing their circle as they converged on the unimpressive and unlovely ruins. Those on the Scheidenau side had neither seen nor heard anything of note since the discovery of the car, and were still merely carrying out their orders with proper attention, and no immediate expectation of incident, when their colleagues from the Bregenz side were already below the flagstones of the unkempt courtyard and battering at the first locked door. Their turn, however, came some minutes later.

The snaggle-toothed outline of what had once been a bastion, now reduced to a ragged stone wall no more than six feet high at any point, and overgrown with grass and weeds, reared from the smooth dark side of the hill ahead of them. And out of it, vaulting the wall at a low place, burst suddenly the figure of a man, running head-down for the gully of trees below. After him surged another, and another.

Gladly the police closed in. The first shout of challenge caused the foremost fugitive to swerve away towards the lake, where willing hands gathered him in without resistance, and the later ones to balk, break in various directions, and open fire. The police returned the fire, picked off the enemy singly and undamaged where they could, and shot to bring them down where they must. Five in all, but the fifth was no more than poised on the wall when the volley of shots broke out. He was notably quick and resolute in making up his mind. The bullet he put through the left upper arm of the nearest policeman was meant to do worse than wound, if the marksman's stance had not been so unstable. The policeman, firing back almost in the same instant, saw his opponent fall backward into the rubble and undergrowth inside the wall. But whether because he was hit or merely because he lost his balance no one was then clear.

By the time they had the other four secured, and came to look for the fifth, he had disappeared, though everyone was sure he had not emerged again anywhere round the perimeter. He had gone back, presumably, by the same way all five had come.

In the rank growth of early autumn it took them some time to find the broken place in the flooring within, and the steps leading down to the new, strong, locked door beneath.

He lay for a moment with the key still in his hand, feeling the waves of faintness approach and recede, and the slow drain of his blood seeping out of him. Here he could scarcely hear the shots from outside, and had no idea how long the skirmish continued; but he knew that they were all lost, every man of them. And he as certainly lost as they, though to another victor. All round the hill, waiting for them, the law. Down here in the rock, waiting for him . . .

How could it have happened, so unexpectedly and so finally?

Suddenly there were no continents left outside Europe, and Europe was crumbling away under his feet. All that carefully constructed kingdom, so firmly established, so long immune, wiped out in a night.

And all because of *her*. *She* had done this to him.

589

He did not know where the bullet in him had lodged, but he knew it was somewhere high in his chest, probably in the lungs. Bright red blood running out of his mouth, staining his hand, and the world sliding irrevocably away from him, and all at once this budding, proliferating pain where no pain had been, filling and overfilling him to the lips until he overflowed in blood.

He had always lived for his own advantage, pleasure and amusement, and in their cause everyone else had been expendable; and now that all these came down so catastrophically into one last small but sweet indulgence, he might as well continue consistent to the end, and rate himself as expendable, too. In any case he was all but spent. He knew he had not much time left, but he had time at least to kill the woman who had destroyed him.

With the last of his strength he set out along the passage, to crawl the ninety or so yards that separated him from Maggie Tressider.

Maggie, stiff and cold on the flagged floor by the open grave, holding Francis on her breast with his head carefully inclined and her thumb wedged hard down into the hollow of his collarbone, heard the key grate in the lock of the rear door, clumsily and for some seconds abortively. She turned her head as if in a dream, without belief, and watched the door swing open, and no one come in. Nothing was quite real any more, except Francis, and the necessity to keep her thumb rammed into his gaunt flesh, and the awful, spurting flow stemmed. She did not move, even when she looked down from the place where the arriving face should have been, down below the lock, down to the creature who lay sprawled black and red across the threshold, with nothing live or human about him but the round, greenish-gold eyes in the ruined face, bent inexorably on her, and the right hand that still clutched the gun.

She raised her voice, not out of panic, but to reach the ears stretched to receive it beyond the other door, where the lock-breaker had been working now for many minutes:

'He's coming back!'

Someone outside cursed terribly. The door shook. George Felse shouted: 'For God's sake try the gun . . .'

'He's come for me,' she called clearly and calmly. It was there in his face. She watched Robin, and cradled Francis, gently retaining the blood in him, never moving.

Outside the door they were going mad. The solid wood shook and trembled and creaked, but held firm, the first burst of gunfire, from something surely larger than a pistol, splintered the woodwork and scarred the stone wall, but still the lock resisted. Inside the cellar it seemed inordinately still and quiet. They were two separate worlds. Maggie excised from her consciousness the one that was useless to her, and sat still, only following with her eyes the struggles of the creature in the doorway.

The gold eyes never left her. His free left hand reached up laboriously, with the patience, she realised now, that belongs not to angels but to devils, until it got a hold on the latch of the door, and held fast. The right hand that held the gun, so carefully, so tenderly because it was the only treasure he had left, prised him doggedly up to his knees. He shifted the hand then with slow, drunken concentration to the door-frame, where it clung by the side and heel of the palm, frozen to the wood by the icy coldness of his will. Nothing else was now alive in him, except the deep, secret nerve that reacted only to hatred.

With infinite effort he had got one foot flattened to the floor, and with clinging hands and sweating agony he was levering himself upright. It was impossible. But for the burning determination he had to kill her as she had killed him, he would have fallen down long ago and stayed down, and died where he fell. Instead, inch by inch he drove himself upright, and even as she watched him, he took one lurching step away from the wall.

Gently and regretfully she laid down Francis out of her arms, on his face, that the wound might bleed less. Rising, she stepped over his body, and stood between him and their enemy. In this last encounter she had to meet Robin on equal terms. This whole affair had begun with the two of them, and with them it must end.

Neither of them heard the renewed grating of metal at the lock, the shattering gunshot, the impact of massed bodies against the barrier. There was no one left in the world but Maggie, erect and motionless in the centre of the cellar, and Robin Aylwin, propelling himself in dogged agony almost to within touch of her. The levelled gun, as heavy as the world, wavered upwards by inches towards her heart, sank irresistibly twice, and twice was recovered and forced onwards, towards her heart, level with her heart.

With abnormal clarity she saw the crooked finger on the trigger struggling to command the strength to contract, and put an end to her. For an age the muzzle quivered, leaned, sagged from her breast, reared again and shook again, straining and ravenous for her.

The flame went out abruptly. The gun and the hand that held it trembled and sank, in spite of all his almost disembodied fury, sank and reached for the flagstones, subsiding into the dark. He pitched forward at her feet, and lay still. The bright blood from his lips stained her white slipper. The hand with the gun was buried under him.

The lock gave, the police flooded into the room. They saw her standing like a statue in ice and blood, her face as white as the ground colour of her own housecoat, blood on her breast and sleeve, blood on her shoe, where her enemy lay prone as if in worship, his curled lips kissing her instep. George Felse put his arm round her, and she crumpled into it with a huge, hapless sigh, and he picked her up bodily and carried her away, out into the air and the clean night emptied of enemies.

Behind him others at least as expert as he converged upon Francis Killian, and took charge of him until the ambulance came to rush him into hospital at Bregenz, where they would pump into him pints of blood, and stop the loss of his own. But it wasn't a hospital this one needed. George thought, as he always thought when the world closed in, of Bunty. He made for the nearest car of the several that had somehow gathered, and commandeered it without scruple, police driver and all. On the journey back into Scheidenau he held Maggie in his arms like the daughter he and Bunty had never had, and promised her the world and Francis, too, and never stopped holding her until he gave her to Bunty at the Goldener Hirsch.

So it was not until half-way through the next day that he provisionally closed his own case. They had excavated the sitting tenant of the wine cellar by then, naked, almost a skeleton, young, male, the errand-boy who knew better how to run the business than did the managing director. Maggie would clear up the references later, but up to then Maggie was a limp, wondering convalescent just coming to life in Bunty's charge, living on bulletins from the hospital in Bregenz, and not yet fit to be questioned. What mattered about the young man from under the flagstones was that his more durable parts, notably the teeth, bore certain unique characteristics which were ultimately to identify him beyond doubt as Peter Bromwich, the art student of Comerbourne.

And that, combined with the capture of four of the international gang which had been plaguing this corner of Europe for so long, made the nocturnal siege of Scheidenau Castle a highly profitable operation. All the more so as three of the four showed signs of being willing to talk for their own sakes, and possibly to bring in, indirectly, at least half a dozen others from the shattered brotherhood.

Not to mention, of course, their lord and master, Robin Aylwin, sometime 'cellist of Freddy's Circus, listed by the hospital at Bregenz as 'Dead on arrival'.

Chapter 14

'I quite understand,' said Maggie, picking abstracted at the keys of her piano and frowning at the music before her, 'that he doesn't want to see me, after all that's happened. What did I ever do for him, except make use of him, involve him against his better judgment in . . . all that horror . . . and nearly kill him? I don't blame him if he never wants to see me again. I haven't any right to force myself on him. Are you *sure* he's all right?'

'Right as rain.' Bunty stood by the window, looking out upon the placid surface of the lake, pale in a still midday, bright but sunless. It was the ninth day since Helmut's night carnival, and the clear, chill peace of autumn lay over Scheidenau. 'They wouldn't be discharging him in two days' time if they weren't satisfied, especially after all the fuss and all the reporters. Six pints of blood they've got staked in Francis, they're not going to waste that, you may be sure.'

'Bunty, I owe you so much, you and George. *Bunty, help me!*'

'Did I ever say,' wondered Bunty, 'that he didn't want to see you? I said he *said* he didn't want to see you. In fact, I rather gave him to believe that you were going home with George and me, tomorrow. So he's due to come out of care the next day on his own, just the way he claims he wants it. He's ordered a taxi already, to take him back to the Weisses Kreuz. Most of his

594

things are still there. He'll stay overnight, and then arrange his exit. He'll think he's clear of the lot of us. *You, too!*'

'Bunty, couldn't you find out for me what time?'

'I know what time. The taxi's ordered for ten in the morning. *Maggie, are you absolutely sure you know what you want?*'

'Yes, quite sure. *Yes, quite sure!* Oh, Bunty, pray for me!'

'Both of us will be doing that, naturally. For both of you!'

'Your car is here,' they told him, and made their goodbyes with warmth and ceremony, for he had been their prize patient for ten days, and when were they likely to get such another sensation? He packed his few toilet things in the briefcase George Felse had brought in for him from Scheidenau, along with a newly-pressed suit and clean shirt and underclothes to replace the ruins they had stripped from him and burned on arrival. He went down the stairs beside a gay little chattering nurse, and picked up at the desk his wallet and papers, with a note left for him by George and Bunty, wishing him luck and hoping to see him at home in England. Yes, perhaps. Nice people! They had visited him several times in hospital, and kept him informed about Maggie. Nothing from Maggie herself, of course. Well, that had been his intention, hadn't it?

So that was that. She had respected his wish to be left alone, maybe she'd even been grateful to him for taking the issue out of her hands. Back into your proper orbit, Miss Tressider, and I'll skid back into mine. I'll see you, he thought, from the back of the circle occasionally, I'll hear you broadcast and be thankful for that, but that's all the rights I shall ever have or ever expect in you.

He stepped out through the door into the cool, autumnal air, and shivered. He felt light, empty and aimless. The world was a big place, but without savour. He looked along the kerb for his taxi; there was little point in hurrying anywhere, but none in staying here.

There was only one car drawn up by the entrance, and that

was not a taxi. It was an elderly Dodge of a creamy coffee-colour, with a girl sitting behind the wheel.

She didn't get out when she saw him, but she leaned across and opened the passenger door, and waited for him to get in. Her hair was braided into two great plaits and coiled on top of her head, and all those subtle colours that met and married in it matched the leaves of the oak tree as well in autumn as in spring. She was pale but radiant; all the lines of her face were easier and more at peace than he had ever seen them before, and her gentian eyes were no longer straining to see something remote and ominous that would not stand still to be seen. On the contrary, they focused very sharply and resolutely upon him.

'I paid your taximan and sent him away,' she said. 'You don't mind, do you? I'll drive you back to Scheidenau.'

There was nothing to be done but get in beside her. 'I thought you'd gone back to England,' he said, leaning rather gingerly to dispose of his briefcase on the back seat.

'No, not yet.' She started the car, carefully because she wasn't yet used to it, and drove slowly out into traffic, winding her way towards the frontage of Lake Constance. 'I waited for you.'

'That was kind, but you shouldn't have put off going on my account.'

'To be honest,' she said, 'I put it off on my own account. Did you really think I could go away and leave you here alone, after all that's happened?'

'I don't see why not. You'd already done more than enough for me. You knew I was being perfectly well looked after, and making a good recovery. And you must be longing to get back and start work again. I see,' he said, veering resolutely away from the subject, 'they found the Dodge in time.'

'At that mason's yard in Regenheim. And quite a lot of contra-band and stolen property, too, that nobody had time to ditch. When they'd done with the car I asked if I could take it over. I thought you'd be relieved to see it.'

596

'It certainly wouldn't be much fun to have to replace it. It was good of you to think of putting my mind at rest.'

Everything was going to be deference, kindness and gratitude, she could see that, whatever stresses might be gnawing away underneath. She waited until they were out of the town, winding their way along the upland road, and then settled to a gentle forty kilometres, and cast a long, measuring look at him along her shoulder.

'You drive very well,' he said. 'I've never seen you in action before.'

'You'll have plenty of chance, I'm driving you back to Zurich when we go.'

'Maggie . . . now look . . .'

'Well, naturally! With that shoulder *you* certainly shouldn't be driving long distances yet. Though of course we could stay in Scheidenau for a week or two longer, if you like. It might be the best plan, actually.'

'Maggie, look, you shouldn't have done this. I can't let you . . .'

'You can't stop me,' she said gently, and turned and smiled at him. She would have to be very careful of him, she could see, he was still easily shaken. She felt his body tighten and brace itself beside her, and saw his brows draw painfully together over clouded eyes.

'Oh, no!' he said, shaking his head with decision. 'None of that! I know you now. Once you passed by an overture of love, as you thought, without noticing it until it was too late, and spent years of your life paying your substance away in requital of what you took to be a debt. Now you're so mortally afraid of repeating the error that you'll fall over backwards to avoid it. But not with me! I've got too much sense to let that happen, if you haven't. You don't love me, you just feel responsible for me. You owe me nothing, and I'll take nothing from you. Go home, girl, sing, be successful, be happy . . . you've got time even for that, now.'

597

'That,' she said patiently, 'depends on you. That's what I'm trying to tell you.' They were high among the meadows, the hills folding and unfolding before them in bleached green of pasture and blue-black of conifers. She pulled in to the wide grass verge and stopped the car, turning on him a face pale to incandescence with solemnity.

'Francis, I'm not making any mistake this time, and I won't let you, either. I've never loved anyone before, perhaps I couldn't because of him. But I love you now, and if you pass me by I shall have lost everything. Maybe you don't want me, and that I could accept, but I daren't let go of you until I know whether that's really why you want me to go away. If you don't love me, tell me so, and I'll leave you alone. But for pity's sake don't tell me you don't if you do, because that wouldn't be noble, it would be damned ignoble, and I should spend the rest of my life paying for it, as well as you. And if you do love me, then start getting used to my being here, because I'm always going to be here.'

He opened his lips to answer her, and found she had left him nothing to say. Everything he could have produced by way of subterfuge she had anticipated, and now he could not lie to her, even if he'd thought for a moment he could have managed it successfully. How could he live with himself afterwards, if he ever began to suspect she had been right? To send her back to her own world and her own kind might have been almost bearable, as long as he could rest in the conviction that she would be happiest that way, which God knew any sane man would take for granted. But what if the unbelievable turned out to be true, and he was the one who was fooling himself, not she?

He had begun to shake and sweat, between crazy hope and craven fear; this sort of thing wasn't for him yet, he wasn't up to it. He dragged his gaze away from her face with an effort, pressing his fingers deep into his hollow cheeks to clamp the wrong words in until he could find the right ones and somehow get them out. There are hurdles not even love can take without a crashing fall; only the native obstinacy recent stresses had roused in her could make her attempt them, and when the stresses passed, and even the memory of them grew pale, she would regret ever assaying the leap. She was a reasonable being, she would listen. And this wouldn't be lying to her.

'Maggie,' he began laboriously, 'have you really thought what you're suggesting? You know who you are, and what you are, nobody knows it better. A world figure, and going to be even greater . . .'

'I could,' she agreed very quietly, 'given the right circumstances.'

'And I'm the right circumstances? Wake up, girl, for God's sake! I don't have to go into details about myself, and I'm not going to. Don't pretend you can't evaluate well enough to get my number right.'

'Better, perhaps,' she said fiercely, 'than you.'

'All right, let it go. But you know very well what I mean. You belong in a world about which I know nothing, among people with whom I have nothing in common, except, perhaps, a liking for music, and that wouldn't get me far. It's a live, mobile, important world, with no room for hangers-on. You know what I'm talking about as well as I do. Do you think that would be an easy marriage?'

'All right,' she said after a long pause, her eyes wide and watchful on his face, 'I do know what you're talking about, and no, it won't be easy. Did you ever hear of a marriage that was? But this one will be more difficult than most, I know it. And fathoms deeper! I'm not glossing over anything. I don't know any of the answers, those we have to find as we go. I'm simply telling you that there isn't any alternative! Marriage may be difficult, but separation is impossible. After what we've been through together, after what we know about each other, what do you suppose the ordinary pinpricks can do to us? Do you think two people ever drew as near as we have, and managed to pull themselves apart again without bleeding to death?'

He didn't know whether she had reached that argument by a

lucky inspiration or by serious thought, but as soon as she had said it he saw that it was irresistibly true, and thanked God for it, since resistance was becoming unendurable. For better or worse, they had grown together until separation would have been extreme mutilation, a death before death.

Whether she had convinced him, or whether he had surrendered only to his own awful longing to be convinced, however it happened, suddenly she was in his arms. They had, after all, no option but to make their own rules, having strayed so far out of range of any others. Maybe she could never have married anyone now for the ordinary, socially respected reasons. Maybe he would really turn out to be what she wanted, and what she would continue to want, life-long. Please God, he thought. And God help us both, because we're going to need it! But when he kissed her all his lingering forebodings vanished like the mists dissolving over Lake Constance, and there was no room left in him for anything but incredulous gratitude and joy.

After a while they disentangled themselves silently and solemnly, and drove on mute and dazed with achievement into Scheidenau.

Appendix

Text of Maggie Tressider's English Singing Version of
'WHERE THE SPLENDID TRUMPETS BLOW'

'Wo die schönen Trompeten blasen,' from *Des Knaben Wunder-horn*: set by Mahler.

Who's that without there, who knocks at my door,
Imploring so softly, so softly: Sleep no more!?

Your love, your own true love is here,
Rise up and let me in, my dear!
And must I longer wait and mourn?
I see the red of dawn return,
The red of dawn, two stars so bright.
O that I were with my delight,
With mine own heart's beloved!

The maiden arose and let him in.
Most welcome home, my more than kin,
Most welcome home, my own true love,
So long you've watched and waited.
She offered him her snow-white hand,
Far off there sang a nightingale.
The maid began to weep and wail.

O do not weep, love, do not pine,
Within the year you shall be mine.
Ere long you shall be one with me
As never bride on earth shall be,
No, none but you on earth, love!

Across the heath to war I fare,
The great green heath so broad and bare,
For there, where the splendid trumpets blare and thunder,
There is my house, my house the green turf under.